The *Year's Best*
Fantasy and
Horror

ALSO EDITED BY ELLEN DATLOW AND TERRI WINDLING

The Year's Best Fantasy: First Annual Collection
The Year's Best Fantasy: Second Annual Collection
The Year's Best Fantasy and Horror: Third Annual Collection
The Year's Best Fantasy and Horror: Fourth Annual Collection
The Year's Best Fantasy and Horror: Fifth Annual Collection
The Year's Best Fantasy and Horror: Sixth Annual Collection
The Year's Best Fantasy and Horror: Seventh Annual Collection
The Year's Best Fantasy and Horror: Eighth Annual Collection
The Year's Best Fantasy and Horror: Ninth Annual Collection
Snow White, Blood Red
Black Thorn, White Rose
Ruby Slippers, Golden Tears
Black Swan, White Raven

The *Year's Best Fantasy and Horror*

TENTH ANNUAL COLLECTION

Edited by Ellen Datlow
and Terri Windling

ST. MARTIN'S PRESS ⚙ NEW YORK

To James Minz and Cassandra Mahoney.
A nuptial gift.
—E.D. and T.W.

First Edition: July 1997

10 9 8 7 6 5 4 3 2 1

Paperback 0-312-15701-0
Hardcover 0-312-15700-2

A Blue Cows-Mad City Production.

Acknowledgments

I would like to thank William Congreve, Linda Marotta, Alice Turner, Steve Jones, Jo Fletcher, Lawrence Schimel, Nick Royle, Gary Couzens, Gardner Dozois, Ayesha Randolph, and Robert K. J. Killheffer for their recommendations and their help. Thank you to the writers, editors, and publishers who sent me material for this volume.

Special thanks to Terri Windling, my partner in crime.

(Please note: It's difficult to cover all non genre sources of short horror so should readers see a story or poem from such a source, I would appreciate it being brought to my attention. Drop me a line at c/o *Omni Internet*, General Media International, 277 Park Avenue, 4th floor, New York, NY 10172-0003.)

I have used the following publications as sources through the Summation: *Locus* magazine, published and edited by Charles N. Brown: $43 for 12 issues (second class) and $53 for 12 issues (first class) payable to Locus Publications, P.O. Box 13305, Oakland, CA 94661; *Science Fiction Chronicle* published and edited by Andrew I. Porter: $35 for 12 issues (second class) and $42 for 12 issues (first class) payable to Science Fiction Chronicle, P.O. Box 022730, Brooklyn, NY 11202-0056. Also, *Publishers Weekly, Interzone, Eidolon,* and *Aurealis* (for descriptions of books I could not get).

I would also like to acknowledge the following catalogs, all of which enabled me to write capsule descriptions of titles not seen by me as well as being excellent sources for ordering genre material by mail: Mark V. Ziesing Books, P.O. Box 76, Shingletown, CA 96088; DreamHaven Books and Comics, 912 West Lake Street, Minneapolis, MN 55408; and The Overlook Connection, P.O. Box 526, Woodstock, GA 30188.

—Ellen Datlow

I am grateful to all the publishers, editors, writers, artists, booksellers and readers who sent material and shared their thoughts on the year in fantasy publishing with me. *Locus, SF Chronicle, Tangent, Publishers Weekly, The Hungry Mind Review, The Bloomsbury Review,* the *Women's Review of Books,* and *Folk Roots* magazines were invaluable reference sources.

I am particularly grateful to the hardworking and resourceful Editorial Assistants on the fantasy half of this volume: Richard and Mardelle Kunz (book publishing) and Bill Murphy (magazines and journals).

Thanks are also due to Charles de Lint, Robert Gould, and Ellen Kushner for music recommendations; to Ellen Steiber for support above-and-beyond-the-call-of-duty during the annual deadline crunch; and to: Elisabeth Roberts, Delia Sherman, Tappan King & Beth Meacham, Tom Harlan Jr., Sondi Mahoney, Patrick Nielsen Hayden, Jennifer Brehl, John Douglas, Jane Yolen, Lawrence Schimel, and Paul Petrie-Ritchie for various kinds of help. Special thanks go to our St. Martin's editor Gordon Van Gelder and his assistant Corin See; to cover artist and pal Tom Canty; and to my amazing co-editor Ellen Datlow.

—Terri Windling

First among those who make this book possible are our editors; their efforts are Herculean. My assistant, Jim Minz, does a huge job in pulling together the permissions from contributors, publishers, magazines, and other licensers. Also most helpful are our interns, Jenna Burrill, Oliver Kaufman, Rachel Nelson, Lori Pacovsky, and Anthony VanWagner. Key to this year's production was Seth Johnson, who performed double duty. Special thanks to Jessi Frenkel, for invaluable assistance in art direction of the jacket.

—James Frenkel.

Contents

SUMMATION 1996: Fantasy
by Terri Windling

Readers familiar with the field of fantasy literature, and with this anthology series in particular, will need no explanation of the mission we set ourselves when we gathered the following stories and poems into one fat volume. For those new to either, however, the usual introduction is in order:

In this book we have brought together a wide assortment of the best fantasy fiction published in the English language in 1996, drawing our material from the bright dreams of traditional fantasy, the dark nightmares of horror, and the vast, fecund area of storytelling that falls between these two poles. Fantasy is a sturdy limb on the tree of modern literature—not something entirely separate from it, as modern critics (and bookstore catagorizations) often suggest. It is wise to remember that the roots of this tree are sunk in the soil of fantasy tales, for our earliest stories were magical ones: Gilgamesh, the *Odyssey*, the *Mabinogion*, the *Nibelungenlied*, Beowulf, the whole Arthurian cycle, to name but a few . . . and that it is only in quite recent years that the use of phantasmagoric imagery has fallen into disrepute. This is changing, due to two strong influences in particular: the impact of Latin American magic realism on fiction writers around the world, and the fact that two generations now have grown up with the works of Tolkien and his ilk, leaving such readers more amenable to non-realist tales in later years (or "post-realism," as some of the more rebellious young writers are calling it).

In the realm of magical storytelling, "fantasy" and "horror" are sister fields of literature that overlap, inform, and enrich each other. For the purpose of this volume, our definition of what makes a fantasy or horror story tend to be broad and inclusive, not exclusive, ignoring the genre demarcations so beloved by modern publishing companies. My co-editor and I have searched for the stories and poems that follow not only in the abundant genre sources (magazines, anthologies, small press zines, and single author collections), but anywhere magical, mythical, surrealistic or horrific fiction might be found: mainstream magazines and anthologies, works of children's literature, foreign works in translation, literary quarterlies, and poetry reviews. While this volume exists to honor fine stories published in the fantasy genre, we also take particular delight in including work from other sources that the average fantasy reader may never otherwise stumble across.

Last year, I felt a bit concerned about the state of novel-length fantasy, particularly within the genre. The specific area of "imaginary world" fiction was beginning to look mighty tired, and I found—in my own personal reading—that I was turning to mainstream magic realism almost exclusively as a result. This year, I am delighted to report that things are changing for the better. Nineteen ninety-six was a strong year for fine and varied fiction in genre fantasy—and the "imaginary world" form of the literature has just gotten an infusion of fresh new blood. Some of this is coming from talented new writers like Sean Stewart, Sean Russell, J. Gregory Keyes, and Sharon Shinn; some is coming from established writers who are rediscovering this territory, George R. R. Martin in particular. Meanwhile, the fantasy genre continues to nurture highly literate works of contemporary magic realism and mythic fantasy (by the likes of Nancy Springer,

Bradley Denton, and Robert Holdstock), while similar work also appears 'round the corner on the mainstream shelves. If you want to keep up with all the interesting work that appeared in in 1996, you've got your job cut out for you—and a lot of good reading ahead.

I am also pleased to report that two fantasy lines that had become lack-luster in years past—Avon and Ace—have really pulled up their socks recently, turning out fine and innovative work on a more consistent basis. Del Rey, DAW, and Tor continue to be the Big Three in terms of hitting those best-sellers lists: Del Rey specializing in sprawling epics and DAW specializing in fantasy adventures (although each list contains a few surprises), while Tor remains notable for the impressive breadth (and size) of its list. HarperCollins is still carving out a niche for themselves in the fantasy field (although they've gotten off to a promising start); while Baen maintains its particular niche with books that often seem to fall in the fantasy/SF borderland ("fantasy with rivets" they like to call it, appealing to a very specific audience). The downsized lists of Bantam and Roc publish the occasional gem, but fewer of them than in years past. Warner has lost visibility, although they're still releasing a few fantasy titles—unlike the small press White Wolf which has made an aggressive appearance on the market with an extensive publishing program (although most of their titles fall into the dark fantasy/horror catagory, or are reprints). In England, Gollancz and Legend (Random House) maintain particularly strong fantasy programs; Signet (Penguin) released some good work too in the year just passed. In mainstream fiction, Harcourt Brace, Henry Holt, Dedalus, and St. Martin's Press are the publishers with the greatest number of magical books on their '96 lists (in the case of St. Martin's, even their "genre" books have a literary or quirky mainstream feel), but most publishers had at least one or two tucked away in their catalogs somewhere (rarely classified as "fantasy"). Through the hard work of editorial assistants Richard and Mardelle Kunz, we've managed to track down a number of these titles and provide a guide to the best, below.

In nonfiction, there were several good biographies, art compilations and works in the folklore field that fantasy readers will find of interest (see recommendations, below). The most notable publication was Patti Perret's *The Faces of Fantasy* (Tor), a book of photographic portraits and autobiographical statements from writers about their work, their lives, or the fantasy field in general. *Locus* magazine has also been doing a good job at keeping up a critical discourse about the craft of fantasy fiction in the interesting author interviews conducted by Charles N. Brown. Here's a sampling of what fantasy writers themselves have to say about the state of the art (drawn from *The Faces of Fantasy, Locus, Dreams and Wishes:* essays by Susan Cooper, and Darrell Schweitzer's excellent interview of Ellen Kushner in *Marion Zimmer Bradley's Fantasy Magazine*):

"Every book is a voyage of discovery . . . but for me, the making of a fantasy is quite unlike the relatively ordered procedure of writing any other kind of book. I've never actually *thought:* 'I'm writing a fantasy'; one simply sits down to write whatever is knocking to be let out. But in hindsight I can see the peculiar difference in approach. When working on a book which turns out to be a fantasy novel, I exist in a state of continual astonishment. The book begins with a deep breath and a blindly trusting step into the unknown . . ."—Susan Cooper

"Myth and legend work through the familiar being expressed in a new and innovative voice. We retell stories, and that is what makes them so powerful. At the core of most fantasy, and most horror I suppose, is the familiar fear or obsession or intrigue, the curiosity about the world around us. We are a species imbued with an incredible curiosity, and to satisfy curiosity isn't good enough, because there is nothing left to quest for. Therefore we are continually asking questions, continually finding new barriers to worry about, to need to cross. It's the personalized quest we all have."—Robert Hold-stock

"The job of a storyteller is to speak the truth. But what we feel most deeply can't be spoken in words alone. At this level, only images connect. And here, story becomes symbol; symbol is myth. And myth is truth."—Alan Garner

"[Fantasy] has the emotional strength of a dream, it works directly on our nerve endings, whatever age we happen to be, touching heights and depths not always accessible through realism. In fantasy, my concern is how we learn to be real human beings. It's a continuing process."—Lloyd Alexander

"I went through decades of writing fantasy and telling myself 'this has nothing to do with me—it's just fantasy.' Then damned if that book doesn't catch you up somewhere, and you realize suddenly that all these things are crowding into your head from *your* life. . . . You cannot write without writing about yourself, but sometimes it's so disguised you don't recognize it."—Patricia A. McKillip

"We read fantasy to find the colors again, I think. To taste strong spices, and hear the songs the sirens sang. There is something old and true in fantasy that speaks to something deep within us, to the child who dreamed that one day he would hunt the forests of the night, and feast beneath the hollow hills, and find a love to last forever somewhere south of Oz and north of Shangri-La."—George R. R. Martin

"Fantasy broke when Dungeons & Dragons appeared . . . I think Dungeons & Dragons has become *the* biggest influence on contemporary fantasy. When it appeared, it took all the pure fantasy traditions from different cultures and threw them together in one huge, complex mess—high fantasy, sword & sorcery, dark fantasy, all in one sourcebook, with tables so you could look it up. If you go back and look at old classical fantasy, you see how rare magic actually is, and how unsystematized. In *Lord of the Rings*, say, there's very little magic actually going on onstage. If you look at E. R. Eddison, there's very little. But in a Dungeons & Dragons-derived universe, everyone's got magical weapons, everyone's got spells, everyone can be a warrior."—Walter Jon Williams

"Irish writers, influenced by our Celtic heritage, are more familiar than most with the concept of alternate reality. For the Celts, the dividing line has always been very thin. In the Celtic cosmos, the Otherworld lies just beneath the surface of perceived reality and can break through at any time. . . . Fantasy is not merely a 'genre,' that denigrating term. Fantasy is a pinnacle, a mountaintop from which all horizons can be seen."—Morgan Llywelyn

"The example I use for people who are genre-blind—they don't know from science fiction or fantasy. They have this notion that it's junk—I say that that's like saying all romance novels are junk. Now, are you talking about *Jane Eyre* or Harlequins? They both have basically the same tropes in them, and one's good and one's bad. The same is true of fantasy; you've got *Jane Eyre* and you've got Harlequins. People can enjoy them both, but you've got to know the difference."—Ellen Kushner

"I look forward to the day when I can again walk into any bookshop and see only a fiction category, arranged alphabetically so that you can find Jonathan Carroll where you look for Angela Carter, Raymond Carver, or Catullus, or William Shatner sharing a shelf with William Shakespeare. Nobody need be afraid that I, or any other reader, will confuse one with the other—but sometimes taking down either could introduce me to something engrossing, stimulating, and entertaining that I might otherwise never have discovered. In literature, as in society, the more we are divided, the more easily we are controlled. . . ."—Michael Moorcock

Now on to the specifics of the 1996 publishing year. In addition to my own wide reading I have solicited recommendations from the international community of fantasy writers, editors and publishers in order to compile the list below. The following is a Baker's Dozen of the best novels published in 1996 (in alphabetical order):

The Hand I Fan With by Tina McElroy Ansa (Doubleday). Published as mainstream fiction, the latest novel from this popular Southern writer is a bittersweet love story filled with ghosts, spirits, psychics, and Southern folklore. Set in a gossipy African-American community in modern Georgia, Ansa's tale is sensual, mystical and wise.

Little Sister by Kara Dalkey (Jane Yolen Books/Harcourt Brace). This beautiful historical fantasy novel, by the author of *The Nightingale*, was published for Young Adult readers but has an ageless, timeless quality. Set in the Heian period of twelfth-century Japan, Dalkey's tale mixes magic with a solid knowledge of the period, and is laced with the language of poetry and exquisite detail.

Lunatics by Bradley Denton (St. Martin's Press). This is a terrific work of contemporary fantasy and a probable awards contender. Denton portrays the interconnected lives of a group of college friends many years after—and the repercussions when one of them falls in love with an owl-winged moon goddess. This smart, funny, whimsical book about love and relationships is set over a period of thirteen full moons in Texas in 1993.

Tex and Molly in the Afterlife by Richard Grant (Avon). Another contemporary fantasy (published as a mainstream title, although the author's work will be familiar to genre readers), this one is set in Dublin, Maine and follows the ghosts of two recently deceased hippies as they move among the Living, the Dead, and the magical spirits of the land they are not quite ready to leave. Highly original, totally absurd, well-written, it's a whole lot of fun.

Requiem by Graham Joyce (Tor). This dark and provocative novel walks the borderland between fantasy and horror. A man grieving for his wife's tragic death journeys to modern Jerusalem—a city filled, in Joyce's portrayal, with ghosts, djinn, and madmen, and smothered by the weight of its history. This is a gorgeous book, both intimate and erudite, mysterious and unnerving.

Of Love and Other Demons by Gabriel García Márquez (Penguin). This is flawless Latin American magic realism written by the acknowledged master of the form. Márquez's latest is set in the tropics of eighteenth-century South America, involving the love affair between a wild young girl and a quiet, bookish priest. The story examines love in its many guises (a familiar Marquezian theme); it's a generous book, visionary, enchanted, and hard to put down.

The Game of Thrones by George R. R. Martin (Bantam Spectra). This acclaimed writer's new novel is a saga written on an epic scale and entirely delicious. It's a fat book, the first in a series, and filled with all the classic fantasy tropes: kings and courtiers, soldiers and sages, magical creatures and a cruel dragon prince—yet Martin manages to give familiar themes and characters vivid new life. I recommend this one even to readers who have sworn off multi-book series fantasy.

Winter Rose by Patricia A. McKillip (Ace). This deeply magical book (very loosely based on the "Tam Lin" legend) is fey, poetic, and utterly sublime. Two sisters live in a Victorian English village at the edge of a forest . . . where their lives become entwined with that of a beautiful, mysterious stranger. Plot summaries do not do justice to this incredibly gifted writer's work, which ought to be known far beyond the genre. Published in a lovely edition (jacket painting by Kinuko Y. Craft), this one's a gem.

Godmother Night by Rachel Pollack (St. Martin's Press). Pollack's new novel is a unique contemporary fantasy about two gay women, their child, and Mother Night (the angel of death, with her coterie of leather-clad bikers). Working with themes from classic fairy tales (such as Germany's "Godfather Death"), the author examines issues of death, life, love, and identity in this bold, skillfully crafted novel.

Fair Peril by Nancy Springer (Avon). This accomplished writer just gets better with every book. Her latest is an audacious work of contemporary fantasy about a disillusioned middle-aged woman, her daughter, an annoying talking frog, and the magical realm of Fair Peril (which lies between two stores at the mall). Springer's droll adult fairy tale is highly original and totally enchanting.

Clouds End by Sean Stewart (Ace). At last we have some new writers of "imaginary world" fantasy worth getting excited about, and Sean Stewart is one of the best. This beautifully textured book about an island woman and her magical doppelganger is set in a fantasy land so real you can feel the solid earth beneath your feet. I am tempted to make comparisons to early Le Guin—but Stewart has a distinctive voice of his own.

The Scarlet Rider by Lucy Sussex (Forge). This Australian writer has come into her own with a marvelous Victorian ghost tale and literary detection novel. Her protagonist is a modern scholar obssessed by a mysterious female writer of adventure stories from Australia's Gold Rush period. Telling tales from two centuries at once, *The Scarlet Rider* is engrossing, rather chilling, and a real page-turner.

The Silver Cloud Café by Alfredo Véa, Jr. (Dutton). This Chicano-Yaqui writer is the author of one of my all-time favorite magic realist novels (*La Maravilla*) so I am happy to report this his second novel is as luminous as his first—and set on a grander scale. Véa opens with angels hovering over modern San Francisco and weaves his way back to the Mexican Revolution in a story drenched in folklore and myth, with passages of prose so beautiful you could weep. He has written a wonderful, wonderful book.

First Novels:

This was quite a good year for strong first novels. The very best of them was published outside the fantasy genre: *The Journal of Antonio Montoya* by Rick Collignon (Macmurray & Beck). This mischievous little book, set in a small village in northern New Mexico, is about Ramona Montoya (a painter who shares her old house with a number of gently meddlesome dead relatives) and the 1924 journal of a sculptor of religious santos. Funny, warm-hearted, beautifully crafted, this is highly recommended.

The Runner-up position for "Best First Novel of the Year" is a tie between a genre fantasy novel and a mainstream fantasy: *The Waterborn* by J. Gregory Keyes (Del Rey) is a fat "quest" fantasy full of gods, warriors, robust adventures, funny-sounding names and that distinctive "we're aiming for a bestseller here" marketing look—but if you like your fantasy smart, literate and well-crafted, don't let that deter you. Keyes (currently pursuing a Ph.D. in the anthropology of belief systems and mythology) is a genuinely fresh new voice in the field and his work has real power. Highly recommended. *Lorien Lost: A Novel of Artistic Obsession* by Michael King (A Wyatt Book/St. Martin's Press) is a sparkling tale about a Victorian gentleman who is able to walk through the paintings he collects to step into the worlds they portray. King's inventive first novel is deeply magical, comes in a lovely edition, and is also highly recommended.

Other distinctive first novels in '96 include two animal fantasy tales (both written for adult readers): *Top Dog* by Jerry Jay Carroll (Ace) is an odd little saga in which a high-powered executive wakes up as a dog and sets off on adventures through a magical landcape . . . doesn't that sound dreadful? It's not. It's actually wonderful. Trust me on this one. *Cowkind* by Ray Petersen (A Wyatt Book/St. Martin's Press) is another animal fantasy, involving cows and a small New York family farm during the years of the Vietnam War. One reviewer aptly dubbed this "Agrarian Magical Realism," and it's udderly charming. (Sorry, I couldn't resist.)

Other notable debuts in 1996, mentioned in brief: *Luck in the Shadows* by Lynn Flewelling (Bantam). *Anvil of the Sun* by Anne Lesley Groell (Penguin/Roc). *Kingmaker's Sword* by Ann Marston (HarperPrism). *Wind from a Foreign Sky* by Katya Reimann

(Tor). *Mage Heart* by Jane Routley (AvoNova). *The Sacred Seven* by Amy Stout (AvoNova). *Wheel of Dreams* by Salinda Tyson (Del Rey).

Oddities:

The "Best Peculiar Book" distinction of 1996 goes to that master of the peculiar, Nick Bantock. *The Venetian's Wife* (Chronicle Books) is the tale of an art restorer plunged into a mysterious quest involving Indian sculpture, unsolved mysteries of the past, and the nature of art. Told through diary entries, email messages, and illustrations, this book is less intimate than Bantock's bestselling *Griffin and Sabine*, but in some ways is more profound. Recommended. The Runner-up is another Chronicle book, and another one that Bantock apparently had a hand in: *Paris Out of Hand: A Wayward Guide* by Karen Elizabeth Gordon. This bizarre and handsome little book is a tour of "an imagined Paris," a guidebook to streets, cafés and metro stops that only exist in a more magical world. It's delightfully deranged, although probably best appreciated by those with some familiarity with the city. Other oddities of 1996:

Free City by Eric Darton (W. W. Norton & Co.). This quirky little book purports to be the visionary journal of an inventor at the dawn of the Enlightenment. Although a scientist by nature (overseeing the construction of an airship, various automatons, and other wonders), our hero's orderly, rational world is impinged upon by the occult and a talking duck. This odd but well-realized tale is published in a very handsome small edition.

The Law of Love by Laura Esquivel, translated by Margaret Sayers Penden (Crown). This is the much-anticipated new book from the author of the charming Mexican magic realist novel (and movie) *Like Water for Chocolate*. I regret to say that it's a great disappointment. This SF/fantasy tale is set in Mexico in the 23rd Century; it's the story of a woman whose job it is to help people deal with their past lives, which gets her involved in planet-wide politics and strangeness. The novel is called "a multimedia book"; it comes with a CD and is partly told through comic book panels and poetry. The whole thing is rather silly, and intrusively New Age.

The Moon Box (Chronicle) is a boxed set of two books about moon myths and two anthologies: one of which is dark fantasy (*The Were-Wolf*, with literary stories by Angela Carter, Saki and others); the other is science fiction (*"Somnium" & Other Trips to the Moon*). The whole set would make a nice gift, which is no doubt the publisher's intent.

In the "Believe it or Not" catagory, someone has actually published a reader's companion to the long-cancelled TV show *Bewitched: Bewitched Forever* by Herbie J Pilato (Summit Publishing), containing plot summaries of each episode. I am at a loss for words here.

Imaginary World Fantasy:

After the Martin and Stewart novels listed above, the best "imaginary world" fantasy of 1996 is *Sea Without Shore* by Sean Russell (DAW). For people who like big fat series books, and even for those who don't, I recommend this entertaining tale set in a colorful land of mages and magic (the sequel to last year's *World Without End*). Yes, this is a standard fate-of-the-world-rests-on-one-young-man's-shoulders kind of a story, but the engaging hero is a naturalist, not a warrior, and Russell's evocation of the natural world is truly first rate. Also recommended:

Arcady by Michael Williams (Roc). The haunted family manor of the title, Arcady, stands on the Border of a realm of wonders. This is a literate, mysterious tale mixing a classic "high fantasy" quest with themes from Romantic poetry.

Songspinners by Sarah Ash (Orion UK). This highly original fantasy from a relatively new British novelist (I believe this is her second novel) is about the power of music in a war-torn, mythical world.

The Golden Key by Melanie Rawn, Jennifer Roberson and Kate Elliott (DAW). Set in a Renaissance-like world where art and magic intertwine, this collaborative novel is entertaining and cleverly rendered.

The Price of Blood and Honor by Elizabeth Willey (Tor). This is the conclusion of the arch and witty fantasy trilogy that began with *The Well-Favored Man*.

Orca by Steven Brust (Ace). Here's the master of "arch and witty" fantasy (at least since Roger Zelazny's sad passing.) This one is #8 in Brust's entertaining—and thought-provoking—Vlad Taltos series about an assassin with a troublesome social conscience.

The True Game by Sheri S. Tepper (Ace). This is an Omnibus edition reprinting Tepper's exuberantly inventive "True Game" trilogy (her first three books, originally published a decade ago).

Contemporary Fantasy:

In addition to the Denton, Pollack, and Springer books listed above, the best "contemporary fantasy" of 1996 was *Ancient Echoes* by Robert Holdstock (Roc). While not officially part of this British author's gorgeous, mythic "Mythago Wood" series, yet this novel follows a young boy to manhood as he encounters ancient "mythagos" through a series of increasingly disturbing dreams. Highly recommended. Also of note:

The Off Season by Jack Cady (St. Martin's Press). The best one yet from this terrific Northwestern writer—a contemporary fantasy tale about the coastal town of Point Vestal, its ghosts, its curse, and a multilingual cat.

Walking the Labyrinth by Lisa Goldstein (Tor). The latest from this talented, original writer of magic realist tales is about a woman from San Francisco who finds true magic among the vaudeville stage magicians of England.

Treasure Box by Orson Scott Card (HarperCollins). A dark, ghostly, wonderfully eerie tale of contemporary fantasy.

The Wood Wife by Terri Windling (Tor). I can't comment on this one, which is set in the desert of the American southwest; you'll have to judge it for yourself.

Historical Fantasy:

After *Little Sister*, listed earlier, the best "historical fantasy" of 1996 was a very unusual one: *A Mapmaker's Dreams* by James Cowan (Shambhala). Cowan, an Australian writer, has created a striking, imaginative work: the meditations of one Fra Mauro, Cartographer to the Court of Venice in the sixteenth century. As he sits at work in his monastic cell dedicated to making a map that "represents the full breadth of Creation," travellers from far-off lands bring him their stories, dreams and desires. This is a quiet, introspective, and lovely little book. I also recommend:

Goa by Kara Dalkey (Tor). Unlike Dalkey's Japanese tale above, this one was published for an adult audience—and it too is a winner. It's the story of an English apothecary thrust into an alchemical adventure in sixteenth century India. The tale is exotic, passionate, visually evocative, and a real page-turner.

Shards of Empire by Susan Shwartz (Tor). Shwartz is another author who does not skimp on historical research and detail. Her accomplished new novel is set in tenth century Byzantium.

Byzantium by Stephen R. Lawhead (Bantam). This British author's latest is about an Irish monk and the *Book of Kells* in a tale that manages to be both adventurous and scholarly.

King and Goddess by Judith Tarr (Tor). Tarr has made a name for herself with impeccably researched sagas of Egyptian history and myth. Her latest is about the female pharaoh Hatshepsut, and skillfully plotted.

The Notorious Abbess by Vera Chapman (Academy Chicago). This is a smart, sparkling adventure fantasy set during the time of the Crusades—slyly witty and entertaining.

Attila's Treasure by Stephan Grundy (Bantam Spectra). This is a dark, muscular, powerful historic fantasy about a warrior fostered to Attila the Hun.

Manchu Palaces by Jeanne Larsen (Henry Holt). Set in the Imperial Court of China's Qing Dynasty in the eighteenth century, this novel carefully stitches myth and history together into a lyrical tale.

The Minotaur Trilogy by Thomas Burnett Swann (Mathew D. Hargraves, Publisher, Seattle, WA). This is an omnibus edition of three out-of-print fantasy novels based on classical myth and history: *Cry Silver Bells*, *The Forests of Forever*, and *Day of the Minotaur*.

Arthurian Fantasy:

The best new Arthurian novel published in 1996 was *Mordred's Curse* by Ian McDowell (AvoNova)—a first novel, as it turns out, and an impressive debut by this talented writer. The book is a psychological portrait of King Arthur's tormented son, written as an "autobiography"—dark, literate and relentless. Recommended. Other Arthurian titles of note:

The Winter King by Bernard Cornwell (St. Martin's Press). This is a robust and muscular portrayal of the Arthurian mythos set against a fine historical recreation of the Dark Ages. Cornwell dazzles with historical detail in this rather brutal novel.

In a Pig's Ear by Paul Bryers (Farrar, Straus & Giroux). This dark, disturbing mainstream novel is set in a modern Europe haunted by the ghosts of World War II. Using rich mythic imagery drawn from Arthurian legends, the narrator (born in Nazi-occupied Prague) recounts his story into the ear of a pig (just as Merlin did during his time of exile and madness in the forests of Wales) while imprisoned in Berlin for a murder he cannot remember. His is a haunted, demon-driven tale, making interesting use of Arthurian material.

Merlin and Company by Alvaro Cunquiero, translated by Colin Smith (Everyman, UK). This is the first English language publication of this unusual 1955 Spanish fantasy bringing the characters of Celtic legend to Galacia, Spain.

Merlin's Harp by Anne Eliot Cromton (Penguin). This one is told from the point of view of Nimue, the ambitious young woman who ensnares the great magician himself.

Two children's series focusing on Merlin began publication in 1996—each very different, yet equally well done. *The Lost Years of Merlin* by T. A. Barron (Philomel) is the first book of a projected trilogy aimed at Young Adult readers. Barron begins his tale with a boy who mysteriously washes up on the coast of Wales, with no memory and no name. It is beautifully written, magical, and spiritual. *Passager* and *Hobby* by Jane Yolen (Harcourt Brace) are the first two books in a Merlin trilogy meant for younger Middle Grade readers. This master fantasist's portrayal of Merlin's youth is written with the lucent, rhythmic prose of a storyteller whispering in your ear. Completely enchanting.

The Chronicles of the Holy Grail edited by Mike Ashley (Carroll & Graf, Robinson Books; UK) contains the best short Arthurian fiction published in 1996. Ashley presents an impressive mix of original and reprinted stories—ones that manage to be both informative and entertaining. This volume centers on Grail legends, and contains fine stories from Tanith Lee, Phyllis Ann Karr, Brian Stableford, and Parke Godwin. (The latter is reprinted in this volume.) For other short Arthurian fiction, you might also take a look at *Return to Avalon* edited by Jennifer Roberson (DAW): nineteen tales inspired by Marion Zimmer Bradley's bestseller *The Mists of Avalon*. This volume includes nice contributions from Dave Smeds, Judith Tarr, and editor Roberson herself.

Dark Fantasy:

By "dark fantasy" I refer to tales that fall in that shifty borderland between fantasy and horror. After the Graham Joyce novel listed earlier, the best novel of this sort in 1996 was *Nadya* by Pat Murphy (Tor), an unusual werewolf tale set in mid-nineteenth century America on the western frontier. This book beautifully evokes the wild western landscape, and the deep, sensual magic of a young woman who literally runs with the wolves. Highly recommended. Also recommended:

The Vinegar Jar by Berlie Doherty (St. Martin's Press). This award-winning British author's eerie, disturbing novel weaves traditional folktales into a contemporary story about a troubled marriage and an imaginary baby.

The Tooth Fairy by Graham Joyce (Signet UK). In this dark and stylish novel an adolescent boy sees the Tooth Fairy and is haunted by its sinister presence as he grows up. It's a neat twist on this generally benign bit of fairy lore.

Dradin, in Love by Jeff VanderMeer (Buzzcity Press, Tallahassee, FL). This is a richly romantic, darkly magical novella about a missionary in a surrealistic city. It is published in a small press edition nicely illustrated by Michael Shores.

Voice of the Fire by Alan Moore (Gollancz UK). I wasn't able to get hold of a copy of Moore's new book before we went to press; but anything by this amazing British writer (known for his work in the graphic novel field) is bound to be dark—and worth picking up.

Fantasy in the Mainstream:

This was a bumper year for excellent fantasy published as mainstream fiction. In addition to the Ansa, Grant, Márquez and Véa books listed above, here's a guide to what else you can find if you prowl the mainstream shelves:

Martin Dressler: A Tale of an American Dreamer by Steven Millhauser (Crown). Set in late-nineteenth-century New York, this is the tale of a shopkeeper's son and his rise to fame and fortune, filled with all those wonderful Millhauser tropes: conjurerers, charlatans, waxworks, clairvoyants, vampires, castles, enchanted forests. The novel goes in both mundane and phantasmagorical directions at the same time. Highly recommended.

The Hotel in the Jungle by Albert J. Geurard (Baskerville). A magical mystery novel set in southern Mexico, this is the tale of a strange hotel buried deep in the jungle, and of the people whose lives intersect there over a span of a century. Recommended.

The History of Danish Dreams by Peter Høeg, translated by Barbara Haveland (The Harvill Press/Panther). Due to the international popularity of this Danish writer's recent work (*Borderliners, Smilla's Sense of Snow*), Høeg's fascinating early novel is now available in English translation. The author brilliantly weaves folklore and myth into an exploration of Danish culture in the twentieth century. Also available from The Harvill Press: Høeg's *The Woman and the Ape*, translated by Barbara Haveland. This is a weirdly charming morality tale about a woman and an ape who elope to the wilderness. Both books are recommended.

Pfitz by Andrew Crumey (Dedalus). A wonderfully strange post-modern fantasy about an imaginary city created by an obsessive eighteenth-century prince. This slyly witty and erudite book, from one of Scotland's finest young writers, ponders the nature of fiction and fact, fantasy and reality. Recommended.

Exquisite Corpse by Robert Irwin (Dedalus). A dizzying, funny, wicked little novel about love and madness among the English surrealists. Recommended.

The Experience of the Night by Marcel Bélu, translated by Christine Donougher (Dedalus). This French novel, first published during World War II, was something of a cult novel among the French surrealists and then a "lost" work of European literary fantasy. This new edition brings Bélu's very Gallic, kaleidoscopic tale of vision and dream back into print in the English language.

The Manuscript Found in Saragossa by Jan Potocki, translated by Ian MacLean (Penguin). Stories within stories of cabalists and phantoms wandering about eighteenth-century Europe. The book was originally published in France in 1989; this is the first English translation.

The Birth of the World as We Know It; or, Teiresias by Meredith Steinbach (Northwestern University Press). A lucid post-modern novel exploring the life of the Greek seer Teiresias.

Our Lady of Babylon by John Rechy (Arcade/Little, Brown). This wacky but intriguing novel follows the adventures of an eighteenth-century mystic—and of a woman who is the incarnation of Eve, Salome, Mary Magdalene and other "famous whores" of history whom (she insists) received bad press. Here she attempts to set the record straight.

Sporting with Amaryllis by Paul West (Overlook Press). This mythic, erotic and powerful little book (by the author of *Lord Byron's Doctor*) explores creativity and sexuality in the character of John Milton.

The Solitaire Mystery by Jostein Gaarder, translated by Sarah Jane Hails (Farrar, Straus & Giroux). The new novel by the Norwegian author of *Sophie's World* is a contemporary fairy tale that chronicles the journey of a young boy from Norway to Greece . . . and the mysterious things that happen to him along the way.

Automated Alice by Jeff Noon (Crown). This is a weird but enchanting updating of Lewis Carroll's Alice—bringing the nineteenth-century heroine to a skewed version of modern Manchester. Delightful.

Dreamhouse by Alison Habens (Picador). Here's another take on *Alice in Wonderland*, by a much-lauded young British novelist. I found this surreal "Alice on acid" a bit uneven—sometimes funny, sometimes just shrill, and needlessly confusing. Maybe I'm simply too old for this one.

Veronica by Nicholas Christopher (The Dial Press). The second novel from this acclaimed American poet is pure fantasy: on a snowy Manhattan street, a man meets a mysterious woman who takes him into the world of mystics, magicians, time travellers, and a secret society called the School of Night. It's an odd one, but Christopher's novel contains some beautiful prose and imagery.

I Was Amelia Earhart by Jane Mendelsohn (Knopf). This interesting first novel reimagines the life of the famous aviator and her mysterious disappearane in 1937. It is written in the form of an autobiography narrated by Earhart herself—after her death.

The Cure for Death by Lightning by Gail Anderson-Dargatz (A Marc Jaffe Book/ Houghton Mifflin). This tale of a young woman on a remote Canadian farm during World War II reads like a northern version of *Like Water for Chocolate*, complete with recipes. Mysterious, magical, and moving. Recommended.

Fall on Your Knees by Anne-Marie Macdonald (Jonathan Cape UK). A contemporary novel with dark magic realist overtones and fairy tale themes about the nightmarish life of a family in Novia Scotia—complex, incisive, and beautifully rendered.

The Sweetheart Season by Karen Joy Fowler (Henry Holt). An author already beloved by genre readers, Karen Joy Fowler (*Sarah Canary*) may finally get the wider audience she deserves with this elegant, ghostly tale of magic realism set in small town America. Highly recommended.

Serial Killer Days by David Prill (St. Martin's Press). St. Martin's editor Gordon Van Gelder is dead-on when he says that Prill may be on his way to assuming R. A. Lafferty's fictional mantle. This is a weird, wild American fantasy about a town where the annual serial killing has become a town fair event. The story follows an eighteen-year-old girl determined to win the Scream Queen crown. This black comedy is very, very funny.

The Bear Went Over the Mountain by William Kotzwinkle (Doubleday). The unpredictable Mr. Kotzwinkle has come up with yet another iconoclastic and outrageous tale—this time the satiric story of a bear (yes, a bear) caught up in media and publishing worlds. It's a hoot.

Butterfly Weed by Donald Harington (Harvest/Harcourt Brace). This is the latest in Harington's series of folksy magic realist novels set in the Ozarks. I've liked this series in the past, but I found the central premise of this particular volume (a grown man's obsession with a 15-year-old student) to be annoying, not romantic. Be forewarned.

The Legend of Tommy Morris by Anne Kinsman Fisher (Amber-Allen Publishers, San Raphael, CA). This sweet little ghostly romance is based on the true life, and death, of a young Scottish golfer.

Canyon of Remembering by Lesley Poling-Kemps (Texas Tech University Press). A disillusioned Sante Fe artists finds ghosts and milagros in a remote old Hispanic town in the mountains to the north. The landscape is beautifully evoked in this magical tale.

Nightland by Louis Owens (Dutton). This powerful, wonderful book takes place on New Mexico ranches so well-realized you can smell the dry soil; the suspenseful story involves Cherokee myths, ghosts, and bodies falling out of the sky. Cherokee writer Louis Owens is creating a body of work that just gets better—and more magical—with every book. Highly recommended.

The Death of Bernadette Lefthand by Ron Querry (Bantam). I overlooked this one last year—and Querry's witchy murder mystery is too good to miss. Setting his story among the Apache and Navajo tribes of New Mexico and Arizona, this Choctaw writer has created a spooky, entertaining, and beautifully-crafted tale about family and heritage. Highly recommended.

Indian Killer by Sherman Alexie (Grove/Atlantic). Here's a third murder mystery with magic around the edges by a Native American writer (of the northwestern Spokane tribe). I've recommended Alexie with the highest praise in the past, so I feel I should warn you not to waste your money on this as I did. It's a racist book and clumsily written—two things that none of the huge media hype around it at the moment seems to mention. Let's hope Alexie's next one brings back the writer we loved in *The Lone Ranger and Tonto Fistfight in Heaven*.

Fantasy about God, the Devil, Jesus Christ, Angels and Saints:
There is so much "religious fantasy" this year that it makes up a category of its own. The best of these books in 1996 were the following:

The Gospel of Corax by Paul Park (Soho Press). Park's latest is a daring "apocryphal Gospel" following Christ's journey across Asia to the borders of Tibet, as narrated by a runaway slave determined to reach India, his ancestral country. Well written, well researched—and a page-turner too.

The Discovery of Heaven by Harry Mulisch, translated by Paul Vincent (Viking). This novel-of-ideas by an internationally acclaimed Dutch author is a meditation on religion, time, truth, and the history of the twentieth century—involving a gifted child and a rebel angel's plot against God himself. An erudite and impressive work.

The Life of God (as Told by Himself) by Franco Ferrucci, translated by Ferrucci and Raymond Rosenthal (University of Chicago Press). First published in Europe in 1986, this unusual Italian fantasy, written as God's autobiography, follows Him throughout history as He incarnates himself in various bodies and becomes involved with the likes of Dante, Shakespeare, and Freud.

The Devil's Mischief by Ed Marguand (Abbeville Press). In contrast to the book above, this one purports to be written by the Devil, telling his own story in words and (full color) pictures. It's an attractive small edition, with art by the likes of William Blake, Gustav Doré, Giotto and Michaelangelo joined to prose by Dante, Baudelaire, Ambrose Bierce, Vladimir Nabokov, Edgar Allan Poe and many others.

The Master and Margarita by Mikhail Bulgakov, translated by Michael Glenny (The Harvill Press/Panther). This Russian author spins a rather bizarre tale about the devil's personal appearance on the streets of modern Moscow—and the aftermath of his visitation.

The Naked Madonna by Jan Wiese, translated by Tom Geddes (The Harvill Press/ Panther). This historical mystery is a dark tale about the miraculous properties of the of the Madonna and Child altarpiece in Perugia—as recounted from a murderer's cell.

Rapture by David Sosnowski (Villard). This dry and very funny novel is about an epidemic of "angelism" (people wake up to find themselves growing wings) and how modern culture copes with it (self-help groups, militant factions, etc. Just imagine).

Bible Stories for Adults by James Morrow (Harvest/Harcourt, Brace). This collection of twelve biblical (and secular) short stories is by turns dazzling, hilarious, and unnerving. Morrow is one of the best writers working today, and this volume is a gem.

Behold the Man by Michael Moorcock (Mojo Press, Austin, TX). This is a handsome thirtieth anniversary edition of Moorcock's now-classic tale of a time-traveller who goes searching for Christ—and his astonishing discoveries. With a new foreword by Jonathan Carroll. Highly recommended.

Literary Fairy Tales:

For lovers of literary fairy tales, there were several books of interest published in 1996:

Briar Rose by Robert Coover (Grove/Atlantic). A gorgeous, highly literary meditation on the Sleeping Beauty theme, as well as on the nature of desire. Coover's novel is witty, wise, and wistful—told in prose that is dense and thorny as a briar hedge without being inaccessible. Highly recommended.

Beauty by Susan Wilson (Crown). This quietly magical and romantic novel is a contemporary retelling of Beauty and the Beast, set in an isolated house in New Hampshire. The Beast in this case is an aristocratic recluse; Beauty is the woman who has been hired to paint his portrait. It's a gently magical, quietly redemptive little book.

Angel Maker by Sara Maitland (Henry Holt). This collection gathers together the short fiction of one of the very best British writers of literary fairy tales. The volume is about evenly divided between Realist stories and Mythic/Folkloric works; the later includes powerful explorations of Greek mythology, Celtic lore, and tales from the Brothers Grimm. (Maitland's dazzling "Lady Artemis" is worth the price of the volume alone.) If you like Angela Carter and Marina Warner, then don't miss Maitland's collected tales in this handsomely packaged volume.

The Red Shoes and Other Tattered Tales by Karen Elizabeth Gordon (Dalkey Archive Press). I had high hopes for this fairy tale-infused collection by the author of *The Transitive Vampire*, a truly magical book about language. The collection got excellent reviews—yet I have to admit that it left me cold. The stories—billed as "sensual and surreal"—just seem tired, self-conscious, and insubstantial.

On the other hand, *Terrors of Earth* by Tom La Farge (Sun & Moon Press, Los Angeles, CA) weaves surreal and sensual imagery out of traditional fairy tale material with far greater success. This poetic little collection is based on old French "fabliaux," and recommended.

Briefly noted:

The following fantasy novels were bestsellers in 1996. Beloved by large numbers of readers across the country (and abroad), they deserve a mention: *The First King of Shannara* by Terry Brooks (Del Rey), *The Belgariad* by David Eddings (Del Rey), *Rise of a Merchant Prince* by Raymond E. Feist (Morrow), *Stone of Tears* by Terry Goodkind (Tor), *A Crown of Swords* by Robert Jordan (Tor), *Storm Breaking* by Mercedes Lackey (DAW), *The Silver Gryphon* by Mercedes Lackey and Larry Dixon (DAW).

In the field of science fiction there were several works with magical elements that fantasy readers should be sure to take a look at: *The War Amongst the Angels* by Michael Moorcock (Orion), *Humpty Dumpty: An Oval* by Damon Knight (Tor), *Wildside* by

Steven Gould (Tor), and *Infinite Jest* by David Foster Wallace (Little, Brown). (The latter was published as a mainstream title, but is actually a near-future alternate history novel—extraordinary in its originality, its breadth of vision, its wild humor, and its sheer love of the English language.)

Young Adult Fantasy:

The best fantasy for younger readers that crossed my desk this year was Peter S. Beagle's beautiful new book, *The Unicorn Sonata*, illustrated by Robert Rodriguez (Turner). This is a lovely tale of a magic land that lies just beyond the suburbs of modern L.A. infused with music, unicorns, and the magic of friendship. Beagle is too fine a writer to let the potential clichés of the theme get in his way (and he adds a nice Mexican touch to the story in the character of the heroine's grandmother).

For something completely different, I also recommend highly *A Midsummer's Nightmare*, the wicked new novel by British author Garry Kilworth (Bantam UK). Kilworth brings Shakespeare's fairies (Titania, Oberon, Puck, and crew) to modern England, following the fairies' progress from Sherwood Forest to the New Forest in a convoy of New Age Travellers. This is a clever, hilarious, and thoroughly enchanting tale.

The best of the rest (in addition to the Yolen and Barron "Merlin trilogies" listed above):

The Cockatrice Boys by Joan Aiken, illustrated by Jason van Hollander (Gollancz, UK). This one is about two English kids (from London and Manchester) on a remarkable train journey. This is darker than usual for Aiken, and riveting.

Cold Shoulder Road by Joan Aiken (Delacorte). This alternate-history fantasy is the eighth book in Aiken's much-loved Willoughby Chase series.

Zel by Donna Jo Napoli (Dutton). This is a dark, disturbing, and engrossing retelling of Rapunzel—handsomely packaged (cover by Stephen T. Johnson).

The Orphan's Tent by Tom De Haven (Atheneum). Dark contemporary fantasy about a young group of musicians searching for their missing singer—from Richmond, Virginia, to a sinister Otherworld.

Girl Goddess #9 by Francesca Lia Block (HarperCollins). Only a few of the nine pieces in this short story collection (by the author of *Weetzie Bat*) could be considered fantasy . . . but don't let that deter you. If you love tales that are both punky and wise, make you laugh and tug at your heart, don't miss this one.

Sabriel by Garth Nix (HarperCollins). A dark Australian fantasy about a girl who can walk in the lands of the dead. Beautifully written, and beautifully packaged (cover by Leo and Diane Dillon).

Zoe Rising by Pam Conrad (HarperCollins). This sequel to *Stonewords* is a quietly powerful, ghostly tale about a girl called back to another time . . . and coping with difficulties in her own.

The Moorchild by Eloise McGraw (Simon & Schuster/McElderry). This tale about a half-human, half-fairy child is fey, lyrical and lovely.

Book of Enchantments by Patricia C. Wrede (Jane Yolen Books/Harcourt Brace). This is a short story collection from an author who has a devoted following among both children and adult fantasy readers. There are some real gems in this book, including "Cruel Sisters," reprinted elsewhere in this volume.

The Time of the Ghost by Diana Wynne Jones (Macmillan). This hilarious contemporary ghost tale is Jones at her best. It's a treat.

The Great Redwall Feast by Brian Jacques (Philomel). The ninth volume in the author's bestselling series about talking rodents. These are actually pretty damn good, and kids adore them.

The Gathering by Isobelle Carmody (Scholastic, UK). The first UK edition of this well-crafted, award-winning Australian fantasy.

The Road to Irriyan by Louise Lawrence (Collins UK). In this sequel to *Journey Through Llandor*, the straw of standard "quest" fantasy is spun into gold by Lawrence's skillful storytelling.

The Thief by Megan Whelan Turner (Greenwillow). This is also standard "quest" fantasy, but it's sprightly and a lot of fun.

Realms of the Gods by Tamora Pierce (Scholastic). This is the fourth and last of in Pierce's "Wild Magic" series, a colorful "imaginary world" fantasy whose heroine can speak with animals. This is another one kids really love.

The Monster's Legacy by Andre Norton (Simon & Schuster/Atheneum). This is a sweet little tale about an apprentice embroidery maker, packaged (by Byron Preiss Visual Publications) with beautiful illustrations by Jody A. Lee.

The Boy With Paper Wings by Susan Lowell, with art by Paul Mirocha (Milkweed Editions). This charming book about an eleven-year-old boy who builds a paper airship and then sails off on adventures comes complete with paper-folding instructions. Kids adore it.

Certain Poor Shepherds by Elizabeth Marshall Thomas (Simon & Schuster). This Christmas tale, about a sheepdog and a goat present during the birth of Christ, transcends the potentially saccharine theme and evokes a true sense of wonder.

Dread and Delight: A Century of Children's Ghost Stories, edited by Philippa Pearce (Oxford Univerisity Press, UK). This volume contains forty truly spooky ghost stories, seven of them original to this volume.

The sad news for the field of children's fantasy is that the excellent Jane Yolen Books division of Harcourt Brace has been cancelled—corporate downsizing strikes again. Harcourt Brace has now begun a new (and presumably less expensive) line of reprint paperback fantasy titles called Magic Carpet Books. For anyone who misses those old Ace MagicQuest titles, here is a similar—and very welcome—series (with a far more beautiful package), rescuing good works of children's fantasy from out-of-print oblivion. Delighted as we are with this, it in no way makes up for the loss of Yolen's line, which nurtured original works of fantasy (like Kara Dalkey's stunning *Little Sister*, listed above in Baker's Dozen Best Books of the Year.)

Magic Carpet releases for 1996: *The Walking Stones* and *The Smartest Man in Ireland* by Mollie Hunter; *The Forgotten Beasts of Eld* by Patricia A. McKillip; *The Pit Dragon Trilogy* by Jane Yolen; *River Rats* by Caroline Stevermer; The "Wizardry" series by Diane Duane; *Tomorrow's Wizard* by Patricia MacLachlan; *Knight's Wyrd* by Debra Doyle & James D. Macdonald; and *Are All the Giants Dead?* by Mary Norton (don't miss the great illustrations by Brian Froud).

Single-author Short Story Collections:
The most all-out dazzling collection of tales in 1996 was published in mainstream: *Tabloid Dreams* by Robert Olen Butler (Henry Holt). Each story in this dastardly book is a take-off on a tabloid headline . . . but this is not a gimmick or "theme" anthology, not by a long shot. Butler, a Pulitzer Prize winner, has created a cycle of contemporary tales that are by turns hilarious, disquieting, and thought-provoking. Many of them are fantasy tales, like the one reprinted elsewhere in this collection. (For anyone remotely connected to the publishing field "Women Struck by Car Turns into Nymphomaniac" is a very, very funny story indeed.) I cannot recommend this collection too highly.

The best reprint collections of the year were the Sara Maitland book mentioned above (in Literary Fairy Tales) and *Burning Your Boats: Collected Short Stories* by Angela Carter (Henry Holt). Carter was one of the most important and influential fantasists of the late 20th century; her early death a few years ago was a tragic loss. This posthumous volume brings together her wide-ranging short fiction (including adult fairy tales and surrealist work) as well as a couple of unpublished pieces that were found among her papers. The collection is introduced by Salman Rushdie, and highly recommended. I also recommend:

Unlocking the Air by Ursula K. Le Guin (HarperCollins). The eighteen stories in Le Guin's latest book could be considered mainstream fiction, or perhaps magic realism—the author herself avoids such labels and simply considers herself an western American writer. Whatever you want to call these elegant contemporary stories with magic around their edges, they're wonderful.

At the City Limits of Fate by Michael Bishop (Edgewood Press, Cambridge, MA). This is an exuberant collection of stories by a modern master of speculative fiction, handsomely packaged in a small press edition (cover painting by Rick Berry). The fifteen stories herein are reprinted from *Omni* and other magazines, as well as various anthologies. Bishop works with a variety of moods, themes, styles, locals, and classical references—demonstrating an impressive breadth of range.

Common Clay: Twenty-Odd Stories by Brian Aldiss (St. Martin's Press). This reprint collection contains a mix of SF, fantasy, and mainstream stories from another master of speculative fiction known for literary, iconoclastic work. Fantasy readers should look in particular at "A Dream of Antigone" and "Traveller, Traveller, Seek Your Wife in the Forests of This Life."

Quicker than the Eye by Ray Bradbury (Avon). This collection presents twenty-two recent stories by one of the godfathers of contemporary fantasy (author of *Something Wicked This Way Comes* and other classics). This volume includes Bradbury's hilarious "Unterseeboot Doktor," and the poignant "That Woman on the Lawn."

The Pavilion of Frozen Women by S. P. Somtow (Gollancz). This prolific, versatile writer was born in Thailand, educated in England, and now lives in America. All of these influences can be found in the range of Somtow's intoxicating stories: contemporary fantasy, dark fantasy, horror, and completely-unclassifiable works, each one a gem. The title story is worth the price of the book alone.

Other notable collections: *The Bumper Book of Lies* by Chris Bell (Myty Myn, New Zealand). This is the first published collection of tales by a British writer and musician currently living in Germany. Although a bit uneven in quality (some of these were published in small press zines and could have used more rigorous editing), at his best Bell is very, very good indeed. His work is smart, mythical, intimate, and wonderfully international in flavor. An impressive debut, and I look forward to seeing more of Bell's work. *Interior Design* by Philip Graham (Scribner). This mainstream collection contains a number of stories that cross the line into contemporary fantasy (see "Angel," reprinted in this volume). This is a beautifully textured book, and well worth seeking out for both its realist and fantasy tales. *CivilWarLand in Bad Decline* by George Saunders (Random House). Saunders is a writer with a sharp satiric bite. These black comedies set in a transformed American landscape are not for the faint of heart. *El Milagro and Other Stories* by Patricia Preciado Martin (University of Arizona Press). This is a slim collection of sparkling, joyous stories about life in a Mexican-American neighborhood. Ghosts, saints and miracles haunt these otherwise Realist tales, along with the spices of cooking and the lyrical cadences of Spanish. If you loved *Like Water for Chocolate*, this is a better book to pick up than Esquivel's own disappointing new novel. *Yolk* by Josip Novokavich (Greywolf). In this collection of bizarre contemporary folktales, a Croatian writer-in-exile explores life in his deeply troubled homeland using the diction of traditional oral stories. *The Great Shadow (and Other Stories)* by Mário de Sá Carneiro, translated by Margaret Jull Costa (Dedalus). This volume contains eight literary fantasy stories from the Portugese, evocative and unusual. *Demon and Other Tales* by Joyce Carol Oates (Necronomicon Press, West Warwick, RI). This slim chapbook edition contains seven mysterious, disquieting tales by this master of dark fantasy; illustrated by Jason Eckhardt. *Far Away & Never* by Ramsey Campbell (Necronomicon Press, West Warwick, RI). This chapbook contains seven bold fantasy tales, two of which have never seen print before. A *Spell for the Fulfillment of Desire* by Don Webb (Black Ice Books, Normal, IL). Webb's surrealist work is on the cutting edge of speculative fiction. This volume comes in an attractive slim edition from a small midwestern press. *Where They Are Hid* by Tim Powers (Charnel House, Lynbrook, NY). This attractive limited small press edition contains an inventive long story, with illustrations by the author, about a man who can jump through time. *The Book of Lost Places* by Jeff VanderMeer (Dark Regions Press, Concord, CA). Another good small press edition, collecting "the selected works" of this highly original fantasist. It's worth the price for the stories "London Burning" and "The Bone Carver's Tale" alone. *Green Monkey Dreams* by Isobelle Carmody (Viking Penguin Australia). This collection of stories comes from an award-winning writer of Young Adult fantasy novels far better known in her native Australia than on these shores. Carmody's short fiction is darkly magical, hard-hitting, and seems aimed at a more adult audience. I predict we're going to see a lot more of this writer's work in this country. Recommended. *Uncovered! Weird, Weird Stories* by Paul Jennings (Viking). This nutty collection from an Australian storyteller was published as Young Adult fiction—but don't let that deter you. I loved these stories, which are weird, yes, but also oddly moving. Jennings must be Australia's answer to Daniel Pinkwater. Recommended. *Tales from the Empty Notebook* by William Kotzwinkle (Marlowe & Co., New York, NY). Four fantasy tales, filled with the usual wonderful Kotzwinkle madness, are connected by a frame story about a magic notebook. *Tales from Watership Down* by Richard Adams (Knopf). I think you have to love Richard Adams's bestselling novel deeply in order to read these tales "about the great folk stories known to all rabbits." I expected to be charmed by them (all right, I admit it, I have a soft spot for rabbits), but I was disappointed. The appeal of these bunnies is wearing thin. *Boy in Darkness* by Mervyn Peake (Hodder Children's Books, UK). This long story about Titus Groan (from Peake's classic "Gormenghast" trilogy) was first published in 1956, and is reprinted now for the first time. *Tales of the South* by William Gilmore Simm (University of South Carolina Press, Columbia, SC). This edition brings twelve stories from this nineteenth-century Southern writer back into print. Many of the tales have strong folkloric and/or magical elements. *The Fairy Tales of Herman Hesse* by Herman Hesse, translated by Jack Zipes (Bantam). Collecting Hesse's marchen into one volume, editor/translator Zipes (a well-known folklore scholar) does an excellent job presenting this lesser-known side of Hesse's work. It's a fascinating book, particularly since many of these tales have never been translated into English before. *The Hashish Man and Other Stories* by Lord Dunsany (Manic D Press, San Francisco, CA). This is a welcome reprint collection of twenty-five classic Irish fantasy stories that have fallen out of print. *The Gifts of the Child Christ & Other Stories and Fairy Tales* by George MacDonald (Eerdmans). This thick, handsome edition collects this English clergyman's classic nineteenth-century fantasy tales, out of print for the last fifteen years. *Legally Correct Fairy Tales* by David Fisher (Warner). This book of fairy tales transformed by modern "legalese" is a cute idea . . . but nowhere near as brilliant in execution as Ian Frazier's "Coyote v. Acme" (*The New Yorker*, 1990/*The Year's Best Fantasy & Horror: Fourth Annual Collection*).

Anthologies:

The following two volumes were the best short fiction anthologies of 1996, one from the fantasy genre, and one from the mainstream:

The Sandman: Book of Dreams edited by Neil Gaiman and Edward E. Kramer (HarperPrism). This book contains nineteen original dark fantasy stories based on Gaiman's hugely popular Sandman series; it's a terrific collection, with strong stories by Gene Wolfe, Tad Williams, Susanna Clarke, and Delia Sherman. (The latter is reprinted in this volume.) The snobs among us may question whether a volume based on a comic book series could really be this good. It is. But then, so are Gaiman's comic books. . . . Trust me and check it out.

Blue Dawn, Red Earth edited by Clifford E. Trafzers (Doubleday Anchor). This gathering of original fiction by Native American writers contains quite a number of excellent stories that could be considered magic realism, mythic fiction and/or dark fantasy. I picked Gerald Vizenor's superlative Trickster tale to reprint here—but had we more room I would have happily selected stories by Kimberly M. Blaeser, Anita Endrezze, Craig S. Womack, Misha, Annie Hansen, Patricia Riley, or Richard van Camp as well. They are all among the year's very best, and the anthology as a whole is highly recommended.

I also recommend: *Modern Classics of Fantasy* edited by Gardner Dozois (St. Martin's Press). A solid reprint collection (solid in both literary quality sheer sheer size) filled with stories that haven't been anthologized to death, ranging from classics by Avram Davidson, Roger Zelazny, and L. Sprague de Camp to recent works by John Crowley, Lucius Shepard, Tanith Lee, James P. Blaylock, and Michael Swanwick. This is a great book to give to those readers who seem stuck in pre-1980s fantasy (. . . you know the ones). *Starlight 1* edited by Patrick Nielsen Hayden (Tor). This volume kicks off what promises to be an excellent anthology series featuring original stories of "science-by-god fiction, blatant fantasy, 'magic realism,' and who knows what else" (to quote its editor). There's enough fantasy work in this volume to be of interest to fantasy readers— and all of it is of high quality. I particularly recommend the contributions by Andy Duncan, Susan Palwick, Martha Soukup, and Susanna Clarke. (The latter is reprinted in this volume.) *The Resurrected Holmes* edited by Marvin Kaye (St. Martin's Press). This anthology is priceless. The editor purports to have uncovered a wealth of Sherlock Holmes tales written by a variety of authors after Conan Doyle's death—authors from Somerset Maugham and Ernest Hemingway to H. P. Lovecraft and Jack Kerouac. For fantasy readers, Lord Dunsany's contribution (actually written by Darrell Schweitzer) is pretty hilarious; I supposed you can consider the whole idea of the book a fantasy of sorts.

Other 1996 anthologies, briefly noted: *Intersections: The Sycamore Hill Anthology* edited by John Kessel, Mark L. Van Name, and Richard Butner (Tor). This is a nice collection of speculative fiction coming out of the well-known Sycamore Hill writing workshop. Of particular note to fantasy readers is Gregory Frost's fine contribution, a long historical fantasy. *Otherwere: Stories of Transformation* edited by Laura Anne Gilman and Keith R. A. DeCandido (Ace). This book explores transformations other than the standard man-into-werewolf theme. It contains fifteen original stories, including good work from Nina Kiriki Hoffman, Esther M. Friesner, and Adam-Troy Castro. *The Shimmering Door* edited by Katharine Kerr & Martin H. Greenberg (HarperPrism). Thirty-two original stories about magic-workers, includes good work from Nina Kiriki Hoffman, M. John Harrison, Gregory Feeley and Dave Smeds. *Castle Fantastic* edited by John DeChancie and Martin H. Greenberg (DAW), sixteen original fantasy tales, with Roger Zelazny's very last Amber story and other good work by Charles de Lint, and Nancy Springer. *Tarot Tales* edited by Rachel Pollack and Caitlín Matthews (Ace). This is a reprint of an anthology that didn't get the attention it deserved the first time around. Filled with magical tales built around the imagery of tarot cards, the volume contains fine work by Michael Moorcock, Gwyneth Jones, and editor Rachel Pollack herself. *Pawn of Chaos* edited by Edward E. Kramer (White Wolf). I haven't seen a copy of this one, but according to the press it contains twenty-three original tales set in the universe of Michael Moorcock's fiction, including a new story by Moorcock himself. *Fantasy Stories* edited by Mike Ashley (Robinson UK). A Young Adult anthology from England, mixing reprint and original material. I highly recommend the contributions by Garry Kilworth and Keith Taylor. (The former is reprinted in this volume.) A *Nightmare's Dozen* edited by Michael Stearns (Harcourt Brace). This Young Adult anthology falls more squarely into the dark fantasy/horror camp—but I highly recommend Nancy Springer's spooky tale and Lawrence Watt-Evans's deeply disturbing story (which you may not want to read if you're a serious cat lover).

There were two collections of "magical cat" tales in 1996. For sheer literary quality, and stories that transcend the potential limits of the theme, I highly recommend:

Twists of the Tale: An Anthology of Cat Horror edited by Ellen Datlow (Dell), containing particularly memorable fiction by Joyce Carol Oates, Stephen King, A. R. Morlan, Storm Constantine, Douglas Clegg, Nancy Kress, and Michael Marshall Smith. (The latter is reprinted in this volume.) *Catfantastic IV* edited by Andre Norton & Martin H. Greenberg (DAW), contains eighteen original feline stories, including nice work from Andre Norton herself, and Elizabeth Ann Scarborough.

For readers interested in fantasy tales with female protagonists, there were several offerings in 1996. The very best of them was *She's Fantastical: Australian Women's Speculative Fiction, Magical Realism and Fantasy* edited by Lucy Sussex and Judith Raphael Buckrich, introduced by Ursula K. Le Guin (Sybylla Feminist Press, Ross House, 247–251 Finders Lane, Melbourne 3000, Australia. This was actually released in 1995, but didn't make it to us on this side of the world until '96.) It's a varied and strong anthology, demonstrating the vitality of fantasy fiction by women Down Under. The best contributions are by Isobelle Carmody, Petrina Smith, and editor Lucy Sussex. Another strong anthology is *Sisters in Fantasy II* edited by Susan Shwartz and Martin H. Greenberg (Roc). The volume contains particularly good work from Pamela Dean and Ru Emerson, a heart-breaker of a coyote tale from Beth Meacham, and a splendid work of contemporary fantasy from Patricia A. McKillip. (The latter is reprinted in this volume.) You might also take a look at *Sword & Sorceress XIII* edited by Marion Zimmer Bradley (DAW), containing twenty-two fantasy adventure tales including good contributions by Jo Clayton and Stephanie Shaver. *Warrior Enchantresses* edited by Kathleen M. Massie-Ferch and Martin H. Greenberg (DAW), contains fifteen fantasy adventure tales; check out the stories by by Tanith Lee and William F. Wu.

Bending the Landscape edited by Nicola Griffith and Stephen Pagel (White Wolf) is an anthology of original stories exploring gender issues of various kinds. The book has a 1996 copyright, but a 1997 publication date; thus we'll review it more thoroughly in next year's volume. For now, let me just say that it's well worth taking a look at. For those interested in fantasy (and SF) on gay and lesbian themes, you might also take a look at *Swords of the Rainbow* edited by Eric Garber and Jewelle Gomez (Alyson Publications, Los Angeles, CA). Not all of the stories are of professional quality, but I can recommend the contributions by Dorothy Allison, Samuel R. Delany (a reprint), Lawrence Schimel, and Tanya Huff.

For readers interested in fantasy erotica, there were several collections published in 1996 you might want to seek out. These volumes contain some stories that are not entirely well-polished, but at least someone is making an attempt to tackle a form of prose that is notoriously difficult to write. Try: *Once Upon a Time*, a book of lesbian tales (Masquerade), *Happily Ever After*, gay fairy tales (Masquerade); and from Circlet Press (Cambridge, MA): *Erotica Vampirica* edited by Cecilia Tan; *The Beast Within: Erotic Tales of Werewolves* edited by Cecilia Tan, and *Forged Bonds: Erotic Tales of High Fantasy* edited by Cecilia Tan.

Short Fiction in the Magazines:
Now that *OMNI* magazine has gone to an on-line format, the only reliable sources for short fantasy fiction on the newstands are *Realms of Fantasy Magazine* (edited by Shawna McCarthy), *The Magazine of Fantasy & Science Fiction* (edited by Kristine Kathryn Rusch) and *Asimov's Science Fiction* (edited by Gardner Dozois)—however, very few of the stories in this volume actually came from these magazines this year. *F&SF* announced a change of editors at the end of 1996: Gordon Van Gelder (of St. Martin's Press) took over the editorial direction of this digest-size magazine as of January 1997—although due to an extensive inventory of stories it will probably be a while before we see this change reflected in the magazine itself. As a book editor, Van Gelder favors inventive and highly literate work; I anticipate good things in pages of *F&SF* to come.

In mainstream publications, there was less fantasy to be found than usual in *The New Yorker*, *Harper's*, *Playboy*, and *Esquire* (although we did choose one story from the latter), but the small press literary journals continue to be a valuable source for magic realist stories and poetry. In particular, take a look at *Conjunctions*, the "Biannual Volume of New Writing" edited by Bradford Morrow (Bard College, Annandale-on-Hudson, NY, 12504). Issue #26, "Sticks and Stones," contained magical work by Angela Carter, Rikki Ducornet, Robert Coover, and others; Issue #27 was devoted to New Caribbean Writing.

There seem to be a million-and-one small press magazines publishing fantasy, dark fantasy, and horror fiction—but all too many of them are fairly uneven in quality or downright amateurish I'm afraid. There are two that are well worth supporting (and I heartily urge you to do so): *Century* (edited by Robert K. J. Killheffer, published by Meg Hamel, P.O. Box 9270, Madison, WI, 53715–0270) and *Crank!* (edited by Bryan Cholfin, Broken Mirrors Press, P.O. Box 1110, New York, NY 10159). These are the speculative fiction field's two literary journals, publishing quality fiction in "little magazine" formats—god bless them. (*Century* ran into publishing problems in 1996, but promises to be back on schedule in 1997.) Also of note this year was volume one of *Leviathan*, an interestingly quirky journal of cutting edge fiction edited by Luke O'Grady and Jeff VanderMeer, Mule Press/The Ministry of Whimsy, P.O. Box 4248, Tallahassee, FL, 32315.

If you are interested in seeking out small press zines that publish fantasy fiction, the best of the rest are: *Marion Zimmer Bradley's Fantasy Magazine* edited by Marion Zimmer Bradley, published by Rachel E. Holmen, P.O. Box 249, Berkeley, CA, 94701; *Tomorrow* edited by Algis Budrys, Tomorrow Speculative Fiction, Box 6038, Evanston, IL, 60204 (just gone online); *The Urbanite* edited by Mark McLaughlin, Urban Legend Press, P.O. Box 4737, Davenport, IA, 52808; *The Year's Best Fantastic Fiction* edited by Rosenman & Olsen, Dark Regions Press, P.O. Box 6301, Concord, CA, 94524; *The Silver Web* edited by Ann Kennedy, Buzzcity Press, Box 38190, Tallahassee, FL, 3231); *Transversions* edited by Sally McBride and Dale L. Sprovle, Island Specialty Reports, 1019 Colville Road, Victoria, B.C., Canada, V9A 4P5; *Pirate Writings* edited by Ed McFadden, P.O. Box 329, Brightwaters, NY, 11718, and *Albedo*, Albedo One, 2 Post Road, Lusk, Co. Dublin, Ireland.

Poetry:
Alas, one rarely finds book-length sources for magical poetry; volumes like Anne Sexton's *Transformations*, Sandra Gilbert's *Blood Pressure*, or Lisel Mueller's *Waving from the Shore* are few and far between. Most fantasy, fairy tale, and mythic poems must be sought, one by one, through the pages of literary journals and mainstream collections. But here are a few 1996 volumes in which you will find more magical work than in most:

Meadowlands by Louise Glück (The Ecco Press). This Pulitzer Prize-winning poet often works with mythic and folkloric themes. In her new collection, she has turned to Greek myth for inspiration.

The Owl in the Mask of the Dreamer by John Haines (Greywolf). A newly updated and expanded edition of these beautiful, subtly mythic poems.

Conditions of Sentient Life by Bruce Boston (Gothic Press, Baton Rouge, LA). A nice chapbook edition of Boston's recent work, much of it dark fantasy, with illustrations by Margaret Ballif Simon.

In a different vein entirely, check out: *Archyology* by Don Marquis (University Press of New England). Marquis (a *New Yorker* columnist in the 1920s and '30s) is best known as the creator of Archy the philosophical cockroach—and his feline friend Mehitabel. These "lost" poems about the famous duo have been tucked away in a trunk since Marquis's death in 1937. Recently rediscovered, they've been published in a slim, delightful volume with illustrations by Ed Frascino.

Picture Books:
Children's picture books are a wonderful source of fantasy tales and some of the most magical artwork produced today. Here's a Baker's Dozen of the very best published in 1996:

Nutcracker, text by E. T. A. Hoffman, illustrations by Roberto Innocenti (Creative Editions/Harcourt Brace). Italian painter Roberto Innocenti is one of the very finest late-twentieth century book artists. His rendition of this classic tale by the nineteenth-century German writer E. T. A. Hoffman is an utterly gorgeous—a Christmas treat. (I also recommend Innocenti's *Rose Blanche*, with text by Christophe Gallaz (Creative Editions/Harcourt Brace), a haunting tale of a child in Europe during World War II.)

Tales of Mystery and Imagination, text by Edgar Allan Poe, illustrations by Gary Kelly (Creative Editions/Harcourt Brace). Gary Kelly's art work (which appears regularly in *The New Yorker* and *Rolling Stone*) is more modernist in flavor than Innocenti's (above), but equally impressive. Don't miss this dark and deliciously rendered book.

Cleo and the Coyote, text by Elizabeth Levy, illustrations by Diana Bryer (Harper-Collins). This charming tale about a city dog from Queens, New York, and a coyote from Utah is one of my very favorites of the year due to the magical paintings by Bryer, rendered in a distinctive style influenced by the Hispanic and Native folk arts of the Southwest. Highly recommended.

The Six Servants, text by the Brothers Grimm (translated by Althea Bell), illustrations by Sergei Goloshapov (North-South Books). This is a strange and mesmerizing version of a dark German fairy tale. The long, oversized format does justice to the extraordinary paintings by Goloshapov, a splendid Russian artist.

Voyage of the Basset by James Christensen (with Renwick St. James and Alan Dean Foster; The Greenwich Workshop). This is more an art or gift book than a simple picture book—published in the format that made *Dinotopia* such a commerical success. The story follows a nine-year-old girl as she sails into adventure on the H. H. S. *Basset*. The story is serviceable, but the paintings are outstanding—and a lot of fun.

Here There Be Angels, text by Jane Yolen, illustrations by David Wilgus (Harcourt Brace). In the fourth in a series (*Here There Be Dragons, Here There Be Unicorns, Here There Be Witches*), master storyteller Jane Yolen once again transcends the clichés of the subject to create a splendid collection of angelic stories and poems—with lovely, delicate black-and-white drawings by Wilgus.

Cupid and Psyche, text by M. Charlotte Craft, illustrations by K. Y. Craft (Morrow Junior Books). Kinuko Craft's jewel-like paintings of this classical myth are utterly beautiful. The painting of Psyche's reflection in the lily pond is worth of the price of the book alone.

Flowers and Fables, text by John Gruen, illustrations by Rafal Olbinski (Creative Editions/Harcourt Brace). These fourteen delicately surrealistic tales are by a writer better known as a dance critic. The tales are nice—but check out the book for Olbinski's haunting surrealistic paintings.

If, text and illustrations by Sarah Perry (The J. Paul Getty Museum/Children's Library Press). In another gorgeous, gently surrealistic book, cats have wings, frogs swallow rainbows, and whales live in outer space. Enchanting.

Favorite Norse Myths, text by Mary Pope Osborne, illustrations by Troy Howell (Scholastic). An exceptional edition of old Norse legends. Osborne's text is magical and Howell's art takes you into another time, another world.

A Treasury of Princesses, text by Shirley Climo, illustrations by Ruth Sanderson (HarperCollins). Ruth Sanderson is an artist known for her rich, highly rendered, intricately detailed work. Her latest is a lovely collection of folktales from cultures around the globe.

Sacred Places, text by Jane Yolen, illustrations by David Shannon (Harcourt Brace). A collection of poems and paintings "honoring twelve magical and holy places throughout the world". Also take a look at: *Between Earth and Sky*, text by Joseph Bruchac, illustrations by Thomas Locker (Harcourt Brace), a collection of poems and legends about Native American sacred places (by an Abenaki writer).

Other picture books, briefly noted:

Starry Messenger, text and illustrations by Peter Sis (Farrar, Straus & Giroux): a book about Galileo, his life and times; exquisite. *Monday's Troll*, poems by Jack Prelutsky, illustrations by Peter Sis (Greenwillow): a hilarious collection from this mad duo. *The Jade Horse, the Cricket and the Peach Stone*, text by Ann Tompert, illustrations by Winson Trang (Boyds Mill Press): an enchanting folktale from ancient China. *Tales from the Mabinogion*, text by Gwyn Thomas and Kevin Crossley-Holland, illustrations by Margaret Jones (The Overlook Press): the first US publication of this nicely presented edition of ancient Welsh tales (originally published by the Welsh Arts Council). *The White Goblin*, text and illustrations by Ul de Rico (Thames and Hudson): the long-awaited sequel to de Rico's popular first book, *The Rainbow Goblins*. *The Magic of Spider Woman*, text by Lois Duncan, illustrations by Shonto Begay (Scholastic): a traditional Navajo tale illustrated with spirited paintings by an accomplished Navajo book artist. *The Girl Who Lived with the Bears*, text by Barbara Diamond Goldin, illustrations by Andrew Plewes (Harcourt Brace): a nice rendition of this magical northwestern Native tale, charmingly illustrated. *Ahaiyute and Cloud Eater*, text by Vladimir Hulpach, illustrations by Mark Zawadzki (Harcourt Brace): a traditional Zuni tale from the American Southwest, with lucent illustrations by an Eastern European artist. *Mother and Daughter Tales*, text by Josephine Evetts-Secker, illustrated by Helen Cann (Abbeville Press): the mythic tales in this collection come from all around the globe. *Ever Heard of an Aardwolf?* text by Madeline Moser, illustrations by Barry Moser (Harcourt Brace): a bestiary of obscure and unusual animals with engravings by this master book artist, text by his daughter. *O Jerusalem*, poems about a city at the heart of three world religions, written by Jane Yolen, illustrated by John Thompson (The Blue Sky Press). *The Snow Queen: A Christmas Pageant*, adapted by Richard Kennedy, illustrated by Edward S. Gazi (HarperCollins): a dramatic version of Hans Christian Andersen's classic tale, beautifully adapted by Kennedy, complete with songs and dramatic advice.

Nonfiction and Folklore:

The Faces of Fantasy by Patti Perret (Tor). A collection of photographic portraits of fantasy writers across the US, England and Ireland, ranging from children's book authors like Madeleine L'Engle and Alan Garner, to genre writers like Charles de Lint and Michael Moorcock, to mainstream writers like Joyce Carol Oates and William Kotzwinkle. The book also contains a long introduction by me about the history of fantasy literature. Perret's photographic work is beautiful, and revealing.

The St. James Guide to Fantasy Writers by David Pringle (St. James Press/Gale Research, Detroit, MI). A bibliographic guide to more than four hundred writers from the seventeenth century to the present.

A *History of Reading* by Alberto Manguel (Potter). An erudite history, compendium of information, and philosophical mediation on the subject of books (by the editor of those wonderful fat *Blackwater* fantasy anthologies).

A *Spell of the Senses* by David Abram (Pantheon). This ecological and philosophical book meditates on the power of words, of stories, and the language of the land beneath our feet. I highly recommend it.

Children's Books and Their Creators, edited by Anita Silvey (Houghton Mifflin). A thorough reference source for American children's literature, with articles about books, authors and illustrators—including terrific autobiographical sketches by Lloyd Alexander, Margaret Mahy, Susan Cooper, and others.

Dreams and Wishes: Essays by Susan Cooper (Simon & Schuster/McElderry). Fourteen essays about fantasy and children's fiction by the author of the now-classic "Dark is Rising" series—as well as an interview with Cooper. This is highly recommended.

The New Arthurian Encyclopedia edited by Norris J. Lacey (Garland Publishing, New York, NY). This revised edition of *The Arthurian Encyclopedia* is a large and vastly informative reference volume—a guide both to the ancient legends and to modern Arthurian fiction (including fantasy genre fiction). It contains some pictorial sources (in black and white) and six hundred pages of entrys. Highly recommended. *Feminist Fairy Tales* by Barbara G. Walker (HarperSanFrancisco). As a feminist and lover of fairy tales, as well as a fan of Walker's previous book, *The Women's Encyclopedia of Myths and Secrets*, I had high expectations of this beautifully packaged volume—and was disappointed. Instead of seeking out the wealth of traditional material with strong female heroines, Walker recasts more familiar tales (Snow White, Beauty and the Beast, etc.) in a fashion that comes off as heavy-handed and moralistic. Save your money and pick up one of the Angela Carter "Old Wives Fairy Tale" books instead. *Wonder Tales* edited by Marina Warner (Farrar, Straus & Giroux). This luminous collection is a must for all fairy tale lovers. It contains six "French stories of enchantment" translated by Gilbert Adair, John Ashbery, Ranjit Bolt, A. S. Byatt, and Terence Cave. Warner contributes a concise and informative introduction worth the price of the book alone. Highly recommended. *Grimm Tales*, adapted by Carol Ann Duffy (Faber & Faber). Tim Supple, Artistic Director of the Young Vic Theatre, asked Scottish poet Carol Ann Duffy to retell several classic Grimms' tales which he then dramatized for the stage. The resulting dramatic pieces—although ostensibly staged for children—are dark, lyrical, and powerful. Now they've been collected and published in this slim edition illustrated by Melany Still. Highly recommended.

Other nonfiction titles, briefly noted: *Inventing Wonderland* by Jackie Wullschläger (Simon & Schuster/Free Press). A critical examination of Victorian childhood as seen through the works of Lewis Carroll, J. M. Barrie, Edward Lear and others. *Blake* by Peter Ackroyd (Knopf). A thorough, insightful look at this mystical eighteenth-century poet's life by one of the best biographers working today. *Ash of Stars: On the Writing of Samuel R. Delany* edited by James Sallis (University of Mississippi Press, Jackson, MS). Ten critical essays about a writer who has pushed the envelope of speculative fiction writing (as well as writing about gender issues). *Myth Maker: J. R. R. Tolkien* by Anne Neimark (Harcourt Brace). A lucid biography of this English fantasist, written for children. *A Cast of Friends* by Bill Hanna and Tom Ito (Taylor). This biogaphy of a famous cartoonist (half of Hanna-Barbera Productions) offers a behind-the-scenes look at the Hollywood cartoon industry. *The Munchkins of Oz* by Stephen Cox (Cumberland House, Nashville, TN). A weirdly fascinating book about midgets and munchkins in the 1938 movie *The Wizard of Oz.* This book contains over three hundred photographs, interviews with living munchkins, and all kinds of Oz trivia. *Behind the Crystal Ball* by Anthony Aveni (Random House). A history of magic and the occult from antiquity to modern times (and the modern "New Age" movement) by a professor of astronomy and anthropology. *King Arthur: A Casebook* edited by Edward Donald (Garland Publishing, New York, NY). A scholarly look at Arthurian legends (including literary renditions) in sixteen essays. *The Knight of Two Swords* translated by Ross G. Arthur and Noel L. Corbett (University Press of Florida). This is the first English translation of this "lost" thirteenth-century French epic, a fascinating addition to the body of Arthurian legend extant today. This edition includes notes and commentary by the translators, both prominent medievalists. *Old Norse Images of Women* by Jenny Jochens (University of Pennsylvania Press). Explores the women of the mythic lore shared by peoples in Germany, Great Britain, Scandinavia, and Iceland from AD 500 to 1500. *Celtic Women: Women in Celtic Society and Literature* by Peter Berresford Ellis (Eerdmans). Explores the lore and cultural status of Celtic women in Great Britain and Brittany. Ellis's text is both scholarly and highly readable. You might also take a look at *Land of Women* by Lisa M. Bitel (Cornell University Press), an exploration of medieval Irish women. *Little Folk: Stories from Around the World* by Paul Robert Walker (Harcourt Brace). A charming children's collection of tales from Japan, Denmark, Hawaii, and other sources, with illustrations by James Bernardin. *The Living World of Faery* by R. J. Stewart (Gothic Image Publications, Glastonbury, UK). A very New Age approach to faery lore, complete with step-by-step instructions for rituals with which to summon them, written in exceedingly purple prose. Much of the book is really quite loony—yet it contains some good folkloric information and charming anecdotes of faery sightings in old Britain. *The Art of the Turkish Tale, Vols. I & II* by Barbara K. Walker (Texas Tech University Press). A collection of over one hundred Turkish folktales, with a foreword by Talat Sait Halman. *Ukranian Folk-tales* retold by Christina Oparenko (Oxford University Press). A nice edition of traditional tales from the Ukraine, part of the Oxford Myths and Legends Series. *The Wonder Child and Other Jewish Fairy Tales* selected and retold by Howard Schwartz and Barbara Rush (HarperCollins). Magical Jewish tales from Europe and the Middle East. *Mysterious Tales of Japan*, retold by Rafe Martin, illustrated by Tatsuro Kiuchi (G. P. Putnam). This is a very beautiful edition of ten haunting tales, plus notes. Kiuchi's artwork is exquisite. *Daily Life of the Egyptian Gods* by Dimitri Meeks and Christine Favard-Meeks, translated by G. H. Goshgarian (Cornell University Press). An excellent book translated from its 1993 French edition. *The Dancing Palm Tree* by Barbara K. Walker (Texas Tech University Press). A reissue of this award-winning book of eleven Nigerian folktales, illustrated by Helen Siegl. *The World of Spirits and Ancestors* by Elizabeth Skidmore Sasser (Texas Tech University Press). This beautiful book examines traditional art, culture, and the entwined roles of ceremony and creativity in the tribal life of Sub-Sahara West Africa. *The Spirits Speak* by Nicky Arden (Henry Holt). A vivid account of one white African woman's training as a sangoma, which are shamans (mostly female) and healers in traditional Zulu society. Arden's study of native medicine traditions is insightful and free of New-Age-ism. *The Children Who Sleep by the River* by Debbie Taylor (Interlink Publishing, Northampton, MA). A poetic account of the lives of black women in rural Zimbabwe, where magical lore is woven into the fabric of life. *Kabloona: Among the Inuit* by Gontran de Poncins (Greywolf). A fascinating look at traditional Inuit life, culture and folklore; beautifully written. *Tales of*

Native America by Edward W. Huffsteler (Friedman/Fairfax Publishers: "Myths of the World" Series). This handsome oversized volume provides an excellent introduction to the varied traditions of Native American myths and legends. Beautifully illustrated with many photographs and full-color art, this book is highly recommended. *Bury Me Standing: The Gypsies and Their Journey* by Isabel Fonesca (Vintage). A colorful, thoroughly fascinating account of the life of European Gypsies by a New York journalist who has spent a great deal of time in Eastern Europe. Highly recommended. *A Desert Bestiary* by Gregory McNamee (Johnson Books). Folklore, literature and ecological thought from the world's dry places, modelled on medieval bestiaries. *Beasts and Saints*, translated by Helen Waddell, edited by Esther de Waal (Eerdmans). Stories of animals and saints drawn from medieval sources.

Art Books:

Myth, Magic and Mystery: One Hundred Years of Children's Book Illustration by Trinkett Clark and H. Nichols B. Clark, with an introductory essay by Michael Patrick Hearn (Roberts Rinehart Publishers, Boulder, CO). This excellent full-color volume contains over two hundred pages of illustrations (from Walter Crane and Arthur Rackham to Trina Schart Hyman and Gennady Spirin), as well as a lengthy, informative text. Highly recommended.

Strange Stains and Mysterious Smells is the latest art book by the extraordinary British artist Brian Froud (the madman behind *Lady Cottington's Pressed Fairy Book*), along with hilarious text provided, once again, by Monty Python's Terry Jones (Simon & Schuster). Froud gives faery form to all those mysterious creatures that plague our lives: steal our socks, grow in the back of the 'fridge and plague our dreams at night. This is a highly original and wonderful book, utterly endearing. *Faeries*, Froud's most famous book, illustrated in collaboration with Alan Lee, is now finally back in print again too (from Bantam)—a book that has influenced a whole generation of artists, writers and filmmakers in the fantasy field. Also available in 1996: *The Goblin Companion: A Field Guide to Goblins* by Brian Froud and Terry Jones (Turner)—a funny, magical, charming little volume of sketches, field notes, and goblin sightings. All three Froud titles are recommended highly.

Maxfield Parrish: A Retrospective by Laurence S. Cutler and Judy Goffman Cutler (Pomegranate Press). A compendium of the life's work of this major American illustrator, this is a beautifully produced volume with over 130 color plates (including never-before-published works), as well as black-and-white illustrations and historical photographs. The artist's granddaughter, Joanna Maxfield Parrish, has contributed an essay to the book, and the Cutlers (of the American Illustrators Gallery in New York) provide a thorough, informative text. Highly recommended.

Spectrum III: The Best in Contemporary Fantastic Art edited by Cathy Burnett, Arnie Fenner, and Jim Loehr (Underwood Books, Grass Valley, CA). This is an annual compilation volume of works judged to be outstanding in the field of the fantastic arts (from among those specifically submitted to the volume by artists and publishers), published in an oversized trade paperback, full-color edition. The jury for this year's volume was: Garry Ruddell, Bill Nelson, Mike Mignola, Terri Czeczko, Jill Bauman, Denis Kitchen, and Harlan Ellison. This year leaned more heavily to science fiction works than fantasy, but one could still find some good magical illustration and fine art in the volume by Kinuko Y. Craft, Mel Odom, James Warhola, John Jude Palencar, Rick Berry, and others. For artists aspiring to work in the commercial field of fantasy book illustration, this volume is indispensable.

21st World Fantasy Convention Program Book, edited by the World Fantasy Award Committee (The Baltimore Gun Club, Baltimore, MD). This publication, distributed at the 1995 World Fantasy Convention, contains an impressive full-color portfolio section of thirty works by the Artist Guest of Honor, Boston painter Rick Berry, with an appreciation by Phil Hale.

A *Christmas Carol* by Charles Dickens (MCE Publishing). This lavishly illustrated new edition of Dickens's ghostly tale is published with forty-five "lost" engravings by Gustav Doré, as well as one hundred and fifty other Victorian illustrations.

Charles Rennie Mackintosh edited by Wendy Kaplan (Abbeville Press). This Glaswegian architect/designer, in partnership with his equally talented wife, was at the forefront of the Scottish Art Nouveau movement at the turn of the century—a movement that often incorporated the themes of folklore and fantasy. This lavish, full-color publication is a catalogue of the Mackintosh retrospective recently exhibited at the Metropolitan Museum of Art in New York.

Dorothea Tanning by Jean Christophe Bailly (George Braziller, Publisher, New York, NY). This is the first comprehensive overview of the fantastical work of this important American surrealist artist. Her work is strange, disturbing, fascinating.

The World of Edward Gorey by Clifford Ross and Karen Wilkin (Abrams). This is a lavish and handsome book about a marvelous strange and fascinating artist.

Music Releases of Note:
Traditional folk music is of interest to many fantasy lovers because the old folk ballads (particularly in the Celtic tradition) are often based on the same folk-or fairy-tale roots as many fantasy stories. Contemporary "world music" working with traditional rhythms is the musical equivalent to mythic fantasy stories: these creative artists (musicians and writers alike) are updating ancient folkloric themes for a modern age.

My favorite release of the year is by a musician who could have stepped straight from the streets of Borderland: Ashley MacIsaac, a brilliant, punky Scottish fiddle player whose new release, *Hi, how are you today?* (A&M Records), is wild and infectious. Cherish the Ladies, a terrific Irish band of women musicians, released *New Day is Dawning* (Green Linnet). Also from Ireland, Arcady's *Many Happy Returns* is a completely gorgeous CD of tunes and songs (Shanachie). Brother is a band from Down Under mixing celtic music with Australian didg, and vocals that sound like a cross between Not Drowning, Waving, and Crosby, Stills, Nash & Young; their new release is *Black Stone Tramp* (Rhubarb Records). For fans of the Celtic harp, *Gan Ainm* is a lovely release that comes from Canada, Sheila White on flutes, Joanne Meis on harps (White Mice Music). *When Juniper Sleeps* is a stunningly beautiful CD of instrumental music by the talented Seamus Eagan from Ireland (Shanachie). Equally stunning, although very different, is *Stor Amhran*, mystical songs sung in ancient Irish by the Gaelic soprano Noirin Ni Riain (Sounds True Audio). The lively new release from Ireland's Patrick Street is *All in Good Time* (featuring the band's strong original line-up once again, from Green Linnet). Also available from Green Linnet: *A Heart Made of Glass* from the Irish singer/guitarist Daithi Sproule; *Skin and Bone*, British roots music from two masters: Martin Carthy and Dave Swarbrick; and *Mad World Blues*, passionate, unique British roots music from Peter Morton.

Two CDs I just can't stop playing this year, with very different moods indeed, are Anonymous Four's *Voices of Light*, and *Vasos Vacios* by Los Fabulosos Cadillacs. The first is Richard Einhorn's Oratorio inspired by the film *The Passion of Joan of Arc*—an absolutely sublime piece of music beautifully performed (Sony Classical). The second is a combination of Latin rock-and-roll infused with ancient hispanic rhythms—the kind of music you can't possibly listen to and stay sitting down (Sony Latin). I also recommend *Songs of the Spirit* highly, an excellent compilation of contemporary Native American music by R. Carlos Nakai, Coyote Oldman, Joanne Shenandoah and others (Triloka Records). R. Carlos Nakai (a Navajo/Ute flute player) has also joined up with Peter Kater in *Improvisations*, a recording of a spirited live performance (Silver Wave Records). Also from Silver Wave: *Matriarch: Iroquois Women's Songs* sung by Joanne Shenandoah; *Warrior Magician* by the magical flute player Robert Mirabal; *Aras*, the new release from Curandera, mixing Flamenco and Indian traditions in one dynamic recording; *Hand Woven*, Celtic harp music and chants from Lorin Grean; and *Track to Bumbliwa*, a bizarre and enchanting musical journey to the heart of Australia by Tom Wasinger and Jim Harvey. I also recommend *Nights of Passage* by Mariam—slightly on the New Age side but still pretty powerful, using world music to explore the initiation rites of many cultures (Silver Wave). On another note entirely, don't miss *Harp of Wild and Dreamlike Strain* by British harpist Elizabeth Jane Baudry—a collection of lost nineteenth-century "fairy" music for the harp (available in this country through the Sylvia Woods Harp Center, CA; phone: (818) 956-1363).

Charles de Lint is a fantasy writer whose books are richly infused with music, and also a professional Celtic musician (with the Canadian band Jump at the Sun). Here are his picks for 1996: "This year's top Celtic/Worldbeat album has to be Scotland's Shooglenifty's *A Whiskey Kiss* (Greentrax), their brilliant follow-up to 1994's *Venus in Tweed*. It's a mix of acoustic and electric instruments playing traditional and original music, and I haven't been able to get it off my player all year. 1996 also saw a live recording from the band Live at Selwyn Hall, *Box* (Womad Select), but good as it is, it can't hold a candle to *A Whiskey Kiss*. In a similar vein are *Mellowosity* by the Peatbog Faeries (Greentrax) and *March, Strathspey, & Surreal* by the Simon Thoumire Three (Green Linnet). The most fascinating mixture of musical genres this year came from a co-operative billing themselves as Afro Celt Sound System. Their first album, *Sound Music* (RealWorld), features Celtic and African musicians singing and playing traditional instruments against an industrial trance-dance backdrop.

"In the United States, the two outstanding traditional albums were . . . *Like Magic* by piper Todd Denman and fiddler Bill Dennehy (Aniar Music), which has all the fire and spirit of the early Bothy Band, and Solas's self-titled album (Shanachie) featuring the gorgeous vocals of Karan Casey and the inimitable skills of multi-instrumentalist Seamus Egan. In Canada, duo Loretto Reid and Brian Taheny released a second album this year: *Celtic Mettle* (Reta Ceol Productions) is again mostly made up of original material written in a traditional vein, only this time the performances are far more adventurous, including everything from step-dancing and electric guitars to scat singing. And lastly, what might be the most eclectic traditional release of the year: Ashley MacIsaac's *Hi, how are you today?* (A&M) which takes Cape Breton music from its traditional setting and thrusts into the worlds of heavy metal, rap and industrial dance. Although originally released in 1995, it didn't really break until this year, which also saw the release—for the more purist among us—of *fine, thank you very much* (A&M), an album of traditional music on fiddle, back with piano and guitar."

Literary Conventions and Conferences:
The World Fantasy Convention (an annual professional gathering of writers, illustrators, publishers, and readers of both fantasy and horror fiction) was held in Schaumburg, Illinois this year, October 31–November 3. The Guests of Honor were authors Katherine Kurtz and Joe R. Lansdale; artist Ron Walotsky; editor Ellen Asher; and toastmaster, author Brian Lumley. The World Fantasy Awards were presented at the convention. Winners (for work published in 1995) were as follows: *The Prestige* by Christopher Priest for Best Novel; "Radio Waves" by Michael Swanwick for Best Novella; "The Grass Princess" by Gwyneth Jones for Best Short Fiction; *The Penguin Book of Modern Fantasy by Women* edited by A. Susan Williams and Richard Glyn Jones, for Best Anthology; *Seven Tales and a Fable* by Gwyneth Jones for Best Collection; Gahan Wilson for Best Artist; editor Richard Evans for Special Award—Professional; Necronomicon Press pub-

lisher Marc Michaud for Special Award—Non-Professional; Gene Wolfe for Life Achievement. Judges for the awards were Bryan Cholfin, Kathryn Cramer, Moshe Feder, Roz Kaveney, and Christopher Schelling. For information on the next World Fantasy Convention, to be held in London, England, October 31-November 2, 1997, write: Box 31, Whitby, North Yorkshire, YO2 4YL, United Kingdom.

The Fourth Street Fantasy Convention (an annual literary convention devoted specifically to fantasy) was not held this year. But the show will go on next year; for information on the 1997 convention write: David Dyer-Bennet, 4242 Minnehaha Avenue S., Minneapolis, MN 55406.

Mythcon (a scholarly convention sponsored by the Mythopoeic Society and devoted to fantasy) was held July 26–29 at the University of Colorado in Boulder, Colorado. The Guests of Honor were Ted Nasmith and Doris T. Myers. The 1996 Mythopoeic Awards were presented July 28; winners were as follows: Adult Literature: *Waking the Moon* by Elizabeth Hand; Children's Literature: *The Crown of Dalemark* by Diana Wynne Jones; Scholarship Award/Inkling Studies: Wayne G. Hammond and Christina Scull for *J. R. R. Tolkien, Artist & Illustrator*; Scholarship Award/Myth and Fantasy Studies: Marina Warner for *From the Beast to the Blonde: Fairy Tales and Their Tellers*. Next year's awards will be announced at Mythcon '97, to be held in Los Angeles, August 8–11, 1997. For information write: Dr. Michael Collings, Humanities/Fine Art Division, Pepperdine University, Malibu, CA 90263.

The Seventeeth International Conference on the Fantastic in the Arts was held in Fort Lauderdale, Florida March 20–24. Guest of honor was Greg Bear, Guest scholar was Tom Shippey, Robert Holdstock special guest author, film guest was Scott MacQueen, art guest was Sarah Clemens, and Brian Aldiss was present in his post as permanant special guest. For information on the conference, write: IAFA, College of Humanities, 500 NW 20th, HU-50 B9, Florida Atlantic U., Boca Raton, FL 33431.

That's a brief look at the year in fantasy fiction, art and music—now on to the stories themselves.

As usual, there are stories (particularly lengthy ones) that we are unable to include even in a volume as fat as this one. I consider the following tales to be among the year's very best, and urge you to seek them out:

In alphabetical order. . . .

Peter S. Beagle's lovely "The Last Song of Sirit Byar" from *Space Opera*.

Suzy McKee Charnas's luscious "Beauty and the Opéra or the Phantom Beast" in *Asimov's Science Fiction*, March issue.

Robert Coover's wonderfully baroque "Briar Rose" in *Conjuctions 26: Sticks and Stones*.

Gregory Frost's delightful historical fantasy "That Blissful Height" in *Intersections: The Sycamore Hill Anthology*.

I hope you will enjoy the stories and poems that follow as much as I did. Many thanks to the authors, agents, and publishers who allowed us to reprint them here.

—T. W.
Devon/New York/Tucson
1996–1997

Summation 1996: Horror
by Ellen Datlow

This anthology series is now ten years old. When Terri and I edited the first volume we were covering 1987. Horror was just beginning to boom and book publishers were starting up horror lines. Tappan King, T. E. D. Klein's successor at *Twilight Zone Magazine* (after the short tenure of Michael Blaine) had been at the helm a full year. *The Horror Show*, edited by David B. Silva, was publishing early work by A. R. Morlan, Poppy Z. Brite, and Bentley Little. Splatterpunk was starting to hit its peak. The Horror Writers of America was incorporated. An air of optimism was apparent in the field. The only sour note was the death of *Night Cry*, *TZ*'s sister magazine edited by Alan Rodgers, after barely being given a chance at success.

Since then HWA has been renamed the Horror Writers Association in order to acknowledge the organization's international character and the organization itself has undergone as much chaos, animosity, and changes as the one it was modeled on, Science Fiction Writers of America. Splatterpunk, a term made up almost as a joke by a few young writers with no specific agenda, was embraced and taken up as a rallying cry by other writers who should have known better, creating a self-defeating and dangerous schism between certain "kinds" of horror writing, by being exclusive rather than inclusive.

The demise of *Twilight Zone* in 1989 rang alarm bells, but the fact is that there has always been a dearth of professional magazine markets for horror fiction. Even ten years ago the best markets for short fiction were anthologies rather than magazines. Was there ever an abundance of horror magazines? Certainly, in the past ten years there have been many small press ventures that lasted a few issues, then went under. But short horror fiction has always popped up in the oddest places. After all, Shirley Jackson's classic "The Lottery" was first published in *The New Yorker*, and *Playboy* magazine regularly published Robert Bloch, Charles Beaumont, Ray Russell, and Richard Matheson. I know, because one of my favorite anthologies as a child was *The Playboy Book of Horror and the Supernatural* and I still have my much reread, dogeared copy. A good deal of Harlan Ellison's short fiction over the years has been horror and was often published in men's magazines. Today, anthologies (reprint and original) are still where you'll find the best short horror.

My horror selections are not meant to be representative of the state of the field or to cover the full range of horror subgenres. (For example, if I don't love any of the ghost stories I've read during the year I won't pick one just for the sake of publishing a ghost story.) But I do try to give a feel for what's going on in the field in my overview of the year. Plain and simply, the stories I've chosen are those I feel are the best of the year. How do I define best?

Smooth, powerful writing with arresting images and believable characters grab me initially, but other things keep me reading. In horror, I judge a story effective if it follows through on its initial premise, particularly if it's supernatural—I think it's harder to write an effective "logical" supernatural horror story than a psychological horror story because most readers have to suspend their disbelief. This, in my opinion, is why so few supernatural horror novels work. The long form is incredibly difficult to pull off.

Most supernatural novels fail because of the "idiot" plot—i.e., the characters behave in a manner that is unbelievable as it ensures their destruction and is merely a way to further the plot. If characters ignore things that point to danger, if they don't leave when they can, if they go somewhere that no one in their right mind would go, etc., it's difficult for the reader to ignore the fact that she's reading a horror novel. So it's especially crucial to give characters good reasons for their behavior.

Some of the stories I have chosen are of the short sharp shock type, others gain power on their rereading. And what I judge worthy to put in the the *Year's Best* must have another element—not just one that causes discomfort, unease, terror, and, occasionally, repulsion, but one that on a deeper level, stays with me and disturbs me and continues to disturb. Generally, the story must have a resonance and must hold up over several readings because by the time I make my choices I have read each story I'm considering at least twice.

Based on what I've chosen, I think you'll find there's still lots of excellent short fiction out there. And it's useful to look outside the genre labels, particularly for some of the best longer horror. I agree with Douglas E. Winter's definition of horror as an emotion rather than a genre. Which is why non-supernatural material is as important to the field as is supernatural. Horror fiction feeds on our fears. As our fears change, our tastes mutate and evolve. So of course the horror field is in flux. It should be.

News of the year:

Omni magazine went completely online after its January 1996 issue. General Media (which also owns *Penthouse*) let about seventy people go late in 1995 and early in 1996, including most of the staff of *Longevity* magazine, and most of the Greensboro, NC, *Omni* staff. By the beginning of May, the Greensboro office was closed, and *Omni* online was being run by a new editor, Pamela Weintraub. Her mandate was to create a successful online magazine—an amalgam of paper and electronic formats. The fiction area under Ellen Datlow was meant to become a hub for the science fiction, fantasy, and horror communities. The reason given for the move to electronic publishing was the rise in paper costs. *Penthouse* lost money for the first time in thirty years in 1995. *Omni* was started by Bob Guccione and his wife Kathy Keeton as a science fact/fiction magazine in October 1978 and continued monthly until 1995 when it went quarterly. General Media went online early, inspired by Keeton's optimism about the new electronic publishing.

By March it was official although there had been rumors for months: Bantam Doubleday Dell shed its Dell Magazines group, selling the assets to Penny Press, Inc., a family-owned puzzle magazine publisher based in Norwalk, Connecticut. The sale included *Asimov's Science Fiction Magazine* and *Analog Science Fiction/Fact, Ellery Queen Mystery Magazine, Alfred Hitchcock Mystery Magazine*, its crossword puzzle and horoscope magazines. The sale removed BDD from the magazine publishing business. The staff of Dell Magazines became employees of Penny Press.

After nine years, Pulphouse Publishing officially shut down. Publisher and editor Dean Wesley Smith announced the closure in February, noting that all scheduled books and magazines, including *Pulphouse: A Fiction Magazine*, would be canceled. Pulphouse Publishing produced a total of 230 books and magazines. Smith decided to pursue his writing career full-time; in addition, Smith, formerly a professional golfer, decided to prepare for the Seniors' Professional Golfing Tour (for which he'll be eligible in three years).

Tomorrow Speculative Fiction, edited by Algis Budrys, announced that it would move to electronic publication after its twenty-fourth print issue; Kristine Kathryn Rusch resigned her part-time job as editor of *The Magazine of Fantasy & Science Fiction* in order to write full-time. She held the position for six years. Gordon Van Gelder, editor at St. Martin's Press, was named to replace her as of January 1, 1997. Van Gelder continues as a full-time editor at St. Martin's but is cutting his list from approximately twenty titles a year to about twelve per year; *Into the Darkness*, published and edited by David Barnett, ceased publication indefinitely. His company Necro Publications continues to publish books. Deadline Press ceased publication of *The Scream Factory* and their book line. *Dead of Night* edited by Lin Stein suspended publication for an indefinite period of time; Senior fiction editor Michael Andre-Driussi of *Aberrations* magazine left the magazine to pursue his writing career. The magazine is continuing to publish its fiction inventory under the direction of managing editor Richard Blair; Gordon Linzner's *Space & Time* lost its financial backer, who in addition to pulling out, demanded repayment of money already spent. Linzner arranged a loan through another small press to cover current expenses. *Space & Time* is being redesigned and plans to start publishing again in 1997; *Terminal Fright* edited by Ken Abner folded after thirteen issues; the excellent cross-genre magazine *Back Brain Recluse* edited by Chris Reed will become an anthology after its twenty-third issue; *Aboriginal SF* edited by Charles Ryan is back after a two-year hiatus; *The End*, edited by Jeffrey Thomas, has been bought by Jon C. Gernon of Zero Publishing, and is scheduled to go quarterly with issue #5.

In early 1996 White Wolf Publishing laid off about fifteen people and everybody else "voluntarily" took an across-the-board 15% temporary pay cut because of a cash flow problem. White Wolf had expanded very quickly in 1995, hiring more than forty people and buying numerous properties. The cuts came primarily in the games and fulfillment departments. White Wolf originally planned to publish five books per month but officially cut back to four, and occasionally fewer. Game Designers' Workshop announced its closing; operations shut down entirely in February. Over the years GDW published a number of book tie-ins with their gaming materials, including some fiction. Wizards of the Coast cut back in January, firing over thirty people and aborting its planned publishing program (headed by former Bantam editor, Janna Silverstein); Marvel Entertainment laid off 275 people in its comics and games divisions.

In a surprise move, HarperCollins president and CEO George Craig resigned his post as of April. His replacement, Anthea Disney, a six year veteran of parent company the News Corporation, is a newcomer to book publishing. Craig's departure came after a worldwide drop of 6 million pounds sterling in HC operating profit for the six month period ending December 1994, a 24% drop in overall 1995 second-quarter earnings for the News Corporation as a whole (blamed in part on weak sales from HC), and rumors that corporation owner Rupert Murdoch was displeased with the way HarperCollins was being run; John Silbersack was promoted from vice-president, editor-in-chief of HarperPrism to Publishing Director of that imprint. He is now in charge of marketing and merchandising, as well as editorial; Amy Stout resigned as executive editor from Roc Books in April to pursue a writing career. Laura Anne Gilman, SF and fantasy editor at Ace, succeeded Stout; in August, Amy Stout was named consulting editor for Del Rey Books; Peter Mayer, who has lead Penguin for eighteen years, left the company at the end of the year to run Overlook Press, a small publishing house he founded a number of years ago with his late father. Michael Lynton, who headed Disney Publishing and most recently Disney's Hollywood Pictures unit was appointed to succeed Mayer by the Pearson Group, the parent company, at Mayer's recommendation; At the end of 1996 the Pearson Group signed an agreement to acquire the Putnam Berkley Publishing Group from MCA for $336 million in cash. The combination of the two companies will create the nation's fourth largest trade publisher, with sales in 1996 projected to be about $650 million. Under the merger, Michael Lynton became Chairman and CEO of the combined Penguin/Putnam company worldwide. Phyllis Grann, Putnam Chairman, becomes President of the combined Penguin/Putnam US operations and reports to Lynton; Thomas McCormack, CEO and Editorial Director of St. Martin's Press for 26 years, announced that he would retire January 5, 1997. He named John Sargent, 38, CEO of Dorling Kindersley Publishing, his successor, to start in October 1996; Charles Haywood, President and CEO of Little, Brown since 1991, left the company; William Morrow finally replaced Elizabeth Perle McKenna, who resigned over a year ago, as Publisher, with Paul Fedorko, who was most recently Associate Publisher and Marketing Director at Dell. He took over in mid-August as Senior Vice-President and Publisher.

Jane Yolen Books, an imprint of Harcourt, Brace & Company children's books, was discontinued. The final books in the imprint, which was started in 1990 by Yolen, will be published in 1997. Future projects by Jane Yolen Books authors will be published in the Harcourt Brace Children's Books imprint and edited by Michael Stearns; James Turner, editor/packager of Arkham House for over twenty years, was dismissed by the Derleth management after arguments about money and responsibilities. He is launching his own press, Golden Gryphon, in 1997. Arkham House Operations Manager Karen Ganser is handling day-to-day business; Zebra Books officially discontinued its horror line. Only books scheduled though April 1997 and already in the publishing pipeline will appear.

In October UK publisher Serpent's Tail announced the December closing down of Ira Silverberg's High Risk Books imprint. Silverberg stayed on through the end of the year to help publish books under contract. The closing was "due to difficult trading conditions and excessive and unpredictable returns." High Risk published William S. Burroughs, Pagan Kennedy, Gary Indiana, Kathy Acker, and Lynn Tillman; Ira Silverberg was subsequently appointed a senior editor at Grove Atlantic; Creation Books of the United Kingdom opened a New York office in September, managed by Michele Karlsberg. Creation specializes in underground and non-mainstream film books such as *Killing for Culture*, the history of death film, *Deathtripping*, about cinema of transgression, and in quality classic erotica; Dragon's World, Ltd., best known for its Paper Tiger artbook imprint, has gone bankrupt. Its assets were taken over by Collins & Brown, with all twelve employees served "redundancy notices." Artists, authors, and most other unsecured creditors are unlikely to receive any payments against Dragon's World's debts, which totaled over 2.2 million pounds sterling. Collins & Brown can sell the company's backstock, and may issue further publications under the imprint; Creed, the horror imprint from Signet UK, was dropped.

RE/SEARCH, the avant garde publisher that covered subjects from J. G. Ballard to "Incredibly Strange Music," has folded, with the split of partners V. Vale and Andrea Juno. The backlist is still available. Juno has started a new imprint, Juno Books, with Walter Keller. And Vale has started V/Search.

Richard Evans, respected genre editor at Victor Gollancz, unexpectedly died of pneumonia after successfully fighting off a severe illness in 1994, leaving the British SF world in shock. Jo Fletcher was appointed Senior Commissioning Editor with sole responsibility for the SF, fantasy, and horror list. Humphrey Price took over the other part of Evans's responsibilities as Editorial Director of Vista, the Gollancz mass-market paperback line.

The Bram Stoker Awards were given out by the Horror Writers Association in NYC June 8th at the Warwick Hotel. The winners for superior achievement in 1995 are: Superior Achievement in a Novel: *Zombie* by Joyce Carol Oates (Dutton); Superior Achievement in First Novel: *The Safety of Unknown Cities* by Lucy Taylor (Silver Salamander Press); Superior Achievement in a Novelette or Novella: "Lunch at the Gotham Café" by Stephen King (*Dark Love*, Roc Books); Superior Achievement in a Short Story: "Chatting with Anubis" by Harlan Ellison (*Lore* #1 /*Harlan Ellison's Dream Corridors*

#4, Dark Horse Comics); Superior Achievement in a Fiction Collection: *The Panic Hand* by Jonathan Carroll (HarperCollins-UK); Superior Achievement in Nonfiction: *The Supernatural Index* by Michael Ashley and William Contento (Greenwood Press).

The Horror Writers Association is a useful organization to look into for professional and aspiring writers. For information, write to HWA Info, Robert Weinberg, P.O. Box 423, Oak Forest, IL 60452-2041.

Novels:

Celestial Dogs by Jay Russell (Robinson UK/St. Martin's Press) is the first novel of a writer who has published a couple of nasty zombie stories as J. S. Russell. Although the prologue is unnecessary (they usually are), the rest of the novel is notable for the author's sharp, colorful use of language. A former child star turned seedy private eye searches for a pimp's girlfriend, who has disappeared. The PI becomes involved in forces for GOOD and EVIL from ancient Japan. Good details of everyday life and the author seems very knowledgeable on all the dirt of Hollywood. Highly readable popcorn with some terrific writing.

The World on Blood by Jonathan Nasaw (Dutton) initially caught my attention because I liked the protagonist. In this vampire novel, the drinking of blood creates a "high" similar to other addictive drugs, and detox is the same, too. No wonder there's a Vampires Anonymous twelve-step program. But one of the vampires resents the "intervention" and vows to destroy the group. The rest of the novel follows his efforts. Unfortunately, the numerous orgies leave the reader yawning. There are some nice touches, but most of the characters are ciphers. I wanted to like this novel more than I did.

On the other hand Todd Grimson's *Stainless* (HarperPrism), another vampire novel, is more successful. Genuinely moving as well as suspenseful, it's about a female vampire and her evolving relationship with a former musician whose hands have been crippled. He is her human amanuensis. She cannot live without him or someone like him to take care of things for her in the daytime. For once, most of the characters are likable, and the book is a very satisfying read. The present tense might put the reader off initially but stick with it, it works. Highly recommended.

The Skin Palace by Jack O'Connell (Mysterious Press) is a very strange book. This third novel (I enthusiastically recommend *Box 9* and *Wireless*) starts out with a seemingly straightforward story about the film-obsessed teenage son of an eastern European gangster emigré to the US and an aimless young woman with a yen for taking photographs—and their connection to the "skin palace," a huge, ornate motion-picture palace now showing pornography. But . . . about halfway through, slowly and subtly, the landscape alters and we're in Jonathan Carroll territory, complete with a cult honoring a mysterious photographer and a "suppressed version" of Judy Garland's *Wizard of Oz*. Highly recommended for the adventurous.

The Web by Jonathan Kellerman (Bantam) is an entertaining psychological thriller tinged with horror, the tenth book of a series about psychologist/detective Alex Delaware. Delaware is offered a temporary job on a pacific island paradise by one Dr. Moreland, who requests help organizing twenty years worth of files on his work. A potent mix of government conspiracy, cannibalism, an insect zoo, and native superstitions help turn what should be a relaxing assignment into a mysterious and macabre little horror show.

The Green Mile by Stephen King (Signet) is a six-part serial novel. King brilliantly sets the time and place from the get-go—the scene is the green mile (death row) in a southern prison during the depression. A convicted rapist/murderer of two little girls is brought in. The entire series, a look back at death row during his stay there, presents characters that come alive and renders a superb sense of time and place as the story shifts between the 1930s and the 1990s. King proves again that he is one of America's major writers. Despite his fame and success he still experiments with style and content and continues to provide entertainment. Highly recommended.

Becker's Ring by Steven Martin Cohen (Crown) is a macabre police procedural/serial killer novel. An ex-convict is dumped from a car with his hands amputated, his arms surgically joined in front of him to form a loop, and his mouth sewn shut. He is just the first victim of what appears to be a vigilante who knows an awful lot about surgical techniques. As the police use computers and old-fashioned legwork to discover the perpetrator, some of the victims are persuaded to cash in on their fifteen minutes of fame doing the talk show circuit. Despite some slow spots, the book is grotesque, funny, and suspenseful.

First Love: A Gothic Tale by Joyce Carol Oates (Ecco) is a short novel, beautifully illustrated by Barry Moser, about an eleven-year-old girl who, with her mother, moves to upstate New York to stay with family. There she encounters her cousin, on leave from a seminary, and over the summer she is drawn to him. A film of unease veils the story from the start as their unhealthy relationship unfolds. Oates explores sexual obsession, psychological manipulation, masochism, religious fanaticism, adolescent fantasy, and child abuse.

The Prestige by Christopher Priest (Touchstone/Simon & Schuster UK 1995/St. Martin's Press) is an elegant work of dark fantasy by an author completely in control of his difficult material. The novel is about magic and illusion and the lifelong rivalry between two stage magicians. Highly recommended. Winner of the 1996 World Fantasy Award.

The Debt to Pleasure by John Lanchester (Henry Holt) is a first novel that is a joy to read—elegant, insidious, and compulsively readable. The unreliable narrator is obsessed with food, its history, its preparation, and its consumption. A dark mystery with recipes to die for. Highly recommended.

The End of Alice by A. M. Homes (Scribner) is a fascinating novel about the epistolary relationship initiated by a nineteen-year-old college student with a convicted pederast and murderer. The convict lives out his obsessions through the young woman's relayed tales of her own forbidden acts, creating an uneasy complicity between them. Because the story is told filtered through the mind and voice of the narrator/prisoner there is an eroticism and explicitness that is especially disturbing. The "Alice" of the title cannot help but echo Lewis Carroll's Alice, particularly because Homes uses a quote from Carroll as an epigraph. *Appendix A:* by A. M. Homes (Artspace), the companion volume to *The End of Alice*, is a strange bit of hyperfiction, in which the narrator (presumably of *Alice*) confesses the guilt he feels over his mother's death when he was nine. It's an exercise in character development by Homes with made-up FBI files, pages from the criminal's diary, samples of evidence, photographs of Alice and the narrator's own family, etc. Fascinating literary experimentation. These two books got some very negative reviews from the mainstream press when they were released. All the more reason for readers interested in horror to take a look.

Exquisite Corpse, Poppy Z. Brite's third novel, (Simon & Schuster), also focuses on sexual predators and the darker side of human sexuality. A vicious serial murderer (based on the infamous Dennis Nilsen case) escapes from English prison and flees to New Orleans, where he encounters his American soulmate. This is a love story, a book full of anger about AIDS, and a remarkably graceful depiction of really bad behavior. Brite's writing is beautiful and her prose never falters—she has complete control over her material. I was surprised at how much I liked the novel because the two story excerpts I read were unrelievedly grisly and repulsive vignettes. In hindsight, those out-of-context excisions did not do Brite's work justice. Highly recommended but beware the grisly bits.

Zod Wallop by William Browning Spencer (White Wolf) is a fine novel that I only just got to. An acclaimed author of children's books is consumed by grief at the death of his little girl and breaks down. As therapy, he writes an extremely dark book called *Zod Wallop* that he never intends to publish, and later rewrites it in a sunnier form. But the original manuscript survives and begins to influence the world through a group of fellow patients at the sanitorium where the author resided during his illness. Spencer is a marvelous fantasist, perfect for those who love Jonathan Carroll. Highly recommended.

Kink by Kathe Koja (Henry Holt) continues the author's exploration of relationships—their boundaries/obsessions and transformations. Horror readers with an open mind should enjoy the novel because even though much of it reads like mainstream there is an undercurrent of anxiety that by the last third of the book blossoms into a very dark vision. A happy, goofy couple innocently open to new experiences brings a wild card into their lives—shifting the landscape in a way they don't expect. The kink of the title has a meaning other than the obvious, which *does* manifest itself also in a type of voyeurism. But the male narrator means it to be the something special in a relationship that keeps it fresh, growing, and just different from other relationships. And there *is* a non-supernatural, non-serial killer monster in this story—a Kali/destroyer of relationships.

Brand New Cherry Flavor by Todd Grimson (HarperPrism) is the author's second novel in one year. *Brand New Cherry Flavor* takes some well-aimed pokes at Hollywood and features voodoo, zombies, sex, and drugs. The director of a small independent film is awaiting her big break. Her lover's promise to get her the assistant director's job on a major film falls through and in anger she yearns for—and gets—revenge. Big time. The book is engrossing but ultimately aggravating. The protagonist is passive, unfocused, and has no idea what she's doing. She dreams through her life, literally at times, and when is given great power squanders it. Still, it's good, dirty, nasty fun.

The 37th Mandala by Marc Laidlaw (St. Martin's Press) is an accomplished Lovecraftian novel by the author of four quirky novels, including the SF satire *Dad's Nuke* and the horrific *The Orchid Eater*. Derek Crowe has made his name "reinterpreting" occult material he stole. He doesn't take his career seriously, he's just out to make a buck. His cynical use of the thirty-seven mysterious sentient mandalas allows these beings into our world. Unfortunately, Crowe is utterly despicable and as he's most often the point of view character it's hard to root for him. A young believer swallows Crowe's line hook and all and when the mandalas find a "home" in his nonbeliever wife, the couple take to the road to seek out Crowe and his "expertise." The last forty or so pages really pop—if only the entire book were as fast-paced.

Requiem by Graham Joyce (Tor) has already won the British Fantasy Award for Best Novel of 1995 and it's not difficult to see why. A guilt-ridden British widower quits his job and flees to Jerusalem and the comfort of a woman who has been his friend for many years. Joyce uses the rich porridge of faith and beliefs focused on the city holy to three religions to create a truly multicultural haunting. A suspenseful ghost story that works.

Neverwhere by Neil Gaiman (BBC Books) is a charming dark fairy tale by the writer of the Sandman series of graphic novels. A young man on his way up the ladder of success does a good deed and his life is altered beyond his wildest dreams—or nightmares. By aiding a young girl he becomes involved in a bizarre underground London where people speak to and understand rats, encountering two cutthroats who have plied their trade for centuries and strange women, all of whom want to take his life. It's a classic quest novel imbued with Gaiman's wit and poetry. His first solo novel, it was simultaneously made into a TV series in the UK.

Lunatics by Bradley Denton (St. Martin's Press) is a complete change of pace from the author's serial killer novel, *Blackburn*. Jack, a sad widower, falls in love with Lily, a beautiful winged woman he believes is a moon goddess. He meets her monthly, and must wait for her outside naked, in the light of the full moon in order for her to find him. Their relationship and the way it affects his small group of friends make for a gentle, satirical story about the ways of men and women. Highly recommended but not horror.

Father and Son by Larry Brown (Algonquin) is a very dark mainstream novel that comes with a pedigree—both Lucius Shepard and David J. Schow recommended it independently. It takes place in Mississippi in the mid-sixties. Three years in prison on a vehicular homicide charge doesn't seem to have done the bad seed member of the Davis family any good at all. Home less than two days he's already committed theft, rape and murder, and is unable or willing to take responsiblity for any of his actions. The troubled sheriff, a man he considers his nemesis, follows in his wake, cleaning up after him. The tension increases gradually and inexorably until the inevitable blow-up occurs. Terrific storytelling, excellent, believable characterization, and a fine sense of place creates a psychological novel that horror readers should enjoy. Highly recommended.

Manhattan Nocturne by Colin Harrison (Crown) is an entertaining *noir* novel about a successful and happily married tabloid columnist tripped up by his love of a good story and for a femme fatale. The protagonist loves New York City, its dark side as well as its glitter. When a beautiful and mysterious woman tempts him both professionally and personally, he's sunk. The writing captures the rhythms of the city beautifully and there are some nice, convoluted plot moves here but I'm afraid the attraction to the selfish female creature with no morality or sense of self is unconvincing.

The Intruder by Peter Blauner (Simon & Schuster) is an engrossing thriller about a successful lawyer with a wonderful family juxtaposed with the life of a former subway motorman, who after a personal tragedy hits the skids in a spiral of drug addiction, insanity, and homelessness. The reader senses immediately that the two are bound to meet. I almost stopped reading around page 80—parts of the story were utterly depressing and I was *sure* I knew where it was going—but before I gave up I admit I started skimming, discovering that the plot had some twists I hadn't expected. So I went back and read the whole thing. And am glad I did. A nice feel for urban paranoia, good characterizations, and compassion puts it levels above the average thriller.

Novel listings:

Godmother Night by Rachel Pollack (St. Martin's Press); *Darker* by Simon Clark (Hodder & Stoughton UK); *The Burning Altar* by Frances Gordon (Headline UK); *The Last Girl* by Penelope Evans (St. Martin's Press/Dunne); *The Devil's Churn* by Kristine Kathryn Rusch (Dell); *Leanna: Possession of Woman* by Marie Kiraly (Berkley); *As One Dead* by Don Bassingthwaite and Nancy Kilpatrick (White Wolf); *Witch-Light* by Melanie Tem and Nancy Holder (Dell); *Servant of the Bones* by Anne Rice (Knopf); *Lizard Wine* by Elizabeth Engstrom (Delta); *Prototype* by Brian Hodge (Dell); *Stolen Angels* by Shaun Hutson (Little, Brown UK); *The Pillow Friend* by Lisa Tuttle (Borealis); *The Cockatrice Boys* by Joan Aiken (Tor); *Dark Cathedral* by Freda Warrington (Creed); *The Gods are Thirsty* by Tanith Lee (Overlook Press); *When the Lights Go Out* by Tanith Lee (Headline UK); *Killjoy* by Elizabeth Forrest (DAW); *Touched* by Carolyn Haines (Dutton); *Motherfuckers: The Auschwitz of Oz* by David Britton (Savoy UK)—follow-up to the banned novel *Lord Horror* of 1989; *Portent* by James Herbert (HarperPrism); *Rook* by Graham Masterton (Severn House UK); *The House That Jack Built* by Graham Masterton (Carroll & Graf); *The House on Nazareth Hill* by Ramsey Campbell (Headline UK); *Cage of Night* by Ed Gorman (Borealis/White Wolf); *Walking Wounded* by Robert

Devereaux (Dell); *Blood of Mugwump* by Doug Rice (Black Ice); *Night Calls* by Katharine Eliska Kimbriel (HarperPrism); *Desperation* by Stephen King (Viking); *The Regulators* by Richard Bachman (Dutton); *The Hanging Tree* by David Lambkin (Counterpoint); *Mirage* by F. Paul Wilson and Matthew Costello (Warner); *Bite* by Richard Laymon (Headline UK); *Supping with Panthers* by Tom Holland (Little, Brown UK); *The Tooth Fairy* by Graham Joyce (Signet UK); *Nadya* by Pat Murphy (Tor); *Santa's Twin* by Dean Koontz (HarperPrism); *The Sword of Mary* by Esther M. Friesner (White Wolf); *Spares* by Michael Marshall Smith (HarperCollins UK); *A Dozen Black Roses* by Nancy A. Collins (White Wolf); *Big Thunder* by Peter Atkins (HarperCollins UK); *In the Valley of the Shadow* by Leonard Sanders (Carroll & Graf); *The Grid* by Philip Kerr (Warner); *Blade Runner 3: Replicant Night* by K. W. Jeter (Bantam Spectra); *A Sudden Wild Magic* by Diana Wynne Jones (Gollancz UK); *Sex Crimes* by Jenefer Shute (Doubleday); *Blood* by Jay Russell (Raven-UK); *Dispossession* by Chaz Brenchley (Hodder & Stoughton); *Shadowdance* by Robin Wayne Bailey (Borealis/White Wolf); *Stiff Lips* by Anne Billson (Macmillan UK); *Madeline: After the Fall of Usher* by Marie Kiraly (Berkley); *The Darker Passions: The Picture of Dorian Gray* by Amarantha Knight (Masquerade); *The Insult* by Rupert Thomson (Knopf); *The Resurrectionist* by Thomas F. Monteleone (Warner Aspect); *Going Under* by Trevor Wright (Gollancz UK); *The Time of Feasting* by Mick Farren (Tor); *A Single Shot* by Matthew Jones (Farrar, Straus & Giroux); *Martin Dressler: A Tale of an American Dreamer* by Steven Millhauser (Crown); *Lord of the Dead* by Tom Holland (Pocket Books); *Equation for Evil* by Philip Caputo (HarperCollins); *The Cure for Death by Lightning* by Gail Anderson-Dargatz (A Marc Jaffe Book/Houghton Mifflin); *Mental Case* by James Neal Harvey (St. Martin's Press); *Cheap Ticket to Heaven* by Charlie Smith (Henry Holt); *December* by Phil Rickman (Berkley); *A Personal History of Thirst* by John Burdett (William Morrow); *False Allegations* by Andrew Vachss (Knopf); *The Judas Glass* by Michael Cadnum (Carroll & Graf); *Mind Games* by C. J. Koehler (Carroll & Graf); *Seahorse* by Graham Petrie (Soho Press); *The Siege* by Graham Petrie (Soho Press); *Crota* by Owl Goingback (Donald I. Fine); *Privileged Conversation* by Evan Hunter (Warner); *Hood* by Emma Donaghue (HarperCollins); *The King of Babylon Shall Not Come Against You* by George Garrett (Harcourt Brace); *The Returns* by Dennis Barone (Sun & Moon Press); *Dark Specter* by Michael Dibdin (Pantheon); *Beyond the Shroud* by Rick Hautala (White Wolf); *The Frog* by John Hawkes (Viking); *Marabou Stork Nightmares* by Irvine Welsh (Norton); *Acts of Revision* by Martyn Bedford (Doubleday); *The One Safe Place* by Ramsey Campbell (Tor); *Shank* by Roderick Anscombe (Hyperion); *The Poet* by Michael Connolly (Little, Brown); *Footsucker* by Geoff Nicholson (The Overlook Press); *Indian Killer* by Sherman Alexie (Grove Atlantic); *The Eternal* by Mark Chadbourne (Gollancz UK); *Dream of a Falling Eagle* by George C. Chesbro (Simon & Schuster); *The Undine* by Michael O'Rourke (HarperPaperbacks); *Serial Killer Days* by David Prill (St. Martin's Press); *Amnesiascope* by Steve Erickson (Henry Holt); *Magazine Beach* by Lewis Gannett (HarperPrism); *Mr. Bad Face* by Mark Morris (Piatkus UK); *The Guardian* by Bill Eidson (Tor); *Quantum Moon* by Denise Vitola (Ace); *Dr. Neruda's Cure for Evil* by Rafael Yglesias (Warner); *The Girl With the Botticelli Eyes* by Herbert Leiberman (St. Martin's Press); *A Gathering of Saints* by Christopher Hyde (Pocket Books); *Fearful Symmetries* by Greg Bills (Dutton); *Cause of Death* by Patricia Cornwell (Putnam); *Dark Ride* by Kent Harrington (St. Martin's Press); *Uncertainty* by Michael Larsen (Harcourt Brace).

Original Anthologies:

High Fantastic edited by Steve Rasnic Tem (Ocean View Books) is beautifully produced, with regional SF, fantasy, horror, and crossover fiction showcasing the many talented writers who live or have lived in Colorado including Edward Bryant, Lucy Taylor, Connie Willis, Robert Devereaux, Don Webb, Dan Simmons, Melanie Tem, and others. Illustrated in b&w and with an essay by Ed Bryant on the history of genre writers and writing in the state and an essay on Coloradan artists by Lee Ballantine. Limited and trade. The book is beautiful and hefty: Almost 500 pages in a slightly oversized hardcover with excellent design by Lee Ballantine. Ocean View Books, P.O. Box 102650, Denver, CO 80250.

Dante's Disciples edited by Peter Crowther and Edward E. Kramer (Borealis) contains solidly entertaining stories relating to hell. The outstanding story by Michael Bishop is only barely fantasy—it's about southern snake-handlers.

Night Screams edited by Ed Gorman and Martin H. Greenberg (Roc) is the third in the "stalkers" series. There are some very good stories here.

Night Bites edited by Victoria A. Brownworth (Seal Press) contains vampire stories by women. The best one can say is that its ethnic mix gives the book a multicultural flavor. But despite claims in the introduction, the book neither "stakes new ground" nor "expands the bounds of the genre." This is one of those "literary" anthologies that knows little of what's gone before or going on around it. The assertion by the editor that "Most vampire anthologies include only one or two stories by women" shows her ignorance.

The Hot Blood Series: Fear the Fever edited by Jeff Gelb and Michael Garrett (Pocket Books) is the best of the series in some time with mostly good, if not necessarily memorable stories including Graham Masterton's incredibly disturbing story reprinted herein.

Sisters in Fantasy 2 edited by Susan Shwartz & Martin H. Greenberg (Roc) contains some excellent darker stories.

Unusual Suspects edited by James Grady (Vintage) is the best original crime/suspense anthology I've read in several years. (It does contain two reprints.) The range of stories here proves that there is no excuse for the staleness and predictability of the long-running mystery pulps. There are contributions by Joyce Carol Oates, Jonathan Lethem, George P. Pelecanos, and Andrew Vachss among others.

Not quite as successful is *Noirotica*, edited by Thomas S. Roche (Rhinoceros). The problem in this combination original and reprint anthology of erotic crime stories is that most of the pieces read like erotic vignettes instead of stories. I find that many writers of erotica concentrate on erotic effect to the detriment of storytelling. Nonetheless *Noirotica* is entertaining, and there are some very good stories in it.

Phantoms of the Night edited by Richard Gilliam and Martin H. Greenberg (DAW) is a solid and entertaining anthology of original ghost stories.

It Came from the Drive-In edited by Norman Partridge and Martin H. Greenberg (DAW) is a clever and often amusing anthology of monster stories inspired by the type of horror movies that often played in drive-ins. A few are even horrific.

Gahan Wilson's The Ultimate Haunted House edited by Nancy A. Collins (HarperPrism/A Byron Preiss Book) is disappointing, from the surprisingly vague Gahan Wilson drawings to the stories themselves. The book doesn't match in either look or format the other "Ultimates" in the series and the Wilson connection seems tenuous. Less than two hundred pages of thirteen stories is rather thin. There are a few good stories.

Heliocentric Net edited by Lisa Jean Bothell is now a hefty one-hundred-page annual with fiction and poetry by Jessica Amanda Salmonson, Edward Lee, and other writers, most of them familiar from the small presses. There is some good fiction and some good illustration work. Bast Media, 17650 1st Avenue S. Box 291, Seattle, WA 98148.

Darkside: Horror for the Next Millennium edited by John Pelan (Darkside Press) has over 450 pages of original horror fiction by a solid roster of horror writers and an excellent frontispiece by Alan M. Clark (major typo on spine). It had a limited edition of 350 copies, but this book has some very powerful stories and should be picked up by a mainstream publisher. Darkside/Silver Salamander Press, 4128 Woodland Park Avenue N., Seattle, WA 98103.

Diagnosis: Terminal, an anthology of medical terror edited by F. Paul Wilson (Forge) is more suspense than horror. Horror readers, will, I suspect, feel a little short-changed, even though the cover gives an horrific feel to the book. The best story is a SF reprint by Ed Gorman from his 1995 collection *Cages*.

Dark Terrors 2: The Gollancz Book of Horror edited by Stephen Jones and David Sutton (Gollancz UK) is one of the few non-theme horror anthology series published and is the continuation of the venerable *Pan Book of Horror* series. Fifteen originals and three reprints, it's a solid bet for literate and chilling psychological and supernatural horror stories. The Dennis Etchison and Jay Russell stories are reprinted in this volume.

A *Nightmare's Dozen* edited by Michael Stearns with illustrations by Michael Hussar (Harcourt, Brace/Jane Yolen Books) is an excellent original young adult horror anthology.

White House Horrors edited by Martin H. Greenberg (DAW) with Ed Gorman's name on the copyright page is pretty undistinguished but has a handful of decent stories.

Monster Brigade 3000 edited by Martin Harry Greenberg and Charles Waugh (Ace) has a good selection of seven original stories and six reprints about future monsters.

Women Who Run with the Werewolves: Tales of Blood, Lust and Metamorphosis edited by Pam Keesey (Cleis) contains stories of transformation and female empowerment rather than of actual terror; some of the stories are very good.

Sons of Darkness: Tales of Men, Blood and Immortality edited by Michael Rowe and Thomas Roche (Cleis) is a solid combination original/reprint vampire anthology with gay themes. The editors have done an admirable job in keeping the erotic vignettes to a minimum.

The Dedalus Book of Polish Fantasy edited and translated by Wiesiek Powaga (Dedalus/Hippocrene) is a fascinating anthology of strange fictions, most published in English for the first time. Surreal, but not all that dark, even filled as it is with tales with the devil as a character. Only a handful of the contributors are still alive.

Miskatonic University edited by Martin H. Greenberg and Robert Weinberg (DAW) is a entertaining anthology of original stories that helps keep Lovecraft's worlds alive.

David Copperfield's Beyond Imagination created and edited by David Copperfield and Janet Berliner (HarperPrism) isn't as good as their first collaborative anthology, last year's *David Copperfield's Tales of the Impossible*, but it has a few excellent stories, including Ed Bryant's which is reprinted herein.

Twists of the Tale: An Anthology of Cat Horror edited by Ellen Datlow (Dell) contains twenty-one original stories by Lucy Taylor, A. R. Morlan, Michael Cadnum, Storm Constantine, and others and two reprints. As might be obvious from the title, cats are the focus. The Michael Marshall Smith story is reprinted here.

Lethal Kisses edited by Ellen Datlow (Orion UK) is an anthology of revenge and vengeance with orginal stories by Joyce Carol Oates, Michael Marshall Smith, Jonathan Lethem, Michael Cadnum, Thomas Tessier, Christopher Fowler, Pat Cadigan, David J. Schow, and others. Stories by A. R. Morlan and Douglas Clegg are reprinted herein.

Other Anthologies:

Dark Destiny III: Children of Dracula edited by Edward E. Kramer, is limited by its narrow focus—the White Wolf role-playing games; *Murder for Love* edited by Otto Penzler (Delacorte) is a good crime anthology with original tales by Ed McBain, Elmore Leonard, James Crumley, Mary Higgins Clark, Joyce Carol Oates, and Bobbie Ann Mason among others; *Off Limits: Tales of Alien Sex* edited by Ellen Datlow (St. Martin's Press) has SF, fantasy, and horror stories about male-female relationships. Two pieces, a poem by Neil Gaiman and a collaboration by Kathe Koja and Barry N. Malzberg have been reprinted herein; *Ghost Movies II* collected and introduced by Peter Haining (Severn House UK) reprints stories that were the basis or inspiration for classic TV productions—including stories by Dean Koontz, M. R. James, and George A. Romero; *The Time of the Vampires* edited by P. N. Elrod and Martin H. Greenberg (DAW); *Worthy Foes: Differently Abled Heroes* edited by Gary Bowen has three stories in an attractive paperback format from Obelisk Books, P.O. Box 1118, Elkton, MD 21922–1118; *The 1995 SPGA Showcase*, edited by David Barnett and Bobbi Sinha-Morey and produced by the Small Press Genre Association, is a collection of fiction, poetry, and artwork, a mixture of fantasy, science fiction, and horror; *Otherwere* edited by Laura Anne Gilman and Keith R. A. DeCandido (Ace); *Future Net* edited by Martin H. Greenberg and Larry Segriff (DAW) is mostly SF but has a dark story by Matthew Costello; *Night Terrors: Stories of Shadow and Substance* edited by Lois Duncan (Simon & Schuster Books for Young Readers) is very dark and has a fine story by Joan Aiken; *Pawns of Chaos* edited by Edward E. Kramer (White Wolf); *The Sandman: Book of Dreams* edited by Neil Gaiman and Edward E. Kramer (HarperPrism) contains stories based on various characters from Gaiman's graphic novel series of the same name. The best stories use the thematic material as a starting point from which to imagine something completely different. There are some good dark fantasies, but little feels like horror; *Leviathan, Volume One: Into the Grey* edited by Jeff VanderMeer and Luke O'Grady (Mule Press/The Ministry of Whimsy) is the first in a projected anthology series to be published every eighteen months. This first volume has some excellent cross-genre material but not much would be considered horrific. The cover art, by Alan M. Clark, is a knockout. The Ministry of Whimsy, P.O. Box 4248, Tallahassee, FL 32315; *Mexican Ghost Tales of the Southwest* by Alfred Avila (Piñata); *Seductive Spectres* edited by Amarantha Knight (Rhinoceros) contains eleven original erotic ghost stories. It includes authors John Mason Skipp, Nancy Kilpatrick and Michael A. Arnzen (not seen); *A Book of Two Halves: New Football Short Stories* edited by Nicholas Royle (Gollancz UK)—British football, that is. While mostly mainstream and veddy veddy British there are stories by some of the more interesting contemporary UK writers, including M. John Harrison, Christopher Fowler, Michael Marshall Smith, Simon Ings, Irvine Welsh, Iain Sinclair, Geoff Nicholson, and Kim Newman, among others; *Fresh Blood* edited by Mike Ripley and Maxim Jakubowski (The Do-Not Press UK) co-launches the Bloodlines imprint with this worthwhile volume of original crime stories by some of the bright new British stars of the genre. Definitely worth a look; *The Tiger Garden: A Book of Writers' Dreams* edited by Nicholas Royle (Serpent's Tale) collects dreams from Dennis Etchison, Kathy Acker, A. S. Byatt, Madison Smartt Bell, Robert Holdstock, Neil Gaiman, Joan Aiken, Ramsey Campbell, Doris Lessing, and many others. Royalties to go to Amnesty International; *Mythos Tales & Others* edited by David Wynn (Mythos Books) contains eleven original stories, two essays, and eleven poems in a Lovecraftian vein. Mythos Books, 218 Hickory Meadow Lane, Poplar Bluff, MO 63901–2160; *Year 1: A Time of Change* edited by Edward J. McFadden and Tom Piccirilli (Pirate Writings Publishing) contains original stories (mostly SF) about the first year after a major cataclysm by several writers mostly known from the small press. Pirate Writings Publishing, P.O. Box 329, Brightwaters, NY 11718.

Reprint Anthologies:
Isaac Asimov's Vampires edited by Gardner Dozois and Sheila Williams (Ace) reprints vampire stories that appeared in *Asimov's Science Fiction* and has a fine line-up by Pat Cadigan, Susan Palwick, Tanith Lee, Connie Willis, Greg Frost, and others; *Backstage Passes: An Anthology of Rock and Roll Erotica from the Pages of Blue Blood Magazine* edited by Amelia G (Rhinoceros) has an original vignette about Ghost and Steve from Poppy Z. Brite's *Lost Souls; Dinosaurs* edited by Martin H. Greenberg (Donald I. Fine) includes stories by Ray Bradbury, Arthur C. Clarke, Edward Bryant, Howard Waldrop,

Pat Cadigan, and Robert Silverberg; *Tales of Terror from Blackwood's Magazine* edited by Robert Morrison and Chris Baldick (Oxford University Press); *The Oxford Book of Twentieth Century Ghost Stories* edited by Michael Cox (Oxford University Press) states its mission as: to "show how ghost stories have successfully utilised the landscape, technologies, and consciousness of contemporary life to adapt to the modern age with imagination and flair"; *Bonescribes: Year's Best Australian Horror: 1995* edited by Bill Congreve and Robert Hood (Mirrordanse Books) is an important new entry meant to become an annual. It's an attractive perfect-bound 5"×7" size book with ten stories and a history of Australian horror by Congreve, Sean McMullen, and Steve Paulsen (based on an article in *Aurealis* in early 1995, and columns in *Bloodsongs*). The stories are reprinted from Australian magazines and anthologies, one British anthology, and one is a photo-copied story passed around to students; *Living with Ghosts: Eleven Extraordinary Tales* by Prince Michael of Greece and translated by Anthony Roberts (Norton). Owners of haunted castles and palaces of Europe tell their ghostly stories; *Scottish Ghost Stories* edited by James Robertson (Little, Brown UK); *The Vampires Hunter's Casebook* edited by Peter Haining (Little, Brown UK); *The 1996 Rhysling Anthology: The Best Science Fiction, Fantasy, and Horror Poetry of 1995* edited by David C. Kopaska-Merkel (Science Fiction Poetry Association) contains thirty-six poems; *Prize Stories 1996: The O. Henry Awards* edited by William Abrahams (Doubleday) includes Stephen King's World Fantasy Award-winning story "The Man in the Black Suit"; *Best New Horror* edited by Stephen Jones (Robinson UK/Carroll & Graf) overlapped with our own *Year's Best* on three stories and one poem. The volume contains 250,000 words of horror fiction, enabling Jones to reprint novellas occasionally. With an overview and necrology of the field; *The Year's 25 Finest Crime and Mystery Stories: Fifth Annual Edition* edited by the staff of *Mystery Scene* with an introduction by Jon L. Breen (Carroll & Graf) contains stories from such diverse sources as the anthologies *London Noir, Cat Crimes Takes a Vacation*, and *Dark Love*, the magazines *Phantasm* and *Playboy*, and one from a collection by Richard T. Chizmar; *Supernatural Sleuths* edited by Charles G. Waugh and Martin H. Greenberg (Roc) collects stories by William F. Nolan, Manly Wade Wellman, William Hope Hodgson, and Larry Niven, among others; *Ghost Stories* selected by Giles Gordon (Bloomsbury Classics UK); *New Masterpieces of Horror* edited by John Betancourt (Barnes & Noble) has stories by Peter Straub, S. P. Somtow, Connie Willis, and Joyce Carol Oates; *American Gothic Tales* edited and with an introduction by Joyce Carol Oates (Plume/Penguin) follows the links in the literature of the macabre from Nathaniel Hawthorne, Edgar Allan Poe and Herman Melville, through Anne Rice, Stephen King, and Peter Straub up to authors less familiar to readers outside of the genre field, contemporary writers such as Kathe Koja and Barry N. Malzberg, Bruce McAllister, and Nancy Etchemendy. Oates's vision encompasses stories that are indubitably science fiction as well as stories by writers either not known for or acknowledged for their macabre writing such as Ursula K. Le Guin, John Crowley, Don DeLillo, and Steven Millhauser. It contains a wonderful array of the unusual; *The Cthulhu Cycle: Thirteen Tentacles of Terror* edited by Robert M. Price (Chaosium) has four original stories and a very good cover illustration by Harry Fassl; *The Disciples of Cthulhu*, second revised edition, edited by Edward P. Berglund (Chaosium) has one original; *Cybersex: Aliens, Neurosex and Cyberorgasms* edited by Richard Glyn Jones (Carroll & Graf) has a foreword by Will Self, some dark material, and one original story by Storm Constantine; *Roald Dahl's Book of Ghost Stories* (The Noonday Press), originally published in 1983, has been reissued with Dahl's introduction telling how he came to the project; *The New Lovecraft Circle* edited by Robert M. Price (Fedogan & Bremer) follows up *Tales of the Lovecraft Mythos*, which collected stories by Lovecraft's contemporaries. The new book reprints seldom seen stories by most of the seven members of the new Lovecraft circle as defined by Lin Carter as well as by new writers such as Thomas Ligotti and Mark Rainey. Two originals. Fedogan & Bremer, Publishers, 4325 Hiawatha Avenue, #2115, Minneapolis, MN 55406; *A Treasury of Ghost Stories* edited by Kenneth Ireland (Kingfisher) contains eighteen Young Adult ghost stories by Joan Aiken, Margaret Mahy, and others; *Murder Intercontinental* edited by Cynthia Manson and Kathleen Halligan (Carroll & Graf) reprints stories from *Ellery Queen's Mystery Magazine* and *Alfred Hitchcock Mystery Magazine*. Patricia Highsmith and Ruth Rendell are among the contributors; *Classic Ghost Stories* edited by Molly Cooper (Lowell House Juvenile) is an anthology of six ghost stories by Stoker, Henry, Dickens, Wilde, and two others; *Classic Vampire Stories: Timeless Tales to Sink Your Teeth Into* edited by Molly Cooper (Lowell House Juvenile) is an anthology of six vampire stories, plus an excerpt from Bram Stoker's *Dracula*. Other contributors include F. Marion Crawford and E. F. Benson; *Virtuous Vampires* edited by Stefan R. Dziemianowicz, Robert Weinberg, and Martin H. Greenberg (Barnes & Noble) contains eighteen vampire stories by Suzy McKee Charnas, Ray Bradbury, Robert Bloch, and Roger Zelazny among others; *Rivals of Dracula* edited by Robert Weinberg, Stefan Dziemianowicz, and Martin H. Greenberg (Barnes & Noble) contains nineteen vampire stories by Dan Simmons, F. Paul Wilson, Tanith Lee among others; *100 Tiny Tales of Terror* edited by Robert Weinberg, Stefan Dziemianowicz, & Martin H. Greenberg (Barnes & Noble) contains short horror stories by Nancy A. Collins, Joe R. Lansdale, Ambrose Bierce, and others; *The Resurrected Holmes* edited by Marvin Kaye (St. Martin's Press) contains fifteen Sherlock Holmes pastiches supposedly ghostwritten by Ernest Hemingway, H. P. Lovecraft, and others; *The Giant Book of Fantasy Tales* edited by Stephen Jones and David Sutton (Magpie/Robinson Australia) is a distillation of thirty-four stories, five poems, and two articles from *Fantasy Tales'* three year incarnation as a paperback book.

Collections:

The Nightmare Factory (Raven/Carroll & Graf) is an omnibus edition of Thomas Ligotti's first three collections: *Songs of a Dead Dreamer*, *Grimscribe*, and *Noctuary* plus several unpublished and one uncollected story. Ligotti is an original with his baroque sensibility. One story is reprinted herein. Highly recommended.

Tales of the South by William Gilmore Simms (University of South Carolina Press) collects twelve nineteenth-century stories about the American South, some supernatural, most with folk tale elements. Introduction by Mary Ann Wimsatt.

Pieces of Hate by Ray Garton features more than 70,000 words of new fiction by Garton, including a short novel, *A Gift from Above*. Garton is passionate about intolerance, but too often uses a bludgeon rather than a scalpel to make his points. Limited to five-hundred signed, numbered, slipcased copies. Full-color dustjacket art by Keith Minnion; *A Fist Full of Stories (and Articles)* by Joe Lansdale is a batch of odds and ends from Lansdale's *oevvre* that he doesn't mind seeing reprinted (there are others, he asserts, that he never wants to see print again), curiosity pieces that are meant to be a "stop gap between the next novel, and what I hope will be a collection of my more recent, ambitious, and best work." Trade hardcover edition and there's also a limited edition. CD Publications, P.O. Box 190238, Burton, Michigan 48519.

Bad Intentions is the first hardcover collection of stories by Norman Partridge. The author's first collection *Mr. Fox and Other Feral Tales* won the Bram Stoker Award. Among the 25,000 words of new material is an excellent follow-up to last year's chapbook "The Bars on Satan's Jailhouse" and the title story. Limited to 500 copies signed by Partridge and Joe R. Lansdale, who wrote the introduction. Subterranean Press, P.O. Box 190106, Burton, MI 48519.

The Masterpieces of Shirley Jackson (Raven/Robinson UK) collects two of her novels, *The Haunting of Hill House* and *We Have Always Lived in the Castle* plus the collection,

The Lottery, with a lovely little introduction by Donna Tartt about Jackson, and about Bennington, Vermont, site of the original Hill House.

Minor Arcana by Diana Wynne Jones (Gollancz UK) collects seven of this fantasist's stories published over the years 1982—1995.

A signed limited 45th anniversary edition of *The Illustrated Man* by Ray Bradbury (Gauntlet Press). Limited to 500 copies with preface by Bradbury, introduction by William F. Nolan, and afterword by Ed Gorman, signed by all three. The cover art is by Bradbury. A fifty-two-copy deluxe lettered leather edition is available. *Midnight Promises* (Gauntlet Press) by Richard T. Chizmar is the first collection by the editor of *Cemetery Dance.* It contains twelve reprints, four original short stories and a new novella, and a comic adaptation of Chizmar's first published story by artist Russ Miller. Introduction by Ed Gorman and afterword by Ray Garton. Cover art by Alan M. Clark. Limited to five-hundred numbered copies signed by Chizmar, Gorman, and Garton. Chizmar is quite good at depicting the non-supernatural horrors of everyday life; also a four story chapbook (one original) by publisher Barry Hoffman called *Firefly . . . Burning Bright.* A very attractive little book with cover art and interior illustrations by Harry O. Morris. Introduction by Ronald Kelly. Limited to 350 copies, signed by Hoffman, Morris, and Kelly. Gauntlet Publications, 309 Powell Road, Springfield, PA 19064.

Ash-Tree Press has been reprinting, often in facsimile editions, an excellent series of hardcover and paperback out-of-print-classics, and occasionally new books. During 1996 Ash-Tree published *Conference with the Dead,* World Fantasy Award-winner Terry Lamsley's second collection in a beautiful hardcover edition limited to 500 copies. The striking black-and-white dust jacket was designed and illustrated by Douglas Walters. It contains four reprints and six original stories of "supernatural terror." One of the reprints, "Screens," was published in last year's volume of the *Year's Best.* Another is elsewhere in the current volume. Highly recommended; *Randall's Round* by Eleanor Scott reprints the extremely rare collection of nine supernatural tales and is especially notable for being perhaps the only collection of tales in the Jamesian mode written by a woman. Introduction by Richard Dalby, whose efforts have uncovered most of what is known of Scott. An original Douglas Walters illustration graces the cover. L. T. C. Rolt's *Sleep No More* first published in 1948, has been reissued with two stories not included in the original edition and with Rolt's essay "The Passing of the Ghost Story." Introduction by Christopher Roden; an essay by Hugh Lamb, and seven new illustrations by Paul Lowe; David Rowlands's supernatural fiction short fiction is collected in *The Executor and Other Ghost Stories; Old Man's Beard,* H. R. Wakefield's second collection (uniform with their first Wakefield title, *They Return at Evening* (OP)). Cover illustration by Paul Lowe; *Forgotten Ghosts: The Supernatural Anthologies of Hugh Lamb* edited by Barbara and Christopher Roden is a booklet that celebrates the work of ghost story anthologist Hugh Lamb. It contains five rare stories from Lamb's early anthologies, with their original notes and new ones written for this volume. Introduction by Mike Ashley, and a complete bibliography of Lamb's collections; *Ghosts in the House* by A. C. Benson and R. H. Benson gathers for the first time in one volume nineteen of the best supernatural tales of these two brothers from the famous Benson family. Also included is a rare 1913 article, "Haunted Houses" by R. H. Benson, reprinted for the first time; *The Stoneground Ghost Tales* by E. G. Swain is a collection by the vicar of the parish of Stanground from 1905 to 1916. This edition restores Swain's original text, and includes an introduction by Cardinal Cox; *A Book of Ghosts* by S. Baring-Gould was first published in 1904, and according to the publisher is one of the classic titles of the field of supernatural literature. The author's life-long fascination with myths, legends, folktales, and the supernatural culminated in *A Book of Ghosts,* which contains twenty-one stories.

The new volume uses all the original texts and adds two other supernatural tales never before published in book form. Introduction by Richard Dalby. The original illustrations by D. Murray Smiths from the 1904 edition are included with a new cover design by Douglas Walters; *The Occult Files of Francis Chard: Some Ghosts Stories by A. M. Burrage* is the second volume of Burrage's weird fiction edited by Jack Adrian. It features twenty-six stories, half of which have never appeared in book form before; Ash-Tree Press, P.O. Box 1360, Ashcroft, B.C., VOK 1AO, Canada.

Count Stanislaus Eric Stenbock: The Complete Weird Tales includes seven stories that make up *Studies of Death: Romantic Tales* (1894), translations of two tales by Balzac, plus one other reprinted weird short story. Also, a revised bibliography from Timothy d'Arch-Smith. Reproduces the format of the original, highly rare *Studies of Death*. Published as a 400-copy numbered edition by Durtro Press, a new imprint from the publishers of the Ghost Story Press. Also from Ghost Story Press comes *The White Road: the collected supernatural stories of Ron Weighell*. With thirty-three stories, four previously published in *Ghosts & Scholars*, this is the first collection of his work. Full color dustjacket and ten b&w illustrations by Nick Malloret. Limited to 400 numbered copies. Ghost Story Press, BM Wound, London WC1N 3XX, England.

Demon and Other Tales by Joyce Carol Oates is an attractive seven story chapbook illustrated by Jason Eckhardt. Tales of religious mania, madness, and the supernatural; *The Sealed Casket and Others* by Richard F. Searight, a six story, twelve poem chapbook of work in the weird/Lovecraftian vein, with an introduction by Franklyn Searight; and Hugh B. Cave's *Bitter/Sweet*, a collection of two original stories with illustrations by Jason C. Eckhardt; Necronomicon Press, P.O. Box 1304, West Warwick RI 02893.

Painfreak: Ten Stories of Pure Erotic Horror by Gerard Daniel Houarner is a powerful first collection with three reprints and seven original stories by a writer to keep an eye on. Introduction by Tom Piccirilli. Cover art by Debbie Tomasetti. The perfect bound paperback is a signed edition limited to 500 copies. Necro Publications, P.O. Box 540298, Orlando, FL 32854-0298.

Beyond the Lamplight, by Donald R. Burleson, is the first publication from Jack O'Lantern Press. The collection contains stories from 1986 up through 1995, two of which were reprinted in the *Best New Horror* series edited by Stephen Jones and Ramsey Campbell. Campbell provides an introduction. Cover and two interior illustrations by Robert H. Knox. Trade paperback. Jack 'O Lantern Press, P.O. Box 1185, Lockport, NY 14095-1185.

With Wounds Still Wet by Wayne Allen Sallee (Silver Salamander Press) with an introduction by Kathe Koja and Illustrations by H. E. Fassl. Sallee's best fiction surprises you in the way it draws you into his characters' world. Invariably they lead sad, desperate lives. And they are often damaged, emotionally and/or physically. One almost feels as if you're catching his characters in an arbitrary moment of their lives; Brian Hodge's first collection, *The Convulsion Factory* (Silver Salamander Press) has an eerily effective photographic cover art and frontispiece by Dolly Nickel and an introduction by Philip Nutman. Five originals and seven reprints; *Shadow Dreams* (Silver Salamander Press), a new collection by the talented Elizabeth Massie includes nine reprints and five original stories. Gary A. Braunbeck has written a graceful and moving introduction and Alan M. Clark has provided some eerily beautiful art for the cover and frontispiece. All three titles have been published in three editions: Deluxe leather, limited hardcover, and trade paperback editions of 500 signed but unnumbered copies. Address under anthologies.

The Great Shadow (and Other Stories) by Mário de Sá Carneiro translated from the Portugese by Margaret Jull Costa (Dedalus) by an author who committed suicide in 1916 at the age of twenty-six and left, according to the blurb, "an extraordinary body of work which dealt obsessively with the problems of identity, madness, and solitude."

Edgeworks 2 by Harlan Ellison (White Wolf) is an omnibus of the crime novel *Spider Kiss* and collection *Stalking the Nightmare* with a new introduction by Ellison. Volume 2 of 20 in "The Collected Ellison."

Quicker Than the Eye (Avon Books), Ray Bradbury's first new collection in almost a decade. Bradbury is still a dazzling magician. Some excellent darker stories, almost half original to the collection.

Ruth Rendell's *Blood Lines* (Crown) collects eleven psychological suspense stories, most published originally in *Ellery Queen Mystery Magazine.*

Dancing Fish by Michael Wilkinson, is a poetry collection from Spout, "a British publisher that exists to publish writers involved in writing workshops and projects run by the Word Hoard, the literature development agency based in the Borough of Kirklees, West Yorkshire." An excellent collection of cross-genre poetry.

Uncovered! by Paul Jennings (Viking) is the newest in this reliably entertaining series of weird and sometimes scary tales for young adults. As usual, a nice mix of the strange and bizarre with a a perfect cover illustration by Blair Dawson.

The Pavilion of Frozen Women by S. P. Somtow (Gollancz UK) collects some of this writer's best short work including the remarkable title story and "Chui Chai," each of which were chosen for a previous volume of *The Year's Best Fantasy and Horror.*

The Curious Room: Collected Dramatic Works by Angela Carter (Chatto & Windus UK) collects several unpublished plays and screenplays including reworkings of *Puss in Boots* and *Dracula*, a draft for an opera of Virginia Woolf's *Orlando*, and film scripts of *The Magic Toyshop* and *The Company of Wolves.*

Terrors of the Sea by William Hope Hodgson (Donald M. Grant, Publisher, Inc.) is a marvelous collection of unpublished and uncollected short works of fantasy and horror by the author of the classic novel *The House on the Borderland*. The cover illustration and interiors are by Ned Dameron. Designed by Thomas Canty. Edited by and with an introduction by Sam Moskowitz. A really lovely collector's item. Donald M. Grant, Publisher, Inc., 19 Surrey Lane, P.O. Box 187, Hampton Falls, NH 03844. Highly recommended.

Moonchasers and other stories by Ed Gorman (Forge) collects seventeen stories of crime, suspense, and the supernatural by this versatile writer. One original. Afterword by Dean R. Koontz.

The Mortal Immortal: The Complete Supernatural Short Stories of Mary Shelley collects five stories with an introduction by Michael Bishop in which Mary Shelley comes for a visit while he's writing the introduction. Limited trade paperback edition of 900 copies and also, a hardcover edition signed by Bishop limited to 100 copies. Tachyon Publications, 1459 18th Street, San Francisco, CA 94107.

Forms of Heaven: Three Plays by Clive Barker (HarperPrism) the follow-up volume to his first collection of plays, *Incarnation*, published last year. Introduction by Barker with production notes for each play.

The Horror in the Museum and Other Revisions by H. P. Lovecraft and Others (Carroll & Graf) collects twelve collaborations by Lovecraft with younger pulp writers.

D. G. Valdron has published several collections of his own short stories, most previously unpublished, in chapbook form under the overall series title "Dark Icons." *Bad Magic, A Solitude of Monsters* and *An Atrocity of Serial Killers* are pretty good. Badlands Press, 304-314 Broadway, Winnipeg, Manitoba R3C OS5 Canada.

Wraiths and Ringers by A. F. Kidd is a collection of ten ghost stories, most original. Self-published in the UK.

Jonathan Lethem's wonderful first collection, *The Wall of the Sky, the Wall of the Eye*, (Harcourt Brace) with two originals, shows off his unique voice and startling images; *A Dusk of Idols and Other Stories* by James Blish (Severn House UK) with an introduction by Francis Lyall; *Common Clay* by Brian Aldiss (St. Martin's Press) was published in the UK in 1995 under the title *The Secret of This Book* and contains a few original stories and some horrific work, including the controversial "Horse Meat"; Christopher Kenworthy's first collection, *Will You Hold Me?* (The Do-Not Press) has several original stories and includes "Because of Dust," which appeared in last year's volume of *The Year's Best*. Mostly mainstream with a definite edge; *Violins in the Void* by Cliff Burns collects some bits and pieces of poetry and vignettes by this Canadian writer. Black Dog Press, 1142-105th Street, North Battleford, SK S9A 1SG, Canada. Pirate Writings Publishing brought out collections by Sue Storm and Paul Di Filippo. The Storm collection *Under the Lizard Trees* is mostly fantasy and has one original story in it. The Di Filippo *Destroy All Brains!* is SF. See address under "anthologies." Several Tom Piccirilli stories are collected in *The Hanging Man and Other Strange Suspensions*. Primitive production values but good fiction. Wilder Publications, Inc., P.O. Box 707, Greenfield, MA 01302-0707; *The Book of Lost Places: The Selected Works of Jeff VanderMeer* is a nicely produced 116 page cross-genre collection by a talented young writer. Illustrations by Rodger Gerberding with an introduction by Mark Rich. Collects nine stories from various SF, fantasy, and horror magazines. Dark Regions Press, P.O. Box 6301, Concord, CA 94524; *The Bumper Book of Lies* by Chris Bell (Myty Myn New Zealand) is a collection of twenty very odd, occasionally fantastic stories including five originals. The stories were originally published in mostly UK magazines. Numbered and limited to 500 copies, and signed by the author. Nice production and an attractive hefty, little paperback of 251 pages. Chris Bell, Redderplatz 8, Haus 4, 22337 Hamburg, Germany.

Werewolves by Daniel Cohen (Cobblehill Books); *A Whisper in the Dark: Twelve Thrilling Tales* by Louisa May Alcott (Barnes & Noble) edited by Stefan Dziemianowicz, with an introduction by Susie Mee; *The Mask of Cthulhu: Horrifying Tales of the Cthulhu Mythos* by August Derleth (Carroll & Graf) collects six stories originally published by Arkham House in 1958; *Tales of Titillation and Terror* by Mel D. Adams (Mosaic Press, 85 River Rock Drive, Suite 202, Buffalo, NY 14207); *The Ghost Feeler* by Edith Wharton (Peter Owen UK/Dufour) collects nine stories of "terror and the supernatural" edited and with a critical and biographical introduction by Peter Haining; *Spectral Snow* by Jack Snow (Hungry Tiger Press, 15 Marcy Street, Bloomfield, NJ 07003-3814) is a collection of eight stories, most dark fantasy, and one "Oz" story. Illustrated by Erin Shanower; *Carmilla and Other Classic Tales of Mystery* by Sheridan Le Fanu (Penguin/Signet Classic) collects thirteen stories, edited and with a biographical/critical introduction by Leonard Wolf; *The Transition of H. P. Lovecraft: The Road to Madness* (Del Rey) collects twenty-nine horror stories, including many early or fragmentary works. Introduction by Barbara Hambly. With a beautiful/eerie cover illustration and interior illustrations by John Jude Palencar; *The Collected Ghost Stories of E. F. Benson* edited by Richard Dalby with a foreword by Joan Aiken (Carroll & Graf); *The Last Pin* by Howard Wandrei (Fedogan & Bremer Mystery) collects Wandrei's hard-boiled detective short fiction and inaugurates a new series dedicated to pulp and crossover mystery writers. Edited and introduced by D. H. Olson and illustrated by Gary Gianni. Hardcover available in a trade and a limited edition. And in conjunction with *The Last Pin*, F&B Mystery published a chapbook called *Saith the Lord*, which collects the story (on which "The Last Pin" is based) in its original version for the first time plus a letter to the author's father while he was living in New York City and some biographical material he was asked to provide to go with various story publications. One hundred copies bound and inserted into the slipcase of the limited edition of *The Last Pin*. Address earlier in this section; *Fables and Fantasies* by Brian Stableford (Necronomicon Press)— nine very short pieces with cover and interior art by Joey Zone; *Far Away & Never* collects eight fantasy stories of Ramsey Campbell (Necronomicon Press); *The Book of*

Hyperborea by Clark Ashton Smith (Necronomicon Press) collects fourteen related stories, edited by Will Murray. A substantially revised edition of *Hyperborea*, originally published by Ballantine in 1971; *Scary Stories from 1313 Wicked Way* by Craig Strickland (Lowell House Juvenile) is ten stories about a haunted house; *The Yellow Wallpaper and Other Stories* by Charlotte Perkins Gilman (Oxford University Press UK) edited and with an introduction by Robert Schulman.

Poetry Collections:
Revelations of the Hot Conquered Darling by Wayne Edwards has dark and occasionally erotic poetry. (Merrimack Books, P.O. Box 83514, Lincoln, NE 68501-3514. $3.00); *La Morte D'Amoureuse* by Tippi N. Blevins and illustrated by Chad Savage has some good dark poetry and one story; *Hunger* by David C. Kopaska-Merkel has some good dark material but the typeface makes for difficult reading (Preternatural Press, 8510 16th Street #101, Silver Spring, MD 20910. $6.50 payable to Meg Thompson); *Speaking Bones* by Denise Dumars (Dark Regions Press) collects this poet's dark fantasy poetry. Introduction by W. Gregory Stewart. Illustrations and cover by Roman Scott; *Variations of Sleeping Alone: The Selected Poetry of Herb Kauderer* (Dark Regions Press) Illustrated by Linda Michaels. Introduction by David Lunde. Both books are available in limited editions of 125 copies signed by author and artist. $4.95 payable to Dark Regions Press, P.O. Box 6301, Concord, CA 94524.

Three mostly SF collections that might be of interest to horror readers: *The Exploded Heart* from Stephen Brown's newly started Eyeball Books is the third collection by John Shirley. Beautiful and disturbing cover by Rick Berry. *The Invisible Country* (Gollancz UK), Paul McAuley's second collection, contains some material verging on the horrific such as the British Fantasy Award-winning "Temptation of Dr. Stein"; *At the City Limits of Fate* by Michael Bishop (Edgewood Press) collects fifteen stories of SF and fantasy some with horrific overtones. Another beautiful cover by Rick Berry.

Mainstream collections: *Follow Me* by Paul Griner (Random House); *Grey Area* by Will Self (Grove/Atlantic); *Coyote v. Acme* by Ian Frazier (Farrar, Straus & Giroux); *Toddler-Hunting and Other Stories* by Kono Taeko, translated by Lucy North (New Directions) collects odd Japanese stories of dark sexuality, such as S&M and child molestation—some very sharp edges; *Will You Always Love Me? and Other Stories* by Joyce Carol Oates (E. P. Dutton/A William Abrahams Book) collects this prolific author's recent work; *Traplines* by Eden Robinson (Metropolitan Books/Henry Holt) is a debut collection of four stories of violently dysfunctional families set in British Columbia, Canada; *Getting It in the Head* by Mike McCormack (Jonathan Cape UK).

Nonfiction Magazines:
The Gila Queen's Guide to Markets edited by Kathryn Ptacek continues to provide a solid listing of current markets in all genres plus news of the field, and short useful essays about writing. A subscription is $30 (12 issues) payable to Kathryn Ptacek, *Gila Queen Guide to Markets*, P.O. Box 97, Newton, NJ 07860-0097. Highly recommended.

The Heliocentric Network edited by Lisa Jean Bothell is published bimonthly. It's a useful newsletter that concentrates on the small press and has interviews, writers' tips and resources, news, and reviews, all in about sixteen pages. $12.00 a year (6 issues), $2.00 sample issue. P.O. Box 68817, Seattle, WA 98168-0817.

Scavenger's Newsletter is a long-lived resource for information about the small press. Edited by Janet Fox; $21 per year (twelve issues) payable to Janet Fox, 519 Ellinwood, Osage City, KS 66523-1329.

Necrofile: The Review of Horror Fiction is crucial for any serious reader of horror. It is the only critical magazine we have and it's a good one. Edited by Stefan Dziemianowicz, S. T. Joshi, and Michael A. Morrison. There's a regular column by Ramsey

Campbell, in-depth reviews and mini-reviews of contemporary and classic horror, and listings of British and American titles. Subscriptions to this quarterly are $12 for one year (U.S.), $15 (Canada), $17.50 (overseas). *Other Dimensions* edited by Stefan Dziemianowicz also published one issue, with an incisive article by Brian Stableford about goth music and the vampiric influence on it, an excellent analysis of the *Alien* trilogy by Scott Briggs, and other nonfiction pieces on non-print horror. $5 an issue; *Crypt of Cthulhu* edited by Robert M. Price and published by Necronomicon Press continues to be a major source of nonfiction on Lovecraft. It now publishes nonfiction exclusively. $4.50; *Studies in Weird Fiction* 18 edited by S. T. Joshi reprints three stories by Ambrose Bierce for the first time, an essay on Stephen King's novel *Christine*, a critical piece on Robert Aickman's theory of weird fiction, and two pieces on Clark Ashton Smith. $5.00. Address under "collections."

Horror: The News Magazine of the Horror and Fantasy Field is back, now published by Dark Regions Press and edited by Joe Morey and John B. Rosenman, who have taken over from John Betancourt. Interviews with King and Koontz. Some of the news items and reviews are dated, presumably awaiting publication during the transition. Hopefully, the new publisher/editors will succeed in making the magazine a viable operation, because a magazine of this type (modeled on *Locus*) is much needed by the horror community. $19 for one year (six issues). See address under "collections."

The Scream Factory: The Magazine of Horrors Past, Present, and Future, edited by Bob Morish, Peter Enfantino, and John Scoleri, is an important and always entertaining horror quarterly. The magazine covers all aspects of horror including books, soundtracks, movies, videos. There's usually at least one piece of fiction. Issue 17 is a theme issue on the British Invasion, an overview of British horror in books and film, and television. As usual, pretty thorough and quite interesting. Unfortunately the magazine and Deadline Press have ceased publication. Highly recommended—look for back issues if you can find them.

Scarlet Street: The Magazine of Mystery and Horror edited by Richard Valley is a quarterly that reached its 21st issue in winter 1996. Always looks professional and always has an attractive slick cover. This issue has a tribute to Jeremy Brett, one of the best loved Sherlock Holmeses. And there's an excellent interview with Farley Granger, much of it about his work with Hitchcock on *Strangers on a Train* and *Rope*.

Fangoria edited by Anthony Timpone is published monthly except February and December and hit its 150th issue in early 1996. It covers all the major studio horror films and is particularly good in showing gore special effects.

Filmfax: The Magazine of Unusual Film and Television edited by Michael Stein and Ted Okuda is the place to read about and see photo stills of *The Outer Limits*, Mexican monster movies, the burlesque films of pin-up Bettie Page, and articles about the people in front of the cameras and behind the scenes of the grade B's and C's. Bimonthly, the magazine has just celebrated its tenth year of publication; *Outré: The World of UltraMedia*, also from Stein and Okuda, seems to cover some of the same territory as its sister magazine. The premiere issue celebrates the career of Jayne Mansfield and has an excellent piece on horror writer Charles Beaumont. The second issue's cover story is about Walt Disney's TomorrowLand and includes a piece on Joi Lansing. In more contemporary coverage, there are articles on Hong Kong movie heroes Jackie Chan and Chow Yun-Fat.

Cinefantastique, the monthly film magazine edited by Frederick S. Clarke, generally has the most in-depth articles on films of the fantastic. E.g.: An analysis of *The Texas Chainsaw Massacre* as an inverted fairy tale, a detailed article on the making of *12 Monkeys*, and an interview with the screenwriter of *Seven*.

Psychotronic Video® edited by Michael J. Weldon is probably the most fun of the movie magazines that cover B-movie (and lesser) videos. This quarterly always has amusing covers and interviews with almost-stars of yesteryear such as Dolores Fuller (who acted in many Ed Wood films and then went on to write music). It also provides good coverage of movie books. Subscriptions are $22 in the U.S.A., $24 in Canada payable to Michael J. Weldon, Psychotronic®, 3309 Rt. 97, Narrowsburg, NY 12764-6126.

Video Watchdog: The Perfectionist's Guide to Fantastic Video edited by Tim and Donna Lucas is a *must* for the sheer entertainment of their detailed analyses of the differences among variant versions of hundreds of videos. Bimonthly, a subscription is $24 (bulkmail) or $35 (first class) payable to Video Watchdog, P.O. Box 5283, Cincinnati, OH 45205-0283.

Gauntlet: Exploring the Limits of Free Expression edited by Barry Hoffman attacks censorship and what it perceives as political correctness. The two 1996 issues contained an article about a body painter at a pagan festival who got into trouble for doing full body painting on children (with their parents' permission!) and one on how Howard Stern got into trouble with the FCC because his sex talk might be heard by children. Also, a piece on the touchy subject of statutory rape. There's also a series of articles on the witch hunts started by those purporting to protect children from abuse. Usually provocative. One year (2 issue) subscription is $18+$4 p&h payable to Gauntlet, Inc, Dept. SUB96A, 309 Powell Road, Springfield, PA 19064.

Nova Express edited by Lawrence Person is a fine, irregularly published nonfiction fanzine that concentrates mostly on science fiction. The fall/winter issue had an excellent bunch of reviews of Hong Kong cinema by Walter Jon Williams and various staff members of the zine, an article on Lovecraft by Don Webb, and reviews of several novels that could be considered dark fantasies. $12 for four issues ($16 in Canada and Mexico, $22 for International) payable to Nova Express, P.O. Box 27231, Austin TX 78755-2231. Highly recommended.

Dark's Art Parlour: The Periodical of Dark Art is up to its third issue but I've just seen it for the first time. It's an art magazine dedicated to horror. Highly recommended for anyone interested in seeing what can be done with horror art—the best work is by Kevin Rolly, Stephen Kasner, and Ross Amador. Photographic manipulation and collage art, painting, and mixed media. Issue 3 contains an excerpt from the next Tim Powers novel, *Earthquake Weather*. Subscription is $25 for six issues payable to Dark's Art Parlour, 5249 Lankershim Boulevard, North Hollywood, CA 91601.

Magazines:
Instead of mentioning artists who worked mostly in the small press under each magazine, I'm listing those I think did the best work over the year.

Alan Casey, GAK, David Grilla, Cathy Buburuz, Alex Nathan Shumate, Keith Minnion, Michael Apice, Bob Crouch, Timothy Patrick Butler, H. E. Fassl, Harry O. Morris, Richard de Lago, Rodger Gerberding, Peter H. Gilmore, Eric M. Turnmire, Randy Broecker, Liam Kemp, Russell Morgan, Martin McKenna, Alan M. Clark, Richard Corben, Jeffrey Thomas, Paul Lowe, Douglas Walters, Gary McCluskey, Andy Tubbesing, Kevin Duncan, R. M. Copley, Stacy Drum, Gerald Gaubert, John Barrick, Shelly Baki, Frank Forte, Doug Yamada, Dan Smith, Tracy Vaughn Moore, Tom Simonton, Bob E. Hobbs, Roman Scott, Michael Betancourt, Mark Wilcox, Scott Eagle, R. H. Phister, Wayne Miller, Chad Savage, Petri Sinda, Stephen M. Rainey, Frances Byer, David Lyttleton, Carl Flint, Trudi Canavan, and Robert Schoolcraft.

There was more original short horror fiction to be read than ever before and most of it was terrible. By terrible I mean badly written, with poor characterization, nonexistent or unbelievable plots, etc. In order to feel the frisson that typifies good horror, the terror, the chill, whatever, the reader must be able to relate to at least one character in the piece. I don't necessarily mean "like" a character but if the reader isn't drawn in by a believable character, forget it. It also helps to have a story to tell—not just a scene/vignette. Lillian Csernica, reviewer for *Tangent* is right on the money in her gentle dissections of individual stories in her regular column.

While there are several professional magazines that occasionally publish horror, there are none that run horror exclusively. By professional I mean those on a regular publishing schedule with professional pay rates, and a circulation of five figures or more. Most of the small press magazines mentioned below are on very erratic schedules and only a handful last longer than two years.

Cemetery Dance edited by Richard Chizmar is back after 1½ years' hiatus. One of the horror field's best fiction magazines, it was sorely missed. This issue has a heartfelt essay on what being a writer means to Charles L. Grant, along with some very good fiction. The summer issue had an excellent piece by Bob Morrish, following up on the status of various small press publishers who have been interviewed in *CD* over the past few years and how they've fared. A one year subscription (four issues) is $15 payable to CD Publications. Address under "Collections."

Deathrealm edited by Stephen Mark Rainey is the other important regularly published horror fiction magazine. The fiction is reliably readable. Issue #30 had the best fiction and poetry overall. Good regular columns and reviews, and interviews with William F. Nolan, F. Paul Wilson, Poppy Z. Brite, Clive Barker, Stephen Jones, and Tom Piccirilli. The eerie cover art on #27 by Ian McDowell was apparently cause for the magazine's censorship in Canada. $16.95 for a four issue (one year) subscription. $4.95 for a single issue, payable to Deathrealm, 2210 Wilcox Drive, Greensboro, NC 27405.

Worlds of Fantasy and Horror edited by Darrell Schweitzer is meant to be triannual but has been off schedule for quite some time. There were two issues in 1996—the first with a good splashy cover by Ian Miller and a good interview with Joe Lansdale. One contained a dynamite story by Thomas Ligotti, but unfortunately missed out on its first publication (Ligotti's collection came out first). In general, good fiction and a well-done interview with Peter Straub. $4.95 for a single issue, $16 for four issues payable to Terminus Publishing Co., Inc., 123 Crooked Lane, King of Prussia, PA 19406-2570.

Grue Magazine edited by Peggy Nadramia claims to publish three times yearly yet I've only seen one issue a year for the past couple of years (that I remember). A generally solid horror mix. You can buy the current issue (Number 18) for $5 or buy a three issue subscription for $14 ($16 Canada, $20 overseas), payable to Hell's Kitchen Productions, P.O. Box 370, Times Square Station, New York NY 10108-0370.

Phantasm edited by J. F. Gonzalez is back after a year's hiatus. It looks very good and has good fiction. This is the reborn *Iniquities* and is worthy of your support. A two-issue subscription is $6.50 and a four-issue subscription is $14.00 payable to Iniquities Publishing, 235 E. Colorado Blvd., Suite 1346, Pasadena, CA 91101.

Night Terrors, a new horror magazine edited by D. E. Davidson, is well-designed; the fiction is good but some of the art is pretty cheesy. Two issues were published in 1996 but their production schedule is not clear. A single issue is $5.00. A two-issue subscription is $9, a four-issue subscription $16 (Ohio residents add 5.75% sales tax) payable to D. E. Davidson, 1202 West Market Street, Orrville, OH 44667-1710. A magazine to watch.

Stygian Articles edited by Jeremy E. Johnson is a new one to me and worth a look. Some good art and some good fiction. A single issue is $5; $18 for a quarterly four-issue subscription, payable to Jeremy E. Johnson, 3201 Sun Lake Drive, St. Charles, MO 63301-3012.

The Silver Web edited by Ann Kennedy tries to publish semiannually. Issue 30 is billed as the "music issue" and has a fine-art portfolio by up-and-coming horror artist

Carlos Batts as well as an interview with him. A good mix of highly readable fiction. This is a cross-genre magazine that is always worthwhile. Perfect-bound magazine size with 120 pages and good production values. $12 for a one year subscription (two issues), $14 foreign, payable to *The Silver Web*, P.O. Box 38190. Tallahassee, FL 32315.

Realms of Fantasy edited by Shawna McCarthy finally began to hit its stride with the February 1996 issue with two excellent darker stories. And there was a smattering of dark fantasy/horror thereafter. The best, by Robert Silverberg, is reprinted herein. Bi-monthly. Subscription is $14.95 for six issues (one year) payable to *Realms of Fantasy*, P.O. Box 736, Mount Morris, IL 61054-8130.

Transversions edited by Dale L. Sproule and Sally McBride continues to publish a stimulating mix of SF, fantasy, and horror two to three times a year. Single issues: $4.95 (U.S. or Canadian), subscriptions: $18 (US or Canadian) for four issues, payable to *Transversions*, 1019 Colville Road, Victoria, BC Canada V9A 4PS.

Kimota edited by Graeme Hurry is an excellent little magazine published twice yearly by the UK's Preston SF Group. Single issues £2.50; four-issue subscription £9 ($23.00 surface—or $31.00 airmail with international money order) payable to Graeme Hurry, 52 Cadley Causeway, Preston, PR2 3RX, England.

Phantoms edited by W. J. Johnson has teeny tiny type that's barely readable, some literate fiction, weird facts, reviews, and good design sense. Bi-monthly, a single issue is £2.80 or six issues for £16 payable to Phantoms, 91 Peartree Road, Derby PE23 6QB, England.

Talebones: Fiction on the Dark Edge edited by Patrick J. Swenson debuted in October 1995 but I only started seeing copies in early 1996. It's a quarterly with good production values including some very good interior art and good cover art on the fall issue. Good fiction by newer writers including some experimental and cross-genre stylists. $16.00 yearly, payable to Fairwood Press, 10531 SE 250th Place, H 104, Kent WA 98031.

Squane's Journal edited by Simon Wady is an excellent fanzine from England. The second issue (first I saw) had two excerpts from novels by Mark Morris and Peter James, one original story, two interviews and an overview of Mark Morris's fiction. £2.50 check payable to S. Wady, 209 Beacon Road, Chatham, Kent ME5 7BU, England.

The Third Alternative edited by Andy Cox is one of the best of the cross-genre quarterlies with generally excellent art on the covers and interiors and interesting, if occasionally opaque, fiction. The magazine has been running a series of profiles of writers such as Joyce Carol Oates, Jeanette Winterson, Poppy Z. Brite, and Geoff Ryman. $22.00 for four issues or $6.00 an issue payable to TTA Press, 5 Martins Lane, Witcham, Ely, Cambs CB6 2LB England.

Skin Tomb edited by Rod Williams hails from Australia. Although only published annually now, this mix of nonfiction and fiction gives an excellent overview of the horror scene from a different perspective with reviews of movies, books, small press magazines, etc. And a regular "censorshit" column. The fiction isn't bad but it's the nonfiction that really impresses. P.O. Box 97, Southland Centre, Cheltenham VIC 3192 Australia. $5.00 Australian per issue.

Visionary Tongue: Dark Fantasy for the Millennium edited by Eloise Coquio is an intriguing idea for a fanzine—several professional British writers have volunteered to critique/edit the contributions. I believe it was begun with the encouragement of Storm Constantine. Other pros offering advice are Brian Stableford, Graham Joyce, Kim Newman, and Freda Warrington. Kind of a magazine workshop. Each issue has an essay by a professional writer. £15 for four issues, 6 St. Leonard's Avenue, Stafford ST17 4LT, England.

The Edge: A Magazine of Imaginative SF, Fantasy, Horror and Slipstream edited by Graham Evans has excellent book and movie reviews, some good fiction, and a lousy attitude. The editor, in his inability or unwillingness to accept criticism and his trashing of competitors, brings the whole enterprise down to a fannish level. Also, in order to demonstrate the magazine's "cutting edge" credentials, the editor makes the provocative and unsubstantiated statement that a particular story "was considered too strong for the American magazine market." Despite these problems the magazine is one to keep an eye on. Meant to come out five times a year it published four issues in 1996. Issue 3 had Dave McKean cover art. $6 an issue (cash). Or for four issues $20 (check acceptable) payable to The Edge, 1 Nichols Court, Belle Vue, Chelmsford, Essex, CM2 0BS UK.

The next two periodicals are musts for aficionados of the ghost story: *All Hallows: the Journal of the Ghost Story Society*—the Ghost Story Society and Ash-Tree Press officially moved from the UK to Canada in early 1997 with Barbara and Christopher Roden, but this should not affect either the society or the publication of magazines. The $23.00 membership fee includes thrice yearly issues of *All Hallows*, which contains fiction, essays, and reviews of material relating to ghost stories. Payable to the Ghost Story Society, P.O. Box 1360, Ashcroft, British Columbia, V0K 1A0, Canada. Issue #12 was disappointing because almost every story was well written, wonderfully atmospheric yet each ending was a letdown . . . too bad. Issue #13, on the other hand, was an excellent issue.

Ghosts & Scholars edited by Rosemary Pardoe specializes in the M. R. Jamesian ghost story, and features fiction, essays and reviews on the subject. Subscriptions are £11 or US $22 (sea) or £17 or US $32 (air)—US orders, cash only. One issue is £4 or US $7 payable to R. A. Pardoe, Flat One, 36 Hamilton Street, Hoole, Chester, CH2 3LJ England. Both periodicals are highly recommended.

Peeping Tom edited by Stuart Hughes remains one of the more important fiction magazines running dark material. Issue #21 had excellent cover art by Pete Queally and some very good fiction. A four-issue subscription is £8.00 payable to *Peeping Tom* Magazine, Yew Street House, 15 Nottingham Road, Ashby de la Zouch, Leiscestershire LE65 1DJ, United Kingdom.

Psychotrope edited by Mark Beech is in its second year. Issue 4 was excellent, with a number of interesting, well-written stories. A four-issue subscription is £7.50 or $20. It's definitely worth a shot. Payable to *Psychotrope*, Flat 6, 17 Droitwich Road, Worcester, WR3 7LG, England.

Tomorrow edited by Algis Budrys began as a science fiction magazine but wisely, I think, Budrys expanded to include fantasy and some horror. The magazine went exclusively online at the end of 1996: http://www.tomorrowsf.com.

Not One of Us edited by John Benson is a good horror/weird magazine that celebrates its tenth anniversary issue with #16. A three issue subscription is $10.50 payable to John Benson, 12 Curtis Road, Natick, MA 01760. Benson also published *In Your Face*, his annual one-off with stories and poetry. $3.00.

Bloodsongs edited by Steve Proposch continues to publish interesting reviews, articles and fiction, and features good art and splashy color covers. Issue 7 contained a welcome interview with David Borthwick, creator of the cult movie *The Secret Adventures of Tom Thumb*. Issue 8 was stalled and the magazine has been taken over by Dave Bauer, US publisher of *Implosion: Journal of the Bizarre and the Eccentric*. Although the magazine will be produced in Orlando, Florida, Proposch will continue to "control the majority of the fiction content" and the regular columns will remain the same. Issue 8 was scheduled for April 1997 and the magazine will be will be going quarterly. Subscriptions (four issues: $14, six issues: $20) payable to *Implosion*, P.O. Box 533653, Orlando, FL 32853.

Aurealis: Australian Fantasy & Science Fiction edited by Dirk Strasser and Stephen

Higgins continues to publish a rich mixture of science fiction and fantasy, although little horror, and also book reviews and good coverage of the Australian genre scene. The format is digest-sized, with a attractive and readable design and excellent cover art by Shaun Tan. Published twice yearly. Subscriptions: four issues A$34 (seamail), A$37 (airmail). All payment must be made in Australian dollars. Credit card payment allowed. Chimaera Publications, P.O. Box 2164, Mt. Waverley, Victoria 3149, Australia.

Eidolon: The Journal of Australian Science Fiction and Fantasy is a uniformly readable and entertaining quarterly edited by Jonathan Strahan, Jeremy G. Byrne, and Richard Scriven. The 20th issue, in honor of Harlan Ellison's visit, contains mostly reprints. It also included a long essay about women (or the percieved lack thereof) in Australian SF. And a useful wrap-up of the year (1995) in Australian horror by Steve Proposch (who inappropriately raves about his own publications). The sixth anniversary 21st issue contains the usual eclectic mix of SF, fantasy, and dark fantasy. Well-designed by Byrne and excellent art direction by Shaun Tan. #22/23 sports an excellent Tan cover illustrating 22nd Western Australian Science Fiction Convention guest of honor Howard Waldrop's "You *Could* Go Home Again." It's a double issue and quite good. A$45 (air) A$35 (surface) for four issues payable (only in Australian dollars) to *Eidolon* Publications, P.O. Box 225, North Perth, West Australia 6006.

Interzone, the important British monthly edited by David Pringle, while concentrating on science fiction, generally has some excellent darker stories during the year. Subscriptions (one year) $56 payable to *Interzone*, 217 Preston Drove, Brighton BN1 6FL, England. This is the magazine responsible for the resurgence of SF and fantasy in the UK. It finally and deservedly won the Hugo Award for Best semi-prozine in 1995.

Bones of the Children edited by Paula Guran was the first and last issue of that magazine. It debuted at the World Fantasy Convention with a good slick cover, literate fiction, and an overwhelming number of psychopaths in the first issue along with book, movie, video, net, and music review columns. Guran has announced that the magazine will be reemerging in March 1997 as *Wetbones*, and that CFD Productions will not have any connection to the new magazine. For information, write Paula Guran at P.O. Box 5410, Akron, OH 44334.

The Urbanite: The Strange Transformation Issue edited by Mark McLaughlin. As always, *The Urbanite* has an entertaining selection of surreal-bizarre fiction. This issue features Joel Lane and Lawrence Schimel for their fiction and poetry respectively. $5 per issue, or three issues for $13.50 payable to Urban Legend Press, P.O. Box 4737, Davenport, IA 52808. US funds only.

Night Dreams published in England and edited by Kirk S. King is up to its fourth issue but this is the first I've seen it. There are some unusual stories and some dead-end ones by writers who should know better. Worth a look. £10.50 ($24.50 US) for a four issue subscription $6.50 for one issue. Payable to K. S. King, 47 Stephens Road, Walmley, Sutton Coldfield, West Midlands B76 2TS, England.

Chills, a publication of the British Fantasy Society is discontinuing after issue 10. *Dark Horizons* will continue, increasing in frequency. *Chills* edited by Peter Coleborn and Simon MacCulloch was excellent and will be missed. The British Fantasy Society is open to membership by anyone. It publishes a regular newsletter and several magazines containing fiction and nonfiction about fantasy and horror and organizes the annual Fantasycon in the UK. £15 payable to the British Fantasy Society, The BFS Secretary, c/o 2 Harwood Street, Stockport, SK4 1JJ, UK A US membership is $32.00.

Cthulhu Codex Number 7 edited by Robert M. Price has taken over the fiction mantle from *Crypt of Cthulhu*, also edited by Price, which no longer publishes fiction, concentrating instead on articles, parodies, and essays. From now on *Cthulhu Codex* will feature Cthulhu Mythos fiction, poetry, and art.

Midnight Shambler edited by Robert M. Price is a good little magazine for Lovecraftian fiction fans. #4 had some very good stories. $4.50 from Necronomicon Press. See address under nonfiction magazines.

Two interesting horror poetry magazines debuted in 1996: *Frisson* and *Contortions*. *Frisson: Disconcerting Verse*, edited by Scott H. Urban is a quarterly. Annual subscriptions: $5.00 payable to Scott H. Urban, 1012 Pleasant Dale Drive, Wilmington, NC 28412. *Contortions: Poems of Extraordinary Dislocation* calls itself a chapbook and is edited by Brandon W. Totman. The first issue features H. E. Fassl's art. $5.00 per copy, payable to Brandon W. Totman, Shark Attack Publications, 3492 L. K. Wood Boulevard #A, Arcata, CA 95521.

Nonfiction:

The Mammoth Book of Oddities by Frank O'Neil (Robinson UK/Carroll & Graf) is a browser's delight, jam-packed with bizarre facts and feats divided into ten categories including sexual oddities, animal oddities, odd people, medical oddities, etc. The UK edition is a lot cuter with its small, plump paperback format and effective cover design. I can't vouch for the accuracy of these "facts" but I do know that at least one, about the history of Chinese footbinding, is suspect. In any case, if you don't take the material too seriously you can read and laugh, be amazed, or scoff at the man given a concrete enema by his lover, the woman who trains insects. . . .

Sacred Monsters: Behind the Mask of the Horror Actor by Doug Bradley (Titan Books UK) is an intelligent and accessible history of the use of masks and make-up by the actor best known for his performances as Pinhead in Clive Barker's *Hellraiser* movies. Beginning with the use of masks by ancient shamans, continuing with their use in theater throughout the world Bradley takes the reader up to the great masters of disguise in the movies: Lon Chaney and Boris Karloff; and others later who occasionally used disguises: Vincent Price, Fredric March, Charles Laughton, Lon Chaney, Jr.; and in the present day: the actors who have played Freddy Krueger, Jason Voorhees, and Michael Myers. Personable and informative, with good photographs.

Necronomicon Book One: The Journal of Horror and Erotic Cinema edited by Andy Black (Creation Books) changes from magazine to book format with this issue. First time I've seen it and it looks good, covering everything from Lovecraft in the movies to Abel Ferrara's *oeuvre* and lesbian vampire art films. Excellent reproduction of b&w still photographs.

A Dark Night's Dreaming: Contemporary American Horror Fiction edited by Tony Magistrale and Michael A. Morrison (University of South Carolina Press) is an excellent introduction to the field in eight essays. The first, by Magistrale, gives a wide-ranging overview of the topic, and the others by academics and critics including Douglas E. Winter discuss the work of Peter Straub, Anne Rice, Thomas Harris, Stephen King, William Blatty, and Whitley Strieber. Written in clear, non-academic prose. While not every essay is brilliant, all are serviceable and a few show exceptional insight. Highly recommended for anyone interested in putting horror since the 1970s into context. At only 135 pages including bibliography I would have loved for the book to have been twice that length.

The Illustrated Werewolf Movie Guide by Stephen Jones (Titan Books) is a short history of werewolf and other films of transformation from the silents up to last year's sixth version of *The Island of Dr. Moreau*. A useful reference book that includes ratings.

The A-Z of Serial Killers by Harold Schecter and David Everett (Pocket Books) is a useful compendium that covers all aspects of the phenomenon: historical, biographical, criminological, psychological, and cultural. Readable and entertaining, especially considering the subject matter.

Fragments of Fear: An Illustrated History of British Horror Films (Creation) is lovingly compiled by Andy Boot, who means to redress the lack of books covering the whole range of British horror movies. Detailed and entertaining.

Death Scenes: A Homicide Detective's Scrapbook text by Katherine Dunn (Feral House) edited by Sean Tejaratchi was acquired from the estate of Jack Huddleston, a detective from southern California between the years c. 1925–1945. Dunn traces the history of the man behind the book. Huddleston collected photographs of people with leprosy, elephantiasis, and hydrophobia, as well as of crime and suicide scenes. Graphic, even more so than Luc Sante's *Evidence* of a few years ago, and *not* for the squeamish.

Nonfiction listings (film books):

The Gore Galore Video Quiz Book: Terrifying Fun with 800 Horror Movie Trivia Questions & Puzzles by Stephen J. Spignesi (Signet); *Lon Chaney, Jr.: Horror Film Star, 1906–1973* by Don G. Smith (McFarland) is a scholarly biography with a complete filmography and photographs; *Hammer Films: An Exhaustive Filmography* by Tom Johnson and Deborah Del Vecchio (McFarland); *Spaghetti Nightmares* by Luca M. Palmerini and Gaetono Mistretta (Fantasma)—forty years of Italian horror films. Producers, directors, screenwriters, make-up artists, and actors in a series of interviews. Color and b&w stills; *Shock Masters of the Cinema* by Loris Curci (Fantasma: 800-544-2020); *A Thousand Faces* (Vestal Press: 607-797-4872) is Michael Blake's sequel to his biography *Man Behind the Thousand Faces* about Lon Chaney; *Guilty Pleasures of the Horror Film* by Gary and Susan Svehla (Midnight Marquee); *The Psychotronic® Video Guide* by Michael J. Weldon (St. Martin's Griffin) is the huge, updated and revised edition of this guide to the weird, wild, and wonderful world of exploitation, SF serials, slasher movies, etc. Buy it. You need it; *Hammer: House of Horror* by Howard Maxford (Overlook Press) is an illustrated history of the famous British studio known for its horror films from its beginnings in the 30s through the horror cycles of the 50s, 60s, and 70s; *The Dread of Difference* edited by Barry Keith Grant (University of Texas Press) maintains that horror is always rooted in gender, particularly in anxieties about sexual difference and gender politics. Essays by Carol J. Clover, Robin Wood, and others discuss the work of David Cronenberg, Dario Argento, and George A. Romero.

Nonfiction listings:

The Unauthorized Anne Rice Companion by George Beahm (Andrew & McMeel); *Conversations with Anne Rice* by Michael Riley (Ballantine); *Bram Stoker: A Biography of the Author of Dracula* by Barbara Belford (Knopf); *The Work of Stephen King* by Michael R. Collings (Borgo Press) appears to be an expanded version of the 1986 Starmont House *Annotated Guide to Stephen King*. This edition has an annotated bibliography and guide to King's work through 1994. (Borgo Press, P.O. Box 2845, San Bernardino, CA 92406-2845; *American Supernatural Fiction: From Edith Wharton to the Weird Tales Writers* edited by Douglas Robillard (Garland) is a critical examination of supernatural fiction in the US. With eight essays by Brian Stableford, Sam Moskowitz, and S. T. Joshi about Wharton, F. Marion Crawford, H. P. Lovecraft, and others. (Garland Publishing, 717 Fifth Avenue, Suite 2500, New York, NY 10022-8101. *The Work of Gary Brandner* by Martine Wood (Borgo Press) is an annotated bibliography and guide to the work of Brandner. Foreword by Richard Laymon and introduction by Kim Greenblatt, and postscript by Brandner; *Ghosts: Appearances of the Dead and Cultural Transformation* by R. C. Finucane (Prometheus Books); *Witches and Neighbors: A History of European Witchcraft* by Robin Briggs (Viking); *Vampires, Mummies, and Liberals: Bram Stoker and the Politics of Popular Fiction* by David Glover (Duke University Press); *Jack the Ripper—First American Serial Killer* by Stewart Evans and Paul Gainey (Random House UK); *Mama's Boy: The True Story of a Serial Killer and His Mother* by Richard T. Pienciak (Dutton); *John Saul: A Critical Companion* by Paul Bail (Greenwood Press); *Evil: Inside Human Violence and Cruelty* by Roy F. Baumeister (Freeman), an inquiry into the causes of evil by a social psychologist who challenges the traditional view that low self-esteem causes violence and aggression; *Lord High Executioner: An Unashamed Look at Hangmen, Headsmen, and Their Kind* by Howard Engel (Firefly); *Dean Koontz: A Critical Companion* by Joan G. Kotker (Greenwood Press); *Writing Horror and the Body: The Fiction of Stephen King, Clive Barker, and Anne Rice* by Linda Badley (Greenwood Press), a critical examination of contemporary horror; *Depraved: The Shocking True Story of America's First Serial Killer* by Harold Schecter (Pocket); *Peter Underwood's Guide to Ghosts and Haunted Places* by Peter Underwood (Piatkus UK); *Art of Darkness: A Poetics of Gothic* by Anne Williams (University of Chicago Press) is pretty dry for the layperson. Williams attempts to bring the "gothic" back into respectibility and show it's never been gone from popular literature but really, who cares? The general reader of horror literature already knows this; *Frankenstein* by Mary Shelley edited by J. Paul Hunter (Norton), a critical edition using the 1818 Lackington first edition, with notes, a section of "Nineteenth-century Responses" and twelve modern essays. Also, chronology, and selected bibliography, and related writings; *Shocked and Amazed* Vol. 2 by James Taylor (Dolphin-Moon Press, Box 22262, Baltimore, MD 21203) is about freak shows; *Caverns Measureless to Man: 18 Memoirs of H. P. Lovecraft* edited by S. T. Joshi (Necronomicon Press), mostly written after Lovecraft's death, but they certainly show the respect and love he inspired in his fellow writers and friends; *H. P. Lovecraft: A Life* by S. T. Joshi (Necronomicon Press) is a major new biography written from a sympathetic but critical perspective. *Unholy Hungers: Encountering the Vampire in Ourselves and Others* by Barbara E. Hart, Ph.D. (Shambhala), a sophisticated self-help book using Jungian psychology and vampires as archetypes of bad relationships. Not much fun; *Guide to the Gothic II: An Annotated Bibliography of Criticism 1983–1993* by Frederick S. Frank (Scarecrow Press), a supplement to the original *Guide to the Gothic* with over 1500 new entries. Includes separate studies on Stephen King and Joyce Carol Oates, and sub-sections covering criticism of "special subjects"; *Bizarre Beasts and Other Oddities of Nature* (Abrams—not seen), text by Anita Ganeri and 32 pages of illustrations; *Cold-Blooded: The Saga of Charles Schmid, the Notorious "Pied Piper of Tucson"* by John Gilmore (Feral House) inaugurates the True Crime Series. Reprint from 1970 with added material; *Haunted Places: Ghostly Abodes, Sacred Sites, UFO Landings, and Other Supernatual Locations* by Dennis William Hauck (Penguin) is organized by state and gives instructions on how to get to the various cemetaries, public buildings, etc.; *Spell of the Tiger* by Sy Montgomery (A Peter Davison Book/Houghton Mifflin) is about the man-eating tigers of Sundarbans, a great mangrove swamp that stretches between India and Bangladesh. The tigers kill hundreds of people a year yet are not hunted down by the populace. About the relationship between the tigers and their prey; *V is for Vampire* by David J. Skal (Plume) calls itself "The A-Z Guide to Everything Undead," and that's just what it is, with armadillos (an animal associated with vampires, for some reason) and Jack Kerouac (he wrote a fantasy with a vampire in it), among the more unexpected entries; *The BFI* (British Film Institute) *Companion to Horror* edited by Kim Newman (Cassell) concentrates mostly on film but does have a few entries on writers, murderers, and actors. Some of the contributors to the volume are Neil Gaiman, Stephen Jones, Anne Billson, Tim Lucas, Douglas E. Winter, Steve Laws, and Maitland McDonagh; *The World of Edward Gorey* by Clifford Ross and Karen Wilkin (Abrams) is the book all Gorey fans have been waiting for—chock full of illustrations, sketches of works-in-progress, and a lengthy interview conducted over two days. The interview is about Gorey's tastes in art and literature, as well as his influences. There's also a critical essay on his work by Wilkin. Highly recommended; *Dead Meat* by Sue Coe (Four Walls, Eight Windows) is about the meat industry, specifically slaughterhouses. Coe spent six years visiting the sites of and drawing every aspect of the process that brings meat to our tables—and they're not pretty pictures. Also includes an introductory essay by Alexander Cockburn on the history of the meat industry. Will certainly make you think before you eat pork, beef, or eggs; *Lustmord* edited by Brian King (Bloat) is a compilation of essays, short stories, memoirs, confessions, letters, photographs and other works created by serial killers, mass-murderers, cannibals, necrophiles, sexual sadists, psychopaths, and assassins; *Skin Shows: Gothic Horror and the Technology of Monsters* by Judith Halberstam (Duke University Press), an examination of the monster as cultural object; *Gothic* by Fred Botting (Routledge) explains the transformations of the genre through history; *Passing Strange* by Joseph A. Citro (Chapters) collects true tales of New England hauntings and horrors; *The Invisibles: A Tale of the Eunuchs of India* by Zia Jaffrey (Pantheon) is the author's journey to understand the cultural tradition and other forces that allow the hijras to persist into modern times; *Tales from the Crypt* by Digby Diehl (St. Martin's Press) is a must for anyone who grew up reading EC comics. It's a tribute to the Crypt Keeper and a history of the comic book with lots of cover art and some sample strips. Also, color stills from the TV incarnation; *Raising Hell* by Robert Masello (Perigee) is a history of the black arts and those who practiced them; *The Oxford Book of Creatures* by Fleur Adcock and Jacqueline Simms (Oxford University Press) is an anthology of writings about all kinds of creatures from the iguana to the Loch Ness monster; *Nightmares of Nature* by Richard Matthews (HarperCollins) has color photographs of a cane toad swallowing a mouse, scarring from a rattlesnake bite, and a hippo with wide open, tusked mouth; in *The Complete Book of Devils and Demons* by Leonard R. N. Ashley (Barricade) you'll find all the names of Lilith and a formula for exorcism; *Inventing Wonderland* by Jackie Wullschlager (Free Press) is a book on Victorian childhood as seen through the lives and fantasies of Lewis Carroll, Edward Lear, J. M. Barrie, Kenneth Grahame, and A. A. Milne; *Evil Sisters* by Bram Dijkstra (Knopf) is about how, in popular culture, the female came to be portrayed as a regressive, primitive force whose sexuality could destroy the social order, undermining the supremacy of the white male. This book notes repercussions of this unfortunate phenomenon; *On Monsters and Marvels* by Ambrose Paré, translated by Janis L. Pallister (University of Chicago Press). Paré, born in France around 1510, was chief surgeon to Charles IX and Henry III. The book is an illustrated encyclopedia of curiosities, bizarre beasts, monstrous human and animal births, and natural phenomena; *Cult Rapture* by Adam Parfrey (Feral House) exposes the sordid story of Walter Keane (painter of those big-eyed children), sex cults of the physically deformed, and other cultish topics. This is the follow-up to *Apocalypse Culture*.

Chapbooks and other Small Press Items:
Gauntlet released a 25th anniversary edition of Richard Matheson's *Hell House*. Limited to 500 copies, signed and slip-cased edition with an introduction by Dean Koontz and an afterword by Richard Christian Matheson. $65 plus $5.00 postage. Also, a twenty-six-copy deluxe lettered leather edition is $150. See address under "Collections."

CD Publications published *The Mountain King*, a new novel by Rick Hautala. This is Hautala's first hardcover publication. Full color-dust jacket artwork plus interior illustrations by Steve Bissette. Five hundred signed, numbered and slipcased copies. $50 see address under "collections."

Charnel House published an odd new short story by Tim Powers called *Where They Are Hid*. Book and handmade slipcase bound in Japanese fabrics, illustrated and signed by the author. Limited to 350 numbered copies. $85 plus $5.00 shipping. A twenty-six-copy lettered edition is also available. Nominated for the 1996 World Fantasy Award (despite the fact that the book actually appeared in 1996).

Donald M. Grant, Publishers, Inc. brought out some beautiful editions in 1996: Stephen King's novel *Desperation* was brought out in two editions illustrated by Don Maitz with five full-color paintings and five b&w drawings. This first edition was published in a 2,000-copy Deluxe traycased edition signed by King and Maitz and a 4,000-copy slipcased Gift edition. $175.00 plus $5.00 insured shipping each. The Deluxe edition was sold first to owners of *Dark Tower III: The Wastelands* and the rest by lottery. Address under "collections."

The Hunger and Ecstasy of Vampires by Brian Stableford (Mark V. Ziesing Books) has a beautiful cover painting and design done by Arnie Fenner. A signed, slipcased edition limited to 300 copies is available for $60.00. The trade edition is $25.00. Address under "Acknowledgments."

A *Binscombe Tale For Summer* a.k.a. "Oh, I Do Like to Be Beside the Seaside (Within Reason)" by John Whitbourn, (A Haunted Library Publication). Whitbourn is the author of A *Dangerous Energy, Popes and Phantoms*, and *To Build Jerusalem*. This is a nasty and clever little tale illustrated by Alan Hunter. $4.00 payable to Richard Fawcett, 61 Teecomwas Drive, Uncasville, CT 06382.

Mojo Press published *dead heat*, a first novel, about zombies, by Del Stone, Jr. Illustrated by Dave Dorman and Scott Hampton. $24.95; Also, the thirtieth anniversary edition of Michael Moorcock's classic *Behold the Man*. With an introduction by Jonathan Carroll; *Atomic Chili: The Illustrated Joe R. Lansdale* is a collection in graphic novel form of some of Lansdale's best work including "By Bizarre Hands," "Tight Little Stitches in a Dead Man's Back," "Steel Valentine," "Night They Missed the Horror Show," and others. Dave Dorman did the excellent cover; various artists illustrated each story. Introduction by Timothy Truman. $24.95. P.O. Box 14005, Austin, TX 78714.

Jeffrey Thomas's Necropolitan Press published an anthology of seven original vampire stories in an attractive volume entitled A *Vampire Bestiary*. Illustrations by different artists. $4.00 payable to Jeffrey Thomas, 65 South Street, Westborough MA 01581-1628.

Forest Plains, a dark fantasy by Peter Crowther, was published in an attractive signed limited hardcover edition by Hypatia Press. Charles de Lint wrote the introduction. $35.00 payable to Blue Moon Books, 360 West First, Eugene, OR 97401.

Necro Publications brought out *Goon*, a new collaboration by Edward Lee and John Pelan. It's a rasslin' story that takes place in the south where the women are hot, the wrestlers are impotent, and the killing goes on and on. A signed, limited edition comes in hardcover ($35.00) and trade paperback ($9.95) with an introduction by t. winterdamon and cover illustration by Alan M. Clark.

Darkside by Dennis Etchison (American Fantasy/Airgedlámh Publications), was brought out in hardcover for the first time in the author's preferred edition. Signed, limited to 750 copies for $35.00 payable to Robert T. Garcia, P.O. Box 41714, Chicago, IL 60641.

A *Plague on Both Your Houses* by Scott Edelman is a zombie play published for Halloween in a limited edition of 125 copies. I'm not sure it's for sale.

Dradin, in Love by Jeff VanderMeer (Buzzcity Press) and illustrated by Michael Shores, is the first book in a new line of trade paperback first editions. It's a very attractive little book of the surreal. $11.50 payable to Buzzcity Press, P.O. Box 38190, Tallahassee, FL 32315.

Jack Ketchum's novel, *The Girl Next Door*, has been reissued by The Overlook Connection with the author's preferred text plus introductions by Stephen King and Ketchum, afterwords by Christopher Golden, Lucy Taylor, Philip Nutman, and Edward Lee. The volume also includes an interview with the author by Stanley Wiater. Signed by all contributors. A 500-copy limited slipcased edition for $75.00 plus $5.00 shipping. Also, a lettered fifty-two-copy edition with a mahogany case, featuring a door with brass hinges, a brass knob, and laser etched plates. Red leather bound, gold foil stamped on the front and spine of binding. Color cover frontispiece of Neal McPheeters's dustjacket. $300 plus $15 shipping. (check for availability of the latter). Payable to The Overlook Connection. See address on acknowledgment page.

Graphic Novels:

The Silent City by Erez Yakin with an introduction by Yevgeny Yevtushenko (Kitchen Sink) is a devastating nightmare look at a totalitarian state (much like the former Soviet Union) in the expressionistic style. Without text, the harsh b&w images speak for themselves. The author, born in New York, was eighteen when he created this remarkable work; *The Comic Strip Art of Lyonel Feininger* (Kitchen Sink) is an important collection by the German artist better known for his painting than his comic strips. Feininger created the innovative and underappreciated *The Kin-der-Kids* and *Wee Willie Winkie's World* for the *Chicago Tribune* in the early 1900s. Gorgeous color reproduction in an oversized format. Not horror but highly recommended nonetheless.

Doma: A Child's Dream by Katsahiro Otamo (Dark Horse) is a chilly story of extrasensory terrorism written by the author of the acclaimed Japanese comic *Akira*. *Doma* takes place in a huge housing complex where a series of strange deaths have occurred over a couple of years. A little girl confronts the evil with unexpected results. This excellent predecessor to *Akira* won the Grand Prix Award in 1983, given by the Japanese SF Writers Asssocation, the only time it has been won by a graphic novel.

Michael Cherkas and Larry Hancock capture all the suburban paranoia of the 1950s with their series *Suburban Nightmares* (NBM) in which *The Twilight Zone* meets *Leave It to Beaver*. The three stories in "Volume 2: Childhood Secrets" reflect the US preoccupation with Communism and aliens at the time. In stark, effective black and white.

Lucius Shepard has authored a new graphic novel series titled *Vermillion*, for DC's new Helix line. Al Davison did the art. A literate science fiction/horror tale about a city that encompasses the exotic, the monstrous, and the fantastic.

Children's Books:

Monday's Troll, poems by Jack Prelutsky and pictures by Peter Sis (Greenwillow) is a sweet, harmless picture book of weird ceatures for young children. Older children might be disappointed if they're looking for a scare, but adults might like the book if they collect Sis's colorful art.

Madame La Grande and Her So High to the Sky Uproarious Pompadour by Candace Fleming illustrated by S. D. Schindler (Knopf) is a charming and funny illustrated book about a woman's vanity. When Madame of the title, a slave to style, reads that pompadours are the new sensation of Paris, she simply must have the biggest and most extravagant. Follow her and her magnificent pompadour on their adventures enroute to the Paris Opera.

The Six Servants by Jacob and Wihelm Grimm, pictures by Sergei Goloshapov (North-South Books), tells the story of a nasty enchantress queen who challenges the suitors of her beautiful daughter with hopeless tasks then has them killed. One wily prince, who has picked up six odd servants on his way to win the princess, of course succeeds at all the tasks then humiliates the princess for being haughty before they both go off to live happily ever after. The art is colorful and reminiscent of Breughal and the book is beautifully designed.

Starry Messenger by Peter Sis (Farrar, Straus & Giroux/Frances Foster Books) is a wonderful and beautiful introduction to the great astronomer for older children. The text is straightforward biography plus, in script, excerpts from Galileo's journal of his observations of the night sky, called *The Starry Messenger*. The art is sly and often very beautiful. Published on October 31, four years to the day after the church pardoned Galileo 360 years after he was found guilty of heresy by the Inquisition.

My Little Sister Ate One Hare by Bill Grossman and illustrated by Kevin Hawkes

(Crown) is perfect for young children with its "ick" factor. Little sister, who seems quite the adventuress, continues her eating spree with snakes, bats, ants, and other critters, to no apparent ill affect.

William Wegman's Mother Goose by William Wegman (Hyperion) features Weimaraners in dresses and bonnets holding storybooks and bowls with human hands. Wegman's mixing his dogs with human body parts creates an eerier, edgier book than usual. Highly recommended for children and adults with a taste for the bizarre.

Klutz by Henrik Drescher (Hyperion) is another winner by the author of *The Boy Who Ate Around*. The colorful Klutz family is a hopeless bunch of, well, klutzes—after a little car accident they find meaning in their lives, join a circus, discover something surprising about themselves, and well—read it. It's fun.

Wayne Anderson's Horrible Book (Dorling Kindersley) is a joy for children. A brave little spider follows a bodiless monster from the grave as it gathers material to recreate itself. Kind of a pop-up book, with startled fish and snails possessing very sharp teeth. . . .

Lisbeth Zwerger illustrates L. Frank Baum's *The Wizard of Oz* (North-South Books) with very untraditional drawings: Scarecrow is rather pear-shaped and sports a dunce cap, the Wicked Witch of the West is all stomach and scarf. A lovely collector's item for children or adults. Green glasses included.

Sleepless Beauty by Frances Minters and illustrated by G. Brian Karas (Viking) a very hip urban variation on the sleeping beauty fairy tale, seems a little sophisticated for the 3-8 year olds at whom it's aimed. Although I very much like the illustrations at times I wasn't sure why some were included—a jazz saxaphonist playing his heart out and a couple of gossips (I think) are intermittent images that have nothing to do with the story. Cool though, for collectors of fairy tale variations and children's book art.

Creepy, Crawly Baby Bugs by Sandra Markle (Walker and Co.) is a colorful and charming introduction for children to the world of bugs. Markle nicely describes bug mother love and the growth of the young. While some of the bugs are cute, others aren't, which might give squeamish adults a difficult time. However, this is the perfect vehicle with which to teach children not to be afraid of bugs. Useful glossary and index of terms in back.

Ever Heard of an Aardwolf? by Madeline Moser and illustrated by Barry Moser (Harcourt Brace Children's Books) is a sophisticated-looking collaboration by this father and daughter team that introduces eighteen odd, mostly unfamiliar animals to children. Included are color engravings of each animal, a short description, and in the back of the book, a more detailed description. Some of the animals previously unknown to me are the viscacha, the babirusa, the solenodon, and the bush dog. In addition to being perfect for children, this is an item for Barry Moser collectors.

The Ghost of Nicholas Greebe by Tony Johnston with pictures by S. D. Schindler (Dial Books for Young Readers) is notable more for its art than its scares. An old man dies, is buried, and one of his bones is dug up by a dog, disturbing Greebe's rest for a hundred years. Greebe's ghost isn't very frightening and is barely in the story. It's the bone that's more fun to watch. Only for very young children.

James and the Giant Peach by Roald Dahl (Knopf) takes Dahl's first novel for children, published in 1961, and adds quirky illustrations by Lane Smith. The illustrations were used by Disney as the basis for the animation in their movie of the same title. Charming.

Art Books:

Neurotica by J. K. Potter (Paper Tiger UK/Overlook Press) is a beautiful new book by a master horror artist. Among his acknowledged influences are his mentor the late New Orleans photographer Clarence John Laughlin, Weegee, and Hans Bellmer. Many of the pieces are from Potter's private collection and use some of his favorite models, including punk diva Lydia Lunch (who also writes the introduction). Some of the transformations jar and shock and while these are certainly effective in creating a particular effect, my own favorites are those pieces that are more fluid and subtle, showing human and animal melding together to create an entirely new reality that seems completely natural in their unreality. A dreamlike eeriness that is difficult to shake off imbues his best work.

Tales of Mystery and Imagination by Edgar Allan Poe with nineteen illustrations by Gary Kelly (Creative Editions/Harcourt Brace) collects "The Cask of Amontillado," "The Black Cat," and "The Fall of the House of Usher" in a beautiful new oversized edition perfect for young adults and adults. The cover art, taken from "The Black Cat"—a skull-like head with the eponymous cat perched on top—is worth the price of the book.

River of Mirrors: The Fantastic Art of Judson Huss (Morpheus International) Huss is an expatriate American living in France. Obviously influenced by the Fantastic Realist school of Vienna, particularly Ernst Fuchs and by Hieronymus Bosch, the Flemish fabulist, Huss juxtaposes lush beauty with the grotesque. The intersticial autobiographical material and one piece about the process of creating his art are fascinating; the captions are not. Terry Gilliam provides a foreword.

The Nutcracker by E. T. A. Hoffman based on a new translation by Aliana Brodmann and illustrated by Gennady Spirin (Stewart, Tabori, and Chang) is a treat for young adult readers and art lovers. This dark fairy tale takes place on Christmas Eve and is about a Nutcracker that turns into a prince and must fight the Mouse King. Tchaikovksy's wonderful ballet of the same name was inspired by this tale. The production of this book is gorgeous, with its rich, saturated colors, its luscious endpapers, and delicate typeface. A perfect gift book.

Something in My Eye by Michael Whelan (Mark V. Ziesing Books) collects the horrific art of this multi-Hugo-Award-winning artist in glorious full color large format book available in both hardcover and paperback. Whelan is versatile, producing memorable work in several different styles, from photo-realism to the stylized broader images of comic-book art. An excellent collection.

Myth, Magic, and Mystery: One Hundred Years of American Children's Book Illustration by Michael Patrick Hearn, Trinkett Clark and H. Nichols B. Clark (Roberts Rinehart Publishers in cooperation with the Chrysler Museum of Art) is a beautiful, informative volume developed in conjunction with a nationwide tour. A plethora of art from Kate Greenaway, Kay Nielsen, and Edmund Dulac (who never made it to America but whose art did), N. C. Wyeth, Barry Moser, Charles Santore, and Edward Gorey. The book misses a few notable children's artists such as Lane Smith and Henrik Drescher but nonetheless is highly recommended.

Spectrum III: The Best in Contemporary Fantastic Art edited by Cathy Burnett and Arnie Fenner with Jim Loehr (Underwood Books). If you want to know what's happening in the visual area of fantasy and horror this is the book to buy. Fenner's introduction provides a useful overview of the year and the book is a cornucopia of fantasy and horror art by newcomers as well as already established artists. Highly recommended.

Animal Farm by George Orwell (Harcourt Brace)—the 50th anniversary edition with new illustrations by the talented Ralph Steadman. A collectible for Steadman fans.

H. R. Giger's Film Design (Morpheus International) is another beautiful book with an introduction by Ridley Scott and ongoing commentary about each project (many of which were never filmed) by Giger.

Barlowe's Guide to Fantasy with text by Neil Duskis (HarperPrism) demonstrates Barlowe's keen imagination and versatility creating colorful visual interpretations of creatures ranging from the Golem and Grendel and Mr. Toad (from *The Wind in the*

Willows) to monsters created by Clive Barker and Dan Simmons. Also, concise commentary on the background of each character and beast.

Beautiful Death: Art of the Cemetery by David Robinson with text by Dean Koontz (Penguin Studio) is filled with color photographs of the beautiful funerary art of European cemeteries.

Odds and Ends:

Spineless Wonders: Strange Tales From the Invertebrate World by Richard Coniff (Henry Holt) is a marvelous book in which the author goes on about his subject with all the enthusiasm and zeal of a convert—which he is. He only became enamored of the creatures after leaving his job as a journalist. Coniff dares the normal reader not to become caught up in this world with him and frankly, the book is perfect for lovers of horror. In his introduction he says *"Formification* is the feeling that ants and other creeping things are crawling over one's flesh. Much as we crave the thrill of horror movies ("bug" and "bogeyman" come from the same Welsh word, meaning "ghosts") so too, does good natural history writing give us the chance, vicariously, and often covertly, to find pleasure in this sensation." So you can read about flies, leeches (there's a man who so loves leeches that he started to farm them for medicinal use, creating a booming business), the giant squid, fire ants, and all manner of spineless creatures. Marvelously entertaining.

The Book of the Spider by Paul Hillyard (Random House) actually overlaps slightly with the above in its mention of tarantula lover and expert Rick West. But Hillyard concentrates on all kinds of spiders. The interesting things to note are that spiders are among the most feared creatures and that they are *all* venomous, (that's how they paralyze their prey) although relatively few are harmful to humans. Usually spider bites are painful but not harmful—but the bite of the brown recluse is necrotic, which can cause gangrene. There's a true, horrific story in the book about a housewife outside of LA who was bitten and went into a coma from an extreme allergic reaction after developing toxic shock syndrome. The rest of the story is even worse. But most of the book is dedicated to learning to love the spider and appreciate it, and even eat it. (The blue-legged tarantula of Laos is supposed to be especially tasty—recipe included).

The Earth Dwellers: Adventures in the Land of Ants by Erich Hoyt (Simon & Schuster) is an in-depth look at the drama of the ant. And it *is* dramatic, from birth to death. Hoyt accompanies field biologists Edward O. Wilson and William L. Brown, Jr. to the tropical jungle of Costa Rica to study different kinds of ants. Hoyt follows individual ants while they scout, forage, fight wars, and sacrifice themselves for their queens. More detail and heavier going than the other books here but fascinating. For the serious student of the ant.

Backyard Bugs text and photographs by Robin Kittrell Laughlin with a foreword by Sue Hubbell (Chronicle Books) is another wonderful book about bugs. In this one Laughlin, who has been interested in bugs since she was a child, started photographing those she found in and around her home outside of Santa Fe, New Mexico. Friends from around the US began to send her interesting bugs for her project, and she eventually ended up with the forty bugs in the book. The bug models are the center of attention on their white backgrounds. Laughlin describes how she came to photograph each bug (and tells how she released them all after they did their duty for her). A beautful, witty little companion volume to the above.

The Beauty of the Beastly by Natalie Angier (A Peter Davison Book/Houghton Mifflin) is by an award-winning science writer who grew up terrified of roaches—she still isn't wild about them but has come to terms with and learned to respect them. Her book is a collection of short, lively essays about the intimate lives of different beasties, a new theory of menstruation, why veggies are good for you, and other topics. According to her research, scorpions fully deserve their rotten reputation—"they're nasty and they're not afraid of anybody . . . strange lives, violent nights, and brutal loves"—and hyenas not only possess unusual sexual organs, but their behavior completely contradicts certain assumptions researchers have made about the effect of testosterone on agressive behavior.

The Compleat Cockroach by David George Gordon (Ten Speed Press) is a book about everything you ever wanted to know concerning the world's most universally despised creature: their life cycle, the different types, how they mate, how they taste, their habits, and the best ways to rid your abode of them. Also, cockroaches in literature, in theater, and in the movies. Suitably illustrated.

The Wonder Book of Sex by Glen Baxter (Villard) is in typical bright Glen Baxter colors and nonsequitors. Baxter is an American cartoonist living in England. His stuff has gotten pretty British of late but is still entertaining for fans of his work. As befits the title, this one is a bit bawdier than his usual with naked bodies, sexual aids, and a doctor dispensing words of wisdom throughout.

The Devil's Mischief: In Which His Own Story Is Told in Words and Pictures by Ed Marquand (Abbeville) is a clever celebration of the devil in all his cleverness rather than his uglier aspects. Abundant art, quotes, excerpts, and entire stories from writers like Mark Twain, Charles Baudelaire, Vladimir Nabokov, William Thackeray, Billy Graham, and Mikhail Bulgakov.

The Devil: A Visual Guide to the Demonic, Evil, Scurrilous, and Bad by Genevieve Morgan and Tom Morgan (*Chronicle Books*). What's the first thing I saw when I opened this attractive volume? A photograph of one of William Wegman's Weimaraners dressed in a red devil costume. Gorgeously designed, with an abundance of illustrations (many of which are not the usual). The text begins with the origin of Hell and follows the development of the devil from an historical perspective; there's a chapter defining and describing all the types of demons and subcreatures; a guide to demons from all over the world; superstitions about the devil, etc. Highly recommended.

The Devil by Peter Stanford (Henry Holt) is in a more serious vein (with no illustrations) but quite interesting. Stanford explores the history of what is now considered the mostly Christian view of the devil. His book and the next book are interesting and useful reading on the subject.

A History of the Devil by Gerald Messadié (Kodansha) researches the genealogy of the devil among the world's major civilizations. His conclusion is that "we live under the sign of a nonexistent diety cobbled together twenty-six centuries ago by power-hungry Iranian priests."

The Book of Dragons and Fabulous Beasts by Violet Wharton (credited only on copyright page) from Prospero's Library (Chronicle Books) is a charming and colorful little item with drawings and fine art in miniature and concise explanations of the minotaur, Chinese dragons, the kraken, the roc, etc. Great little gift book.

Even Weirder by Gahan Wilson (Forge) is a very enjoyable collection of cartoonist Wilson's most recent grotesqueries. For lovers of the macabre.

Freak Show: Sideshow Banner Art by Carl Hammer and Gideon Bosker (Chronicle Books) is another marvelously packaged book by the press that has revolutionized book packaging (since its surprise bestseller, *Griffin and Sabine*). A pictoral and text history of the art of sideshow banners, those gaudy, sometimes creepy visual come-ons created to get the rubes in to see various freaks of nature in circuses and carnivals. A great American art form that has died along with the sideshow.

Torture Garden: A Photographic Archive of the New Flesh from Bodyshocks to Cybersex edited by David Wood (Creation Books) is a lot less interesting than it sounds although the cover photograph of a red-haired woman in bondage gear with exposed breasts and lots of *things* in her nose is quite striking. Torture Garden is a London fetish club that opened in 1990. The book is a large format trade paperback with lots of photographs of people dressed up as if for a sexual Halloween party. The more interesting photographs are the close-up portraits of people with odd piercings (I mean like spikes in their facial cheeks and bones through their noses) by Alan Sivroni. Some of the stuff looks faked (at least I hope so, particularly the guy whose face seems to be skinned with its muscles exposed—I don't believe someone would survive very long without infection setting in). There are some interesting quotes throughout about the body, the new flesh, sexuality, etc.

Infamous Manhattan: A Colorful Walking History of New York's Most Notorious Crime Sites by Andrew Roth (Citadel Press) is perfect for the native or tourist who wants to stroll down the avenues with a sense of the criminal history of each location. Inside are listings and brief descriptions of restaurants and bars where mob hits have taken place, the bar on which *Looking for Mr. Goodbar* is based, the bar where Jennifer Levin was picked up by her murderer, Robert Chambers, etc. Informative and fun for dipping into, even if you don't want to visit New York.

Amok Journal Sensurround Edition: A Compendium of Psycho-Physiological Investigation edited by Stuart Swezey (Amok) is divided by chapters covering eight outré subjects from autoerotic fatalities to self-trepanation (drilling a hole in your skull as a means to a permanent "high"), cargo cults, self-mutilation and amputee fetishes. The subjects are covered in a serious but non-academic manner with case histories, texts by experts, and occasionally testimony or interviews with the participants (apparently, though, there are very few survivors of repeated autoeroticism via hangings and other dangerous practices). Also, an interview with Gualtiero Jacopetti, the maker of the documentary *Mondo Cane*. Fascinating, often disturbing reading and photographs.

Thirteen by Jonathan Cott (Doubleday) examines the number thirteen—the superstitions revolving around it, the famous people obsessed with it (Schoenberg). One of the more interesting chapters involves the Philadelphia Friday the Thirteenth Club, founded in 1936. When its thirteen members meet, they walk under ladders, break mirrors, and do other things in public disturbing to certain phobics. Entertaining.

Medical Blunders by Robert Youngson and Ian Schott (Robinson) sounds like it should be filled with examples of scalpels left in patients' stomachs, wrong teeth pulled, etc.—one time screw-ups. But the book is more concerned with "quacks" and medical tragedies throughout history—for example, the Greek physician Galen decided that bloodletting was a great method of healing. He had no knowledge of anatomy because at the time no one was allowed to dissect human corpses. His mistaken belief killed thousands of people for centuries. A depressing but informative chapter on Walter Freeman's enthusiastic embrace of lobotomy as the cure for far too many mental problems, human experimentation, etc. These are ongoing, deliberate actions rather than "accidents," which is how I would define a "blunder."

The Customized Body by Ted Polhemus and Housk Randall (Serpent's Tale) continues where *Modern Primitives* (RE/SEARCH) left off. Divided into chapters on body painting and make-up, piercing, tattooing and scarification, hair and nails, shoes and feet, masks, body modification, and gender transformation. The engrossing commentary and photography by Polhemus and Randall respectively, draws the reader/viewer into a world theoretically accessible to anyone (that is, if you don't want a 9-5 type job). The piercings go way beyond mere nipple and genital piercings—here are people with sticks and spikes stuck into their noses, their cheeks, their lips, etc., with plugs in their ears, many many earrings or studs. Then there's Pearl, a man who has, by corsetting himself for four years, reduced his waist from thirty to seventeen inches. He can only use the top half of his lungs to breathe, which only allows him to speak a little above a whisper and to eat very small amounts of food. He has no real explanation for his obsession other than enjoying helping his grandmother lace up her corsets and his dressing up in her clothes.... A fascinating book. Highly recommended.

La Jetée by Chris Marker (Zone Books) is a book based on the revered twenty-two minute experimental film made in 1962, on which the feature film *12 Monkeys* was based. The film was made, frame by frame, with still photography, and has only one tiny movement within it. I saw it recently and found it pretentious and the antithesis of good filmmaking—but it *is* an interesting experiment. Perhaps not so surprisingly, the book is far more successful—the still images work. Check it out to see what all the fuss was about.

America's Strangest Museums: A Traveler's Guide by Sandra Gurvis (Citadel Press) is a terrific guide for travelers bored with the usual, organized by state. My only complaint is the use of terrible puns. Check out the Nut Museum, for which a nut is part of the price of admission and the exhibits often get stolen by chipmunks and squirrels; the Crayola Hall of Fame, which honors those colors recently taken out of commission; the Mütter Museum (which has discontinued its marvelous calendars as "presenting the wrong image," according to the executive director of the College of Physicians of Philadelphia, owner of the museum—spoilsport).

Paris Out of Hand by Karen Elizabeth Gordon, author of *The Transitive Vampire* (Chronicle Books), in collaboration with Barbara Hodgson and Nick Bantock, creates a very weird and amusing fake guide to Paris. Take your dog to the Patte à la Main (Paw in Hand) for a snack and learn the French for "My Airdale is foaming at the mouth. What did you put in his ragout?" A beautiful little gift for your favorite traveler.

The Dark Progress 1997 Horror Writers Calendar, third in the series co-published by Dark Delicacies and Fool's Progress, priced at $16.95, $2 of which goes to the Make-A-Wish Foundation. The cover art is by Steve Montiglio and the calendar was designed by Jill Heck. Thirteen writers (of course) are represesented by b&w photographs, their "epitaphs," biographies, and bibliographies. The writers featured include Peter Straub, Lucy Taylor, Yvonne Navarro, David J. Schow and Christa Faust, Douglas E. Winter, William Relling Jr., Douglas Clegg, Robert Devereaux, William F. Nolan, and Edward Bryant. Lots of good horror dates noted. Signed and limited to 250 numbered copies, and twenty-six lettered copies. Dark Delicacies, 3725 Magnolia Boulevard, Burbank, CA 91505 or Fool's Progress, P.O. Box 591596, San Francisco, CA 94118; *Days of Blood* is the Dracula Centennial Calendar, a one-shot produced by the same as above. This one features fiction and nonfiction authors of vampire literature and $2 of every sale goes to the National Blood Foundation. Cover art by Daerick Gross, Sr.

Morpheus International's Fantastic Art Calendar for 1997 is also an ongoing series and has beautiful art by Hieronymus Bosch, Ernst Fuchs, H. R. Giger, Jacek Yerka, Clive Barker, and some lesser known but very talented fantasy and dark fantasy artists. The notable dates are rather sparce but this is definitely a worthwhile buy at $12.95; *The H. R. Giger Calendar of the Fantastique* is beautiful, dramatic, and disturbing to look at but not very practical with its black background.

Perhaps not as attractive but certainly more useful is *Autonomedia's Calendar of Jubilee Saints*, abundantly adorned with photographs, paintings, and illustrations of the famous and not-so-famous around the edges, leaving the actual dates clear for notes. As usual, anyone can nominate someone for Jubilee Sainthood. Info is on the calendar. The 1998 calendar can be ordered for $10 postpaid from Autonomedia, P.O. Box 568, Williamsburgh Station, Brooklyn, NY 11211-0568.

Horror and Fantasy in the Media: 1996
by Edward Bryant

Independents' Day:

The theme music for this year's essay is courtesy of Marilyn Manson *(Antichrist Super-star)* and Beck! *(Odelay)*—but more about them later. First there's the matter of all that fantastical darkness I detect in what many purists might dismissively slough off as the movie mainstream. This year's fair-haired candidates in the Oscar races mostly fit into this essay on the basis of tone and treatment rather than any arbitrary genre clas-sification. Now don't get me wrong—I'm not going to argue on behalf of including *Jerry Maguire*, though, come to think of it, the fantasy element of a born-again ethical sports agent seems terribly sunk in the realm of imaginative fiction . . .

But look at *Sling Blade*, Billy Bob Thornton's auteur approach to gothic Southern fiction in which he wrote, directed, and starred. His depiction of a mildly retarded adult released from an Arkansas institution where he's been confined for decades since the childhood murder of his mother and her lover, is absolutely sensational. Remember Thornton as a crazed killer in *One False Move*? He's a marvelous actor. One way to look at *Sling Blade* is to consider it as a Deep Southern variant on the Frankenstein myth. Thornton's character lurches about the landscape in a manner that makes the locals nervous. Is he "cured"? Is it a good idea for him to be befriended by and hang out with a young boy (Lucas Black)? Is he a monster? Works for me. The supporting cast, with walk-ons by such as Robert Duvall, is first rate. And Dwight Yoakum, the film's antag-onist, is an astonishment. It takes real guts for a country music sex symbol to doff his hat and display his male pattern baldness in action. *Sling Blade* will rip your heart out in more ways than one.

Then there's *The English Patient*, directed by Anthony Minghella from Michael On-daatje's well-received literary novel. An out-and-out horror flick? Well, not exactly. But it does possess two horrifying scenes few viewers will soon forget. One's quiet (the prospect of the heroine dying alone and lonely in an isolated desert cave while her lover struggles vainly to reach her); the other's loud (poor Willem Dafoe faced with losing both thumbs to a forceful Moslem nurse with a straight razor, egged on by a German officer). And the finely crafted, highly complex, onion-peeling structure of the rest of the movie? I cried at the end of *Sling Blade*, but not at the closing credits of this one. *The English Patient* is finely crafted and technically admirable but, it seems to me, never quite communicates honestly from the heart.

Breaking the Waves holds a dark view of life in the provinces . . . more specifically on an isolated island off Scotland. Emily Watson is wonderfully tragic as a wife in a difficult position. She has visions and speaks with God—and gets replies from Himself. This is a film that intimately connects sexuality and the divine. You get a convincing view of personal relationships being sucked down by the same sort of psychic maelstroms you find in Kathe Koja novels. The word for *Breaking the Waves* is *devastating*. The usually harmless syndicated columnist Liz Smith sniped cattily, in regard to all the relative unknowns from indie productions appearing on the Oscar ballot, "Who's going to tune in the Oscars to see what dress Emily Watson is wearing?" Well, Liz, me for one.

Trainspotting is a nonjudgmental portrait of heroin-addicted youth in contemporary urban Scotland, a horror for many viewers. It also possesses, along with sly nods to Beatles movies of yore, a queasily hilarious scene of a kid diving into a toilet bowl in the dirtiest, most disgusting loo in all the British Isles. It's an attention grabber—an *Alice in Wonderland* image for a new generation.

Let's not forget the Coen brothers' *Fargo*, that only slightly exaggerated portrait of what most non-North Dakotans and -Minnesotans might view as a truly alien landscape. Frances McDormand as the pregnant Sheriff Marge was to die for. Film historians may eventually note *Fargo* as the first mainstream American film to expose equally mainstream audiences to the special use of rural wood chippers more usually found in direct-to-video exploitation flicks.

In *Lone Star*, director John Sayles created a dramatic structure less romantic than *The English Patient*, but a great deal more convincing. The film evocatively demonstrated the defensible view that time is a patient entity that simply sits back and waits for precisely the right moment to rear up and bite; something of a philosophical trapdoor spider. Then there was *Antonia's Line*, the charming Dutch import depicting several generations of a lusty, lively, politically (particularly in terms of gender) complex family. It included such great fantasy (or magic realist, if you prefer) touches as a stone angel in a graveyard leaning down to pummel with its marble wings a collaborator priest.

Let's not forget classic fantasy from the Bard. Kenneth Branagh's four-and-a-half-hour *Hamlet* retained every last line and scene often cut from the customary abridged stage versions. The ghost was still there. And so were a lot of fascinating expansions of the play's political backdrop. *William Shakespeare's Romeo & Juliet* gave us something of an MTV version of the classic love story. The movie's conceit was to update the settings and dress to the present, but to retain the Shakespearean language; much the same approach as S. P. Somtow's version of *A Midsummer Night's Dream, Ill Met by Moonlight. R&J* was vastly more successful financially.

And so on. All in all, it was good year for independent productions, and a banner year for darkness.

Genre Features: Adventures in the Big Screen Trade:
1996 launched in a big, splashy (well, perhaps *gooshy* would be a more appropriate adjective) way with Robert Rodriguez directing *From Dusk Til Dawn* from an old Quentin Tarantino script. George Clooney and Tarantino himself star as a pair of criminal brothers on the lam after a botched bank job. Guess which bro is the genuine psycho and which one the classic good guy with rough manners? The Gecko brothers kidnap disaffected preacher Harvey Keitel and his two kids and use them as a cover to sneak into Mexico. The Geckos have a rendezvous with getaway consultants at a notorious Mexican bar called the Titty Twister. What none of our heroes knows is that the club is a Sawney Beane–style hangout for vampires who delight in draining and dismembering unwary travelers.

This is a film with a definite multiple personality. Some viewers much preferred the straightforward pursuit and escape crime drama of the first half. Others just lay back, said "go for it," and dug the exceedingly graphic second half when a lot of vampire and human ass became (bloody) grass. Special treats included Selma Hayek's sensual snake dance (in real life, she is terrified of serpents) and appearances by such as Cheech Marin, who played three roles, and the seldom-seen Fred Williamson. Over-the-top? Yeah. Lots of fun? Ditto. The movie ends with a visual tweak that doesn't make a heck of a lot of sense, but it's cute anyway. Allegedly Tarantino and Rodriguez are planning both a sequel and a prequel.

The very beginning of the new year also brought us *Screamers*, based on Philip K. Dick's chilling classic short story, "Second Variety." This was a Canadian production, with that north-of-the-border chilly look that we so frequently see in Cronenberg movies. *Screamers* was directed by Christian Duguay from a script cowritten by Dan O'Bannon. Peter Weller, Roy Dupuis, and Jennifer Rubin headed the cast. In a nice updating of Dick's Cold War extrapolation, it's the year 2078. A distant mining planet has been devastated by war. The survivors of the corporate factions find themselves united by desperation. The "screamers"—intelligent, self-replicating, able-to-mimic humans, highly lethal robot weapons—are well on the way to exterminating all humanity on this world. It's grim, cold, violent terrain, and most of the film works well as intelligent action melodrama. The O'Bannon influence seems clear, though, and it appears to be both a benefit and a liability. The action seems to play in the same gritty universe as *Alien*, which is fine. But the ending also seems highly derivative of *Alien*, and it plays badly here. I won't give everything away, but imagine the cat was a teddy bear . . .

Two of the biggest films of the year were invasion spectaculars. One was a triumph of economics; the other, a triumph of aesthetics. I think you know which category *Independence Day* fell into. Roland Emmerich directed the quarter-billion dollar success. *ID4*, as it was abbreviated in the promotions, gave us a whole raft of moderately high-profile actors, all thoroughly upstaged by the special effects. By now, there's probably no one on Earth who hasn't seen at least the trailers depicting gigantic ships shadowing Terran cities, and death rays blowing the hell out of the White House and the Empire State Building. Bill Pullman did well as the Gulf War vet–U.S. President we all wish we had, Jeff Goldblum sufficed as the brilliant geek scientist who first figures out the aliens are less than benign, Will Smith played the top-gun fighter pilot role to the hilt, and Randy Quaid, as a drunk crop duster, saw the best part of his crucial role cut to pieces. *ID4* worked best with the viewer's higher faculties switched off. As SF, it was a hellacious compilation of clichés, leavened with a series of brain-dead encounters with illogic. It really wouldn't have cost any more to have it make sense. But that presumably was not the point. . . . This one sold the Mother Ship's mass in popcorn.

The conceptually more ambitious alien invasion flick was Tim Burton's *Mars Attacks!* Some moviegoers, not too swift at figuring out relative production schedules and release dates, thought this must surely be a spoof of *ID4*. Well, it could have been, but truly, folks, it was a coincidence. Tim Burton audaciously based a major picture on the notorious Topps bubblegum cards that graphically depicted a Martian invasion three decades ago. Every big invasion movie's got to have a president; here, it was Jack Nicholson (who then got to play a dual role as a Vegas wheeler-dealer). Glenn Close was in this, as was Michael J. Fox and a whole passel of others, climaxing in a startling appearance by Tom Jones himself! This was a very funny movie, though I suspect most of the younger viewers (well, under thirty-five) didn't get a lot of the jokes. The Martians, when they spoke, sounded like a weird impression of Jerry Lewis. There were plenty of in-jokes and references to '50s SF movies. The truth be told, though, probably nothing in the movie surpassed *Mars Attacks!*'s initial and powerful image, a shot of a stampeding herd of burning cattle, though Lisa Marie's strikingly choreographed role as a Martian warrior masquerading as a sexy Earth babe with a huge bouffant came close. Burton fans can usually expect a powerfully off-trail achievement. This filled the bill.

Earlier I mentioned two Shakespeare fantasies; now I'll cite a truly first-rate Shakespeare science fiction political epic. Yes, really! I've got to call Richard Loncraine's updating of *Richard III* the best alternate-world picture of the year. Set during a Fascist coup in 1930s England, *Richard III* spectacularly captures the complex political plotting, royal wrangling, and violent turmoil of colliding worlds. All the Bard's language is here, the production being based on the stage production by Richard Eyre and Ian McKellen. McKellen plays the title role with icy, serpentine precision. He's backed by a wonderful cast including the likes of Kristin Scott Thomas, Annette Bening, Maggie Smith, Robert Downey, Jr., and many more. It's ingeniously mounted, and it all makes sense—showing how timeless Shakespeare's insights can be. Of course you do have to get used to the tanks, the occasional fighter plane, and the action scenes that would do justice to a Schwarzenegger action epic. Culture? Absolutely. This is guiltless pleasure.

Would you believe a biographical drama about one of the century's greatest fantasists, a pulp magazine writer who galvanized the fantasy lives of generations of young men and women before killing himself in 1936? Yep, *The Whole Wide World* marvelously brought to life the final years of Robert E. Howard, Cross Plains, Texas's favored son. Dan Myers directed from a script by Michael Scott Myers, and Myers based his script on Novalyne Price Ellis's memoir, *One Who Walked Alone*. What a surprise, and a pleasant one at that, to see a Donald Grant small-press original volume turned into a well-received art-house flick! Ellis, née Price, was a schoolteacher and aspiring writer herself when she met Howard. She found herself in a quiet but powerful emotional battle with Howard's ailing mother for the creator of *Conan the Barbarian*'s fierce affections. Vincent D'Onofrio plays Robert Howard with a great deal of empathy; Renée Zellweger gives her character, Novalyne Price, a great and convincing insight into the powerful, but largely platonic, forces that drew these two together. Expert sound design cleverly devised a way to portray Price's attempt to immerse herself in a Conan epic. This was clearly a film that wouldn't have been produced, at least in this form at this time, without considerable backing from Vincent D'Onofrio. He—and everyone else connected with the production—should be congratulated. *The Whole Wide World* automatically joins a select group of films that empathically and powerfully explore the world of the creative act, a category that includes such works as *All That Jazz*, *Reuben, Reuben*, and *My Left Foot*. Robert Howard makes a perfect centerpiece. Can you imagine a similar film about the life of any of today's well-marketed crafters of thick heroic-fantasy-epic series?

Without a doubt, the best *Star Trek* picture of the year was the only *Star Trek* picture, that one being *Star Trek: First Contact*. There's a modern piece of urban folklore that says that it's the odd-numbered Trek pictures that are the good ones; or is it the even? At any rate, *First Contact* was pretty good. Directed by Jonathan Frakes, this feature starts with those implacable hive-minded adversaries, the Borg, setting their big cubical ship against Star Fleet in Earth's local space. Disregarding the Borg admonition that "Resistance is futile!" the Captain Picard–helmed *Enterprise* rushes to help, only to be sucked into a Borg plot to return through time to the devastated Earth of the twenty-first century, there to sabotage the shaky test flight of humankind's first experimental warp-drive craft (based in rural Montana!) and spoil Earth's initial contact with the Federation. It's solid, serviceable space opera with some good effects and touches. The Borg are, as ever, implacably devious cyborgs, even scheming to get Data (Brent Spiner) laid. As I recall, Data's brief liaison with the Borg queen is his second sexual experience in the Trek universe. The queen is played with thoroughly weird Clive Barkeresque sensuality by Alice Krige, the South African actress most of us first noticed when she appeared as the malevolent spirit in *Ghost Story*, back in 1981. Gene Roddenberry's legacy continues to chug along profitably, even as private space enterprise rockets a portion of the de-animated producer's ashes into space.

Every year there's a best Stephen King–related film. 1996 didn't disappoint. "Well, okay," I said after I saw Stephen King's *Thinner*, "you're right." Horror writer Dawn Dunn had summed up the adaptation of the Richard Bachman novel as a "low budget version of *Moby-Dick*." You know something? She's right. There's no sailing ship or great white whale (well . . . I could make a comment about the "before" phase of the protagonist, but I will forbear), but there is a relatively sophisticated and complex treatment of why Revenge Is Bad. And that pretty much sums up Melville's great novel as well. Back in the old days, this would have been a Laurel Entertainment project. It was still produced by Richard Rubenstein and Mitchell Galin, but appeared under the Spelling imprint. Robert Paul Burke stars as the sleazy New England criminal lawyer successfully defending Mafioso Joe Mantegna (surprisingly restrained).

Burke's initial fat suit is just as neato as Eddie Murphy's in *The Nutty Professor*. Burke's triumph is, however, short-lived after he accidentally runs down the aged daughter of a 106-year-old Gypsy chief who then puts a curse, becoming "thinner," on Burke, as well as on the police chief and judge who help whitewash the affair. Burke starts to lose weight, spiraling down from three hundred pounds at a rate of about a percent per day. The other two guys develop horrendous deteriorative skin conditions. People start to die classily offstage. Burke panics. He finds the old Gypsy, but there's no forgiveness in the offing. Meantime, he suspects his wife of having an affair with the family doctor. Things get dire, then desperate. Burke enlists the aid of the thug he got off.

The whole movie's strikingly restrained, probably in large part due to the script by classy writer Michael McDowell and director Tom Holland. The location filming in coastal Maine helps, too. The dramatic suspense is a touch flaccid, but the developing grimness makes up for a lot of deflated melodrama. By the time the film ends, just about everyone, it seems, guilty and innocent alike, has died because of the protagonist's obsessive behavior. Ambiguity keeps us from firmly placing some victims in either the guilty or innocent category. And the really bad guy appears to have gotten away scot-free. So there's a great deal of ambiguous moral dilemma—oh, and did I mention political incorrectness? If the movie didn't fare tremendously well at the box office, it may have been because of the Gypsy curse placed on it by offended Romany. Complaints may also have been lodged by Italian Americans, animal lovers, doctors, lawyers, and fat people. Ah, well. I still think Herman Melville would have found something to talk about over coffee once he'd seen this one.

I think my personal favorite horror movie all year was Peter Jackson's *The Frighteners*. This New Zealand production didn't have the visceral quality of Jackson's 1992 serio-comic zombie-film-to-end-all-zombie-films, *Dead Alive*, but it had many terrific moments. For the sake of the American market, it starred Michael J. Fox as a not too tightly wired exorcist, actually a scam-inclined psychic working in league with a few disaffected, if genial, spirits to set up hauntings and then defuse them for cash. Director Jackson cowrote the script with Fran Walsh. The plot of *The Frighteners* wrapped around the ambitions of a genuinely malign spirit, the ghost of a hopeful world-class mass murder bucking to make the level of a Guinness Book killer, though momentarily stalled by physical death. The production didn't do the box office the makers hoped for, obviously, possibly because of thwarted audience expectations. The ad campaign could never seem to figure out exactly what sort of movie this was—chiller or yuk-fest. Actually it was neither one. In the classic Shakespearean tradition it was, by turns, comic and serious, letting tension build from each quality playing off against the other. These days the mass commercial audience seems to have some real problems if a film marketed as general entertainment doesn't confine itself to a single mode. Just as director Jackson's *Dead Alive* was funny serious, a perfectly legitimate artistic oxymoron, so was *The Frighteners*. But a lot of viewers didn't seem to get it. John Astin, Dee Wallace Stone, Jake Busey, and the rest of the cast, were all very good. I've reserved a particular place in my heart for Jeffrey Combs's (remember *Reanimator*?) over-the-top turn as an FBI agent who is certainly no Fox Mulder. . . .

A vastly more successful experiment in combining tones was *Scream*, a phenomenal commercial success that once again revived director Wes Craven's intermittently faltering career. Made for less than $10 million, *Scream*, largely through audience word of mouth, made close to $90 million, then returned in a rerelease early in 1997. Releasing studios don't usually do that . . . *Scream* was essentially a tony summation of the last quarter century of teen slasher flicks. It was also a compilation of recursive jokes, trivia, and uncountable references to any number of earlier pictures. Sometimes the reference was verbal, sometimes visual, and, as in the extended first scene, structural. *Scream* begins with Drew Barrymore playing a teen girl in the house alone, menaced in a tone of escalating terror by a psycho voice on the phone. Psycho it is, and *Psycho* is the filmic reference. Most of the audience is too young to know or care about what all the references mean. For them, the attraction is a fast, smart, scary melodrama of a small-town society terrorized by a crazed killer, a movie that avoids dumbness, a scenario in which characters generally recognize the rules of bad horror flicks as survival tips for this movie: Don't have illicit sex in a cabin if you're a teen, Don't go off alone to the basement if you hear a mysterious noise, etc. The marketers say that about 20 percent of *Scream*'s tickets have been going to people who have already seen it. Nobody could have predicted this. Wes Craven gave us all a breath of fresh graveyard air. Be sure to give a lot of credit to screenwriter Kevin Williamson, as well as a wonderful repertory cast (mainly young) including the villainous Skeet Ulrich and the surprising Courteney Cox. A real treat was seeing Henry Winkler all grown up as the local high school principal. The villain's Edvard Munch–style mask should market exceedingly well next Hallowe'en.

City of Lost Children was certainly the most wondrous fantasy feature of the year. Back in 1991 I praised quite highly Jean-Pierre Jeunet and Marc Caro's black comedy of a decrepit future France, *Delicatessen*. Well, the guys returned with flash and dazzling imagery in *City of Lost Children*, a terrific quest to rescue abducted kids amid all manner of magical twists and weird science. In a genuinely surprising development, Jean-Pierre Jeunet will be (as *Variety* would put it) helming the fourth *Alien* movie, the one in which Ripley returns courtesy of the cloning labs. It could be very, very good. Or—

Woody Allen's *Mighty Aphrodite* was a successful contemporary fantasy. As ever, Allen crafted a first-rate complex of human relationships, at the same time funny and serious. This picture could initiate a new fad in Hollywood—giving each new feature its own literal Greek chorus. It's better than subtitles.

Dragonheart was a good fantasy, but not quite up to the expectations of many. After all, it starred Sean Connery as the voice and personality of a (computer-animated) dragon named Draco. Dennis Quaid was the medieval fantasy-world rogue who teamed with Draco to scam the locals: Draco would menace the community, toast a sheep or two with his breath, buzz the village square, then the "knight" would come along to take a healthy fee for getting rid of the pesky reptile. A lot of design and programming time went into attempting to construct Draco so that he would, to some degree, mimic actor Connery's facial expression and body language as he delivered his lines. It was a great experiment, but produced only mixed results. Perhaps credit Rob Cohen's direction and Charles Edward Pogue's script. This one was determinedly lightweight.

Also lightweight was David Twohy's break from movie writing to movie writing and directing, *The Arrival*. This had a strong '50s feel about it: a maverick scientist, played by Charlie Sheen, stumbles onto an extraterrestrial radio signal that suggests intelligent life. Everyone he trusts proceeds to mess him over. And so, just how widespread *is* the alien conspiracy? The conspiracy's broad enough, but the paranoia isn't nearly so effective as in many of the movie's predecessors. It simply lacks conviction.

For flat-out funny fantasy, I have a soft spot in my dark reviewer's heart for *Joe's Apartment*. Based on John Payson's popular MTV short film, the feature version took the same premise: nice ordinary guy from the sticks (Jerry O'Connell) moves to New York and takes the only apartment he can find—a dump that turns out to be massively infested with cockroaches. So far, highly realistic, right? The roaches turn out to be quite intelligent, personable, and civilized. They just want to live in a happy symbiotic relationship with the new guy. Viewers with extreme bug phobias never got through the theater doors. But many of the rest of us found ourselves laughing aloud more than once, at bits that were deliberately and calculatedly hilarious. Don Ho (!) and Robert Vaughn play the bad buys. Reginald Hudlin and Billy West play the voices of two of the most personable roaches. The literal "cast of thousands" is a stand-out, incorporating live, animatronic, and computer-generated insects.

My sense of nostalgia was greatly pleased by Billy Zane's convincing playing of *The Phantom*. Simon Wincer directed from Jeffrey Boam's script. I think justice has been done to comic book artist Lee Falk's classic "ghost who walks." This is bright, vigorous, highly unlikely, action-never-slacking, comic book adventure. It is so much better than Alec Baldwin's stint two years ago as *The Shadow*. Just shut down your sense of disbelief and try to forget that there's no convincing reason why the isolated, jungle-bound, Phantom should spend his working days clad in a bright purple leotard! Treat Williams apparently has a ball as the villain, and Kristy Swanson and Catherine Zeta Williams do well as light and dark female interests. Seaplanes, crystal skulls, a spectacular white horse, hey, this movie's got it all.

My favorite animated feature for the year was Henry Selick's *James and the Giant Peach*, adapted from Roald Dahl's typically dark and droll children's novel. Actually I should be a touch more precise and say this was my favorite blending of live action and stop-motion animation for 1996. The visuals were absolutely terrific as young James screws up, spills a magic potion, and has to deal with big bugs, a huge peach, and an arduous transoceanic voyage/quest. Voices included those of Susan Sarandon, Paul Terry, and Richard Dreyfuss. Alas, this didn't quite measure up to the same director's Tim Burton–produced *Nightmare Before Christmas*, but then the 1993 modern classic would be a hard act to equal, much less beat.

As a neat mix of animation and live action, *Space Jam* worked, even for us viewers who aren't basketball fans. Though one might be suspicious that this was merely a hyperannuated athletic shoe commercial, Michael Jordan played himself ingenuously as the abducted-by-aliens NBA player most likely to save the Earth. Of course he had a great deal of help from his thespian allies, Bugs Bunny, Daffy Duck, the Tasmanian Devil, et al. Joe Pytka directed; Ivan Reitman produced. This was a corporate confection, absolutely, but it still amused.

The Disney Studios did their best to expunge some of the darkness from *The Hunchback of Notre Dame*, and didn't do too badly, though all singing, all dancing, all genial gargoyles is a concept whose time may not have truly arrived. Tom Hulce and Demi Moore lent their voices to the roles of Quasimodo and Esmeralda. Good jobs both, though Moore will have to commit a lot more penance to soften the memories of *The Scarlet Letter* and *Striptease*. It was a brief, small breath of noxious air in the politically correct '90s to see a local McDonald's with this hand-lettered poster in the window: NOW!!! HUNCHBACK TOYS!

Okay, so you wanted some serious, adult, cyberpunk animé? Then I trust you took in the US release of Japanese animator Mamoru Oshii's *Ghost in the Shell*, an adaptation of the manga by Masamune Shirow. In the year 2029, the world has been made borderless by the Net, claims the picture. Quite a lot of nasty, violent, brutish maneuvering is going on involving high-tech, morphing agents. The dialog and the dubious cultural parallax between Japan and the United States militates against much viewer involvement on the emotional level. But on the intellectual—this one's fascinating, if a touch off-putting.

For deliberate oddness, Jim Jarmusch's fantasy Western, *Dead Man*, determinedly strayed from any mainstream track. Johnny Depp played a callow Easterner stranded in the nineteenth-century American West after his job offer falls through. What's a guy to do except learn to shoot extremely well and become a tormented myth figure? Especially when his name is William Blake. Gary Farmer's a standout as an Indian, a spiritual guide, and a William Blake fan. This starkly shot feature boasted a wonderfully eclectic cast (Iggy Pop in drag?), a wholly sardonic outlook, and a pace more, well, stately than some of the audience might want. Do not expect a John Wayne Western— and that's all to the good. Enjoy the caustic wit.

In *Multiplicity*, Michael Keaton missed the Dolly the Sheep cloning bandwagon. This was that variety of lame science fiction high concept that swipes part of the cloning idea, but ignores all the reality. A comedy? To some . . . especially Michael Keaton fans. The bloom was off Arnold Scharzenegger's two features for the year. *Eraser* had lots of gunfire, laser zapping, and explosions, but the excitement ran sluggishly. And the holiday release, *Jingle All the Way*, never came to full consciousness, even with costar Sinbad and some astute observation of superhero toy marketing.

Oddness that didn't quite work—that was the bottom line for *Mary Reilly*, the Julia Roberts vehicle directed by Stephen Frears. Based on Valerie Martin's fine novel, this should have hit on more cylinders than it actually did. It was a literary dark fantasy with a perfect high concept: recount the Jekyll and Hyde story from the point of view of Dr. Jekyll's housekeeper, the eponymous Mary Reilly. Good idea; dubious execution. John Malkovich was a decently ominous Jekyll, but didn't really look all that different from his alter ego. Glenn Close added a sense of solidity with her role as a nasty madam. Alas, Julia Roberts wasn't fully up to the task. To give her credit, she didn't deep-six the production the way Demi Moore did in *The Scarlet Letter* and *Striptease*. But she still could not bring her character to sufficient and needed life. The movie was dark indeed, but torpid.

If you wanted a quick fix for depression bred by *CNN Headline News* or the daily newspaper, *Phenomenon* probably filled the bill. Jon Turteltaub, directing from Gerald DiPego's script, showcased John Travolta as a thirty-something good guy in a sleepy California town. On the night of his thirty-seventh birthday, Travolta maybe gets zapped by a mysterious brilliant light in the sky; or maybe he suffers a micro-aneurism or something similar. Whatever the cause, it's *Flowers for Algernon* time as Travolta's character starts ascending to genius level. The solid surrounding cast (Kyra Sedgwick, Forrest Whitaker, Robert Duvall, and others) gives this Capra-esque light drama a feeling of solidity. But ultimately it seems a bit air-puffed. I probably didn't really appreciate *Phenomenon* following so closely on the heels of the vastly more affecting *Powder*, last year's similarly themed film by Victor Salva.

John Travolta was rather more endearing in *Phenomenon* than he was in the high-tech thriller, *Broken Arrow*. As a psychopathic Air Force pilot stealing nuclear weapons from an inflight Stealth bomber to sell to international terrorists, he slavered a lot but didn't really convince. Christian Slater did his considerable best to compensate as a good guy.

Edward Norton earned his Academy Award supporting actor nomination for his role as the psycho altar boy in Gregory Hoblit's *Primal Fear*. Poor Richard Gere was hard-pressed to compete in his lead role as an ambitious and opportunistic attorney who thinks he's lucked into a dream case after Norton's accused of savagely murdering the local archbishop. Most of the movie's sharp and edgy enough, but it simply goes on too long.

H. G. Wells has supplied material for quite a few adaptations now; not so many as Shakespeare, of course, but Bill's been around a lot longer. Give Herbert George time . . . John Frankenheimer's *The Island of Dr. Moreau* was no *Food of the Gods/Village of the Giants*, thank God, but neither was it George Pal's *The Time Machine*. It was something of a mixed bag—or perhaps more accurately, metaphorically and otherwise, a mixed breed. The script, credited to a quartet that included Walon Green and Richard

Stanley, updated the science to the realm of gene-splicing. David Thewlis is a marooned UN official somewhat taken aback by Moreau's groundbreaking scientific efforts. The Good Doctor is played by a papal Marlon Brando, steeped in weirdness all the way to the top of his bizarre hat. Val Kilmer plays Moreau's middle manager; Fairuza Balk plays the ever-popular cat woman (wasn't it the sensual Barbara Carrera the last time around in 1977?). This is an okay production with lots of neat tropical vacation cinematography and a variety of camp moments. It will probably not go down in history as the defining melodrama of the biological revolution.

Disaster movies? In the summer's first biggie, *Twister*, director Jan De Bont and writers Michael Crichton and Anne-Marie Martin took us into the noisy, special effects-riddled world of tornado-chasing researchers. The effects were all the movie had to offer. The visual joke of a cow aerially circumnavigating a funnel cloud was a true example of Midwestern humor. Later in the autumn, Roger Donaldson's *Dante's Peak* mixed a few civics lessons from *Jaws* and some background from the Mount Saint Helens's disaster to show us a little northwestern town in the line of fire from a long dormant volcano. Linda Hamilton stood out as the town's careworn mayor. Lots of things blew up real good—except whenever the script screeched to a halt to espouse conventional American nuclear family values.

Just as the audience seemed to have a tough time interpreting *The Frighteners*, they also seemed confused by Ben Stiller's dark seriocomedy, *The Cable Guy*. If viewers were expecting a typical Jim Carrey laff-riot, they were sorely disappointed. There were funny moments—including some hysterical sequences at a medieval-themed restaurant when Carrey's character did a genuinely deranged impression of Anthony Hopkins's Hannibal Lecter—but primarily this was a muted, moody portrait of a disturbed and lonely cable installer (Carrey) who obsesses on Matthew Broderick as a potential friend. Writer Lou Holtz, Jr. created an edgy script that apparently didn't have enough of that "endearingly wacko" Ace Ventura shtick. It's not wholly successful, but the movie's also a bit better than you probably heard.

Tom Shadyak's remake of *The Nutty Professor*, a more mainstream, straightforward comedy, succeeded wildly at the box office. This project also resuscitated Eddie Murphy's lurching career. If you saw the 1963 original, you may find Murphy a much more endearing actor than Jerry Lewis as the poor overweight, lonely, frustrated college professor Sherman Klump. A Dr. Jekylloid formula changes his life radically, both in terms of weight fluctuation and by transforming him into the testosterone-jazzed Buddy Love. Murphy plays a total of seven characters in this film, including the entire cast of a Klump family meeting. The Rick Baker makeup and the "fat suits" will take away your breath—and your appetite.

Less than wholly successful Walter Hill features are better than no Walter Hill pictures. *Last Man Standing*, a hard-boiled melodrama of rival bootlegger gangs in a small Texas town in the distant heart of Prohibition, had something of a detached fantasy-world feel to it. Bruce Willis did well as the lone stranger who comes to town for his own reasons, and then finds himself trapped in any number of physical and metaphorical crossfires. You won't be surprised to learn this is yet another homage to *Yojimbo*. The cinematography is stunning; the treatment of female characters is a touch less than enlightened.

Though not trumpeted in this category, *The Ghost and the Darkness* made a valiant effort to be a mainstream monster movie in the tradition of *Jaws*. In the late nineteenth century, construction engineer Val Kilmer is dispatched to East Africa to oversee the completion of a critical railroad bridge. All this is essential to the well-being of the British empire. The trouble is, a pair of people-eating lions are depleting and terrorizing the construction crews. Kilmer finds an ally in a great white hunter (Michael Douglas). The two deadly big cats (130 victims and counting) are given their eponymous names by the local natives. Directed by Stephen Hopkins from a William Goldman script, this picture should have been a lot more effective than it turned out to be. Based on a real-life case in which reality never came up with an explanation for the preternaturally deadly lions' killing spree, Goldman's script doesn't speculate either. It's all a bit frustrating.

I had a lot of hopes for *Bad Moon*. Writer/director Eric Red's always done best, though, when he's worked as writer with someone else directing. Witness *Near Dark* and *Blue Steel* with Kathryn Bigelow. *Bad Moon*'s a Morgan Creek/Warner Bros. production filmed in scenic Vancouver. First we see Michael Pare as Ted, a guy who loses his girlfriend to a werewolf deep in the heart of Asia. He's wounded by the beast before blowing off its head with a shotgun. He returns to the States and turns up without warning in the neighborhood of his loyal sister Janet (Mariel Hemingway). She's a single mom lawyer raising her young son apparently just outside some little town in the Pacific Northwest. There's not a lot of mystery here. Poor Uncle Ted's become a murderous werewolf himself, though he's still attempting to find a way out of his dilemma. Medical science can do nothing, so his last chance is the power of family love. Unfortunately either the theory's not working or the family's too dysfunctional. Uncle Ted just gets meaner and noisier. The only one in the family who cottons quick to his true nature is Thor, the German shepherd. The dog can discern the werewolf hiding in human's clothing. The movie's based on G. Wayne Miller's novel, *Thor*. It's a scenic little film with reasonable shapeshifter F/X by Steve Johnson. The wonderfully named Hrothgar Matthews, better known in the Lower 48 as the Alien Bounty Hunter on *The X-Files*, does a nice turn as the flopsy, a sleazy door-to-door con man. It all looks good. But unfortunately *Bad Moon* comes a cropper because it never really comes to grips with the apparent core issue—whether or not there's some way to stop Uncle Ted's descent into lycanthropy. Eric Red tries to get some mileage out of showing a clip of *Werewolf of London* within the film, but it never quite coheres. Another *Wolf*, this isn't. Too bad.

For high-tech contemporary adventure, Keanu Reeves tries again (it's hard to forget *Johnny Mnemonic*) in Andrew Davis's *Chain Reaction*. It seems scientists in Chicago figure out how to get an inexhaustible, nonpolluting energy supply from water. This leads to all sorts of murder, mayhem, and corporate and governmental chicanery. It's an energetic melodrama that generates its own high energy, but still doesn't really make much sense. And it has that new staple of movie effects, a human being (in this case, Reeves on a motorcycle) outdistancing a fireball blast.

1996 brought a number of sequels. Vincent Perez replaced the late Brandon Lee in *City of Angels: Crow 2*. Once again a benign (if you're not a bad guy) revenant returns to seek revenge. The filming is again dark and rainy; the music, loud and raucous. The fabricated cityscapes are enthralling. But the movie itself is slight. *Slight* is also the appropriate adjective for *The Craft*, a slender thriller about teenage girls dabbling in witchcraft. Be patient. In 1997, tune in *Buffy the Vampire Slayer* . . .

The third sequel to *Hellraiser* was *Bloodline: Hellraiser IV*. Kevin Yagher directed, but eventually took his name off the credits. Peter Atkins, I think, didn't particularly like what happened to the scenes shot from his script, but left his name on the movie. Originally this was to be something of an anthology approach to the history of the Lament Configuration, and that damnable puzzle box, depicting three chronologically disparate generations of the puzzle-making family. What eventually hit the screen had been through some mighty peculiar editing mills. It was, unfortunately, hash. Still, it was interesting seeing Pinhead on a futuristic spacecraft.

Bordello of Blood was the latest *Tales from the Crypt* feature. Not nearly so taut as

Demon Night, the last installment, *Bordello* concerned itself with a self-interested business establishment set up by a reconstituted vampire queen. Dennis Miller was funny, but not often enough.

The year's most remarkable rerelease was 1975's Jack Hill B movie classic, *Switchblade Sisters*, a politically astute portrait of gang life that holds up just fine two decades later. This picture made the art-house circuit, thanks to Quentin Tarantino's intervention, cutting a deal with Miramax to rerelease some of his favorite old B flicks. Camp? Well, sure. But the last third, when city streets run loud with the gunfire of revolution, is awe inspiring.

You could also call *Mystery Science Theatre 3000: the Movie* a rerelease, sort of. The acerbic *MST3K* crew turned their attention on *This Island Earth* with mixed results. I mean, really, what's there to make fun about with an interocitor kit? Anyone who'd make jokes about the dire situation on Metaluna would probably make light of Serbian atrocities. At any rate, the *MST3K* feature kept us all occupied until the TV series finished its suspenseful negotiations and moved from the Comedy Channel to the Sci-Fi Channel.

Television: Bright Pixels, Small Screen:
The amount of SF, fantasy, and horror presently broadcast on the small screen is phenomenal. It's also a highly volatile quantity. Blink twice and an intriguing new series arriving via network or syndication is gone.

Conversely, stare in your unblinking, pixilated fashion, universal remote squeezed in your fingers, and any number of series you wished would go away, simply won't. To put it another way, buy stock in Sky, Rupert Murdoch's new satellite media conglomerate, and you'll get your fill of the fantastic beamed to your small screen. You'll never need to pick up a book or venture out to a movie theater again. Consider it a transitional larval state carrying you from the advent of digital video disk technology to the home installation of hi-res virtual reality equipment. Get those IV drip snacks ready!

Meanwhile . . .

Early in the year, ABC's compelling supernatural series, *American Gothic*, went belly up and that was a genuine shame. Child actor Lucas Black recovered nicely, though, playing opposite Billy Bob Thornton in the magnificent feature, *Sling Blade*.

Another sad casualty was Fox's VR5, the high-tech, near-future drama featuring Lori Singer as a smart, capable, vulnerable tech-head trying to survive a world of dark conspiracy and treacherous virtual reality. Singer's plucky protagonist carried an added benefit of being a good role model for computer-shy female viewers.

A third unfortunate loss was the SF military adventure series, *Space: Above and Beyond*, the *X-Files* alums Wong and Morgan's attempt to mix a little Haldeman and Heinlein. Although it sometimes seemed to resemble a Gulf War *China Beach*, the show carried its weight with an effective young cast thoroughly mixed in ethnic and gender roles. It did a particularly good job using the distorting lens of science fiction to treat discrimination issues. The metaphor was artificially created, vat-grown human beings.

A lot of standbys hung around for another season. *Highlander* completed a fifth season, with Adrian Paul still dealing with a multitude of enemies wishing to lop off his potentially immortal head. The theme for the year seemed to be "who shall judge?" The series' audience appears to be both a devoted and a high-powered lot. Popular novelist Jennifer Roberson reputedly took a 90 percent cut from her usual advance so she could write *Highlander: Scotland the Brave* for Warner Books. And a good tale it was.

J. Michael Straczynski's epic SF novel in TV series form, *Babylon 5* continued into its fourth season. Momentum for the show continues to build. At the World Science

Fiction Convention in Anaheim, the episode "Coming of Shadows," written by Strac-zynski, won a Hugo Award for dramatic achievement. With what seem like scores of important characters and dozens of plotlines, the show bustles with activity. With roots sunk deep in classic science fiction, *Babylon 5* seems steeped in a familiarity that in-creasingly attracts a body of traditional SF viewers. Unlike the various series of the *Star Trek* universe, Straczynski's show suggests and reflects the reality that what's going on at the front of the CRT stage is an integral component, but certainly not the entire reality, of what's happening politically and culturally in the rest of the galaxy.

John Lithgow continues to provide the ignition spark for the ensemble cast of the comedy *Third Rock from the Sun*. It's good sitcom, but it's still sitcom. I liked the out-of-school comment in a *Details Magazine* interview of nubile alien Kristen Johnson: "I know that I'm biting the hand that feeds me, but TV can really suck the brains right out of your body."

Chris Carter's *X-Files* leads the Fox Network pack and has survived a change of scheduling day from Friday to Sunday. FBI agents Mulder and Scully (David Duchovny and Gillian Anderson) continue to divide their time between UFO/alien abduction/massive government conspiracy plots and more freestanding episodes involving super-natural plots and freaks of nature. Probably the most striking episode of the 1996 season was "Jose Chung's from Outer Space," in which Charles Nelson Reilly played the epon-ymous character, a best-selling writer researching a book on UFOs and alien abduction. With complete tongue in cheek, all manner of conspiracy lore was spooned into the broth, including a pair of Men in Black played by professional wrestler Jesse Ventura and game show host Alex Trebeck. Something of a metafictional spoof of the series, "Jose Chung" was a pure delight. TV series are rarely this brave.

Chris Carter's new series, *Millennium*, took over the old *X-Files* Friday night slot. Starring the wonderful Lance Henriksen as a semipsychic ex-FBI criminal profiler named Frank Black, the character now lives in Seattle and works for the Millennium Group, a shadowy law enforcement agency that's allegedly trying to stem the tide of psychotic frenzy that might increasingly engulf the US population as we wind down to the year 2000. At least that's the stated premise. The season started out with all too many similar "serial killer of the week" shows. The filming is striking, the production values high, but the tone has tended to be grim in the extreme. This is not exactly a feel-good show. One national columnist referred to the star as "the glum Lance Henriksen." Episodes have contained some remarkably powerful material about violence and death. The at-titude is unremittingly grim, though a broadening of focus to include some active par-ticipation by Frank Black's wife (Megan Gallagher) has helped leaven the show. Another welcome change was an open-ended episode (come to think of it, most of the episodes are fairly open-ended) about genetic engineering, identical bright clones, and a crazed plan to provide the right crew for the metaphorical millennial ark. Naturally Brad Dourif was the guest star. In both of Chris Carter's shows, composer Mark Snow's scores are an evocative, atmospheric pleasure. I hope that *Millennium* increasingly confronts the real issues of millennial fever and begins to realize its apparent stated ambition. It's got the tone down fine; now it just increasingly needs a vision. Interestingly, *Millennium* is probably second only to *Touched by an Angel* in terms of imparting Christian instruction to the audience. Each episode bears an epigraph, usually biblical, customarily from the Old Testament. These Christian homilies are never good news. But do they ever strike a tonal chord!

Sliders has continued, taking the adventurous cast (and us) each week to a parallel universe where a divergent reality has taken hold and created a world familiar yet ul-timately alien. The shtick frequently seems to borrow from movies as diverse as *Twister*, *Tremors*, and *Night of the Living Dead*.

The Outer Limits and Poltergeist: the Legacy continue to originate on Showtime, then migrate to Fox. The new Outer Limits—well, while the show occasionally adapts existing SF stories and employs prose writers who can also handle scripts, the series has yet to exceed its classic predecessor and produce a "Demon with a Glass Hand." Poltergeist frequently surmounts its limiting premise of attempting to fit freestanding narratives into a framework concerning a Bay Area network of operatives working to keep the World-as-We-Know-It safe from dark magical phenomena. It screened some particularly peachy episodes dealing with a vengeance-driven Chinese fox demon and a haunted railroad man.

Sam Raimi's team continues to bring us antipodean delights from Down Under with Hercules: the Legendary Journeys and Xena: Warrior Princess. Both series mix with abandon contemporary attitude and language with the tropes of classical mythology. Kevin Sorbo still maintains his Herculean hunkdom effortlessly. Each series amuses. They're not Great Art, but they pursue their own individual seriocomic courses with panache. These days, Xena appears to be getting the lioness's share of attention. Xena was only momentarily slowed this season when actress Lucy Lawless broke her pelvis while practicing a horseback stunt for the Tonight Show. Whether Xena is a "post-feminist" hero for a new generation is certainly open to debate. Xena's a tough, smart, highly competent barbarian warrior. But that doesn't preclude her adhering to the classic definition of a feminist: someone who practices the heretical notion that women are people too. There are doubtless those who would rather see her settle more plot issues with reasoned discourse than lethal weapons—and that does indeed happen from time to time. But that isn't really the point. What's more critical is that Xena clings to freedom and independence as though it really means something. Brava!

NBC turned Saturday nights into a three-hour prime-time smorgasbord of the fantastic, but unfortunately also saw fit to burden it with an odious neologism, the "Saturday night thrillogy." The block led with Dark Skies, a (literally) '50s SF series about aliens lurking about here on Earth. The government is, of course, trying to keep everything secret so as not to panic the voters. J. T. Walsh does a fine job as Frank Bach, the leader of Majestic 12, the covert program to mislead American presidents and hoodwink the public. It's fun seeing actors playing actual historical figures such as Robert Kennedy, Allen Dulles, and J. Edgar Hoover, though the novelty wears thin after a while. I have to wonder whether a significant portion of the viewing audience have no idea at all who these apparently significant people are. I particularly enjoyed (for its cockeyed grotesquery) the episode in which the female half of the young couple who discover the Truth and have to run has her head invaded by a nasty parasitic alien. Her husband finds out the untried, but highly touted by the discoverer, solution. We get to see the couple in an abandoned house, the woman tied to a chair. Her husband feeds her a big glass of Bromo-Seltzer, then figures out a source for acetone (ah, the nail polish remover all American women then carried in their purses . . .). He fills a big syringe with the chemical, then wings it, apparently trusting to blind luck that when he sticks the needle into her neck, he'll put the acetone right into the ET. Of course he lucks out. She starts to cough like a kitty hacking up a hairball, and finally a worse-for-wear critter pops out of her mouth and expires on the floor. I liked that. Maybe I've been watching Beavis and Butt-Head way too much. Though it shares neither the tone nor the craft, Dark Skies acts like something of a prequel to the X-Files.

In the middle of the "thrillogy" is The Pretender, which boasts the shaky premise that if someone's smart enough, he can be a quick enough study to master any discipline (paramedic, lawyer, Indian chief . . .) and pass himself off convincingly through an hour of melodrama. Michael Weiss, a former soap opera star, has a great set of weird eyes that help make his role convincing. It seems he is an escapee from the secret government project aiming at creating really smart people who can be used as resources or weapons. In this one, the villains are also quite good.

The "thrillogy" tops out with *Profiler*, a more conventional, less stylish, far less moody version of *Millennium*. Call it Millennium Lite. The woman who plays the usually-in-jeopardy ex-FBI profiler of the title, tries for intensity with varying degrees of success. The real cast standout is Robert Davi, who plays her cop mentor. He's very good.

And no, I haven't forgotten that both *Star Trek: Voyager* and *Deep Space Nine* continue to chug along where no man has gone before. Hardcore Trekkers continue to stand loyally by their shows. Other, less partisan viewers seem to have drifted over to *Babylon 5*. This being a theoretical democracy, however, it's not a Tory or Whig dichotomy. You are allowed to enjoy and follow both the Roddenberry and the Straczynski universes if you so choose.

For really wacky SF, you needed to follow UPN's *The Burning Zone*, an attempt at a thriller showcasing operatives for the Centers for Disease Control. One of my favorite episodes involved an in-flight transoceanic 747 flight on which a virulent disease is erupting among the passengers. One badass passenger wants to open a door and dump the afflicted into the ocean before the contagion spreads. Later he redeems himself by confessing he had been a chemical engineer before he was an oil company executive. The CDC people by then (who by lucky coincidence are on the plane) are wondering how to get a certain antiviral agent. The chemical engineer has them collect all the packets of salted almonds from first class, grind 'em up, and then extract the salient substance using, you guessed it, acetone gathered from ladies' purses. Another amusing episode concerned kids spontaneously combusting at an underprivileged high school unfortunately located right beside an evil pharmaceutical company's research facility. Guess who needed test subjects?

Let's see . . . what else helped keep indigent actors off the streets? *The Sentinel* gave us an ex–Special Forces dude whose jungle experience juiced up his natural senses so he could see and hear better than us normal people. Then he put these powers to good work as a law enforcement guy in the Pacific Northwest. Trouble is, the writers could rarely figure out a plot where the story wouldn't have worked out if the protagonist had simply possessed . . . normally acute powers of observation.

Touched by an Angel continued to give us Wonder Bread for the soul. *Sabrina the Teenage Witch* and *Lois and Clark* gave us more mainstream mythology. *Homeboys in Outer Space*, needless to say, did not draw in Nichelle Nichols or Avery Brooks as guest stars. But it was one of those guilty pleasures that occasionally provided a funny line or a hilarious image. But not often. *Nowhere Man* was another paranoid clone of *The Prisoner*. Unfortunately it never seemed to have the courage of its convictions and tended to underplay surrealism for torturous reality.

It's hard not to think of *Baywatch Nights* as *Kolchak* with large breasts . . . but hey, there was a real bravery in matching up David Hasselhoff with vampires, werewolves, and the like. Who would have thought it? *Psi Factor*, hosted by Dan Aykroyd, reminds me of the old *Science Fiction Theater*, hosted by Truman Bradley. There's something endearingly old-fashioned about a program of alleged scientific wonders, more or less explained by a knowledgeable-sounding host. I watched an episode in which a mini-black hole mysteriously appeared in a house in a Central American city and started sucking things in. Never mind plot or drama. It was all the wonder of extremely close event horizons, mysterious collateral phenomena on the exact other side of the globe, and sucking.

Viper did its high-tech car thing. And *Strange Luck* ran out of good fortune. *The Cape* was a pretty darned good series about Canaveral and the space program. A great view from a height . . . If you like YA material, you should have checked out Peter David and Bill Mumy's *Space Cases*.

Vampire lovers were pulling for *Kindred: the Embrace*, adapted from White Wolf's best-selling role-played game, *Vampire: the Masquerade*. Unfortunately it lasted only for about six episodes. The Nosferatu family of bloodsuckers was particularly effective in their portrayal. Stephen J. Cannell's *Profit*, a nasty little black comedy about the consummate young business shark, played by Adrian Pasdar as a guy whose father had effectively raised him in a Skinner Box, sadly expired after only four episodes. Pasdar slept, as an adult, in an empty packing crate. It was nicely done.

On the animation front, Fox's *The Simpsons* moved maniacally along. One episode featured characters modeled suspiciously after FBI agents Mulder and Scully from the *X-Files. Beavis and Butt-Head*'s creator, Mike Judge, masterminded *King of the Hill*, a weekly series about suburban Texas life that is both very funny and a deeply telling and affecting commentary about how real people live and relate. *Gargoyles* is hard to find in some cities, but it's well worth the effort. And let us not forget the new *Jonny Quest*, about which rumors swirl that this latest incarnation is specifically jiggered so there can be no audience suspicion of any homosexual hanky-panky . . .

In made-for-TV movies, *Dr. Who* had a new vehicle, and there was a pair of new *Alien Nation* films. With its emphasis equally spread between action melodrama, clever writing and commentary, and the characters' interrelationships, *Alien Nation* has been far more effective on the small screen than it was in its initial feature film outing. There are rumors of perhaps one more TV feature before the franchise folds its tent. *Roger Corman Presents* gave us cable remakes of some of his vintage inventory: *Alien Avengers, Last Exit to Earth*, and *Humanoids from the Deep*.

Accomplished SF writer Melinda Snodgrass created a UPN pilot called *Star Command*, a far-future melodrama of politics and military action. It was unfortunately undercut by some peculiar production decisions. In a projected future egalitarian military establishment, the female officers sport dress uniforms that include white miniskirts and go-go boots. Ah, well, maybe so. The future is not easy to predict.

Nor are next season's ratings . . .

Performance: Oh So Live and In Person:

Being a far distance from any of the greatest of white ways, I often have to settle for seeing touring performances of *Cats* or *Phantom of the Opera* when they show up in their own sweet time. But every once in a while, something remarkable turns up in timely fashion in live performance here in Denver. Here are two events that definitely startled the locals—and invigorated my life.

A couple of years ago I reported on the *Jim Rose Sideshow*. As I recall, that was long after Rose had made a big national splash touring with the *Lollapalooza* show, and not long after guest-starring with his colleague the Enigma in an *X-Files* episode. Millions of adventurous Fox TV viewers came away from their screens permanently psychically scarred by their encounter with Rose's warped P. T. Barnum persona and the exotically tattooed countenance and body of the Enigma. Hey, I wanted to caution them. You ain't seen nothing yet.

Lately the *Jim Rose Circus* has toured the nation with some old material, tried and true, and a good selection of new marvels. If you've never seen a Rose show, here's how it works: Jim Rose has gathered an amazing road troupe of human freaks and weirdos. These are not the genetic mishaps of older, more traditional sideshows. These are human beings who have deliberately cultivated their own sets of wondrously variant characteristics and talents. There is the Enigma, the tattooed man. There is Mr. Lifto, the performer who suspends and swings heavy objects, such as car batteries, from rings piercing such body parts as ears, nipples, and penis. Added this year were two wrestling ring events. First were the cross-dressing Mexican wrestlers, playing heavily to comedy with their masked super-hero costumes and huge strap-on plastic dildos. Then there were the female sumo wrestlers, neither of whom was probably within a hundred pounds of the announced weights. That's part of the fun—ringmaster Jim Rose's running patter, a hyperbolic, overheated, often obscene, usually hilarious routine that stitches all the rest of the stage activity into a continuous tapestry of complete weirdness. Rose performs as well. He does the old stage illusion of swallowing razor blades and a ball of string, contorts his mouth and throat painfully, and then withdraws a sequence of the blades nicely strung on the twine. He also allows his Beautiful Assistant to throw steel darts into his back. In short, he pays his dues.

And if he wants to say the heavyweight female sumo contender weighs in at 450 pounds, who are we to argue? It's all part of the fun. The last time Mr. Lifto performed in Denver, he finished his penile suspension stunt without benefit of the translucent modesty sheet. Some bluenose called the police. This time the sheet stayed in place and all was cool, if not so dramatic. At the *Rose Circus's* next stop in Lubbock, Texas, the cops busted the show. I have my suspicions . . . or it could simply have been the matter of all the female performers leaving their breasts bare save for strategic Xs of black electrician's tape. It's always hard to guess which ways community standards will be most affronted.

I have to admit that my favorite bit was the tasteful but exciting sequence in which a hooded chainsaw artist had a volunteer from the audience hold an apple in his mouth, then carved the guy's initial into the fruit. In this case the initial was a *T*. I couldn't help wondering how the episode would have played had the volunteer's name been Quentin or William—or Jean-Claude. When all was done, the entire cast came out to the edge of the stage to greet the audience, sign autographs, and schmooze. This was billed as "the human petting zoo." All in all, it was an evening of fun, wonderment, and awe. Forget another retread of Stephen Sondheim—this was entertainment.

Then there was the night Crispin Glover came to town, his appearance being billed as "a rare spoken word performance." You know Glover, right? His acting performances have been first rate in everything from *River's Edge* to *The People vs. Larry Flynt*. He appeared at the Aztlan Theater, an old, run-down venue in an old, run-down part of town. You don't really need an Uzi to fight your way from your distant parked car to the theater, but you feel like you do.

Glover's presentation was in two parts. First he screened an hour of rough cut of his on-going do-it-yourself feature film, *What Is It?* I'm tempted to yield to the smart-ass response of answering the titular question, "Beats me." But I'm kinder than that. Suffice it to say that the movie is weirdly fascinating in its imagistic way, but is not exactly a tightly structured plot engine. I'll be curious to see what it turns into as Glover finishes it. I have a strong suspicion that *What Is It?* is destined never to be perceived by anyone as a rigidly linear work.

Ah, but the second half of Glover's presentation—now that was a genius-level surprise. After a brief intermission, he narrated his *Big Slide Show*. Standing at stage left, he provided the voice track as slides replicated the pages of six of Glover's peculiar books. As a writer and performance artist, he has produced a series of small-press volumes combining facsimile art and text from vintage nineteenth-century books, often highly modified with ink and new text, as well as twisted doodle-art. *Rat Catching* is a prime example. The result is surreal, visually provocative, and often outlandishly funny. It's thoroughgoing fantasy. Watching and listening to Glover live is much like listening to Harlan Ellison or Joe R. Lansdale reading their stories aloud—the authentic auctorial voice lends a transforming new dimension to the work.

Crispin Glover, it must be said, is a highly accomplished performance artist and a born storyteller. I can make only a theoretical comparison—beholding him is like, I can only surmise, listening to artist Edward Gorey narrate his own strange books. It was a marvel, and I commend the experience to any reader who happens to be in the right place at the right time for Crispin Glover's *Big Slide Show*.

The Music of the Fears:

No major SF or dark fantasy concept albums found their way to me in '96, but there was still some interesting material that had the feel of what this essay generally treats. Writer Mark Barsotti suggested two quite dissimilar albums, Marilyn Manson's *Antichrist Superstar* (Nothing/Interscope) and Beck's *Odelay* (DGC).

Marilyn Manson is this year's lineal descendant of Kiss, at least in the sense that they aim their music and appearance to appeal to younger listeners' core desire to shock the bejeezus out of their elders. With selections such as "Wormboy," "Irresponsible Hate Anthem," and "Man That You Fear," *Antichrist Superstar* comprises three song cycles that evoke plenty of horrific angst. I particularly liked "Tourniquet"; the video for this song is especially disquieting—the makeup and the general tone are flat-out disturbing. Manson and his musical cronies are highly proficient at evoking subversive creepiness.

Beck—in the person of Beck Hansen—comes across as something of a Dylan for the slacker generation. *Odelay*'s music is hard to classify. With "Devil's Haircut," "Derelict," and "Sissyneck," you might think of the album's eclectic nature as something categorizable as punk-rock-folk-rap . . . or something like that. Beck's flights of fantasy cast a wide net, one that's gained Beck a growing and loyal listening audience over the last few years. *Odelay* has shipped better than a million copies. He's got the chops; but if he just weren't so nonthreatening . . . perhaps one can think of Beck as the anti-Marilyn, and vice versa.

Horror writer and historical novelist Trey Barker suggested a wide rainbow of tunes: The Chieftains' "The Foggy Dew," was a cool Irish death song from *The Long Black Veil* (RCA). Sinead O'Connor participates on this track. The album is intriguing in part for the range of artists who sit in on various selections: Mick Jagger, Mark Knopfler, Ry Cooder, Van Morrison, even Tom Jones.

Jackson Browne's "Information Wars" is on *Looking East* (Asylum). It's scary Big Brother stuff. Better Than Ezra's "The Killer Inside" is just what you might suspect. It appears on *Deluxe* (Elektra). Clint Black's "Cowboy Jack Favor" is included on his Greatest Hits compilation (RCA). It's a very, very cool tune about murder and frame-ups. On Sting's *Mercury Falling* (A&M), check out "Hounds of Winter," evoking dead, lost love, and "I Hung My Head," a ballad about killing a man and getting to hang for it. The titles tip you with Rusted Root's "Virtual Reality" and "Voodoo" from their album, *Remember* (Mercury). In a similar vein, check out "Virtuality" by Rush, appearing on *Test for Echo* (Atlantic).

Two more special treats: blues harmonica blower James Cotton does a typically fine job with "Down at Your Buryin'," "Dealin' With the Devil," and "Two Trains Runnin' " on *Deep in the Blues* (Verve). Also, Cassandra Wilson's incredible version of Son House's "Death Letter" on *New Moon Daughter* (Blue Note). Part of the effect is the great guitar by Brandon Ross and hopping drum and percussion work by Doughie Bowne.

I'd like to pass along the recommendation for a quarterly magazine called *Asterism*, a publication that calls itself "the journal of science fiction, fantasy and space music." Published and edited by Jeff Berkwits, *Asterism* covers a remarkable bandwidth of speculative sound. Write to the magazine at P.O. Box 6210, Evanston, IL 60204. When last heard from, *Asterism* subscriptions charged a quick $8 for four issues. And worth every dime.

Ever wonder what your faithful essayist listens to when he's putting all this together? It varies. Certainly I check out the music my informants recommend. But a lot of the background mood texture is albums such as *Shelter* by Lone Justice (Maria McKee's voice is always to die for—and in), Pierce Turner's *The Sky and the Ground*, *Thunder and Fire* by Jason and the Scorchers, Brian Eno's *Taking Tiger Mountain*, and, let's see, Wall of Voodoo and Rosanne Cash and the Iron City Houserockers and so it goes . . . okay, okay, I admit it. I'm hopelessly retro.

By next year I expect to have submerged myself in the new albums from the Panther Moderns (fronted by horror and SF novelist John Shirley) and Curse of Horseflesh (the Canadian prairie-surf band with horror writer Tia Travis on bass). And a lot more. Music's a drug of choice.

It's a Wrap:

Let me suggest another fine resource for those who have not yet discovered it. *Video Watchdog* is published bimonthly by Tim and Donna Lucas, P.O. Box 5283, Cincinnati, OH 45205-0283. It costs $6.50 per issue and bills itself as "the perfectionist's guide to fantastic video." It's solid, free-range, no-bullshit journalistic coverage that can help us all out. In 1997, the magazine made the Horror Writers Association's Bram Stoker Award final ballot for achievement in nonfiction.

So what have I learned about the fantastic in the nonprint media in 1996? Well, I've been reminded of two important things. The first is that the mass of output is incredible in its profusion. I can't see everything—not while still having a minimal life and career (as generous as this anthology is, it sadly cannot keep me installed year-round in the life to which I've become accustomed). So, the quantity of material is enormous. And, as one might suspect, the quality still falls along the bell curve. There's plenty of genuine wonder, novelty, innovation, and mature, provocative work—and there's a lot more outright crap in the middle of the bulge.

My second lesson seems to be that genre lines are continuing to blur ever more: genres slide into the mainstream, even as mainstreamed material feeds back into category work. Which will be reinvigorated hybrid work, and which an unstable mutation that will collapse of its own grotesque weight? You pays your money, and you takes your choice.

My final observation is to report on two havens for the fantastic I don't usually cover.

1. Toys. Dolls, to be exact. Many of you keep up with the wonderful world of Barbie and her friends, and you're aware of the San Francisco gallery that's been ringing such changes on that all-American girl as creating the "White Trash Barbie." Well, now there's suddenly a new nostalgic relapse. Chatty Cathy's back. A whole generation's favorite talking doll is now thirty-seven, and she has her own Web site at www.ttinet.com/chattycathy. Mattel's buck-toothed, pull-string babe is suddenly highly popular (and very collectible) again. These days there are Chatty Cathy repair surgeons who go in with knives and a small hammer to fix the voice box in the doll's belly. There are also rumors that some droll technical types are altering the recorded phrases in some individuals. Can you contemplate a Chatty Chuckie in drag?

2. Billboards. Altoids, "the original celebrated curiously strong peppermints," Britain's great gift to cleaning up throat pollution and mouth odor, has been erecting advertising billboards in American cities that proclaim: Refreshes Your Breath While You Scream . . .

Ah, an advertising slogan to take us into the millennium.

Comics: 1996
by Seth Johnson

It has been a tumultuous year in the comics industry: distributors have been bought, sold, and gone out of business; creative alliances have been formed and broken; comic shops across the nation have opened and closed; and in the last days of 1996 the Marvel Entertainment Group, the largest publisher of comics, filed for Chapter 11 bankruptcy protection. But none of this has prevented the writers, artists, and editors working to create the comics from producing some wonderful work in the past year.

Foremost among today's fantasy comics is Jeff Smith's *Bone* (Cartoon Books), following the cartoonish Bone cousins on a journey that alternates between Tolkienesque fantasy and slapstick comedy. Smith has completed twenty-five issues so far (available in both reprints of single issues and four trade paperback collections), what he calls "Act I." And what a first act it's been, from the Bone cousins' flight out of Boneville to the Great Cow Race to the invasion of the Rat Creatures. *Bone* is epic fantasy in the mold of a Sunday comic strip, grand adventure fit for all ages.

Akiko (Sirius) by Mark Crilley is named for a fourth-grade girl taken off to the planet Smoo on a journey to help rescue a young prince. Akiko travels with an odd but lovable crew of companions, working together to overcome each incredible obstacle Crilley dreams up. This is a comic that parents and children will have to read together—if only to avoid arguing who gets to read it first.

A comic that will appeal to fantasy readers who tend to frequent the bookstore instead of the comic shop is *Harlan Ellison's Dream Corridor* (Dark Horse), where the award-winning author's stories are adapted into comics form. A comics fanatic, Ellison hand-picks the creative teams, a wonderful diversity of talented writers and artists from within and outside the comics field ranging from Nancy A. Collins and Heinrich Kipper, who do a beautiful adaptation of Ellison's "Pride in the Profession," to Diana Schutz and Teddy Kristiansen and their dark, haunting adaptation of "Knox." Ellison also contributes an original short story to each issue based on the cover painting; his Bram Stoker Award-winning story "Chatting with Anubis" had its first appearance in *Dream Corridor*. Initially a bimonthly comic, *Dream Corridor* has now gone quarterly and to a perfect-bound format, so that it reaches beyond comic shops and into bookstores. It's well worth looking for.

This year brought two milestones in fantasy comics. The first: Dave Sim's epic story *Cerebus* (Aardvark-Vanaheim) reached issue #200. What began as a simple aardvark-as-Conan parody has evolved into heavy social commentary on topics ranging from politics to religion to relationships between the sexes—it just happens to be set in a fantasy milieu. While *Cerebus* can be alternately funny, brilliant, or infuriating, it never ceases to be engaging.

The other milestone was the end of Neil Gaiman's best-selling series *The Sandman* (DC/Vertigo). Over the course of the series, Gaiman and a bevy of talented artists have told stories that are wonderfully literary and mature, bringing a whole new audience to appreciate the power of comics. Luckily, for those who may have missed it (or if you want to protect your issues from becoming too dog-eared from reading and re-reading), the series is collected in both hardcover and trade paperback editions. Simply one of the best comic series ever.

One of the projects Gaiman has gone on to (along with *Bone*'s Jeff Smith and non-comic writers such as Delia Sherman, Jane Yolen, and Charles de Lint) is Charles Vess's *Book of Ballads and Sagas* (Green Man Press). This is an ambitious series, with Vess providing black-and-white illustrations for the writers' adaptations of classic folk songs and folktales ranging from "Thomas the Rhymer" to "Barbara Allen." This is what *Classics Illustrated* should be; Vess's exquisite art adds a whole new level of beauty and vitality to the age-old words. A rare gem of a title that might be hard to find but is worth seeking out.

Moving on to horror: *From Hell* (Kitchen Sink), Alan Moore's in-depth investigation of Jack the Ripper, ended this year, sixteen chapters collected into ten issues. Although the story's narrative may be fiction, its factual framework is not: Moore is a dedicated Ripperologist who put in an incredible amount of research, evidenced by the copious footnotes accompanying each chapter and a thick companion book to the series that brings together Moore's scripts for the series with even more detailed notes and references. Combined with the pen-and-ink artwork of Eddie Campbell (who also writes and illustrates his own tale of modern mythology, *Bacchus* (Eddie Campbell Comics), it is a scholarly work that, as with most of Moore's work, will leave readers in awe.

Another terrific horror comic is Mike Mignola's *Hellboy* (Dark Horse/Legend), released as one-shot specials and mini-series, each telling a single tale, rather than as a continuing series. An investigator for the Bureau for Paranormal Research and Defense, Hellboy is a half-man, half-demon fighting against ghosts, demons, frogs, giant dogs, and the machinations of the undead Rasputin. Mignola's art is dark and dynamic—a perfect complement to his stories, which crash together pulp adventure and a wide variety of classic mythologies. A quirky but fun book.

This year Mojo Press, the same folks who brought us the hardcover horror-comics anthology *Weird Business* a few years back, have collected a good chunk of Joe R. Lansdale's horror comic work into *Atomic Chili*. Lansdale has an obvious affinity for horror and western comics, and this collection is evidence of the casual ease with which he manages not only to work within the two genres but to combine them. A trip through Lansdale territory provides sights from the offbeat to the macabre, and although at times it may be disturbing, it's a worthwhile journey.

Not everyone has a dark take on horror. *Yikes!* by Steven Weissman is, almost oxymoronically, a *funny* horror comic, the Peanuts gang pureed with the Universal Monsters. The result is a hilarious gang of kids ranging from Li'l Bloody and Pullapart Boy to Kid Medusa and X-Ray Spence, who go around causing trouble from the mythic (wanna know who really gave the apple to Adam and Eve?) to the simply odd.

Leave It to Chance by James Robinson with Paul Smith (Homage) is a straightforward adventure series steeped in horror—the daughter of a monster hunter trying to fill her father's boots—as is *Coventry* (Fantagraphics), the latest series by Bill Willingham, who a few years back brought out the cult classic erotic fantasy *Ironwood* (now collected by Eros Comix). The monsters in these may range more toward the absurd than the terrifying (an invasion of toads is part of the first plotline of each), but even if they may not necessarily be keep-the-lights-on scary they're still a lot of fun.

The last comic in the horror category is here primarily due to shock value and its often provocative subject matter: *Preacher* (DC/Vertigo), by Garth Ennis and Steve Dillon, is the story of Jesse Custer, a Texas minister searching for a God who has quit His post in Heaven. But before Jesse can complete his quest he'll have to deal with his ex-lover, an Irish vampire, a serial killer, an albino pervert, and his own malevolent grandmother—and that's apparently just the beginning of the story. It's definitely a comic for mature (and, perhaps, slightly twisted) readers—the "sexual investigators" featured in one storyline are par for the course, along with extreme and graphic violence—but it's also one of the most gripping comics currently on the shelves and another feather in Vertigo's cap.

1996 was the tenth anniversary of two works that influenced almost every comic of the last decade, Frank Miller's *The Dark Knight Returns* (DC) and Alan Moore and Dave Gibbons's *Watchmen* (DC). They have often been imitated, but very few attempts have managed to approach their level of storytelling—instead, the attempts to follow *Dark Knight* gave us the trend of "grim 'n' gritty," heavily-armed, over-violent vigilantes that swamped the field in the late '80s and early '90s. Both series are still available in trade paperback (while *Dark Knight* was also recollected in a lavish hardcover anniversary edition), and both are highly recommended.

Even darker than *Dark Knight* are Miller's ongoing tales of *Sin City* (Dark Horse/Legend), a hard-boiled, two-fisted crime comic that deserves to be described in those terms. In stories like this year's *Sin City: That Yellow Bastard*, Miller tells tales from the gutter that resonate with deeper meaning—honor, betrayal, greed, love—once you manage to peer through the hail of bullets.

Joining Miller on the stage of crime comics is David Lapham's increasingly popular *Stray Bullets* (El Capitan). Lapham has gathered well-deserved praise and awards galore as he tells tales of the all-too-human side of crime and violence ranging from a young girl's violently interrupted Halloween to the life of Amy Racecar, the world's most beloved bank robber. Each issue is a wonderful story that stands on its own, but as the series continues they are slowly being revealed as threads in a larger, more intricate tapestry whose design has yet to be revealed.

A different reaction to the trend of "grim 'n' gritty" comics is the current renaissance of the heroic superhero. Writers are taking up the task of explaining exactly why it is that superheroes do what they do, and a few are doing it very well. *Leave It to Chance*'s James Robinson brought out *The Golden Age* (DC) to wide acclaim a few years ago and now writes *Starman* (DC). The journey of Jack Knight, son of the former Starman, has seen him evolve from shunning the Starman mantle to embracing it, along the way finding out more about his father, the city the Starmen defend, and the hero that lies hidden within himself. Unlike many writers, who often discard a character or title's past so as to begin with a *tabula rasa*, Robinson doesn't bulldoze the past to make progress. Like Jack, he embraces the past and incorporates it, bringing together the disparate comic book Starmen of the past, from the Knights to an alien in another galaxy, into one coherent picture and one terrific story.

In 1994's *Marvels* (Marvel) Kurt Busiek gave readers a whirlwind trip through the early days of the Marvel Universe. Now he has returned to Marvel's glory days in *Untold Tales of Spider-Man* (Marvel), telling all-new and quite fine stories of the Webbed Wall-Crawler's high school days, when he was still dealing with bullies and learning that "with great power comes great responsibility." Busiek is also gaining acclaim for *Astro City* (Homage), a series drawing on the wellspring of comic-book history and set in the Busiek-created title city, where everything is surprisingly original while remaining tantalizingly familiar. Like *Marvels*, the stories in *Astro City* are told from a down-to-earth point of view: a thug who accidentally learns a superhero's secret identity, a country boy come to the big city who yearns to be a superhero's sidekick, a single father trying to decide if a city rife with superhumans is a place to raise children. Whether you've been a fan of comics since the Silver Age or are picking one up for the first time, this is one of those comics that somehow manages to appeal to everybody.

A couple of other great comics weighing in on what it means to be a superhero: Mike Allred's hip and zany *Madman Comics* (Dark Horse/Legend) cranks back the clock to a time when giant robots and zombie beatniks were all the rage, and Jim Krueger's *Foot Soldiers* (Dark Horse, later Maximum Press), the story of street kids in a dystopic future who uncover and rob a superhero graveyard to become heroes for a world that has none. Both comics are perfect material for the big screen; hopefully some aspiring producer will find them on the shelves. Keep an eye on the multiplexes. . . .

In 1997 writer Mark Waid will take a year-long hiatus from his excellent run on *Flash* (DC) so that he can concentrate on other projects. Hopefully they'll be as good as *Kingdom Come* (DC), where Mark teamed up with *Marvels* artist Alex Ross to tell a tightly crafted—and thanks to Ross, beautifully and almost photorealistically painted—story about a possible dark future for the DC Universe, where Superman and other aging heroes must come out of retirement to save the world from "grim 'n' gritty" vigilante heroes who have become more terrible than the villains they pursue.

For more than ten years Paul Chadwick has been telling stories of *Concrete*, an eight-foot-tall superstrong man of rock in an otherwise ordinary world. Concrete's stories are not ones of beating up the bad guys, or saving the world—at least not in the traditional sense. In this year's thoughtful and enjoyable *Concrete: Think Like A Mountain* (Dark Horse) Concrete joins Earth First! and has to deal with the repercussions of getting involved in pro-environment monkeywrenching. Once you look beyond his alien appearance, Concrete is among the most human of all characters in comics, one worth getting acquainted with by tracking down a trade paperback collection of Chadwick's stories.

If you're looking to get a taste of things on the cutting edge of comics, a good place to look is one of the several anthology comics on the racks. These are the breeding grounds for comics' future: *Sin City* and *Concrete* first appeared in *DHP: Dark Horse Presents* (Dark Horse), now celebrating its tenth anniversary and still featuring great work like Paul Pope's "One Trick Ripoff" and Evan Dorkin's "Hectic Planet." New and talented writers and artists appear monthly in *DHP*, Caliber's *Negative Burn* and *New Worlds*, and the infrequently-appearing *Blab* (Kitchen Sink); experienced pros also publish some of their finest work in these anthologies, projects that wouldn't or couldn't appear in mainstream venues—or perhaps have yet to catch the fickle public's fancy.

One final recommendation is the *Acme Novelty Library* (Fantagraphics) by Chris Ware. Ware is a bundle of talent; he's a wonderful cartoonist, a brilliant designer—as evidenced by the intricate design and layouts of each issue, which have ranged in size from Little Golden Book to larger than tabloid—and a darkly humorous storyteller. The ongoing and tragic life story of "Jimmy Corrigan, Smartest Boy on Earth" can be at times riotously hilarious and achingly poignant, and often manages to be both at once. And his parodies of classic comic book and magazine ads are dead on target.

The comics mentioned in this essay should be available at your local comic shop, along with many other wonderful titles that there wasn't room to mention. If you don't frequent a comic store, you can find one by checking the Yellow Pages or calling the Comic Shop Locator Service toll-free at 1-888-COMIC-BOOK.

Thanks to the all the folks at Pic-a-Book in Madison, WI and the late, lamented Capital City Distribution for their help in completing this essay.

Obituaries: 1996
by James Frenkel

Each year we note the passing of talented people from the scene. While it is, of course, a melancholy task, this exercise also gives us a chance to recognize the talent and contributions of many who perhaps were not appreciated in recent years, those who have been among us for a long time and may have been better known earlier in their lives. Let's celebrate, then, those who are no longer here, but who have left indelible marks on our lives with their work and their genius.

Evangeline Walton, 88, was an important American fantasy writer. Her novel *The Virgin and the Swine* (1936), reprinted in Ballantine Books' Adult Fantasy series in 1971 as *The Island of the Mighty,* was but the first of her wonderful retellings of Welsh myths known collectively as *The Mabinogian.* The other three books were also published by Ballantine in the 1970s. These four books alone confirm her status as one of the great fantasists of the twentieth century. She also wrote a seminal novel, *Witch House,* which for years was hidden under a "gothic" (as in romantic suspense with a supernatural tinge) package. There were other works, but the *Mabinogian* books were what made her special, and probably what earned her the Life Achievement Award at the 1989 World Fantasy Convention. She was a remarkable woman, and overcame health problems to write books that would inspire and enthrall generations, and which are still as fresh and sensuous and powerfully magical today as they were when she first wrote them.

Burne Hogarth, 84, an illustrator best known for his "Tarzan of the Apes" adventure comic strip, was a dynamic innovator in the field of comic strip illustration. Known for strict attention to anatomy and his vivid, energetic style, Hogarth created a distinctive body of work that inspired a generation of artists in the 1950s and '60s. **Garth Williams,** 84, was a wonderful illustrator of children's books. His distinctive style created a sense of innocence and wonderment that enchanted generations of children and adults. Some of his most famous works were the illustrations for *Charlotte's Web* and *Stuart Little,* both by E. B. White.

Jerry Siegel, 81, was the cocreator of Superman. He drew the comic, which was written by Joe Shuster. Both were young comics fans when they created what was to become arguably the most popular comic-book character of all time. Siegel and Shuster sold Superman to DC comics after trying for five years to publish it otherwise. For ten years they created the comic book, after which DC, which had bought all rights to the character, fired them. They created other characters, but none nearly so successful. After a long period of obscurity, the two were finally recognized by DC's new owners, Warner Inc., and given residual income. Shuster died in 1992.

Elsie Wollheim, 85, was the wife of publisher, editor, and writer Donald A. Wollheim. A woman of enormous energy and dedication, she was a true partner to her husband in the running of DAW Books, handling many of the business aspects of their family company. Married for nearly fifty years, the Wollheims were a real team. Short and fierce, Elsie Wollheim (née Balter) was also extremely loyal to those she loved, and she loved the entire field of science fiction and fantasy. Those who knew her also knew that she was a very kind and generous person, a side of her personality that was often obscured by her keen business sense. She and her husband, their daughter Elizabeth, and

Sheila Gilbert have published and fostered the careers of many fine fantasy writers, including Tanith Lee, C. J. Cherryh, Thomas Burnett Swann, Jo Clayton, Melanie Rawn, Jennifer Roberson, Marion Zimmer Bradley and many others.

Gene Kelly, 83, was a dancer who did things that had never been done before, primarily on film. Like Fred Astaire, the acknowledged master of film dance before Kelly, he was a perfectionist and an innovator. Utterly unlike Astaire in style and affect, Kelly was known for his athleticism and energy, where Astaire was known for his ease and smoothness. Kelly was, however, like Astaire in that he wanted to do things that nobody thought could be done. He appeared in what may be the most famous dance on film, the "Singing in the Rain" sequence that became his signature piece. He also acted in serious films, but nothing will ever eclipse his joyous, wonder-filled dancing across the silver screen. **Marcello Mastroianni,** 72, was in a way the object of fantasy. He was a leading man and international symbol of the Latin Lover. He appeared in a number of films by Federico Fellini, and was a fine actor in serious, comic, and romantic roles, garnering two Cannes Best Actor awards and three Oscar nominations for Best Actor. **George Burns,** 100, was a vaudevillian, a star of radio, television, stage, and screen. Primarily a comedian, he was also an actor in the fantasy films that started with *Oh, God!*. For most of his career he was straight man for his brilliant wife, Gracie Allen, but after her death he had a fine solo career, even garnering an Oscar.

Brian Daley, 48, was a writer of fantasy and science fiction best known for his novels *The Doomfarers of Coramonde* (1977) and its sequel, *The Starfollowers of Coramonde* (1979), and a series of "Han Solo" novels. He also wrote in collaboration with Jim Luceno as "Jack McKinney" on Robotech novelizations. He wrote other fantasy and science fiction novels, as well as other novelizations, virtually all of his books appearing under the Del Rey imprint. He also wrote a number of radioplays, including those for the *Star Wars* radio series. His work tended to be strong adventure stories with likeable characters and well-realized backgrounds. He had a natural storytelling gift. **Richard Condon,** 81, was a novelist of great intensity, which he used to portray the abuse of power and its effects on society in such varied novels as the brilliant political thriller made into a chilling film, *The Manchurian Candidate* (1950) and *Prizzi's Honor* (1982), a comic novel of the Mafia in America. His work could only very loosely be called fantasy, but he always saw reality in a unique and twisted way that pried loose any illusions one might have about the innocence of life.

P. L. Travers, 93, was the author of many children's books and other fantasy novels. Her most famous creation must be *Mary Poppins* (1934), which spawned a number of sequels, adaptations, and finally, the well-known film. She also wrote fantasy novels not for children, including *The Fox at the Manger* (1963), *Friend Monkey* (1971), and *About the Sleeping Beauty* (1975). In addition, she wrote folktales, collected in *Two Pairs of Shoes* (1980), and nonfiction about myth and folktales. Born in Australia, she was a poet and journalist early in her life, and danced and acted professionally for a time. **Vera Chapman,** 98, was a writer of fantasy best known for her Arthurian novel, *The Three Damosels* (1978), and other fantasy works. She didn't start to write until late in life, but was quite prolific and irrepressible. Her novel *The Wife of Bath* (1978) was a saucy retelling of Chaucer's story. She also wrote several children's books. **Caio Fernando Abreu,** 48, was a Brazilian writer, internationally known for his fiction, including some works in magic realism. His best known work was *Morangos Mofados* (1982). **Eleanor Butler Campson,** 84, wrote SF and fantasy, most notably *The Wonderful Flight to the Mushroom Planet.*

Albert "Cubby" Broccoli, 87, was a film producer best known for his work on the James Bond films, fantasies in a very real sense. **Greer Garson,** 88, was an actress in many Hollywood films, including several with fantasy themes. She won an Oscar for her role in *Mrs. Miniver*. **Saul Bass,** 76, was a graphic designer who created a new style of film title sequences in such films as *Psycho* and others. He also did very creative work with film posters. **Dorothy Lamour,** 82, was an instant star after appearing in *Hurricane* (1937), famous for wearing a sarong very attractively. She was also an accomplished comedienne in the Bing Crosby–Bob Hope "Road" film fantasy adventures, and acted in a number of other movies, including *Creepshow 2* (1987). **Jack Weston,** 72, was an actor on stage, screen, and television. Never a big star, he was a fine character actor, and appeared in, among hundreds of roles, a number of *Twilight Zone* episodes. **Martin Balsam,** 77, was a character actor who was ubiquitous throughout the 1950s and 1960s on television in a great variety of roles, including many roles on *Alfred Hitchcock Presents*, among other shows. **Claudette Colbert,** 93, was a versatile, charismatic actress primarily on screen, for over thirty years. Famous for the scene in *It Happened One Night* (1934) where she bared her leg to hitch a ride, she was a great presence in dozens of films, including some with fantasy motifs. **Greg Morris,** 62, played a master of espionage on the fantasy/suspense/adventure series *Mission: Impossible*.

Ella Fitzgerald, 79, was a great jazz singer, one of the best scat singers, creating fantasy in sound. She won bunches of Grammy Awards, was voted best female jazz singer by *Downbeat* eighteen years running, and was a versatile, subtle singer for more than fifty years. **Gerry Mulligan,** 72, was a jazz saxaphonist and composer of innovative improvisational music. **Morton Gould,** 82, was a composer whose range encompassed classical, jazz, pop, and musical theater.

Cheri Lynn "Tomi" Lewis, 44, was a bookseller. She and her husband Doug owned and ran The Little Bookshop of Horrors, and Roadkill Press, in Arvada, Colorado. She was the kind of bookseller who made customers feel special and took great pains also to make sure that every author who came to the store to do a signing or reading felt well loved, regardless of his or her sales history. Personal attention by booksellers is something many people don't notice, especially if the only store in your area is a chain store, but if you have an independent bookstore near you, check it out. There may be someone there like Tomi who could change your life. She will be missed.

Richard Evans, 46, was a British book editor who worked at a number of houses, most notably Macdonald/Futura, Arrow, Headline, and Victor Gollancz. He published a lot of very good science fiction and fantasy, and was one of the most caring and personally involved editors on the British SF/fantasy scene. He discovered some major authors and more than that was a real developer of authors, often working painstakingly with the author through numerous drafts. He was a friend to many on both sides of the Atlantic and notable for his ability to find American authors who would be embraced by the British audience, where other editors couldn't see the connection. **Walter M. Miller Jr.,** 73, was best known for his novella and novel *A Canticle for Leibowitz*. Published as a book in 1960, this quietly powerful novel must be called science fiction, but there is a quality of spirituality in this and Miller's other work that makes his writing of importance in the spectrum of imaginative literature. **Leon Garfield,** 75, was a noted writer of children's books, including a number with supernatural elements in them, such as *Black Jack* (1968), *Mr. Corbett's Ghost*, also 1968, and others. The novel *The God Beneath the Sea* (1970), which he wrote with Edward Blishen, based on Greek myth, won the Carnegie Medal. He was an excellent writer with a marvelous range of subject and capable of great emotional power. **Pam Stampf Conrad,** 48, was a well known children's book writer. Her novel *Prairie Songs* (1985), won the Golden Spur Award from the Western Writers of America.

Mark Gruenwald, 43, was a writer and longtime editor at Marvel Comics. He was a strong believer in the necessity for maintaining a sense of continuity and consistency in the universes of various comics creations. He worked with a number of different series, including *The Avengers* and others. **Mike Parobeck,** 31, was a comics artist mainly for DC comics, best known for his work on the *Batman Adventures* series. **Jack Abel,** 69, was a longtime inker and proofreader. He worked for various companies, including, for a long time, Marvel Comics, inking many of their best series. **Bernard Baily,** 75, co-creator of the Spectre, and artist on a number of other comics. **Nestor Redondo,** 68, was a Philippine-born comics artist who penciled and inked such series as *Swamp Thing, Tarzan, House of Mystery,* and others for DC Comics.

L. A. Taylor, 56, was primarily a mystery writer, but also wrote some fantasy and science fiction, including the fantasy *Catspaw* (1995). She did some self-publishing in recent years with her Allau Press. **George H. Smith,** 73, was primarily a science fiction writer, but he also wrote fantasies, including *Druid's World* (1967) and several sequels. **Sam Merwin Jr.** 85, was an author and editor of science fiction and fantasy. He was a major editor of SF in the pulps during the 1930s and '40s, and discovered a number of important writers, chief among them Jack Vance. He bought major works by a number of writers, including C. L. Moore and Henry Kuttner, as well as Ray Bradbury, from whom he bought the first "Martian Chronicles" story, among others. He wrote, under his own and other names, SF, mystery, and gothic horror/suspense.

William Keith Everson, 67, was a film historian and critic who wrote hundreds of articles and more than twenty books on cinema, including *Classics of the Horror Film* (1974) and a sequel (1968). **Claudia Peck,** 43, was the author of *Spirit Crossings* (1991), a horror/fantasy novel, and many short stories, as well as mystery fiction. **Collin Wilcox,** 71, was a well-known mystery writer who wrote some short fantasy for pulp magazines as well. He wrote a number of successful series books involving a varied cast of protagonists, ranging from a homicide lieutenant to an eccentric theater director. **Willis Conover,** 75, was an early fan and correspondent of H. P. Lovecraft, and published a major book on Lovecraft, *Lovecraft at Last* (1974). He also gained considerable fame as a jazz expert and host of the Voice of America radio station for many years. **Frank H. Parnell,** 79, was an extremely knowledgeable collector of fantasy and science fiction, often consulted by professionals who were researching stories for anthologies. He also sold some fiction in the 1950s. **Charles Burbee,** 81, was a fan who wrote innumerable fanzines and articles for other people's zines. He was for a time editor of the Fantasy Amateur Press Association. **Maria Casares,** 74, was a French actress who played in a number of films and stage productions, including some of Jean Cocteau's great fantasy films, such as *Orphée,* among others. **William N. Copley,** 77, was an American Surrealist painter.

Curt Swan, 76, was a comics artist who for many years was a mainstay of DC comics, defining the look of Superman and other comics. **Jim Davis** was a cartoonist for over five decades, working for the Max Fleischer studio in the 1930s and going on to create many funny animal cartoons, both as cartoons, and also in comic books.

In the Fantasy-is-Reality-is-Fantasy Department: **Timothy Leary,** 75, was a professor of psychology at Harvard University until his experiments with the hallucinogenic drug LSD drew the attention of those who felt that his activities were not in the best interests of the University. He was the most visible proponent of the use of hallucinogens to expand human consciousness, encouraging the youth of the 1960s to, "Tune in, turn on, and drop out." He became perhaps *the* symbol of the '60s counterculture, but didn't stay in a single mode for long. He was interested in many other areas of "new age" concern, including the exploration of space and, more recently, in cyberspace.

These and many others brought the wondrous, the strange, and the transcendant into our lives. Their memory and their works will endure as long as people laugh, cry, or think about life in ways affected by their works.

THE LAST RAINBOW
Parke Godwin

Parke Godwin is a playright, an actor, and a novelist. In the latter role, he has shown a particular interest in British history and myth. He has published two excellent Arthurian novels to date *(Firelord* and *Beloved Exile)*, as well as two novels about Robin Hood *(Sherwood* and *Robin and the King)* and a novel based on the Beowulf saga *(The Tower of Beowulf)*. Godwin also has edited the Arthurian collection *Invitation to Camelot*.

In the enchanting and entertaining story that follows, Godwin explores the Arthurian legend of the Holy Grail—still a powerful mythic symbol in this magical England of the Middle Ages. The story, first published over fifteen years ago in *The Magazine of Fantasy & Science Fiction*, comes from Mike Ashley's anthology, *The Chronicles of the Holy Grail*, a fascinating collection of original and reprinted material.

—T. W.

The legend goes something like this:

Once upon a time a princess caught a faerie, one of the little folk, and demanded his treasure, since it was well known that all faeries had fabulous wealth hidden under some hill and were legend-bound to render it on request. The faerie reluctantly waved his hand, the hill opened up, and there was the treasure, its dazzle rivalling the sunlight. But, according to tradition, the little folk always ask something in return. . . .

Thus the legend. The truth is more fun.

Once upon a time there was a girl named Brangaene . . . but "once" is vague; we can be more specific. It was rather well on in the Middle Ages, late enough for dragons and quests to be quite *passé*, late enough for Brangaene to be literate and even over-read in that narrow, romantic field. She was the daughter of a harried baron who held a very small castle in a very small and agriculturally uninspired corner of England. His liege lord was both an earl and a bishop, which meant the earl could demand his secular rights and, if not forthcoming, the bishop could close the gates of heaven.

Such was the case one spring when Brangaene was fifteen. The earl had declared war on a neighbouring tenant and ordered Brangaene's father to send help or money. Since the baron depended heavily on his neighbor's grain mill, had no money and not enough men to populate a decent garden party, he declined with apologies.

The earl-bishop thundered and threatened excommunication. The poor baron was in up to his neck, and since his life had gone much this way for a long time, his temper was understandably short.

Brangaene longed to be of help, but the bishop was only peripheral to her enchanted world. She hunted for unicorns in the forest beyond their moat, nosed for faeries on moonlit nights, and though she never found either, her faith was undented by failure. As pure and good a man as Lancelot hunted the Grail, and Percival even saw it. More than one historical knight had slain a dragon or a giant; it said so in her books. Unicorns might be scarce and shy, but scarce was not non-existent. Faeries might be elusive—

"But so are foxes," she reasoned, turning to canonical precedent. If bushes could burn, seas part, tombstones roll aside and the dead rise, this fortuitous by-pass of natural law could not logically be confined to the Middle East. So her catechism and belief. The unicorns would come, white and willing, the little folk would be caught, their treasure demanded. Faith would be rewarded.

"I mean, Father, we only have to look for them."

"Ye gods." The baron brooded over his soup, the bishop's tyranny, and his daughter's mind. "What have I done to deserve this?"

Brangaene looked like her mother. This did not endear her to him. That pious woman had departed the world leaving behind an unfinished tapestry on the life of St. Paul and, as his enduring penance for marrying a Celt, this unworldly, star-eyed, faerie-chasing wisp of a girl. Her marriage value declined with his own fortunes. Once he might have bargained for a prince or dukeling, later a baron's son or even a plain knight. Now as he watched Brangaene running through the garden and tripping over her own dainty feet, he longed for a decent kidnapping.

She was forever racing up the steps with the news of (maybe) unicorns sighted across the moat, or (they looked like) faerie-folk peeping from behind trees in the forest. He had tolerated this until her twelfth birthday and then announced his incredulity by kicking her down the stairs. As Brangaene persisted in her optimism, his placekick and her nimbleness improved with time. She was even able to gauge her father's temper by the manner and sound of the kick. Mild irritation: side of the foot, a flat *bup!* Genuine wrath: point of the toe and swung from the hip with a resounding *poonk!* And as she became airborne, floating down towards the scullery, Brangaene meditated on the treasures and principles of her own, private, shining and utterly undeniable world. She was an unusual child.

Though her latest idea was truly inspired, Brangaene couldn't have chosen a worse day to break it to the baron. They were at dinner in the hall, the dogs rooting in the rushes for scraps and the baron dipping his bread in the soup and wishing it was the bishop's innards. That worthy had made good his threat. The baron was now excommunicate. The clerk in his soul quailed at the red tape involved: audiences with the archbishop, letters to the king and even to Rome, all for reconciliation with the earl-bishop, might he strangle in his own *pallium*. Heaven aside, the re-elevation from goat to lamb would cost a bundle.

"But, Father." Brangaene pushed her bowl away and went on earnestly, "That's my plan. We'll give the bishop and the Church the greatest treasure they could wish. No, not the bishop, he's too small. We'll *allow* him to take it to Rome, and the Pope himself will reward you, and the king will make you an earl."

"And what had you in mind to present to His Holiness?" asked the baron with deceptive patience.

"Such a treasure," she bubbled. "I thought of it as I was reading in the garden. The Holy Grail, Father."

The baron sighed. "Oh yes, the Holy Grail." He dropped his bread in the soup where it sank like the rest of his luck. "You've seen it lately?"

"No one has seen it since Sir Percival."

"Some centuries back, I gather, and somehow mislaid since then."

"All we have to do is find it," she asserted. "The faerie have it without doubt—they steal everything. And today I found little footprints smaller than my own in the woods across the moat. I'll take the dogs and trap them, and say 'caught caught caught' three times for the charm, and—"

Thoughtfully the baron laid aside his spoon. Pensively he rose, tenderly he guided his only begotten child to the head of the stairs. Brangaene knew what was coming, but she was finished eating anyway.

Poonk! went the baron's full-inspired toe.

But Brangaene dreamed as she flew, and her dreams were not to be denied.

From the forest, the two small men in worn green tunics contemplated the unimpressive castle. Wary, dark and sharp-featured, they were accomplished thieves, and their present disagreement over method was conducted in a dialect ancient when the first Druids came to wild Britain.

Malgon, slightly the elder, held that the small keep was poor pickings: best steal two horses and be gone. Young Drust thought it shrewder to ask for a meal at the scullery door, tell a fortune or two, and filch from within. They strolled back into the copse that had sheltered them since yesterday and considered it.

"Yon's a starveling lord," Malgon guessed. "If a's got a horse, steal it now before a has to eat it himself."

Drust stretched out on the soft, marshy turf, grinning up at him. "Thee's so fond of sleeping on rock, will pass up soft straw?"

"I want my own bed," Malgon wished disconsolately.

"And I. How many days to home, Malgon?"

"Four, five, an thy mother's not moved our tents."

"Hast counted the time since we left her? A full year."

"The leaving was thy madness, not mine."

Arms behind his head, Drust squinted up at the sunlight filtering through the treetops. "But hast not travelled? Hast not seen armies and great battles and the lords of the tallfolk and learned their speech? Hast not thieved in glorious and honourable fashion for a year?"

Malgon snorted. "Hast not *worked* as well?"

"Aye, true," Drust admitted with a tinge of shame. "Too often hast been reduced to that. We'll not tell my mother."

Their kind did not mingle much with the tallfolk of the valleys and towns. They were upland dwellers, following their cattle and goats where the grazing led them, as their folk had done since the first of them tracked the reindeer when the land was half ice. Then the tallfolk had come with their bronze swords and their planted fields, taking the best lands, forcing the faerie ever further into the hills and heaths. They never planted grain like the bigger folk; if they had, how could they follow the herds? In hard times—and times were very hard now—they hung about the edges of the towns or hovered like Drust and Malgon about the twopenny barons' wars, and over the ages an unspoken contract grew up between faerie and tallfolk based on mutual distrust and fear. The tallfolk came to Drust's people for their magic and their gaiety, and even married them sometimes, though this was rare.

It was taken for granted that they stole as a way of life, but worked well when necessity drove them to it. Drust and Malgon could mend anything from harness to boots and clothing with a lasting skill denied bigger hands. Knowing their shyness, the work was left outside at night with a few coins or a little food carelessly placed about so that the bit of paid work could seem the whim of the little folk and the coins honourably filched. It paid to be on good terms with the faerie. The cattle blight that they could cure, they could bring again. They had the magic.

And they *were* small. They lacked the crossbreeding and the grain diet that lengthened the lowlanders' bones, but already legend and fireside tale were shrinking them further into Lilliputian creatures with shining wings, and faerie no longer meant what it had. They were men, but few and fading out, fading into the hills and fanciful stories. There was little left of their magic but the tallfolk's dread of it. If Drust had learned anything in the year away from his mother's tents, it was this.

He turned to face his friend, "Malgon, I think—"

A dry stick cracked nearby; his head swivelled round, and then down into the copse poured a conquering avalanche of three men-at-arms, four huge dogs, and a blonde girl yipping with delight.

"Caught!" she bounded at them. "Caught—" She tripped over a root and went down spectacularly as a fallen empire in a puddle. Undismayed, she leaped up, muddy but victorious.

"Caught! Three times is the charm, and you must yield to me or my men will chop you up and the dogs will eat you."

Drust and Malgon considered there seemed no future in the vagaries of courage. The guards were shabby but armed, and the lean dogs of most uncertain benevolence.

"Yours, lady," Drust acceded in English.

She held onto him, not sure he wouldn't vanish if she let go. "You're faerie folk?"

"Aye, but—"

"And have the magic and yield it to my service?"

Drust glanced at the undernourished dogs. "My God, yes."

"Including all hidden treasures—"

"Well, there's sixpence in my—"

"And the whereabouts of dragons to be slain?"

"What's a dragon?"

"Be large and scaly, I think," Malgon ventured, "and dost fly."

Brangaene's free hand clamped on his arm. "Then you have seen them?"

"Not this far north," Malgon hedged.

"*Aargh*," snarled the largest dog, and Malgon shut up.

"No," said Brangaene, "you must uncover every lair, every trove of treasure, and grant me three wishes, or one at least, and if I just get one, it's going to be a crusher, and then," she paused for breath, "you must recommend my good fortune to the Queen of Faerie and bring me the Holy Grail.

She released them and waited, as it were, for wonders.

"A's mad," Malgon trembled. "Speak gently, Drust. Thee has the better English."

"Lady," Drust began, "it's true we're faerie and do a bit of trading, but—"

"But you will do magic?" Brangaene prompted.

Some of his composure regained, Drust managed a feeble smile. Even if Brangaene were an inch taller than he, her eyes were not difficult to look into, and he had seen very few blonde women.

"Not before dinner, lady."

"Of course, of course." She turned, gesturing to the guards. "To the hall. Our plans are perilous and there's not much time. Away!"

"Truly a sweet lass," Drust whispered as they were trundled towards the bailey bridge over the moat. "Such golden hair. None of our girls have golden hair."

"Dost cleverly hide the shape of her skull," Malgon hissed. "And but for that, would swear a was dropped on her soft little head at birth. Oh, if thy mother could see thee now: taken by a mad girl—"

"And three men."

"It retches me!"

"And four dogs, very large."

"Aye, and four dogs," Malgon glanced apprehensively at the drooling of the nearest hound, "and unreasonable at that."

They were hustled over the bridge, across the bailey and up the steps to the hall, Brangaene urging them on. "Hurry! Hurry!"

If prudence were Brangaene's long suit, she would not have disturbed her father just then. The baron had few good days, but this one was a negative gem. The earl-bishop had descended on his delinquent neighbor, seized his lands, including the all-important mill, and now perched only two hours away to chastise the baron for his breach of fealty. Thus, his beleaguered lordship was not only excommunicate, he was technically under siege. Prices were going up.

"I can promise God," the baron moaned to Rainier, his steward, "but the bishop wants cash. Bishop, hell; he's a broker! I've got to buy him off when I couldn't afford his horse."

Rainier tried to be helpful. "Is there a crusade forming?"

"We lost the last two."

"Perhaps a pilgrimage to the Holy Land."

"Full of sandflies and Arabs selling pieces of the Cross. Rainier, we're sunk."

Voices, thumping feet, a skittering of hounds and then the stairwell erupted with Brangaene and her guards, four baying hounds and two rather stunted strangers. Caught up in the excitement, the dogs careered about, slipping on the rushes, *owoo*-ing in a frantic quartet until Rainier booted them into silence. The baron fixed his daughter with a dangerous eye.

"What is this?"

Brangaene's eyes shone. "Father!Guess what I have!"

"Bad manners and mud in your hair."

"I fell down."

"Again? I ought to put you on wheels."

"But I found them!" She tugged Drust and Malgon forward by their wrists, presenting them with a flourish. "They're ours."

Her father studied the two prisoners. "Indeed?"

Drust essayed a tentative smile. "How do you, sir?"

"Miserably, and shut up. Brangaene, your eye for value seems keener than my own. Found what?"

"The little folk."

"Their lack of height is apparent."

"But they're faerie!"

The baron looked again. They did not improve with definition. "These two . . . rabbit-droppings?"

Brangaene nodded, jubilant. "And they've been charged to give up their treasures and three wishes and find the Grail as I told you."

Her father turned away, suffering. "Ye gods."

"They look like thieves," Rainier judged. "What are they doing so close to the keep?"

Drust spoke up. "Just trying to get home, sir. We stole nothing from you."

"Which I take not as innocence but oversight," said the baron. "I ought to hang you—"

"That would be nice," said Rainier.

"But I'm at war and very busy. Brangaene, you and your treasures will accompany me to the head of the stairs."

She winced. "The *side* of the foot, father. They're really quite nice."

"Of course." He prodded Drust forward. "Come along now—no, wait. What's this?"

He fingered at the neck of Drust's tunic, opened it and extracted a heavy gold chain. From it, winking in the light, dangled a fair-sized emerald. Drust's hand caught his.

"That's mine. My mother gave it me."

"Where would your mother get a chain like that? Look, Rainier. Worth a warhorse at least."

Brangaene clapped her hands. "I knew it. I knew it."

Drust held on. "My mother gave it me."

"And who's she?" the baron demanded.

"Why, Queen Olwen," said Malgon.

The baron's eyebrows rose. "Who?"

"Queen of Faerie." Malgon struggled imperfectly with English. "Hast not stolen them; did give me one, too." He opened his tunic. "See?"

Rainier examined the rich chains and the undeniably precious stones. "This is not English work, my lord. Nor French or German, nor any I can recognize. Extremely antique."

The baron was a practical man, not given to unexamined belief; practical, but in deep trouble. And he had eyes. He turned to Drust. "I've heard those treasure stories from every passing witch and gypsy all my life. Are they true, then?"

"Remember my wishes," Brangaene jiggled urgently. "Oh, please, please, we need them so much."

The two little men looked at the floor and were silent. Then Drust spoke quietly. "Take the chains, but let us go."

"Oh, no," the baron decided. "No, that was hasty. Rainier, deposit my guests in the tower room, it has a workable lock. Golden geese, you're laying in *my* barnyard now."

Standing tiptoe on a stool, Drust viewed the bustling bailey fifty feet below. The bars were meant to constrain larger men; they might wriggle through, but the drop would be terminal. No way out.

"There must be," said Drust.

Malgon hugged his knees on the straw pallet. "Thee's the fleet mind among us. Tell me how."

"By wit and wile. Am I Olwen's son for nothing?"

"Hast not heart? Thee's the property of that great, scowling man, the golden goose to drop eggs like breadcrumbs. And must not forget the mad lass with a's caught-caught-caught and the wishes and the grails." Malgon threw up his hands. "A thinks we're a mill for magic."

Drust studied him with a slow, thoughtful smile. "Then we will be one. The great baron wants treasure—"

Malgon's eyes flashed a stern warning. "Impossible."

"Just so," Drust nodded, "and therefore . . ."

They heard footsteps on the stone steps beyond their cell. A key groaned in the lock, then the door swung back and Brangaene hurried in with a tray. Two guards waited at the door. She placed the tray on a stool and closed the heavy door. She placed the tray on a stool and closed the heavy door. The faerie men inspected their dinner: two apples, two slices of black bread, but only one bowl of leek and barley soup.

"There were two," Brangaene explained, "but I dropped one."

"Did guess." Malgon fell hungrily to the bread and apples. Brangaene noticed how he offered the soup first to Drust. Clearly this was Queen Olwen's son, a genuine faerie prince, and her luck was almost as great as her imminent need. The bishop would not be put off.

"You must give me my wishes very soon."

Drust spooned the soup, careful to leave half for Malgon. "Oh yes, the treasure."

"And the Grail."

"That's two."

Brangaene blinked. "Don't I get three?"

"Magic's hard, lady, and treasure's rare. There's the bargaining yet." Drust laid down the spoon and offered the bowl to Malgon without taking his eyes from Brangaene. "For a treasure, I'll ask value in return."

Brangaene gazed back at him, and suddenly found it a little hard to breathe. She ascribed it to his magic aura—and let that suffice for an answer. Inexperienced as she was, her glands worked very well, thank you, and Drust was something new. She had never seen hair so sleekly black or eyes so dark, or a male figure, though diminutive, so perfectly formed. He was her gleaming opposite, and the attractive force of that juxtaposition is magic of a very palpable cast. No man had ever looked at her quite like that before, especially one who came so close and took both of her hands.

"It won't be easy, Brangaene. It will take time."

"We don't have time!" she wailed. "The earl-bishop is coming, and he'll want just buckets of money."

"The road itself is hard to find, the road of the gods."

"We're in trouble with God, too. Father's excommunicated." Brangaene fluttered to the door. "There's no time for roads. You must wave your hand and make the hill open. Forget the dragons; father doesn't hunt much anyway. Just one treasure, just a small one, and the Holy Grail. You're bound to do it. The books said."

"What books?" Malgon wondered.

"All of them," she said. "The tales of faerie."

Malgon bit into his apple. "Was't *writ* by faerie?"

"Well, no, but—"

"Did think not. Lies."

Drust frowned. "Peace, Malgon."

"It . . . *can't* be a lie," Brangaene said in a small voice.

Malgon chewed placidly. "Why not?"

"Because—because I need it so much. Because I've searched for you all my life."

"Yes," said Drust. "I see that."

"It *is* true . . . isn't it, Drust?"

Drust glanced once at Malgon. "Tell your father we will bargain."

The color came back to her cheeks. "Oh, yes!"

"And bargain has two sides."

"Yes, yes," Brangaene flung open the door and plunged out. "And quickly, because the bishop—" She tripped over a guard's pike and went flying. Malgon winced.

The footsteps died away, the apparently unbreakable Brangaene in the van. "Hurry! Hurry!"

Malgon sighed. "Now thee's done it. Nay, don't cock thy brow or frown at me who swore to look after the queen's only son. A will whip me from her tent! And thee's no better than tallfolk with the mooning at yellow hair and watery blue eyes. 'May leave out the dragons. Just a small treasure and the Grail,' a says. Ha! What'll thee give little Sure-Foot and her greedy da but the lone, lorn sixpence between us?"

But Drust grinned from ear to ear. He threw himself down on the straw, glowing with satisfaction. "An impossible bargain, Mal: what I can't give for what the baron won't give up."

His mother's guess at the high birthrate of fools—one a minute—was rather informed, Drust realized. There were not one but two keys to their freedom, the baron's greed and the girl's belief.

Malgon was sceptical. "What won't a give up?"

"Brangaene."

With Adam's innocence, he bit lustily into his apple. As with Adam, it was only the prelude to his enlightenment.

The political axiom of the times was "every man must have a lord"—which is to say that no matter how big you were, someone had your number. Someone very definitely had the bishop's.

"Lord, hear Thy servant in his hour of need!"

By the altar of a small, roadside chapel, the earl-bishop prayed very earnestly. He had attached the goods of one baron, his men waited outside amid the snorting of horses and the clank of mail to do the same thing to Brangaene's father, and all out of necessity. The earl-bishop was in the same trouble as the baron, but larger.

By chance he was related to the king; by misfortune he was ambitious, since it led him to accept his bishopric from his royal cousin. The king thought it sound policy, in view of Rome's persuasive power, to have a bishop or two he could count on. Unfortunately, the bishop accepted his *pallium* of office from the crown and didn't wait, as was customary, to have one blessed and sent from Rome. This political oversight has filled volumes; suffice to say His Holiness took umbrage and a flurry of letters coursed between the crown, the bishop and the Vatican. When the diplomatic smoke cleared away, the bishop was regarded as unreliable in London, quite temporary in Rome, and had to decide which to placate first.

He prayed now for guidance with honest intensity. Truly conscientious, even dogmatic, in his holy office, he was less intelligent than shrewd and above all less fervent than superstitious. He could always feel the heat of hell and was not about to fan the flames. The king was a mere relative; he could wait. To pay Peter, Paul would be cheerfully robbed. The gift must be large and of noble intent, one grand gesture of faith.

He and Brangaene had more in common than either realized.

The earl-bishop crossed himself, rose and strode out to take his horse from the groom. He mounted in a rattling of mail and an aura of sanctity.

"Quickly on. We'll raise his keep before vespers."

It was late afternoon and rather warm for April when the baron came into the hall carrying the two gold chains. Drust waited by the trestle table guarded by one man, all the baron could spare from the gates and watch towers. The baron dropped the chains on the table, sat and poured wine into a silver cup.

"Brangaene says you're willing to bargain for your freedom."

Drust sat and indicated the wine. "May I?"

"Please do. Tell me, how much are you prepared to pay?"

Drust sampled the wine pleasurably. "How much will you ask?"

"A heap, little man. The lot, the bundle. Where is it?"

"Oh, now, now, sir. That's not how it's done. The cup of wine begins the bargaining. Aye, there's treasure, but the way to it is a matter of when, not where."

The baron picked up the gold chains; the emeralds flashed in the light. "Did these come from that hoard?"

Drust sipped his wine dreamily. "Mother always liked those. The stones are like the green of wild Britain when we first found it. And the gold—is there any colour goes so well with green as gold? Like sunlight it is. But when you talk money to us, you talk of wives and cattle and goats. These we value, these bring children and make food. We love gold only because it's so pretty."

"And yet you steal it."

"A hard word, sir. Very hard. We were the first men in Britain, and the land belongs to us. We only charge you rent."

The baron choked on his wine. "You what?"

"My lord taxes his own tenants, doesn't he, for the use of the land? The earl-bishop charges you, the great king takes from him. A clear logic."

Drily, the baron asked, "What do you charge the king?"

"Mother's rates go up for him. For you, we will be reasonable."

"That's gracious for a man who has no choice. Now, this treasure. How much is there?"

"Your wine is lovely." Drust settled back in his chair, helping himself to more. "How much? That's hard to say. And the road of the gods . . . not where it is, but when. This is April, a fortnight yet to Beltane-fire—aye, could be soon, could be. But your king strikes his coin in silver, and we don't deal in that."

The baron frowned. "You don't?"

"Oh, a wee bit." Drust shrugged. "The larger pieces. It's not pretty as gold. Must think in silver weight; let me see. Fifty . . . sixty . . . aye, the chest of pearls, large ones only . . . perhaps eighty—"

His host blinked. "Pearls?"

Drust's brow furrowed in concentration. "Eighty-five . . ."

"Eighty-five *what*, damn it!"

"No, there's the rubies. I always forget them."

"You forget—"

"We don't like red. It's the colour of rage. That makes ninety . . . and some trifles, cups, ewers and jewelled plate that Mother holds dear for the charm of them. Yes," Drust set down his cup. "Near a hundred thousand marks of silver."

Luckily, the baron's cup was empty, because he dropped it. He gasped. "A—hundred—thousand—"

"Oh, and the Grail." Drust snapped his fingers. "Lady Brangaene asked for it."

The baron was still stunned. "Part of the . . . rent, I take it."

"Collected from Glastonbury church by Mother's own ancestor these thousand years gone. The Grail, the Cup of the Last Supper. Mother calls it her Jerusalem Cup. She may not wish to part with that."

The baron found his aplomb. "Quite, quite. Now, as to delivery—"

"But my lord, there's my bargain."

"Well, what is it? What do you want?" A good question. If the gold chains were only appetizer to a hundred thousand marks of silver, what could he toss in to humor this improbable pixie?

Drust picked up a candlestick, admiring the workmanship. When he spoke, his voice was gentle with an old sorrow. "Bronze: we learned from the first tallfolk how to make it, and that gave us swords to match theirs. Then others came with the iron we couldn't make or match. We don't like iron. But gold is beautiful, and beauty is what we love. Will you give me one thing with gold in it, even a little, for trade?"

"Done," said the baron.

"And if you fail me, your fields will blight and your cattle perish."

"Done. And if you cheat me—well, *media vita in morte sumus*. In the midst of life, eh? You're rather young to die."

Drust rose and gravely placed his small hand in the baron's. "Done for the third time and the charm. I want your daughter Brangaene for my wife."

The baron dropped his cup again—full, this time. "What?"

"Just that, sir. Not a jot more, not a hair less."

The baron began to chuckle, then to roar with it. Even the guard laughed. "My daughter marry *you?* I'll die laughing."

"Laughing and poor, alas." Drust rose. "Since there's no bargain—"

"Wait a minute!" The baron pushed him down again. "In the midst of life, remember? Ever see a man hanged, drawn and quartered?"

Drust regarded him imperturbably. "That will leave you with two gold chains and my mother's very long memory for injustice. Thy cattle will be Britain's wonder for their mortality." He tried to rise again; this time the guard quashed him back into the chair.

The baron thought: the earl-bishop was imminent. Two dead faeries and two gold chains would benefit no one. He was still thinking furiously when Brangaene pattered up the stairs into the hall.

"Men, Father, a whole line of them on the west road. Good day, Drust, are you working on my wishes? At least five hundred men, Father, all in iron. When can I have the Grail, Drust?"

He shook his head. "There's no bargain made, lass. 'Done' my lord says and takes my hand on it, then 'undone' says he when he learns what I want. Alas— no Grail, Brangaene."

She flew at her father, stricken. "Why not? It has to be a bargain. The book said. Give him something."

"Don't tempt me." Her father drew her close with an acerbic smile. "He's asked for the single rose among my weeds, the hope of my declining years."

She hopped up and down with the urgency. "So *give* it to him!"

"He wants you."

It caught Brangaene on the upswing of a hop. She came down with a thud. "Huh?"

Drust favoured her with what he hoped was a winning smile. "You'll be the only golden-haired girl among my people, a bright star in a midnight sky. No longer dreaming of faerie folk, but a princess among them, sharing their lives, learning to herd and milk goats—"

Rainier panted up the stairs and rushed across the hall. "My lord! The earl-bishop is at the gate with five hundred men, five times what we have on the walls. What defence can we make?"

"Against five hundred? What would you do, Rainier?"

"I'd bloody well let him in, sir."

"Precisely," the baron sighed. "Surrender politely, invite his grace to dinner and hope he chokes on it."

Rainier hurried away, his orders trailing behind him through the air like a ragged banner. "Open the gates. Open the gates. . . ."

"Goats?" Brangaene said. "Smelly goats?"

Drust smiled. "The most fragrant in Britain. Will learn to skin cattle and scrape hides—"

Brangaene swallowed. "Scrape hides?"

"And wear them as our women do, and pitch and strike our tents when we follow the herds to graze. But look at you! So pale and startled." Drust held out his arms. "What do I offer you but your own dreams?"

"I never dreamed goats. Father—"

"Peace, child. Would I marry you to this?"

"I thought not." Drust rose with confident regret. "So, of course . . ."

Footsteps again. Rainier burst out of the stairwell, even more breathless. "Ruin, my lord! Poverty, destruction and the end of all! His grace is taking the cattle and swine and all that's not nailed or mortared down—"

There was a growing uproar in Rainier's wake, voices, dogs, dozens of feet tramping up the stairs into the hall. The earl-bishop appeared out of breath, out of sorts, and perfunctory. Hardly an imposing figure, either as noble or man of God, he looked like a tax collector whose books were not yet balanced. Behind him came his entourage—soldiers, the almoner, the clerks already listing on vellum the valuables attached, one of them with a voice like deep-knelling doom reciting aloud as he scribbled: "Four ivory chests . . . one oaken *prie-dieu.*"

Brangaene wailed to heaven "*I hate goats!*"

The bishop nodded to her. "Then you won't mind that I've removed yours."

"Eight goats," verified the clerk. "Seventeen hens . . ."

"I can't stay for supper, baron. I'm dispossessing you. Look to that table, you men. And the chairs, all of them."

Drust was picked up by two brawny soldiers and the chair swept out from under him.

"Five chairs . . ."

"Sorry about this, baron, but you wouldn't help when I needed, so I must foreclose."

The baron mopped his brow. "Your grace is known to be just. Can't we negotiate?"

"Your troubles are minuscule to mine." The bishop swept up the candlesticks. "That's it, men, all of it. Everything."

The hall was growing quite crowded with soldiers lugging out furniture and chests, and since it was near suppertime, the quartet of dogs elected to charge musically through the procession, eddying about the fringes of the activity. "Four . . . dogs," noted the clerk, but the bishop kicked him.

"Not them, you idiot!"

"Blot . . . four dogs."

"Not my goldware," moaned the baron. "It belonged to the baroness."

"One chest goldware."

"I'm ruined; I'm a poor man."

"*I hate tents!*" Brangaene screamed.

"Tent?" The clerk paused, looking up. "Did I miss a tent?"

"*Keep your Grail!*"

The baron muttered brokenly, "At a time like this . . . grails." Instantly the bishop was at his side. "What is this? What Grail?"

"Grail," the baron echoed in feeble despair. Then, slowly, he said it again. "Grail!" A dawning purpose lit his eye, already tinged with the madness to match a desperate hour. "Grail! Yes, look!" He thrust the two gold chains with their emerald pendants before the bishop. "Treasure, your grace. Gold, silver, pearls, a hundred thousand marks of it. Look at these!"

The earl-bishop looked, but he had heard something that faded the emeralds to green clay. "The Holy Grail, did you say?"

It was to the baron's credit that he could think on his feet, and he knew how to play a trump. "*The* Holy Grail." His arm swept out to point triumphantly at the bewildered Drust. "He has it all and promised it to me."

"The Grail," whispered the bishop, sepulchral as his subject.

"But my *own* goods," the baron reminded him delicately.

The earl-bishop looked, but he had moment. "Bring it all back! Everything!" And far down the stairs the order coursed and echoed. *Bring it back. Bring it back. . . .* The trudging feet paused, turned and started back up the stairs, the dogs dodging around and among them, baying for supper. One of them nibbled at the clerk.

"Brangaene," said her father tenderly, "I'm a man of my word. Prepare yourself."

"Wait!" Drust looked hopelessly from father to weeping child. "You mean—"

"*I hate cows!*"

"So don't drink milk." The baron took her hand and placed it in Drust's, the world once again in place and revolving nicely. "I mean you made a bargain, you demented elf. You're getting married."

Malgon understood none of it as he waited by the saddled horse watching the approach of Drust and the great bishop. The world had turned turvy. The bishop's men peered from every casement and cranny of the small keep while their lord loped about muttering feverishly of grails. The baron looked doubtful. Drust and Brangaene were betrothed and miserable.

But Queen Olwen—he shuddered to think of *her* when he broke the news. Her merest irritation could blister paint, but her rage was lethal as it was silent and patient. Malgon shivered a little with the memory.

Drust seemed different, too. His open good nature was now masked with sober purpose and a kind of sorrow. It wasn't right for faerie to be so serious.

Drust halted by him, the earl-bishop hovering over them both like a thundercloud.

"Malgon, hast the message clear, what to ask the queen?"

"Clear, Drust."

"Her leave to follow the road of the gods."

"And the Grail," said the earl-bishop. "That above all. Her son's life in exchange."

Drust favoured him with an inscrutable look. "And the Jerusalem Cup," he verified. "Tell Olwen I would drink from it."

The bishop's mouth dropped open. "*Drink* from it? You would profane— are you serious?"

"Most gravely so," Drust assured him. "It is old custom. The queen would demand it if I didn't. Faerie are innocent—as the world goes—and when we travel out among tallfolk, we drink from the Grail on our return to show we are still God's first children. There are dangers . . . your grace is a man of learning. Surely you know the legend of this holy vessel?"

The troubled bishop knew only too well. The most sacred relic in Christendom could not be touched or even approached by the impure without instant death. To drink from it as this vagrant pixie proposed was not only sacrilege but madness that beggared adjectives.

And yet the thought came unbidden—he would make confession of the pride—if he himself could be allowed . . .

He shelved the thought. Devout he was, but the product of a suspicious world. Faerie were notorious deceivers. He knew not only the legends but the factual history of the relic. A few subtle questions would show the truth of it.

"Where was this stolen?" he demanded.

"Acquired," Drust amended tactfully. "At Glastonbury."

"The abbey, of course?"

"No, the old wattle church. No more than a mud hut it was then."

The bishop felt himself begin to sweat. "Where hidden? Behind the altar? Under the floor?"

"In a well, my mother said."

The earl-bishop swallowed hard. His heart skipped a beat. "Wh-why should it be brought to Britain at all?"

Drust answered easily. "The merchant had friends here."

"What friends? What friends would a poor Jew have in Britain?"

Drust smiled at Malgon. "Mark how dost try to catch me out. Your grace knows Joseph was a friend of the governor of Judea and a merchant in tin. Who needs hearsay when common knowledge will do? Every port in the Middle Sea, from Rome to Thebes on the Nile, shipped its tin from Cornwall. Is not Joseph still remembered and sung about there? Belike he made the journey more than once."

The earl-bishop hid his trembling hands in the folds of his robe. "You have seen the Grail?"

"Olwen told me of it. 'Tis kept masked."

"Describe the jewels set in the vessel."

"There be no jewels," Drust shook his head. "No, *those* stories were writ in French, and not even your grace would trust a Frank. The Christ-man wasn't rich. Bronze it is and plain as truth. Mother wouldn't prize it else." His glance flicked over the bishop's rich mantle filigreed in cloth-of-gold. "Gaudy's not to her taste."

The bishop turned away to hide his excitement. He looked up at his men perched like predatory birds on the walls, the baron and his daughter waiting at the hall entrance. Most of the Grail stories were maundering, allegorical romance, and over the centuries a thousand liars claimed to have seen it. They all described a cup or bowl too rich for most kings let alone the simple dwelling that housed the yet-obscure band of the Nazarene on the night of the Last Supper.

Now, the bishop was a religious man—as those things went—though he could not believe the Grail had been withdrawn into heaven or simply disappeared from mortal sight. Lost, stolen or strayed, it had to be somewhere.

"Bring it." He turned and bustled away towards the chapel.

Drust embraced Malgon. "Haste thee back. The tower will be lonely."

Malgon studied him closely. "Thee looks sad as death."

"No matter. Go."

But Malgon caught his arm. "Nay, tell. Hast been thy servant; hast not been thy friend as well?"

Drust's eye twinkled with the ghost of his old merriment—and an elusive something else behind it. "And will be when bishop and baron be long forgot. Faerie's dealt with greedy men before, else why our saying that one thing worse than wanting . . ."

"Is getting," Malgon finished it. "True, they be all stupid and mad. Help me to shorten this stirrup, Drust; 'twas set for a giant."

Drust watched him across the bridge and onto the north road, then turned back toward the keep. Brangaene left her father and hurried across the bailey toward him. Drust's mouth curved ironically; this wishing business was quite beyond her now. She looked like someone who'd conjured a rose and received a thorn.

"Drust, what happened to the bishop? Runs past us without a word, talking to himself. Not even vespers yet, and he's in chapel praying for all he's worth."

"That won't take long."

"What did he ask of you?"

His expression was strange, but the words were gentle when they came, as if he were teaching a child.

"What you all want of faerie: wishes granted, dreams come true, death put off till some far time when the world's lost all of its sweet. He wants magic in a bronze bowl. And what's your pleasure today?"

Brangaene saw the thing he had tried to conceal from Malgon, the pain. She might have missed it a week before, but even unicorn hunters, when they grow up, have to start somewhere.

"Poor Drust. I didn't mean to . . ."

"Ladybug, don't be sad. I was like you once. Because I couldn't see any further than a frog, I thought my lily pad was the world. Then I saw how big the world really was, and how little and how few we are. Olwen has less folk to call her queen than the great bishop brought here with him. Our cattle are scrawny, our children starve, and we have no land. What little graze is left the tallfolk's sheep tear away bit by bit, year by year. We move from poor to worse and must keep on moving until there's nothing left. Gold, jewels—" he spread his hands helplessly "—these buy *things*, Brangaene. They can't—there's a word in my tongue that means *what was then*, but more than that. It means the good, green time, all the good things that were. My mother will never understand. Malgon will never understand. And it's not in my poor pudding of a heart to tell them." After a moment, Drust took her hand and kissed it. "And *you* want magic?"

"Not any more," she confessed. "Not that you're not *very* nice, Drust, just . . ."

"Not entirely what you wished."

"I guess it's the goats."

Drust surveyed her, his manner changing abruptly. "Look, lass, when you make a gown, you don't just cut and stitch away with no thought to it. You measure what's needed. Well, it's the same with wishes: they have to fit *you*. I'll guess you've never done it right. Would you like to try?"

Brangaene hesitated; the whole phenomenon had proved hazardous. "Should I?"

"You have one left. Close your eyes and think of something you want so deep you never even whispered it."

Eyelids squeezed tight around the effort, Brangaene concentrated.

"Oh dear." She giggled. "Oh, my goodness!"

"You see?"

"I didn't even wish. It was just—there."

"No dragons or grails?"

"No," Brangaene blushed—rather more with anticipation than embarrassment. "No, indeed."

Two men-at-arms marched out from the hall, halted, flanking Drust like falcons bracketing a sparrow. "The baron wants a word with you. Quick *march!* One-two-one-two-step *out*, you horrible little man! One-two . . ."

Drust tried to keep up with them.

The baron met them, rubbing his hands together nervously. "No problems? Your servant will return, of course?"

Drust nodded. "Until then, back to jail, I suppose."

"Just to keep things regular. The *cuisine* will not stint. There'll be a good supper."

"And wine," Brangaene prompted from behind the soldiers.

"Of course, he's our guest." The baron stepped close to Drust, lowering his voice. "My abbreviated friend, I don't know how you take to metaphor, but you and I are ripe wheat." He inclined his head significantly toward the chapel. "And *he* has a very large scythe."

"Just so, my lord," Drust said expressionlessly. "And what price wishes now?"

"Eh?"

"The Grail and treasure make two. 'Twas not in the bargain, mind, but if I *could* eke out a third . . ."

In the elogent silence of understanding, they listened to the interminable Latin braying forth from the chapel where the bishop was, as it were, covering his bet.

The baron sighed. "If indeed."

"Just a thought." Drust let it hang in the air between them. The guards in his wake, he started up the tower stairs.

A week passed, eight days, nine. Then a morning came when the sun climbed only half-heartedly into the sky, sulked and then hid its face in thick cloud. On the tenth day, the small world of the keep was wrapped in fog, and out of it came Malgon on the same manor horse, leading two of Olwen's ponies. Drust watched him across the bailey bridge. Within minutes, he heard the heavy tread of the soldiers counterpointed with the light patter of Brangaene's feet.

"Drust! To the hall and quickly. Malgon's come with a letter from your mother, and the bishop's angry because no one can read it, and—oh, hurry!"

The guards hustled him away in the backwash of her haste. In the hall were the earl-bishop, the baron and Rainier, and in the center of their regard, like a spaniel pup among irritable greyhounds, the weary Malgon.

"This fool of yours can barely speak English," the bishop growled.

"Here, read." The baron thrust a rolled parchment at Drust. "I didn't think anyone still wrote on sheepskin."

"And a palimpsest at that." Rainier peered at it. "Ancient as those chains they wore. This queen doesn't write very often."

The heavy parchment was tied with a strip of worn linen. Drust undid it, speaking to Malgon in faerie, "How did the queen at this?"

"Cold," Malgon murmured. "So cold and quiet, would swear 'twas winter and not spring in a's tent. Then a smiles like death and sits down to write this."

Drust glanced at the rounded Gaelic script and the scrawled, looping signature. His mother styled herself, as her ancestors did, with a title that had not appeared on any map for a thousand years, if at all. He felt a pang; for Olwen and her people, nothing would ever change.

> To the English who hold Drust:
> I marvel that so many tallfolk can prize cold metal over the real treasures of this world and yet call themselves wise.
> Natheless, my son is precious to me. For his safety, you have my leave to travel the road of the gods and take such fortune as you find there, to the which is added my chiefest possession known as the Jerusalem Cup, excepting only our custom that Drust may prove the innocence of his soul by drinking therefrom.
> I wish only to see my son safe home.
> Olwen, Queen of Prydn

Rainer squinted quizzically. "Queen of what?"

Drust handed him the letter. "It means 'the very old people.' "

The bishop's eyes were fevered. "But the Grail, where is it?"

"Olwen's word is good," said Drust. "Will be with the treasure. And I will drink from it." He went to the casement and scrutinized the air beyond it. "After this fog will come rain," he told them. "And we need the rain to find the road. We must leave now."

The bishop needed no urging. "To horse!" He whirled and hurried to the stairs, his officers in his wake. To *horse!* The relayed orders echoed after him.

"Well, Brangaene." Her father took her arm. "Will you come? It seems only right. This was your inspiration to begin with."

The guards had taken up their parenthetical position around Drust and Malgon. "Yes, ride with us, Brangaene," Drust laughed. "To the end of the road, the end of wishing. Who could miss that?" He shrugged philosophically to the guards. "Come, sirs."

They travelled north all day through a blanketing fog, Drust and Malgon in the lead, the bishop and two guards just behind, then the baron and Brangaene. Behind them, in a train stretching over a quarter-mile, came the bishop's entourage.

The road gave way to forest, the great trees looming up and fading again like ghosts behind them. When the last of the gaunt shapes disappeared in the fog, Brangaene missed them, nothing now but wild gorse, rolling moor and dampness that chilled through her heavy cloak. They pitched their tents in the middle of it before nightfall. The next day was drearier still. Though the fog was gone, heavy clouds loured over the barren hill tops. Before midday, the rain began, gentle at first, then harder, in a steady downpour through which they plodded all afternoon across the monotonous moor in the wake of the faerie men. Before they pitched camp for the night, Brangaene was sneezing with her worst cold in years.

Swathed in blankets, she huddled over a brazier in her small tent, hating quite beyond demure limits the weather, the moor, her father, the bishop and the whole blighted notion of wishes and magic.

"Dab!" she cursed. "Dabdab*dab!*"

"Odd; your da just said that."

Drust stood in the entrance of the tent with a steaming cup. "Magic's hard work, isn't it? Here." He handed her the cup. "Olwen's own tea. Made from honeycomb and flowers."

She sipped at it. "Oh, it's good."

"Some say it's the rose does the trick, some the pimpernel, but we never have colds."

"Where are we bound, Drust? Will this moor ever end?"

He nodded. "Soon enough. Tomorrow we must be in a certain place."

"Why?"

"Not why, lass. When. When the sun comes out."

Like much of what Drust said, Brangaene understood it not at all. She listened to the rain drumming against the tent sides. "What if it doesn't?"

"Then we wait till it does. Nothing is perfect."

An interesting aside: this logical question and answer just might have been the end of the Age of Faith and the beginning of the Renaissance. Everything starts somewhere, and Brangaene was no longer a child of pure belief.

The rain let up towards mid-morning of the next day. Their way ran through uplands now, wave after wave of bare, steepening hills and rocky outcroppings. Drust dropped back to ride at the baron's knee and found him red-eyed as his daughter and definitely out of sorts.

"If you know this treasure to the last pound, why must we look for some damned silly road-of-the-gods?"

"Only Olwen knows the way. I've seen it only once." Drust pointed to the hills, alike as wrinkles in a blanket. "Without the road, I couldn't find it again."

The baron exploded. "There's no bloody road! Nothing but heath and no end to that."

"Will be soon," Drust soothed him. "We must have passed the treasure an hour ago."

"An *hour*—?"

"Or thereabouts. Must go beyond to see back, like a lifetime. Brangaene, lass, how's your cold?"

She snuffled. "Bedder, thag you."

Up ahead, the earl-bishop and his guards were paused over something on the ground. The bishop wheeled his horse and cantered back to Drust.

"There are tracks. They might be your people."

Drust urged his pony forward to the indicated spot. A hundred yards beyond, Malgon was halted, observing the lightening sky.

The prints were those of a single, small horse. Most were obliterated by rain, but they pointed south.

"Faerie horse," Drust confirmed.

The bishop pondered the print. "Should we follow?"

"You'd never find her. That mark in the print there? Olwen's horse. She's brought the Grail for me to drink."

The bishop regarded him solemnly. "You still persist in that madness?"

"The old custom, almost law. My mother expects it of me." Drust smiled quickly as if to dispel any personal doubts. "Will be no danger to your grace, of course, though it might be wise to stand well back and perhaps not stare it straight on."

The earl bishop could no longer choke back the question. "How many . . . men have drunk from the grail?"

"In a thousand years? Many."

"And died?"

"Only a few," said Drust offhandedly. "It may be the Christ-man's more merciful than one thinks."

"Drust!"

It was Malgon ahead, pointing not to the sky now, but the ground. "Be shadow! The sun!"

Abruptly, Malgon kicked the pony into a flat run up a rocky defile. Drust beckoned the others forward in a sweeping wave and galloped after him. The whole column rippled forward in the rush up the narrow pass, the bordering rocks now showing in sharp relief the shadows that raced across them as the last clouds parted and the sun burned through. Up and up they clattered until Brangaene felt the ground level out under her horse. She rounded a sharp bend in the trail; there on the rocky ledge before her stood Drust and Malgon looking away to the south, while the bishop sat his horse with a foolish expression on his face, saying over and over to himself, "I don't believe it. No, I don't believe it. We could have—we should have known . . ."

And Brangaene's heart leaped with the last flicker of an old dream. Sad, because it would never come again. The old tales were not magic, no part of magic, only truth—and a kind of map worn faint with time.

"There, Brangaene!" Drust's voice rang out over the bishop's. "The road of the gods. *Where it goes down!*"

Across the moist prism of the morning sky, the rainbow bent its glory to earth.

The long mound looked like any other low rise in the rolling hills. Only when Brangaene knew what it was could she see that it rose to smoothly, the length of its hundred-foot ridge too even. It had been built of stone like the great circle on Salisbury Plain, Drust told her, and sodded over so long it was truly part of the hills around it.

Now she knew why Drust had stressed *when*. The rainbow lasted no more than a quarter-hour, fading as the sun clouded over again. Before it went, Drust carefully estimated the exact point at which it would touch the earth, selected a series of references, leading to that spot, then led them back along the trail.

Two more hours and the hardest riding of the whole journey, straight up hills, jolting down the other side. The mist rose rapidly, seeping like pale white snakes into the valleys and copses, rising toward the low hill tops. Just after they attained Drust's last reference point, Brangaene spied the figure that might have been a stunted tree or a large bush in the thickening fog, but she thought it moved slightly. Later, she saw it again: off to her left, slipping away into a wall of whiteness like a ghost-wolf padding their flank. But for a moment Brangaene had seen clearly, if only in silhouette, the pony and its small, hooded rider.

She could hardly see the others now in the mist. Drust must be moving on pure instinct. At last the wraith-figures of the two faerie men dipped into one last defile and disappeared briefly. When she and her father drew up on them, they were sitting their horses amid the bishop and his guards, and beyond loomed the long, regular shape of the cairn.

Drust slipped out of the saddle and knelt to examine something in the earth. The bishop followed him.

"What is it?"

Drust pointed to the small hoofprint. "Olwen."

If no one else believed, Brangaene did.

The baron studied the dimensions of the cairn. "This thing goes back for at least thirty yards. Is it all hollow?"

"And goes far down," Drust told him.

The bishop was all business now; "Set my tent here at the entrance . . . this *is* the entrance?"

"Hard by." Drust took several steps to the foot of the mound where a tumbled outcropping of stones rose some six feet above him. He leaned almost casually against one of the stones; with a grinding rumble, the largest boulder in the pile rolled back to reveal an aperture large enough for a man to wiggle through.

"Will need a torch," he said.

"Bring a resin torch, bring them all," the bishop commanded. "A fire here quickly. Set my tent."

Brushwood was collected, rubbed with tallow and lighted in a large brazier. With a great deal of bustle, the bishop's tent was pitched. Drust dipped his torch into the fire, slipped into the black opening and disappeared. Malgon waited by the rocks. Suddenly he knelt close to the opening. Brangaene heard him mumble something, then he rose and shouted to all of them.

"The Jerusalem Cup be here. All may look. Be covered with a cloth."

Drust's arm jutted out of the hole bearing an object swathed in a long dark cloth. "Take it, Mal, so I can climb out."

Malgon shrank back and fell on his knees, turning his face away. "Nay, cannot. Do not ask it of me. Be not shriven or heard mass this fortnight."

Still the arm protruded from the opening. Like that which caught Arthur's sword in the lake, Brangaene thought. All around her, the men were dismounting, sinking to their knees, the sound of their armor eerie and distorted in the mist. Only the bishop remained upright, rooted in front of his tent, gazing at the masked object.

"I need both hands to climb out," the voice came again. "Let him who is without fear of his soul take the Grail from me."

Head bowed over her hands in reverence, Brangaene felt the awed silence. Then a rustle of movement. Her eyes opened. Slowly, deliberately, the bishop moved towards the Grail. Brangaene swallowed hard. There must be fear in him, but the bishop kept going till he stood within reach of the upthrust arm.

He stretched out both hands and took the covered Grail. An exhalation of fright and wonder sighed through the company of his men. When Drust clambered out of the hole, he regarded the earl-bishop with a grave respect.

"Your grace is the holiest of men—and the bravest. They may go in now. The treasure is there." He raised his hand for the watching men and opened it to reveal the rubies lying on his palm. He let them fall like so many pebbles. The men watched carefully where they rolled, their eyes wide, tongues licking out over dry lips.

"The treasure is there!" Drust raised his voice. "Olwen's word is kept."

"Yes . . ." The bishop's voice cracked slightly. He stared at his men and hardly saw them. "Yes, go in. Take the sacks. Get . . . get it all."

A dozen, twenty torches were dipped into the fire. A line of fireflies in the mist, the men squeezed through the opening and vanished into the cairn. The bishop appeared oblivious to it all. With stiff movements, he carried the covered prize to his tent.

Passing Malgon, Drust whispered something, received the other's silent affirmation, then joined Brangaene at the fire, listening with them to the growing clamour of discovery within the cairn.

"Now they're finding it, hear them? Finding out how much there is, how it shines in the light, thinking there's nothing lovelier, not even a fair woman. Feeling it in their hands. Wondering will it all disappear as they've heard tell. You can smell their greed. Don't go in, baron." Drust smiled up at him. "There *is* that third wish."

In his tent, the earl-bishop placed his precious burden on a low chest. He prayed briefly, then contemplated on his—no, his soul's desire.

The first test was past. He was allowed to approach, to touch it, perceive its solidity. The shape under the woolen cloth was a foot and a half across by perhaps six inches deep. He fingered the edge of the cloth, took hold of it—

"Your grace."

Drust moved forward to face the bishop across the chest. "I came to drink, and so grave with the thought of it, I forgot to bring wine. May a frightened man beg that favour?"

"You will still do this?"

"I must," Drust said tonelessly. He indicated a wine skin. "May I?"

The bishop's throat tightened.

"God with us." With a quick motion, Drust jerked the cover from the bowl. As he did, the bishop shut his eyes and crossed himself. Nothing happened; the world churned on. When he looked again, the bowl sat quite mundanely on the chest, feeble light from the one candle darting with unusual brightness over the polished surfaces. He watched in horrified fascination as Drust unstoppered the wineskin and poured a good measure into the vessel. The red wine swashed and sparkled over the polished bottom.

"Your grace will send this to the Pope?"

"What? Yes . . . yes, I will."

"Don't tell him of this act. Would not bring on him the sin of envy." Drust laid hands on the bowl.

"Faerie, are you mad?"

The answer, when it came, was faint and weary. "No . . . no. Only a man from a small, weak people whose green time is gone, who will not walk Britain much longer. Olwen and I be their strength and their conscience, perhaps their soul. The Christ-man could not escape Gethsemane, neither can I."

Yet he hesitated, hovering over the vessel. The tent rustled back, and a beefy sergeant lumbered into view. "Pardon, your grace, but—" He saw the bowl and stopped. "God a mercy!"

"What is it?"

The man tried not to look at the vessel, but his agitation had to do with more immediate problems. "Sir, the treasure—"

"It is there?"

The sergeant's eyes seemed slightly glazed. "Th-there?" he stammered. "God, yes. And there and *there! Yards* of it, levels and stairs of it. Ringlets, plate, torques, jewels. We haven't sacks enough for all there is, and not to the bottom yet. The coins spill out of the chests like pebbles." He thrust out a handful. "See!"

The bishop examined the bronze and silver coins, all very ancient but legible. He turned them over, reading the inscriptions. " 'Agricola', 'Trajanus'. These are Roman."

"For sure," said Drust blandly. "All Roman and writ of in the Saxon books. Some they took away, some they buried should they return. Faerie watched where they dug." He shrugged. "They were here four hundred years; did owe much rent."

The sergeant glanced nervously out of the tent. "Sir, the men outside. They hear those in the cave. They saw the rubies this madman tossed on the ground. I can't hold them back much longer."

The earl-bishop bristled. "If one of them steals so much as one coin—"

"A wise man would let them," Drust observed. "How much can magpies steal from a granary? Let every man fill his pocket before he fills your sacks."

"That bunch?" The sergeant snorted. "They'll steal my lord blind, little man."

"Would do that anyway," Drust countered smoothly. "Your grace, when generosity comes cheap, buy a reputation. Will need them all to carry. Singing your praises will make light work of it. Let them go in."

It took only a moment for the bishop to see the wisdom. How much gold could one man tuck away in a tunic? "Give that order, sergeant."

"Yes, sir. God bless you, sir!" The sergeant hurried out. They heard his muffled, staccato orders, the answering shout and the rush of feet.

But Drust's attention had returned to the bronze bowl. "Was glad your man came in. It forestalled—" He broke off suddenly. "Pity a poor man. I must drink, but I cannot, not before shriving. You are a man of God and most blessed. Will you guard—It—while I pray?"

"It will be here." The bishop looked down at the bowl; the wine shone dark and red as rubies. He barely heard Drust leave the tent.

He looked at the bowl. After a long time, he bent and picked it up.

Drust joined the baron and Brangaene by the fire, a small island of light in the fog. For some minutes they watched the last of the bishop's men struggle through the small opening to the cairn. Brangaene wondered if there was room inside for all of them.

"And more," Drust told her.

Then the last man vanished into the black mouth. They heard his shout of discovery added to the others that faded as the men ran and stumbled from level to level, finding, filling their pockets. Then quiet. The grey-ghost horses stamped and snuffled. Only Drust noted the slight sound that might have come from the earl-bishop's tent, as if something had fallen.

"This is a strange place." Brangaene shivered. "The eyes on those men when they went in . . ."

"Like their master," the baron growled. "And what's that holy hypocrite up to?"

"At war with conscience and need." Drust warmed his hands over the fire. "Will not be long."

"A moment's too long with such as these." The baron spat. "Greedy pigs, let 'em choke on the damned gold."

Drust favoured him with that odd smile—amusement, sadness, more wisdom than the cairn held treasure. "Yes. Your third wish."

He took several quick strides to the rocky outcrop of the cairn entrance. "Mark how faerie keeps his word. Three wishes. One, the gold. Two, the Cup. And three to choke them on it. One stone to open, another to close." Drust pressed against one of the stones. With a grating sound, the cairn was sealed tight again. His dark head snapped up. "And the third—now, Malgon!"

Brangaene looked up with him. On the roof of the cairn, dim with mist, she saw the little figure bend close to to the ground, move something, then run nimbly down one side. Before the booming began, before the earth trembled, she saw another, mounted figure race away behind Malgon. Then the shocks came, and the muffled roar that grew as the ground quaked beneath her feet.

Brangaene gasped, clutched her father's arm. Before their eyes, the long roof of the cairn buckled, went swaybacked and sank as five-ton stones toppled from the first interior level, ruptured the second, and the combined dead weight fell on the third . . . the fourth. The sickening concussions rumbled through Brangaene's feet again and again. At length they weakened, the distant roar faded, the shrieking echoes died. From the entrance stone, a small dust-wraith emerged.

"Good Jesus," the baron managed weakly. "What happened?"

"The end of wishing," said Drust.

Brangaene trembled under her father's arm. "All of them. All the b-bishop's men." The thought struck her like ice water. "The bishop!"

"Let him be," Drust held up his hand. "The thing's done; the queen will be calling me home. Baron, Brangaene, share a cup of wine with me before I go."

The baron stared at him. "But the bishop—?"

"Please," Drust protested mildly. "It is so peaceful now." He cocked an ear. "Aye, they're coming."

"But where is he?" the baron persisted, nervously eyeing the tent. "Is he deaf?"

"Quite."

The soft *clop* of hooves came out of the mist. One horse stopped, the other grew louder until Malgon materialized, leading Drust's pony up to the guttering fire.

"Thy mother wants thee home, Drust."

"Will come." Drust dug in his saddle bag, extracted a plain wooden bowl and gave it to Malgon. "Fetch me wine, Mal. Some of the bishop's best."

Malgon vanished into the tent. Some yards up the defile, barely limned in the fog, the cloaked and hooded rider waited, motionless.

Brangaene wondered. "Drust, is that—?"

"Olwen. Will not come close. Has been hurt too often by tallfolk."

Malgon reappeared with the filled bowl which he placed in his master's hand.

"His grace?" Drust asked delicately.

Malgon shook his head.

"Did drink, then?"

"Did."

The baron put his question very carefully; not that it troubled him overmuch. "The earl-bishop is . . . dead?"

"Dead as pork," Malgon contemplated. "Not even Caesar be so well deceased."

"He was reaching for this from the first day," Drust mused. "Did only help him along." He chuckled softly. "Olwen burnished the bowl to make it shine, and in the burnish was rubbed foxglove and hemlock. Would kill six bishops."

Brangaene caught her breath. "You—poisoned—the Holy Grail?"

"We tempted him with a custom that never was, Brangaene. If that's a sin—well, I think your father will pray for me."

Malgon laughed. Out of the mist came another laugh like a silvery, musical echo. Drust drank from the bowl and passed it to the baron. "Especially when he has five hundred horses and their saddles to sell."

"Faerie," the baron judged, "I never realized, but you command a sterling quartet of talents: philosopher, diplomat, liar and thief. Have you thought of a career at Court?"

"Perhaps some day. If must take up a trade." Drust passed the bowl to Brangaene but she struck it out of his hand.

"*You poisoned the Holy*—"

"Nay, nay, nay, lass." Drust patiently retrieved the battered bowl. "Not the Grail. Olwen never promised the Grail. Did write of the Jerusalem Cup—"

"B-but—but wasn't that—?"

"Which belonged to Joseph's friend, the governor of Judea."

"The gov—" Suddenly the baron saw light. He could believe anything now. "You mean Pilate? *Pontius Pilate?*"

Drust nodded: "Does sound right, yes. 'Twas his wash-bowl."

Monstrously sacrilegious, but the baron had an irrepressible and quite secular urge to laugh. "Ye bloody gods."

"Brangaene," Drust offered her the old bowl again. "This is no great Jerusalem Cup; this was made for common folk like us. But it holds pease porridge well and doesn't leak, old as it is." He pressed it into her hands. "Take it as a favor to Drust. When you eat or drink from it, remember me." He kissed her lightly, gave her a wink. "And leave a supper at your gate for tired faerie men."

He nodded gravely to the baron, then mounted his pony. "Let's go home, Mal."

They rode away. Once, after the fog had swallowed them up, Brangaene heard Drust's joyful shout and again that other voice, low, melodious—welcoming.

That was all. She and her father were alone.

The baron spent some time stringing stallions into a train the mares would follow. He also inspected the tent. Malgon's assessment had been precise; his grace rivalled Caesar, even the pharaohs, for the finality of his past tense. When the baron returned to his daughter, she was pensively turning the ancient bowl in her hands.

"Father . . ."

When you eat or drink from it, remember me.

She recalled the text, almost the same words, written so long ago.

So worn it was. So *very* old . . .

Her voice was tiny, a whisper. "Father—what kind of wood is this?"

"Hm?" He examined it. "Not oak or ash . . . not English at all, I'd say. It's—well, I don't know."

"I do," Brangaene murmured. "Like my chests from Lebanon. This is cedarwood."

So ancient, dark-stained, the rim warped with time. Brangane held it to her heart, and her laugh was tremulous. "That man, that fine, beautiful man. He brought it after all. He brought it." Her eyes glistened with purpose. "Father, do you think the *arch*bishop—"

Her father understood then. "Oh, not again, Brangaene. That? You heard him; it's his porridge bowl."

"Father." There was something rising in Brangaene's voice that the baron should have heeded. "Listen to me. I think we should ask the archbishop—"

But he turned away and spread his arms to the fog. "She's hopeless. Hopeless! Will she never be done wishing?"

He did not see the subtle change of expression levelled at his back. *Just one more,* Branaene thought. Just the one Drust had taught her to realize, the never-even-whispered wish. It was a good day for miracles, and why not one of her own? She sighted coolly on the baron's posterior, wound up with a dainty hop-step and fired from the toe. "One to grow on!"

Poonk!

The baron flew.

As he lacked his daughter's practice his flight was brief and graceless. When he sat up, thoroughly stunned, he faced a new Brangaene—confident, serene and sure. She held up the bowl.

"On second thoughts," Brangaene said crisply. "Tell the archbishop *I* want to see *him.*"

As it turned out, the baron's judgement was suspect on several counts. He thought his arse would never stop aching, but it did. He thought he might come back and dig up the gold, but he never found it. Though after a while, as they rode home, the sun came out and Brangaene sang sweetly.

The archbishop sent the bowl to Rome, where it was studied by ecclesiastic scholars imbued with the new spirit of rationalism. They are studying it yet, as cautious scholars will, though the history-minded may note how suddenly Grail stories went out of vogue. They might have asked Brangaene, but who in the wise new world would credit a girl who told fairy tales and still left a supper by the gate for no one in particular?

LILY'S WHISPER
Jay Russell

Jay Russell's Hollywood horror romp *Celestial Dogs* was recently published in the United States. His revisionist vampire saga, *Blood*, has been published in the UK. Russell's short stories have appeared in the anthologies *Splatterpunks, Still Dead: Book of the Dead 2* and *The King Is Dead: Tales of Elvis Post-Mortem*.

"Lily's Whisper" is quite unlike most of Russell's other work. It's about a family haunted by ghosts. The story was first published in *Dark Terrors 2: The Gollancz Book of Horror*, but is recommended to fantasy and horror readers alike.

—E. D. and T. W.

Sometimes, at the edge of consciousness, on that unsteady divide between my waking and dreaming life, I'll hear her wonderful little song. The spectral voice of memory, I suppose. All in my head. But then, isn't everything?

An orderly asked if anything was wrong. A *lot*, I thought, but I told him I was fine and forced myself to walk on in. I'd been standing, frozen with dread, outside the door to my grandmother's hospital room. I stared at the small white paper with her name in blurry type: **Bernstein, Sally.** No middle initial. When I was little I used to ask her why it was that she had no middle name. She always answered with the same joke: 'We were too poor to afford one.' It drove me crazy because it didn't make any sense, but now I smiled thinking about it. *Okay, Grandma*, I thought, *let's get this over with.*

My Aunt Lily died when I was a kid. She was actually my great-aunt. My mother's aunt. Grandma Sally's sister.

Although she didn't live far away from the house where I grew up, I never knew Lily very well. Once or twice a year someone would bring her along to a family gathering—she couldn't drive—where she always showered the children with fruit candies and cheap but wonderful presents. Unlike my mother's other seemingly born-ancient aunts and uncles, Lily seemed not just to like children, but to understand them. To think like them. Even though she was the only one without kids of her own.

I never much cared for those other relatives, who were somehow sort of scary to me in their sere way, but I was always happy to see Lily. It wasn't just that she treated us differently or better (though she did), she somehow seemed utterly apart from her siblings. Her face betrayed the same harsh, Eastern European stock, but there was a gentle quality to her that none of the others possessed. A humor in her eyes and playfulness to her touch which made the cloying affections of her shrewish kin all the more glaring.

I suppose I realized that there was something unusual about Lily—something secret—from the way the others talked about her. They always lowered their voices when Lily's name came up, as if she was something to hide or to be ashamed of. If not for the fact of our Jewishness, I think they would have crossed themselves at the mention of her name. Even when Lily was in the room the others spoke about her as if she wasn't there. Or as if she was dead. Perhaps the reason the children identified with her so closely was because, among the other adults, she was treated as if she, too, was of no real consequence.

Hospital rooms are like shopping malls in their dislocated uniformity. Stepping into one, whether in Los Angeles or West Palm Beach, removes you from the normal fabric of local time and space and into the antiseptic, spiritually liminal realm of the sick and dying.

The bed nearest the door had been stripped of linens and I had the sudden ominous sense that the last person to occupy it had not walked out on their own. A tall plastic curtain had been drawn around the far bed, the elongated shadows of the guard rails silhouetted like prison bars on the laminated barrier. As I got closer I could hear raspy breathing. The curtain hadn't been pulled all the way around, and as I reached the foot of the bed I saw my grandmother for the first time in almost ten years.

Sally had always been a short, plump woman, but age and illness had shrunk her down so that, lost under her covers, she looked like an old ventriloquist's dummy. She stirred in uneasy sleep and I saw that she was little more than a bag of withered flesh. The sight of her reminded me of a balloon you'd find behind the couch two weeks after a party, limp and wrinkled and only vaguely suggestive of its original shape. Her skin had stretched and sagged beyond the capacity of her diminutive frame. As a child I had always marvelled at my grandmother's upper arms; they were fatty and thick and dangled like jowls, jiggling wildly with every gesture she made. Now I saw that the folds of skin remained, but the meat beneath them had dissolved and the flesh hung limp as a ghost ship's sails.

Her stained dentures swam in a plastic cup on the formica night table and her hollow mouth drooped open. A glistening thread of saliva trailed down her chin and tufts of thin, colorless hair dotted her mottled scalp. In fact, the sight of her made me feel a little queasy and I started to walk back out when her eyes opened, nailing me to the floor.

She stared at me, but I wasn't certain she could see me or if she could, that she recognized who I was. The last time I'd seen her had been at my mother's funeral almost a decade before. Despite her numerous illnesses and various surgeries, I had spoken with Sally only once since then, when she had called on my birthday. It was a hellish call in which she quizzed me accusatorially about my lack of contact with her.

Like all good New York Jews, she and my grandfather had retired to Florida when I was a kid. As a result I had never been particularly close to her—from an adult's point of view, I never knew her at all—though I still carried a certain latent guilt over having ignored her so in her declining years.

Especially after first her husband, then my mother died.

It was primarily that lurking guilt (along with my father springing for the cost of the air fare) which had served to bring me all the way from my home in Los Angeles to her Florida hospital for this reunion. A reunion for which Sally had hysterically and inexplicably begged.

The silence was broken only by my grandmother's fractured breathing. She scanned me up and down, but her only movement was the slight rise and fall of her chest. I shifted nervously and cleared my throat. I was about to identify myself when, with a low moan, she pulled herself up against the pillow and slowly lifted an arthritic hand.

"Brucie," she said.

I came around the side of the bed and took her hand. It felt as light as a Styrofoam coffee cup, the skin hard and cool to the touch.

"Hi, Grandma," I croaked.

She left her hand in mine for a moment then drew it back beneath the covers. Her eyes never left mine.

"You're so thin," she said and coughed. Then she farted wetly. I felt slightly embarrassed, but she didn't seem bothered. "And a beard, yet."

"Yeah," I said, scratching my chin. "That's right."

She didn't reply. The tension could have been cut with oh, say a small sword: six-foot blade.

"So," I said, posing the stupidest question of all time: "How are you?"

Here is everything that I knew about Lily's life:

She was the youngest sibling of the large Petrowski family, something like eight or nine children in all. They were dirt poor and lived like sharecroppers in seriously anti-Semitic Poland at the turn of the century. Neither my great-grandparents nor any of their children were educated and they all worked at maintaining the subsistence-level farm.

Most of the family emigrated to America in the early years of the century with the great human tide that fled the miseries of the Old World. A couple of the older siblings stayed behind, but the rest, including Lily, settled in Brooklyn.

While the various children who became my mother's aunts and uncles started families of their own in America, Lily never married. She lived out her drab life and died, alone, in the basement flat of a Brooklyn tenement. In the end, no one even knew exactly when she died. Her body was found by a stranger because of the stench rising from her corpse.

I only really remember three things about Lily. Once, when she came to visit, she brought along a new puppy. It was a mad, brown ball of energy. In what even at the time I recognized as pure Lily style, she had named it Wolfie. My cousins and I spent a wondrous day chasing the dog around the small yard of my parents' suburban New York house while Lily watched and clapped along in delight. She seemed, I remember, not to handle the dog very well, as if she didn't understand that it was a living thing and not a toy, but her pleasure in its company was clear. A couple of weeks later I overheard my mother tell my father that Wolfie had been run over by a car.

I also remember a simple little song Lily used to sing to us. My mother knew it too—had probably learned it from Lily—and often sang it to me as a lullaby. Lily would sing in Polish mostly, but sometimes in English. My mother only knew the English version. It went:

> *Meet me at midnight, my sweet one.*
> *By the tree in the garden,*
> *Where the white roses grow.*
> *Meet me at midnight, my darling.*
> *But don't let anyone know.*
> *Never let anyone know.*

The song had a tender, happy/sad melody and to this day it summons, however fleetingly, that childhood feeling of utter safeness and security that simply doesn't exist in maturity.

The third thing I remember is not so much about Lily as about myself. It concerns her death and I recall it, even after all these years, with some shame.

I was maybe eight or nine years old and my best friend and I were playing in the house one day when the phone rang. My mother picked it up in the kitchen while I eavesdropped (as usual) from the hall. Sally was on the line and I heard my mother start to cry. I understood that it was because Lily had died. I knew Lily was my mother's favorite aunt. I stood there listening to her cry when my friend came down the hall to see what was up. As soon as he looked at me I began to laugh. He kept asking what was so funny, but each time I tried to tell him the laughter grew more hysterical. I couldn't stop myself. We retreated to the safety of my room and I told him what had happened. I don't think I'll ever forget the look on his face.

In the years since I've tried to rationalize my behavior without real success. I've told myself that the laughter was a child's nervous response to the mystery of death or a cathartic emotional release. Hell, maybe it's even true. For a time I thought that I'd blown the incident out of proportion, but years later, that same friend and I were talking and he asked me about that day and my laughter. It had stuck with him, too. I managed to change the topic of conversation, but I've never forgotten the shame.

I leaned against the hall's cool tiles waiting for a nurse to finish helping Sally with the bedpan. I heard the gulping flush of a toilet and a moment later the nurse came out and nodded at me.

The room stank of shit and piss, but I pretended not to notice. I pulled a chair over next to the bed and as I sat down I saw that Sally had put her teeth in. Her eyes looked a little clearer, too. Her wasted body still suggested the proximity of the scythe, but she seemed more alert and, I hoped, able to explain her desperate need to see me.

"I know you don't care so much for me," she began, and seeing my burgeoning protest held up a finger. "No, no, you don't have to say. It's all right."

I sat back in the chair and exhaled a deep breath. I felt desperately trapped, like being stuck in bumper-to-bumper traffic at the entrance to a long tunnel.

"I know also you're only here because your father insisted, but this I don't care either."

That was true as well. Not only had my father paid for my ticket, he had seriously guilted me into making the haul from California at all.

"I have something to ask you, but first I have a story to tell. It's to do with your Aunt Lily, I don't know if you even remember."

I nodded, suddenly more interested. Though Sally didn't ask, I recited the outline of what I knew and remembered. I didn't mention how I laughed the day that Lily died.

"What you say is right. I don't remember a dog, but with Lily it could be. Always she did such things. But this is like the skin of the apple what you know. The fruit is underneath, but I'll tell you now and you should understand, it's not so sweet.

"Lily we always hated," Sally said. She stared past me, out the window as she spoke. "When she was born she was too small, like to die, and Mama was very sick. They have what to call it today."

"Premature," I said.

"Yes, I think. Always weak Lily was and so tiny. For a long time she didn't walk or talk. A terrible burden she was on us. We lived all of us then in a little house, like you don't know. Always Lily had to have special and we all had to make do with less so she could get. Terrible jealous it made us.

"My father came first to America and sent back money for the children to go one by one, but Mama died soon after we all arrived. But this you probably know. Lily was then a big girl already, but still she was . . . not right. Slow, she was and difficult. But with Mama gone Lily wasn't special any more and terrible mean we could be to her, like how we always wanted."

My grandmother laid back against the pillows and closed her eyes. Her breathing became shallow and even and I thought perhaps she had dozed off, but then she opened her eyes again and stared up at the ceiling.

"When Bella died . . ."

"Whoa! Wait a minute. Who's Bella?"

Sally shook her head. "I forget, Brucie. These people, some you never met. But to me it's all like yesterday. Bella was the oldest sister. She married and stayed yet in Poland."

"You know, I don't think I've ever even heard her name."

Sally only nodded, but somehow communicated to me: *such is the sad nature of time and memory.* She went on:

"Bella died from the typhus, left alone a husband and a little boy. Such could not be in those days and something had be done. We saw then a chance to get rid of Lily. Lily had no husband and who would ever marry such a thing?

Bella's husband we knew from before. A hard man. Like only in Poland you find. We knew it was a bad thing to send Lily to him, but jealousy is—" Sally shook her head "—she went, you know, it was not so long before the war. We didn't know then from Hitler, but even if we did, I can't say sure that we would have done different."

"Christ," I muttered. I'd never heard *any* of this before.

"What happened, who would have thought? Lily married to Bella's husband and took the little boy to her heart. And she was happy. The life there wasn't easy, but Lily made for herself a place. The baby she thought of like her own and Bella's husband she even maybe could love. Who can say?"

Sally laid back again and I could see she was exhausted. She could barely keep her eyes open.

"Maybe you should take a little nap, Grandma," I said, though I was intrigued by her story and puzzled as to where it was leading.

She nodded and offered me a little smile. She was asleep before I could get out of the chair.

I waited around the hospital for a while, ogling the student nurses and drinking bitter coffee from a machine. I saw a nurse go in and out of my grandmother's room and ran after her. She told me that Sally would probably sleep for a few hours at least.

"Can you tell me . . ." I started. I felt a little silly asking, actually.

"What?" the nurse asked.

"What, exactly, is wrong with her?" I knew from my father that Sally had undergone some treatments for cancer a while back, and that at least one hip had been replaced fairly recently, but I didn't actually know why she was hospitalized now.

"Some heart trouble. Bad circulatory problems. Mostly, she's old," the nurse said. "Just plain worn out." She must have seen I wasn't too thrilled with the answer and sort of shrugged. "You're Brucie, aren't you?"

"Bruce," I said, clearing my throat.

"She's been going on and on about you."

"Really?" I asked. "Do you have any idea why?"

"No, she wouldn't say," she said. She started to walk away then half turned around again. "Though maybe if you called her once in a while, you'd know."

I scraped my lower jaw—and my pride—off the floor and walked out of the hospital.

West Palm Beach ain't exactly the thrill capital of the world. That is to say, if you aren't for a rollicking round of Bingo or a day at the jai alai fronton, there's not one heck of a lot to do. There *is* the beach, I reckon, but living in Los Angeles pretty well spoils you for such things.

So I went to visit my cousin.

Beth owned a condo in one of those godawful, prefab developments which litter the Florida landscape like broken shells on the beach. She worked for a bank and wasn't married, which is the extent of what I knew about her life. I had to call my dad to get her address.

I don't even know how long it had been since I'd seen Beth. We'd been close as children—we were born just two months apart—but that was ancient history. She was my mother's sister's only child and had somehow come to serve as kind of caretaker to Sally after my aunt passed away. Neither of us had even bothered to attend the funeral of the other's mom. I didn't even think I'd be able to recognize Beth, but when she opened the door I was pleasantly surprised to find the face of the little girl I remembered etched inside the older-than-her-years lines of the woman I didn't even vaguely know.

I hadn't bothered to call or write, but she wasn't surprised to see me. "Grandma said you'd be coming," she told me. "I didn't believe it though."

"I'm not entirely sure why I'm here," I told her.

We tried the small-talk thing for a while, but it didn't go too well. I found her life in banking as dull as she found mine as a teacher. Neither of us was too keen to talk over good old days which didn't exist, so all that was left was Sally. Beth told me about the old woman's physical decline in rather clinical, unemotional terms. I got the strong feeling that Sally's glacially slow deterioration had worn Beth out. She basically told me what the nurse had said about Sally's health.

"A tumor, some angina there. Old age everywhere," Beth shrugged between chain-smoked cigarettes.

"And you don't know why she's been so adamant about wanting to see me?" I asked.

"Not a fucking clue," Beth said.

I could hear the resentment in her voice, got the feeling that my seeing Sally was somehow treading on territory Beth thought of as her own. I couldn't blame her, really. I wasn't the one who'd been changing the old bag's diapers these past years.

"Apparently it has something to do with Lily," I told her.

Beth coughed out a cloud of smoke. "*Aunt* Lily?" she choked.

"Yeah. She started telling me all about her before she dozed off. I haven't a clue as to why, though."

"Unbelievable," Beth whispered, shaking her head.

"What?" I asked.

"I've been trying to get her to talk about Lily for years. I've asked her time after time and she'd never tell me a goddamn thing."

"Why did you want to know about Lily?" I asked. But somewhere a memory stirred in the back of my head.

"My mom used to talk about her a lot. She always thought there was something important about Lily. I wanted to make a film about her. Once."

I remembered. I remembered from years before that in our very practical and deeply unimaginative family, Beth had been an "artsy" kid with dreams of being a filmmaker. I never quite got it straight how she ended up working for a bank. Looking now at her tired face and nicotine-stained fingertips, I didn't want to ask. A hint of a smile formed at the edge of her lips.

"She was in the camps, you know," Beth said.

"Excuse me?"

"You don't know, do you?" Beth shook her head. "Lily was in a concentration camp for a while during the Second World War."

"No," I said weakly. This was quite the day for family tales. "I didn't know. How did . . . how could she have been in the camps? Who told you this?"

"My mom. But she didn't know much more than that, either. It was something no one ever talked about, apparently."

"I'm not surprised," I said. But I was trying to picture the sweet old lady with candy who I remembered superimposed into one of those archive-issue black and white images of Dachau or Treblinka that we all have stowed in our heads. I couldn't suppress a shudder. "What happened?" I asked. "Do you know?"

Beth got up and rooted around for another pack of cigarettes. She let me dangle while she fiddled with the wrapper, searched for some matches and oh-so-deliberately lit up the smoke.

"You'll tell me what this is all about? Why Grandma wants to see you? What she says about Lily?"

"Of course,' I said. 'Why wouldn't I?"

Beth shrugged and I realized it was information *she* would hoard.

"Come on," I said. "Please?"

"I don't know that much, really. But I guess it's more than *you*." I realized all of a sudden that there was some deep resentment happening here, but I didn't have a clue what it was all about.

"You know that Lily was in Poland right before the war? She went back to like nursemaid her brother-in-law or something."

"Grandma was just telling me about it. She said that Lily married a dead sister's husband. And there was a kid, too."

"Yeah," she said and hesitated again. I summarized what Sally had told me in the hospital. Beth listened and nodded, seemed to think about it for a little while.

"I don't know the details," she finally said. "I don't think any of the family really did. But Lily got rounded up by the Nazis at some point. Just for being Jewish, far as I know. They all got herded into the cattle cars. Lily was separated from the husband and the kid, but apparently she still had American papers or something. Anyway, she was in a camp for a while. I don't know which one. Not a death camp, obviously. But they let her go."

"I didn't think they ever let anyone go."

Beth shrugged again. "Who knows? A US citizen, a woman. They probably just didn't give a shit. Or she was just fucking lucky."

"What about the brother-in-law—the husband, I mean—and the little boy?"

"Soap. Lamp shades. Ash. Whatever."

I winced at the harshness, the casual tone of my cousin's response. "Jesus," I said.

"I don't think old JC was involved," Beth said, sucking in the last of the smoke. "But you never know."

"Do you know anything else?"

"Apparently she waited out the war in Europe. Don't ask me where or how. She waited for the others. She never found them, of course."

"How did you find all this out?" I asked again.

"My mom. She told me the whole story once when she was stoned." I must have looked at Beth oddly, because she laughed and quickly explained. "You never saw her during her post-menopausal hippy phase did you?"

"Uh, no," I admitted.

"Far out. Literally. I'd get home from work and we'd share a joint. Man, you ain't lived till you've had it out with your mom for bogarting a roach."

"I can only imagine," I said. But remembering my aunt as a suburban housewife, I really couldn't. Beth lit up another cigarette and neither of us said a word for a while.

"What must have it been like?" I finally said. Beth raised an eyebrow. "For Lily, I mean. Growing up hated by her brothers and sisters. Treated like a piece of shit. Finally finding a family only to lose it to the . . . you know. What would that do to you?"

Beth didn't have any answer, but for the first time since I arrived, some of the hard edges fell out of her face.

"It's too bad you never got to make your film," I said.

She turned away, ostensibly to reach for another cigarette, but through the swirl of smoke I'm sure I saw a tear in the corner of one bloodshot eye.

I got back to the hospital just after six that evening and walked smack dab into chaos. Sally had become hysterical wanting to know where I was. It seemed they could only dope her up with the mildest of sedatives and she fought it tooth and nail. She had just dozed off again when I arrived, much to the relief of the third-floor staff. I chatted with a couple of nurses who told me Sally had been driving them nuts for weeks. They all seemed to know who I was; Sally had been ranting to them about me and about Lily, though the connection was unclear.

I went back to Sally's room to wait until she stirred. I stared out the window as a thunder squall broke apart the still-hot Florida evening. I listened to the sizzle of the warm rain on concrete and to Sally's graveyard hack. I looked over at her as she began moaning lowly in her sleep, her drawn face contorting.

Suddenly, her eyes shot open and her face took on a frenzied expression. She started to yell, then saw me sitting by the window. The wildness went out of her eyes and she settled back against the rumpled sheets. I asked her if she was all right and she nodded.

"I went to see Beth," I told her.

"A good girl," Sally said, nodding. But her face suggested she didn't entirely believe her own words.

"We talked about what you were telling me. She said that Lily was once in a concentration camp. That she lost her family there."

My grandmother looked up sharply, but wouldn't meet my eye. She nodded again, but looked down into the sheets as she spoke.

"This is true," she said. "Terrible. Terrible." She seemed to want to say more, but I don't think she could.

"So what happened?" I prompted.

"Lily we brought back to New York after the war. . . ."

"Wait,' I said. 'What happened to . . ."

Sally just closed her eyes and started to shake her head. Like a little kid throwing a tantrum. I half-expected her to stick her fingers in her ears and yell "blah-blah-blah" to drown me out. I got the message.

"Lily came back," she continued, "and she was like a child again. We all thought she would be different maybe, but she barely could take care of herself. So a tiny apartment we found for her, cheap but close to where we lived. We took turns bringing her food when we could and your mother . . ." she paused here, choking on the words. I felt a coldness roll through my bowel.

"Your mother liked to go over to Lily and play. She kept Lily company and Lily would sing to her."

I thought I saw Sally's eyes moisten and felt a pang myself. I imagined it was the Polish lullaby that Lily sang to my mother.

"It was later yet that the troubles started. We hadn't been to see Lily for a while and your mother wanted to visit. I made a kugel to take her.

"We knocked on her door, but she wouldn't open. Inside we could hear Lily, talking and laughing, but to us there was no answer. I knocked and knocked and your mother called out to her. We heard her voice, but still the door was shut.

"I began to think something is terrible wrong, so I went to get the super and I made him to open the door."

Sally paused for a moment, her eyes open wide. She seemed to be someplace else, looking at a picture from the past.

"Inside Lily sat at her table, all set with the best china and a beautiful dinner. Two other chairs also she had there and she was serving food and laughing."

Sally looked right at me, now, streaks of moisture cutting across the deep crags in her old face.

"Who was she talking to, Grandma?"

Sally shook her head. "Dolls. Two dolls, like made from *shmates*, she sat up in those chairs. She talked to them like they were people. She never looked at us, never saw. The super, he didn't say a word, just ran away fast as he could.

"I tried to talk to her, but Lily had not to hear. She just kept serving the food and talking to the dolls. One I heard her call Joseph and the other Avram. Such a coldness I felt, you shouldn't know. My heart still doesn't beat like it should when I think about it."

"Were those the names of the husband and the boy? The ones who'd died?" I asked. Sally nodded, painfully.

"For days, only to the dolls Lily would talk, and never to leave the house. We all went, but she didn't see through her eyes. We left her food and cleaned a little, not that she noticed. Finally, one day your grandpa and me went over and the dolls were gone. We tried to ask her about it, but she made like she didn't know. Like a stone she was. Like a golem.

"Long after she would go funny like this. Everything fine, then suddenly she went away to that other place. To be with the dolls."

There was a long silence. I thought about the horrors of Lily's life, of the terrible loss and the place her mind must have fled to escape from her memories. I thought again of my laughter that day so many years before and felt a rush of self-loathing. The nurse came in then and asked me to step out while she changed Sally's IV. I went into the men's room to piss and wash my face, but I couldn't look in the mirror as I stood at the sink.

I settled back into the chair, saw the nurse had smoothed the sheets and fluffed the pillow. Sally still looked uncomfortable, but a fresh glass of orange juice with a flex-straw sat on the tray by the bed.

"Why are you telling me all this now, Grandma? Why did you want me to come here after so many years?"

"It's Lily," she said. "Lily needs you."

I exhaled slowly and deeply. I had no idea how to deal with this, wished more than anything that I was back home in Los Angeles with only earthquakes and riots and semi-literate student essays to worry about.

"Lily's dead, Grandma," I said as softly as I could.

"I see her, Brucie," Sally said. Her eyes took on the most life I'd yet seen. "Every night she comes to me. I see her. Every night she tells me what it is has to be done. It's Brucie, she says, he's the only one who can do it."

I didn't know what else to do but humour her. "Do what, Grandma?"

Sally looked away from me, turned her head towards the tall curtain. She spoke without once looking back my way.

"This what I tell you now no one knows. Your grandpa and the others are all gone. Only me now. Your mother I never told and I don't want you should say to anyone else. Especially not your father."

I was puzzled, but told her okay. Still she wouldn't look at me.

"Before Lily went back to Poland, there was a man. She was a foolish girl, Lily, but not so bad looking. This man, he . . . took advantage. You understand what I mean?"

I swallowed and nodded. I may have blushed.

"There was a baby, but Lily we knew couldn't take care on her own. So we all decided that someone else had to look after the little girl, this child without a father and no kind of a mother.

"It was agreed your grandfather and me should be the ones to take care of her. Always like our own we treated her. Never we told her the truth. We sent Lily away not just for Bella's family in Poland, but for ours. For yours. For your mother."

Senility, I thought. Or drug-induced fantasy brought on by a lifetime of guilt over the mistreatment of her sister. Surely, that explained Sally's belief that the long-dead Lily came to see her.

And this other grotesque fantasy.

I was tired and annoyed that this was what I had come all this way for, inconvenienced my life about. Until Sally turned and faced me and I looked into her eyes.

And I knew, I just knew, that it was all true.

"Oh Jesus, Grandma," I said. "Jesus Christ."

"A terrible thing this has been to keep inside so many years, but it was the only way. Before the war it was a thing that was done. And after . . ."

I was in shock. The thought that Lily was my real grandmother sent me into new paroxysms of guilt. I looked back out the window. The rain had stopped and a setting sun made its final appearance of the day.

"What does Lily want me to do?" I asked, mostly to fill the deadly silence, intending sarcasm.

Sally didn't seem to notice.

"Lily wants you should find her son," Sally said.

I'd already seen the in-flight movie, but sought refuge in it again to avoid my troubled thoughts. After an hour I surrendered and stuffed the cheap plastic headphones back into the seat pocket and stared out at the clouds.

I thought of poor Lily—*Grandma*, for Christ's sake—and the nightmare of her life. I racked my brain till my head ached trying to remember something more about her: the details of how she looked and dressed, the inflections of her voice, the things she said.

Anything.

But it was no use.

It came down, every time, to that damn dog, my hellish laughter and her sweet sad song.

Back in the hospital, Sally had told me that every night it was the same. She'd wake with a start and though she could feel the hospital bed beneath her, hear the blips and bleeps of her various monitors, she could also see her old Brooklyn apartment. The door would open and a youthful Lily stood there, naked and pregnant with the daughter that Sally would claim as her own. Lily would drift in like a balloon and float around the room. Sally would reach out for her, but Lily always bobbed out of reach. As she wafted through the air she rubbed at her swollen belly and tears streamed off her troubled face.

Lily told Sally how her adopted son had survived the Nazi killing machine, had been adopted by a Christian family not very far from the Sobibor death camp which had claimed his father. The boy was a boy no longer, Lily said, but he was in terrible trouble. He lived now not in Europe but in Montreal, where his adoptive parents had emigrated. Her grandson—me—she told Sally, had to go to this place to save him from some terrible thing. What it was, or how it was to be done she would or could not say. But the son of the daughter she had been denied was the only one who could act. Only through the daughter that was stolen, could she redeem the son who had been lost.

As Sally told me the story and no doubt saw my dubious expression she grew increasingly frantic. I tried to convince her that it was just a recurring dream, but she'd have none of it. She insisted it was real and that her nights had become a kind of torture. She clutched at my arm and dug her nails into my flesh, pleading with me to honour Lily's wishes and make good the offences of her past. She gasped for breath like a runner at the end of a marathon and her voice became a shrill chalkboard scratch as she begged me to promise to fulfill Lily's plea.

"What do you expect me to do?" I yelled at her. "What do you expect? Am I supposed to scour a foreign city to find some old Polish guy and tell him his dead mother sent me to be his guardian angel? This is crazy!"

"No," she told me. "His new name Lily told to me. Wajda. Stefan Wajda. And where he lives even. You have to promise me, Brucie, you have to!"

I tried to protest again, but she started to scream. I couldn't believe, frail as she was, that the old lady could muster such intensity. The IV was slipping out of her arm and spittle and mucus exploded from her lips and nose. I feared she was about to stroke out.

"Promise," Sally shrieked, "promise, promise!"

"I promise," I finally said in desperation. "I do, I promise."

She calmed down as soon as the words passed my lips and collapsed back on to the bed.

Yeah, I thought in the merciful quiet, *I promise.*

And I love you and the check's in the mail and I won't . . .

I promise, I thought again, silently mouthing the words as the plane descended into the Christmas-tree fantasy of lights that is Los Angeles.

Shit.

I awoke to the starkest moment of terror in my life. I've always been jealous of people who can remember their dreams because I never do. At most I usually recall an image or a feeling that melts like a vampire in the morning sun. This dream, though, was as real and solid to me as my own name.

It was Lily, of course. In what had to be the horrid Brooklyn tenement where she spent her life after the war. I saw her sitting at a rickety table heaped with plates piled with bones and gristle and rotten fruit. She stood between two high-backed chairs, each with a midget-sized rag doll perched on it. Sawdust stuffing spilled out of gaping holes and button-eyes hung off torn faces by frayed, black threads. One doll had an arm of real flesh with a bluish-black number etched into the peeling skin. The other was slighter, but no less ragged. Lily forced sharpened spoonfuls of greyish meat between their tightly sewn lips. I tried to move towards the table but hung suspended, like an insect in amber, condemned to watch. I looked at Lily, and for a moment, saw my mother's face ripple across her countenance like a slight Florida wave lapping across a sandbar.

Lily looked up at me. Tears of blood flowed from her soft eyes and ran down her cheeks in jagged streaks. She opened her mouth and through blackened teeth the horrid sound that emerged was the world's sorrow.

I woke with a start and dashed into the bathroom to throw up. I ran cold water over my wrists and splashed my face, rinsed my mouth. I stumbled back to bed, but sleep was out of the question. I lay awake thinking and shivering, though the night air was quite warm.

As the first grey finger of dawn poked a hole in the darkness, I got up and went to the phone. I looked up the Montreal area code in the phone book and dialled the number for information. In a voice as dry as a perfect martini I asked if there was a listing for Stefan Wajda, apologized for not having an address. The line was quiet for two unendurable moments. "Thank you," a computer-generated voice said, "the number is . . ."

Fresh doubts assailed me as the plane hit turbulence near Salt Lake. I thought again of the crazy phone call that sent me packing, considered the possibility, the likelihood, that the Stefan Wajda I was going to see was a mere namesake of Lily's lost son. Was Wajda the Polish equivalent of Smith or Jones? Still, I was so shaken by the reality of *someone* by that name in the city of which Sally spoke that in a less than rational moment, I booked the flight. I didn't have a clue what I was going to do when I got there.

I thought again about Sally and about Lily and my terrible dream. I kept coming back to that brief moment in the dream when my mother's face flashed across Lily's and knew that this was about her as much as anything else. My mother had died, rather horribly, of cancer while I was at college, drinking and screwing and having fun. I hadn't wanted to face the horrors of her condition. Just as, at a younger age, I found a way not to face Lily's death, and more recently had avoided dealing with Sally's decline.

The promise I'd made to Sally, I knew, meant nothing in and of itself. I could tell myself that it was the reason for this insane excursion, but in that deep mental pit where we live with our unspeakable truths, I knew that this was about my mother. It was about a kind of expiration, a purging. About the debts—and respect—we each owe to our past.

Ain't guilt grand?

I had called an old college friend named Dornan who lived in Montreal. He met me at the airport. He was a bit puzzled by the sudden visit, but had happily agreed to put me up for a few days. He seemed to sense that I had something on my mind, but didn't pry. We reminisced some about the good old days as we drove back to his apartment. He already had a date arranged for the evening, invited me—sincerely—to tag along, but I told him no, that I had something to do.

I was exhausted physically and mentally, but grew restive shortly after Dornan went out. I snooped among his many bookshelves. I found the city White Pages on the third shelf, wedged between copies of Max Weber's *Protestant Ethic and the Spirit of Capitalism* and Art Spiegelman's *Maus*. I briefly puzzled over his organizational scheme, but my head hurt too much already.

There was only one Wajda, S in the book. The address listed was for Rue Saint-Cuthbert. A quick look at a map showed it to be a street within walking distance of Dornan's place. I stuffed the map in my pocket and carefully shut the door behind me.

Wajda's street was yuppy-ritzy with lots of black Saabs and BMWs parked in front of restored brownstones. It was quiet, with only the omnipresent background rush of the city to break the silence. The house matching Wajda's number stood at the end of the block. A great maple tree by his gate whispered in the warm night breeze, and through a small square of leaded glass in the front door I saw the glow of a dim yellow bulb. The rest of the house looked dark and empty. I leaned on the gate to the entrance path and stared at the door, unsure of what to do. What the hell was I *supposed* to do? It was almost eleven o'clock at night. I could hardly go up and knock at this hour. What would I say? I must have looked pretty damn suspicious lurking out front, but there was no one else on the street and not a single car passed while I waited.

What the fuck am I doing here? I thought. I suddenly felt ridiculous and was prepared to turn around and head back to Dornan's place, discounting the whole trip as temporary insanity, when I noticed the sound of an idling automobile engine. I glanced around at the parked cars, but they were all dark and lifeless. Cautiously, I opened the gate at the front of the house and took a few steps up the path.

The low rumble grew slightly louder.

I found my way around the side of the building and saw that there was a garage in back that opened on to a narrow alley running the length of the block. I pressed an ear to the corrugated steel door and heard and felt a deep bass reverberation from within.

I stood there for a minute, listening to the steady throb of the idle. I tried peering under the garage door, but no trace of light filtered out from inside. I glanced down the dark alley, but like the street, there wasn't a sign of life. Just a long row of locked garages.

As I stood there, a sick feeling overcame me with the suddenness of a heart attack. A sheen of nervous sweat oozed from my pores and my tongue went thick and dry in my mouth. I started to knock, then pound on the garage door and called Wajda's name at the top of my voice. When there was no response but the engine's throaty hum I began to kick at the door with all my strength. I saw some lights go on in nearby windows, but I ignored them.

I tried to turn the handle, but the garage door was locked and wouldn't budge. I kicked it again, trying to force the mechanism. Someone next door leaned out the window and yelled at me in French, but I didn't stop to respond. Instead, I dashed back around the house and leapt up the steps to the front door. I tried the knob, but of course it too was locked. I pounded on the door and stabbed repeatedly at the bell without result.

I stopped and thought carefully about my choices.

If I was wrong Dornan would likely be bailing me out of a Montreal jail and I was going to have to make up one hell of a story.

But if it was what I feared . . .

I saw a small garden spade among the shrubs and used it to break the thin square of glass in the front door, knocking jagged shards into the hall. I snaked my arm through the window and opened the locks, cutting my elbow on a tiny piece of glass.

I dashed about the house looking for the way in to the garage. I ran madly from room to room until I realized that I was one floor *above* the level of the back alley. I tried every door I came to until I found a flight of steps leading down. I couldn't feel the light switch and crashed into a second door at the bottom.

I flung that door open and smashed it into the dark headlights of the idling car. I was nearly overcome by the noxious carbon monoxide fumes. A bare thirty-watt bulb suspended from the ceiling had come on when I opened the door, illuminating the narrow garage. I gagged and covered my mouth and nose, peering through the smoke towards the driver's side. Slumped over the wheel of a Mercedes I saw the wan outline of a figure, one hand dangling out of the open window.

Coughing and retching, I ran around to the driver's door, but I could only open it a few inches before it scraped against the garage wall. I tugged at the limp body but he was too heavy for me to pick up. I touched his hand. It felt warm, but I couldn't find a pulse. Not that I ever could.

I switched off the engine then squeezed past to the back of the car. At the base of the garage door I saw that sheets and towels had been firmly wedged into all the gaps. I kicked them aside and reached for the handle. The door opened readily from the inside. I heaved it open as far as I could and took a deep gulp of the fresh night air. I hurried back inside and released the car's emergency brake. Then I went around front and, bracing myself against the garage wall, pushed the car backwards with my legs.

It rolled slowly, but the garage floor was on a slight grade. With another shove the car picked up speed and scooted out of the garage and into the alley until it crashed loudly into a solid brick wall across the way. I ran out behind it gasping for a clean breath.

In the alley, several neighbors had come to investigate the ruckus. Through blurry eyes, I saw a thin man in a red bathrobe pull Wajda out of the car and start to administer CPR. I heard the sound of approaching sirens even as I dizzily fell forward, the Mercedes' hood ornament looming in my vision like a harvest moon.

I sat in the back of an ambulance while a uniformed policeman interviewed me and a paramedic dressed the cut on my arm and a small gash in my forehead. I gave them Dornan's address and told them Wajda was a friend of a friend who I didn't know but had been told to look up while I was in town. The cop asked me what led me to check the garage or even suspect that anything was wrong. I glanced away, shook my head and told him the truth.

"I don't know," I said. "Just a feeling."

The cop didn't look happy, but he had one of those faces that probably never did.

The crowd started to disperse as the ambulance sped off. I made eye contact with the man in the red bathrobe and went over to talk to him. He nodded as I approached and cinched his belt. He had bony legs. We watched for a moment as the last of the police pulled out of the alley, then introduced ourselves.

"Hell of a thing this, eh?" he said.

"You have no idea," I said.

"You're a friend of Steve's, then?"

"Relative," I said with a half-smile.

"Is that right? So you must know what this was about then." A-*bewt*, he said, like a good Canadian.

I shook my head nervously. "*Distant* relative. Several times removed, you might say. And then some."

"The wife and kid, I figure," my new friend nodded.

"How's that?" I asked, my gut starting to roil. "What about his wife and kid?"

"Don't you know?" he asked in that special voice reserved for the perversely joyful presentation of lurid news. "Killed. Just a couple of weeks ago. Car accident, don't you know. The boy was quite young. I mean, considering Steve's age. Terrible thing. Just awful. I suppose it was all too much for him."

I must have visibly blanched because the man asked if I was all right. I nodded and mumbled something about the effects of the evening. He clucked sympathetically and patted me on the shoulder as we said goodnight.

I walked for a while—a few hours, actually—until I didn't know where I was and eventually found a cab. I started to give the driver Dornan's address, but suddenly changed my mind. I told him to take me to the hospital. I wanted, needed, to know how Wajda was. To make sure he had made it okay.

I wanted to see him again.

I emptied my mind as we drove, too numb to think or try and understand what had happened, how I got here or what it meant that Sally had really known about what was going to happen. I pressed my bruised forehead against the cool glass of the air-conditioned cab and let the lights of Montreal dance and shimmer in my fuzzy vision.

At the front desk I was told that Wajda's condition was listed as "guarded," but that I would have to wait until morning for more details. I got his room number and thanked the receptionist. Then for reasons I can't entirely explain, I snuck around to a deserted hospital entrance. I tried to appear officious as I walked the quiet halls, but no one even looked at me twice. I hesitated outside his room. With a quick glance around, I eased the door open.

Wajda's wrists were secured to the guard rails as a precaution and an IV dripped into his left arm. I looked carefully at his thin, ashen face in the faint fluorescent glow. It was crazy to expect him to look like Lily—he was, I reminded myself, her blood nephew, not her son—but I thought I detected a trace of the family genes in his sharp-ridged cheeks and deep-set eyes.

He seemed to be breathing well and I somehow felt sure that he was going to be fine. That my bizarre journey of redemption, a trip I could never hope to truly understand, was over.

I started to sneak back out when my cousin's eyes opened and he looked up at me. I froze as I saw a mixture of puzzlement and fear cross his face. I was tempted to bolt, but he dragged his tongue across chapped lips. I really didn't know if he should have water, but there was a cup and pitcher beside the bed so I figured it would be okay. I poured out two fingers' worth and held the cup to his lips. He lifted his head slightly and dabbed at it gingerly with his tongue. I put the cup aside and he smiled at me and for ever so slight a moment I thought I saw my mother's face in his.

I don't know what made me do it, it certainly wasn't a conscious thing.

I started to sing Lily's song.

With the second note, his expression went as wide as a western sky. As I sang, I saw tears pool in his eyes, felt them fall down my own cheeks.

When I got to the last line he sang it, too, in a voice as slight as a rose petal.

Never let anyone know.

I fell asleep almost as soon as I got back home to LA. And I dreamed. At least, I think it was a dream.

It was strange, because I could sort of make out the familiar contours of my bedroom in the background.

I found myself staring at Lily's apartment again, but this time the light was bright and soft and the air rich with the oniony smell of good home cooking.

The table had been set for one, the plate heaped with steaming potato *latkes* and sour cream and a big bowl of borscht. Lily stood in the kitchen fussing over the stove, sweetly humming her little tune. She looked up at me for a moment and passed a wisp of a smile. Then she turned back to her cooking.

The telephone woke me up. I mean if I was asleep. The smell of fresh *latkes* seemed to linger in the air and it made me wonder.

I stumbled over to the receiver and mumbled a hello. It was my father calling from New York. Where had I been, he demanded, he had been calling all night. I made up a story about visiting friends in Santa Barbara and staying over when I hadn't planned to. What was the big deal, I asked. He yelled a little more then calmed himself down.

He was calling, he said, because he had some bad news: my grandmother had died in her hospital in Florida.

I didn't bother to correct him about her identity, but I asked what had happened.

Nothing, he said. She died during the night. Peacefully.

In her sleep.

> The red rose cries, "She is near, she is near";
> And the white rose weeps, "She is late";
> The larkspur listens, "I hear, I hear";
> And the lily whispers, "I wait."
>
> Alfred, Lord Tennyson, *Maud*

THE REASON FOR NOT GOING TO THE BALL
(A Letter to Cinderella from Her Stepmother)

Tanith Lee

British author Tanith Lee has published more than forty highly regarded books of speculative fiction for both adults and children; she has also written for radio and television, and is a talented visual artist. Her novels include *The Secret Books of Paradys, Elephantasm, Eva Fairdeath* and *Reigning Cats and Dogs.* Her stories have been collected in *Forests of the Night, Dreams of Dark and Light,* and other volumes. Her collection of dark adult fairy tales, *Red as Blood,* is particularly recommended. Lee has won the World Fantasy Award and the August Derleth Award. She and her husband live on the sea coast of Great Britain.

"The Reason for Not Going to the Ball," the author's unique and powerful take on the "Cinderella" fairy tale, comes from the October/November issue of *The Magazine of Fantasy & Science Fiction.*

—T. W.

To the Princess, Wife of the Prince
Madam:

The girl will have brought you this, the one you trust. Before you tear it into pieces, remember, never before has she done you a disservice. Rather she has helped you. And, I must tell you now, she has been a friend also to me. This is not to make you hate her. It is to make you pause for a moment. To ponder that, if I have sent her to you, and she has aided you, can *I* have tried to aid you? Please, therefore, read a little further. Perhaps, say to yourself, you will read until I am cruel or insult you, or ask you for something. That is fair, I think. Of course, you suppose, as how should you not, that I have given you only evil. Your world is colored now by trouble, which seemed to begin, I would imagine, with me. But, beautiful Princess, let me have a little time. I promise, I will at least invite your thoughts. And if you read here a word of mine against you—throw this letter in your fire.

Where to begin then, conscious you may lose patience. Shall I provoke your pity? No, for how could you pity me, the wicked step-mother who thrust you from your adoring Father, raised her two ugly daughters over you, exiled you to the dungeon of the kitchens to sweep up the dirt. And finally, worse—withheld you from the famous ball. But then, you went to the ball, despite my efforts. Consider that. Consider what that glorious night has brought you, and read on.

When I was thirteen, my father, a gambler, sold me to a man who offered to pay all the debts. I was very beautiful—so I can speak of she I was, for she was another and not I. The rich man wed me in a modest clandestine service, and then, for a month, he set about me. You know of rape. Naturally you do. I knew nothing. I was terrified. And before I had even grasped what he had done to me, I was with child. When I grew big he was encouraged. He thought I carried a son. But no, it was two daughters. Four days it took me, it took them, to free ourselves from each other. I almost died, and so did they. Probably from this cause they were so ugly. Or else, it was from their father, a hideous man like a gigantic goblin. But they did not have his nature. No, they were in temperament like my own mother. Sweet and gentle, full of laughter. And loving.

Well, you already think me a criminal. Why dissemble? I poisoned the goblin wretch in my twenty-seventh year. He had begun to beat me by then, as he beat his servants. When I could not hide them, he beat his—my—daughters. There was a clever groom. He knew how to procure certain draughts. It looked like a disease of incontinence, and indeed, my husband had given his favors everywhere; no one was surprised, not even he, though he railed against women for a month, before he died.

His estate passed to a brother and I was left with very little. I lived on sufferance in the house of a relation, and my daughters with me. This terrible woman, my aunt, would say to me, in the hearing of my children, "Even though you are poor as mice, and they foul as imps, some man will take you all on, if you act properly."

And to this end she conveyed me about and welcomed suitors. She told me frankly she would expect a gift when I remarried.

Then came your father.

He seemed, of course, like a dream-being, so handsome, so wealthy, so softly spoken and gracious. I was amazed, but even so, now I had the space, I put myself to learning his true nature. I had suffered before, you see, and my daughters had suffered. I did not want them again trapped in the house of a man who would knock them down and spit upon them, calling them pigs and monsters. Your father was, in fact, only courteous to the girls. He even brought them little presents, when he came to call on me—you know his excellent manners. A red rose for me, wound with a tiny golden bracelet. And for them— a sash of scarlet silk and a sash of yellow silk. As if they were pretty, and would soon be popular. I thought myself very mean of spirit to set my faithful groom to learn things of your charming father. But still, I did it.

And so, dear Princess, I learned. And what I learned made me grim but not uneasy. For I was quite selfish and perhaps still am. Me he could do no harm I would notice, and my children would be treated with kindness. Even so, I was loath to marry him—he had by now asked me—until the evening when I saw *you*.

It was, in its way, strange, for I beheld you by accident, going by in his carriage, just in the fashion my first husband had seen me in the carriage of my gambler father. There was only a moment, your pale and perfect face, the glimpse of your raven hair, and then you were gone like a spring flower.

Possibly you have never seen—how would you—that you and I resembled one another. Why that should be I have no notion, and probably now the resemblance is less, or is no more. But you, Princess, were like the girl I had been. And, being selfish, perhaps that is the only explanation for what I did next. Because you were like the child I might have borne. Because I knew— and, to my shame before had never troubled with it—what would become of you.

I wed your father, and I recall how first I met you. You were twelve years old, and came out to greet me hand in hand with him. You leaned on him, in utter trust and love, and his pride in you was evident. At me you looked not shyly, for you are not shy, but carefully, polite and reticent, yet not cold. You were ready, my dear, I saw, to be my friend, if I should prove worthy.

But you, too honorable to speak ill of me, you pined for him. You pined for your loving father who, if he had had one clear thought, would have rescued you, bathed you, dressed you in silk—and raped you over and over.

You thought I was a witch, and my daughters, who sobbed for you every night—I had no need to lie to them—were creatures of the Pit—your tormentors. Obviously, being so ugly, they had nothing to fear. I could let them walk about the upper house in the finest raiment. And I could let them, when they were eighteen and you sixteen, go to a ball.

If you have read so far, and I pray you have, and not thrown my letter in your winter fire, you will now perhaps await, scornfully, bitterly, my excuse for keeping you from that ball of state where, it was said, the roving eye of the glamorous prince might light on any girl, so ostentatiously egalitarian is your kingdom.

To be plain, at first I thought that here might be the answer. I had mused on plans to get you from your father's hands, but there was no one I might rely on, or so it seemed to me, who might assist you. But now, here was this. For you were yet so beautiful, and I could allow you to become more beautiful, if away from the sight of your father. And I had heard of this prince, I had once met him, and he was young and straight, handsome, a warrior and a scholar, a paragon. How could he fail to notice you? How could you fail to respond to him? And so you would escape that dire house where you had been made a slattern rather than an unpaid and incestuous whore.

Yet I had to meddle, had to be certain.

And so I turned again to my clever groom.

Yes, in reply to your question, perhaps your accusation, I paid him with my body. That grimy, cranky little man, always to the windward of the law. And do you know, my Princess, this villain was gentle. He had no imagination as a lover, but also he wished to play no games. He took his pleasure politely, and after it said that he had been proud to have access to my flesh. But also he confessed he loved truly a woman of the slums. I had seen her. She is ten years his senior, with fallen breasts, but when she beholds him, her face lights like the face of a girl. He said he would marry her if ever he had money enough. He had never asked me for a single coin, and refused the little I could offer him.

He, then, made investigation of the paragon, and soon enough I was brought word. The prince was another of a kind. Well, do I need to tell you now? You have, so the servant girl has whispered to me, the marks of his whip engraved upon your back, and where they cut the ring from your finger, after he had broken the bone, there is now another ring of white.

Could I have warned you of it? Only as I had tried to do in the matter of your father.

Instead, I kept you close. I locked you in. You were a slut in the kitchen. How could you go to the ball of the prince who was a beast?

You found a way. I had mislaid, thinking of your loveliness and your vulnerability, that you were intelligent, and, like me, devious after your own fashion.

You wrote to your godmother, that icy ambitious woman, and when she consented to interview you, you found a means to reach her. She saw at once, with her gimlet gaze, your potential under my disguise. So then she had you washed and garnished, and put on you a gown made in a single day by those seamstresses who work until they go blind. It was a sorcerous gown, pure white, and threaded with silver. How many lost the last of their eyesight over it? It was meant to dazzle only one.

She took you to the ball in her own carriage. She introduced you as a relative from a far country. Did she say that, when you were settled, she expected a gift? Perhaps she was more subtle. And anyway, you were grateful, were you not, for he saw you, the beauteous royal young man, and he danced with you. Did his warm possessive hands remind you of the loving touches of your father? And when you kissed, hidden in the vines upon the balcony, were his lips a little parted?

She was very wise, your godmother, whisking you away so decorously on the stroke of midnight. It is said you left him a token, a small glass brooch shaped like a dancing slipper. I imagine that was also her idea. The shoe of a woman is the symbol of her sexual part. That into which one may slip and be a perfect fit.

The rest is well known about the kingdom. That he sought you, claimed you. That he wedded you.

And after that did you hear—I expect they kept it, protectively, from you—that your mad father grew more mad? That he went to the king's court and shouted there that you were a minx and a harlot, and the prince a lecher. Those loyal to the kingly house pursued your father. No one knows who. It was in an alleyway. They cut his throat. And I, of course, was disgraced, because I had ill-treated you. They sent us away, I and my daughters, into exile, beyond the border. But they let me keep a share of widow's money, which was to me a fortune, and we have done very well. It may amuse you to know—or anger you—or gladden you, how can I tell—that both my daughters have married. Their husbands are good men, and very rich. It happened in strange fateful ways. I will not tax you with it, in case I should offend. But, one of these husbands is even handsome, and both value laughter and sweetness. My daughters have blossomed in their care. They do not look ugly anymore, I can even see in them—my younger self. Or, sometimes, you.

So as our path went upwards, lovely girl, sad, lost girl, yours declined. When did he begin to hurt you first? The female servant who has helped me says that it was on your wedding night. She says he chained you in a spiked collar like a dog, and used his boots. And worse. Much worse. Does she lie? How I hope so. Maybe they are even lies about the scars upon you. Though once I came back, yes, hidden in my own disguise, and I watched on the street as you passed in the glass carriage. And you were like a bird in a cage. Your hair so pale a black—is there white in your hair? Your eyes that looked about, seeing nothing. Just a glimpse, then gone, like a spring flower, the snow-drop, that is swallowed by the mud.

Listen to me.

Tonight the clever dirty groom will be at your door, the hidden door your husband uses, but not now, for he is away hunting, is he not, riding down other slender things with his whip and that sack of poison in him called by some his heart. Yes, the groom will be there, and he will have a cloak for you, and papers. And if you go down with him, he will guard you like a child. He knows how, for he too has a daughter now, by his wife that he loves, in their fine house that I have been able to buy for them. You should witness him with this girl child. I think in him, for the very first, I have seen the proper, golden, everyday love of a *father*. Trust this man, if you will trust me. If ever again you can trust anyone. The border is near, and it is lightly snowing now. By dawn, when you can be far away, the snow will be thick as a wall between you and your hell.

I have bought a house for you, also. It is in a valley. A fountain falls from a cliff, and there are pines that smell of balm. In the summer there was never anywhere a sky so blue. And in winter, the sun is like silver. Even if you never live in it, this place is yours.

You need never see me, never look at me. Of course, of course, I love you. I always have. It is the selfish love that finds in another its own self. But I ask nothing of you, only that you will let me set you free. That you will let me set free the one I might have been, the one I was, the one you are.

There is everything I can say. I will put down my pen. The groom takes this to the girl, the girl gives this to you. And now, through the hours of the silent night, I will wait, wondering if you are on the road, flying at midnight, leaving not only a provocative shoe of glass, but all the false and empty dreams behind you, the dreams which became nightmares. Or, since I hid you in cold cinders, have you thrown my letter in your burning fire?

AMONG THE HANDLERS
or,
The Mark 16 Hands-On Assembly of Jesus Risen, Formerly Snake-O-Rama

Michael Bishop

Michael Bishop has published many excellent stories and novels in the speculative fiction field, for which he has won the Nebula Award and the World Fantasy Award. Of particular interest to fantasy readers are *Unicorn Mountain*, a lovely contemporary fantasy novel set in the mountains of Colorado, and *Brittle Innings*, a delightful "southern gothic" novel about baseball and Frankenstein. His stories have been collected previously in *Blooded on Arachne* and *One Winter in Eden*. Bishop lives in Pine Mountain, Georgia, with his wife and family.

Bishop's contribution to this volume could also be called a "southern gothic" tale: a wild, original fantasy about a snake handler in hell. The story originally appeared in the 1995 anthology *Dante's Disciples* (edited by Peter Crowther and Edward E. Kramer), but I only caught up with it in his recent story collection, *At the City Limits of Fate*. Bishop's moving story, "Allegra's Hand," published in the June issue of *Asimov's Science Fiction* magazine, is also one of the year's very best, and I recommend seeking it out.

—T. W.

And He said to them, "Go into all the world and preach the gospel to every creature.... And these signs will follow those who believe: In My name they will cast out demons; they will speak with new tongues; they will take up serpents; and if they drink anything deadly, it will by no means hurt them; they will lay hands on the sick, and they will recover."

—Mark 16: 15, 17-18

Men in soiled workclothes occupied the cracked red leather booths. Some pointed at their cronies with wrist-twisted forks. Two or three ate alone, a folded newspaper at hand or a scowl of wary dragged-out blankness protecting or maybe legitimating their aloneness. None of them any longer took heed of the smells saturating Deaton's Bar-B-Q: scalded grease, boiled collards, sauce-drowned pork. And the sinuous anglings of the sandyhaired kid waiting their tables drew the notice of only one or two.

Becknell, a hulking thirty-two-year-old in a filthy ballcap, said: So how you like a peckerwood that lifts up snakes handlin yore vittles?

His boothmate, Greg Maharry, said: You mean Pilcher?

Course I mean him. Anyways, it ain't my idea of telligent ressraunt policy.

Criminy, Maharry said, who're you to bellyache bout young Pilcher's cleanliness?

Who am I? Becknell squinted at Maharry.

You spend most days up to yore butt in axle grease.

So?

I reckon Hoke knows as well as you to wersh his hands.

Mebbe. But grease's clean gainst them slitherin canebrakes thet Sixteener bunch of his favors.

You ever lifted a snake? I bet you never.

Think I ain't got the sand? Greg, thet's—

Hoke Pilcher eased around the honeycombed divider from the kitchen with his tray aloft. Becknell, bigger than Maharry by a head, released a long sibilant breath while Maharry gave Hoke a queasy smile. Hoke lowered the tray to waistheight so that he could remove to the table the loaded barbecue platters, two sweaty amber longnecks, and two heavyweight mugs bearing icy white fur from Mr. Deaton's walk-in freezer. Holding the tray against the table edge, Hoke began to rearrange the items on it for easier transfer.

Mr. Becknell, he said, I aint been to an assembly out to Frye's Mill Road in moren a month.

Becknell said: You blong to thet bunch, don't you?

Yessir. But I've never lifted a snake there. He wanted to add, Either, but swallowed the impulse.

How come you not to've?

No anointin's ever come on me. So far I've mostly just shouted and raised my hands. Waitin and prayin, I guess. Hoke reached the longnecks onto the table, then the mugs with their dire chiseled coldness.

Becknell said: My golly. Yo're a Mark Sixteener thout the balls to do what you say you blieve.

Leave him go, Albert, Maharry said.

Why?

Minit ago you was blastin him for bein a Jesus Only. Now yo're chewin on him for the contrary.

Thet's where yo're flat wrong, Greg.

Okay. Tell me how.

I'm chewin on him for claimin one thing then actin somethin allover yellowbelly else.

Hoke set Maharry's hubcapsized pork platter in front of him and shifted the tray to unload Becknell's wheel of shrimp and chicken, with onion rings and hot slaw around them for pungent garnish.

Becknell said: And if you really blong to thet bunch, whyn hell don't you go to their services?

It's sorter complicated, Mr. Becknell.

You aint turned heathen?

Nosir. I'm tryin—

A heathen's shore as Judas lost, but a Mark Sixteener thet acts like what he sez mebbe has a chanst. Mebbe.

Hoke felt his grip loosen and the tray tilt. Becknell's chicken, scarletbrown in its breathtaking sauce, slid down his mattress-striped overall bib along with an avalanche of slaw and shrimp pellets. The onion rings flipped ceilingward and dropped about Becknell and Maharry like mudcaked nematodes. A longneck toppled. A razorthin tide of beer sluiced across the table and off it into Becknell's lap. He roared and jumped, catching a falling onion ring on one ear and nearly upsetting Maharry's bottle. Maharry grabbed it in a trembling fist and held it down. Hoke's tray, which had hit the floor, rattled from edge to edge.

My cryin cripes! Becknell said. You summabitch!

It was an accydent, Maharry said. Go easy now.

Using the towel on his belt, Hoke picked chicken and slaw off Becknell. He righted the fallen longneck, daubed at the beer, and turned this way and that between the unbroken platter under the table and the reverberating plastic tray. His boss, Mr. Deaton, burst into the diningroom with so many wrinkles on his forehead's pale dome that Hoke could not help thinking of a wadded pile of linen outside a unit of the Beulah Fork Motel. Deaton, stooped from working under the greaseguard that hooded his stove, unfolded to full height.

Hoke, what you done now?

Ruint my clothes, Becknell said. Ruint my meal. Stole my peace of mind.

It wasn't apurpose, Maharry said.

Thet's the second spill you've had today, Deaton said. The second.

See, Maharry said. He didn't mean it personal.

Albert, Deaton said, I'll bring you replacement eats in ten minutes. He thought about that. No, seven.

Free?

Awright. Spruce up in the ressroom. I'll pay for either yore drycleanin or a new pair of overalls. He turned to Hoke. Criminy, boy. My Lord.

My mind's gone off, Mr. Deaton. I cain't focus.

S thet right? Well. I cain't afford to keep you till you git it right. Ast Maltilda Jack to pay you off.

I'm fired?

Yore word, not mine. Just git yore money and beat it on out of here.

Sir, I need this job.

Mebbe you can git you somethin out to the sawmill.

I done ast.

Ast again. Now git. Have mercy.

Hoke tossed the filthy sodden towel onto the table, amazed that the disaster had scarcely dirtied his hands, much less his clothes. He strode through Deaton's Bar-B-Q under the mirthful or slipeyed gazes of maybe a dozen other customers and wrenched back the frontdoor.

From airconditioning to pitiless summer swelter. Hoke hiked straight across Deaton's parkinglot, filched a cigarette from his shirtpocket. The sky pulsed so starwebbed that the neon sign winking Bar-B-Q, Bar-B-Q, could neither sponge those stars away nor make Beulah Fork's maindrag look like anything other than a gaudy podunk road.

Hoke lit up. Smoke curled past his eyes, settled in lazy helices into his lungs.

*   *   *

Thirty minutes later, still afoot, Hoke stopped on the edge of Twyla Glanton's place, a clearing off Frye's Mill Road. He registered the insult of the jacked-up candyapple-red pickup with chromium rollbars parked alongside the deck of Twyla's doublewide. The truck belonged to Johnny Mark Carnes, a deacon in the Mark 16 Hands-On Assembly of Jesus Risen, a congregation whose tumbledown stone meeting center lay farther along this blacktopped strip. Like Albert Becknell, Carnes had ten years and maybe forty pounds on Hoke.

Almost aloud, Hoke said: Pox on yore hide, Carnes. Then waded through fragrant redclover and sticky Queen Anne's lace toward the deck. He felt gutknotted in a way reminiscent of the cramps after a dose of paregoric. What did he plan to do? No clear notion. None.

His tennis shoes carried him up the treated plank steps of Twyla's deck, anyway, and before he could compute the likely outcome of this showdown, his fist began to pound the flimsy aluminum stormdoor over the cheap wooden one that was supposed to keep Twyla Glanton safe from burglars, conartists, and escaped murderers out here in the honeysuckle-drenched boonies of Hothlepoya County. Yeah.

Carnes himself opened the door, then stood in it like the sentry that Hoke would have hoped for, except that Hoke wanted someone else in the role and took no pleasure in any detail of Carnes' manifestation there but the fact that he still had his britches on. Unless of course . . .

Pilcher, Carnes said. Kinda late to come callin on a lady, ain't it?

You've just said so.

I been here a while. Somethin we can do you for?

Even with the light behind him, Carnes presented a handsome silhouette: narrowheaded, wideshouldered, almost oaken in the stolidity of his planting. Actually, the light's fanning from behind improved his looks, dropping a darkness over his sunken piggy eyes and also the waffleironlike acne scars below and off to one side of his bottom lip.

Could I just talk to Twyla a minit, Johnny Mark?

From somewhere in the doublewide's livingroom, Twyla said: Let him in.

Some folks you let em in, it's nigh-on the War tween the States to git em out again. Carnes stood stockstill, unmoving as a capsized tractor.

Twyla appeared behind him. Her look surprised Hoke. She wore a swallowing purple sweatshirt, luminous green and purple windsuit pants with a band of Navajo brocade down each leg, and pennyloafers. Her sorrel hair had a mahogany nimbus from the backglow, and strands floated about her teased-out helmet like charged spidersilk. Hoke, looking past Carnes at Twyla, felt the pilotlight in his gut igniting, warming him from that point outward.

A pearl onion of sweat pipped out on his forehead.

Never before had he seen a Mark Sixteener woman in any garb but anklelength skirts or dresses. Certainly not Twyla, whose daddy had lifted serpents, and who called out His name at every assembly, and who, at Li'l People Day Care in Beulah Fork, had a steady job, where she so staunchly refused to wear jeans that she often got the other workers' goat. Hoke, though, had given her a private pledge of fidelity.

He said: Colby Deaton fired me tonight.

The jerk, Twyla said. Babes, I'm so sorry.

Tough way for a guy to git him some sympathy, Carnes said.

We've missed you out to church, Twyla said. You orter not stopped comin cuz of me. I'm still yore friend.

Thet ain't it, Carnes said. He's afraid to come.

Not of snakes, though. I wunst saw him grab a pygmyrattler with a stick and a gloved hand.

No, not of snakes, Carnes said. Thisere wiseboy's scairt of me. Cause I'm even more pyzon than they are.

Wadn't afraid to come up here with yore showoffy truck out front. Or to knock on Twyla's door.

Yall stop yore headbuttin! Twyla pushed Carnes aside and the stormdoor out. She laid a cool hand on Hoke's shoulder, bridging him into the double-wide, beckoning him out of the dark to either self-extinguishment or redemption—if these options did not, in fact, mesh or cancel. Go on home, babes. Sleep on it. Tomorry's got to have a perter face.

I'm footsore, Twyla. Bout wore out.

I'll wear you out, Carnes said.

What you'll do, Johnny Mark, is none of the sort.

Then praytell what?

Yo're gonna carry him home. In yore truck.

Play chauffeur for puley Mr. Pilcher here? Dream on.

No dream to it. And do it now. S bout time for me to turn in anyways.

So Hoke sat hugging the passengerside door of the jacked-up candyapple-red truck as Carnes accelerated through the woods and flung back under his tires long humming stretches of asphalt. Possum eyes caught fire in the headlamps. An owl stooped in cascades through a picketing of trees, and a fieldmouse, or a rabbit, or some other fourlegged hider in the leafmulch was rolled to its back and taloned insensate.

Past this kill, through some roadside cane that loblollies deeper in over-towered, a quartet of ghostly deer—two does, two fawns—made Carnes brake. The deer negotiated a quicksilver singlefile crossing. The truck fishtailed hearts-toppingly and squealed to juddering rest on the shoulder in time for Hoke to watch the flags on the deer's rumps bounce into the pines' mazy sanctuary.

Carnes muttered, strangled the steeringwheel, exhaled hard.

Nice job, Hoke said.

Don't talk to me. Carnes took an audible breath.

We could've died if we'd hit just one of em. Hoke spoke the truth. In this part of Hothlepoya County deer on the road comprised an often deadly, year-round hazard. Hoke knew—had known—a highschool girl cut to ribbons by a buck attempting to leap the hood of her boyfriend's car. The buck had landed on the hood and, asprawl there, struggled to free itself from the windshield glass, one bloody leg kicking repeatedly through the glittery hole.

Don't compliment me, Pilcher. Ever.

Awright. I won't.

You aint got the right to tell me nothin. Cept mebbe yo're a sorry excuse for a Sixteener.

Hold it a minit.

And mebbe not even thet. Speak when spoken to. Otherwise, hush it the hell up.

Who made you God?

Carnes pointed a finger, holding its tip less than a wasp's body from Hoke's nose and staring down it like a man sighting a rifle.

I did speak to you, pissant, but I didn't ast you a blessed thing. He dropped the point.

Hoke wanted to say, Up yores, but leaned back against his door instead, shrinking from the despisal in Carnes' face. Who would know or care if Carnes killed him out here on this road, then rolled his body into the cane? Twyla. Thank God for Twyla Glanton.

And thank God Carnes didn't have a row of snakeboxes in the bed of his truck or, even worse, a solitary crate here in the passengerside footwell. Hoke could imagine sitting over an irritated pitviper—copperhead, rattler, whatever— with one foot to either side of the box, the rotting vegetable smell of its scales rising alien and humid to gag him, its heartshaped head searching for a way out. Meantime, though, he had Johnny Mark Carnes less than a yard away, still wired from their close call with the deer, still palpably resentful of Hoke's presence in his truckcab.

Whym I drivin you home, pissant?

Hoke set his teeth and stared.

I ast you a question. You can answer. You better.

Twyla told you to.

Ast me to. Nobody tells me to do anythin, Pilcher, least of all a outtake from the flank of Adam.

Hoke thought a moment. Then he said: You got no bidnus movin in on her.

I had my eye on her first. From all the way back in school, even.

I beg yore pardon.

You heard me.

Losers weepers, huh?

I love her, Johnny Mark.

God loves her. You just got yore hormones in high gear.

I spose you got yores set on idle?

You wisht. Look, pissant, what can you give the lady but puppydog looks and a fat double handful of air?

Somethin thet counts.

Deaton canned you tonight from yore waitressin. You live in a verbital cave.

It's not a cave. Don't say waitressing. Men do it too.

Yore mama died of a lack o faith drinkin strychnine.

No, Hoke said. The Spirit went off her cause strife had fallen mongst the people. She had faith aplenty.

And yore daddy hightailed it to who knows where, Minnesota mebbe. No wonder Twyla took her a second look at you.

Like yo're a prize.

Got me balls enough to uplift serpents to the Lord and make us babies in the marriage bed.

Hoke shut his eyes. Yo're already married.

Not for long. Carnes smiled. Comparisons're hateful, aint they, pissant? Least you've got yore faith, though.

Yes, said Hoke quietly.

Which gives you a family in Jesus. Protection from slings and arrows, snakebites and poison. Right?

Right.

So come on to meetin this Friday. Forgit Twyla's migrated affections. Us Mark Sixteeners want you mongst us. Where else you got to go, Pilcher?

Nowhere.

Aint thet the truth. So come on Friday. I got someone you need to meet there.

Like who?

S name's Judas, Pilcher. He's a longboy. Called for the betrayer cause they aint no trustin when or who he next might bite.

Hoke put his hands on his knees and squeezed. Carnes had him a new diamondback, name of Judas. Well, of course he did. Subtlety had never much appealed to Carnes, else he would have linked with Methodists and driven a white twodoor coupe off a Detroit assemblyline.

Now git out, he said.

Yo're sposed to take me home.

Carried you far as I aim to. You aint but a mile from thet crayfish den of yores anyways. Out.

Hoke got out. Carnes put the boxy truck in gear, flung sod and gravel backing off the shoulder, and shouted out the window after a screechy turnaround: Don't I deserve a nice thanks for totin you this far?

Thank you. Hoke eyed Carnes blankly, then stared away down the blacktop at dwindling taillights and the broken ramparts of pines bracketing it. Shithead, Hoke said, turning to foot it the rest of the way home, morosely aware that he had no idea which of them, Carnes or himself, he had just cursed. Nor did the incessant burring of the cicadas among the cane afford him any clue or solace.

He had never lived in a cave. He lived with Ferlin Rodale, a former schoolmate now doing construction work, in a dugout of bulldozed earth, old automobile tires hardpacked with clay, and plastered-over walls strengthened with empty aluminum softdrink cans. Ferlin had seen such houses on a hitchhiking trip to New Mexico, then brought back to Hothlepoya County—whose director of Department of Community Development had never even heard of such structures—an obsession to build one locally, despite the higher watertable and wetter climate. Anyway, to Hoke's mind, Ferlin's dugout qualified as a house. Even the head of Community Development had allowed as much by issuing Ferlin a building permit even though his tirehouse lay outside every local engineering code. It wasn't finished, though, and wouldn't be for another six to eight months, if that soon, and so Ferlin and Hoke lived in the shell of the place, sleeping in a U-shaped room that faced south under a roof of plywood, black felt, and grimy plastic sheeting.

Mebbe it is a kinda cave, Hoke said, limping home through the woods. Carnes is sorta right, the bastid.

Well, so what? Ferlin had wired it for lights, sunk a well, and laid PVC piping so that both sinks and the cracked and resealed commode had water. Hoke paid fifty dollars a month for a pallet in the lone bedroom and split the electric bill with Ferlin. His own folks had never had so nice a place, only a rented fourroom shack, aboveground, with pebbled green shingles on the walls and a tarpaper roof. If Ferlin's house struck some ornery people as cavelike, well, better a cave than a windbuffeted shanty on lopsided fieldstone pillars. Mama and Daddy Pilcher should've enjoyed such luck—even with the beer cans, bottlecaps, cigarette packages, candywrappers, clamlike fastfood cartons, and other junk littering Ferlin's clayey grounds.

In a footsore trance Hoke shuffled over the murderously potholed drive leading in, a drive lined about its full length with blackberry brambles, dogwoods and pines. He had only starlight and lichenglow to guide him, just those undependable helps and the somewhat less fickle guyings of nightly habit. At length he approached a sycamore, a striated ghost among the scaly conifers, on which Ferlin had hammered up a handlettered placard:

TRESPASERS!!!—
WE AIM to PLEZE But SHOT to KILL!

Hoke stopped, perplexed. Did that mean him? Ferlin had prepared the sign to secure them solitude, even down to the premeditated detail of its misspellings, working on the already frequently borne-out surmise that the image of a surly cracker with a shotgun would scare off uninvited visitors better than a storebought KEEP OUT notice. Hoke, shambling by, gave the sign a fresh twist out of true and chuckled bitterly.

Half the people in Beulah Fork probably thought that Ferlin and he, not to mention every Mark Sixteener in the county, were ignorant sisterswyving mooncalves. Well, damn them too, along with Carnes.

I know a thing or two the President don't, Hoke said. Or a perfessor up to Athens, even.

Like what? he wondered.

Aloud he said: Like I love Twyla and don't want to die in front of her with a snakefang in my flesh.

This saying stirred Ferlin's dogs, a redbone hound named Sackett and a mongrel terrier named Rag that began barking in echoey relay. They came hurtling through the dark to meet the intruder and possibly to turn him.

Hush, Hoke said. S only me.

Sackett took Hoke's hand in the webbing between thumb and forefinger and led him up the trail, his whole ribby fuselage atremble. Rag pelted along behind, kinking and unkinking like an earthworm on a hot paving stone.

From the dugout—doors wide open, plastic scrolled back to the clocking stars—Hoke heard a breathy female voice singing mournfully from Ferlin's totable CD player. It sang about a blockbusted blonde with a disconnected plug at the Last Chance Texaco. Ferlin sang along, overriding the soft female voice, his screechy upndown falsetto an insult to his dogs, to Hoke, to the very notion of singing.

Thank God the Last Chance Texaco cut was fading, drifting like a car whose driver has nodded asleep. But as Hoke crossed the dugout's threshold, into earthen coolness and the glare of one electric bulb swinging on a tarnished chain, the next song began and Ferlin ignored Hoke's arrival to play airguitar and hoot along with Rickie Lee Jones, albeit out of sync and out of tune, the words in his throat (*Cmon, Cecil, take some money! Cmon, Ceece, take you a ten!*) like cogs mangled and flung from the strident clockwork coming-apart of his lungs and throat. Ferlin wore a jockstrap and flipflops, nothing else, and when he finally looked at Hoke, he checked his wrist, which bore no watch, raised his eyebrows, and kept on screeching, his stance hipcocked, showbizzy and questioning at once. At the end of Rickie Lee's cut, he mouthed, *But, baby, don' dish it ovah if he don' preciate it. . . .*

Then Ferlin turned off the player and came over to Hoke with a look of almost daddyish concern on his freckled hatchet face. Squinting and grinning, he said, Home a mite early, aint you?

Deaton canned me. Hoke told Ferlin the whole story, even the parts about stopping at Twyla's and catching a spooky ride in Johnny Mark Carnes' pickup.

But you don't like Carnes, said Ferlin.

I don't like walkin neither.

You walkt in. I didn't hear nothin stop out on 18.

Hoke crumpled into a lawnchair Ferlin had salvaged from the county landfill. Carnes got him a new snake he's callin Judas, he said. Wants me to make the next service out to the assembly so's I can charm it.

Ferlin whistled, a sound like a mortar shell rainbowing in. You aint handled with em yet, and he wants you to lift a serpent name of Judas right out the gate?

Looks thet way.

S why my religion don't include handlin, less a course it's women. Them I'll handle. Devotedly. Ferlin never attended services anywhere, but to willing females he tithed regularly the selfalleged five inflated to ten percent of himself that at this moment he had pouched in his jockstrap.

Such talk. Eddie Moomaw told me to git a new roommate if I planned to stay on a Sixteener.

Ferlin played airguitar. *O mean Mark Sixteener,* he sang: *Climb outta yore rut!*

Hush thet, Hoke said.

But Ferlin kept singing: *You don't like my wiener, So you show me yore butt!*

Didn't I ast you polite to stop it?

Ferlin threw his airguitar at the wall and paced away from Hoke. You got to watch yore fanny. Some of them Sixteeners'll drag you down for pure selfrighteous spite.

Meanin Johnny Mark Carnes?

Him, ol Moomaw, and anyone else over there thet cain't pray a blessing thout first tearin the world a new a-hole.

The world hates us Mark Sixteeners.

It don't understand yall, Ferlin said. Neither do I.

So I shouldn't go this Friday?

You hear me say thet? I just said to watch yore fanny.

So mebbe I orter go?

Ferlin said: I wouldn't visit thet stonecold snakeranch of yall's thout a direct order from God Hisself.

Groaning, Hoke pulled off his tennis shoes and claystained sweatsocks. His feet sang their relief, his anxiety over his lost job, the more judgmental Mark Sixteeners, and Carnes' new diamondback a smidgen allayed by the night air and his roomy's profane straightforward banter.

Then he said: Ferlin, I have to go.

Nigh-on to hatchling naked, Ferlin squatted over his svelte black CD player. Balancing on the spongy toes of his flipflops he punched up a song about Weasel and the White Boys Cool, his wide chocolate irises reflecting a crimson 9 backward from the control console. Ditchfrogs, a cicada chorus and Ferlin all crooned along with the disc (*Likes it rare but gits it well, A weasel on a shoadohdah flo*), but this time so low and softly that Hoke did not feel slighted. Ferlin had heard him, and as soon as cut number nine ended, and before number ten began, Ferlin said:

What would happen if you didn't?

I'm not rightly shore. The Holy Ghost'd probably go off me for good.

Meanin what?

I'd send my soul to perdition for aye and awways.

Better go then, Ferlin said, knobbing down the volume on cut ten. Hell's a damned serious bidnus and forever's a smart jot longern Monday.

Hoke gave him back a forlorn chuckle.

Answer me one thing: Why would a fella with half a brain and a workin pecker take up a pyzonous snake?

To git Spiritjumped and throughblest totally. You won't never know, Ferlin, till you've gone puppetdancin in Jesus' grace yoreself.

Sounds like really rollickin sex.

S a billion times better.

The expert speaks, Ferlin said. Hothlepoya County's Only Still Cherry Stud.

They's moren one kinda virgin, Hoke said. Not bein married I've never slept with a woman. But not being sanctified you've never come under the Spirit's caress.

Ooooooo, Ferlin said. Got me. Got me good. He fell over next to his CD player, writhing as if gutshot. When Rickie Lee finished singing about her gang's all going home, leaving her abandoned on a streetcorner, Ferlin stopped thrashing and lay motionless: a rangy unclad departmentstore dummy, flung supine into a junkroom.

Hoke struggled out of the lawnchair. He hobbled over to Ferlin and around the CD player on whose console a red O had brilliantly digitized. He nudged Ferlin in the armpit with his toe. When Ferlin persisted in his willful unflinchingness Hoke said, Thanks for the words of wisdom, dead man, and retreated to their U-shaped bedroom to dream of Twyla and climbing knots of sullen upraised snakes.

Ferlin drove Hoke in his customized '54 Ford, a bequeathment from Ferlin's daddy, to the Friday-night meeting of the Mark 16 Hands-On Assembly of Jesus Risen farther down Frye's Mill Road, on an island between that road and a twolane branch going who knows where. Ferlin dropped Hoke off near a private cemetery about fifty yards from the church itself, with a nod and a last cry of advice:

Be careful, Pilcher, who you take a rattlesnake from!

Hoke recognized the saying as one of the shibboleths of a wellknown Alabama handler selfbilled the EndTime Evangelist, a big amiable man who preached a foursquare Jesus Only doctrine heavier on redemption than judgment. A year ago he had visited their hall, blessing it with both his message and his serpent handling; and when a longtime Mark Sixteener upbraided an older teenager near the front for wearing a T-shirt printed with the profane logo of a rocknroll band, the evangelist helped avert a nasty dustup, saying:

Leave him go, Brother Eddie. You've got to catch the fish before you can clean em.

Hoke remembered that saying and also the preacher's caution against accepting a pitviper from just anybody. Anyway, even should an anointing drop on him like a garment of spiritwoven armor, Hoke would steer clear of Johnny Mark Carnes. A spirit of deceitfulness and envy in a house of worship could undo even an honest-to-Christ mantling of the Holy Ghost, as his own mama had learned too late to prevent her from dying of a pintjar of strychnine so polluted.

Polluted pyzon? Ferlin had said once, reacting to Hoke's story. Aint thet redundant?

A child of the world would think so, but a Sixteener would know from experience that it wasn't. It wasn't that such petty feelings could defeat God, but rather that the Spirit generally chose not to consort with folks nastily prey to them. If it withdrew when you had fifteen pounds of diamondback looped in your hands, of course, you would probably find beside the point the distinction between a defeated Spirit and just a particular One. . . .

Dented pickups and rattletrap jalopies surrounded the stone church. Years ago—a couple of decades, in fact—it had housed a country grocery and a fillingstation. Then it had closed. It had reopened for three or four summer seasons as a roadside produce market, setting out wicker baskets of peaches, grapes and tomatoes, along with two hulking smokeblackened cauldrons for boiling peanuts. Then the place had closed again. An oil company removed the gaspumps. The owner died, and the owner's family sold out.

A Mark Sixteener from Cottonton, Alabama, purchased the building and turned it into a touristtrap herpetology museum called Snake-O-Rama. This entrepreneur equipped the interior with several long trestletables, furnished the trestletables with three or four glasswalled aquariums apiece, and stocked the aquariums with serpents. For two bucks (for grownups) or fifty cents (for kids), you could go in and ogle diamondbacks, copperheads, cottonmouths, water-moccasins, pygmyrattlers, timberrattlers, kingsnakes, greensnakes, racers, cor-alsnakes, gartersnakes, one sleepy boaconstrictor, and, for variety's sake, geckos, chameleons, newts, an aquatic salamander called a hellbender that resembled a knobby strip of bark with legs, and an ugly stuffed gilamonster.

Hoke had visited Snake-O-Rama on an eighthgrade fieldtrip with Mr. Nye-land's science class, the year before he laid out of school for good. But tourist traffic on Frye's Mill Road was light to nonexistent, and the number of sub-sidized trips from the Hothlepoya County schools fell so dramatically during Snake-O-Rama's second year that the welloff Mark Sixteener who ran the place—most members of the Assembly were collardpoor—arranged to sell the building and land, not including the old family graveyard nextdoor, to a dis-possessed offshoot of his church from west of Beulah Fork.

The Pilchers began attending the new Assembly as a family. Hoke's mama died only months later—a death the coroner ruled an accidental poisoning—and his daddy soon thereafter fled such crazy piety. Hoke, though, had hung on, convinced that these handlers, poisondrinkers, and ecstatic babblers were now kin and that one day Jesus would bless him if he lifted up and chanted over a handful of coiling snakes. For the most part, Hoke had found that belief fulfilled in his association with the Sixteeners, especially in his friendships with Twyla, an elderly couple called the Loomises, and the family of the black preacher C. K. Sermons, whose surname jibed so exactly with his calling that even a few in their Assembly wrongly figured it a pulpit alias.

In fact, of all the twentyodd folks who met regularly in the former Snake-O-Rama, only Johnny Mark Carnes and two other men in their thirties, Ron Strock and Eddie Moomaw, had ever shown him anything other than accep-tance and aid. Their help had included shoemoney, a Bible, and Sam Loomis' appeal to Colby Deaton to give Hoke a job at Deaton's Bar-B-Q.

The trio of Carnes, Strock, and Moomaw, though, saw him as a pretender, a pain in the buttocks, and, in Carnes' case, a misbegotten rival for Twyla Glanton, even though Carnes already had a wife from whom he had separated over her disenchantment with hazardous church practices and his evergrowing inventory of scaly pets. Eddie Moomaw called Hoke the orphan and, in a service not long after Hoke moved into the tirehouse, rebuked Hoke for living with an unredeemed heathen, taking as his text the prophetic recriminations of *Ezekiel* 16:

Then I wershed you in water; yes, I thoroughly wershed off yore blood, and I anointed you with oil! Moomaw had said, his eyes not on Hoke but instead on a wildeyed portrait of Jesus on the Snake-O-Rama's rear wall.

Amen! said many of the unwary Sixteeners, Hoke included. *Tell it, Brother Eddie!*

Brother Eddie told it, at last bringing his eyes down on the target of his rant: You offered yourself to everyone who passed by, and multiplied yore acts of harlotry!

Amen! Woe to all sinners!

Hoke stayed silent, but his napehair rose.

Yet you were not like a harlot, Moomaw said, because you scorned payment! *Sicm, Brother Eddie! Hie on!*

Men make payment to awl harlots, but you made yore payment to awl yore lovers, and hired em to come to you from awl aroun for yore harlotry!

Amen! Go, Brother Eddie! At this point, only Carnes and Ron Strock were seconding Moomaw's quoted accusations. No one else understood the reasons for such condemnation. No one else could follow the argument.

I will bring blood upon you in fury and jealousy! Moomaw said, pointing the whole top half of his body at Hoke, snakily twisting shoulders, neck, and head.

At that point C. K. Sermons rose from his altarchair. His skin the purple of a decaying eggplant, he clapped his enormous hands as if slamming shut a thousandpage book.

I will be quiet n be angry no more, he said. The boy you scold does not deserve such upbraision, Brother Eddie. He goes where he muss to put shelter over his head.

Amen! Twyla said. *Amen!* said the Loomises. *Amen!* said a dozen other Six-teeners.

A course he's a orphan. He's done long since lost his mama n daddy. But didn't Jesus say, I will not leave you orphans, I will come to you?

He said it! Deed He did!

So what if the Pilchers come to us stead of vice versa? So what? They's moren one way fo the body of Jesus to surroun this worl's orphans! Moren one way to stretch comfort to the comfortless!

Amen! Praise God!

Thus rebuked, Eddie Moomaw retreated to his own altarchair grimfaced and blanched, his tongue so thick on the inside of his cheek that its bulge looked like a tumor. And only C. K. Sermons raised snakes heavenward that night. Of course, he had also—alone among the evening's worshipers—tossed back a small mayonnaise jar of strychnine (making a comical pucker at its bitterness), foretold in tongues, and restored Brother Eddie to concord with their fold by exorcising from his body a demon of resentment named Rathcor.

Rathcor! Sermons shouted, one hand hard on Moomaw's chest, the other shoving downward on his head. Rathcor, come ye forth in shame n wretched-ness! *Now!*

And Rathcor had departed Moomaw, half its vileness in a sulfurous breeze from Moomaw's mouth and half in a startling report from his backside. These smells had lingered in the stone building, a stench that Hoke recalled as burnt cinnamon, bad eggs, and decomposed pintobeans.

S awright, Sermons told everyone. Just means the demon's done hightailed it. Means Brother Eddie's free.

Brother Eddie had smiled, lifting his hands into cobwebby shadow and prais-ing the Lord. But his hostility toward Hoke, not to say that of Carnes and Strock, never fully evaporated, and Hoke could only wonder if a portion of Rathcor had lodged in the most secret passages of Moomaw's anatomy—his nose, his ears, his anus, his dick—because Hoke could not imagine, from Moomaw's present behavior, that Sermons had cast Rathcor out of him entire.

Greet one another with a holy kiss.
—Romans 16:16

The closer Hoke drew to the kudzu-filigreed building the louder grew the buzzing syncopated music leaking through its mortared joins. He heard tambourines, trap drums, an electric guitar, a trumpet. This music, pulsing like strobes in the grimy windows, told him he had arrived late, the service had already begun. The stolid rockwalls and the roof of steeply pitched shakes seemed almost to expand and contract with the singing and its jangly backup, like a jukejoint roadhouse in an old Krazy Kat cartoon.

The people crooned: *Oh, weary soul, the gate is neah. In sin why still abide? Both peace n rest are waiting heah, And you are just outside.*

And a fervent chorus: *Just outside the door, just outside the door, Behold it stands ajar! Just outside the door, just outside the door—So neah n yet so far!*

Hoke halted, clammy with the cold suspicion that through this old gospel hymn the Sixteeners were addressing and jeering his tardiness:

Just outside the door, just outside the door—So neah n yet so far!

Then go on in, he told himself. Walk through the gate and face em like one of their forever own.

He did, pushing in more like a gunslinger entering a saloon than a believer in search of his sweet Jesus Only. The ruckus from the toothache-imparting guitar and trumpet, not to mention the rattle of drums and tambourines, smacked him like a falling wall. The handclapping, pogojumping Mark Sixteeners—men to the left of the pewless sanctuary, women to the right—ladled a soupy nausea into Hoke's gut. Usually, such motionful devotion wired him for most of the fiercest God frequencies, but tonight a fretfulness lay on the people, a catching mood of upset, even derangement.

At the end of Just Outside the Door, Sermons leapt to the altardeck from between his wife, Betty, and their thirteen-year-old daughter, Regina, already a jivy trumpeter. The only black male in the building, Sermons wore a sweated-out Sunday shirt and a bolo tie with a turquoise cross on its ceramic slide. He harangued the sweltering room:

I grew up wi the cutaway eyes n the sad caloomniation o folks who figgered me n my kin just a lucky step up from the monkeys.

We hear you, Brother C. K.!

Caw it bigotry, peoples. Caw it hate or ignorance. Caw it puft-up delusion.

Amen!

Whatever anybody caws it, peoples, it hurt—like stones n flails. Sometimes, Lawd Lawd, it still lays me out, even me, faithful servant to our Risen Jesus thet I long since become in my rebornin.

Glory!

Now the chilrens of this worl done started comin after our own. Mockin, namecawin, greedy to troublemake.

Satan has em, C. K.! Satan!

Lissen what they done to Sister Twyla—to make her move off our Risen Jesus to the dead Christ they socawed churches strive to burry eyebrow deep in works n talk!

Preach it!

They bite like unprayed-over snakes! They want to pyzon the chilrens of the light!

God'll repay!

Sister Twyla, cmon up here! Testify to what the heathen n them lukewarm Christians of Beulah Fork's sitdown churches done to knock back yore faith!

C. K. Sermons reached out a hand, and Twyla, modest in a lightyellow anklelength poplin dress, emerged redeyed from the women. She floated across the floor to the platform. She did not mount it, but pivoted to face everyone with a sweet timid smile. People upfront parted to make her visible to worshipers farther back.

Hoke stood admiring. Three nights ago she'd worn her hair in an unrighteous teased-up globe. Now it hung long, reddish streaks flashing in the sorrel every time she moved her head, a small ivory barrette for ornament. Hoke could tell, though, that she'd had a monster bout with tears: Her eyesockets looked scoured, shiny with knuckling.

Bless yall, she said. Praise God.

Praise God!

Yall notice, please, thet Hoke Pilcher's come in. It'd be good if you men greeted him with a holy kiss, like Paul sez to do, and you womenfolk guv him a sisterly nod.

Hoke felt an abrupt heat climb from his chest and settle in his cheeks. The women to his right nodded or curtsied while in their half of the sanctuary the men milled into ranks to bestow on him the holy kiss spelled out in Romans 16. Sermons, Eddie Moomaw and Hugh Bexton leapt down from the altardeck to greet him—mechanically in Moomaw's case, it seemed to Hoke—and Ron Strock and Johnny Mark Carnes used their go-bys to pinch one of Hoke's reddened earlobes or to razz him about the irregularity of Twyla's appeal.

I need to remember this tactic, Carnes said, nudging Hoke's cheek: Big entrance, ten minits late.

Ferlin couldn't git his Ford cranked. I wadn't—

Stifle it, Pilcher, Carnes said. Lady's gonna talk.

Twyla absentmindedly rubbed her palms together. Early Wednesday mornin, she said, I had my car tires slashed and my deck strewn with toy rubber snakes. My trees got toiletpapered and my trailer aigged.

Cry out to God, said Camille Loomis, the Sixteener nearly everyone called Prophetess Camille.

Thet's not all. On Wednesday I went to Li'l People, where I've done worked three years now, and Miss Victoria let me go. Said some of her parents don't want their babies tended to by a known snake handler.

C. K. Sermons said: Christian parents, no doubt.

Sposedly. Anyways, I'm a known handler. Like a known car thief or a known ax murderer.

Yo're a known blessed friend, said Sam Loomis.

I cain't work a minit longer cause I might feed somebody's darlin a bowl of baby rattlers. I might wrap a watermoccasin up in the poor kid's didy.

We'll hep you, said Angela Bexton.

I know yall will. Like Brother C. K. sez, it hurts—this persecution by the world.

Somebody suggested a love offering.

Wait, Twyla said. The world thinks we've gone crazy cause we abide in and by the Word. Thet's what the silly children of this world've come to.

Amen!

But much as I love them little ones I seen to awmost ever day for three years, I love the Word—I love the Lord—more. I won't walk outta the light to satisfy any false Christian I may offend by abidin true.

Praise God!

And as Moses lifted up the serpent in the wilderness, even so must the Son of Man be lifted up.

Amen! Praise God!

Jesus sez thet in the Book. Which is to affirm thet I will lift serpents myself at ever pure anointin.

In His name! Amen!

I will do it to lift up the Word thet is also Jesus Risen, else this brief life will fall out in ashes and I myself blow away like so much outworn dust.

Twyla's speech, carrying news of her persecution and the witness of her resolve, stunned Hoke. He could not move. His embarrassment had drained away, though, and in its place welled pride. His love streamed over and then from Twyla like a flood of rich silt. Others among the Sixteeners did move in response to her testimony, reclaiming their instruments, cranking up a gospel shout, swaying to the acid caterwauling of Ron Strock's guitar and the ripple blasts of young Regina's trumpet, leaping about like stifflegged colts, footstomping and handclapping not in unison but in a great cheerful boil that somehow melded them in faith and triumph. Finally, Hoke absorbed through his pores their backasswards confederating spirit. And then he too began to move.

The bite of the serpent is nothing compared to the bite of your fellow man.
—Charles McGlocklin, the End Time Evangelist

Later C. K. Sermons leapt again to the altardeck. His wife, Sister Betty, a light-skinned AfricanAmerican with the figure and selfpossession of a teenaged gymnast, broke out a video camera. She shouldered it like an infantryman shouldering a bazooka. Hoke had noticed such cameras at other Jesus Risen services, usually in the hands of local TV crews looking for two or three filler minutes for an 11:00 P.M. news broadcast. The red light on Sister Betty's camera glowed like a coal, or a serpent's eye.

Sister Twyla did no preachin tonight, said Sermons. She testified. You see, I just heard some wayward mumblin bout how womens don't blong up here preachin.

They don't, said Leonard Callender.

Nobody disputes it, said Sermons. I know they got no caw to make mens subject to they preachments n foretellins. And Sister Twyla knows it. Futha-more, nothin like thet's happened here tonight. Yall unnerstand?

Praise God we do!

Good. We got new bidnus to tend to, new praises to lift. And none of it'll go Jesus Risen smooth if they's wrong thinkin or foolish resentments mongst us.

A fiftyish man named Darren DeVore bumped Hoke's shoulder. S mazin to me, he whispered, how we got us a nigger preacherman and female testifiers.

Thet so? said Hoke, stepping away.

My daddy woulda cut the fig off thetere fella and led the uppity women outside to catch some rocks.

Whynt you tell it so everybody can hear you?

I ain't my daddy, Brother Hoke. I've changed wi the times. Grinning, he angled off through the other men toward the altar platform.

We need some prayin music, Sermons told the band. We got to pray over these pernicious snakes.

The band struck up a hardrock hymn, Regina Sermons cocking her elbows and blowing out her cheeks like a swampfrog. Twyla, Hoke noticed, had a tambourine. She hipbanged it in proximate time to the hymn's rhythm. Only the women sang:

> *When Judah played the harlot,*
> *When proud Judah mocked her God,*
> *God stripped her of her garments,*
> *Nor did He spare the rod.*

> *Yet His love was such, O mighty such,*
> *Judah He toiled to save:*
> *He proffered her His Jesus touch,*
> *And with sweet rue forgave.*

As the women sang, C. K. Sermons, Eddie Moomaw, and Hugh Bexton prayed over the snakeboxes against the church's rear wall. The boxes showed bright handpainted portraits of Jesus, Mary and the disciples. The men prayed with their eyes shut, hands palm upward at shoulderheight or squeezed into juddering fists at their bellies, their voices either high monotone pleas or low gruff summonses.

Shan-pwei-koloh-toshi-monha-plezia-klek! shouted Prophetess Camille, her head thrown back as if inviting a knife to unhinge it at her wattled throat. *Fehzhka-skraiiii!*

Camille sez they's a demon in here, Sam Loomis told Hoke over the tubthumping music.

A demon? Rathcor?

A betrayer. A worker of hoodoo what'll drag hypocrites and baby blievers straight to hellfire.

Camille turned in a slow circle, her arms hanging down like rusty windowsash weights. *Auvlih-daks-bel-woh-oh-vehm-ah-pih!* she cried. *Neh-hyat-skraiiii!*

Camille sez we got moren one in here! said Loomis. But the betrayer he's done fell to pitdiggin!

Sermons did a solitary congadance from the snakeboxes to the edge of the altardeck with three or four serpents in each hand. He dipped from side to side in an ecstatic crouch as the Jesus Risen band veered into a rave-up of Higher Ground. Eddie Moomaw and Hugh Bexton slid forward to bookend Sermons, the way the thieves on Golgotha had flanked the crucified Jesus, Bexton with canebrakes and pygmyrattlers squirming about his wrists like overboiled spaghetti, Moomaw with only a single snake but that one a silky diamondback of such length that it looped his forearms in countergliding coils.

Hoke knew this snake for Judas even before Carnes took it from Moomaw. Carnes began to handle it in an orgasmic frenzy. He may have even moaned glory in his upright congress with Judas, but the rattle and blare of the Sixteener combo, along with the worshipers' continuing babel, drowned even the loudest utterances of the chief three handlers.

In spite of Prophetess Camille's warning, Hoke could feel a benevolent essence—the Holy Ghost—seeping from overhead and even sideways through the stones into the former Snake-O-Rama. He half expected everyone to sprout plumelike flames from the crowns of their heads, like so many outsized cigarette lighters snapping to radiant point.

It entered Hoke, this Spirit, and, amid the crazy din, he too began to dance, jitterbugging in place, barking praise, reconnecting with his dead mama and his absconded daddy as well as with the raptured majority of the Sixteeners. This was what it was like to open to and be tenanted by the Comforter, Jesus Risen at His ghostliest and most tender.

Yes. It was like a blessèd fit.

Hoke began to stutterstep diagonally through the other happy epileptics, a chess piece on a mission. He could smell the Holy Ghost, Who had now so totally saturated the room that C. K. Sermons and the other handlers pranced about veiled in a haze thick as woodsmoke. The smell was not woodsmoke, though, but cinnamon sourdough and overripe juiceapples, offerings to eat and drink, not to laud. Hoke elbowed through this fragrant haze, seeking its source. He suspected that it had its focus somewhere near C. K. Sermons.

Sermons gave Regina—the band now lacked a trumpetplayer—two snakes; and Regina, more child than woman, lifted them through the layered gauze of the Spirit, to the Spirit, one snake climbing as the other twisted back to flick her pugnose with its quick split tongue. Sister Betty videotaped Regina's performance.

Other Sixteeners began to handle, one man thrusting a snake into his shirt, another tiptoeing over a diamondback as if it were a tightrope, enacting Jesus' promise, Behold, I give you authority to trample on serpents.

Sister Camille fell down ranting. Twyla, Polly DeVore and Angela Bexton knelt beside her with prayercloths and stoppered bottles of oliveoil, dimestore items with which to minister to her as holy paramedics.

Hoke, still dancing, had reached the front, hungry for the boon of a serpent from C. K. Sermons. For the first time since joining the Sixteeners, he knew the Holy Ghost had anointed him to handle, as it had anointed nearly every other person in the church tonight. But Sermons had already distributed his entire allotment of snakes. He stood on the platform with a masonjar of strychnine, praying over it, preparing to drink.

Hoke floated past Sermons and many others . . . to Eddie Moomaw, who still had three or four living bracelets to hand out. He looked peeved that no one had yet come to relieve him of them. Sister Betty, Hoke noted sidelong, recorded the chaos with her video camera, paying as much heed to him and the other congregants as to her own husband and child.

Then Hoke went flatfooted and reached out to Moomaw, his face helplessly grimacing. He mewled aloud. Moomaw handed him a canebrake, a pinkishbeige timberrattler not quite a yard long, a satinback that winched itself up to his chin, shaking its rattles like maracas.

Hoke was anointed, fearless. Gripping the canebrake with both hands, he inscribed 8s with it in the air before him. He slipped into a floating whiteness where the rattler focused his whole attention and no other material body in the Snake-O-Rama impinged on him at all.

Furiously, the snake continued to rattle warning, but Hoke had surrounded and entered it just as the Spirit had done him, and it would not strike. Hoke knew this with the same kind of bodyborne knowledge that made real to him his possession of ears, elbows, knees, even if he made no effort to touch them. He and the snake shared one spellbound mind. In fact, he felt so loose, so brainfree, that he imagined the serpent an extract from his own person: his spinalcord and brainstem in a sleeve of patterned velvet.

Then something in the immaterial sanctuary of Hoke's trance bumped him. *Bumped* him. Someone in the Hands-On Assembly was shouting louder than anyone else, louder even than the scouring racket of the Jesus Only band.

Hoke sensed the soft white pocket of his trance blurring at the edges, breaking down. Forms and voices began to intrude upon him. The timberrattler in his hands separated out of the albino plasma that had sheltered them, taking on the outline and bulk of a realworld menace. Hoke finally understood that the loudest screaming in the room was his own. He clamped his mouth shut, thinning out the sound, and turned to Moomaw to rid himself of the agitated canebrake.

Regina Sermons, still powerfully anointed, stood handling beside him, but even without looking at Hoke, she edged away to allow him to make the transfer.

Eddie Moomaw took the snake from Hoke, smiling mysteriously sidelong. Why the smile? Was he disappointed that Hoke had escaped unbit? sorry that a snake had already come back to him? peeved that no one else had returned one? Hoke shook his head and retreated a step.

C. K. Sermons, holding his masonjar, wiped the back of his hand across his mouth. Good to the last drop! he said. Praise God! He beamed at Sister Betty's camera, spread his arms wide, revolved on the deck like a musicbox figurine.

Hoke decided he had to get some air. He turned to thread his way doorward.

Carnes blocked his path. Welcome back, Pilcher, he said. Here. Have you another. . . .

* * *

Judas folded into Hoke's arms like eight feet of burdensome firehose. Hoke had no time to sidestep the handoff. To keep from dropping it he shifted the diamondback and, as he did, saw on Carnes' face a look of combined glee and despisal. More from surprise than fear, Hoke lost his grip. Judas, suddenly alert and coiling, dropped. Hoke went to one knee to catch the snake, managed a partial grab, and found himself eye to yellow eye with Judas. Fear washed through him, a quickacting venom, and he shielded his face with the edge of his hand. The snake struck, spiking him just below the knuckles of his pinkie and his ringfinger, a puncture that toppled him.

Somebody screamed piercingly, and this time the rising sirenlike wail belonged not to him but to Twyla Glanton. Judas crawled over Hoke's fallen body. It bit him again, this time in the upperarm, then rippled over the concrete in a beautiful coiling glide.

Help him! shouted Twyla, arrowing in. Hush thet racket and help him, else he's bound to die!

Not if he's got faith! said Carnes.

The band stopped playing, the prophets stopped babbling, and Sermons, Bexton and Moomaw hopped down from the altardeck to see about Hoke. He could hear the cicadas outside, whirring dryly, the sad bellyaching of ditchfrogs, and the faraway hum and buzz of pickup tires rolling on asphalt and ratcheting over a cattleguard.

Git him a doctor, somebody!

Now, Twyla, if we do thet, Carnes said, aint we sayin the Word's not the Word? Before Twyla could answer, Carnes looked down at Hoke. Boy, you want a doctor?

Nosir. Just some kinda ease. Hoke sprawled, burning where Judas had fanged him.

He'd say thet, Twyla said. Just to fit in better here at th Assembly.

He won't ever fit in better if he truckles to this world's medicine, said Carnes.

Sermons knelt beside Hoke. He don't want a doctor, Sister Twyla, cause he knows from whence comes his hep.

Praise God!

Look here, said Twyla. Thet's a big Judas of a snake. It spiked him twyst. Thet much venom'd drop a buffalo, much less a peakèd skinny boy.

Faith can toss mountains into the sea, Carnes said.

Twyla grimaced. When was the last time yore faith tossed a mountain into the sea?

Kept me safe handlin thatere serpent, Carnes said. S moren anybody can say for Brother Hoke.

Hoke'd done handled, Sermons said. You caught m when the Spirit'd gone off him.

Hugh Bexton returned with Judas around one shoulder like a great drooping epaulette braid. He stood directly over Hoke, and Hoke could see Bexton and the snake looming like paradefloats against the cracked ceiling. Judas seemed to probe about for a baseboard chink or a skylight, a way to escape. Occasionally, though, it coiled the upper portion of its length floorward and flicked its tongue, swimming over Hoke with the airy loveliness of a saltwater eel.

If Brother Hoke dies faithless, said Camille Loomis, he'll go straight to—

—hellfire, Sam Loomis finished for her.

It was told me from on high, said Camille.

What happens to the hoodoo workers here amongst us? Twyla said. Do those betrayers go to hellfire too?

Not till they die, Camille said.

But they laid the hoodoo on Judas and got poor Hoke bit.

Camille sounded sad or embarrassed: No, missy, them hoodoo workers just showed up his weakness.

What garbage, Twyla said. What backasswards crap.

The Loomises looked at each other and backed away. Hoke watched Judas swimming, climbing, loopsliding in dimensionless emptiness. The Loomises' curse—*straight to hellfire*—rang in his head. The faces of those still hovering over him revealed a peculiar range of passions, Twyla's running from cajolery to outrage, Carnes' from amusement to satisfaction. Sermons made a series of increasingly sluggish peacemaking gestures. Judas bobbed down in a slowmotion arc and once again laid its yellow gaze on Hoke.

Somewhere beyond the diamondback's scrutiny glowed a single pulsing red dot.

Hoke thought: I'm going straight to hellfire.

Like Jesus, Hoke rises from himself and strides out of the cooling tomb of his own bones.

He leaves Twyla, Carnes, Moomaw, Sermons, and all the other Sixteeners and ambles into the quiet darkness—no cicadas, no frogs, no trucks—outside the Hands-On Assembly of Jesus Risen, formerly Snake-O-Rama. He walks and walks. In less time than it takes to leap a ditch he comes to a steeppitched road lined with blackberry brambles, dogwoods, pines.

A sycamore almost concealed by this other foliage bears a handlettered sign:

TRESPASERS!!!—
WE AIM to PLEZE But SHOT to KILL!

He has come home to his roommate Ferlin's tirehouse in a hard-to-reach pocket of Hothlepoya County. Neither Sackett nor Rag rushes out to greet him. The house itself blazes like a firebombed tiredump, turbulent coalback smoke billowing away, climbing into the sky's midnight fade.

The conflagration does not devour the house, but surrounds, dances on, and leaps from it. Pungent smoke skirls ceaselessly from the twoply radials and the halfburied whitewalls. Hoke calmy observes the fire, then cuts painlessly through its pall, and enters the dugout's U-shaped livingroom.

Ferlin! he shouts. You to home?

The interior startles him. It looks like an immense tiled lavatory. The walls glitter like scrubbed kitchen appliances, even if their white enamel faintly reflects the movement of fire and rippling smoke. Although he has no trouble breathing here, he must hike forever—longer than it takes to leap a ditch—to reach the glass cage, a bulletshaped capsule, across from Ferlin's frontdoor.

Hoke rides the capsule down. Flames twist in the glass or clear hardplastic shaping it, flickering from side to side as well as up and down. Beyond these flames the countryside (yes, countryside) looks infinitely hilly. Figures—faceless sticks dwarfed by the buttes and spires in the brickbrown landscape—cower in halfhidden rock niches or flee over plains like fiery icefloes.

Occasionally a longnosed fish, or a mutant parrot, or a parachuting man-of-war drifts past the capsule, each with some raw disfigurement: a gash, an extraneous growth, an unhealthy purpling of its visible membranes. Hoke wants to pull these wounded critters inside the capsule and heal their wounds with hands-on prayer.

Can God dwell in any of these freaks? In any part of this infernal canyon? Hoke thinks so. How could he have trespassed here without help?

In the subbasement the capsule halts. Hoke emerges, and an ordinarylooking man in a chambray shirt and a pair of designer jeans meets him. The man does not speak. His sunglasses lenses betray neither friendliness nor hostility. Hoke discovers his name only because it is stitched in flowing script—JUDAS—over his heartside shirtpocket (if he has a heart). He greets Hoke with a crooked thrifty bow.

This man, this Judas, leads Hoke through a tunnel lit at distant intervals with baseboard lights fashioned to resemble lifesized Old and New World serpents: cobras, mambas, pythons, shieldtails, eggeaters, rattlesnakes, vipers and so on, each of these sinuous devices plugged in at ankleheight and aglow with an icy radiance that both animates and eerily Xrays the shaped light. Hoke can see the skull, vertebrae, and tubelike organs of each makebelieve serpent.

Leading the way, Judas lists to one side or the other of the tunnel, but Hoke walks straight down its middle, trying to ignore the threat implicit in the baseboard lamps. The tunnel—itself a hollow, kinking serpent—goes on and on. Sometimes its twisty floor and curved walls seem to tremble, as if bombs have fallen close to hand.

At length the tunnel opens into a chamber—Hoke regards it as a satanic chapel—with a crooked wingless caduceus where the cross would hang in most decent Protestant churches. Ringing the chamber's squat dome are bleak stainedglass windows whose cames outline serpents in a stew of motifs, all colored in deep brown, indigo, or slumbering purple, with intermittent shards of crimson or yellow to accent the snakes' hooded or bulgingly naked eyes.

In these cames Hoke sees the same kinds of snakes in two dimensions that he saw rendered in the tunnel in three, except that here the serpents are all venomous cobras or pitvipers. The conflagration outside the chamber inflicts a sullen glitter on the dome's glass, but Hoke draws some comfort from it, as he would from a fire on a stone hearth.

Unlike the church on Frye's Mill Road, Judas' antichapel has pews. Three rows of benches face the pulpit, each one covered in snakeskin. Behind the pulpit, a choir loft made of long white bones and ornate ivory knobs faces outward beneath a stainedglass triptych.

With a gesture, Judas urges Hoke to find a place among the pews. Hoke chooses the curved middle pew and sits halfway along its scaly length. Judas mounts to the pulpit, growing two feet in height as he uncoils from a deceptive stoop. For the first time since arriving down here, Hoke can study Judas' face.

It is the machinemolded face of a departmentstore dummy, with just enough play in the blockfoam to permit the creature to smile faintly or to twitch a lip corner. When he removes his sunglasses, he reveals yellow eyes like a diamondback's and his face deforms into the soft triangle of a pitviper's head, with severe dents in the cheeks and a smile that has widened alarmingly. The rest of Judas' body maintains a human cast, and, hands gripping the pulpit's sides, he leans forward to regale Hoke, his lone congregant, with a stemwinding sermon. Outside, bombs or depth charges continue to explode, and Judas responds to the tremblors by rubbernecking his head around and whiteknuckling the lectern that seems to hold him erect. Hoke pays close heed.

Judas' sermon has no words. It issues from the creature's smile as hisses and sighs. Flickers of a doubletipped tongue break the sibilance, and at each pause Judas seems to rethink the next segment of his message. Then, as the crux of his text demands, a quiet or a vigorous hissing resumes, along with more tongueflickers and sighs. Sometimes Judas pounds the lectern or ambles briefly and shakily away from it. Hoke can make no sense of any of it, but Judas' voiceless sermonizing continues without relent. Hoke would like to make a getaway back through the tunnel, but his dead mama taught him never to walk out on a preacher and so he sits longsufferingly in place. Maybe Judas wants to torment him the way Carnes and the handlers tormented their spiritdrugged snakes.

Long into this sermon, a blue film creeps over Judas' eyes, turning them a sickly green. This milky film thickens. As it does, Judas' eyes go from green to seagreen to turquoise to a dreamy cobalt. These cobalt veils blind Judas, but he goes on hissing his wordless rant.

When Hoke thinks he can take no more, Judas stops hissing and rubs his snout with his human hands. The skin over his snout loosens all the way back to his capped eyes. Judas grabs this scaly layer and peels it back. Then the skin on his hands splits, and the new hands beneath these glovelike husks break through to peel away the old skin, including his chambray shirt and designer jeans.

With one reborn hand on the pulpit for support, Judas steps out of this old covering and sets it aside. The husk rocks on its feet like a display mannikin fit only for junking. The new Judas, meanwhile, clings to the pulpit in the guise of a human female: another mannikin, but an animated one for the women's department. With chestnut hair that cascades down and trembles over her shoulders, this female version of Judas picks up her discarded skin by the shoulders, carries it to the choir loft, and places it in one of the five chairs there. The integument of this molt rattles dryly, its snaky head deforming again into something recognizably human, as if its serpentshape had never really taken.

Hoke sits mesmerized. He no longer wants to run, simply to understand. At the lectern again, the female snakeperson goes on changing, her face shrinking and triangulating, her tresses pulling back into her skull and weaving into satiny snakeskin. Looking past her, Hoke sees that the molt in the choir has come to resemble his daddy, who ran out on his mama and him shortly after she had yoked them with the Sixteeners.

You bastid! Hoke shouts at the thing.

Outside, very near, a bomb falls. The explosion rocks the domed chamber, audibly warping the stainedglass in its cames, swaying the pulpit and rattling the hollow imago of his daddy, which totters in its chair. The imago has no eyes, only gaping vents, but it stares at Hoke without love, remorse, or any plea for understanding. It sits, merely sits, teetering whenever ordnance detonates.

The snakeperson at the pulpit ignores Hoke's daddy and launches into another harangue—a hissyfit, Hoke thinks—that expands and expands. Usually Hoke's bladder, given the length of these speeches, would expand too, threatening rupture and flood, but here in Ferlin's subbasement his bladder has lots of stretch and he too much endurance.

At last, though, the second Judas' eyes grow a milky film and a second shedding occurs, revealing a new snakeperson and leaving behind a female husk that the third version of Hoke's guide places in the choir loft next to his daddy. The face of this shell takes on the features of his mama, while the third snaky preacher begins a brandnew tirade.

Hoke nods. At length, a third molt puts a fresh male husk in the loft with his folks. This tedious process occurs twice more. By the end of the diamondback's fifth hissyfit, every seat in the choir is occupied. The choir now comprises five false human beings whom Hoke sees as wicked likenesses of his daddy, his mama, Johnny Mark Carnes, Twyla Glanton and Ferlin Rodale. They rustle to their feet, and the sixth Judas sheds its preacherly garments to join them in the loft as an immense coiled rattler.

How can they sing an anthem when they have no voices? Why does the sixth Judas lace her long anatomy among the other five betrayers, then raise her triangular head above the zombie face of Johnny Mark Carnes?

Ulo-shan-pwei-koloh-ehlo-scraiiii! says the sixth Judas in a female voice familiar to Hoke. *Neh-hyat-kolotosh-mona-ho!* Her split tongue flits among these syllables like a hummingbird sampling morningglory blossoms. Then, on her warning rattle, the choir, once mute, joins her in pealing out a hymn that Hoke well knows:

O for a thousand tongues to sing. . . .

Hands pressed against him, their warm palms on his chest, upperarms, forehead. One pair had a viselike grip on his temples, flattening his ears and struggling to touch fingertips behind his head.

Here he comes, a voice said. Glory.

Bring m out, Jesus. Bring m on out.

Hoke let the faces surrounding him clarify in the glare of a ceilinglamp. As his pupils narrowed, even the darker faces among the four took on definition. He recognized Twyla Glanton and then every member of the Sermons family.

Praise God.

Twyla's face came toward him, and she placed one ear less than an inch from his lips. Say again, she said. Her sorrel hair touched his face.

Lift him from the pit n set him upright midst us, said C. K. Sermons. Bless his ever goin forth n comin home.

Say again, Twyla said again.

Hoke tried—no sound, but his lips quirked.

Looky there, said Regina Sermons. He be smilin.

Hoke stayed with the Sermonses the next three days. They prayed with and over him, often laying on hands. They fed him unsalted rice, applesauce, bananas, and tea made of chamomile flowers, passionflower leaves, and crushed rosebuds. With no other medical attention but this food and prayer ("Antivenin is the antichrist and doctors are its antifaith disciples," Carnes had liked to say), Hoke recovered quickly.

On Sunday morning, the Sermonses held an outdoor service on the decks of the splitlevel gazebo in their backyard. No one brought snakes into it, although Hoke knew that the Sermonses kept a dozen or more in crates along the rear of their double garage. Twyla, Ferlin Rodale, and Sam and Camille Loomis (who had forgiven Twyla her words at the Friday-night snakehandling service) attended this informal gathering. Oddly, though, no other member of the congregation showed up, and Hoke began to suspect that something more dire than his own rattlerbites had disrupted Friday's worship.

The Sermonses refused to talk about such matters while his body went about healing itself. When not praying or reading the Bible with him, they gave him his space, including free run of their house and grounds.

Their brick house sat on an acre off White Cow Creek Road, ten miles west of Beulah Fork. It appeared to have been lifted from a hightone suburban subdivision and set down again in the sharecropper boonies. It had three bedrooms, a study, and a den with a hightech entertainment center: largescreen TV and VCR combo, multideck stereophonic CD soundsystem, and, because none of the Mark Sixteeners were teetotalers, a wellsupplied wetbar. The Sermonses could afford such a place because C. K. sold insurance as well as preached, and Betty worked a deskjob in the Hothlepoya Country Health Department, even if her job struck Hoke as peculiarly at odds with the noninterventionist doctrines of their Hands-On Assembly.

On Monday evening, Twyla, Ferlin, and the Loomises came for another call. This time, though, C. K. herded everyone into the den to watch the videotape that Betty had shot three evenings earlier. Hoke understood that C. K. had organized the gathering as a small party in honor of his recovery. If it had any other purpose, beyond showing off Betty's skills as a camerawoman, he could not have named it.

This past Friday a true anointin came on Brother Hoke, C. K. said. Yall watch n see.

Somebody had wound the tape exactly to the point at which Eddie Moomaw passed Hoke a timberrattler. The tape showed Hoke handling, there among the other Sixteeners. The hopping and stutterstepping of the worshipers, the clangy music, the scary inscrutability of the snakes—everything on the tape united to make Hoke see himself and his friends as part of an outlandish spectacle, separate somehow from their everyday selves. He recognized himself, and he didn't. He recognized Twyla and the Sermonses, and he didn't. Betty's tape tweaked the familiar old church and the ordinary folks inside it into a gaudy circus tent, with jugglers, acrobats and clowns.

My Lord, Ferlin said.

You know you'da loved to been there, Twyla said.

F yall think this's gonna work on me like a recruitin film, yall just don't know Ferlin Rodale.

Where is it? Hoke said. I don't see it.

Betty Sermons leaned over and patted his forearm. Where's what, baby?

The Spirit, Hoke said. Thet night it was so thick in there you coulda bottled it.

It don't tape, Betty said. Never has.

Hush, Prophetess Camille said. This's where Brother Hoke passes his serpent on back to Eddie Moomaw.

Hoke watched himself hand off the timberrattler. Then he watched C. K. take a hearty swig of poison and Carnes explode into view to unload an even bigger snake on the video image of himself. On the Sermonses' largescreen, Hoke accepted and then almost dropped the diamondback.

Yall're flakier than a deadman's dandruff, Ferlin said.

From a threestage recliner, Sam Loomis leveled a hard gaze on Ferlin. Who taught you yore manners, young man?

Beg yore pardon, sir. I've just never liked snakes.

They've awways spoken well of you, Twyla said.

The videotape continued to unspool, flickering and jumping in testimony to Betty's active camera technique.

Here comes the bites! Regina said.

Hoke flinched. So did Ferlin, who looked off at the framed underwriter certificates on the wall. Hoke kept watching and soon saw himself sprawled on the concrete floor, surrounded by Twyla, the Loomises, Sermons, Moomaw, Bexton, and two bigeyed little boys—the Strock twins—who had wriggled free of their mama's restraining arms to hunker next to Hoke and gawk at him in cheerful expectation of his demise.

Brats, thought Hoke.

Aloud he said: This's where I died. Then walked home to Ferlin's. And rode a elevator straight to hell.

Except, of course, the largescreen showed no sequence of events like that at all. Instead they saw Judas writhing above Hoke in Hugh Bexton's arms, and Twyla saying, *What backasswards crap*, and the Loomises moving stiffly out of view. Then the screen showed a dozen worshipers milling, smoke rolling over the floor from beneath the altardeck, a painted churchwindow shattering, and a fractured brick tumbling end over end on the concrete.

Sermons and the others raised their heads to register the broken-out window. Smoke began to rise through the church from baseboards, closets, windowsills, and the junkrooms behind the altar. The pictures of the outbreaking fire careened even more madly than Betty's earlier shots. Folks scrambled to flee the building. A sound like the amplified crumpling of Styrofoam dominated the audio; shouts, children crying, and the slamming of car and pickup doors echoed in the background.

C. K., Darren DeVore, Leonard Callender, and Ron Strock—there to shoo away his twins as much as to assist Hoke—picked Hoke up and hustled him in a hammockcarry to the door. Other men crated up and rescued their snakes, sometimes appearing to put their decorated boxes and the creatures inside them before their own wives and kids. The tape's last poorly exposed shots included a pan from the church's burning facade to the gleaming asphalt road going past it.

What was thet all about? Hoke said.

A fire got goin in the dry kudzu behind the church, Twyla said. It burnt us out, comin through the back.

How? Why?

Somebody done set it, C. K. Sermons said. A enemy like unto them crop-burners in the gospels.

Only part standin today is walls, Betty said.

Twyla allowed that the fire could have started from a flungaway cigarette, but that C. K.'s investigation on Saturday morning did make it look that somebody had piled dry brush and maybe even two or three wheelbarrows of waste lumber, ends and pieces, against the church's rear wall. Then the sleazes had soaked the piles with kerosene, covered them with kudzu leaves and evergreen branches, and sneaked up during the snakehandling to drag the brush away and light the kindling.

Why'd anybody try to kill yall? Ferlin said. Yall're in a damnfool hurry to do it yoreselves.

Rathcor had his claws in it, said Camille. And whilst them snakes were out, I bet you cash money thet Carnes, Moomaw and DeVore awl played divil's innkeeper.

You don't know thet, Twyla said.

She sez it she's nigh-on certain, Sam Loomis said.

Plus it looks like Carnes's done skedaddled outta thisere county, C. K. said.

Hoke cavecrawled into himself. The Mark Sixteeners had lost their meeting-hall, Johnny Mark Carnes had vamoosed without a faretheewell, and a disagreement of fierce consequence had split the Assembly—Eddie Moomaw and his cronies arguing that the fire bespoke a judgment for allowing a descendant of Ham to preach and handle snakes amongst them; the Loomises, Twyla, and their friends adamant that Moomaw had laid a vile scapegoatment on the Sermonses for reasons having less to do with theology than with low blood, covetousness, and whitetrash pride. There had been no full Mark Sixteener fellowship on Sunday morning not merely because their church had burnt, but because a schism along skewed racial and maybe even economic lines had cleft the Assembly.

Why'd Johnny Mark run? Hoke said.

I tracked him, Betty Sermons said. Taped his ever step wi thet big Judas snake of his. He figgered if you died, we'd put it out to Sheriff Ott thet he murdered you.

Then the bigger fool he, C. K. said. Law aint gonna squash no Sixteener for killin a Sixteener.

Why not? Regina said.

Same reason it aint like to vestigate our church fire as a arson, said C. K. dyspeptically, as if the strychnine he'd drunk had soured his stomach.

Or look too hard at the mischief out my way, said Twyla.

Rewind, said Regina.

Mam? said C. K. Sermons.

Rewind. Show me playin wi them ol snakes again.

Betty Sermons rewound the tape, and everyone watched Regina handle her rattlers again. Then the TV rescreened Hoke's work with the canebrake. Was that Hoke Pilcher? he wondered. Yes, but Hoke Pilcher under a throughblest anointing. In spite of everything else—snakebite, hellfire, schism—the sight of this miracle poured a tart joy into him, and Hoke perched before it, utterly rapt, oblivious to his surroundings.

That autumn Twyla Glanton moved from Hothlepoya County to Cottonton, Alabama. There she found a job as assistant city clerk and joined a small off-shoot of the Hands-On Assembly of Jesus Risen. In early October Hoke got Ferlin to drive him to Cottonton to see her, but Twyla had begun to date a surveyor in the Alabama highway department, and Hoke's visit brought down embarrassment on everyone but Ferlin.

Johnny Mark Carnes, according to Eddie Moomaw, had opened an uphol-stery shop near Waycross. In this shop, he recovered easychairs, divans, carseats, footstools, threestage recliners, and a variety of other items from pewcushions to the padded lids of jewelryboxes. Occasionally, according to Moomaw, he used snakeskin, for which reason he made frequent unauthorized jaunts into the Okefenokee Swamp.

The Mark Sixteeners in Hothlepoya County remained divided. The Moomaw faction held brush arbor services on New Loyd Hill until the first frost in October. The Sermons family met with the Loomises, the Callenders, and the Bextons in either their garage or the splitdeck gazebo in their backyard, de-pending on the weather. Both groups suffered snakebites over these weeks, but no one died. Neither faction attracted anyone new to its meetings except the occasional media reporter and GBI agents in scruffy but futile disguise.

Hoke attended the services of neither group. He had gone to hell in a dis-orienting feverdream, but the conflicts among the local Sixteeners, especially in the absence of Twyla, had tormented him a thousand times worse than either his snakebite or his resultant delirious trip to the sheol tucked away under Ferlin Rodale's tirehouse. Why attend services if a spirit of feud and persnicketiness held the real Spirit at bay? Hell had nothing on a holeful of serpents or an assembly of quarrelsome believers. Hoke would gladly risk eternal judgment if he could avoid the latter two kinds of snakes.

Aside from spiritual issues and Twyla's leavetaking, Hoke's biggest worry was putting money in his pockets. Ferlin forgave him rent shortfalls and overdue payments for the electric bill, but Hoke cringed to impose and even in his exile from Deaton's Bar-B-Q often ventured into Beulah Fork to prune shrubbery, cut grass, sweep parkinglots, or carry out groceries. Sometimes he went with Ferlin on roofing or carpentry jobs, earning his hire by toting shingles, bracing ladders, and sorting nails into the pockets of canvas aprons.

In December, Colby Deaton rehired him to bus tables, wash dishes, and run errands, and Hoke stayed with this job—despite the ragging of halfwit good ol boys like Albert Becknell—until early March, when he quit to begin a new line of work, catching and selling poisonous snakes.

A Japanese tuliptree had flowered in the wilderness among dogwoods and red-buds still under winter's spell. Hoke stopped with his crokersack to marvel at it. The tuliptree had set out its pink blossoms on whitespotted grey limbs altogether bare of leaves. These flowers danced like ballerinas against the naked boughs. Another coldsnap, no matter how brief, would kill the flowers; a violent rainstorm would knock them to the leafmulch, and no one would ever guess that they had bloomed.

At the base of an uglier tree nearby—Hoke took it for a blighted elm—a timberrattler slithered languidly up into the day from a hole down among the tree's roots. Hoke had come for just this event, the emergence of a congregation of snakes from their hibernating place. Because it was still early, he could expect more snakes to follow this one to the surface. Dens in which to pass safely an entire winter commanded allegiance, and snakes that had successfully hibernated returned to them fall after fall. Many serpents slept coiled together in the same den, moccasins with cottonmouths, diamondbacks with canebrakes, an immobile scrum of pitvipers in coldblooded wintersleep. And this first rattler, Hoke knew, signaled like a robin the coming of even more of its kind.

In his lowcut tennis shoes he crept up to the elm, seized the canebrake behind its head, and quickly bagged it. Then he crouched and waited. This strategy brought results. In an hour, with the latewinter sun steadily climbing to the south, he caught four more snakes, bagging them as efficiently as he had the first.

Even this small early haul promised a decent payoff. He could get ten dollars a snake from some of the Sixteeners and possibly as much as fifty if he captured a rattler longer than six feet. Snakes died over the winter, or escaped, or emerged from their crates bent like fishhooks from clumsy handling. Conscientious handlers would replace and retire their injured snakes. That turnover meant a career of sorts, if Ferlin would allow him to breed members of like species inside or near the tirehouse. And Sam Loomis had told Hoke of a research center in Atlanta that bought pitvipers for their venom, yet another likely customer and income source.

Hoke caught three more emerging snakes, and then there was a lull. Well, fine. All work and no lolligagging made Hoke a dull dude. His gaze wandered to the tuliptree again and to the pink chalicelike blossoms fluttering in it—pretty, so pretty. Then Hoke started. A human figure sat in an upper crook of the tuliptree, balanced there as shakily as an egg on an upended coffeecup. The figure shifted, and Hoke recognized her as his dead mama, Jillrae Evans Pilcher. He stood up.

Good to see you again, Hoke.

You too, Hoke told his mama. He meant it.

What day is it, honey?

Sunday, he said.

Well. You orter have yore tail over to the Sermonses then, shouldn't you?

Hoke explained about Rathcor and Carnes and Judas and the schism that had come to the Mark Sixteeners in the aftermath of the fire at the former Snake-O-Rama. He explained why he would never encounter the Holy Spirit among either of the church's contending factions and how attending the services of one or the other turned him into an angry uptight nitpicker, a heathen nearlybout. God, he said, would more likely happen to him here in the woods.

My me, said Jillrae Pilcher. The classic copout.

Mama, I cain't do everthin the same blest way you would.

Look quick, she said. They's more comin.

Hoke looked. A halfdozen pitvipers had boiled up through the tunnel from their den. They burst forth into the dappled noon in a slithery tangle. Hoke chuckled to see them, but made no sudden grab to catch one. He glanced back at the tuliptree, his awkwardly perched mama, and the pink blossoms stark against the reawakening woods. His mama faded a little, but because he held his glance, the pink grew lovelier, the sunlight crisper, and the separate trees beyond the tuliptree both more distinct and more mysterious, a pleasant contradiction. Then a snake raced over Hoke's instep. He had no need to look away from the tuliptree at the escaping serpents because their touch told him nearly everything and the woods into which he continued to peer told him the rest.

What is it? said his mama, clinging to the forking branches over her head.

Hoke smiled and blew her a kiss.

The woods behind the tuliptree filled with a haze like a cottony pollen, and this haze drifted through the dogwoods, redbuds, and conifer pillars until it hung from every limb of every tree within a hundredfoot radius of Hoke's dying elm. The awakening snakes boiled out into the haze. Hoke knelt and picked up pitviper after pitviper, two or three to each hand. Standing again, he handled them in the enabling white currents of the drifting pollen grains. His mama, looking on, faded toward invisibility. Hoke lifted a handful of serpents to her in heartfelt farewell. The woods rang with a shout, his own, and the haze pivoting around Hoke's blight elm either drifted or burned away.

Ferlin burst into the clearing.

My God, he said. Way you uz yellin, I figgered somebody'd done kilt you.

No, said Hoke, bagging the snakes in his hands. I'm just out here laudin God.

Alone? said Ferlin, closing the distance between them.

Only takes two or three, said Hoke.

Not countin them divilish snakes there, who's yore second, Pilcher?

Hoke gestured at the tuliptree, realizing as he did that Ferlin was unlikely to have seen his mama stranded amid its blazing pink flowers. He set his crokersack down and dropped a friendly arm over Ferlin's shoulder.

How bout you? he said.

[Author's note: I owe a significant debt to Dennis Covington's *Salvation on Sand Mountain: Snake Handling and Redemption in Southern Appalachia* for much of the background of this story. Charles McGlocklin, the End-Time Evangelist, whom I quote three times from Covington's book, is a real person, but all the other characters and situations are imaginary; resemblances to real human beings, living or dead, or to actual situations in the histories of real snakehandling congregations are entirely coincidental.]

THE PHANTOM CHURCH
Ana Blandiana

Romanian author Ana Blandiana began publishing poetry and fiction as a college student in the 1960s, although her work was often judged subversive and suppressed by Ceausescu's government. Her collection of poetry for children, *Events on My Street*, was perceived as a satire on the authorities and Blandiana was forbidden to publish again until 1989. Since then, Blandiana has won both national and international awards for her work. Her publications include *The Four Seasons* and *Projects for the Past* (two volumes of fantasy tales), *A Drawerful of Applause* (a novel), and *The Quality of Witness* (a collection of essays). In addition to writing, Blandiana is one of the leaders of the Civic Alliance, an organization working to restore Romania's civil society.

"The Phantom Church" ("Biserica fantoma") was first published in Romania in *Projects for the Past*. In 1996, it was translated into English by Georgianna Farnoaga and Sharon King, and published in *The Phantom Church and Other Stories from Romania* (The University of Pittsburgh Press). This deeply mysterious story, set in a small village in the Transylvanian mountains, is one of my very favorite fantasy finds of the year. I hope you will agree.

—T. W.

There are so many kinds of fantasy it is no wonder that some of them may pass for reality. Sometimes reality itself arrogantly extends its borders and the overlapping zones remain ambiguous, uncertain of status for years, decades, even centuries. And then—who knows how, perhaps simply through the natural erosion of time—either the fantastic or the real blurs and slips to the other side, astonished it could ever have appeared otherwise. Of course neither the trickling of reality into the molds of fantasy nor fantasy's invasion of the real can have overly serious consequences for anyone trained to see beyond appearances; the mere occurrence of an event cannot remove it from the bounds of the imaginary, any more than fantasy's shading of an incident is sufficient to oust it from the realm of actuality. Since Creation, a line has been drawn between the real and the unreal, and transgressing it signifies a desire to test its strength rather than an intention to defy it, in the same way that taking a drug means not so much underestimating its effects as being willing to experience them. Most of the time the real and the unreal coexist in parallel spheres, independent of and even indifferent to one another. Yet in the rare moments when they do come together, their union brings forth a mutual revelation: having passed through reality, an element of the fantastic returns to the imaginary world strengthened by the authority of the test, while an element of the objective universe that joins fantasy becomes charged with a new significance capable of transforming the existence from which it escaped, if only for a moment.

The extraordinary journey of the wooden church that began in the village of Subpiatră in the Transylvanian Mountains of Bihor in the late eighteenth century, more precisely in the winter of 1778, is one of those occurrences which, though having actually taken place, belong by nature to the domain of fantasy. Yet having passed through reality, even if under the sign of the miraculous, they bring to the imaginary world a prestige all the more undeniable for being unnecessary.

The story, which began as verifiable history, is as follows.

The serfs of Subpiatră, having no legal right to construct a church for themselves, decided to bring to their village a church already built. Such an unusual idea might never have crossed their minds had there not been an abandoned wooden church some ten kilometers away in Lugoşu de Jos, a village of free peasants who had managed to build themselves a new stone church. The idea of hauling a church ten kilometers—from the valley of the Crişul Repede River to the Carpathian Mountains—as well as setting it up hundreds of meters higher, complete with porch, spire, roof, vestibule, nave, altar, benches, icon screen, and even icons, may today seem an exclusively literary idea, a clever symbol not to be taken seriously (and thus an aberration). At the time, however—it was before the peasant uprising led by Horea—the people about to revolt might well have deemed it possible. The legend, though detailed, does not say whether or not the villagers of Subpiatră voiced any doubts about the feasibility of the move at the outset. It merely describes the negotiations for purchasing the church, the difficulties encountered in raising the money, and the fashioning—more toilsome than the move itself—of a an immense saw, as long as the church was wide, to sever the building from the place where it had been erected more than a century before.

For that is how the church was wrested from its foundations of thick logs, thrust into the ground like deep roots: it was felled with the saw as if it were a tree, hewn down at its base like one of the countless fir trees—crisscrossed and pegged together—that had brought the church to life so many years before. It was not in fact difficult to cut, as the saw's teeth passed gently through the wood; it was only hard to keep it standing, the thin arrow of the spire pointing up and the porch pillars supporting the infinitely high roof. The age-old skill of loggers had to be called upon for the twenty pair of oxen, yoked in an elaborate web on three sides of the church, to extricate it from its foundation and make it slide evenly, centimeter by centimeter, without toppling. The journey, or more precisely, the first part of it, took almost a year. They could advance no more than a few meters a day, and only on days when the ground was dry. After careful planning, they decided to avoid the winding roads and go instead straight across the slopes and woods, opening new trails and clearing whole forests. The weighty frame of the church, plowing through the dust, dug deep and wide furrows into the ground, leaving behind scars visible even today on the ancient face of the land. In time the trail became a road, a highway even (a strange kind of highway, one gouged into the earth, with inexplicably high banks). Covered with asphalt now, it still bears the name (a name absurd to anyone unfamiliar with the story) of the Church's Furrow. Today you can reach Subpiatră from Lugoşu de Jos either by the Lane—the old country road that no one uses any more, where grass grows idyllically in the deep ruts made over the centuries—or by the Church's Furrow, the asphalt highway, which is much shorter and steeper and cuts the forest in two.

In that year of 1778 spring had come early, Easter too, and by Saint George's Day the earth was dry and covered with lush grass. The serfs began hauling the church on the patron saint's name day, April 23. Though advancing only a few meters a day, they managed to bring it out of the cemetery by Ascension Day, and by Whitsunday they had reached the higher end of the village. The church moved more easily than they had dared to hope, and they dragged it carefully, lest the bottom of the porch, with its wide swath of carvings one handbreadth above the saw cut, should wear off. They were in no hurry; they knew it was no use reaching the Criş River before the frosts of winter: only over the hard-frozen riverbed could they hope to make the church glide like a sled.

But there were long summer months until then, months in which the church progressed without swaying, scarcely betraying its motion, so slowly and imperceptibly did it inch forward. But for the yawning furrow left behind and the teams of oxen tangled in their yokes and ropes and brought to their knees with the effort, one might have said, glancing at the cross barely stirring on the horizon, that the church was ascending the mountain by itself. This impression grew even stronger when the church entered the woods and proceeded along the deforested path, only its eerily thin spire still visible both from the village below, now left behind, and the village above, not yet reached. The steeple thrust up above the tops of the fir trees, not like an object resisting the laws of gravity but like a creature growing from the earth, floating above the peaks of the other firs, unadorned with crosses.

Consequently, though no one forgot how hard the labor was (and how could they when they had all taken part in it?), the more the weeks and months passed, the more people thought of the church's progress as some thing of a miracle. Thus, on major holidays, streams of believers from neighboring villages—or perhaps merely curious onlookers—would converge on the church. Smaller groups, like envoys on reconnaissance missions, came from the other side of the mountain. It would have been hard to say whether those who came from afar were paying homage to the miraculous relocation of the church or to the human effort that had made it possible. Be that as it may, the fame of the church making its way from one village to another burgeoned, its legend gradually taking shape, though nothing out of the ordinary had yet happened. Whenever a holiday caught the church on the road, it would come to a halt, and the priest—his chestnut beard flying in the wind, his voice reverberating from tree to tree—would perform the service on the porch stairs, bystanders swelling the ranks of the moving team. By August 15, the Day of Our Lady, the church had reached a clearing in the hills, where shepherds' gatherings and festivities had taken place for centuries. The large bright meadow looked like an elegant anteroom, its flooring the short, coarse, brushy grass of Alpine pastures. Not until they saw the crowds surround the church (and overflow into the forest, since even the wide meadow could not contain all of them, as they stood there respectfully in their bright clothes) did the peasants from Subpiatră really begin to believe in the miracle of the move. They looked at Father Nicola, the priest who had started it all, with new eyes, full of astonishment and awe. Thus everything that followed not only failed to surprise anyone but even seemed expected, as if predestined by forces beyond human control.

The church reached the Criş River at the onset of winter, as planned. They now had to wait for the river to freeze over so they could slide it across to the opposite bank and haul it up the mountain through the thick, soft snow. By Saint George's Day the next spring the church would have finished its course, ending its journey at its future home. But that year the snows may have come early, falling deeply and deceptively; perhaps, since everything had gone so well until then, the men had started to rely on miracles rather than on doing their duty; or perhaps they wanted to push the church within the village borders by Christmas. In any case, they did not wait for the Criş to freeze over. The ice had not had time to thicken between the nervous restlessness of the water and the pacifying sleep of the snow. It held up as the dozens of teams of oxen, their yokes adorned with fir twigs and colored woolen threads, crossed over, but then, with a prolonged, ominous sound, as if gnashing against its own powerlessness, it cracked, at first invisibly, then split and broke apart, causing the church to go down erratically, tilting it to one side and finally depositing it majestically, under the terrified gaze of the crowd, on the gravelly riverbed. For a few long moments the sharp spire continued to sway, like a bent branch beating the air, fighting to regain its place. Then the flowing water surrounded the church with unconditional acceptance, as if it were an island suddenly submerging. The water in fact barely covered two of the three steps of the porch, and the topmost row of carvings could still be seen, its flowery motif coiling like a plaited rope. Having reached the other bank, the oxen strained to look behind them, not comprehending why they were no longer being goaded and sensing they should not move. A few men, roused from their stupor as from a heavy sleep, rushed to unyoke the beasts. The slightest mishap could topple everything. It was getting dark; they would have to wait until morning.

But by the next day the church seemed to have taken root, as if it had been built there from the beginning. After a night of hard frost, the hardest of the winter, the ice had sealed it in completely, clasping it jealously like a gift it refused to give back. As nothing could be done until spring, the parish celebrated Christmas and Epiphany right there, in the middle of the Criş, the voice of Father Nicola rising in tune with the water pounding below the ice, stronger than the howling winds and the snowstorms. Thus he stood on the porch all winter, in raging wind or blizzard, officiating to the crowds gathered on the frozen surface. Meanwhile the church's renown continued to grow, its fall through the ice, though unexpected and unforeseen, soon being interpreted as a new sign of its extraordinary destiny.

Father Nicola was the only person not carried away by the miracle that seemed more and more in control of the move. Instead he acted as a cautious steward, closely overseeing the details of his charge and continually repairing one thing or another with such unusual skill that his parishioners soon exaggerated it in their eagerness to make it part of the miracle. All that winter he worked on the church's floor, replacing it with long, carefully planed boards that he joined together almost seamlessly. He worked alone, requesting no help yet never saying no when a bystander offered to fetch some tool he needed.

For there were always spectators—after the initial astonishment and timorous questions about the priest's daily visits to the church had worn off, after the first expedition had surged through the snow to see what was going on— sometimes only a few, sometimes more, but all of them striving to discern some hidden meaning in the priest's strenuous labor and uncommon skill. They had no doubt (at least this was the conclusion they had reached in the village, where they talked of nothing else) that the priest knew something they could not yet fathom, that there was an order to things they could not yet grasp. Otherwise, why would Father Nicola be working in the biting cold, trudging for hours through waist-high drifts, some days not even returning home but sleeping on the bare floor of the church, wrapped only in his homespun woolen cloak? True, there were those who said, albeit guardedly, that since the priest had no family or household, he might be restless in the village, while his work on the church trapped in the ice would occupy his time and make him feel less lonely. Of course, no one paid any heed to such an absurd explanation. The mystery taking shape before their eyes could no longer be separated from the tall, slightly bent figure of the priest.

Once he had finished the new floor, Father Nicola set to carving the altar screen, an altar screen such as had never been seen before. Then came the benches with notched patterns and high backs, like thrones for voivodes. When he asked the women to weave piles of strong white linen cloth, the villagers took it as a sign that the repairs were coming to an end and that the priest was certain the church would be raised from the riverbed in the spring. The women thought the linen was to serve as altar cloths and window drapings, and they wove eagerly and diligently, not surprised by the priest's request. Later, much later, when tidings of their church reached them from foreign lands, tidings so fantastic they surpassed the realm of human imagination, the cloth was seen in a different light and the priest's request interpreted as proof of his prescience.

By the time the ice started to thaw, at a frantic pace, the women had finished weaving the cloth and brought it to the church. The way the ice melted that year has been retold by the people of Subpiatră for the past two hundred years, and although there have been no eyewitnesses for a long time now, the villagers still relate it in the minutest detail, as if each narrator had actually been there. So great is the number of details and so rapid their proliferation that, in time, as you listen to the storytellers, you begin to wonder whether there ever were any eyewitnesses, whether the whole extraordinary tale of the church is not merely unfolding before the transfixed eyes of the storyteller each time he retells it, as if he were under the spell of his own vision. But such is not the case. The peasants' account is reinforced by place names dating back two hundred years: the ford of the Criş, for example, is called the Ice Hole of the Church. The excess of local color at this point in the story stems from the fact that, though real, the event had none of the dimensions of reality. And though certain of their truth, people sense how unbelievable it sounds when they relate it and start piling up details, trying to evince a reality the very details deny.

In fact, there was nothing unusual about the way the ice melted that year. Spring had given fair warning, and long before the ice began to thaw the church had been anchored with plaited ropes that coiled around the sturdy fir trees on the banks or were tied to posts laboriously pounded into the snowy ground. Once the thawing began the oxen would replace the posts; they would pull the church off the river bottom as soon as the spring torrents loosened it from its miry place of rest. For weeks that moment had been carefully watched and waited for. Men took turns keeping vigil on the banks, and Father Nicola never left the church, day or night. The women looked after him, bringing him pots of stew and slices of *mămăligă*, which they would find barely touched a day or two later when they came to bring more. During those last few days Father Nicola grew more and more silent, seized by an anxiety far greater than they would have expected. His long beard flowing wildly, he seemed consumed by a terror known only to himself. The villagers—especially the women—hovered around him, awed by a suffering they could not comprehend but which they promptly associated with the miracle, calling it after the fact a premonition or even a preparatory ritual.

For several days the layer of ice had been thinning, growing transparent, and the sun, emerging from time to time from among the fluffy clouds, shone its rays here and there on the river, turning cracks into ice holes. Finally, the water spilled over the surface of the ice, gushing up as from a spring. Overnight it froze again, but the frail, hurried freeze only proved that the cold had lost its power, that these were its death throes. The morning before, the water had begun lapping against the sides of the church, and twice the church had swayed slightly. Less than an hour before the ice finally broke, Father Nicola came out on the church porch and shouted at the sentries on the banks to come to him, at the same time urging the women about to set off in the boats to bring him food that they should stay where they were. His voice sounded harsh and strong above his wind-whipped beard; his eyes impatiently searched upriver. The men clambered into the boats, seized in turn by the urgency of his summons.

That was the last the women saw of their husbands before everything sank into confusion: the boats striking against ice floes as the men hurried to reach the priest, who was still staring anxiously and restlessly upriver. No one ever found out what Father Nicola told the twelve men he had called to his side. The women waited on the bank—patiently at first, then apprehensively—as they gazed at the water swelling up like dough. Now the ice was pouring down in chunks that screeched wildly and rebelliously, smashing into one another and leaping into the air like huge glossy fish, only to crash down again ominously. When the women finally screamed out to their husbands, it was too late. The roar of the river was stronger than their voices. In the space of the one hour the men had been in the river, everything had changed. Crying and shouting at the top of their lungs, deafened by their own wailing and the mad whirling of the waters, the women never knew whether the men had chosen not to answer or whether they had not heard the answers the men had shouted to them. This is the most debated point in the story, the moment that is open to the most diverse interpretations, the juncture at which the narrators have to declare their position, either trying to grasp the facts or boasting that those facts are incomprehensible, as if the nobility of the epic were in direct proportion to its mystery. And this moment of decision is, quite naturally, followed by the moment of truth, the dénouement.

Seeing the church tilt slightly to one side, then turn upright, then list almost playfully to the other side, the women ceased weeping. Mute, they kept their eyes riveted on the steeple, which swung like the clapper of an overturned bell, as if trying to cry out to the walls of sky and water imprisoning it, then changing its mind before making itself heard. For a moment there seemed to be a pause in the river's tumultuous clamor, and in the unnatural, suspended vacuum of silence one could hear a long, searing shriek, as if all the fir trees sacrificed in the body of the church had heaved a deep moan, a single note, almost human, of pain. The very next moment the ice swelled up to the sky with a thundering roar, releasing the church and sending it viciously downriver. For an instant the steeple made an astonishing bow, almost touching the water, and the sides of the porch were exposed indecently. But just when all hope seemed lost the spire miraculously righted itself again, as if brought round by the steady hand of a helmsman. The church, standing straight as a frigate, its mast perfectly vertical, started snaking down the pebbly surface of the waters. The ropes that had held it in place stretched to their fullest to keep it back, then gave way, uncoiling gracefully from the posts and trees and turning the church loose. On this point all narrators agree: the ropes uncoiled effortlessly, as if of their own volition, and whether this is explained away vaguely, as due to the driving force of the ice, or stated proudly, as part of the miracle, nobody overlooks the moment when the ropes let go of the church. Astounded beyond terror, the women watched the church grow smaller and smaller as it proceeded downriver. At times, through the din of the torrents and the thawing of the ice, they thought they could make out voices, voices that could only belong to the men inside. And though what they heard could only be cries of despair or pleas for help, the women stubbornly insisted, themselves amazed at their words, that the sounds coming from within the church and echoing down the water were songs, that the men sailing off were singing horas.

On this bewildering note (which would have been impossible to accept had the storytellers themselves not presented it as incredible and thereby, paradoxically, made it seem unequivocally believable) the historically verifiable account (down to the most outlandish detail) of the church of Subpiatră comes to an end. Everything I have related so far was seen by eyewitnesses and retold by their children, grandchildren, and great-grandchildren. The proofs are in evidence to this day—the bare foundation of the church still visible in the old cemetery of Lugoşu de Jos, the deep ruts in the road called the Church's Furrow, the place that goes by the name of the Ice Hole of the Church, the unnaturally deep ford at the narrow headwaters of the Criş, where even now a child will sometimes drown. Everything I have related so far actually took place. All the rest is hope—a dream belonging not to me but to the villagers who were both the heroes and the bards of the events. And if I can reproduce all the richness of detail of their story, it will be because of my fascination—from the beginning—with the absence of boundaries between the real and the imaginary. Reality flowed into dream, according to God knows what mysterious laws, as unexpectedly and dramatically as gall can seep into the bloodstream.

At first, the sensation that something was terribly wrong overcame even the feeling of sorrow—not so much because the misfortune appeared incomprehensible as because it seemed so intentional. The sense of the miraculous that had filled the village with its euphoria went through a crisis of confidence; people started to give interpretations, mundane and harmful to all concerned, of facts that up to then had required no interpreting. A strange reversal occurred: as long as everything had been unquestionably real, the outcome of their own work, they had considered it fantastic, but the moment things went out of control and took a turn for the fantastic, they analyzed them, as if suspecting a fraud. Father Nicola's expectant glance upriver, his summons to the men on the bank, and especially the strange singing coming from the church—all these led them to believe that the events had been somehow foreordained. Things were complicated even further by the ropes uncoiling of their own will (though what if they had been cut?) and by the church sailing confidently down the river (heading where?), ambiguities that cast a shadow over the grief of the village mourning its lost men. The peasants' sorrow mingled incongruously with doubt, anger, and curiosity, feelings that together formed a fertile terrain, rich in omens, for the dream that was to follow.

In the spring of 1779, five years before the great peasant uprising led by Horea, soldiers of the emperor in Vienna, together with agents of the Hungarian landowners, were combing the villages of the western Carpathians in search of that notorious agitator *(ille famosus agitator)*. Eventually they reached Subpiatră. I cannot claim that the inhabitants of Subpiatră had never heard of Horea or were ignorant of the exaggerated tales—verging on legend—about him, but they believed they had never seen him, and it was only that spring that they heard the facts about him, facts they later mulled over in secret gatherings.

The emperor's men were looking for a certain Nicola Ursu, nicknamed Horea, a builder of churches and a skillful singer from the village of Albac. They asked the people of Subpiatră if Horea had paid them a visit and offered to build them a church or address grievances to the emperor on their behalf, if he had sung for them or urged them to revolt. Strangely, as if by unspoken agreement, the villagers said nothing, either about the extraordinary journey of their church or about Father Nicola. Only after the soldiers had left did they begin to put the facts together (amazed at their own reaction, which they could only attribute to the miracle they had been honoring for over a year), and came to the conclusion—by a swift, firm shift in their collective psyche—that Father Nicola was none other than Nicola Ursu from Albac, the man called Horea. They reached this conclusion with evident, almost radiant, relief, as if it suddenly made everything logical and clear.

Soon thereafter news began pouring into the village. The more incredible it was, the more promptly and enthusiastically it was reported. First it was rumored that a church had been seen cruising like a ship down the Criş River, its sails, fastened to a steeple-mast, billowing in the wind. Then they heard that Horea had set off to see the emperor with the people's petitions. That settled the matter. The women recalled the linen they had woven at Father Nicola's behest and were proud to have been involved in so daring an adventure. Facts fell into place and took on a design that—it was increasingly obvious—had long before been masterminded by Father Nicola. The priest's name, which everyone now accepted as Horea, was pronounced with true conspiratorial pleasure, both as a sign of the mystery that united them all and as a token of the undeniable importance that secret had conferred on them. After weeping for many days and many nights, the women whose husbands had been called to the church were now respected and looked upon—by virtue of their suffering—as equal participants in the expedition. None of the villagers doubted that their church had been chosen from the start for the journey which, from the Criş down the Tisa, from the Tisa down the Danube, was to take the delegation of mountain peasants to the emperor in Vienna. Of course, the miraculous transformation of a church into a ship and its miraculous advance down the thin thread of water lost none of their significance by joining forces with the true wonder that was the birth of a leader. The miracle no longer required separate acceptance: if you believed in Horea's strength, you took everything about his acts or existence for granted, without any possibility of doubt or need for proof.

The legends from Subpiatră do not say whether the men who left with the church ever returned after Horea, back from Vienna, urged the people to revolt, but the documents of the uprising do mention an unusually large number of rebels from this particular village in the western Carpathians following their leader to the bitter end in the terrible winter of 1785. When it was all over, the peasants of Subpiatră, the few that were left, returned in silence, as if awakened from a dream they had taken for reality and continued to believe in, while choosing to view reality as a harsh and incomprehensible slumber. Reports of the executions in Alba Iulia found the villagers locked in an impenetrable silence, gazing on the outside world with an unwavering, untrusting eye from behind bolted doors and drawn-up bridges. And though they never spoke, they seemed to say, "Your attempts to frighten us are in vain. We know that everything is only part of this bad dream. Reality is otherwise; we have just returned from it. And things are quite different there." Only when they were alone—beyond the ultimate wall, the wall of silence that shielded them from themselves—did they shut their eyes, daring to face the deep and slippery place where doubt lived, chained and gagged, but still babbling on and on, "Which is the true reality?"

And just when too much time had elapsed for doubt to lie hidden any longer, just when, in its deep and slippery vault doubt had grown stealthily and threatened to break its chains at any moment, to erupt in the rotting silence of uncertainty, a rumor came from the other reality, hard to believe yet impossible not to accept, and started the debate all over again. A man journeying back to the Romanian Lands from the great sea had come upon the church floating down the Danube, its sail joined to a cross-topped mast, and he spoke of the event with awe, not knowing it was their church. He had seen it clearly one evening as it floated gently on the lazy surface of the water, and described not only the porch with its notched pillars and carved panels running like a twisted rope around the base of the church but also the candles burning inside as if on Easter morn. He had seen no one, the traveler hastened to add, seized with a wonder akin to dread, nor would he have expected to. The scene was so tranquil and serene that the church might have seemed deserted had it not been for the deep manly voices singing secular music, not hymns but haunting strains filled with anxiety, which made sense only later, when he realized what he was hearing from the unseen men in the church lit up as for Easter was a *hora*.

After the stranger left (never suspecting the turmoil he had wrought in the souls of his listeners, who accepted his story greedily, as those denied hope always accept the miraculous), the news he had brought so molded the spirit of that mountain hamlet that even now, two centuries later, it is utterly different from its neighboring villages. A quiet but stubborn pride—its source the deep mystery that could not be disclosed but that illuminated everything from within—lends to this day a defiant and enigmatic grace to the women, a secret vigor to the men. Even now, when the days of the revolt are lost in the mists of history and the church's voyage is but a legend recounted to tourists, the inhabitants of Subpiatră (forest rangers, workers in the furniture factory, commuters to the towns of Ştei or Beiuş, hurried passengers crowding into dusty, rickety buses, people for whom history exists only in long-forgotten schoolbooks and on the television screen that they doze in front of) have a secret of their own that shows in their laconic words and penetrating gaze: "That's right, everything is as you see it—not very good and nothing to be done about it. But it doesn't really matter. There's another reality in which things are completely different." Obviously, the villagers themselves are unaware of their uniqueness; they would be the first to express surprise at what I have just said, just as they would be amazed if I mentioned the touch of unmistakable defiance, absent in other country people, that characterizes their gestures, words, and demeanor. To me it is evident that, unbeknownst to them, some of the shock of unquestioningly accepting the miracle as part of their existence— everyday reality thus becoming a mere deviation, a secondary projection, easy to ignore—has transformed the very core of their being. The people who (smiling ironically, their emotion barely surfacing) tell the story of the strange traveler and its influence on the psychology of their village at the end of the eighteenth century show the unconditional acceptance of the tale in their own psyche and behavior. I have always been fascinated by the impossibility of establishing facts in an absolute manner, the sensation that anything, no matter how simple and indisputable, can acquire (as it basks in the bright light of that unconscious, bewildering defiance) complex connotations, contradictory interpretations, new meanings. Throughout their long history, tragic and devoid of hope, flowing down paradisiacal valleys topped by fairy-tale peaks, the villagers' absurd yet profoundly optimistic belief that miracles do exist ultimately made miracles occur over and over again.

I was a child when I first heard about the church floating down the river, saving its heroes from martyrdom and the people's faith from disbelief. It happened one summer many years ago, when I was accompanying my father—a passionate hiker—on one of those treks that delighted my early years. Everything I learned then is still intact and intangible within me, crowned by misty haloes of wonder and uncertainty. When I went back to Subpiatră as an adult, I feared that nothing would be left of the tale that had so charmed my childhood: it might have all been just a flower blossoming on the threshold of sleep, a perfect fruit ripening in the orchard of dreams. It would not have been the first time I discovered how utterly incongruent the images in my memory were to reality.

Aware of my tendency (which I concealed and cherished like a vice) to let fantasy mingle illicitly with the truths surrounding it and take on their hues and shapes so that no alien glance, no matter how profound, could distinguish between them, I passed through adolescence with a persistent feeling of guilt, a lasting fear that I might be found out. The less I could tell the difference between fantasy and reality, the greater my guilt became. Before going to bed at night or while painfully trying to take a nap during the long afternoons, I would review the day's occurrences in my mind, correcting their shameful or embarrassing aspects so that, as I recast them for filing in my memory, the central character, me, gained in intelligence, kindness, and daring, without losing credence. Then I would finally fall asleep, whereupon everything took a definite shape in its subtly revised version. After a while I would forget the original, though a dim glow of guilt remained, a guilt that I carried throughout my childhood and that sometimes envelops me even now.

To my surprise, however, the beautiful tale did not exist solely in my mind: as an adult prepared to accept even the most prosaic of accounts, I came across the story almost word for word among the recitations offered to tourists by the inhabitants of Subpiatră. I relished revisiting the tale, whose improbability had given it the courage (or prudence) to arm itself with so many proofs of its veracity. I relished driving along the Church's Furrow and bathing (together with West German hikers pausing for a rest) in the Ice Hole of the Church. These topographical traces, like markers on the road to the Surreal, strengthened my feelings of certainty. It was as if my own private experiences gained credibility by being linked to the truthfulness of the events. But no matter how much the storytellers' personalities caught my attention and my own recollections colored the story's fantastic outline, I still believed only in the spirit, not the letter, of the account. I was moved, yes, but with admiration for its mysterious and timeless naïveté. The adult's nostalgic superiority surrounds even the final episode of the journey of the church of Subpiatră, with its confusing interplay between real and unreal, possible and impossible.

A few years ago, during a very mild September, I traveled to the Danube Delta to write about its magnificence for a foreign tourist magazine. But what impressed me most, more than the unsurpassed strength of its waters and land and the unrivaled beauty of its birds and fish, which I described for the benefit of septuagenarian American women and tottering Scandinavian men (so they would gratefully spend their currency in Romanian hotels, restaurants, and fisheries), were the residents of this swampy terrain, halfway between water and dry land. Bearded and taciturn, they kept themselves aloof from civilization as well as history, obeying mysterious laws that rarely coincided with those of the uncaring world around them and many times vehemently opposed them. In those villages, so stable in their beliefs, though lying on land so unstable, my wordless queries were unable to break the people's tight-lipped silence, a silence like a door slammed in my face.

One morning, well before dawn (in fact, just after two o'clock, when the moon had set), I went fishing with the crew of the Timofteanu family, father, sons, and sons-in-law. They seemed indifferent to my presence, with the almost insulting indifference that closed communities display toward strangers. Yet I could not say that their silence bothered me. I was grateful to them for accepting me among them; I could not ask for more. They talked among themselves without paying me the slightest heed, totally unconcerned about having excluded me. As far as I could make out, there was something troubling them, some cause for anxiety I was ignorant of. But something—I don't know what— made me sense it was of a mysterious nature, out of the ordinary even for them, perhaps supernatural.

"Stepan saw it," one of them remarked. "He swears he saw it. And he hadn't touched a drop of vodka for two days."

"He was dead drunk last night," another voice rejoined, distrustful, withdrawn.

"True, but he got drunk afterwards. He swears by everything sacred," insisted the first, as if something vital to them all were tied up with Stepan's credibility.

"God, who'd have thought it!" said a third voice, bursting into laughter. But he said nothing more, his mirth ending abruptly.

My back turned to them, I stood looking at the Danube, its waters a quivering mirror for the setting moon. I was trying to guess what it was all about. It was like a game. Their fears had no power over me.

"Victor saw it too," the old man said, breaking the long silence. I could tell it was his voice by its hollow hoarseness and by the deferential quiet that followed. But it was not merely respect for the old man that had made the others listen to him in awe. His words had disturbed them profoundly. If Victor had seen what Stepan had, then everything was suddenly different; the event had taken on a much greater significance.

"When was it?" one of them asked.

"Last night."

There seemed to be nothing more to say. The ensuing pause was so long that I involuntarily turned my head to see what was going on. They were all staring down the river, scrutinizing the vast expanse of water. Some stood erect; others were bent forward, though they could have seen nothing even if there had been something to see: the moon had set and the stars that were still visible, though brighter now, were too feeble to illuminate the night.

"We'd better go back," someone said. No one answered, and the suggestion remained suspended in a night that was growing thinner, more apprehensive. The weather was calm; clearly it was not a storm that had given them cause for alarm. And since I was a mere spectator, unable to take part in their drama, I could only stand back and watch, the heightened suspense enhancing the value of the performance.

"Did they hear it too?" somebody else queried, then quickly added: "Did Victor hear it too?" And since no response came I guessed that someone had nodded or shaken his head.

"What were they singing?" a voice close to me whispered, one I had not heard before.

"What they always sing," the old man answered, almost with a snarl.

There was no way I could find out what they meant, and that both annoyed and excited me. I felt involved in a great adventure, yet I hoped I would never have to discover the reason for their mute, anxious terror. I only wanted to take back with me, unaltered, their restless silence, like a gift that the universe, its mysteries parceled out in trivial realities, sometimes decides to offer us. This did not happen, but the solution to the puzzle exceeded by far my need for the miraculous.

Day had not yet broken, but vague contours loomed in the darkness of the disintegrating night. The dim outlines of the riverbanks looked strangely expressive. The air smelled saltier, felt colder; we were approaching the sea. No one had said a word for over an hour; only the engine whirred at times, like a teased, maddened cat. Then, all of a sudden, someone turned off the engine and the men started rowing. In the eerie stillness, interrupted only by the rhythmic splash-splash of the oars as they rose in the gray air and sank eagerly back into the water, we heard the song. At first I paid no heed to it; I thought it might be a transistor radio left on in the boat. Maybe I didn't really think about it at all: a song from nowhere is just another banal reality, one that no longer registers in our dulled minds. It was the unnatural tension I felt behind me, the oars pausing oddly in midair, that made me listen more intently. The singing rose in an uncanny crescendo, as if someone were turning up the volume, slowly but steadily, on an invisible radio. In an instant I became aware that the sound couldn't possibly be coming from anywhere near me. Nobody was singing, nothing was playing in our boat, and there was no other boat either up-or downstream.

"There she is," I heard the old man say, almost in a whisper, yet clearly, over the rising song. What surprised me was not so much his tone, in which awe verging on joy had replaced terror, but the use of the feminine to describe a reality that had nothing feminine about it. The song we were hearing (though it may have been just a tune, since it was hard to say whether there were words in its tumultuous waves) was sung by deep male voices in a pitch so low that it sounded like a murmur weirdly amplified by night and wind. I turned and stared at the fishermen. By now it was light enough for me to distinguish their features. Their faces were more than half covered by untrimmed beards, and matted hair grazed their bushy eyebrows, but their eyes burned from beneath the rebellious mass of hair with a brightness that stood out against the dull thatch. The expression in the men's eyes, as they strained to see what they could only hear, was one of intense expectancy, as if they knew what was about to happen yet did not fear it in the least. By now I could tell that the mysterious "she" did not refer to the song we were hearing, which was only secondary in importance, but to what was about to be revealed, to what they shuddered yet waited impatiently to see. Our boat had been slowly making its way down the Danube, drifting along with the current, when all at once it veered sharply around a bend in the river. As I stood gazing upstream I suddenly knew that the curve in the river's course had disclosed something. The fishermen's eyes widened, lighting up with a mixture of elation and dread. But there was joy in their dread, if that can be believed—a dread almost relieved that it could finally be expressed. I realized that at long last they had seen "her," and I turned to see for myself.

It must have been four o'clock by then, and the atmosphere, halfway between day and night, was oppressive, uncertain. Yet under the smooth gray sky and in the pearly, fluorescent dawn the view had broadened considerably. The river's banks had spread out, and in the distance, where sky and water merged, the sea seemed to be breathing deeply, like a beast not yet roused from its slumber. There, where landscape ended and dream began, a church rose above the waters, silhouetted against the horizon. It looked so familiar to me that at first I was neither surprised nor frightened, and my gaze subconsciously traveled beyond it. Only seconds later did it strike me that this church from the western Carpathians, with its carved porch and slender spire, did not belong here, at the mouth of the Danube, in the gentle caress of the morning sea breeze. And the moment I realized it, the story came back to me. I cannot say if the windows were lit by the rising sun or by burning tapers, but in the grayish morn the dark silhouette of the church swaying on the waves seemed to glow from inside, as on holy days, with a joyful fire that yet did not consume it. And the dancing flames formed the very image of the *hora*, the dance whose melody had swept over us, the more disquieting as not a soul could be seen in the church.

And I knew at once it was the church from Subpiatră. I stared as we approached it at unusually high speed (had the water accelerated its course all of a sudden, or did it merely seem faster because the church itself was getting closer?) as if I had seen her before, as if I knew her well. Now she was revealing herself to me, as if I were a long-lost relative, one of her own. Even when I realized she did not belong there (no matter how strange it might seem), I still wasn't surprised. It was as if I had expected the apparition, as if I, too, had always believed the story of the church's journey. In the meantime she had pulled up alongside us, her advance raising waves so high that they lifted and lowered our boat like a walnut shell. The song could still be heard, dizzyingly, maddeningly, a *hora* sung in perfect rhythm, suggesting the syncopated movements of the dance. Yet her festively lit interior was empty. When she passed us, so near I could have reached out and touched her, she looked incredibly tall. I leaned back to see her top. To my astonishment, an immense sail towered above the porch, billowing in the wind. It may have been too far away for me to see before, or it may not have unfurled until she started upriver. For without a doubt the church was heading upstream, fast enough for her progress to be seen with the naked eye, her bulk stirring up ever greater waves in the resistant waters, waves forcing our boat in toward shore. As she glided along her steeple swayed almost imperceptibly, and once or twice it tilted so much it made the whole church list precariously. Then we caught a glimpse of the ancient base of the church, now covered with moss and barnacles, deep down in the water. I don't know why this indecent display of the innermost parts of the being that the church of Subpiatră had become for me troubled me more than her very presence. For while her advance up the river was clearly a miracle, those old beams, furry with moss, were a telling detail that forced me to consider everything in a logical sequence. The image of the smooth mountain wood strangely overgrown with algae and shells kept bothering me until I remembered the logs that the church (felled like a living tree) had been cut from, far away in Lugoşu de Jos, logs blanketed in moss as thick as lamb's wool. And once I connected the two, I suddenly grasped the concrete nature of the facts. One thing was certain: there was nothing subjective about the church's passage alongside our boat. Its laborious progress, with its steeple turned mast, gave no hint of the ethereal or intangible. It was real, utterly real. And it was only such indisputable reality that would be able to enter the realm of the supernatural.

Once the church had passed us, my companions seemed exhausted and confused, as if having received a message they didn't know what to do with and whose meaning was beyond them. I sat down facing them, certain that the trial by fire of this apparition had overcome the abyss of silence that had made us feel we belonged to different species. To be honest, the most astonishing part had not been the appearance of the church itself—that was familiar, something I had long known—but its significance for this colorless world, so far removed from my own. It astounded me not so much that they had seen the church as that she seemed to belong to their universe, possess an importance I could not grasp. Moreover, I could not fathom how much of the church's true story was known here in the Danube Delta, how much had remained unchanged within the changed conditions of the community's spirit. I had trouble imagining the Timofteanu crew talking about Horea or having even a vague idea about the village in the western Carpathians to which their phantom rightfully belonged. For I only had to look into the fishermen's somber eyes to understand that they had seen a ghost, a ghost whose ominous significance was clear to them. Surprisingly, when I asked them about it, they spoke of it simply, with no reticence, as if by having seen the floating church together we had somehow become related, as if I had become part of their universe and they were amazed that I too had been vouchsafed the vision.

Some time later I returned to the western Carpathians as if to a spring, eager to tell about the distant places its waters had reached. The villagers of Subpiatră were stupefied to hear that their miraculous church was known as the Dead Church at the mouth of the Danube. What distinguished their place of worship from all others in the eyes of these mountain peasants was its intense, even supernatural vitality: the sailing church was not only alive, incredibly alive, she was a savior of life. While for the Danube fishermen she was a phantom, inhabited by corpses and presaging death, for the people of Subpiatră she was a denial of death, counteracting, annulling the rebels' execution on Hanging

Forks Hill in Alba Iulia. I hastened to tell them what I had seen, certain that it would please them and reconfirm their belief in the miracle. But I discovered that my account saddened them: what they needed was not so much outside confirmation as acknowledgment of their own truth.

One warm evening that smelled of smoke, milk fresh from the cow, and *mămăligă* (a smell that remains for me the most ineffable definition of the Romanian village—as long as it exists, the village itself exists, no matter how "commuterized" its inhabitants may have become), I was sitting on the porch of the parish house in Subpiatră, talking with the young priest, just out of seminary, who, with his long blond hair, thick beard, and checked shirt, and rolled-up sleeves, looked more like a nonconformist artist than a cleric. He had been born in the very house where he was now master, and was following his father into the pulpit. His decision had been sudden and unexpected, as he had almost finished his degree in architecture. His father, the village priest for over forty years, was also the son of the village priest. (Such dynasties were once quite common in Transylvania, but few have survived to the present.) I had known the young priest since childhood—we were about the same age—and I remember even today the prestige he gained in my eyes when, the day after I heard the story of the church, he took me to visit the places that proved its reality: the furrow, the ford, the cut-off foundation. I never forgot it, and ever since I have considered myself related to him by virtue of the tale.

"What is life to some is death to others. It's very natural," the young priest said, his gaze fixed on the village church, perched high on a hill and surrounded by a churchyard where the sun was decorously setting among the crosses. "The revolt that brings death in its wake and thus leads to immortality—that is, to life—is open to both interpretations, without changing any facts or distorting any meanings."

His words sounded both bewildering and familiar. Maybe I had heard them before or thought of them myself. Yet I sensed that the story of the church was more complicated than his summary made it out to be. The church taken by the waters was the sign of the uprising's defeat, and at the same time, of its profound, though barely perceivable, victory. All its meanings were gathered forever in the elliptical, inflexible line of the legend; the rest was ideology. I followed the young man's gaze. His little wooden church stood out against the reddish dusk, incredibly graceful and fragile, its tall pillars carved masterfully, its dagger-thin steeple topped by a cross that softened the sharpness, its notched swath of wood winding around it like a tightly knotted rope. It looked exactly as I had always pictured the other one.

"I've never asked you," I said to my friend, using that casual conversational tone one resumes at the end of serious discussions to signal that they are over, "I've always meant to ask you—when was the present village church built?"

"It wasn't built," he replied matter-of-factly, though slightly startled by my question. "It was brought here."

I turned to him, at first not understanding his meaning, then not daring to pursue my thought. He looked at me, almost amused at my confusion, yet puzzled as well and curious to know what I was thinking.

"This is the church," he said smiling. And only then did he express his astonishment. "Didn't they ever tell you how the story ended?"

THE SNOW PAVILION
Angela Carter

British author Angela Carter was one of the most important fantasists of this century; her early death of cancer in 1992 was a blow to both genre and mainstream readers, beloved as she was by both. Carter published many acclaimed novels, stories, and essay collections including the award-winning *Nights at the Circus, Several Perceptions* and *The Magic Toyshop*. Of particular interest to fantasy readers are her dark and groundbreaking adult fairy tales, most of which were published in her collection *The Bloody Chamber*.

"The Snow Pavilion" was found among Carter's unpublished papers after her death. It was published in the U.S. last year in *Burning Your Boats: The Collected Short Stories of Angela Carter* (introduced by Salman Rushdie). This gothic tale is vintage Angela Carter: sensual and disquieting. It is an honor to present Ms. Carter's work in the *Year's Best Fantasy and Horror* series one last time.

—T. W. and E. D.

The motor stalled in the middle of a snowy landscape, lodged in a rut, wouldn't budge an inch. How I swore! I'd planned to be snug in front of a roaring fire, by now, a single malt on the mahogany wine-table (a connoisseur's piece) beside me, the five courses of Melissa's dinner savorously aromatising the kitchen; to complete the décor, a labrador retriever's head laid on my knee as trustingly as if I were indeed a country gentleman and lolled by rights among the chintz. After dinner, before I read our customary pre-coital poetry aloud to her, my elegant and accomplished mistress, also a connoisseur's piece, might play the piano for her part-time pasha while I sipped black, acrid coffee from her precious little cups.

Melissa was rich, beautiful and rather older than I. The servants slipped me looks of sly complicity; no matter how carefully I rumpled my sheets, they knew when a bed hadn't been slept in. The master of the house had a pied-à-terre in London when the House was sitting, and the House was sitting tight. I'd met him only once, at the same dinner party where I'd met her—he'd been off-hand with me, gruff. I was young and handsome and full of promise; my relations with husbands rarely prospered. Wives were quite amother matter. Women, as Mayakovosky justly opined, are very partial to poets.

And now her glamorous motor car had broken down in the snow. I'd borrowed it for a trip to Oxford, ostensibly to buy books, utilizing, with my instinctual cunning, the weather as an excuse. Last night, the old woman had been shaking her mattress with a vengeance—such snow! When I woke up the bedroom was full of luminous snow light, catching in the coils of Melissa's honey-colored hair, and I'd experienced, once again, but, this time, almost uncontrollably, the sense of claustrophobia that sometimes afflicted me when I was with her.

I'd said, let's read some snowy poetry together, after dinner tonight, Melissa, a tribute of white verses to the iconography of the weather. Any excuse, no matter how far fetched, to get her out of the house—too much luxury on an empty stomach, that was the trouble. Always the same eyes too big for his belly, as grandma used to say; grandma spotted the trait when this little fellow lisped and toddled and pissed the bed before he knew what luxury was, even. Cultural indigestion, I tell you, the gripe in the bowels of your spirit. How can I get out of here, away from her subtly flawed antique mirrors, her French perfume decanted into eighteenth-century crystal bottles, her inscrutably smirking ancestresses in their gilt, oval frames? And her dolls, worst of all, her blasted dolls.

Those dolls that had never have been played with, her fine collection of antique women, part of the apparatus of Melissa's charm, her piquant originality that lay well on the safe side of quaint. A dozen or so of the finest lived in her bedroom in a glass-fronted, satinwood cabinet lavishly equipped with such toyland artefacts as miniature sofas and teeny-tiny grand pianos. They had heads made of moulded porcelain, each dimple and bee-stung underlip sculpted with loving care. Their wigs and over-lifelike eyelashes were made of real hair. She told me their eyes had been manufactured by the same craftsman in glass who made those terribly precious paperweights filled with magic snowstorms. Whenever I woke up in Melissa's bed, the first thing I saw were a dozen pairs of shining eyes that seemed to gleam wetly, as if in lacrimonious accusation of my presence there, for the dolls, like Melissa, were perfect ladies and I, in my upwardly social mobile nakedness—a nakedness that was, indeed, the essential battledress for such storm-troopers as I!—patently no gentleman.

After three days of that kind of style, I badly needed to sit in a public bar, drink coarse pints of bitter, swap double entendres with the barmaid; but I could hardly tell milady that. Instead, I must use my vocation to justify my day off. Lend me the car, Melissa, so that I can drive to Oxford and buy a book of snowy verses, since there's no such book in the house. And I'd made my purchase and managed to fit in my bread, cheese and badinage as well. A good day. Then, almost home again and here I was, stuck fast.

The fields were all brim-full of snow and the dark sky of late afternoon already swollen and discolored with the next fall. Flocks of crows wheeled endlessly upon the invisible carousels of the upper air, occasionally emitting a rusty caw. A glance beneath the bonnet showed me only that I did not know what was wrong and must get out to trudge along a lane where the mauve shadows told me snow and the night would arrive together. My breath smoked. I wound Melissa's husband's muffler round my neck and dug my fists into his sheepskin pockets; his borrowed coat kept me snug and warm although the cold made the nerves in my forehead hum with a thin, high sound like that of the wind in telephone wires.

The leafless trees, the hillside quilted by intersections of dry-stone walling— all had been subdued to monochrome by the severity of last night's blizzard. Snow clogged every sound but that of the ironic punctuation of the crows. No sign of another presence; the pastoral cows were all locked up in the steaming byre, Colin Clout and Hobbinol sucked their pipes by the fireside in pastoral domesticity. Who would be outside, today, when he could be warm and dry, inside.

Too white. It is too white, out. Silence and whiteness at such a pitch of twinned intensity you know what it must be like to live in a country where snow is not a charming, since infrequent, visitor that puts its cold garlands on the trees so prettily we think they are playing at blossoming. (What an aptly fragile simile, with its Botticellian nuance. I congratulated myself.) No. Today is as cold as the killing cold of the perpetually white countries; today's atrocious candor is that of those white freckles that are the stigmata of frostbite.

My sensibility, the exquisite sensibility of a minor poet, tingled and crisped at the sight of so much whiteness.

I was certain that soon I'd come to a village where I could telephone Melissa; then she would send the village taxi for me. But the snow-fields now glimmered spectrally in an ever-thickening light and still there was no sign of life about me in the whole, white world but for the helmeted crows creaking down towards their nests.

Then I came to a pair of wrought-iron gates standing open on a drive. There must be some mansion or other at the end of the drive that would offer me shelter and, if they were half as rich as they ought to be, to live in such style, then they would certainly know Melissa and might even have me driven back to her by their own chauffeur in a warm car that would smell deliciously of new leather. I was sure they must be rich, the countryside was lousy with the rich; hadn't I flattened a brace of pheasants on my way to Oxford? Encouraged, I turned in between the gate-posts, on which snarled iron gryphons sporting circumcision caps of snow.

The drive wound through an elm copse where the upper limbs of the bare trees were clogged with beastly lice of old crows' nests. I could tell that nobody had come this way since the snow fell, for only rabbit slots and the cuneiform prints of birds marked surfaces already crisping with frost. The drive took me uphill. My shoes and trouser bottoms were already wet through; it grew darker, colder, and the old woman must have given her mattress a tentative shake or two, again, for a few more flakes drifted down and caught on my eyelashes so I first saw that house through a dazzle as of unshed tears, although, I assure you, I was out of the habit of crying.

I had reached the brow of a hill. Before me, in a hollow, magically surrounded by a snowy formal garden, lay a jewel of a mansion in a voluptuous style of English renaissance and every one of its windows blazed with light. I imagined myself describing it to Melissa—'a vista like visible Debussy.' Enchanting. But, though lights streamed out in every direction, all was silent except for the crackling of the frosty trees. Lights and frost; in the winter sky above me, stars were coming out. Especially for my cultured patroness, I made an elision of the stars in the mansion of the heavens and the lights of the great house. So who was it, this snowy afternoon, who'd bagged a triad of fine images for her? Why, her clever boy! How pleased she'd be. And now I could declare the image factory closed for the day and get on with the real business of living, the experience of which that lovely house seemed to promise me in such abundance.

Yet, since the place was so well lit, the front door at the top of the serpentine staircase left open as for expected guests, why were there still no traces of arrivals or departures in the snow on which my footprints extended backwards to the lane and Melissa's abandoned car? And no figures to be glimpsed through any window, nor sound of life at all?

The vast empty hall serenely dominated by an immense chandelier, the faceted pendants of which chinked faintly in the currents of warm air and stippled with shifting, prismatic shadows walls wreathed in white stucco. This chandelier intimidated me, like too grand a butler but, all the same, I found the bellpull and tugged it. Somewhere inside a full-mouthed bell tolled; its reverberations set the chandelier a-tinkle but even when everything settled down again, nobody came.

I hauled again on the bellpull; still no reply, but a sudden wind blew a flurry of snow or sleet around me into the hall. The chandelier rocked musically in the draught. Behind me, outside, the air was full of the taste of snow—the storm was about to begin again. Nothing for it but to step bravely over the indifferent threshold and stamp my feet on the doormat with enough éclat to announce my arrival to the entire ground floor.

It was by far the most magnificent house I'd ever seen, and warm, so warm my frozen fingers throbbed. Yet all was white inside as the night outside, white walls, white paint, white drapes and a faint perfume everywhere, as though many rich women in beautiful dresses had drifted through the hall on their way to drinks before dinner, leaving behind them their spoor of musk and civet. The very air, here, mimicked the caress of their naked arms, intimate, voluptuous, rare.

My nostrils flared and quivered. I should have liked to have made love to every one of those lovely beings whose presence here was most poignant in her absence; it was a house built and furnished only for pleasure, for the indulgence of the flesh, for elegant concupiscence. I felt like Mignon in the land of the lemon trees; this is the place where I would like to live. I screwed up sufficient wincing courage to shout out: "Anyone at home?" But only the chandelier tinkled in reply.

Then, a sudden creak behind me; I spun round to see the door swing to on its hinges with a soft, inexorable click. At that, the chandelier above me seemed to titter uncontrollably, as if with glee to see me locked in.

It is the wind, only the wind. Try to believe it is only the wind that blew the door shut behind you, keep a strong hold on that imagination of yours.

Stop that shaking, all at once uneasy; walk slowly to the door, don't look nervous. It is the wind. Or else—perhaps—a trick of the owners, a practical joke. I grasped the notion gratefully. I knew the rich loved practical jokes.

But as soon as I realised it must be a practical joke, I knew I was not alone in the house because its apparent emptiness was all part of the joke. Then I exchanged one kind of unease for another. I became terribly self-conscious. Now I must watch my step; whatever happened, I must look as if I knew how to play the game in which I found myself. I tried the door but I was locked firmly in, of course. In spite of myself, I felt a faint panic, stifled it . . . No, you are *not* at their mercy.

The hall remained perfectly empty. Closed doors on either side of me; the staircase swept up to an empty landing. Am I to meet my hosts in embarrassment and humiliation, will they all come bouncing—"boo!"—out of hidey holes in the panelling, from behind sweeping curtains to make fun of me? A huge mirror behind an extravagant arrangement of arum lilies showed me a poor poet not altogether convincingly rigged out in borrowed country squire's gear. I thought, how pinched and pale my face looks; a face that's eaten too much bread and margarine in its time. Come, now, liven up! You left bread and margarine behind you long ago, at grandma's house. Now you are a houseguest of the Lady Melissa. Your car has just broken down in the lane; you are looking for assistance.

Then, to my relief but also my increased disquiet, I saw a face behind my own, reflected, like mine, in the mirror. She must have known I could spy her, peeking at me behind my back. It was a pale, soft, pretty face, streaming blonde hair, and it sprang out quite suddenly from the reflections of the backs of the lilies. But when I turned, she—young, tricksy, fleet of foot—was gone already, though I could have sworn I heard a carillon of giggles, unless my sharp, startled movement had disturbed the chandelier, again.

This fleeting apparition let me know for sure I was observed. ("How amusing, a game of hide-and-seek. All the same, do you think, perhaps, the chauffeur could . . .") With the sullen knowledge of myself as appointed clown, I opened the first door I came to on the ground floor, expecting to discover my tittering audience awaiting me.

It was perfectly empty.

A white on white reception room, all bleached, all pale, sidetables of glass and chrome, artifacts of white lacquer, upholstery of thick, white velvet. Company was expected; there were decanters, bowls of ice, dishes of nuts and olives. I was tempted to swallow a cut-glass tumbler full of something-or-other, to snatch a handful of salted almonds—I was parched and starving, only that pub sandwich since breakfast. But it would never do to be caught in the act by the fair-haired girl I'd glimpsed in the hall. Look, she's left her doll behind her, forgotten in the deep cushioning of an armchair.

How the rich indulge their children! Not a doll so much as a little work of art; the cash register at the back of my mind rang up twenty guineas at the sight of this floppy Pierrot with his skull-cap, his white satin pajamas with the black buttons down the front, all complete, and that authentic pout of comic sadness on his fine china face. *Mon ami Pierrot*, poor old fellow, limp limbs adangle, all anguished sensibility and no moral fiber. I know how you feel. But, as I exchanged my glance of pitying complicity with him, there came a sharp, melodious twang like a note from an imperious tuning fork, from beyond the half-open double doors. After a startled moment, I sprang into the dining room, summoned.

I had never seen anything like that dining room, except at the movies—not even at the dinner where I'd met Melissa. Fifteen covers laid out on a tongue-shaped spit of glass; but I hardly had time to take in the splendor of the fine china, the lead crystal, because the door into the hall still swung on its hinges and I knew I had missed her by seconds. So the daughter of the house is indeed playing "catch" with me; and where has she got to, now?

Soft, softly on the white carpets; I leave deep prints behind me but do not make a sound. And still no sign of life, only the pale shadows of the candles; yet, somehow, everywhere a sense of hushed expectancy, as of the night before Christmas.

Then I heard a patter of running footsteps. But these footsteps came from a part of the house where no carpets muffled them, somewhere high above me. As I poised, ears a-twitch, there came from upstairs or downstairs, or milady's chamber, a spring of thin, high laughter agitating the chandeliers; then the sound of many, many running feet overhead. For a moment, the whole house seemed to tremble with unseen movement; then, just as suddenly, all was silent again.

I resolutely set myself to search the upper rooms.

All these rooms were quite empty. But my always nascent paranoia, now tingling at the tip of every nerve, assured me they had all been vacated the very moment I entered them. Every now and then, as I made my increasingly grim-faced tour of the house, I heard bursts of all kinds of delicious merriments but never from the room next to the one in which I stood. These voices started and stopped as if switched on and off and, of course, were part and parcel of the joke; this joke was, my unease. In what, by its size and luxury, must have been the master bedroom, the polar bearskin rug thrown over the bed was warm and rumpled as if someone had just been lying there and now hid, per-haps, in the ivorine wardrobe, enjoying my perplexity. And I could have wrecked their fun if only—if only!—I had the courage to fling open the pale doors and catch my reluctant hosts crouching, as I thought, among the couture. But I did not dare do that.

The staircarpets gave way to scrubbed boards and still I had not seen any-thing living except the possibility of a face in the mirror, although the entire house was full of evidence of life. These upper floors were dimly lit, only single lights in holders at intervals along the walls, but one door was standing open and light spilled out onto the passage, like an invitation.

A good fire glowed in a neat little range where nightclothes were warming on the brass fender. I felt a sudden, sharp pang of disappointment to find her trail lead me to the nursery; I had been duped of all the fleshly adventures the house had promised me and that, damn them, must be part of the joke, too. All the same, if I indulged the fancy of the child I'd seen in the mirror, perhaps I might engage the fancy of her mother, who must be still young enough to enjoy the caress of a bearskin bedstead; and not, I'd be bound, inimical to poetry, either.

This mother, who had condemned even the nursery to whiteness, white walls, white painted furniture, white rug, white curtains, all chic as hell. Even the child had been made a slave to fashion. Yet, though the nursery itself had succumbed to the interior designer's snowdrift that had engulfed the entire house, its inhabitants had not. I'd never seen so many dolls before, not even in Melissa's cabinet, and all quite exquisite, as if they'd just come from the shop, although some of them must be older than I was. How Melissa would have loved them!

Dolls sat on shelves with their legs stuck out before them, dolls spilled from toychests. Fine ladies in taffeta bustles and French hats, babies in every gradation of cuteness. A limp-limbed, golden-haired creature in pink satin sprawled as if in sensual abandon on the rug in front of the fire. A wonderfully elaborate lady in a kitsch Victorian pelisse of maroon silk, with brown hair under a feather straw bonnet, lay in an armchair by the fire with as proprietorial an air as if the room belonged to her. A delicious lass in a purple velvet riding habit occupied the saddle of the wonderful albino rocking horse.

Now at last I was surrounded by beautiful women and they were dumb repositories of all the lively colors that had been exiled from the place, vivid as a hot-house, but none of them existed, all were mute, were fictions and that multitude of glass eyes, like tears congealed in time, made me feel very lonely.

Outside, the snow flurried against the windows; the storm had begun in earnest. Inside, there was still one threshold left to cross. I guessed she would be there, waiting for me, whoever she was, although I hesitated, if only momentarily, before the door that lead to the night nursery, as if unseen gryphons might guard it.

Faint glow of a night light on the mantelpiece; a dim tranquillity, here, where the air is full of the warm, pale smells of childhood, of clean hair, of soap, of talcum powder, the incenses of her sanctuary. And the moment I entered the night nursery, I could hear her transparent breathing; she had hardly hidden herself at all, not even pulled the covers of her white-enamelled crib around her. I had taken the game seriously but she, its instigator, had not; she had fallen fast asleep in the middle of it, her eyelids buttoned down, her long, blonde, patrician hair streaming over the pillow.

She wore a white, fragile, lace smock and her long, white stockings were fine as the smoky breath of a winter's morning. She had kicked off her white kid sandals. This little hunter, this little quarry, lay curled up with her thumb wedged, baby-like, in her mouth.

The wind yowled in the chimney and snow pelted the window. The curtains were not yet drawn so I closed them for her and at once the room denied tempest, so I could have thought I had been snug all my life. Weariness came over me; I sank down in the basketwork chair by her bed. I was loath to leave the company of the only living thing I'd found in the mansion and even if Nanny brusquely stormed in to interrogate me, I reassured myself that she must know how fond her little charge was of hide-and-seek indeed, must have been in complicity with the game, to let me wander about the nursery suite in this unconventional fashion. And if Mummy came in, now, for goodnight kisses? Well so much the better; I should be discovered demonstrating the tenderness of a poet at the cradle of a child.

If nobody came? I would endure the anti-climax; I'd just take the weight off my feet for a while, and then slip out. Yet I must admit I felt a touch of disappointment as time passed and I was forced reluctantly to abandon all hope of an invitation to dinner. They'd forgotten all about me! Careless even of their own games, they had left off playing in the middle of the chase, just as the child had done, and retired into the immutable privacy of the rich. I promised myself that at least I'd help myself to half a tumbler of good whisky on my way out, to see me warmly back to the lane and the stark trudge home.

The child stirred in her sleep and muttered indecipherably. Her fists clenched and unclenched. Her cheeks were delicately flushed a pale, luminous pink. Such skin—the fine texture of childhood, the incomparable down of skin that has never gone out in the cold. The more I watched beside her, the frailer she looked, the more transparent. I had never, in my life before, watched beside a sleeping child. The milky smell of innocence and sentiment suffused the night nursery.

I had anticipated, I suppose, some sort of gratified lust from this game of hide-and-seek through the mansion if not the satisfaction of lust of the flesh, then that of lust of the spirit, of vanity; but the more I mimicked tenderness towards the sleeper, the more tender I became. Oh, my shabby-sordid life! I thought. How she, in her untouchable sleep, judges me.

Yet she was not a peaceful sleeper. She twitched like a dog dreaming of rabbits and sometimes she moaned. She snuffled constantly and then, quite loudly, coughed. The cough rumbled in her narrow chest for a long time and it struck me that the child, so pale and sleeping with such racked exhaustion, was a sick child. A sick, spoiled little girl who ruled the household with a whim, and yet, poor little tyrant, went unloved; they must have been glad she had dropped off to sleep, so they could abandon the game she had forced them to play. She had fairy-tale, flaxen hair and eyelids so delicate the eyes beneath them almost showed glowing through; and if, indeed, it had been she who secreted all the grumbling grown-ups in their wardrobes and bathrooms and wound me through the house on an invisible spool towards her, well, I could scarcely begrudge her her fun. And her game had been as much with those grown-ups as it had been with me; hadn't she tidied them all away as if they'd been dolls she'd stowed in the huge toychest of this exquisite house?

When I thought of that, I went so far in forgiveness as to stroke her eggshell cheek with my finger. Her skin was soft as plumage of snow and sensitive as that of the princess in the story of the princess and the pea; when I touched her, she stirred. She shrugged away from my touch, muttering, and rolled over uneasily. As she did so, a gleaming bundle slithered from between her covers on to the floor, banging its china head on the scrubbed linoleum.

She must have tiptoed down to collect her forgotten doll while I went prowling about the bedrooms. Here he was again, her Pierrot in his shining white pajamas, her little friend. Perhaps her only friend. I bent to pick him up from the floor for her and, as I did so, something caught the light and glittered at the corner of his huge, tragic, glass eye. A sequin? A brilliant? The moon is your country, old chap; perhaps they've put stars in your eyes for you.

I looked more closely.

It was wet.

It was a tear.

Then I felt a succinct blow on the back of my neck, so sudden, so powerful, so unexpected that I felt only a vague astonishment as I pitched forward on my face into a black vanishment.

When I opened my eyes, I saw a troubled absence of light around me; when I tried to move, a dozen little daggers serrated me. It was terribly cold and I was lying on, yes, marble, as if I was already dead, and I was trapped inside a little hill of broken glass inside the wet carapace of Melissa's husband's sheepskin coat that was sodden with melting snow.

After a few, careful, agonising twitches, I thought it best to stay quite still in this dank, lightless hall where the snow drove in through an open door whose outline I could dimly see against the white night outside. Slow as a dream, the door shifted back and forth on rusty hinges with a raucous, mechanical, monotonous caw, like that of crows.

I tried to piece together what had happened to me. I guessed I lay on the floor of the hall of the house I could have sworn I'd just explored, though I could see very little of its interior in the ghostly light—but all must once have been painted white, though now sadly and obscenely scribbled over by rude village boys with paint and chalks. The despoiled pallor reflected itself in a cracked mirror of immense size on the wall.

Perhaps I had been trapped by the fall of a chandelier. Certainly, I had been caught in the half-shattered glass viscera of the chandelier that I thought I'd just seen multiplying its reflections in another hall than the one in which I lay and every bone in my body ached and throbbed. If time had loosened the chandelier from its moorings in the flaking plaster above me, the chandelier might very well have come tumbling down on me as I sheltered from the storm that howled and gibbered around the house but then it might have killed me and I knew by my throbbing bruises that I was still alive. But had I not just walked through this very hall when it was warm and perfumed and suave with money? Or had I not.

Then I was pierced by a beam of light that struck cold green fire from the prisms around me. The invisible behind the flashlight addressed me unceremoniously in a cracked, old woman's voice, a crone's voice. Who be you? What be you up to?

Trapped in the splintered glass, the splintered light, I told her how my car had broken down in the snow and I had come here for assistance. This alibi now seemed to me a very feeble one.

I could not see the old woman at all, could not even make out her vague shape behind the light, but I told her I was staying with the Lady Melissa, to impress her old country crone's snobbery. She exclaimed and muttered when she heard Melissa's name; when she spoke again, her manner was almost excessively conciliatory. She has to be careful, poor old woman, all alone in the house; thieves come for lead from the roof and young couples up to no good come and so on and on. But, if I am the Lady Melissa's guest, then she is sure it is perfectly all right for me to shelter here. No, there is no telephone. I must wait here till the storm dies down. The new snow will have blocked the lane by now—we are quite cut off! she says; and titters.

I must follow her carefully, walk this way; she gives me a hand out of the mess, so much broken glass . . . take care. What a crash, when the chandelier came down! You'd have thought the world had come to an end. Come with her, she has her rooms; she is quite cosy, sir, with a roaring fire. (What weather, eh?)

She lit me solicitously out of the glass trap and took me past our phantoms moving like deep sea fish in the choked depths of the mirror; up the stairs we went, through the ruins of the house I thought I had explored in my waking faint or system of linked hallucinations, snow induced, or, perhaps, induced by a mild concussion. For I am shaky and a little nauseous; I grasp the banisters too tight.

The doors shudder on their hinges. I glimpse rooms with the furniture spookily shrouded in white sheets but the beam of her torch does not linger on anything; her carpet slippers go flipperty-flopperty, flipperty-flopperty, she is an intrepid negotiator of the shadows. And still I cannot see her clearly, although I hear the rustle of her dress and smell her musty, frowsty, second-hand clothes store, typical crone smell, like grandma's smell, smell of my childhood women.

She has, of course, ensconced herself in the nursery. And how I gasped, in my mild fever, to see so many dolls had set up camp in this decay!

Dolls everywhere higgledy-piggledy, dolls thrust down the sides of chairs, dolls spilled out of tea chests, dolls propped up on the mantelpiece with blank, battered faces. Had she gathered all the dolls of all the departed daughters of the house here, around her, for company? The dolls stared at me dumbly from glass eyes that might hold in suspension the magic snow-storm that trapped me here; I felt I was the cynosure of all their blind eyes.

And have I indeed met any of these now moth-gnawed creatures in this room before? When I first fainted in the hall, did I fall back in time to encounter on a white beach of years ago this young lady, whose heavy head drops forward on her bosom since her limp body has lost too much sawdust to continue to support it? The struts of her satin crinoline, stove in like a broken umbrella. Her blousy neighbor's dark red silk dress has faded to a thin pink but she has not lost her parasol because it had been sewn to her hand and her straw bonnet with the draggled feathers still hangs by a few threads from the brunette wig now awry on a china scalp. And I almost tripped over a poor corpse on the floor in a purplish jacket of balding velvet, her worn, wax face raddled with age, only a few strands left of all that honey-colored hair. . . .

Yet if any of the denizens of that imaginary nursery were visiting this one, slipped out of my dream through a warp of the imagination, then I couldn't recognise them, thank God, among the dolls half loved to death and now scattered about a room whose present owner had consecrated it to a geriatric cosiness. Nevertheless, I felt a certain sense of disquiet, not so much fear as foreboding; but I was too preoccupied with my physical discomfort, my horrid aches, pains and scratches, to pay much attention to a prickling of the nerves.

And in the old woman's room, all was a comforting as a glowing fire, a steaming kettle could make it, even if eldritchly illuminated by a candle stuck in its own grease on to the mantelpiece. The very homeliness of the room went some way towards restoring my battered spirits and the crone made me very welcome, bustled me out of the sheepskin coat with almost as much solicitude as if she knew who it belonged to, set me down in an armchair. In its red plush death-throes, this armchair looked nothing like those bleached, remembered splendors; I told myself the snow had got into my eyes and brain. The old woman crouched down to take off my wet shoes for me; poured me thick, rich tea from her ever-ready pot; cut me a slice of dark gingerbread that she kept in an old biscuit tin with a picture of kittens on the lid. No spook or phantom could have had a hand in the making of that sagging, treacly, indigestible goody! I felt better, already; outside, the blizzard might rage but I was safe and warm, inside, even if in the company of an authentic crone.

For such she undeniably was, bent almost to a hoop with age, salt and pepper hair skewered up on top of her head with tortoiseshell pins, a face so eroded with wrinkles it was hard to tell whether she was smiling or not. She and her quarters had not seen soap and water for a long time and the lingering, sour, rank odour of uncaredforness faintly repelled me but the tea went down like blood. And don't you remember the slops and old clothes smell of grandma's kitchen? Colin Clout's come home again, with a vengeance.

She poured tea for herself and perched on top of the pile of old newspapers and discarded clothing that cushioned her own chair at the other side of the fire, to sip from her cup and chatter about the violence of the weather whilst I went on thawing myself out, eyeing—nervously, I must admit—the dolls propped on every flat surface, the roomful of bedizened raggle-taggles.

When she saw me looking at the dolls, she said: "I see you're admiring my beauties." Meanwhile, snow drove against the curtainless window panes like furious birds and blasts echoed through the house. The old woman thrust her empty cup away in the grate, all at once moved as if by a sudden sense of purpose; I saw I must pay in kind for my kind reception, I must give her a piece of undivided attention. She scooped up an armful of dolls and began to introduce them to me one by one. Dotty. Quite dotty, poor old thing.

The Hon. Frances Brambell had one eye out and her bell-shaped, satin skirt had collapsed but she must have been a pretty acquisition to the toy cupboard in her day; time, however, has its revenges, the three divorces, the voluntary exile in Morocco, the hashish, the gigolos, the slow erosion of her beauty . . . how it made the old woman chuckle! But how enchanting the girl had looked when she was presented, the ostrich feathers nodding above her curls! I looked from the old woman to the doll and back again; now the crone was animated, a thick track of spittle descended her chin. With an ironic laugh, she tossed the Hon. Frances Brambell to one side; the china head bounced off the wall and her limbs jerked a little before she lay still on the floor.

Seraphine, Duchess of Pyke, wore faded maroon silk and what had once been a feathered hat. She hailed, initially, from Paris and still possessed a certain style, even in her old age, although the Duchess had been by no means a model of propriety and, even if she carried off her acquired rank to the manner born, there is no more perfect a lady than one who is no better than she should be, suggested the old woman. In a paroxysm of wheezing laughter, she cast the Duchess and her pretensions on top of the Hon. Frances Brambell and told me now I must meet Lady Lucy, ah! she would be a marchioness when she inherited but had been infected with moth in her most sensitive parts and grown emaciated, in spite of her pretty velvet riding habit. She always wore purple, the color of passion. The sins of the fathers, insinuated this gossipy harridan, a congenital affliction . . . the future held in store for the poor girl only clinics, sanatoria, a wheel-chair, dementia, premature death.

Each doll's murky history was unfolded to me; the old woman picked them up and dismissed them with such confident authority I soon realized she knew all the little girls whose names she'd given to the dolls intimately. She must have been the nanny here, I thought; and stayed on after the family all left the sinking ship, after her last charge, that little daughter who might, might she not? have looked just like my imaginary blonde heiress, ran off with a virile but uncouth chauffeur, or, perhaps, the black saxophonist in the dance band of an ocean liner. And the retainer inherited the desuetude. In the old days, she must have wiped their pretty noses for them, cut their bread and butter into piano keys for them . . . all the little girls must once have played in this very nursery, come for tea with the young mistress, gone out riding on ponies, grown up to come to dances in wonderful dresses, stayed over for house parties, golf by day, affairs of the heart by night. Had my Melissa, herself, danced here, perhaps, in her unimaginable adolescence?

I thought of all the beautiful women with round, bare shoulders discreet as pearls going in to dinner in dresses as brilliant as the hot-house flowers that surrounded them, handsomely set off by the dinner-jackets of their partners, though they would have been far more finely accessorized by me—women who had once filled the whole house with that ineffable perfume of sex and luxury that drew me greedily to Melissa's bed. And time, now, frosting those lovely faces, the years falling on their head like snow.

The wind howled, the logs hissed in the grate. The crone began to yawn and so did I. I can easily curl up in this armchair beside the fire; I'm half asleep already—please don't trouble yourself. But, no; I must have the bed, she said. You shall sleep in the bed.

And, with that, cackled furiously, jolting me from my bitter-sweet reverie. Her rheumy eyes flashed; I was stricken with the ghastly notion she wanted to sacrifice me to some aged lust of hers as the price of my night's lodging but I said: "Oh, I can't possibly take your bed, please no!" But her only reply was to cackle again.

When she rose to her feet, she looked far taller than she had been, she towered over me. Now, mysteriously, she resumed her old authority; her word was law in the nursery. She grasped my wrist in a hold like lockjaw and dragged me, weakly protesting, to the door that I knew, with a shock of perfect recognition, led to the night nursery.

I was cruelly precipitated back into the heart of my dream.

Beyond the door, on the threshold of which I stumbled, all was as it had been before, as if the night nursery were the changeless, unvaryingly eye of the storm and its whiteness that of a place beyond the spectrum of colours. The same scent of washed hair, the dim tranquillity of the night light. The white-enamelled crib, with its dreaming occupant. The storm crooned a lullaby; the little heiress of the snow pavilion had eyelids like carved alabaster that hold the light in a luminous cup, but she was a flawed jewel, this one, a shattered replica, a drawing that has been scribbled over, and, for the first time in all that night, I felt a pure fear.

The old woman softly approached her charge, and plucked an object, some floppy, cloth thing, from between the covers, where it had lain in the child's pale arms. And this object she, cackling again with obscure glee, handed to me as ceremoniously as if it were a present from a Christmas tree. I jumped when I touched Pierrot, as if there were an electric charge in his satin pajamas.

He was still crying. Fascinated, fearful, I touched the shining teardrop pendant on his cheek and licked my finger. Salt. Another tear welled up from the glass eye to replace the one I had stolen, then another, and another. Until the eyelids quivered and closed. I had seen his face before, a face that had eaten too much bread and margarine in its time. A magic snow-storm blinded my eyes; I wept, too.

Tell Melissa the image factory is bankrupt, grandma.

Diffuse, ironic benediction of the night light. The sleeping child extended her warm, sticky hand to grasp mine; in a terror of consolation, I took her in my arms, in spite of her impetigo, her lice, her stench of wet sheets.

BIRTHDREAM
Laurie Kutchins

Laurie Kutchins is a member of the department of English language and literature at the University of New Mexico. Her poetry collection, *The Night Path*, will be published by BOA Editions this year.

Kutchin's provocative dream-poem is one that lingers in the memory long after it is done. It comes from the June 3rd issue of *The New Yorker* magazine.

—T. W.

This time I had given birth
to a child with a dark, remarkable tail.
Part animal, part girl.
I wanted no one to see her,
not even the father. I wanted my privacy
to put her back inside me,
back through the glop of the birth neck,
into the bluish glue my body had made
for her for seven months. It was not time,
she must wait, come back
when the animal had been outgrown. I held her briefly
in my arms, stroked her tail before
we parted, her eyes
nursing the dark moons.

She was never my daughter, and yet
she brought
her own wild light
into the room so that when I opened my eyes

at daybreak
the first thing I saw was snow
spinning small
shoulders in the windows.

The last I saw of her.

DISILLUSION
Edward Bryant

Edward Bryant, though born in White Plains, New York, grew up on a cattle ranch in southeastern Wyoming. He began writing professionally in 1968 and has published more than a dozen books, starting with *Among the Dead* in 1973. Some of his titles include *Cinnabar*, *Phoenix Without Ashes* (with Harlan Ellison), *Wyoming Sun*, *Particle Theory* and *Fetish*. *Flirting With Death*, a collection of his suspense and horror stories, is forthcoming. Bryant's stories have appeared in numerous magazines and anthologies, and he has won two Nebula Awards. He has worked as a guest lecturer, speaker, and writer-in-residence, and frequently conducts classes and writers' workshops. He has been a radio talk host, an actor in two of S. P. Somtow's movies, and currently is the horror host for *Omni VISIONS*, Omni *Internet's* interview show. He's working on a feature film script and a start-up comic book, and trying to finish a novel.

"Disillusion," originally published in *David Copperfield's Beyond Imagination*, is about a man hired to demystify magic, to find the strings. And to his surprise he finds just how fragile illusions can be.

—E. D.

Shining eyes.

The spotlit circle rippled across the audience in the orchestra section, reflected in astonished, delighted eyes. Amazed creatures, snared by the sudden glamor.

First they saw it. Then—a flash of dazzling white light. Now—

"That was absolutely amazing!" said Ingrid. Jack abruptly saw that her mouth was hanging slightly open. He couldn't help but notice the full redness of her lips. He suddenly wished they were back in the room, not here in this garish showroom approximately the size of the Astrodome. But if only she weren't—

He crushed the thought, involuntarily squeezing the attaché case that sat on his lap. Ingrid turned toward him, eyes shining. The audience's wild applause crested around them. "What do you think, darling? Could it *really* be real? I mean real magic?"

"Misdirection," said Jack flatly. "There's no magic, and there are no *Star Trek* transporters. Leopards don't become giant condors—" He was rolling now.

He ran out of breath and had to gulp some air. "And neither one of them turns into nubile young women."

"Well, you could fool me," said Ingrid, her wide smile shining almost as bright as the flashpots that had left dazzle floaters in each's eyes. "And I'm not a fool, Jack."

The words carried just the slightest edge. Jack looked at his new-but-maybe-not-much-longer lover sharply. Her smile softened.

"Watch the show," she said.

The Great Mandragore bounded back to center stage, wide grin dazzling the crowd. The wireless mike, limned in glowing crimson neon, spun slowly through the air from stage left. The eerie baton halted smoothly in front of the magician and parked itself in midair. The man reached out and plucked it from whatever invisible purchase.

"Not bad," breathed Ingrid.

Jack ignored her. "Look," he said. "See that gleam? The reflection?"

Ingrid shook her head impatiently. "I see nothing, Jack. Just another wonderful thing."

"It's a wire," he said. "Very thin. It caught the light." He thought he heard her sigh.

"No, Virginia," she said, almost too softly for him to hear. "There is no magic in this world. There's only wires, and mirrors, and trapdoors, and illusion."

"Deception," he said, recognizing the smug tone only too late, but still making no attempt to disguise it.

"Shut up, Jack." Ingrid said the words with no apparent malice. "Let him amaze me." It was like flipping a light switch. Her attention was . . . gone. It was up *there*. Onstage.

". . . and this is what I call my shell game," the Great Mandragore was saying. As he gestured, the serenely smiling young men and women of the stage crew smoothly pushed a series of what appeared to be clear Lucite pedestals into place. There were three, ranging from about six to ten feet in height. From the flies came what looked like huge hollowed and inverted shells of brown walnuts, each about four feet long. Lowered on wires, they hovered ten feet above the upper platforms of the pedestals.

The Great Mandragore clapped his hands. The leopard bounded smoothly from stage left and easily leapt to the nearest platform. It sat alert on its haunches, pink tongue protruding as it panted.

The magician clapped sharply twice. The rush of great wings buffeted the air from stage right as the condor flapped into sight. The huge bird alighted on the right-most platform and smoothly folded its twelve-foot wingspan. Its flat black eyes followed the Great Mandragore's every motion.

Then the magician clapped three times, the sounds as distinct as whip cracks. The beauty of the young woman who gracefully back-flipped in a blur across to stage center was of a degree to take Jack's breath away. As tall as Mandragore, she vibrated to a stop upright, with arms and hands angled up in a victory pose. Her short, shining, russet hair shimmered in the spotlight. Emerald green eyes seemed to gaze into Jack's own.

"Ladies and gentlemen, Cybele."

The audience was already clapping wildly, and without prompting.

The young woman stepped into the air as two young male stagehands clasped hands below her foot. They snapped her upward; she tucked and flipped twice around—and landed with no wasted movement on the platform ten feet up. The crowd continued to roar.

"Now," said the Great Mandragore. Leopard, condor, and woman held their positions like stone as the magician snapped his fingers and two assistants carried a fourth large walnut-shell construction onstage and set it on the floor beside Mandragore.

The music cranked up.

"Wait!" said the magician. He gestured, and four stagehands staggered out beneath the weight of what appeared to be a four-by-four square of sheet steel. They maneuvered it into place beside the shell, lowered it to a height of about six inches, and then jerked their hands and fingers back, dropping the square. It clanged to the stage with a sound like the tone of doom. Two of the stagehands picked up the shell and set it in place on the steel square.

"*Now* we are ready!" He swept his arms around, and the shells on their wires lowered slowly to the three elevated platforms. The leopard lay down. The condor bowed its reddish head. The woman tucked to hands and knees. All three disappeared beneath their respective shells.

The drums rolled. The music took on a frenetic gypsy beat. While the stage lighting dimmed slightly, bright spots flashed strobelike on the four shells.

The Great Mandragore clapped his hands, this time amplified to a level that set Jack back in his seat. The lights came back up completely.

"So who's where?" called out the magician. He pointed at the shell on the upper right. When the covering rose, the audience gasped at the sight of the leopard. The sleek cat yawned, its tongue lolling.

The Great Mandragore pointed to the upper left. The shell rose. The great condor spread its wings, shaking out its feathers. The bird uttered a piercing, echoing *yawp*.

The magician motioned to the center shell. It rose, revealing no one and nothing on the platform atop the ten-foot transparent pedestal.

The drums thundered, the music and the audience both screamed with anticipation as the Great Mandragore turned his back to the audience and passed his hand over the shell on the metal sheet on the floor by his feet. The shell lifted into the air. A red-furred wolf rose to its haunches. The wild howl spiraled out from the grinning white jaws and filled the auditorium.

The leopard hissed and yowled. The condor shrieked.

A flash of intense light haloed the magician. When he turned to face the audience and take a bow, they realized it was no longer the Great Mandragore. He had, it seemed, become the young woman.

For the first time, she changed expression, grinning at the audience and waving.

The Great Mandragore descended from the flies, moving his arms gracefully, as if gently swimming toward the stage. He landed on his feet beside the young woman.

Taking her hand, he said simply, "Cybele and I thank you."

"No," said Jack under his breath, glancing to his side and seeing Ingrid staring raptly at the stage, "thank *you.*" He squeezed the handle of his attaché case and felt, rather than heard, the *click.*

After the show, when the theater emptied, Jack and Ingrid walked back to their hotel and ordered a late snack in the all-night coffee shop. Jack had the feeling that Ingrid was still viewing the dazzle and mystery of the magic show. He also wondered whether she was seeing the Great Mandragore sitting in Jack's seat.

"It was wonderful," she kept saying.

The waitress brought them both more decaf.

"Good illusions," Jack said grudgingly.

"It was more than that," Ingrid said. "I'm sure of it."

For a quick disorienting moment, Jack thought he saw the russet-haired assistant—Cybele, was it?—sitting in Ingrid's place. Then the blond hair was back, the eyes as blue as the sky at midmorning. Ingrid.

"What's wrong?" she said.

He shook his head. "Nothing."

She cocked her head like a tropical bird. "Are you having flashbacks to the performance tonight?"

"Maybe," he admitted.

"To the gorgeous assistant in the shell game finale?"

He stared at her, startled.

She nodded with some satisfaction, and half smiled. "We've been lovers for—what? A week? Now you're checking out the competition?" She shook her head. "Men." Her tone didn't sound amused.

Jack started to protest, then decided it probably wouldn't do any good. It was as though a voice inside him was telling him not to bother. He suspected everything was already written on his face. "That's not it at all."

Ingrid looked disgusted.

"You're the ace investigative reporter," he said, trying to sound neutral.

"Maybe I should have run a background check on you," she said sharply. "After the first two or three times guys burned me, I've been tempted. It just seems so cold. . . ."

Jack suddenly had the feeling this was running downhill, all of a sudden out of control. He wanted to say the things that would make everything all right. "Ingrid—"

"Never mind." She turned away from him. "I'm on edge, doing this 'death of magic' article for the magazine. I've got to learn to keep my work out of my life, and my life out of my work."

He reached across and took her hand. It felt cold. "Listen," he said, "is this the professional on duty? I mean, you're the big enchilada writer, and I'm the lowly researcher with only a month's tenure at *RealWorld.*"

Her expression softened. She cupped her hand like one of the Great Mandragore's giant walnut shells and set it down on the knuckles of his hand as he clasped hers. "Look, Jack, I don't mean to make things tense. Let's just go back to the room. Okay?" Her voice sounded genuinely hopeful.

But he realized he was looking at her now as a virtual stranger. What had he been thinking all this past week as they planned the Atlantic City junket? He tried to recall what he had felt for her only a few hours earlier. He didn't remember this disorienting sense of chaos before. His thoughts abruptly stalled in confusion. He *knew* he must have confronted situations like this: mutual attractions, kindled love affairs, relationships suddenly accelerating in feeling. Everyone dealt with this. Had Jack? *Hadn't he?*

"Are you going to prove to me that Mandragore's a fake?" she said. And then in exactly the same tone, "Are you going to break my heart?"

"Yes to the first," Jack said. He stared back at her. What was going *on?* With effort, he said, "As for the second—Let's go back to the room."

She looked away from his face again. "If he's a fake, how did he pull off that last trick, the shell game?"

"He's good," Jack said. "He's not a fake. It's just not real magic."

Ingrid's eyes momentarily lost focus. "Magic," she said. "I desperately crave some magic in my life. Not illusion."

Jack put down on the table twice the money he estimated was needed. "Let's go, okay?"

"No illusion," Ingrid repeated. "I don't need that. Jack, you told me last night you loved me. Do you?"

It was all going too fast to register. He couldn't remember last night.

Jack shook his head, feeling suddenly that the hard bone of his skull was a sieve, and the rough-textured fabric of nightmare was filtering into his head. If he could just shake his head fast enough, the nightmare threads would fly out again. This was horrible. It was progressively and rapidly getting worse.

"What's the matter?" said Ingrid. "Have you got a headache?"

Jack massaged his temples. "Sorry. Just felt shaky for a moment. I'm okay." But he knew he wasn't. Okay, that is.

He waited until they were both back in the quiet of the room before he told her that, no, he didn't love her. Fortunately, when he said it, it was spoken only in his mind, and it was said after she'd dropped off to sleep and while he remained terribly awake, staring up in the dark at the invisible ceiling.

What was *happening* to him? For the smallest split of a second, he imagined he was being watched by hidden eyes.

The next day was Sunday and, after a leisurely room service breakfast, they took the train back to the city. They cabbed together from Penn Station. In front of Ingrid's building, with the meter ticking over, Jack argued her into seeing him after supper.

"It's important," he said. "It's something you'll need for the article."

Ingrid wasn't entirely sure she wanted to get together again so soon after the Atlantic City trip.

"I've got so much work this week," she protested. "I'm going to need the time at home."

"I've got something to show you," Jack answered. "I have something you really do need to see."

It took a little cajoling, but she finally agreed. "It's important?" she said doubtfully. "I mean, for real?"

"It is," he assured her.

Ingrid gave him a peck on the cheek and a quick hug, and told him she'd call before coming downtown. A shake of blond hair, a flash of blue eyes, and she was gone.

"Where now?" said the cabbie.

Jack told him.

Once back in his apartment off Sixth Avenue and Tenth, Jack set his overnight bag in the sleeping loft without unpacking it. He returned to the living room and carefully unsnapped the top of the attaché case. Gently he lifted the lightweight video camera out of its vibration-damping cradle and set it on the coffee table.

The tape cassette looked to be in good shape.

Mr. Constantine had quietly lent Jack the secretive camcorder. Mr. Constantine was Jack's boss. If the publisher had a first name, no one at *RealWorld Magazine* seemed to know it. Perhaps "Mister" really was, as the office joke went, Constantine's given name.

Jack used the remote to turn on the Sony big-screen he used as a monitor. He registered that CNN *Headline News* was on the screen. It was close to the bottom of the hour. Feature stuff.

". . . magic or illusion?" the female reporter was saying.

Jack cranked the volume up.

"Tabloids across the country are asserting that the Great Mandragore is everything from a space alien with superhuman powers, to an ordinary sleight-of-hand artist who has a posted Faustian bargain with Satan. Mandragore has twice turned down requests by CNN for an interview opportunity to answer his accusers. A spokeswoman for his booking company offered regrets—but perhaps something more."

The shot cut to a close-up of the woman Cybele. Jack stared, the tape in his hand forgotten for the moment. "For the successful illusionist," she said, "the hand is indeed always quicker than the eye." She looked directly into the camera, green eyes afire. "The truth about the Great Mandragore is right there for all to see—if only you have the quickness of wit to look."

The picture cut back to the reporter, who then signed off.

Jack slipped the videotape cassette into the VCR's slot and punched the play button on the remote. He watched for the better part of four hours, reversing the tape, hitting the pause button, taking notes and timing numbers, running footage in superslow motion, taking more notes.

Finally he stopped when he realized his concentration was edging him close to exhaustion.

"You clever son of a gun," he said toward the Great Mandragore's jovial image frozen on the screen. "I've got you. Gotcha dead to rights. Even Ingrid will believe me now."

"You did *what?*" she said that night.

"I smuggled this into the performance," Jack said, gesturing at the minicam on the table. "Ultralight, completely quiet, autofocus, and perfect for low-light conditions. I taped the whole damned thing."

"I'm not sure this was a good idea," Ingrid said.

Jack stared at her in disbelief. "*Not a good idea?* We're journalists, my love. *Investigative* journalists. We're checking out a stage magician who's so good, half the country thinks he's the real McCoy. Sneaking a camera in may have broken a rule or two, but it's not a hanging offense. For crying out loud, Ingrid, I didn't pay off the leopard or the condor to give me the dirt."

She looked back at him, mute.

"Okay," he said. "I'm done. No more ranting. I just want you to watch some things. The show was about two hours, but I've culled a compilation of footage from all the really amazing stunts. You know, the shell game and all the rest."

Now Ingrid looked disgusted. "Okay," she said. "Show me."

"You'll love it," he said.

But she didn't.

He showed her all the ultraslow, frame-by-frame breakdowns of the vanishings and the transferences and the transpositions. He showed her how the camera could not be fooled by misdirection.

"No," she said.

"Oh, yes."

He pointed out the fractional moments when the lens caught the shine of a wire, the glimmer of a mirror, the suggestion of movement in a hidden compartment when the human eye of the perceiver wouldn't have noticed a thing.

Tears came to her eyes.

And then he showed her how the shell game had been performed.

"You son of a bitch," she said, starting to sob.

He couldn't stop. He showed her absolutely everything.

Then there was something else he could not stop.

He raised her chin with his hands and looked into her tear-glossed eyes. "By the way," he said, "I don't love you."

Her hand. His eye. The hand really *was* quicker. Her slap solidly smacked his cheek.

It echoed in his head for a long time; much longer than the time it took Ingrid to grab her coat and leave.

When Jack went to work at the midtown AusPub Tower the next day, Ingrid wasn't there. Lisa, the short, intense receptionist on the editorial floor of *RealWorld Magazine*, told him that Ingrid had phoned in earlier and said that she'd be working at home the entire day.

Jack stared at the telephone in his cubicle before finally dialing her number.

She answered on the fourth ring. Her voice sounded logy, exhausted.

"It's me," he said.

"What do you want?"

"I'm sorry. I just needed to talk to you." That wasn't what he wanted to say at all, but it was a start. Jack tried to seize fast to the opening.

"Last night," said Ingrid. "Did you mean those things you said at the end?"

He was silent for a while. He wanted to deny what he had told her.

"Jack?"

He started at her prompt.

"Are you there?"

"Yes," he said. Horrified, he realized he had been presented with his agenda. "About last night, yes."

"Jack—" He heard infinite sadness in the single word. Saying nothing more, Ingrid hung up.

He dialed her back after hesitating. What was the use? But he still refused to set down the receiver and terminate the call. Jack got her answering machine and hung up without leaving a message. He stared at the phone long minutes more.

The moving feet of people traversing the wide expanse of offices, the keyboard clatter, the voices speaking urgently into phones, all faded into a soft white noise.

What was going on? The question haunted him. He had come to work at *RealWorld* barely more than a month before. He had met Ingrid, he had wooed her, won her, rejected her, all in that month. What kind of man was he? He didn't remember ever acting like this before.

His own character revelations bloomed in front of him like an endless series of silk handkerchiefs being pulled from a magician's sleeve.

Was it an illusionist's trick?

But this was not a stage in a theater supercharged with shattering sound and disorienting lighting. This was the real world. All the world's a stage. . . . The quotation reverberated in his brain, a basic musical echo that wouldn't go away, a language virus infecting his thoughts.

Which *was* quicker, thought Jack. The hand, or the eye?

Nothing made sense.

So he told the receptionist Lisa that he felt nauseated, he was probably coming down with Tehran A flu, he was going home for the day.

She should log his calls. Which didn't really matter, he thought. In his short tenure at the magazine, he had received few messages.

After leaving the office, he walked over to Forty-second Street, picked a martial arts film at random, and sat through the movie for three consecutive showings.

When he exited the dark theater in late afternoon, Jack realized he could recall nothing of the plot. Sonny Chiba? Some other fierce, lethal hero?

He couldn't remember.

That night, Jack extracted the last TV dinner from the freezer compartment of his refrigerator and cooked it in the oven. He wondered whether his life would be measurably different if he bought a compact microwave unit from the Korean electronic supermarket two blocks away.

He glanced around the apartment. There really were few amenities. The living room held a TV set on a metal folding chair. The windows had no curtains. He had pinned up some flowered sheets to keep the early light out. There were two more folding chairs over behind the nondescript coffee table. A cheap phone was centered on the coffee table.

The kitchen held a coffeemaker and a bag full of paper plates and plastic utensils. A mug with a Boston Red Sox logo rested by the sink. The refrigerator held a pound of ground coffee and a small container of half & half.

There were some clothes on hangers in the closet.

The bathroom contained an extra roll of toilet paper, but held too few towels.

It was, in short, an apartment that *looked* as though he had moved in yesterday and had been living out of a suitcase.

Jack spent much of the evening sitting and staring at the telephone. Should he call Ingrid? What good would it do if he reached her? What would he tell her? What was there at all to say? But he knew he wanted to talk with her.

When he dialed her number, Ingrid let the machine take the call—if indeed she was at home at all.

Jack left no message.

After he finally lay on his mattress in the sleeping loft, Jack quickly slept. He dreamed of his past. At first it was a lucid dream in which he knew he was journeying to his beginnings. Beyond a month, though, the details were frustratingly vague.

He recalled his parents, but they turned their faces inevitably away from him. So did his childhood friends, as well as his college schoolmates and the coworkers at his first job. He couldn't remember what that job was. Something . . . in a warehouse, he thought.

Now he *knew* he was being watched. He saw no watchers at first, but the sensation of being observed was unmistakable. He stood among lush trees and tall flowering plants, and felt certain the foliage hid eyes.

He would see those eyes if only he glanced in the right direction at precisely the right time. Branches moved without wind; bird sounds cooed and raucously cawed. Jack realized this was misdirection.

The next time he was tempted to redirect his vision, he deliberately gazed where he was obviously not supposed to.

That was when he made out the stone-still leopard gazing back at him from deep green eyes. But the more he stared at the great jungle cat, the more its furred outlines wavered and shifted into a huge bird whose shiny anthracite eyes fixed him dispassionately; and then the bird was a red wolf, a creature of long white teeth and hypnotic eyes.

Faces. The wolf's face deformed to a human face. The Great Mandragore grinned back at him. The face of Cybele took form superimposed over the illusionist's features. When she met Jack's eyes, she appeared wary.

Her expression softened, lips parting as though she were going to tell him something.

He awoke.

Jack wanted to return to the dream, but he also knew that was impossible. How he knew . . . he no longer understood.

When Jack walked into the glass-enclosed lobby of the AusPub Tower at nine in the morning none of his coworkers and acquaintances seemed to be meeting his eye.

Lisa, the receptionist on the editorial floor, appeared to gawk at him, startled.

"What's the matter?" he said.

She seemed to gather her wits. "Um, good morning, Jack."

"What's wrong?"

She said nothing, looked beyond his shoulder, and said, "Good morning, Mr. Constantine."

Jack glanced back at the publisher.

"Jack, would you mind coming back to my office for a minute, please?"

He nodded mutely, shooting an accusing glare at Lisa before turning on his heel.

This didn't look good. As they threaded through the maze of desks and cubicles toward Constantine's office, Jack thought that everyone else was studiously ignoring their passage. Or maybe he was just imagining that. But it was true that no one seemed to be looking up or offering a "hi" or "good morning."

They walked past Constantine's secretary, who looked up but didn't offer a greeting. Once in the corner office, Constantine shut the door behind them, gestured to the empty leather chair in front of his immaculately bare desk, and crossed to the west windows. He threw open the curtains with a dramatic rush of air—almost a gust of wind, Jack thought—and stood looking out at the tops of other midtown towers.

"Jack, Jack, Jack . . ." Constantine said. Still with his back turned, he shook his head.

"What?" said Jack tentatively.

"Ingrid turned in the rough of her 'death of magic' article early this morning."

"So how was it?" said Jack.

"Everything I could have hoped for." Constantine stared out over the city's suddenly Gothic-appearing towers.

"Everything?" Jack tried to smile.

"Indeed," said Constantine. "It will play as a wonderfully rationalist analysis of public gullibility and popular hysteria. The Great Mandragore is pictured as a consummate illusionist and nothing more."

"Which is what you wanted."

Constantine nodded. "There is a real tone of acute disappointment, of crushed romance in Ingrid's prose. I'm afraid her sense of joy in the infinite wonder of the universe may have been diminished a bit by this assignment."

"But that's what you wanted, too," said Jack.

The publisher nodded again, slowly. "You've been a good employee, Jack. You've done exactly what I requested of you, and more."

Jack wanted to smile, but couldn't quite manage it. "Is there a problem, sir? You said I'd get the nod for an editorial position if I brought this off."

"I'm afraid," said Constantine, "that I misrepresented matters a bit." He turned back from the window, and Jack saw the man's reflection waver like a desert heat shimmer.

The Great Mandragore faced him, hands palm-first at waist level.

Jack recoiled. A gentle hand touched his arm.

"It's all right, Jack," said Cybele from behind him.

Bewildered, shocked, Jack tried to jerk away from her. Her fingers tightened like spring steel.

"You're going to sleep for just a little while, Jack," said the Great Mandragore in Constantine's voice. "There won't even be a hangover." He nodded at the woman.

Cybele's fingers rose to the back of Jack's head. "Rest," she said.

Jack felt what he imagined a light switch might feel if it were conscious, as it was flipped off.

The light. First he saw it; then he—

Awoke.

Dim light, dust mote-laden light, the kind of light that made him think of late afternoons, light slanting down from high, narrow windows all around him. He stood in a spacious room cluttered on all sides with half-perceived heaps of things, piles of construction materials, vaguely apprehended equipment and tools.

Jack shook his head, trying to clear it. Meaning filtered back into his brain. Ahead and to his left, the thing that at first appeared to be the hummocks left by some sort of giant mole burrowing just under the concrete floor actually translated to a series of large, walnut-shell constructions.

He remembered. The props from the Great Mandragore's shell game.

Behind the shells, a row of Lucite pedestals shone in the window light. Off to the right, he saw shelves diminishing in perspective into the distance. The shelves held a variety of objects he couldn't even identify. What he *could* recognize included ropes, chains, handcuffs, manacles, leather masks. Was this some kind of S&M bondage and discipline emporium? No, he thought, these are props. For escapes.

Directly ahead, he could make out a steel tank on stilts, a container enigmatically labeled NAPHTHA.

Footsteps approached on the hard warehouse floor. Jack saw Cybele and Constantine materialize out of the dimness.

"Are you feeling all right?" said Cybele. It sounded like genuine concern in her voice.

Jack answered the question with his own question. "Where am I?"

"New Jersey," said Constantine. "We cabbed you out from the city."

"Cabbed?"

"I'm a publisher, Jack, not a magician."

"I'm not so sure about that." Jack gingerly touched his own face. "What the hell did you do to me?"

"We let you rest," said Cybele.

"What is this place?" Jack said.

Constantine spread his arms and turned to indicate the whole vast space. "It's a place to work; a place to rest; a place to find sanctuary." The publisher wore loose-fitting black clothes. As he raised his arms, for just a moment, the cloth of his voluminous shirt seemed to extend into wings.

Jack stared. He glanced to the side of the momentary condor-creature and thought he saw Cybele's skin take on the texture of fur as jungle cat rosettes began to pattern her body.

He blinked. Then the publisher and the magician's assistant were only a man and a woman again, and both smiled at him.

"How did you get me out of the building?" said Jack.

"AusPub?" the publisher said. "Why, you walked out under your own steam."

"I don't remember it."

"It seemed like a good idea," said Cybele, "not to debate the matter with you. We simply urged you to come with us."

"*Strongly* urged," said Constantine. "Now," he continued, "please accompany us further."

Jack had the feeling that this would be a bad time—or at least a useless time—to inquire about his promised editorial job. Things seemed to be accelerating quickly and out of all control, much as they had after the performance two nights ago. "Okay," he said. "Are you going to do anything bad to me?"

Constantine shook his head and smiled paternally. Cybele gently patted his cheek, a feather touch that still suggested all the force of a hurricane gale.

The publisher leading, the trio walked a narrow concrete path toward the distant wall.

"We owe you some explanation," said Cybele, her hand gently guiding his elbow to steer him around heaps and stacks of objects in the receding light.

"I guess I'd appreciate that," Jack said. They passed folded tarps and bolts of silk, an antique cannon and a series of nested glass boxes that looked like nineteenth-century aquariums. He frowned and slowed for a moment. "Is that a stuffed elephant?"

"A mammoth, actually."

Jack couldn't help but gawk.

Constantine smiled. "I picked it up as a curiosity awhile back. Mandragore caused it to disappear and then reappear nearly instantaneously in an aisle behind the entire audience."

They reached what had been the distant wall. All three of them stood in front of a heavy plank door. The door was evidently made to be secured with a thick brass padlock. Right now the locking hasp was open, the lock hanging by one post.

Constantine grasped the edge of the heavy door and swung it open with a creaking rasp of complaining hinges. Little light illuminated the inside. The three of them waited for their eyes to adjust.

Cybele said, "You will rest for a while. Then we'll have another job for you."

Jack stopped in some confusion. "Job? What about the editorial position?"

"Perhaps someday," said Constantine.

"Jesus!" said Jack. He realized he was staring at what looked for all the world like a human body dangling limply from a hook on the wall. "Who the hell is that?"

Cybele flicked a wall switch and a low-wattage bulb blinked on. Now Jack could read the sign beside the door. It read, PROPS. "Don't you recognize him?" she said.

Jack looked closer and realized he did, in fact, recognize the limp man hanging on the wall.

Eyes blank, every muscle at rest, the man on the hook was the Great Mandragore.

"Oh my God," said Jack. "The magician. What did you do to him?"

"Nothing," said Constantine. "We just keep him here until we need him."

"Until it's showtime," said Cybele.

"I'm missing something," Jack said. "None of this makes any sense at all."

The magician's assistant and the publisher exchanged glances.

"Conceive of strangers," said Constantine. "Imagine them dwelling in a strange land where they must survive the best way they can devise."

"Imagine strangers," said Cybele, "who perform what most inhabitants of their new home would perceive as wonders."

Jack looked at them, at the slack and suspended Great Mandragore, and then back at his companions again. "You mean—" he started to say, then fumbled for the words. "You mean all the magic's real? Is that what you're saying?"

Cybele nodded. "But we can't let anyone else know that. We'd be imprisoned by the authorities, maybe dissected to see how our powers work."

"Or we would be torn apart by the population," said Constantine, "out of fear. We don't want to take over your reality. Our goals are more modest. We just would like sanctuary."

"So you want the public to be sure to think that the magic is only illusion," said Jack slowly. "That it's all a fake."

"And that is why we needed the cooperation of Ingrid," said Constantine. "And that is why we needed your help."

"You got my help," said Jack. "Ingrid did what you ultimately wanted her to do." He glanced sharply at the two of them. "Why did you make me do what I did to Ingrid?" Pain stabbed deep into him, sharp and edged as ice.

Neither said anything. Constantine looked away, but Cybele met his gaze. In her eyes, in the twist of her lips, Jack saw a flash of what he suspected must be jealously. It was like the light glimmering off a sharpened tooth. "Now what about me?" He abruptly felt more bitter than fearful.

"We'll require you again," said Constantine. "Someday."

"Thank you," said Cybele. Her lips brushed his cheek as she stood on toe tips. Her hair was soft against his face for just a moment; but not as soft as Ingrid's had been. "I'll see you again, Jack," she said, in the doorway of the prop room.

Cybele reached with delicate transforming fingers to turn him off.

The last image he saw was not her eyes, but Ingrid's.

Jack wished futilely for that final wondrous shapechange. *Ingrid*, he thought, *love, if only you knew* . . . The miracle transformed solely in his mind.

He saw her magical eyes.

Disillusioned eyes.

DIANA OF THE HUNDRED BREASTS

Robert Silverberg

Robert Silverberg was born in New York City but has resided in the San Francisco Bay area for many years. He has won multiple Nebula and Hugo Awards for his short fiction and his novels. His most recent novels are *Hot Sky at Midnight*, *The Mountains of Majipoor* and *Starborne*. His short fiction has been collected in several volumes including *World of a Thousand Colors*, *Beyond the Safe Zone*, and *The Collected Stories of Robert Silverberg volume 1: Secret Sharers*. A new novel, *Sorcerers of Majipoor*, has just been published.

Silverberg is best known for his science fiction but is erudite in many fields including history and archeology. His interest in the latter is bound to have influenced this story about ancient gods. For me, the story evokes terror not from the obvious horror trappings, but from the consequences arising from one inconceivable possibility. The story was first published in the February issue of *Realms of Fantasy*.

—E. D.

The two famous marble statues stand facing each other in a front room of the little museum in the scruffy Turkish town of Seljuk, which lies just north of the ruins of the once-great Greek and Roman city of Ephesus. There was a photograph of the bigger one in my guidebook, of course. But it hadn't prepared me—photos never really do—for the full bizarre impact of the actuality.

The larger of the statues is about nine feet tall, the other one about six. Archaeologists found both of them in the courtyard of a building of this ancient city where the goddess Diana was revered. They show—you must have seen a picture of one, some time or other—a serene, slender woman wearing an ornamental headdress that is all that remains of a huge, intricate crown. Her arms are outstretched and the lower half of her body is swathed in a tight cylindrical gown. From waist to ankles, that gown is decorated with rows of vividly carved images of bees and of cattle. But that's not where your eyes travel first, because the entire midsection of Diana of Ephesus is festooned with a grotesque triple ring of bulging pendulous breasts. Dozens of them, or several dozens. A great many.

"Perhaps they're actually eggs," said my brother Charlie the professor, standing just behind me. For the past eighteen months Charlie had been one of the leaders of the team of University of Pennsylvania archaeologists that has been digging lately at Ephesus. "Or fruits of some kind, apples, pears. Nobody's really sure. Globular fertility symbols, that's all we can say. But I think they're tits, myself. The tits of the Great Mother, with an abundance of milk for all. Enough tits to satisfy anybody's oral cravings, and then some."

"An abomination before the Lord," murmured our new companion Mr. Gladstone, the diligent Christian tourist, just about when I was expecting him to say something like that.

"Tits?" Charlie asked.

"These statues. They should be smashed in a thousand pieces and buried in the earth whence they came." He said it mildly, but he meant it.

"What a great loss to art that would be," said Charlie in his most pious way. "Anyway, the original statue from which these were copied fell from heaven. That's what the Bible says, right? Book of Acts. The image that Jupiter tossed down from the sky. It could be argued that Jupiter is simply one manifestation of Jehovah. Therefore this is a holy image. Wouldn't you say so, Mr. Gladstone?"

There was a cruel edge on Charlie's voice; but, then, Charlie is cruel. Charming, of course, and ferociously bright, but above all else a smart-ass. He's three years older than I am, and three times as intelligent. You can imagine what my childhood was like. If I had ever taken his cruelties seriously, I suspect I would hate him, but the best defense against Charlie is never to take him seriously. I never have, nor anything much else, either. In that way Charlie and I are similar, I suppose. But only in that way.

Mr. Gladstone refused to be drawn into Charlie's bantering defense of idolatry. Maybe he too had figured out how to handle Charlie, a lot quicker than I ever did.

"You are a cynic and a sophist, Dr. Walker," is all that he said. "There is no profit in disputing these matters with cynics. Or with sophists. Especially with sophists." And to me, five minutes later, as we rambled through a room full of mosaics and frescoes and little bronze statuettes: "Your brother is a sly and very clever man. But there's a hollowness about him that saddens me. I wish I could help him. I feel a great deal of pity for him, you know."

That anyone would want to feel pity for Charlie was a new concept to me. Envy, yes. Resentment, disapproval, animosity, even fear, perhaps. But *pity?* For the six-foot-three genius with the blond hair and blue eyes, the movie-star face, the seven-figure trust fund, the four-digit I.Q.? I am tall too, and when I reached twenty-one I came into money also, and I am neither stupid nor ugly; but it was always Charlie who got the archery trophy, the prom queen, the honor-roll scroll, the Phi Beta Kappa key. It was Charlie who always got anything and everything he wanted, effortlessly, sometimes bestowing his leftovers on me, but always in a patronizing way that thoroughly tainted them. I have sensed people pitying me, sometimes, because they look upon me as Charlie-minus, an inadequate simulacrum of the genuine article, a pallid secondary version of the extraordinary Charlie. In truth I think their compassion for me, if that's what it is, is misplaced: I don't see myself as all that goddamned pitiful. But Charlie? Pitying *Charlie?*

I was touring Greece and Turkey that spring, mostly the usual Aegean resorts, Mykonos and Corfu and Crete, Rhodes and Bodrum and Marmaris. I wander up and down the Mediterranean about half the year, generally, and though I'm scarcely a scholar, I do of course look in on the various famous classical sites along my way. By now, I suppose, I've seen every ruined Roman and Greek temple and triumphal arch and ancient theater there is, from Volubilis and Thuburbo Majus in North Africa up through Sicily and Pompeii, and out to Spain and France on one side and Syria and Lebanon on the other. They all blur and run together in my mind, becoming a single generic site—fallen marble columns, weatherbeaten foundations, sand, little skittering lizards, blazing sun, swarthy men selling picture postcards—but I keep on prowling them anyway. I don't quite know why.

There are no hotels remotely worthy of the name in or around the Ephesus ruins. But Charlie had tipped me off that I would find, about six miles down the road, a lavish new deluxe place high up on a lonely point overlooking the serene Aegean that catered mostly to groups of sun-worshipping Germans. It had an immense lobby with marble floors and panoramic windows, an enormous swimming pool, and an assortment of dining rooms that resounded day and night with the whoops and hollers of the beefy Deutschers, who never seemed to leave the hotel. Charlie drove out there to have dinner with me the night I arrived, and that was when we met Mr. Gladstone.

"Excuse me," Gladstone said, hovering beside out table, "but I couldn't help hearing you speaking in English. I don't speak German at all and, well, frankly, among all these foreigners I've been getting a little lonely for the mother tongue. Do you mind if I join you?"

"Well—" I said, not really eager for his company, because tonight was the first time I had seen my brother in a couple of years. But Charlie grandly waved him to a seat.

He was a grayish, cheerful man of about sixty, a small-town pastor from Ohio or Indiana or maybe Iowa, and he had been saving for something like twenty years to take an extensive tour of the Christian holy places of the Middle East. For the past three months he had been traveling with a little group of pilgrims, I guess one could call them, six weeks bussing through Israel from Jerusalem to Beersheba, down to Mount Sinai, back up through the Galilee to Lebanon to see Sidon and Tyre, then out to Damascus, and so on and so on, the full Two-Testament Special. His traveling companions all had flown home by now, but Mr. Gladstone had bravely arranged a special side trip just for himself to Turkey—to poky little Seljuk in particular—because his late wife had had a special interest in an important Christian site here. He had never traveled anywhere by himself before, not even in the States, and going it alone in Turkey was a bit of a stretch for him. But he felt he owed it to his wife's memory to make the trip, and so he was resolutely plugging along on his own here, having flown from Beirut to Izmir and then hiring a car and driver to bring him down to Seljuk. He had arrived earlier this day.

"I didn't realize there was anything of special Christian interest around here," I said.

"The Cave of the Seven Sleepers of Ephesus," Mr. Gladstone explained. "My wife once wrote a little book for children about the Seven Sleepers. It was always her great hope to see their actual cave."

"The Seven Sleepers?"

He sketched the story for me quickly: the seven devout Christian boys who took refuge in a cave rather than offer sacrifices in the temple of the Roman gods, and who fell into a deep sleep and came forth two hundred years later to discover that Christianity had miraculously become the official religion of Rome while they were doing their Rip van Winkle act. What was supposedly their cave may still be seen just beyond the Roman stadium of Ephesus.

"There's also the Meryemana," Charlie said.

Mr. Gladstone gave him a polite blank smile. "Beg your pardon?"

"The house where the Virgin Mary lived in the last years of her life. Jesus told St. John the Apostle to look after her, and he brought her to Ephesus, so it's said. About a hundred years ago some Eastern Orthodox priests went looking for her house and found it, sure enough, about three miles outside town."

"Indeed."

"More likely it's sixth century Byzantine," said Charlie. "But the foundations are much older. The Orthodox Christians go there on pilgrimage every summer. You really ought to see it." He smiled his warmest, most savage smile. "Ephesus has always been a center of mother-goddess worship, you know, and apparently it has continued to be one even in post-pagan times."

Mr. Gladstone's lips quirked ever so slightly. Though I assumed—correctly— that he was Protestant, even a Presbyterian was bound to be annoyed at hearing someone call the Virgin Mary a mother-goddess. But all he said was, "It would be interesting to see, yes."

Charlie wouldn't let up. "You will, of course, look in at the Seljuk Museum to see the predecessor goddess' statue, won't you? Diana, I mean. Diana of the Hundred Breasts. It's best to visit the museum before you begin your tour of the ruins, anyway. And the statues—there are two, actually—sum up the whole concept of the sacred female principle in a really spectacular way. The primordial mother, the great archetype. The celestial cow that nourishes the world. You need to see it, if you want truly to understand the bipolar sexual nature of the divine, eh, Mr. G?" He glanced toward me. "You too, Tim. The two of you, meet me in front of the museum at nine tomorrow, OK? Basic orientation lecture by Dr. Walker. Followed by a visit to ancient Ephesus, including the Cave of the Seven Sleepers. Perhaps the Meryemana afterward." Charlie flashed a dazzling grin. "Will you have some wine, Mr. Gladstone?"

"No, thank you," Mr. Gladstone said, quickly putting his hand over the empty glass in front of him.

After the museum, the next morning, we doubled back to the ruins of Ephesus proper. Mobs of tour groups were already there, milling around befuddledly as tour groups will do, but Charlie zipped right around them to the best stuff. The ruins are in a marvelous state of preservation—a nearly intact Roman city of the first century A.D., the usual forum and temples and stadium and gymnasium and such, and of course the famous two-story library that the Turks feature on all those tourist posters.

We had the best of all possible guides. Charlie has a genuine passion for archaeology—it's the only thing, I suspect, that he really cares for, other than himself—and he pointed out a million details that we would otherwise have missed. With special relish he dwelled on the grotesqueries of the cult of Diana, telling us not only about the metaphorical significance of the goddess' multiplicity of breasts, but about the high priest who was always a eunuch. "His title," said Charlie, "meant 'He who has been set free by God' "—and the staff of virgins who assisted him, and the special priests known as the Acrobatae, or "walkers on tip-toe," et cetera, et cetera. Mr. Gladstone showed signs of definite distaste as Charlie went on to speculate on some of the more flamboyant erotic aspects of pagan worship hereabouts, but he wouldn't stop. He never does, when he has a chance to display his erudition and simultaneously offend and unsettle someone.

Eventually it was midafternoon and the day had become really hot. We were only halfway through our tour of the ancient city, with the Cave of the Seven Sleepers still a mile or two in the distance, and clearly Mr. Gladstone was wilting. We decided to call it a day and had a late lunch of kebabs and stewed eggplant at one of the innumerable and interchangeable little bistros in town. "We can go to the cave first thing tomorrow morning, when it's still cool," Charlie offered.

"Thank you. But I think I would prefer to visit it alone, if you don't mind. A private pilgrimage—for my late wife's sake, do you see? Something of a ceremonial observance."

"Certainly," Charlie intoned reverently. "I quite understand."

I asked Charlie if he would be coming out to the hotel again that evening for dinner with me. No, he said, he would be busy at the dig—the cool of the evening was a good time to work, without the distraction of gawking tourists—but we arranged to meet in the morning for breakfast and a little brotherly catching up on family news. I left him in town and drove back to the hotel with Mr. Gladstone.

"Your brother isn't a religious man, is he?" he said.

"I'm afraid that neither of us is, especially. It's the way we were raised."

"But he *really* isn't. You're merely indifferent; he is hostile."

"How can you tell?"

"Because," he said, "he was trying so hard to provoke me with those things he was saying about Diana of Ephesus. He makes no distinction between Christianity and paganism. All religions must be the same to him, mere silly cults. And so he thinks he can get at my beliefs somehow by portraying pagan worship as absurd and bizarre."

"He looks upon them all as cults, yes. But silly, no. In fact Charlie takes religion very seriously, though not exactly in the same way you do. He regards it as a conspiracy by the power elite to remain on top at the expense of the masses. And holy scriptures are just works of fiction dreamed up to perpetuate the authority of the priests and their bosses."

"He sees all religions that way, does he, without making distinctions?"

"Every one of them, yes. Always the same thing, throughout the whole of human history."

"The poor man," said Mr. Gladstone. "The poor empty-souled man. If only I could set him straight, somehow!"

There it was again—the compassion, the pity. For Charlie, of all people! Fascinating. Fascinating.

"I doubt that you'd succeed," I told him. "He's inherently a skeptical person. He's never been anything else. And he's a scientist, remember, a man who lives or dies by rational explanations. If it can't be explained, then it probably isn't real. He doesn't have a smidgen of belief in anything he can't see and touch and measure."

"He is incapable of giving credence to the evidence of things not seen?"

"Excuse me?"

" 'The substance of things hoped for, the evidence of things not seen.' Book of Hebrews, 11:1. It's St. Paul's definition of faith."

"Ah."

"St. Paul was here, you know. In this town, in Ephesus, on a missionary journey. Gods that are fashioned by human hands are no gods at all, he told the populace. Whereupon a certain Demetrius, a silversmith who earned his living making statuettes of the many-breasted goddess whose images we saw today in the museum, called his colleagues together and said, 'If this man has his way, the temple of the great goddess Diana will be destroyed and we will lose our livelihoods.' And when they heard these sayings, they were full of wrath, and cried out, saying, 'Great is Diana of the Ephesians.' And the whole city was filled with confusion. That's the Book of Acts, 19:28. And there was such a huge uproar in town over the things that Paul was preaching that he found it prudent to depart very quickly for Macedonia."

"I see."

"But the temple of the goddess was destroyed anyway, eventually. And her statues were cast down and buried in the earth, and now are seen only in museums."

"And the people of Ephesus became Christians," I said. "And Moslems after that, it would seem."

He looked startled. My gratuitous little dig had clearly stung him. But then he smiled.

"I see that you are your brother's brother," he said.

I was up late reading, and thinking about Charlie, and staring at the moonlight shimmering on the bay. About half past eleven I hit the sack. Almost immediately my phone rang.

Charlie. "Are you alone, bro?"

"No," I said. "As a matter of fact, Mr. Gladstone and I are hunkering down getting ready to commit abominations before the Lord."

"I thought maybe one of those horny Kraut ladies—"

"Cut it out. I'm alone, Charlie. And pretty sleepy. What is it?"

"Can you come down to the ruins? There's something I want to show you."

"Right now?"

"Now is a good time for this."

"I told you I was sleepy."

"It's something big, Tim. I need to show it to somebody, and you're the only person on this planet I even halfway trust."

"Something you discovered tonight?"

"Get in your car and come on down. I'll meet you by the Magnesian Gate. That's the back entrance. Go past the museum and turn right at the crossroads in town."

"Charlie—"

"Move your ass, bro. *Please.*"

That "please," from Charlie, was something very unusual. In twenty minutes I was at the gate. He was waiting there, swinging a huge flashlight. A tool sack was slung over one shoulder. He looked wound up tight, as tense as I had ever seen him.

Selecting a key from a chain that held at least thirty of them, he unlocked the gate and led me down a long straight avenue paved with worn blocks of stone. The moon was practically full and the ancient city was bathed in cool silvery light. He pointed out the buildings as we went by them: "The Baths of Varius. The Basilica. The Necropolis. The Temple of Isis." He droned the names in a sing-song tone as though this was just one more guided tour. We turned to the right, onto another street that I recognized as the main one, where earlier that day I had seen the Gate of Hercules, the Temple of Hadrian, the library. "Here we are. Back of the brothel and the latrine."

We scrambled uphill perhaps fifty yards through gnarled scrubby underbrush until we came to a padlocked metal grate set in the ground in an otherwise empty area. Charlie produced the proper key and pulled back the grate. His flashlight beam revealed a rough earthen-walled tunnel, maybe five feet high, leading into the hillside. The air inside was hot and stale, with a sweet heavy odor of dry soil. After about twenty feet the tunnel forked. Crouching, we followed the right-hand fork, pushing our way through some bundles of dried leaves that seemed to have been put there to block its entrance.

"Look there," he said.

He shot the beam off to the left and I found myself staring at a place where the tunnel wall had been very carefully smoothed. An upright circular slab of rough-hewn marble perhaps a yard across was set into it there.

"What is it?" I asked him. "A gravestone? A commemorative plaque?"

"Some sort of door, more likely. Covering a funeral chamber, I would suspect. You see these?" He indicated three smaller circles of what looked like baked clay, mounted in a symmetrical way over the marble slab, arranged to form the angles of an equilateral triangle. They overlapped the edges of the slab as though sealing it into the wall. I went closer and saw inscriptions carved into the clay circles, an array of mysterious symbols and letters.

"What language is this? Not Greek. Hebrew, maybe?"

"No. I don't actually know what it is. Some unknown Anatolian script, or some peculiar form of Aramaic or Phoenician—I just can't say, Timmo. Maybe it's a nonsense script, even. Purely decorative sacred scribbles conveying spells to keep intruders away, maybe. You know, some kind of magical mumbo jumbo. It might be anything."

"You found this tonight?"

"Three weeks ago. We've known this tunnel was here for a long time, but it was thought to be empty. I happened to be doing some sonar scanning overhead and I got an echo back from a previously uncharted branch, so I came down and took a look around. Nobody knows about it but me. And you."

Gingerly I ran my hand over the face of the marble slab. It was extraordinarily smooth, cool to the touch. I had the peculiar illusion that my fingertips were tingling, as though from a mild electrical charge.

"What are you going to do?" I asked.

"Open it."

"Now?"

"Now, bro. You and me."

"You can't do that!"

"I can't?"

"You're part of an expedition, Charlie. You can't just bust into a tomb, or whatever this is, on your own. It isn't proper procedure, is it? You need to have the other scientists here. And the Turkish antiquities officials—they'll string you up by the balls if they find out you've done a bit of secret freelance excavating without notifying any local authorities."

"We break the seals. We look inside. If there's anything important in there, we check it out just to gratify our own curiosity and then we go away, and in the morning I discover it all over again and raise a big hullabaloo and we go through all the proper procedure then. Listen, bro, there could be something big in there, don't you see? The grave of a high priest. The grave of some prehistoric king. The lost treasure of the Temple of Diana. The Ark of the Covenant. Anything. Anything. Whatever it is, I want to know. And I want to see it before anybody else does."

He was lit up with a passion so great that I could scarcely recognize him as my cool brother Charlie.

"How are you going to explain the broken seals?"

"Broken by some tomb-robber in antiquity," he said. "Who got frightened away before he could finish the job."

He had always been a law unto himself, my brother Charlie. I argued with him a little more, but I knew it would do no good. He had never been much of a team player. He wasn't going to have five or six wimpy colleagues and a bunch of Turkish antiquities officials staring over his shoulder while that sealed chamber was opened for the first time in two thousand years.

He drew a small battery powered lamp from his sack and set it on the ground. Then he began to pull the implements of his trade out of the sack, the little chisels, the camel's-hair brushes, the diamond-bladed hacksaw.

"Why did you wait until I got here before you opened it?" I asked.

"Because I thought I might need help pulling that slab out of the wall, and who could I trust except you? Besides, I wanted an audience for the grand event."

"Of course."

"You know me, Timmo."

"So I do, bro. So I do."

He began very carefully to chisel off one of the clay seals. It came away in two chunks. Setting it to one side, he went to work on the second one, and then the third. Then he dug his fingertips into the earthen wall at the edge of the slab and gave it an experimental tug.

"I do need you," he said. "Put your shoulder against the slab and steady it as I pry it with this crowbar. I don't want it just toppling out."

Bit by bit he wiggled it free. As it started to pivot and fall forward I leaned all my weight into it, and Charlie reached across me and caught it too, and together we were able to brace it as it left its aperture and guide it down carefully to the ground.

We stared into the blackest of black holes. Ancient musty air came roaring forth in a long, dry whoosh. Charlie leaned forward and started to poke the flashlight into the opening.

But then he pulled back sharply and turned away, gasping as though he had inhaled a wisp of something noxious.

"Charlie?"

"Just a second." He waved his hand near his head a couple of times, the way you might do when brushing away a cobweb. "Just—a—goddamn—second, Tim!" A convulsive shiver ran through him. Automatically I moved toward him to see what the matter was and as I came up beside him in front of that dark opening I felt a sudden weird sensation, a jolt, a jab, and my head began to spin. And for a moment—just a moment—I seemed to hear a strange music, an eerie, high-pitched wailing sound like the keening of elevator cables far, far away. In that crazy incomprehensible moment I imagined that I was standing at the rim of a deep ancient well, the oldest well of all, the well from which all creation flows, with strange shadowy things churning and throbbing down below, and from its depths rose a wild rush of perfumed air that dizzied and intoxicated me.

Then the moment passed and I was in my right mind again and I looked at Charlie and he looked at me.

"You felt it too, didn't you?" I said.

"Felt what?" he demanded fiercely. He seemed almost angry.

I searched for the words. But it was all fading, fading fast, and there was only Charlie with his face jammed into mine, angry Charlie, terrifying Charlie, practically daring me to claim that anything peculiar had happened.

"It was very odd, bro," I said finally. "Like a drug thing, almost."

"Oxygen deprivation, is all. A blast of old stale air."

"You think?"

"I know."

But he seemed uncharacteristically hesitant, even a little befuddled. He stood at an angle to the opening, head turned away, shoulders slumping, the flashlight dangling from his hand.

"Aren't you going to look inside?" I asked, after a bit.

"Give me a moment, Timmo."

"Charlie, are you all right?"

"Christ, yes! I breathed in a little dust, that's all." He knelt, rummaged in the tool sack, pulled out a canteen, took a deep drink. "Better," he said hoarsely. "Want some?" I took the canteen from him and he leaned into the opening again, flashing the beam around.

"What do you see?"

"Nothing. Not a fucking thing."

"They put up a marble slab and plaster it with inscribed seals and there's nothing at all behind it?"

"A hole," he said. "Maybe five feet deep, five feet high. A storage chamber of some kind, I would guess. Nothing in it. Absolutely fucking nothing, bro."

"Let me see."

"Don't you trust me?"

In fact I didn't, not very much. But I just shrugged, and he handed me the flashlight, and I peered into the hole. Charlie was right. The interior of the chamber was smooth and regular, but it was empty, not the slightest trace of anything.

"Shit," Charlie said. He shook his head somberly. "My very own Tutankh-amen tomb, only nothing's in it. Let's get the hell out of here."

"Are you going to report this?"

"What for? I come in after hours, conduct illicit explorations, and all I have to show for my sins is an empty hole? What's the good of telling anybody that? Just for the sake of making myself look like an unethical son of a bitch? No, bro. None of this ever happened."

"But the seals—the inscriptions in an unknown script—"

"Not important. Let's go, Tim."

He still sounded angry, and not, I think, just because the little chamber behind the marble slab had been empty. Something had gotten to him just now, and gotten to him deeply. Had he heard the weird music too? Had he looked into that fathomless well? He hated all mystery, everything inexplicable. I think that was why he had become an archaeologist. Mysteries had a way of unhinging him. When I was maybe ten and he was thirteen, we had spent a rainy evening telling each other ghost stories, and finally we made one up together, something about spooks from another world who were haunting our attic, and our own story scared me so much that I began to cry. I imagined I heard strange creaks overhead. Charlie mocked me mercilessly, but it seemed to me that for a time he had looked a little nervous too, and when I said so he got very annoyed indeed. Then, bluffing all the way, I invited him to come up to the attic with me right then and there to see that it was safe, and he punched me in the chest and knocked me down. Later he denied the whole episode.

"I'm sorry I wasted your time tonight, kid," he said, as we hiked back up to our cars.

"That's OK. It just might have been something special."

"Just might have been, yeah." He grinned and winked. He was himself again, old devil-may-care Charlie. "Sleep tight, bro. See you in the morning."

But I didn't sleep tight at all. I kept waking and hearing the wailing sound of far-off elevator cables, and my dreams were full of blurry strangenesses.

*   *   *

The next day I hung out at the hotel all day, breakfasting with Charlie—he didn't refer to the events of the night before at all—and lounging by the pool the rest of the time. I had some vague thought of hooking up with one of the German tourist ladies, I suppose, but no openings presented themselves, and I contented myself with watching the show. Even in puritanical Turkey, where the conservative politicians are trying to put women back into veils and ankle-length skirts, European women of all ages casually go topless at coastal resorts like this, and it was remarkable to see how much *savoir-faire* the Turkish pool-side waiters displayed while taking bar orders from saftig bare-breasted grand-mothers from Hamburg or Munich and their stunning, topless granddaughters.

Mr. Gladstone, who hadn't been around in the morning, turned up in late afternoon. I was in the lobby bar by then, working on my third or fourth post-lunch *raki*. He looked sweaty and tired and sunburned. I ordered a Coke for him.

"Busy day?"

"Very. The Cave of the Seven Sleepers was my first stop. A highly emotional experience, I have to say, not because of the cave itself, you understand, al-though the ancient ruined church there is quite interesting, but because—the associations—the memories of my dear wife that it summoned—"

"Of course."

"After that my driver took me out to the so-called House of the Virgin. Perhaps it's genuine, perhaps not, but either way it's a moving thing to see. The invisible presence of thousands of pilgrims hovers over it, the aura of centuries of faith." He smiled gently. "Do you know what I mean, Mr. Walker?"

"I think I do, yes."

"And in the afternoon I saw the Basilica of St. John, on Ayasuluk Hill."

I didn't know anything about that. He explained that it was the acropolis of the old Byzantine city—the steep hill just across the main highway from the center of the town of Seljuk. Legend had it that St. John the Apostle had been buried up there, and centuries later the Emperor Justinian built an enormous church on the site, which was, of course, a ruin now, but an impressive one.

"And you?" he said. "You visited with your brother?"

"In the morning, yes."

"A brilliant man, your brother. If only he could be happier, eh?"

"Oh, I think Charlie's happy, all right. He's had his own way every step of his life."

"Is that your definition of happiness? Having your own way?"

"It can be very helpful."

"And you haven't had *your* own way, is that it, Mr. Walker?"

"My life has been reasonably easy by most people's standards, I have to admit. I was smart enough to pick a wealthy great-grandfather. But compared with Charlie—he has an extraordinary mind, he's had a splendid scientific career, he's admired by all the members of his profession. I don't even have a profession, Mr. Gladstone. I just float around."

"You're young, Mr. Walker. You'll find something to do and someone to share your life with, and you'll settle down. But your brother—I wonder, Mr.

Walker. Something vital is missing from his life. But he will never find it, because he is not willing to admit that it's missing."

"Religion, do you mean?"

"Not specifically, no. Belief, perhaps. Not religion, but belief. Do you follow me, Mr. Walker? One must believe in *something*, do you see? And your brother will not permit himself to do that." He gave me the gentle smile again. "Would you excuse me, now? I've had a rather strenuous day. I think a little nap, before supper—"

Since we were the only two Americans in the place, I invited him to join me again for dinner that night. He did most of the talking, reminiscing about his wife, telling me about his children—he had three, in their thirties—and describing some of the things he had seen in his tour of the Biblical places. I had never spent much time with anyone of his sort. A kindly man, an earnest man, and, I suspect, not quite as simple a man as a casual observer might think.

He went upstairs about half past eight. I returned to the bar and had a couple of raw Turkish brandies and thought hopeful thoughts about the stunning German granddaughters. Somewhere about ten, as I was considering going to bed, a waiter appeared and said, "You are Mr. Timothy Walker?"

"Yes."

"Your brother Charles is at the security gate and asks that you come out to meet him."

Mystified, I went rushing out into the courtyard. The hotel grounds are locked down every night and nobody is admitted except guests and the guests of guests. I saw the glare of headlights just beyond the gate. Charlie's car.

"What's up, bro?"

His eyes were wild. He gestured at me with furious impatience. "In. *In!*" Almost before I closed the door he spun the car around and was zooming down the narrow, winding road back to Seljuk. He was hunched over the wheel in the most peculiar rigid way.

"Charlie?"

"Exactly what did you experience," he said tightly, "when we pulled that marble slab out of the wall?"

My reply was carefully vague.

"Tell me," he said. "Be very precise."

"I don't want you to laugh at me, Charlie."

"Just tell me."

I took a deep breath. "Well, then. I imagined that I heard far-off music. I had a kind of vision of—well, someplace weird and mysterious. I thought I smelled perfume. The whole thing lasted maybe half a second and then it was over."

He was silent a moment.

Then he said, in a strange little quiet way, "It was the same for me, bro."

"You denied it. I asked you, and you said no, Charlie."

"Well, I lied. It was the same for me." His voice had become very odd— thin, tight, quavering. Everything about him right now was tight. Something had to pop. The car was traveling at maybe eighty miles an hour on that little road and I feared for my life. After a very long time he said, "Do you think there's any possibility, Tim, that we might have let something out of that hole in the ground when we broke those seals and pulled that slab out?"

I stared at him. "That's crazy, Charlie."

"I know it is. Just answer me: Do you think we felt something moving past us as we opened that chamber?"

"Hey, we're too old to be telling each other spook stories, bro."

"I'm being serious."

"Bullshit you are," I said. "I hate it when you play with me like this."

"I'm not playing," Charlie said, and he turned around so that he was practically facing me for a moment. His face was twisted with strain. "Timmo, some goddamned thing that looks awfully much like Diana of Ephesus has been walking around in the ruins since sundown. Three people have seen her that I know of. Three very reliable people."

I couldn't believe that he was saying stuff like this. Not Charlie.

"Keep your eyes on the road, will you?" I told him. "You'll get us killed driving like that."

"Do you know how much it costs me to say these things? Do you know how lunatic it sounds to me? But she's real. She's there. She was sealed up in that hole, and we let her out. The foreman of the excavations has seen her, and Judy, the staff artist, and Mike Dornan, the ceramics guy."

"They're fucking with your head, Charlie. Or you're fucking with mine."

"No. No. No. No."

"Where are we going?" I asked.

"To look for her. To find out what the hell it is that those people think they saw. I've got to know, Tim. This time, *I've absolutely got to know.*"

The desperation in Charlie's voice was something new in my experience of him. *I've absolutely got to know.* Why? Why? It was all too crazy. And dragging me out like this—why? To bear witness? To help him prove to himself that he actually was seeing the thing that he was seeing, if indeed he saw it? Or, maybe, to help him convince himself that there was nothing there to see?

But he wasn't going to see anything. I was sure of that.

"Charlie," I said. "Oh, Charlie, Charlie, Charlie, this isn't happening, is it? Not really."

We pulled up outside the main gate of the ruins. A watchman was posted there, a Turk. He stepped quickly aside as Charlie went storming through into the site. I saw flashlights glowing in the distance, and then four or five American-looking people. Charlie's colleagues, the archaeologists.

"Well?" Charlie yelled. He sounded out of control.

A frizzy-haired woman of about forty came up from somewhere to our left. She looked as wild-eyed and agitated as Charlie. For the first time I began to think this might not be just some goofy practical joke.

"Heading east," the woman blurted. "Toward the stadium or maybe all the way out to the goddess sanctuary. Dick saw it too. And Edward thinks he did."

"Anybody get a photo?"

"Not that I know of," the woman said.

"Come on," Charlie said to me, and went running off at an angle to the direction we had just come. Frantically I chased after him. He was chugging uphill, into the thorny scrub covering the unexcavated areas of the city. By moonlight I saw isolated shattered pillars rising from the ground like broken teeth, and tumbledown columns that had been tossed around like so many toothpicks. As I came alongside him he said, "There's a little sanctuary of the Mother Goddess back there. Wouldn't that be the logical place that she'd want to go to?"

"For shit's sake, Charlie! What are you saying?"

He kept on running, giving me no answer. I fought my way up the hill through a tangle of brambles and canes that slashed at me like daggers, all the while wondering what the hell we were going to find on top. We were halfway up when shouts came to us from down the hill, people behind us waving and pointing. Charlie halted and listened, frowning. Then he swung around and started sprinting back down the hill. "She's gone outside the ruins," he called to me over his shoulder. "Through the fence, heading into town! Come on, Tim!"

I went running after him, scrambling downhill, then onward along the main entrance road and onto the main highway. I'm in good running shape, but Charlie was moving with a maniacal zeal that left me hard pressed to keep up with him. Twenty feet apart, we came pounding down the road, past the museum and into town. All the dinky restaurants were open, even this late, and little knots of Turks had emerged from them to gather in the crossroads. Some were kneeling in prayer, hammering their heads against the pavement, and others were wildly gesticulating at one another in obvious shock and bewilderment. Charlie, without breaking stride, called out to them in guttural Turkish and got a whole babble of replies.

"Ayasuluk Hill," he said to me. "That's the direction she's going in."

We crossed the broad boulevard that divides the town in half. As we passed the bus station half a dozen men came running out of a side street in front of us, screaming as though they had just been disemboweled. You don't expect to hear adult male Turks screaming. They are a nation of tough people, by and large. These fellows went flying past us without halting, big men with thick black mustaches. Their eyes were wide and gleaming like beacons, their faces rigid and distended with shock and horror, as though twenty devils were coming after them.

"Charlie—"

"Look there," he said, in an utterly flat voice, and pointed into the darkness.

Something—*something*—was moving away from us down that side street, something very tall and very strange. I saw a tapering conical body, a hint of weird appendages, a crackling blue-white aura. It seemed to be floating rather than walking, carried along by a serene but inexorable drifting motion almost as if its feet were several inches off the ground. Maybe they were.

As we watched, the thing halted and peered into the open window of a house. There was a flash of blinding light, intense but short-lived. Then the front door popped open and a bunch of frantic Turks came boiling out like a pack of Keystone Cops, running in sixty directions at once, yelling and flinging their arms about as though trying to surrender.

One of them tripped and went sprawling down right at the creature's feet. He seemed unable to get up; he knelt there all bunched up, moaning and babbling, shielding his face with outspread hands. The thing paused and looked down, and seemed to reach its arms out in fluid gestures, and the blue-white glow spread for a moment like a mantle over the man. Then the light withdrew from him and the creature, gliding smoothly past the trembling fallen man, continued on its serene silent way toward the dark hill that loomed above the town.

"Come," Charlie said to me.

We went forward. The creature had disappeared up ahead, though we caught occasional glimpses of the blue-white light as it passed between the low little buildings of the town. We reached the man who had tripped; he had not arisen, but lay face down, shivering, covering his head with his hands. A low rumbling moan of fear came steadily from him. From in front of us, hoarse cries of terror drifted to us from here and there as one villager or another encountered the thing that was passing through their town, and now and again we could see that cool bright light, rising steadily above us until finally it was shining down from the upper levels of Ayasuluk Hill.

"You really want to go up there?" I asked him.

He didn't offer me an answer, nor did he stop moving forward. I wasn't about to turn back either, I realized. Willy-nilly I followed him to the end of the street, around a half-ruined mosque at the base of the hill, and up to a lofty metal gate tipped with spikes. Stoned on our own adrenaline, we swarmed up that gate like Crusaders attacking a Saracen fortress, went over the top, dropped down in the bushes on the far side. I was able to see, by the brilliant gleam of the full moon, the low walls of the destroyed Basilica of St. John just beyond, and, behind it, the massive Byzantine fortification that crowned the hill. Together we scrambled toward the summit.

"You go this way, Tim. I'll go the other and we'll meet on the far side."

"Right."

I didn't know what I was looking for. I just ran around the hill, along the ramparts, into the church, down the empty aisles, out the gaping window-frames.

Suddenly I caught a glimpse of something up ahead. Light, cool white light, an unearthly light very much like moonlight, only concentrated into a fiercely gleaming point hovering a couple of yards above the ground, thirty or forty feet in front of me.

"Charlie?" I called. My voice was no more than a hoarse gasp.

I edged forward. The light was so intense now that I was afraid it might damage my eyes. But I continued to stare, as if the thing would disappear if I were to blink for even a millionth of a second.

I heard the wailing music again.

Soft, distant, eerie. Cables rubbing together in a dark shaft. This time it seemed to be turned outward, rising far beyond me, reaching into distant space or perhaps some even more distant dimension. Something calling, announcing its regained freedom, summoning—whom? *What?*

"Charlie?" I said. It was a barely audible croak. "Charlie?"

I noticed him now, edging up from the other side. I pointed at the source of the light. He nodded.

I moved closer. The light seemed to change, to grow momentarily less fierce. And then I was able to see her.

She wasn't exactly identical to the statues in the museum. Her face wasn't really a face, at least not a human one. She had beady eyes, faceted the way an insect's are. She had an extra set of arms, little dangling ones, coming out at her hips. And, though the famous breasts were there, at least fifty of them and maybe the hundred of legend, I don't think they were actual breasts because I don't think this creature was a mammal. More of a reptile, I would guess, with leathery skin, more or less as scaly as a snake's, and tiny dots of nostrils, and a black slithery tongue, jagged like a lightning bolt, that came shooting quickly out between her slitted lips again and again and again, as though checking on the humidity or the ambient temperature or some such thing.

I saw, and Charlie saw. For a fraction of a second I wanted to drop down on my knees and rub my forehead in the ground and give worship. And then I just wanted to run.

I said, "Charlie, I definitely think we ought to get the hell out of—"

"Cool it, bro," he said. He stepped forward. Walked right up to her, stared her in the face. I was terrified for him, seeing him get that close. She dwarfed him. He was like a doll in front of her. How had a thing this big managed to fit in that opening in the tunnel wall? How had those ancient Greeks ever managed to get her in there in the first place?

That dazzling light crackled and hissed around her like some sort of electrical discharge. And yet Charlie stood his ground, unflinching, rock-solid. The expression on my brother's face was a nearly incomprehensible mixture of anger and fear.

He jabbed his forefinger through the air at her.

"You," he said to her. It was almost a snarl. "Tell me what the hell you are."

They were maybe ten feet apart, the man and the—what? The goddess? The monster?

Charlie had to know.

"You speak English?" he demanded. "Turkish? Tell me. I'm the one who let you out of that hole. Tell me what you are. I want to know." Eye to eye, face to face. "Something from another planet, are you, maybe? Another dimension? An ancient race that used to live on the Earth before humans did?"

"Charlie," I whispered.

But he wouldn't let up. "Or maybe you're an actual and literal goddess," he said. His tone had turned softer, a mocking croon now. "Diana of Ephesus, is that who you are? Stepping right out of the pages of mythology in all your fantastic beauty? Well, do me some magic, goddess, if that's who you are. Do a miracle for me, just a little one." The angry edge was back in his voice. "Turn that tree into an elephant. Turn me into a sheep, if you can. What's the matter, Diana, you no spikka da English? All right. Why the hell should you? But how about Greek, then? Surely you can understand Greek."

"For Christ's sake, Charlie—"

He ignored me. It was as if I wasn't there. He was talking to her in Greek, now. I suppose it was Greek. It was harsh, thick-sounding, jaggedly rhythmic. His eyes were wild and his face was flushed with fury. I was afraid that she would hurl a thunderbolt of blue-white light at him, but no, no, she just stood there through all his whole harangue, as motionless as those statues of her in the little museum, listening patiently as my furious brother went on and on and on at her in the language of Homer and Sophocles.

He stopped, finally. Waited as if expecting her to respond.

No response came. I could hear the whistling sound of her slow steady breathing. Occasionally there was some slight movement of her body, but that was all.

"Well, Diana?" Charlie said. "What do you have to say for yourself, Diana?"

Silence.

"You fraud!" Charlie cried, in a great and terrible voice. "You fake! Some goddess you are! You aren't real at all, and that's God's own truth. You aren't even here. You're nothing but a fucking hallucination. A projection of some kind. I bet I could walk up to you and put my hand right through you."

Still no reaction. Nothing. She just stood there, those faceted eyes glittering, that little tongue flickering. Saying nothing, offering him no help.

That was when he flipped out. Charlie seemed to puff up as if about to explode with rage, and went rushing toward her, arms upraised, fists clenched in a wild gesture of attack. I wanted desperately to stop him, but my feet were frozen in place. I was certain that he was going to die. We both were.

"Damn you!" he roared, with something like a sob behind the fury. "Damn you, damn you, damn you!"

But before he could strike her, her aura flared up around her like a sheath, and for a moment the air was full of brilliant flares of cold flame that went whirling and whirling around her in a way that was too painful to watch. I caught a glimpse of Charlie staggering back from her, and I backed away myself, covering my face with my forearm, but even so the whirling lights came stabbing into my brain, forcing me to the ground. It seemed then that they all coalesced into a single searing point of white light, which rose like a dagger into the sky, climbing, climbing, becoming something almost like a comet, and—then—

Vanishing.

And then I blanked out.

It was just before dawn when I awakened. My eyes fluttered open almost hesitantly. The moon was gone, the first pink streaks of light were beginning to appear. Charlie sat beside me. He was already awake.

"Where is it?" I asked immediately.

"Gone, bro."

"Gone?"

He nodded. "Without a trace. If it ever was up here with us at all."

"What do you mean, *if?*"

"*If,* that's what I mean. Who the hell knows what was going on up here last night? Do you?"

"No."

"Well, neither do I. All I know is that it isn't going on any more. There's nobody around but me and thee."

He was trying to sound like the old casual Charlie I knew, the man who had been everywhere and done everything and took it all in his stride. But there was a quality in his voice that I had never heard in it before, something entirely new.

"Gone?" I said, stupidly. "Really gone?"

"Really gone, yes. Vanished. You hear how quiet everything is?" Indeed the town, spread out below us, was silent except for the crowing of the first roosters and the far-off sound of a farm tractor starting up somewhere.

"Are you all right?" I asked him.

"Fine," he said. "Absolutely fine."

But he said it through clenched teeth. I couldn't bear to look at him. A thing had happened here that badly needed explanation, and no explanations were available, and I knew what that must be doing to him. I kept staring at the place where that eerie being had been, and I remembered that single shaft of light that had taken its place, and I felt a crushing sense of profound and terrible loss. Something strange and weirdly beautiful and utterly fantastic and inexplicable had been loose in the world for a little while, after centuries of— what? Imprisonment? Hibernation?—and now it was gone, and it would never return. It had known at once, I was sure, that this was no era for goddesses. Or whatever it was.

We sat side by side in silence for a minute or two.

"I think we ought to go back down now," I said finally.

"Right. Let's go back down," Charlie said.

And without saying another word as we descended, we made our way down the hill of Ayasuluk, the hill of St. John the Apostle, who was the man who wrote the Book of Revelations.

Mr. Gladstone was having breakfast in the hotel coffee shop when Charlie and I came in. He saw at once that something was wrong and asked if he could help in any way, and after some hesitation we told him something of what had happened, and then we told him more, and then we told him the whole story right to the end.

He didn't laugh and he didn't make any sarcastic skeptical comments. He took it all quite seriously.

"Perhaps the Seal of Solomon was what was on that marble slab," he suggested. "The Turks would say some such thing, at any rate. King Solomon had power over the evil jinn, and locked them away in flasks and caves and tombs, and put his seal on them to keep them locked up. It's in the Koran."

"You've read the Koran?" I asked, surprised.

"I've read a lot of things," said Mr. Gladstone.

"The Seal of Solomon," Charlie said, scowling. He was trying hard to be his old self again, and almost succeeding. Almost. "Evil spirits. Magic. Oh, Jesus Christ!"

"Perhaps," said Mr. Gladstone.

"What?" Charlie said.

The little man from Ohio or Indiana or Iowa put his hand over Charlie's. "If only I could help you," he said. "But you've been undone, haven't you, by the evidence of things seen."

"You have the quote wrong," said Charlie. " 'The substance of things hoped for, the evidence of things not seen.' Book of Hebrews, 11:1."

Mr. Gladstone was impressed. So was I.

"But this is different," he said to Charlie. "This time, you actually *saw*. You were, I think, a man who prided himself on believing in nothing at all. But now you can no longer even believe in your own disbelief."

Charlie reddened. "Saw *what*? A goddess? Jesus! You think I believe that that was a goddess? A genuine immortal supernatural being of a higher order of existence? Or—what?—some kind of actual alien creature? You want me to believe it was an alien that had been locked up in there all that time? An alien from where? Mars? And who locked it up? Or was it one of King Solomon's jinn, maybe?"

"Does it really matter which it was?" Mr. Gladstone asked softly.

Charlie started to say something, but he choked it back. After a moment he stood. "Listen, I need to go now," he said. "Mr. Gladstone—Timmo—I'll catch up with you later, is that all right?"

And then he turned and stalked away. But before he left, I saw the look in his eyes.

His eyes. Oh, Charlie. Oh. Those eyes. Those frightened, empty eyes.

LA LLORONA

Yxta Maya Murray

In last year's volume of *The Year's Best Fantasy & Horror* we published Pat Mora's poetic version of the myth of La Llorona; this year we have a stunning prose retelling of the same myth by Chicana author Yxta Maya Murray. According to Southwestern folklore, La Llorona is a frightening horse-faced, claw-fingered creature found haunting dry riverbeds. She is the ghost of a woman abandoned by her lover who then killed her own children in grief and rage. An encounter with the spectral Wailing Woman of the West is deemed to be fatal.

Yxta Maya Murray's dark rendition of the tale falls on the border between fantasy and horror. It comes from the November/December issue of *The North American Review*. The author, a law professor at Loyola Law School in Los Angeles, recently published a novel, *Locas*, which focuses on the lives of Mexican women in East L.A.

—T. W. and E. D.

I could have cooked them up and eaten them with some fine dark wine, a few dry crackers. Like a mad greek goddess, searching out the bones, searching her sons' blank eyes for a last song then gulping them down like that, ferociously.

Instead I fed them to the water. There is a deep, silty river by my house, it is purple black at night with strains of shaded blue like royal velvet beneath the surface. The fish live here, quietly, staring up at the light during the day with their small electric eyes, gulping in the watery air with their fishy mouths opening and shutting, their gills fluttering in the current. You can skim your hand through the force of the water, then plunge it in and feel the hard rushing push as it runs back toward the sea.

A man never knew how angry a woman could be until the very last moment, the last second when he glanced up at her and saw nothing but red, hot volcanoes. How could he love another, with his smooth skin and hard legs, his hands as strong as river rocks, and as soft? A husband is forever, he belongs to you, as do his children. They cannot leave no matter how hard they try, it will turn them into beasts, it will make you into a monster.

I have green gills now, I breathe the water as the fish do, as my children did, living down here at the bottom of the river, caressing myself and remembering.

I was once like you are. I spoke quietly, my head turned down and my mouth bending up slightly into a small smile, satisfied. I cooked warm, spicy meals with meat and rice and beans in them, milk on the table and spirits for my husband after. Putting the children to bed with stories of an Aztec king, a Mayan princess living among jaguars and wild horses, fighting in their bloody wars. My sons would sleep like trees.

What is a woman? A woman is waiting. Waiting for the day to begin and then the lights to dim at night. A woman is praying to God. To think of the things that will happen to you, that you will let others do to you, it is madness. There is a limit to those things, but it stretches on and on, like a desert, like you are dying of thirst in the sandy ocean, seeing nothing all around but a thin, grey line at the horizon.

I have black eyes, big like a deer's. And a nose so sharp it can sniff out a beetle. My hands would have turned into claws if anyone threatened my family, I would have died for them, spread out my body like a blanket, opened to any knife, just to keep them safe, to keep them mine forever. And then the lies came, and I had to protect myself. I had to do the hardest things, and sing and cry and let the heavens know that I was doing them.

My husband began turning away from me in bed. Cold sheets of air between us, between our bodies. A woman may not ask, not ever, she must keep to herself, patient until the time when the man reaches over, when he decides that it is time for love. So I did not ask. I said nothing, only lying there surrounded by the whispering air, my skin lonely, my eyes open all through the night, seeing the black walls, listening to the rats gather their food in the dark corners of our home.

And so I was the dying person in the desert, stretching myself out over the horizon, a vast sheet of skin and blood and bone, of endless hope, of patience. I would wait forever until this time passed, until he would want me again.

Once a woman like me waited until there was no more time. Then she gathered herself like the brown bear, collected all her strength and made a gold ball-gown, with fine filigree and a headdress, with jewels on the sleeves and bodice, gold lace, gold petticoat, gold slip, air-spun and weightless. She sat in her small sewing room and bent over the sheets of fine, burning gold, so careful not to tear it with her thin fingers, pulling the needle in and out, the thread only a gold breath, invisible, like the thoughts in her mind.

It was her finest craft. And it was so beautiful on her husband's lover, who had the same shade of hair, the same jewel-tone lips like fine rubies. The girl smiled when she saw her wedding present and offered her body to its fiery cloth, letting it burn her into ash. There were colors then, more than in any art, there was the color of vengeance, blood red and bone-white, and the stinking pull of pale skin folding over.

But I would take my creation home. I would become it. Because it is in the blood, in the soil from where we grow our food, in the black, southern dirt, with our darker skin. The women are only their families, and their husbands and sons feel every drop of them.

* * *

He would not have me, he said. He would not have me any more, and he hid his washed hands in his pockets. I looked over at our home with its thick wooden walls, the stone floors, my small garden with the flowers and the herb plants for making teas, the quiet and beauty of the rooms, each holding us like a mother.

I will wait, I told him.

He was gone many nights, and then there was more than a cool sheet of air around me in bed, it was a tornado, and I was sinking. My children still laughed and played out by my garden, squeezing the flowers with their hands, wanting more food, as they grew and widened, expanded into broader, demanding men. I saw how they would only become bigger, how they would grow dark shadows above their lips, their voices getting harder and thicker, their footfalls heavy.

I would pray to God.

The sky will not forgive stones, if you toss one up in the air it will be thrown back to you, harder and faster than before. God is like that, He is like the sky with your stones. He is like an echo, only giving back the same, spare thing, without a sign.

I burnt sage and candles and sprinkled the house with my holy water, purifying myself with it, praying from my books with a low whisper. We have many devices for calling on God. There are the plants to tuck into pillows and to burn in small clay pots, there is starvation, turning from food and water until the day gets clearer, until everything has a crisp, silver outline. You may kill small animals, breathing in the mist from their hot bodies in the morning, leaning over them after your knife has done its work. God may speak with you then, if you are lucky.

But He saw what was in me, what was rightly mine, and He turned away from the sight with the same cool force as all my nights alone in my swallowing bed.

My sons lengthened, their legs stretching out like watered weeds.

I became a mongoose. Secret and moving at night. My skin leathered and my eyes narrowed from sifting through the darkness to see the sleeping world. I burrowed through the dirt faster than a running horse, with my ugly humped back and my spiky dirt-colored fur.

There are deceptions for the quiet ones to see, the small silent animals traveling at midnight. I wandered through my neighbors' homes, splintering their wood floors with my digging claws. I saw how other men take their lovers in different houses, the noise of their sex filling the late sky, sweeter than the simple duty of home. I saw the married women who lay like stone in their sleeping beds. These women were not like me any more.

My husband would return some days, giving me his old smile. He would tell me lies with a slick voice. That he had fallen asleep at a bar, drinking with his friends, playing cards, discussing the new regime. He wanted me to see him there in my mind, on an old wood stool with a cognac, smoking cigars with the other good men. To believe.

But I had hardscrabbled my small, spindly animal body over the floor boards of his new woman's house. With my raw fangs I had nibbled on her linen sheets while they slept, listening to the pace of their breathing, and had seen their breath twining up in the cold night in a pale, lingering fog. His lover is the color of parchment, pale against him.

He would tell me these things, how he had lost track of time with his friends, and I would stare into his flat, familiar face.

He has the look of our lost people, the old bloodlines, with his flint sharp nose and widening cheeks, his skin a weathering bronze. We are twins, I used to say, my face mirroring his with the color of an ancient pot buried under the sand. I would smile with my teeth shining out. We are the same.

But now I am dark skinned like the mongoose, like the brown bear, and not like him any longer. I am not like any woman or man, only godless, and I was digging tunnels in the dirt and preying on grasshoppers, small mice. Practicing.

And as with the other woman who sewed night and day to make a beautiful burning gown, there came a day when I saw that all the time in the world would run out. It bled out of me, flowing and rushing out of my body like this river, the night and the day, the dark and the light became the same, and there was only a flat, dank grey to the world. The wind ceased. I could not hear it any more, nor the birds, any laughter or music, and I wondered if I would die, quieter than dust.

Children are their mothers. They can only belong to the women. We kiss their faces and feed them, we know the fresh scents of their heads, their questions. When they will cry. Children belong to mothers, because they are of the same body. They do not become separated from us until a certain age, until they lose that gleam, the shining of their simple, pure faces. When they become like the other people all around.

My sons were still only mine, they were unformed yet and simple minded. And they were the only path to my wandering husband, who was reaching past me faster and farther. I could barely see him then, only the top of his head down the road, and I knew it would be over soon, that I would fold into the earth with no more sound.

Women are weak like glass. Life will offer them only few gifts, a drawer full of trinkets. The memories of our children, of our husband and our home, the scent of a clean room, a fine meal. They will be offered for a handful of years, and then they are gone.

And so I brought my sons to the edge of the river bank, stroked their beautiful heads, their ink black hair and sturdy frames, and whispered into their ears of my love for them. They reached for me with their small hands, curved like beach shells. I saw that my own hands against their gleaming heads were starving, the meat shrunk away, only a few sticks and a layer of bark, and I remembered my husband with his clove skin, his lover's white face.

My sons did my bidding then, and swam under the river with the strength of a shark, their faces becoming its same grey color. They asked no questions, only smiling up at me until the very end, the sounds of the water rushing and their raised cheeks, letting me fold them into the murk, into the cold water like the sky in the dark night. My arms were like iron, my teeth set in a stone line while I plunged them in, and I shrieked to the sky with all the sound of the wind and the roaring ocean, all the music of rain. I thought I might grow blind, with the black water in my eyes, my hair wet ropes like eels, and the thick feel of silt on my face as I tried to swim too.

At the river bed there are the copper coins that the children throw in for luck, and the small sucking bottom fish and tangled feathery plants. The men and the women refuse to come near, they whisper about what I did. How my husband fell ill with the news of me, of our sons, how he cried and screamed just as a woman would, a woman with a heart in her. He would kill himself, he said, and I held my breath at this news, waiting and watching at this small shore. Then he came and took our sons away from me, he dredged up their hard bodies, their little heads with their open eyes and mouths, their few baby teeth showing. He showed no fear as he did this, but I let him feel my presence, the ice of it, as I draped my shadowy body over his and laughed into his ear.

But men live. They live without the blood running through them to keep them alive, somehow they stay on the earth to walk and work and eat and sleep just like before, only now their eyes are round and blank like eggs. My victory was small, taking life from the living, but he could not smile again with the memory of us.

There was that day when all the time poured out of me like the ocean, and now time feeds in and out of me the same as the wind, winding its way down my spine, through my fingers, it wraps its thick cloak about my body. I sit by this river and sing out loud, so that my boys might hear me, so that my husband will stop what he is doing and look up, a dazzled look on his face.

Women are weak but now I am the strong one, here in the river with the sucking fish. The townsfolk say that I hated men, that I would kill all men and boys with a cutting smile, my hands like scythes. The women cluck their tongues when they hear my singing, calling me *bruja, llorona*. They tell their own sons to behave, to not wander, warning them that I will kill them with my knife and tear them with my big teeth. I am the rumor now, the thing that they will whisper about, and I torture them with my songs, my voice a low violin, a grand piano, a symphony full of men in tuxedos, their heads bent over their instruments, their eyes closed.

The dirt on the river bank is green and dust brown, it is wet with the river water, a thick muck where I sleep. I will sing the people my songs, and I appear to them, dressed in green plants and old skirts, my hair these wild wet ropes around my breasts, wrapping my hips, coiling my legs like snakes. I see my old friends' frightened white-egg eyes, their open mouths, and I love to hear them speak my name out loud in the living world. But there are the times when I will remember and cry, seeing the grey faces of my two sons like stone, their teeth like pebbles just showing out of their open mouths, as they were with me that small while, here at the bottom of the river.

It shadows my joy, a dark bog, when I remember the time before I was a mongoose, when I could not yet become a jaguar, a muskrat, a beetle. Before

I could make myself heard as the thunder is and have the whole sky tumble down like weeds. I felt different then, I could let my hands linger on my husband's back, I could kiss him below his hair, my children would rush to me, like the water does. Those pictures are my ghosts now, haunting me as I will haunt all of you.

I would have a war here. If I could summon men I would bring them here with their pistols and their drums, and they would fight before me and die only for my amusement, waving their silly flags and their trumpets. I know the world works like that. But here at the marshy river my voice only carries into a few small homes, my legend travels a short distance, and the small brown fish and the spiders, the plants and the flies around me are my only family now.

They say I hate all the men and the small boys, that I drowned my sons here and will walk along this bank until the sun dies, singing and crying like a hard wind. If I could have done it again, I would have been a cannibal, eating them all like lunch. If my husband had given me a daughter I would have forced her in me like that, even harder than I tucked my sons under the lapping water. I would want to breathe in the air with her same nose, her same lungs, to see the clouds with the eyes I imagine she would have had. I would want to take them all in, my husband, my sons, my daughter, one by one until they were gone.

TEATRO GROTTESCO
Thomas Ligotti

Thomas Ligotti was born in 1953 in Detroit, Michigan. His short stories have been published in a host of horror and fantasy magazines and anthologies, and collected in *Songs of a Dead Dreamer, Noctuary, Grimscribe: His Life and Works* and *The Nightmare Factory*, from which this story is taken.

Ligotti's unique voice can be heard in all of his work. His baroque weird fictions are often convoluted, with tales within tales. In the following tale (as in many of Ligotti's stories) there is a mystery at the heart of a poor, misguided fool's quest.

—E. D.

The first thing I learned was that no one *anticipates* the arrival of the Teatro. One would not say, or even think, "The Teatro has never come to this city— it seems we're due for a visit," or perhaps, "Don't be surprised when you-know-what turns up, it's been years since the last time." Even if the city in which one lives is exactly the kind of place favored by the Teatro, there can be no basis for predicting its appearance. No warnings are given, no fanfare to announce that a Teatro season is about to begin, or that *another* season of that sort will soon be upon us. But if a particular city possesses what is sometimes called an "artistic underworld," and if one is in close touch with this society of artists, the chances are optimal for being among those who discover that things have already started. This is the most one can expect.

For a time it was all rumors and lore, hearsay and dreams. Anyone who failed to show up for a few days at the usual club or bookstore or special artistic event was the subject of speculation. But most of the crowd I am referring to lead highly unstable, even precarious lives. Any of them might pack up and disappear without notifying a single soul. And almost all of the supposedly "missing ones" were, at some point, seen again. One such person was a film-maker whose short movie *Private Hell* served as the featured subject of a local one-night festival. But he was nowhere to be seen either during the exhibition or at the party afterwards. "Gone with the Teatro," someone said with a blasé knowingness, while others smiled and clinked glasses in a sardonic farewell toast.

But only a week later the filmmaker was spotted in one of the back rows of a pornographic theater. He later explained his absence by insisting he had been in the hospital following a thorough beating at the hands of some people he had been filming but who did not consent or desire to be filmed. This sounded plausible, given the subject matter of the man's work. Yet for some reason no one believed his hospital story, despite the evidence of bandages he was still required to wear. "It has to be the Teatro," argued a woman who always dressed in shades of purple and who was a good friend of the filmmaker. "*His* stuff and *Teatro* stuff," she said, holding up two crossed fingers for everyone to see.

But what was meant by "Teatro stuff?" This was a phrase I heard spoken by a number of persons, not all of them artists of a pretentious or self-dramatizing type. Certainly there is no shortage of anecdotes that have been passed around which purport to illuminate the nature and workings of this "cruel troupe," an epithet used by those who are too superstitious to invoke the Teatro Grottesco by name. But sorting out these accounts into a coherent *profile*, never mind their truth value, is another thing altogether.

For instance, the purple woman I mentioned earlier held us all spellbound one evening with a story about her cousin's roommate, a self-styled "visceral artist" who worked the night shift as a stock clerk for a supermarket chain in the suburbs. On a December morning, about an hour before sun-up, the artist was released from work and began his walk home through a narrow alley that ran behind several blocks of various stores and businesses along the suburb's main avenue. A light snow had fallen during the night, settling evenly upon the pavement of the alley and glowing in the light of a full moon which seemed to hover just at the alley's end. The artist saw a figure in the distance, and something about this figure, this winter-morning vision, made him pause for a moment and stare. Although he had a trained eye for sizing and perspective, the artist found this silhouette of a person in the distance of the alley intensely problematic. He could not tell if it was short or tall, or even if it was moving— either toward him or away from him—or was standing still. Then, in a moment of hallucinated wonder, the figure stood before him in the middle of the alley.

The moonlight illuminated a little man who was entirely unclothed and who held out both of his hands as if he were grasping at a desired object just out of his reach. But the artist saw that something was wrong with these hands. While the little man's body was pale, his hands were dark and were too large for the tiny arms on which they hung. At first the artist believed the little man to be wearing oversized mittens. His hands seemed to be covered by some kind of fuzz, just as the alley in which he stood was layered with the fuzziness of the snow that had fallen during the night. His hands looked soft and fuzzy like the snow, except that the snow was white and his hands were black.

In the moonlight the artist came to see that the mittens worn by this little man were actually something like the paws of an animal. It almost made sense to the artist to have thought that the little man's hands were actually paws which had only appeared to be two black mittens. Then each of the paws separated into long thin fingers that wriggled wildly in the moonlight. But they could not have been the fingers of a hand, because there were too many of them. And the hands were not paws, nor were the paws really mittens. And all of this time the little man was becoming smaller and smaller in the moonlight of that alley, as if he were moving into the distance far away from the artist who was hypnotized by this vision. Finally a little voice spoke which the artist could barely hear, and it said to him: "I cannot keep them away from me anymore, I am becoming so small and weak." These words suddenly made this whole winter-morning scenario into something that was too much even for the self-styled "visceral artist."

In the pocket of his coat the artist had a tool which he used for cutting open boxes at the supermarket. He had cut into flesh in the past, and, with the moonlight glaring upon the snow of that alley, the artist made a few strokes which turned that white world red. Under the circumstances what he had done seemed perfectly justified to the artist, even an act of mercy. The man was becoming so small.

Afterward the artist ran through the alley without stopping until he reached the rented house where he lived with his roommate. It was she who telephoned the police, saying there was a body lying in the snow at such and such a place and then hanging up without giving her name. For days, weeks, the artist and his roommate searched the local newspapers for some word of the extraordinary thing the police must have found in that alley. But nothing ever appeared.

"You see how these incidents are hushed up," the purple woman whispered to us. "The police know what is going on. There are even *special police* for dealing with such matters. But nothing is made public, no one is questioned. And yet, after that morning in the alley, my cousin and her roommate came under surveillance and were followed everywhere by unmarked cars. Because these special policemen know that it is artists, or highly artistic persons, who are *approached* by the Teatro. And they know whom to watch after something has happened. It is said that these police may be party to the deeds of that 'company of nightmares'."

But none of us believed a word of this Teatro anecdote told by the purple woman, just as none of us believed the purple woman's friend, the filmmaker, when he denied all innuendos that connected him to the Teatro. On the one hand, our imaginations had sided with this woman when she asserted that her friend, the creator of the short movie *Private Hell,* was somehow in league with the Teatro; on the other hand, we were mockingly dubious of the story about her cousin's roommate, the self-styled visceral artist, and his encounter in the snow-covered alley.

This divided reaction was not as natural as it seemed. Never mind that the case of the filmmaker was more credible than that of the visceral artist, if only because the first story was lacking the extravagant details which burdened the second. Until then we had uncritically relished all we had heard about the Teatro, no matter how bizarre these accounts may have been and no matter how much they opposed a verifiable truth or even a coherent portrayal of this phenomenon. As artists we suspected that it was in our interest to have our heads filled with all kinds of Teatro craziness. Even I, a writer of nihilistic prose works, savored the inconsistency and the flamboyant absurdity of what was told to me across a table in a quiet library or a noisy club. In a word, I delighted in the *unreality* of the Teatro stories. The truth they carried, if any, was immaterial. And we never questioned any of them until the purple woman related the episode of the visceral artist and the small man in the alley.

But this new disbelief was not in the least inspired by our sense of reason or reality. It was in fact based solely on fear; it was driven by the will to negate what one fears. No one gives up on something until it turns on them, whether or not that thing is real or unreal. In some way all of this Teatro business had finally worn upon our nerves; the balance had been tipped between a madness that intoxicated us and one that began to menace our minds. As for the woman who always dressed herself in shades of purple . . . we avoided her. It would have been typical of the Teatro, someone said, to use a person like that for their purposes.

Perhaps our judgment of the purple woman was unfair. No doubt her theories concerning the "approach of the Teatro" made us all uneasy. But was this reason enough to cast her out from that artistic underworld which was the only society available to her? Like many societies, of course, ours was founded on fearful superstition, and this is always reason enough for any kind of behavior. She had been permanently stigmatized by too closely associating herself with something unclean in its essence. Because even after her theories were discredited by a newly circulated Teatro tale, her status did not improve.

I am now referring to a story that was going around in which an artist was not *approached* by the Teatro but rather took the first step *toward* the Teatro, as if acting under the impulse of a sovereign will.

The artist in this case was a photographer of the I-am-a-camera type. He was a studiedly bloodless specimen who quite often, and for no apparent reason, would begin to stare at someone and to continue staring until that person reacted in some manner, usually by fleeing the scene but on occasion by assaulting the photographer, who invariably pressed charges. It was therefore not entirely surprising to learn that he tried to engage the services of the Teatro in the way he did, for it was his belief that this cruel troupe could be hired to, in the photographer's words, "utterly destroy someone." And the person he wished to destroy was his landlord, a small balding man with a mustache who, after the photographer had moved out of his apartment, refused to remit his security deposit, perhaps with good reason but perhaps not.

In any case, the photographer, whose name incidentally was Spence, made inquiries about the Teatro over a period of some months. Following up every scrap of information, no matter how obscure or suspect, the tenacious Spence ultimately arrived in the shopping district of an old suburb where there was a two-story building that rented space to various persons and businesses, including a small video store, a dentist, and, as it was spelled out on the building's directory, the Theatre Grottesco. At the back of the first floor, directly below a studio for dancing instruction, was a small suite of offices whose glass door displayed some stencilled lettering that read: T G VENTURES. Seated at a desk in the reception area behind the glass door was a young woman with long black hair and black-rimmed eyeglasses. She was thoroughly engrossed in writing something on a small blank card, several more of which were spread across her desk. The way Spence told it, he was undeterred by all appearances that seemed to suggest the Teatro, or Theatre, was not what he assumed it was. He entered the reception area of the office, stood before the desk of the young woman, and introduced himself by name and occupation, believing it important to communicate as soon as possible his identity as an artist, or at least imply as best he could that he was a highly artistic photographer, which undoubtedly he was. When the young woman adjusted her eyeglasses and asked, "How can I help you?" the photographer Spence leaned toward her and whispered, "I would like to enlist the services of the Teatro, or Theatre if you like." When the receptionist asked what he was planning, the photographer answered, "To utterly destroy someone." The young woman was absolutely unflustered, according to Spence, by this declaration. She began calmly gathering the small blank cards that were spread across her desk and, while doing this, explained that T G Ventures was, in her words, an "entertainment service." After placing the small blank cards to one side, she removed from her desk a folded brochure which outlined the nature of the business, which provided clowns, magicians, and novelty performances for a variety of occasions, their specialty being children's parties.

As Spence studied the brochure, the receptionist placidly sat with her hands folded and gazed at him from within the black frames of her eyeglasses. The light in that suburban office suite was bright but not harsh; the pale walls were incredibly clean and the carpeting, in Spence's description, was conspicuously new and displayed the exact shade of purple found in turnips. The photographer said that he felt as if he were standing in a mirage. "This is all a front," Spence finally said, throwing the brochure on the receptionist's desk. But the young woman only picked up the brochure and placed it back in the same drawer from which it had come. "What's behind that door?" Spence demanded, pointing across the room. And just as he pointed at that door there was a sound on the other side of it, a brief rumbling as if something heavy had just fallen to the floor. "The dancing classes," said the receptionist, her right index finger pointing up at the floor above. "Perhaps," Spence allowed, but he claimed that this sound that he heard, which he described as having an "abysmal resonance," caused a sudden rise of panic within him. He tried not to move from the place he was standing, but his body was overwhelmed by the impulse to leave that suite of offices. The photographer turned away from the receptionist and saw his reflection in the glass door. She was watching him from behind the lenses of black-framed eyeglasses, and the stencilled lettering on the glass door read backwards, as if in a mirror. A few seconds later Spence was outside the building in the old suburb. All the way home, he asserted, his heart was pounding.

The following day Spence paid a visit to his landlord's place of business, which was a tiny office in a seedy downtown building. Having given up on the Teatro, he would have to deal in his own way with this man who would not return his security deposit. Spence's strategy was to plant himself in his landlord's office and stare him into submission with a photographer's unnerving gaze. After he arrived at his landlord's rented office on the sixth floor of what was a thoroughly depressing downtown building, Spence seated himself in a chair looking across a filthy desk at a small balding man with a mustache. But the man merely looked back at the photographer. To make things worse, the landlord (whose name was Herman Zick), would lean towards Spence every so often and in a quiet voice say, "It's all perfectly legal, you know." Then Spence would continue his staring, which he was frustrated to find ineffective against this man Zick, who of course was not an artist, or even a highly artistic person, as were the usual victims of the photographer. Thus the battle kept up for almost an hour, the landlord saying, "It's all perfectly legal," and Spence trying to hold a fixed gaze upon the man he wished to utterly destroy.

Ultimately Spence was the first to lose control. He jumped out of the chair in which he was sitting and began to shout incoherently at the landlord. Once Spence was on his feet, Zick swiftly maneuvered around the desk and physically evicted the photographer from the tiny office, locking him out in the hallway. Spence said that he was in the hallway for only a second or two when the doors opened to the elevator that was directly across from Zick's sixth-floor office. Out of the elevator compartment stepped a middle-aged man in a dark suit and black-framed eyeglasses. He wore a full, well-groomed beard which, Spence observed, was slightly streaked with gray. In his left hand the gentleman was clutching a crumpled brown bag, holding it a few inches in front of him. He walked up to the door of the landlord's office and with his right hand grasped the round black doorknob, jiggling it back and forth several times. There was a loud click that echoed down the hallway of that old downtown building. The gentleman turned his head and looked at Spence for the first time, smiling briefly before admitting himself to the office of Herman Zick.

Again the photographer experienced that surge of panic he had felt the day before when he visited the suburban offices of T G Ventures. He pushed the down button for the elevator, and while waiting he listened at the door of the landlord's office. What he heard, Spence claimed, was that terrible sound that had sent him running out in the street from T G Ventures, that "abysmal resonance," as he defined it. Suddenly the gentleman with the well-groomed beard and black-rimmed glasses emerged from the tiny office. The door to the elevator had just opened, and the man walked straight past Spence to board the empty compartment. Spence himself did not get on the elevator but stood outside, helplessly staring at the bearded gentleman, who was still holding that small crumpled bag. A split second before the elevator doors slid closed, the gentleman looked directly at Spence and winked at him. It was the assertion of the photographer that this wink, executed from behind a pair of black-framed eyeglasses, made a mechanical clicking sound which echoed down the dim hallway. Prior to his exit from the old downtown building, leaving by way of the stairs rather than the elevator, Spence tried the door to his landlord's office. He found it unlocked and cautiously stepped inside. But there was no one on the other side of the door.

The conclusion to the photographer's adventure took place a full week later. Delivered by regular post to his mail box was a small square envelope with no return address. Inside was a photograph. He brought this item to Des Esseintes' Library, a bookstore where several of us were giving a late-night reading of our latest literary efforts. A number of persons belonging to the local artistic underworld, including myself, saw the photograph and heard Spence's rather frantic account of the events surrounding it. The photo was of Spence himself staring stark-eyed into the camera, which apparently had taken the shot from inside an elevator, a panel of numbered buttons being partially visible along the righthand border of the picture. "I could see no camera," Spence kept repeating. "But that wink he gave me . . . and what's written on the reverse side of this thing." Turning over the photo Spence read aloud the following hand-written inscription: "The little man is so much littler these days. Soon he will know about the soft black stars. And your payment is past due." Someone then asked Spence what they had to say about all this at the offices of T G Ventures. The photographer's head swivelled slowly in exasperated negation. "Not there anymore," he said over and over. With the single exception of myself, that night at Des Esseintes' Library was the last time anyone saw Mr. Spence.

After the photographer ceased to show up at the usual meeting places and special artistic events, there were no cute remarks about his having "gone with the Teatro." We were all of us beyond that stage. I was perversely proud to note that a degree of philosophical maturity had now developed among those in the artistic underworld of which I was a part. There is nothing like fear to complicate one's consciousness, inducing previously unknown levels of reflection. Under such mental stress I began to organize my own thoughts and observations about the Teatro, specifically as this phenomenon related to the artists who seemed to be its sole objects of attention.

Whether or not an artist was approached by the Teatro or took the initiative to approach the Teatro himself, it seemed the effect was the same: the end of an artist's work. I myself verified this fact as thoroughly as I could. The film-maker whose short movie *Private Hell* so many of us admired had, by all accounts, become a full-time dealer in pornographic videos, none of them his own productions. The self-named visceral artist had publicly called an end to those stunts of his which had gained him a modest underground reputation. According to his roommate, the purple woman's cousin, he was now managing the supermarket where he had formerly labored as a stock clerk. As for the purple woman herself, who was never much praised as an artist and whose renown effectively began and ended with the "cigar box assemblage" phase of her career, she had gone into selling real estate, an occupation in which she became quite a success. This roster of ex-artists could be extended considerably, I am sure of that. But for the purposes of this report or confession (or whatever else you would like to call it) I must end my list of no-longer-artistic persons with myself, while attempting to offer some insights into the manner in which the Teatro Grottesco could transform a writer of nihilistic prose works into a non-artistic, more specifically a *post-artistic* being.

It was after the disappearance of the photographer Spence that my intuitions concerning the Teatro began to crystalize and become explicit thoughts, a dubious process but one to which I am inescapably subject as a prose writer. Until that point in time, everyone tacitly assumed that there was an intimacy of *kind* between the Teatro and the artists who were either approached by the Teatro or who themselves approached this cruel troupe by means of some overture, as in the case of Spence, or perhaps by gestures more subtle, even purely noetic (I retreat from writing *unconscious*, although others might argue with my intellectual reserve). Many of us even spoke of the Teatro as a manifestation of super-art, a term which we always left conveniently nebulous. However, following the disappearance of the photographer, all knowledge I had acquired about the Teatro, fragmentary as it was, became configured in a completely new pattern. I mean to say that I no longer considered it possible that the Teatro was in any way related to a super-art, or to an art of any kind, quite the opposite in fact. To my mind the Teatro was, and is, a phenomenon intensely destructive of everything that I conceived of as art. Therefore, the Teatro was, and is, intensely destructive of all artists and even of highly artistic persons. Whether this destructive force is a matter of intention or is an epiphenomenon of some unrelated, perhaps greater design, or even if there exists anything like an intention or design on the part of the Teatro, I have no idea (at least none I can elaborate in comprehensible terms). Nonetheless, I feel certain that for an artist to encounter the Teatro there can be only one consequence: the end of that artist's work. Strange, then, that knowing this fact I still acted as I did.

I cannot say if it was I who approached the Teatro or vice versa, as if any of that stupidness made a difference. The important thing is that from the moment I perceived the Teatro to be a profoundly anti-artistic phenomenon I conceived the ambition to make my form of art, by which I mean my nihilistic prose writings, into an anti-*Teatro* phenomenon. In order to do this, of course, I required a penetrating knowledge of the Teatro Grottesco, or of some significant aspect of that cruel troupe, an insight of a deeply subtle, even dreamlike variety into its nature and workings.

The photographer Spence had made a great visionary advance when he intuited that it was in the nature of the Teatro to act on his request to utterly destroy someone (although the exact meaning of the statement "he will know about the soft black stars," in reference to Spence's landlord, became known to both of us only sometime later). I realized that I would need to make a similar leap of insight in my own mind. While I had already perceived the Teatro to be a profoundly anti-artistic phenomenon, I was not yet sure what in the world would constitute an anti-*Teatro* phenomenon, as well as how in the world I could turn my own prose writings to such a purpose.

Thus, for several days I mediated on these questions. As usual, the psychic demands of this meditation severely taxed my bodily processes, and in my weakened state I contracted a virus, specifically an *intestinal virus*, which confined me to my small apartment for a period of one week. Nonetheless, it was during this time that things fell into place regarding the Teatro and the insights I required to oppose this company of nightmares in a more or less efficacious manner.

Suffering through the days and nights of an illness, especially an intestinal virus, one becomes highly conscious of certain realities, as well as highly sensitive to the *functions* of these realities, which otherwise are not generally subject to prolonged attention or meditation. Upon recovery from such a virus, the consciousness of these realities and their functions necessarily fades, so that the once-stricken person may resume his life's activities and not be driven to insanity or suicide by the acute awareness of these most unpleasant facts of existence. Through the illumination of analogy, I came to understand that the Teatro operated in much the same manner as the illness from which I recently suffered, with the consequence that the person exposed to the Teatro-disease becomes highly conscious of certain realities and their functions, ones quite different of course from the realities and functions of an intestinal virus. However, an intestinal virus ultimately succumbs, in a reasonably healthy individual, to the formation of antibodies (or something of that sort). But the disease of the Teatro, I now understood, was a disease for which no counteracting agents, or antibodies, had ever been created by the systems of the individuals—that is, the *artists*—it attacked. An encounter with any disease, including an intestinal virus, serves to alter a person's mind, making it intensely aware of certain realities, but this mind cannot remain altered once this encounter has ended or else that person will never be able to go on living in the same way as before. In contrast, an encounter with the Teatro appears to remain within one's system and to alter a person's mind permanently. For the artist the result is *not* to be driven into insanity or suicide (as might be the case if one assumed a permanent mindfulness of an intestinal virus) but the absolute termination of that artist's work. The simple reason for this effect is that there are no antibodies for the disease of the Teatro, and therefore no relief from the consciousness of the realities which an encounter with the Teatro has forced upon an artist.

Having progressed this far in my contemplation of the Teatro—so that I might discover its nature or essence and thereby make my prose writings into an anti-Teatro phenomenon—I found that I could go no further. No matter how much thought and meditation I devoted to the subject I did not gain a definite sense of having revealed to myself the true realities and functions that the Teatro communicated to an artist and how this communication put an end to that artist's work. Of course I could vaguely imagine the species of awareness that might render an artist thenceforth incapable of producing any type of artistic efforts. I actually arrived at a fairly detailed and disturbing idea of such an awareness—a *world-awareness*, as I conceived it. Yet I did not feel I had penetrated the mystery of "Teatro-stuff." And the only way to know about the Teatro, it seemed, was to have an encounter with it. Such an encounter between myself and the Teatro would have occurred in any event as a result of the discovery that my prose writings had been turned into an anti-Teatro phenomenon: this would constitute an *approach* of the most outrageous sort to that company of nightmares, forcing an encounter with all its realities and functions. Thus it was not necessary, at this point in my plan, to have actually succeeded in making my prose writings into an anti-Teatro phenomenon. I simply had to make it known, falsely, that I had done so.

As soon as I had sufficiently recovered from my intestinal virus I began to spread the word. Every time I found myself among others who belonged to the so-called artistic underworld of this city I bragged that I had gained the most intense awareness of the Teatro's realities and functions, and that, far from finishing me off as an artist, I had actually used this awareness as inspiration for a series of short prose works. I explained to my colleagues that merely to exist—let alone create artistic works—we had to keep certain things from overwhelming our minds. However, I continued, in order to keep these things, such as the realities of an intestinal virus, from overwhelming our minds we attempted to deny them any voice whatever, neither a voice in our minds and certainly not a precise and clear voice in works of art. The voice of madness,

for instance, is barely a whisper in the babbling history of art because its realities are themselves too maddening to speak of for very long . . . and those of
the Teatro have no voice at all, given their imponderably grotesque nature.
Furthermore, I said, the Teatro not only propagated an intense awareness of
these things, these realities and functionings of realities, it was *identical* with
them. And I, I boasted, had allowed my mind to be overwhelmed by all manner
of Teatro stuff, while also managing to use this experience as material for my
prose writings. "This," I practically shouted one day at Des Esseintes' Library,
"is the super-art." Then I promised that in two days time I would give a reading
of my series of short prose pieces.

Nevertheless, as we sat around on some old furniture in a corner of Des
Esseintes' Library, several of the others challenged my statements and asser-
tions regarding the Teatro. One fellow writer, a poet, spoke hoarsely through
a cloud of cigarette smoke, saying to me: "No one knows what this Teatro stuff
is all about. I'm not sure I believe it myself." But I answered that Spence knew
what it was all about, thinking that very soon I too would know what he knew.
"*Spence!*" said a woman in a tone of exaggerated disgust (she once lived with
the photographer and was a photographer herself). "He's not telling us about
anything these days, never mind the Teatro." But I answered that, like the
purple woman and the others, Spence had been overwhelmed by his encounter
with the Teatro, and his artistic impulse had been thereby utterly destroyed.
"And *your* artistic impulse is still intact," she said snidely. I answered that, yes,
it was, and in two days I would prove it by reading a series of prose works that
exhibited an intimacy with the most overwhelmingly grotesque experiences and
gave voice to them. "That's because you have no idea what you're talking
about," said someone else, and almost everyone supported this remark. I told
them to be patient, wait and see what my prose writings revealed to them.
"Reveal?" asked the poet. "Hell, no one even knows why it's called the Teatro
Grottesco." I did not have an answer for that, but I repeated that they would
understand much more about the Teatro in a few days, thinking to myself that
within this period of time I would have either succeeded or failed in my attempt to provoke an encounter with the Teatro and the matter of my nonexistent anti-Teatro prose writing would be immaterial.

On the very next day, however, I collapsed in Des Esseintes' Library during
a conversation with a different congregation of artists and highly artistic persons. Although the symptoms of my intestinal virus had never entirely disappeared I had not expected to collapse the way I did and ultimately to discover
that what I thought was an intestinal virus was in fact something far more
serious. As a consequence of my collapse, my unconscious body ended up in
the emergency room of a nearby hospital, the kind of place where borderline
indigents like myself always end up—a backstreet hospital with dated fixtures
and a staff of sleepwalkers.

When I next opened my eyes it was night. The bed in which they had put
my body was beside a tall paned window that reflected the dim fluorescent
light fixed to the wall above my bed, creating a black glare in the windowpanes
that allowed no view of anything beyond them but only a broken image of
myself and the room around me. There was a long row of these tall paned

windows and several other beds in the ward, each of them supporting a sleeping body that, like mine, was damaged in some way and therefore had been committed to that backstreet hospital.

I felt none of the extraordinary pain that had caused me to collapse in Des Esseintes' Library. At that moment, in fact, I could feel nothing of the experiences of my past life: it seemed I had always been an occupant of that dark hospital ward and always would be. This sense of estrangement from both myself and everything else made it terribly difficult to remain in the hospital bed where I had been placed. At the same time I felt uneasy about any movement *away* from that bed, especially any movement that would cause me to approach the open doorway which led into a half-lighted backstreet hospital corridor. Compromising between my impulse to get out of my bed and my fear of moving away from the bed and approaching that corridor, I positioned myself so that I was sitting on the edge of the mattress with my bare feet grazing the cold linoleum floor. I had been sitting on the edge of that mattress for quite a while before I heard the voice out in the corridor.

The voice came over the public address system, but it was not a particularly loud voice. In fact I had to strain my attention for several minutes simply to discern the peculiar qualities of the voice and to decipher what it said. It sounded like a child's voice, a sing-songy voice full of taunts and mischief. Over and over it repeated the same phrase—*paging Dr. Groddeck, paging Dr. Groddeck*. The voice sounded incredibly hollow and distant, garbled by all kinds of interference. *Paging Dr. Groddeck*, it giggled from the other side of the world.

I stood up and slowly approached the doorway leading out into the corridor. But even after I had crossed the room in my bare feet and was standing in the open doorway, that child's voice did not become any louder or any clearer. Even when I actually moved out into that long dim corridor with its dated lighting fixtures, the voice that was calling Dr. Groddeck sounded just as hollow and distant. And now it was as if I were in a dream in which I was walking in my bare feet down a backstreet hospital corridor, hearing a crazy voice that seemed to be eluding me as I moved past the open doorways of innumerable wards full of damaged bodies. But then the voice died away, calling to Dr. Groddeck one last time before fading like the final echo in a deep well. At the same moment that the voice ended its hollow outcrying, I paused somewhere toward the end of that shadowy corridor. In the absence of the mischievous voice I was able to hear something else, a sound like quiet, wheezing laughter. It was coming from the room just ahead of me along the right hand side of the corridor. As I approached this room I saw a metal plaque mounted at eye-level on the wall, and the words displayed on this plaque were these: Dr. T. Groddeck.

A strangely glowing light emanated from the room where I heard that quiet and continuous wheezing laughter. I peered around the edge of the doorway and saw that the laughter was coming from an old gentleman seated behind a desk, while the strangely glowing light was coming from a large globular object positioned on top of the desk directly in front of him. The light from this object—a globe of solid glass, it seemed—shone on the old gentleman's face, which was a crazy-looking face with a neatly clipped beard that was pure white and a pair of spectacles with slim rectangular lenses resting on the bridge of a slender nose. When I stood in the doorway of that office, the eyes of Dr. Groddeck did not gaze up at me but continued to stare into the strange, shining globe and at the things that were inside it.

What were these things inside the globe that Dr. Groddeck was looking at? To me they appeared to be tiny star-shaped flowers evenly scattered throughout the glass, just the thing to lend a mock-artistic appearance to a common paperweight. Except that these flowers, these spidery chrysanthemums, were pure black. And they did not seem to be firmly fixed within the shining sphere, as one would expect, but looked as if they were floating in position, their starburst of petals wavering slightly like tentacles. Dr. Groddeck appeared to delight in the subtle movements of those black appendages. Behind rectangular spectacles his eyes rolled about as they tried to take in each of the hovering shapes inside the radiant globe on the desk before him.

Then the doctor slowly reached down into one of the deep pockets of the lab coat he was wearing, and his wheezing laughter grew more intense. From the open doorway I watched as he carefully removed a small paper bag from his pocket, but he never even glanced at me. With one hand he was now holding the crumpled bag directly over the globe. When he gave the bag a little shake, the things inside the globe responded with an increased agitation of their thin black arms. He used both hands to open the top of the bag and quickly turned it upside down.

From out of the bag something tumbled onto the globe, where it seemed to stick to the surface. It was not actually adhering to the surface of the globe, however, but was sinking into the interior of the glass. It squirmed as those soft black stars inside the globe gathered to pull it down to themselves. Before I could see what it was that they had captured and surrounded, the show was over. Afterward they returned to their places, floating slightly once again within the glowing sphere.

I looked at Dr. Groddeck and saw that he was finally looking back at me. He had stopped his asthmatic laughter, and his eyes were staring frigidly into mine, completely devoid of any readable meaning. Yet somehow these eyes provoked me. Even as I stood in the open doorway of that hideous office in a backstreet hospital, Dr. Groddeck's eyes provoked in me an intense outrage, an astronomical resentment of the position I had been placed in. Even as I had consummated my plan to encounter the Teatro and experience its most devastating realities and functions (in order to turn my prose works into an anti-Teatro phenomenon) I was outraged to be standing where I was standing and resentful of the staring eyes of Dr. Groddeck. No matter if I had approached the Teatro, the Teatro had approached me, or we both approached each other. I realized that there is such a thing as being approached in order to force one's hand into making what only appears to be an approach, which is actually a non-approach that negates the whole concept of approaching. It was all a fix from the start, because I belonged to an artistic underworld, because I was an artist whose work would be brought to an end by an encounter with the Teatro Grottesco. And so I was outraged by the eyes of Dr. Groddeck, which were the eyes of the Teatro, and I was resentful of all insane realities and the excruciating functions of the Teatro. Although I knew that the persecutions of the Teatro were not exclusively focused on the artists and highly artistic persons of the world, I was nevertheless outraged and resentful to be singled out for *special treatment*. I wanted to punish those persons in this world who are not the object of such special treatment. Thus, at the top of my voice, I called out in the dim corridor, I cried out the summons for others to join me before the stage of the Teatro. Strange that I should think it necessary to compound the nightmare of all those damaged bodies in that backstreet hospital, as well as its staff of sleepwalkers who moved within a world of outdated fixtures. But by the time anyone arrived Dr. Groddeck was gone, and his office became nothing more than a room full of dirty laundry.

My escapade that night notwithstanding, I was soon released from the hospital pending the results of several tests I had been administered. I was feeling as well as ever, and the hospital, like any hospital, always needed the bedspace for more damaged bodies. They said I would be contacted in the next few days.

It was in fact the following day that I was informed of the outcome of my stay in the hospital. "Hello again," began the letter, which was typed on a plain, though waterstained sheet of paper. "I was so pleased to finally meet you in person. I thought your performance in our interview at the hospital was really first rate, and I am authorized to offer you a position with us. There is an opening in our organization for someone with your resourcefulness and imagination. I'm afraid things didn't work out with Mr. Spence. But he certainly did have a camera's eye, and we have gotten some wonderful pictures from him. I would especially like to share with you his last shots of the soft black stars, or S.B.S., as we sometimes refer to them. Veritable super-art, if there ever was such a thing!

"By the way, the results of your tests—some of which you have yet to be subjected to—are going to come back positive. If you think an intestinal virus is misery, just wait a few more months. So think fast, sir. We will arrange another meeting with you in any case. And remember—*you* approached *us*. Or was it the other way around?

"As you might have noticed by now, all this artistic business can only keep you going so long before you're left speechlessly gaping at the realities and functions of . . . well, I think you know what I'm trying to say. I was forced into this realization myself, and I'm quite mindful of what a blow this can be. Indeed, it was I who invented the appellative for our organization as it is currently known. Not that I put any stock in names, nor should you. Our company is so much older than its own name, or any other name for that matter. (And how many it's had over the years—The Ten Thousand Things, Anima Mundi, Nethescurial.) You should be proud that we have a special part for you to play, such a talented artist. In time you will forget yourself entirely in your work, as we all do eventually. Myself, I go around with a trunkful of aliases, but do you think I can say who I once was *really*? A man of the theater, that seems plausible. Possibly I was the father of Faust or Hamlet . . . or merely Peter Pan.

"In closing, I do hope you will seriously consider our offer to join us. We can do something about your medical predicament. We can do just about anything. Otherwise, I'm afraid that all I can do is welcome you to your own private hell, which will be as unspeakable as any on earth."

The letter was signed Dr. Theodore Groddeck, and its prognostication of my physical health was accurate: I have taken more tests at the backstreet hospital and the results are somewhat grim. For several days and sleepless nights I have considered the alternatives the doctor proposed to me, as well as others of my own devising, and have yet to reach a decision on what course to follow. The one conclusion that keeps forcing itself upon me is that it makes no difference what choice I make, or do not make. You can never anticipate the Teatro . . . or anything else. You can never know what you are approaching, or what is approaching you. Soon enough my thoughts will lose all clarity, and I will no longer be aware that there was ever a decision to be made. The soft black stars have already begun to fill the sky.

THE SECRET SHIH TAN

Graham Masterton

Graham Masterton lives in England and is the author of twenty-eight novels, including *Master of Lies, Death Trance, Spirit,* and *Burial,* a sequel to *The Manitou.* He has written a new horror-thriller, *St. Xavier's Day,* set in Warsaw. His short fiction has been collected in *Fortnight of Fear, Flights of Fear* and *Faces of Fear.* He edited the anthology *Scare Care.*

Masterton is a master storyteller, as "The Secret Shih Tan" proves. The story, originally published in *Fear the Fever: The Hot Blood Series,* is clever, erotic, and quite chilling.

—E. D.

Men eat the flesh of grass-fed and grain-fed animals, deer eat grass, centipedes find snakes tasty, and hawks and falcons relish mice. Of these four, which knows how food ought to taste?

—Wang Ni

Craig's father had always told him that cooking was just like sex: It aroused you. It empowered you. It enabled you to play God with other people's senses. Afterward it left you feeling sweaty and exhausted, but the first inklings of what you might cook next were already teasing you like a girl who wouldn't stop playing with your softened penis.

Tonight Craig had cooked over 112 covers since the Burn-the-Tail restaurant had opened at six o'clock, and now he was sitting on an upturned broccoli box in the back yard, drinking ice-cold Evian water out of the bottle and listening to the clattering and clamoring of dishes being washed.

He smeared his eyes with the back of his hand. He was so tired that he couldn't even think of anything to think. But he knew that fresh carp would be delivered in the morning, and there were so many amazing things you could do with fresh carp: carp with dry white wine, horseradish, and prunes; carp with celeriac and leeks simmered in lager beer and dry white wine; carp stuffed with scallions and ham and winter bamboo shoots.

Craig didn't look at all like somebody who had been obsessed by cooking ever since he was old enough to stand on a chair and reach the stovetop. He was twenty-eight years old, as gangly as a stork, with a thin, sharply etched face and short hair that stuck up like Stan Laurel's. But both his parents were brilliant cooks and had inspired him to play in the kitchen in the same way that other kids used to take piano lessons.

His father, George, was French-Canadian, and used to cook for La Bella Fontana at the Beverly Wilshire Hotel. His mother, Blossom, was half Chinese and had taught him everything from the four levels of flame to the eleven shapes by the time he was nine. Between the two of them, they had given him the ability to turn the simplest ingredients into dishes about which *Los Angeles* magazine had said, "There's no other word for Craig Richard's cooking except 'erotic.' " The *Los Angeles Times* had been even more explicit: "This food is so indecently stimulating that you almost feel embarrassed about eating it in public."

Craig had opened the Burn-the-Tail on Santa Monica Boulevard a few days after his twenty-third birthday, and now its endlessly surprising juxtaposition of classic French and Asian cooking meant that it was booked solid almost every night, mainly with movie people and lawyers and record executives. But unlike Ken Hom and Madhur Jaffrey and other celebrity chefs, Craig had shied away from television appearances and cookbook offers. Whenever he was asked to give cooking tips, he always shook his head and said, "Ask me in ten years' time. I'm not good enough yet."

All the same, he had plenty of faith in himself. Almost too much faith. He believed that he was more highly skilled than almost any other chef in Greater Los Angeles, if not in all of California. But he had an idea in his mind of food that would arouse such physical and emotional sensations in those who ate it that they would never be able to touch any other kind of food again. He had an idea of food that would literally give men erections when they put it in their mouths, and make women tremble and squeeze their thighs together. He could cook better than any chef he knew, but until he had cooked food like that, he knew that he wasn't good enough.

He swigged more Evian. On a busy night he could lose up to three pounds in fluid. He had six assistants working with him, but his style of cooking was furious, fast, and highly labor-intensive. That was attributable to the Chinese influence: the pride in slicing marinated duck livers so that they looked like chrysanthemum flowers, and cutting sea bass into the shape of a bunch of grapes.

Tina, his cocktail waitress, came out into the yard. Tina didn't know Escoffier from Brad Pitt, but Craig liked her. She was very petite, with a shiny blond bob and a face that was much too pretty. She wore a tight blue velvet dress with a V-shaped décolletage that gave customers a brief but startling view down her cleavage whenever she bent over to serve them a drink. Tina was proud of her cleavage. She had appeared in two episodes of *New Bay Watch* and had sent pictures of herself to *Playboy*.

"Almond Head's asking to see you," she said.

"Tell him I've been bitten by a rabid dog." Craig hated it when customers asked him to come out of the kitchen so that they could congratulate him. They would kiss their fingertips and say things like, "that *feuilleté* of scallops, that was just . . . *mwuh!*" while all the time Craig knew that the *feuilleté* of scallops was not just *mwuh*. It was made from sparkling fresh scallops that he had bought himself from W. R. Merry, the exotic fish wholesalers, and had poached in eggs and cream and served with a cognac-flavored lobster sauce that had taken him three years to perfect.

"Almond Head seemed kind of insistent. Here." She handed him a visiting card. It was slightly larger than the usual type of visiting card, and printed with severe, dark letters: Hugo Xawery, The Sanctuary, Stone Canyon Avenue, Bel Air.

Craig turned the card over. On the back, four words were scrawled in fountain pen: *"The Secret Shih Tan."*

He stared at the words and found that he could hardly breathe, let alone speak. Their effect on him was the same as the words "The Ark of the Covenant" would have been on a devout Christian, if he had known for sure that whoever had written those words had actually found it.

And there was no doubt in Craig's mind that Almond Head had found *The Secret Shih Tan*, because scarcely anybody knew of its existence.

Craig had never seen a copy. It had been written only for private circulation among a privileged number of chefs; and after its publication its author had suffered such deep remorse that he had tried to retrieve and burn every copy. But two copies had eluded him, and *The Secret Shih Tan* had been reprinted in a strictly limited edition in Shanghai in 1898, under the liberal regime of the young emperor Kuang Hsü. Only one hundred days later, however, Kuang Hsü had been deposed by the Dowager Empress Tzu Hsi, and *The Secret Shih Tan*, along with hundreds of other books, had been banned and destroyed. It was rumored that a single copy had been smuggled out of China by the emperor's personal chef, the legendary K'ang Shih-k'ai, but that was the last that anyone had heard of it. As far as Craig knew, the book now existed only in legend.

Craig first heard about it from one of his Chinese uncles when he was fourteen. His mother had found a copy of *Penthouse* under his mattress. His uncle Lee had laughed and said, "At least it wasn't *The Secret Shih Tan!*" Blossom Richard had been unaccountably disgusted; and George had warned Craig's uncle not to mention it again. But later, Craig had asked his uncle what it was, and his uncle had told him.

Now here was the title again, on this stranger's visiting card, and Craig was seized by the same feeling of dread and excitement that had gripped him all those years ago when his uncle had sat smoking by the window, murmuring all those forbidden and alluring things that *his* uncle had once murmured to him, and his father before him.

"Are you okay?" asked Tina. "You look as if you've *really* been bitten by a rabid dog."

Craig swallowed. "I'm fine. Thanks. Tell Mr. Xawery I'll be right out."

"You're going to *see* him?"

"Why not? You have to kowtow to the customers some of the time. It's *their* money, after all." After Tina had bounced her way back into the restaurant, Craig went to the men's room, stripped off his sauce-splashed whites, and vigorously washed his hands.

Jean-Pierre, one of his sous-chefs came in. He was plump and unshaven, and mopped sweat from his forehead with a crumpled T-shirt. "We had idiots tonight, yes?" he asked Craig, in his erratic, up-and-down French accent. "Those people on table five sent back that Columbia River caviar because it was yellow. 'We know caviar,' they said. 'And caviar is black.' "

Craig was trying to comb his hair. He was trembling so much that he had to grip the rim of the sink to steady himself.

"Hey, you're not sick, are you?" asked Jean-Pierre.

"No, no," Craig told him.

"You're shaking like jellies."

"Yes. Yes, I'm shaking." He hesitated for a moment, then said, "What's the most terrible thing you've ever done?"

Jean-Pierre blinked at him. "I don't understand the question."

"What I mean is, have you ever deliberately hurt another human being in order to fulfill a wish that you've always cherished?"

"I don't know. I stole quite a lot of money from one of my girlfriends once. Well, I say 'stole.' She kept buying me clothes and presents, thinking that I was going to marry her, but I knew I never would. She had a . . . what do you call it? A wart. Do you know, I am not fond of warts."

Craig laid a hand on Jean-Pierre's shoulder and said, "Sure. I understand. I don't like warts either."

"Are you certain you're not sick?" Jean-Pierre frowned.

"I don't know. It's hard to diagnose your own sickness, isn't it? What's sick to one person is right as rain to somebody else."

Craig dressed in jeans, a button-down oxford-cloth shirt, and his favorite sand-colored Armani jacket. Then he walked through the kitchen, turned left, and went through the swinging door into the restaurant.

It was nearly one o'clock in the morning, and almost everybody had left. The restaurant was decorated in a pale, restrained style, with lots of natural-colored woods and concealed lighting. The only distinctive decorative motif was a steel-and-enamel mural of carp leaping across the main wall, with their tails ablaze.

The man whom the waitresses called Almond Head was sitting with a young girl at table nine, the most discreet table in the restaurant, but the table with the best view. He was very tall and swarthy, with a narrow skull and ears that lay flat back against his head. His hair was jet black and combed in tight oily ripples; his forehead was deeply furrowed too. His eyes disturbed Craig more than his almond-shaped head. They were hooded and withdrawn and as expressionless as two stones. For all that they communicated, he might just as well not have had eyes at all. He wore an expensive gray suit, and his black shoes gleamed as bright as his hair. On his hairy wrist hung a huge gold wristwatch.

It was the girl who commanded Craig's attention, however. She looked part Asian and part European. She was very slight, all arms and legs, and she wore a short dress of flesh-colored silk that made her look from a distance as if she were naked. As it was, it concealed very little. Her nipples made little shadowy points, and the silk clung to her thighs as if it was trying to ride up all by itself and expose her. Her face was extraordinary. She had black hair cut in a severe cap, and beneath this cap she had the features of a sphinx—slanted eyes, a narrow nose, and lips that looked as if she had just finished fellatio. She was deeply suntanned. Her skin was so perfect that Craig found it hard to resist the temptation to touch her shoulder, just to see what it felt like.

"I wish to congratulate you on a very exciting meal," said Hugo Xawery. His voice was deep, but his speech carried no trace of a European accent. On the phone, you might have thought he came from Boston.

"You had the beef tendon," said Craig.

"That's right. It takes great skill and patience to make a piece of gristle into one of the finest dishes in the city. 'If one has the art, then a piece of celery or salted cabbage can be made into a marvelous delicacy, whereas if one has not the art, not all the greatest delicacies and rarities of land, sea, or sky are of any avail.'"

"Wang Hsiao-yu," said Craig. "Quoted by the scholar Yüan Mei."

"You're a very gifted man. I have searched for more than eleven years for a chef as skillful as you. Why don't you sit down? I wish to make a proposition."

Craig remained standing and passed over Hugo Xawery's visiting card. "Is it this?"

Hugo Xawery's eyes gave away nothing.

Craig said, "I've heard about it, for sure. But I didn't think there were any copies of it still in existence. Besides, it wouldn't exactly be legal to try cooking from it, would it?"

"Some things are so pure in their purpose that they are above illegality."

"You could never say that this book is pure."

Hugo Xawery gave an infinitesimal shrug. "You haven't read it. I myself have read it more than a hundred times. I know it by heart. If I ever lost it, or if it was stolen, I could rewrite it from cover to cover. It is the single greatest cookbook ever compiled. The nature of the recipes takes nothing away from its single-minded purity of purpose."

"I don't know whether everybody would see it the same way."

Hugo Xawery leaned forward a little. His watch was of a very strange design, with a brand name that Craig had never seen before. "How would you see it?" he asked.

"Academically, I guess."

"How could a chef of your brilliance read a book like *The Secret Shih Tan* and not have a burning desire to try it out?"

Craig let out a little humorless bark. "Well, you know why. The ingredients are something of a problem, to say the least. And I have my restaurant to think of, my career."

"Ah, yes," said Hugo Xawery. "Your career."

Craig waited, but Hugo Xawery said nothing more. He sat with his stone-dead eyes, his watch ticking away the seconds, one of his hands resting on the girl's bare thigh, far higher up than most restaurant patrons would have considered decent.

"I'd certainly like to see it, though," said Craig after a moment.

"You may see it," Hugo Xawery replied. "And that is a part of my proposition."

"Go on."

"You may come to my house and read it. You may read it all the way through, if you so wish. But there is one condition."

"What? That I don't steal any of the recipes and serve them up here? Not very likely! Ha!"

Hugo Xawery turned to the girl. His hand was very high on her thigh now, and his little finger had disappeared under the hem of her dress. God, she was alluring, thought Craig. She was so erotic and so vulnerable that he could hardly believe she was real.

"Mr. Richard here has named his restaurant Burn-the-Tail," Hugo Xawery said to her, almost murmuring. "This comes from the story told in the Tang dynasty of how the carp used to swim up the Huanghe River to spawn. They did well until they reached the Dragon Gate, which was narrow and turbulent, and the current was too strong for them to go any farther—that is, until one of them learned to leap."

When he said this, he turned back and stared at Craig with such an expression of power and dark intensity that Craig felt a cold shrinking sensation in his spine.

"One of them learned to leap, and so all the others followed, and as they leaped, they flew in shimmering arcs through the spray. The gods were so impressed by their beauty and their courage that they burned their tails gold and changed the carp into scaly dragons who could fly wherever they wanted. In Chinese, if anybody says you have a burned tail, it means you have a glittering future."

He almost smiled, and then he said, "Mr. Richard could be the first carp to make the leap through the Dragon Gate."

"So what's your condition for reading the book?" asked Craig. He still couldn't bring himself to say its title out loud.

"Very simple, Mr. Richard. You may read the book, but then, having read it, you must choose one recipe and cook it for me."

Craig hesitated. "Is this a joke? You're not pulling my leg or anything?"

Hugo Xawery's face made it utterly clear that he found even the word "joke" to be offensive.

"I'd be using substitute ingredients, right?"

"Do you use substitute ingredients here at the Burn-the-Tail? Do you use small-mouthed bass instead of mandarin fish? Do you use collard greens instead of Chinese broccoli? Or pig's-liver pâté instead of *foie gras?*"

"Of course not."

Hugo Xawery said, "I will provide the ingredients. Whatever you ask."

Craig smiled and shook his head, then stopped smiling.

"Very well," Hugo Xawery told him. "If you won't do it, then I will have to continue my search for someone who will. I have to confess that I am gravely disappointed. You are one of the greatest chefs whose creations I have ever had the pleasure to eat."

Tina came up and said brightly, "Can I bring you some refreshment?"

Hugo Xawery stood up. He was unusually tall—almost six feet five. "I do need refreshment, yes. But not wine. I need to have my soul refreshed. I need to taste . . . I need to taste *God.*"

Craig escorted him to the door. The girl silently followed. She brushed past Craig, and he felt as if they were both naked.

"Listen, I'm sorry I couldn't help you," he said, as Hugo Xawery buttoned up his coat.

"Don't be sorry, Mr. Richard. Only the weak are ever sorry."

When they had gone, Craig went over to the bar and asked Tina to pour him a vodka on the rocks.

"Weird people," she remarked. "That girl looks young enough to be his daughter."

"Maybe she is."

"And do you know what's strange about her? I mean, apart from the fact that you couldn't stop staring at her with your mouth hanging open?"

"Go on, tell me."

"She wasn't wearing any perfume. None at all. No makeup, either. Don't you think that's strange?"

"Maybe she's allergic."

"I don't know," said Tina. "My grandmother used to say that women can smell fear in other women, even when they're laughing and smiling and trying to show everybody that they're having a great time. That girl wasn't wearing any perfume, but she smelled of fear."

Craig lay alone that night in his pale, sparsely decorated apartment on Mulholland Drive, unable to sleep. He kept thinking of Uncle Lee, sitting by the window, smoking. He could see him now, his eyes lowered, his voice little more than a dry, crackly whisper: "*The Secret Shih Tan* was written by the scholar Yüan Mei during the Ching period. He was a great intellectual, you know, a great philosopher. For him, food was a world in itself. He loved everything about it and its preparation and the way in which it was served. He delighted in such tiny nuances as the fact that the word for 'fish' in Chinese sounds exactly like the word for 'more than enough.' He had written *Shih Tan,* a famous book of recipes that was published all over the world. But his fame became so great that he was introduced to a secretive order of chefs from the province of Shandong, on the east coast of China on the Yellow Sea. They were all master chefs. But they had another interest. Like you, they were interested in the pleasures of a woman's body."

Craig switched on the light and sat up. He kept trying to imagine what *The Secret Shih Tan* looked like, what it was like to turn the pages of the most forbidden book in the Western world.

His uncle had blown out smoke and said, "Some meat is traditionally taboo. Ch'en Ts'ang-ch'i said that you should never eat the flesh of a black ox, a goat with a white head, a single-horned goat, any animal that had died facing north, a deer spotted like a leopard, horse liver, or any meat that a dog had refused to eat."

Craig could remember staring at his uncle, speechless, waiting for the words that were almost too dreadful to think about.

His uncle said, "Yüan Mei tasted the chefs' food, and it affected him forever. After the first time, he went to a house in Jinan near the Qianmen and lay face down on the floor of an empty room for two days and two nights, eating nothing more, because he didn't want his mouth or his body to be affected by the taste of anything else until the food had passed completely through him. Only at the end of this time did he start to write a second *Shih Tan,* known as *The Secret Shih Tan.*"

Craig had swallowed. "What did he eat?"

And that was when his uncle had put his lips close to Craig's ear and fired his imagination with *The Secret Shih Tan* forever.

The Sanctuary was a large white house set well back from the road on Stone Canyon Avenue; it was fenced, gated, and almost invisible behind dark, prickly-looking shrubs. Craig drove up to the gate in his red Mercedes and pressed the intercom button.

"Xawery residence." A girl's voice, light and expressionless.

"Hi, this is Craig Richard. I'd like to talk to Mr. Xawery."

"Do you have an appointment?"

"No, I don't. But you can tell Mr. Xawery I accept his condition."

"You'll have to wait."

He waited, listening to Beck singing about being screwed up and life's a toilet and why don't you kill me. After a long while, the gates hummed open, and Craig drove up the steeply angled driveway to the house.

It was large, but it was also oddly proportioned and deeply unwelcoming. A Rottweiler barked insanely at him as he approached the porch, hurling itself from side to side on its chain. When he rang the doorbell, a small grille opened up, and he was examined for a ridiculously long time by a disembodied pair of glittering eyes.

"You satisfied?" he said impatiently.

At last he heard bolts being shot back, and the door was opened by an unsmiling Mexican in a black uniform. Inside the house, the air was startingly chilly. The floor was polished marble, and there was scarcely any furniture. No flowers, either. Without a word, the Mexican turned and walked off across the hallway, his shoes squeaking. Craig followed him, although he wasn't sure that he was supposed to. They walked all the way down a long, gloomy corridor until they reached a sunroom—or what would have been a sunroom if all the drapes hadn't been drawn. Instead, it had a kind of papyrus-colored light, as if it were an ancient tomb.

Hugo Xawery was sitting in a large armchair, reading. He was dressed in white pants and a collarless white shirt. The girl was kneeling on the floor next to him, one arm on his knee. She was wearing a plain white sleeveless dress, as square as a sack.

"Well," said Hugo Xawery. "It seems that you have changed your mind."

"As a matter of fact, no, I don't think I have. I think I was always going to have to do this, no matter what."

"Of course."

"I'd just like to know how you knew."

"What? That you were interested in seeing *The Secret Shih Tan?* I met your Uncle Lee Chan the second time I had dinner at the Burn-the-Tail. He's a well-educated man, your uncle, but he shouldn't smoke so much. It ruins the palate, smoking. I like your Uncle Lee, though. I don't like many Chinese. We talked about your talent, you see, and the conversation went around to Paul Bocuse and nouvelle cuisine, and then to some of the great modern chefs in China. I praised your skill in using difficult ingredients and said something like 'He's probably cooked everything except the dishes described in *The Secret Shih Tan.*' That was when your uncle said, 'Yes, but he *knows* about it.' And that was when I was satisfied that I had found my man. You have only to know about it to want to cook from it."

Craig said, "I want to ask you something. Have you ever . . . well, have you ever tasted the dishes made from any of those recipes?"

Hugo Xawery gave him a closed, stony look. "What happens in this house is private, Mr. Richard."

Craig hesitated. A molting white parrot was perched in a cage, nodding at him with horrible intimacy. Craig knew that what he was about to do was wrong. It was probably the most terrible thing that he would ever do. But he also knew that if he turned around and walked out of Hugo Xawery's house without seeing *The Secret Shih Tan*, his career as a chef would be finished. He would wonder for the rest of his life what he could have done, what he could have been.

He wanted to cook a meal that would make Hugo Xawery want to lie face down on the floor for forty-eight hours, sobbing because he was digesting it and because when he had excreted it, it would be gone forever.

"Show me the book," he said in a throaty voice.

Hugo Xawery put down his book and stood up. "Very well," he said, and extended his hand. "So long as you remember what you have solemnly agreed to do."

"I won't forget."

Hugo Xawery led the way along another dark, echoing corridor until they reached a bare, marble-floored room with nothing in it but a rectangular steel desk, a plain office chair, and a gray-painted safe. A greenish bamboo shade was drawn most of the way down the French windows. Beneath the shade, Craig could see part of a patio and the feet of a stone cherub, a reminder of the world that he had now decided to leave behind.

Hugo Xawery walked across to the safe, produced two keys, and opened it. Inside, there was nothing but the book itself, wrapped in plain white tissue. Hugo Xawery brought it over, laid it on the desk, and unwrapped it.

It wasn't much to look at. A maroon fabric-bound book with a Chinese character stamped into the cover.

"No," said Hugo Xawery, "it isn't very impressive, is it? This edition was published in Paris in 1911. I've seen only one other English edition, and that was much older, and illustrated. But I don't think you need illustrations in a book of this nature, do you?"

Craig sat down in the chair. Hugo Xawery said, "I'll leave you to it. Tell me when you've had enough. My man will bring you coffee or wine or anything else that you'd care for."

He left, and Craig was alone. He sat looking at the book for a long time without opening it. The moment he turned to the first page, he would be committed. He glanced around the room. He wondered if Hugo Xawery was watching him on closed-circuit television. Maybe he should stand up, and walk out now. There was always the Burn-the-Tail; there was always business and chatter and laughter, buying produce, devising new menus, cooking with sauces and sizzling shallots and flames.

But there was nothing like *The Secret Shih Tan*; and here it was. It was probably the only copy in America. He laid his hand on the cover. Still he didn't open it.

He knew all of the arcane secrets of great French cookery, right down to roast camel's hump, which the Algerians prepare with oil, lemon juice, salt, pepper, and spices, roasted like a sirloin of beef, and served on a bed of watercress. He knew all of the Chinese recipes that the bravest of his customers couldn't face, like *bêche-de-mer*, the sea slug, which had no flavor whatsoever and the consistency of a jellyfish; and bird's-nest soup, made out of cliff swallows' nests, a combination of bird spit, sea moss, and feathers.

But this was something else. This was the moment when food, sex, and death came together in the darkest challenge that any chef could face. Food is sex, his father had always told him. But food was death, too. Every time something was eaten, something had to die.

Craig felt as if he were standing with his toes on the edge of a terrible abyss. It was too late to turn back; and because it was too late to turn back, he opened the book.

The recipes were written with grace and subtle charm, but that only served to make their horror more intense. Craig started with the simplest of them, in the beginning, but he hadn't read more than three before he began to feel as if he were no longer real, as if the room around him were no longer real. What heightened his feeling of unreality was knowing that he had agreed to prepare one of these dishes, that he would actually be following the instructions in one of the recipes.

YOUNG GIRL'S BREAST, BRAISED

The breast should first be soaked in cold water, blanched, cooled in cold water, and carefully flattened under pressure so that its youthful curves are not lost when it is braised. Place the breast in a clay casserole. Cut two thin slices of smoked thigh meat into ½-inch squares and add to the casserole with 6 soaked dried black mushrooms. Make horizontal slashes along one side of each of two bamboo shoots, like a fan. These will make decorative angels' wings to surround the breast when it is served. Add salt, sugar, 3 tablespoons rice wine, and 2 slices peeled fresh ginger. Braise very gently for 3 to 4 hours. Slice thin so that each diner receives a full curve showing the shape of the breast. The most honored guests will receive a slice with a section of the nipple on it. Serve with braised asparagus and rape hearts. Breast can be served fresh, cold, or smoked.

There were over a hundred recipes in all, every one of them using male or female sexual parts, sometimes accompanied by other organs, such as liver or pancreas or stomach lining. Some of the dishes were plain—sexual interpretations of everyday Chinese dishes such as zha yazhengan, which was nothing more than duck gizzards deep-fried and served with a dip of prickly ash—a mixture of salt and Szechuan peppercorns. In *The Secret Shih Tan*, however, the gizzards were replaced by deep-fried testicles.

Woman In Man was a sausage made from penis skin and filled with a mixture of finely chopped labia, seasoned with mao-tai liquor, salt, sugar, sesame oil, and fat from the pubic mound.

There were elaborate preparations of male and female organs, marinated, steamed, and served in the act of disembodied coitus. Man Takes Many Lovers was a penis stuffed into rigidity with scores of nipples and encircled with six or seven anal sphincters, like quoits. These should be cooked in the same way as jellyfish, the book advised, and in the same way they required "spirited, vigorous chewing."

As he turned the pages, Craig didn't notice the room gradually growing darker. He was lost in a world where every meal required the death or mutilation of a human being—sometimes eight or nine people sacrificed for one tantalizing side dish.

Toward the end of the book, some of the dishes were so perverse that Craig left the table and stood on the opposite side of the room, almost too horrified to continue reading. But eventually he returned and sat down and read the recipes to the very end.

The last recipe was the most challenging of all. It was called, simply, Whole Woman Banquet. A young woman was to be carefully eviscerated, and every organ cleaned, marinated, and cooked in a different way, including her eyes and her brains. Everything would then have to be returned to the body and her original shape restored as perfectly as possible. Then she would be steamed.

It was the footnote that riveted Craig more than any of the lengthy descriptions of how to poach lungs in the same way as soft-shelled turtle. The author Yüan Mei had written, "It is essential for this dish that the woman be as beautiful as can be found and that the chef should make love to her the evening before the banquet. The lovemaking endows both the food and its creator with spiritual tenderness and is a way that a chef can pay homage to his ingredients."

Craig closed the book. It was dark now, and he hadn't realized that Hugo Xawery was standing in the doorway, patiently waiting for him.

"What do you think?" he asked in a voice like brushed velvet.

"It's everything I ever imagined it would be."

"Did it shock you?"

"I'd be lying if I said it didn't."

"But the technique . . . what do you think of the technique?"

"Very difficult, some of it."

"But not beyond you?"

"No."

Hugo Xawery circled the table. "Have you decided what you're going to cook?"

"I don't know. You'll have to give me some time to think about it."

"Not too long. I have to find you the ingredients, you understand, and they must be fresh."

Craig stood up. "I'll call you tomorrow."

"Yes. You will," Hugo Xawery said, with an imperative tone in his voice.

"Don't you trust me?" asked Craig.

"I don't know. You could cause me a great deal of embarrassment as well as disappointment. I've already promised this treat to several very influential people."

"I've given you my word. What more can I do?"

"You don't have to do anything more. Because I've taken one simple precaution, in case you renege on your agreement. Somewhere in one of your freezers, among the rest of your meats, there are human remains—packed, of course, in anonymous freezer bags just like all of your other meat. I'm sure the police would be interested in rummaging among your livers and your kidneys and your loin chops."

"You didn't have to do that," said Craig tersely. "I don't have any intention of reneging on my agreement."

"Let's just call it insurance. And they're high-quality remains. Even if you cook them and serve them up, they won't harm anybody."

On the way out, Craig saw the girl standing in a half-open doorway at the end of the corridor. She was wearing nothing but the thinnest of silk slips, so short that it scarcely covered her. She was watching him with those slanted, sphinxlike eyes, her skin shining smooth in the lamplight. He stopped and stared back at her. She made no attempt to turn away or to close the door.

"You like her?" asked Hugo Xawery.

"She's beautiful."

"I call her Xanthippa. Of course that's not her real name. Her mother and I lived together for a while, in Carmel. One day her mother left and never came back. So I suppose you could call me Xanthippa's guardian."

Craig took one last look at Xanthippa and then walked across the hallway to the front door, where the Mexican servant was waiting with undisguised displeasure to show him out.

Early the next morning, he found his Uncle Lee in his back yard in Westwood, hosing his roses. Uncle Lee was over seventy now, and his face was wrinkled like an aerial view of Death Valley. He wore a coolie hat and a loose blue shift.

"Uncle Lee?"

"Hallo, Craig. I was wondering when you would come."

"I've read it, Uncle Lee. *The Secret Shih Tan.* I read it yesterday evening, from cover to cover."

"Then today you will be different."

"Yes, I'm different." He watched the hose water splattering into the flower bed, and then he said, "Why did you tell Hugo Xawery that I knew about it?"

"Because *The Secret Shih Tan* is as far as any chef can go, and you would never have been satisfied with anything less."

"Hugo Xawery let me look at it on one condition."

Uncle Lee looked up at him, his eyes slitted against the seven o'clock sunlight. "Don't tell me. You have to cook one of the recipes for him."

Craig nodded. "I've been awake all night. I don't know which one to choose."

"Which do you *wish* to choose? The greatest of all the recipes or the recipe that will cause the least human suffering?"

"I don't know. It's not just gastronomy, is it, *The Secret Shih Tan?* It has so many inner meanings. We kill thousands of people in war, and that's supposed to be moral and glorious, even though war is totally destructive. But if we sacrifice half a dozen human beings to create one of the greatest meals in gastronomic history, that's supposed to be so goddamned evil that we're not even allowed to *talk* about it."

"So which dish are you going to choose?" Uncle Lee repeated.

"I don't know. I'm still trying to work out what it is that *The Secret Shih Tan* is trying to tell me."

Uncle Lee turned off the faucet, and laid a withered hand on Craig's shoulder. "If you do not see it for yourself, then I cannot tell you."

"You can't even give me a clue?"

"All I can say is that whatever you decide to cook, you must make sure, above all, that you do it justice."

Craig didn't open the Burn-the-Tail restaurant that day, although he spent a half hour in thick insulated gloves, sorting through the foods in his freezers. He couldn't find any packages of meat that looked human, but how could anyone tell if there was one human kidney among thirty lamb's kidneys, or one escallope of human thigh among ten escallopes of veal? He would either have to throw away his entire stock or wait until he had fulfilled his promise to cook Hugo Xawery's meal.

Later in the afternoon he drove up to Stone Canyon Avenue. Hugo Xawery was sitting alone in the sunroom behind tightly drawn shades. Through the open door, however, Craig could see Xanthippa sitting on the patio under a large green parasol.

"Ah, Mr. Richard," said Hugo Xawery. "What a pleasure to see you so soon. Have you come to a decision?"

Craig nodded. "There's no point in playing around with *hors d'oeuvres*," he said. "I'm going to cook the Whole Woman Banquet."

Hugo Xawery's face slowly lit up with unholy relish. "The banquet! I knew you would! The greatest challenge that any chef could ever face! The greatest feast that any gastronome could ever imagine!"

"You won't be able to eat it all on your own, will you?"

"I have no intention of eating it on my own. I have . . . friends."

"Can you get in touch with them? I'd like to start making preparations right away."

"Of course I can get in touch with them. And I can procure your main ingredient, too. In fact, I have it already."

Craig looked out onto the patio. "Xanthippa?"

"Isn't she beautiful? You can't make the banquet of banquets out of inferior raw materials."

"You know what it says at the foot of the recipe?"

"About the chef making love to his uncooked banquet? Of course. And you shall. Xanthippa has been expecting this day for many years."

"You mean she already knows what you're going to do to her?"

Hugo Xawery smiled. "She lives only to serve me; she always has. Her greatest pleasure has always been to know that one day I shall ingest her. Why do you think she never wears perfume or cosmetics? She doesn't wish to taint the taste of her flesh."

"How about tomorrow evening?" Craig suggested. "Or is that too soon?"

Hugo Xawery wrapped his long arm around Craig's shoulders. "Tomorrow evening will be perfect. Expect six for dinner, including me. You can stay here tonight, with Xanthippa, and early tomorrow morning you can start your preparations. You will, of course, allow me to watch you at work?"

"You're very welcome, Mr. Xawery. In fact, I'd be disappointed if you didn't."

"How about . . . the butchery? Do you need any assistance?"

"I prefer to do my own, thanks."

Hugo Xawery gripped Craig's shoulder and stared into his eyes with such emotion that Craig thought for a moment he was going to weep. "You're a great, great chef. Do you know that? After tomorrow, your name will rank with the very finest."

"We'll see," said Craig.

Without taking his eyes off Craig, Hugo Xawery called out, "Xanthippa!"

She turned and frowned at him.

"Xanthippa, I have a surprise for you!"

The bedroom that Hugo Xawery lent him was silent and painted a silky gray. In the center stood a massive carved-oak bed heaped with Moorish-style cushions. It was a warm night, so Craig left the French windows open. The net curtains billowed silently in the breeze, like the ghosts of nuns.

Craig was sitting up in bed reading *The Secret Shih Tan* when the door quietly opened and Xanthippa came in. She was wearing nothing but a thin shirt of aquamarine linen and small brown beads around her wrists and ankles. She came across the room and climbed onto the bed next to him. She smelled of nothing but the natural biscuity aroma of an aroused young woman.

"You're reading that book," she said, although not accusingly.

Craig closed it and dropped it down by the side of the bed. "I'm sorry," he said.

"Why should you be?"

"It isn't in very good taste, is it, considering what I'm supposed to do to you tomorrow?"

"You don't understand. I'm looking forward to it. Hugo is one of the greatest men in the world. He's intellectual, he's refined, but he doesn't believe in limits. With Hugo, everything is possible. I've already had enough pleasure for five lifetimes. Why should I worry if my life ends now?"

Craig gently touched her cheekbones and then traced the outline of her lips. *Carefully remove the eyes and set aside on a dish.* Then he leaned forward and kissed her.

"You're very beautiful," he told her.

She smiled and kissed him back. She kissed him like no woman had ever kissed him before, sucking and teasing his lips and then sliding her tongue into his mouth and stimulating nerve endings he hadn't even known he had. Underneath the blanket, his penis stiffened.

Xanthippa crossed her arms and took off her shirt. She was lean and small-breasted, but her skin was so exquisite that Craig couldn't stop himself from sliding his hands up and down her bare back. Her pubic hair was shiny and black, and she plaited it tightly and decorated it with small colored beads, so that the lips of her vulva were exposed.

She said, "Lie back . . . you can taste me first."

He lay back on the pillow and Xanthippa drew aside the blanket. She climbed astride him, with her back to him, and then she lifted her bottom so that he was confronted with her vagina. He kissed all around it, and then he ran the tip of his tongue down the cleft between her buttocks and tasted her tightly wrinkled anus. She sighed and kissed him all around his penis in return.

The room was so quiet that he heard the moistened lips of her vagina opening, like the softest click in the Xhosa language. He slid his tongue into her wetness and warmth, and tasted saltness and sweetness and something else as well, like highly purified honey. At the same time, she slowly sucked his penis, flicking it and drumming it with her tongue.

They made love for hours, and she showed him all of the tastes of love. He licked her perspiration-beaded armpits and the soles of her feet. He swallowed her vaginal juices when they were thick with early arousal, and again when they thinned out, just before orgasm. He tasted her saliva when she was excited, and again when she was drowsy. She had eaten a salad for lunch with wildflowers in it, and he could actually taste it.

Eventually, as it began to grow light, she rubbed his penis so that he climaxed into her mouth, and she drank his sperm with long, appreciative swallows. "Did you know that you can *chew* sperm and that it actually changes texture as you chew it?"

They lay together in silence for a long while. At last Craig sat up and said, "Would you do something for me? Something really special?"

"I'm yours now," she said, her voice husky. "You know that."

"Well, that's the point. I feel as if you're not really mine at all. I'm just the chef. I'm a craftsman, not a lover. If you belong to anybody, you belong to Hugo."

She propped herself up on one elbow. "So what do you want me to do?"

"The recipe says that there should be lovemaking before the meal is prepared, to give it spiritual tenderness. But I can't give you anything like the spiritual tenderness that Hugo can give you. I mean, think of it, Hugo's the one who's actually going to—"

"You think I should make love to Hugo?"

"Yes, I do."

She smiled, and kissed him. "If you want me to make love to Hugo one last time, then I will."

It was nearly six o'clock in the morning. The house was already bright. Craig stood silently outside the door of Hugo Xawery's enormous white-carpeted bedroom. The door was ajar only a half inch, but that was enough for him to be able to see Hugo Xawery lying on his back on the white silk sheets while Xanthippa rode up and down on his dark, erect penis as if she were taking part in some dreamlike steeplechase.

He didn't know if either of them knew he was there until Hugo Xawery looked over Xanthippa's shoulder toward the door and gave a wide, knowing, lubricious smile.

Craig watched his purple glans disappearing into Xanthippa's stretched-open vagina and tried to think of all the spiritual tenderness that was passing between them, one to the other. Hadn't Yüan Mei said that spiritual tenderness flows both ways?

At eight, Craig was awakened by a soft knock at the door. Hugo Xawery came in and stood over the bed. "Good morning, Mr. Richard. It's time for the kitchen."

"I'm ready," said Craig.

"Xanthippa . . . was she enjoyable?"

"Oh, she was more than enjoyable. She was a revelation."

Blood hurried down the grooves in the butcher's table, and he carefully collected it for blood puddings and gravies. His knives slit open skin and fat and sliced through connective tissue.

On the stove, pans of stock were already simmering, and the ovens were warming up. The kitchen echoed to the sound of chopping and dicing.

By the middle of the day, the house was already filled with extraordinary fragrances—frying liver, poaching lungs, heat-seared filet of human flesh—mingled with the aroma of basil and rosemary and coriander and soy sauce.

Craig worked nonstop, swallowing ice-cold Evian to keep himself going. By six o'clock in the evening he was almost ready when the Mexican servant knocked at the door and announced that the first two guests had arrived.

They sat at the long mahogany dining table, none of them speaking. The room was lit only by candles, and the plates and glasses gleamed and sparkled. The cutlery shone like shoals of fish. The sense of drama was immense.

At last, the double doors opened, and Craig appeared, in immaculate whites. Behind him, the Mexican servant was pushing a long trolley, more like a paramedics' gurney than a serving wagon.

Craig recognized at least two of the guests as customers from the Burn-the-Tail, and a famous face from one of the movie studios. They must have recognized him, too, but they gave no hint of it. Their eyes were fastened on the long trolley, with its cover of highly burnished silver.

Craig said, "I welcome you on behalf of Mr. Xawery, who has spent eleven years of his life preparing for this moment, when *The Secret Shih Tan* becomes more than a book of recipes, but a reality, which you can eat.

"I always thought *The Secret Shih Tan* was nothing more than the ultimate cookbook. But, you know, it's much more than that. It's a book of thought, justice, and devastating truth. Yüan Mei never intended that any of its recipes should ever be cooked. He just wanted us to understand what we are—that we are foodstuffs, too, for anybody or anything who finds us good to eat. He wanted to put us in perspective."

Craig beckoned the manservant to wheel the wagon right up close to the end of the table. Even though the lid was tightly closed, the fragrance of flesh and herbs was overwhelming, and one of the guests was salivating so copiously that he had to cram his linen napkin into his mouth.

Craig said, "I learned about life while I was cooking this meal. I learned about death. I learned about ambition, too, and vanity. But most of all I learned about love."

The studio director said, "Shouldn't we wait for Hugo? This is Hugo's moment, after all."

Craig took off his chef's hat. "We don't need to wait for Hugo. Hugo's already here."

With that, he rolled back the shining cover on top of the wagon, and there was a human body—glossy, plump, gutted of every organ, braised, fried, steamed, and poached, and restored to its original shape. The greatest recipe that man had ever devised. It smelled divine.

Craig laid his hand on the body's belly. "Do you see this? It was my uncle who first told me about *The Secret Shih Tan*. It was my uncle who gave me the clue to what it meant. Cook your meal, he told me, and do it justice. And this is what this is. Justice."

He turned and beckoned, and Xanthippa appeared, wearing an impossibly short linen dress, a black bandanna tightly braided around her forehead. She stood beside the body, but she wouldn't look at it.

"This is my new sous-chef," said Craig. "She gave me the inspiration to cook this meal, and help in preparing it, and she also gave it the spiritual meaning that Yüan Mei demanded. Not just an eye for an eye, but a heart for a heart, a spleen for a spleen, and a liver for a liver. She was the last person to make love to Hugo Xawery, and here she is, to serve him to you. Enjoy."

Three weeks later Craig took Xanthippa to Shanxi Province in China, where the Huanghe roars and froths between two mountainous, cloud-swathed peaks called the Dragon Gate.

It was a chilly, vaporous day. The skies were the color of slate. Xanthippa stood a short distance away while Craig climbed right to the edge of the river, carrying the book.

He looked around him, at the mountains and the clouds. Then he ripped the pages out, six or seven at a time, in clumps, and threw them into the river.

He had almost expected them to catch fire, to burn, to leap in the air. But the Huanghe swallowed them and swamped them and carried them away. He tossed in the book cover last of all.

"Are you satisfied now?" she asked him. She was wearing a pink ribbed roll-neck sweater and tight blue jeans, and she looked almost good enough to eat.

"I don't know," he said. "I don't think I ever will be."

"Aren't you going back to Burn-the-Tail?"

"What's the point? Jean-Pierre is as good as I am; he'll keep it going. Once you've cooked from *The Secret Shih Tan*, how can you cook anything else?"

"But what will you do next?"

"Try to understand you."

She touched him and gave him an enigmatic smile. He could never forget that she had been willing to be cooked.

"What about the human meat that Hugo hid in your freezers?" she asked him. "What are you going to do about that?"

"Well . . . I looked for it, but I couldn't find it, and I think Hugo was lying. Even if he wasn't lying, it doesn't matter. Human meat is the very best there is. It's one thing to eat an animal. It's another thing to eat an animal that you can talk to and make love to."

Xanthippa linked arms with him and kissed him, and together they walked back down the hillside to the waiting tourist bus.

In the Burn-the-Tail restaurant that evening, Morrie Walker, the restaurant critic from *California* magazine, ordered the seared liver with celeriac. He jotted on his notepad that it was "pungent, strange . . . a variety meat lifted to a spiritual level . . . almost sexual in its sensuality.

"Without being blasphemous," he wrote, "I felt that I was close to God."

IN THE MATTER OF THE UKDENA

Bruce Holland Rogers

Bruce Holland Rogers has published short fiction in a number of magazines and antholgies including *Century, The Magazine of Fantasy & Science Fiction, Diagnosis: Terminal, Enchanted Forests* and *Monster Brigade 3000.* His story "Enduring as Dust" was nominated for an Edgar Award by the Mystery Writers of America and he recently won a Nebula Award for his "Lifeboat on a Burning Sea." Rogers lives in Eugene, Oregon.

"In the Matter of the Ukdena" is an "Alternate History" fantasy—a beautifully crafted, thought-provoking and spirit-filled tale. The story explores what might have happened if the European conquest of North America had taken a very different turn . . .

—T. W.

Spiral Mind turns in on itself,
thinking about the story
of its own nature.

There are many versions
of the story Spiral Mind
is thinking.

Here is one.

Of course, the story can't begin
until there is a universe to contain it.
Spiral Mind says,
Manifestation began in formlessness.
That's how the story gets started,
with the making of a place,
a sky above.

This story begins in the time
when everyone lived in the sky.

Spiral Mind names this time
The First World of the original era.

Clearly, geography is destiny, and a rivalry between the Super-
powers was clear as far back as 1850 when Alexis de Tocqueville
wrote that he foresaw the development of two principal powers in
the world: Imperial Russia, and the United Nations of Turtle Island. "Both countries control an abundance of natural resources,"
de Tocqueville wrote after his visit to North America, "but the exploitation of those resources is a matter of command in Russia.
In the United Nations, the use of resources is controlled by dem-
ocratic forces and elaborate religious restraints."

It was crowded in the sky.
The human beings, the spirits, the gods,
the two-leggeds and the four-leggeds,
people with wings like Eagle and the crawling people like Ant
and the digging people like Badger
and swimmers like Box Turtle,
the grasses and trees,
even the stone people
all crowded in
together.

Aluminum extraction relies on a process devised simultaneously
by Charles Martin Hall in the U.N.T.I and Paul Héroult France. In
this process, alumina (aluminum oxide) is dissolved in molten cry-
olite and electric current is passed through the solution. At the
cathode, metallic aluminum is liberated while oxygen collects at
the anode. For the sake of clarity, this chapter will concentrate
entirely on the technical aspects of the process. Spiritual consid-
erations on the extraction of metals from the earth, our mother,
will be covered in the chapter to follow.

Water Beetle came down to look around
before there was any land.
He dove under the waves
and surfaced with mud
in his jaws.
The Creator Spirits
rolled the mud in their hands.
It grew. It became islands.
Everyone came down.

The human beings came down.
They were red and brown and black,
they were white and yellow,
and they started in their own places,

but did not stay there.
They spread themselves out
as far as possible.
Wherever they were,
they walked until oceans stopped them.
Even back when this
world was new,
that's how
they were.
That's how
human beings
have always been.

Aroism (from Spanish, *aro*, hoop), European term for the plurality of religious beliefs and practices to which the vast majority of the North Americans adhere. Arising initially as a synthesis of indigenous beliefs and the religions brought to the Americas by Europeans, Aroism has developed in syncretism with the religious and cultural evolution of the hemisphere. Aroist belief is generally characterized by sacralization of all phenomena, but special emphasis is given to particular sacred locales and to Mother Earth in general. Similar in some aspects to **Animism,** Aroism calls upon believers to communicate with the natural world as they interact with it so that their actions may be in harmony with the natural order. As Western technological practices such as mining and deep-furrow agriculture were introduced, Aroist beliefs evolved to allow for resource exploitation consistent with sacred regard for the earth. Most Aroists adhere to traditions of **Vision Quest, Ritual Purification** and, for women, **Moon Lodge.**

The white tribes
on their part of the world
were as varied as any people,
but there were some things
most of them believed.

"I'll tell you," said the keynote speaker at the Conference for Spiritual History, "what the white nations of Europe believed. They believed that children were little bags of sin to be redeemed by beatings. They believed in the authority of a God King, in the authority of human kings, in the authority of men over women."

The white tribes believed in a universe divided
between good and evil,
in a world that was theirs to master
if they could only destroy enough
of the evil.

> Don't get the idea
> that these people were creatures of darkness.
> Any human being can carry light.

From: V. Adm. David Many Bears
Fleet Operations

To: Capt. Henry Jefferson
U.N.S. Nimitz

Hank, this is going to come down to you through channels, but before it does I wanted you to have some advance notice of the new policy regarding Navy fighter jets for use in vision quests. NAFCOM acknowledges the right of pilots and their RIOs to use any means at their disposal to seek a vision, but loss of an Ukdena in the Sixth Fleet's carrier group has lead us to formulate what you might call Rules of Engagement with the Great Mystery.

The F-4 Ukdena is rated at a service ceiling of 43,000 at power, but the crew of the Sixth Fleet mishap had throttled up hard and gone to 56,000.

Hank, you and I both know how imminent the Great Mystery must be at ten miles above the earth, but we also know that this was a thousand feet above the fleet-configured F-4's maximum rating. A pilot in combat won't make a mistake like that, but a pilot who's flying into the sun can get a little lost up there.

From now on, each crew is allowed one official quest flight per deployment, and they aren't to climb above the military-power service ceiling. I know that there will be some grumbling about this, and I know that there will be covert questing beyond what we're officially sanctioning, but this will at least make it clear that the pain of the sundance is meant for the body, not the airframe of a fighter plane.

> The red tribes
> on this Turtle Island
> were as varied as any people,
> but most of them tried to discover
> right relation to one another
> and to the earth.

> The red tribes believed in
> the spiral,
> the circle,

and everything
was alive.

Don't get the idea
that these people were flames of enlightenment.
Any human being drags a shadow.

Sequoyah, 1766-1843, Tsalagi. First president of the **U.N.T.I.**,
commander in chief of the Continental Army in the **War of Union**,
called the Father of His Country. He created a syllabary for the
Tsaiagi language, based on the characters he saw for English
and Spanish writing, providing the model for the Universal Writing
System.

New Etowah, capital of the **U.N.T.I.**, co-extensive with the District
of Sequoyah.

Andrew Jackson, 1767–1832. White separatist leader. After his
defeat by units of the Creek Nation in the battle of Horseshoe
Bend, Jackson escaped and continued to lead Europeans opposed to national assimilation. Convinced that his vision of a Eu-
ropean-dominated culture could take root in the west, he led his
erstwhile followers on an ill-fated forced march. See **Trail of
Tears.**

In those times
before the white people came to Turtle Island
the Tsalagi, the Principal People,
lived in the mountains
that were at the middle of the earth.

They wanted
peace at the center of all things.
At the center of all things,
harmony.

Late in the last year of the eleventh heaven,
seven generations before the first hell
of the Fifth World,
the days and nights came into
balance
and the cornstalks grew heavy
with grain,
so the Principal People began the Green Corn Ceremony
that would preserve harmony for all beings.

In the council houses of many villages,
the Tsalagi danced and made offerings

to the sacred fire.
In the rivers
they bathed seven times for purity
and held rituals to turn aside any anger
left over from the year they were about to finish.

"What can we reliably say about Spiritual History in pre-literate times?" said the keynote speaker. "To a large extent, we must rely upon the oral tradition. Spiral-thought does not record events with the same emphasis that Arrow-thought does, of course, so we do not remember the details of the political discussions, the names, dates, and exact locations of the debates. But we know, generally, what was decided in the matter of the Ukdena, and we know that it was probably decided in Green Corn time. To this day, that remains the best time for establishing national policy."

Before we went to sleep after the fifth day of deliberations, Walks the River made an offering of cedar smoke to the four directions, to heaven, and to earth. The open eaves of his wife's summer house let the smoke drift away, but the scent remained behind to clear his thoughts and purify his dreams. Though the fire was low, he could see that his wife was watching him with the same expression she had worn during the council, a mixture of discomfort and expectation. There might have been impatience in that gaze, too, except that she was an old Tsalagi woman, a Bird clan woman. She knew how to master herself. She knew how to turn impatience aside, for the sake of harmony.

Silently, Walks the River asked for dreams that would help him carry light. Then, with limbs stiffened by the chill air, he lay down beside his wife.

"It has been five days," she said. She said it gently, sleepily, as if in answer to a question.

"Yes," he said, keeping his voice level. "I have counted them, too."

If she divorced him, he could always go live in his sister's house. It pained him to think such a thought, and he doubted that his wife would turn him out, but who would blame her if she did? What was worse than for a man to seem stubborn and argumentative at the holiest time of the year?

He waited, but she said nothing more. Soon she was breathing the breath of sleep. He heard one of his daughters whisper to her husband in a far corner of the lodge, and an ember popped in the fire.

Give me a dream, he prayed again. Let me see them in my dream.

And then he let the night sounds carry him, the sounds of dark water in the river and wind moving through the trees. Those sounds were still in his ears when he crossed into the dream side of the world and found himself standing on an unfamiliar mountain's grassy bald. Around him were other mountains, covered with fir and spruce. He raised his hands into the dream sky, asking for bountiful life, a prayer for his arrival.

Light dazzled him. Something huge was there in front of him, making the air near him hiss with its passing, and then it was far away. It moved partly in the air and partly along a mountain ridge, making the trees sway. He wanted to see it clearly, but it was not a thing the eyes could easily hold.

"Ukdena," he said.

"Ukdena," he prayed.

The presence swirled high into the air. It was not one being, but a group. They twisted and twined together, parted, and rushed together again. They moved from one side of the sky to the other. Walks the River squinted.

Their scales flashed like facets of crystal. Their bodies were long, sinuous, humping and curving as though even in the sky they had to follow the lines of the mountain ridges below. Once, he thought he caught a glimpse of transparent wings, and for a moment there seemed to be an eye that gazed at him, cold and brilliant.

For a long time he dreamed this dream. Claws. They had terrible claws, glittering like ice, opening and closing on the wind.

"What do you want us to do?" he asked them. "What do you want?" They danced their dance and glittered and burst into flames that didn't harm them. They roared like a forest on fire.

When he awoke, he was careful not to move. That way he could hold the memory a little longer. Then at last he sat up, filled with sadness because he was more firmly trapped than ever. This would be the sixth day of council, but the dream had only strengthened his resolve. He rose quietly and dressed, slipping out of his wife's house before she and her daughters could wake up to repeatedly ask no one in particular when the council would be over.

He went to watch the river. There was, as far as he could see, no right way to act. If he continued to argue, he brought discord into the council house. If he withdrew, he betrayed both the Ukdena and his own heart.

Of course, if he no longer had the support of his clan, then the matter would come to an end. What mattered was not his opinion, but the consensus of the village's Wild Potato clan. Perhaps his people could no longer bear the shame of contentious words spoken in their name.

He went to his sister's lodge to eat breakfast, rather than returning to the Bird clan household of his wife, and then he began to test the opinions of his people. His sister and her grown daughters supported him, but there was certainly more to the clan than his closest family.

He greeted White Clay Woman by the doorway of her house, working in the morning light.

"Good day, Beloved Man," she answered as she sewed feathers onto her new cape. At her feet were songbirds, not yet plucked of feathers for the cape's fringe. "Has your heart changed in the night?"

"No," he told her. "But I am afraid that it is time for us to withdraw."

"Is that what your dreams told you?"

"No," he admitted.

"Then speak to your heart," White Clay Woman told him. "I am with you."

Eye Covered, who was guarding her corn from crows, said she had no opinion and just kept asking Walks the River to bring her water to drink, or to watch the field while she fetched it herself. He brought her water, and then she told him he should follow his heart in the matter of the Ukdena. He asked her again, just to be sure she was not merely being polite. "What do your dreams say?" she said.

With the men who were catching fish, it was the same. Walks the River watched them dam the fishing stream, and then a man named Runner threw ground horse chestnuts into the shadowed pools of still water where the fish hid themselves.

"The other clans are in agreement," Walks the River said. "We are the only holdouts. I begin to feel that we are not behaving well."

The men waiting for the fish asked him if his dreams had changed, and he said again that they had not.

"Every night," one young man said as he stirred the water, "I pray for all my relations. The Ukdena, too, are my relations."

The first of the paralyzed fish floated to the surface. The young men began to choose the ones they wanted and loaded them into baskets. Soon they had all they wanted.

Walks the River looked through the foliage, seeing light from the ridge line glint between the trees. He had never seen the Ukdena in the waking world, but the priests saw them all the time. "The Ukdena are our relations," he agreed. "But I will not shame the clan."

"Do not stand aside until you are almost moved to anger," advised Runner. "We are all of one heart. The Ukdena should be maintained." He opened the dam, and fresh water rushed into the pools. The remaining fish soon recovered and dove back down into the deeper water.

"People think impatient thoughts," Walks the River said.

"As long as you do not become angry," another man said, "there is only a little shame. We can bear it."

So it was that on the sixth day of the council Walks the River sat in the circle of seven Beloved Men with his resolve unbent. Behind him sat the people of the Wild Potato clan, and he could feel their support still flowing to him, even in the face of unified opposition.

In the center of the circle of Beloved Men stood the principal priest, the second priest, and Red Fox, who was the secular officer.

As if he had not already put the question to them a score of times already, the principal priest said, "In the matter of the Ukdena and a third priest, how are we resolved?"

"As we have heard," said Woods Burning, the Beloved Man of the Deer clan, "The Ukdena are growing fewer." He looked at Walks the River and the Wild Potato clan behind him. "We acknowledge that this is true. And fewer priests train to control the energies of the Ukdena. That also is true. But is this bad? The Ukdena are dangerous, so it is a good thing that there are fewer of them. And since there are fewer of them, we need fewer priests to control them. Therefore, in the matter of a third priest for the village who would learn the ways of the Ukdena and carry the objects that control them, let it be resolved that we shall not support such a priest. We have two priests already. That is enough."

The other Beloved Men spoke in turn. For the Wolf clan and the Long Hair clan, they spoke. For the Paint clan and the Blue clan and the Bird clan. All agreed that the village would not support a third priest, that maintaining the Ukdena was too costly a task for a village of their size to take on.

"I have considered," said Walks the River, "and I have dreamed." For a moment, he could feel the hope that filled the lodge, the expectation that he was going to throw in with the rest and make the opinion unanimous and harmonious at last.

"The Ukdena are growing fewer because there are fewer priests to master them and hold them to the earth. Yes, the Ukdena are dangerous, but under the control of the Principal People they are dangerous only to our enemies."

The disappointment filled the room like bad air.

"All right," said the second priest. His job was to manage the discussion, and he was allowed no opinion of his own. "Let us consider again the nature of the Ukdena."

"We all know their nature," said Holds the Corn Up, Beloved Man of the Long Hair clan. "They are anger and fear. That is their energy."

"They are the unmastered anger and fear of all the world's people," said Walks the River. "And why does this energy come here, to the Principal People, if not to be guided by us? Why are we together, Tsalagi and Ukdena, in the same place, the middle of the world, if not so that the Principal People might direct those energies safely? We must hold in trust all the powers that attach to us."

"I have had a dream," said the Paint clan's Beloved Man. "In my dream, I saw the Great Bear dancing, stomping."

Everyone had that dream sooner or later, and everyone understood what it meant. The Great Bear was stamping out fear and ignorance from the world.

"I think," the man continued, "that the Ukdena are the very thing that the Great Bear is trying to drive out of the earth with his dancing."

"No power is all good or all bad," said Walks the River. "In my dreams, I have seen the Ukdena, and they are beautiful."

The secondary priest said, "The man who has not mastered himself looks at the Ukdena and sees demons. But the man who knows his heart and masters clear thought will see angels instead. The Ukdena are the same Ukdena." This was not opinion, but simply a review of the facts.

"It's just a question of one priest," Red Fox reminded everyone.

"Ours is the Very Middle village," said Walks the River, "in the middle of the world. We are at the center of many circles. Already, the science that communicates with the Ukdena and guides them for us is in decline. Our decision may travel from the center like a stone in still water. If we will not maintain the Ukdena, how do we know anyone will? I think that if we make the wrong decision, the Principal People will forget how to master the Ukdena. I can imagine a time when the Ukdena pass out of this world with hardly any notice by our people. What if we call to them and they are no longer here to answer us?"

"Why should we call to them?" said Woods Burning. "Why should we bring down fear and anger to the earth? When is fear good? When is anger good?"

"A man without fear cannot be brave," said Walks the River. "As for anger, it is needed for passion. For justice."

"For justice, we have the law," said Woods Burning. "If the Shaawanwaaki raid our village and kill five people, then we will kill five Shaawanwaaki. If a Blue clan man murders someone in the Long Hair clan, then the killer or someone else in his clan must die. The law maintains harmony. Nothing else is needed."

"Walks the River imagines a time without Ukdena," said the Paint clan's Beloved Man. "I imagine instead a time of abundant Ukdena. If there are too many of these beings held here by our medicine, then no one will be able to contain them. They will range farther and farther from the middle of the world. Other people do not train themselves as we do. Who knows what the wandering Ukdena might do in the lands of people who do not see as clearly as we must see?"

"Neither thing has happened," said Red Fox. "We have always held the Ukdena here in harmony."

"The Ukdena grow fewer," said Walks the River. "That is certain. Who knows what turn the future will take?"

"Is the future singular," said the Beloved Man of the Blue clan, "or is it multiple? Is there one future, or many?"

"The future shall unfold according to prophecy," said Holds the Corn.

"Yes," agreed Woods Burning, "but many paths are possible to the same point in prophecy."

The principal priest said, "In the matter of the Ukdena and a third priest, how are we resolved?"

Again, the Beloved Men of the majority clans spoke their positions. Nothing had changed. Walks the River looked at his bony hands and bit his lip. What else was there to do? All of his arguments had been repeated many times. He had not moved any of the others, and he had not himself been moved to join them.

Politeness dictated that he should withdraw now. He and all of his clan should leave the council house so that the decision could be made unanimously in their absence. That was not what he wanted to do, but how could he stay and still believe himself a reasonable man?

Clearly he must withdraw.

But he waited. He thought of what the Blue clan speaker had just said. Was there one future, or many? Perhaps he was now at the place where the futures divided like channels of a river moving around a great stone. He was the great stone. If he leaned one way, this channel would be the greater. Lean the other way, and the other channel would determine how prophecy would be fulfilled.

And what prophecy was it that was flowing around him? What futures might depend on him?

The Ukdena were beautiful. The Ukdena were terrible. Harmony was beautiful and holy, but was it better preserved by defending the Ukdena or by letting the matter drop?

Continue or withdraw? Each choice seemed both right and wrong.

"We will not be moved," he said for his clan.

People in the Council House shifted around, as if feeling for the first time the stiffness of sitting for many days. The Beloved Men of the other clans looked over their shoulders to read the eyes of their people.

After a time the speaker for the Wolf clan turned to face the priests and the sacred fire. "It is the sixth day," he said. "For six days, the Wild Potato clan has not moved. Nothing moves them, and they do not turn aside. Walks the River is a thoughtful and well-mannered man. He bears a lot and does not anger. This begins to change our hearts. We say there shall be a third priest, and he shall learn to master the Ukdena."

That was how the tide turned, but politics flow slowly. It was not until later in the next day that the Blue clan and Deer clan supported the training of a new priest.

"Think of the Great Bear, stamping on the ground," the Paint clan's Beloved Man argued, though the flow had clearly shifted against him. "Fear and ignorance, that's what he tramples down. Let the Ukdena decline. We don't need them. We do not need a third priest."

But it was after this speech that Holds the Corn had brought the Long Hair clan to the other side, in favor of maintaining an additional priest. Woods Burning felt his own clan shift beneath him, and whatever his own feelings, he had to speak for his people. "Let there be a third priest," he said.

The Paint clan held their ground until the end of that seventh day. Their Beloved Man argued about the risks of crowding the skies with Ukdena, but too many Ukdena seemed a less plausible future than a future where the last Ukdena had vibrated itself out of this world. Everyone had already agreed that the Ukdena were in decline.

In the end, the Paint clan could not agree with the majority, but they left the Council House and let the village make a unanimous decision in their absence.

"In the matter of the Ukdena and a third priest," said the principal priest, "how are we resolved?"

"That there shall be a third priest so that we may remember how to hold the Ukdena to the earth," said Red Fox. "That is the decision of all the people."

If any Tsalagi were angry over the outcome, they turned their anger aside and it did not show. The village held the form of harmony, and the sacred fire was extinguished. The last year of the eleventh heaven was over. The priests kindled a new fire in the Council House, and women carried embers from it into each home. The people carried their new clothes to the river, and then they bathed, letting the current carry away their old clothing and the old year with it. When they stepped ashore to dress in new garments, they were themselves renewed. It was the twelfth heaven, seven generations before the first hell of the Fifth World.

Walks the River did not dream of the Ukdena again, and in the year that followed, he died in his sleep. Many Beloved Men died in that year, but they had lived long enough, at least, to see the twelfth heaven.

The keynote speaker said, "The extent to which Ukdena-mind became prevalent on Turtle Island is evident in the report of Bernal Díaz del Castillo, a sailor in Hernando de Soto's 'discovery' voyage, who wrote that the crew saw 'dragons' in the air above Cuba. Some researchers have even speculated that a forgotten earlier explorer, a Genoan called Cristobal Colón, made landfall in the Americas fifty years ahead of de Soto. Ukdena-mind, and the fear and suspicion it often generates if unchecked, could explain what happened to this Colón. As was the case for de Soto, it's almost certain that the Caribs would have welcomed him with arrows. De Soto himself narrowly escaped the destruction of his fleet on his first voyage. But this earlier landfall and contact would explain the arrival of smallpox on the continent two generations before the first significant wave of European invaders. Our history might have been very different if, without two generations of previous exposure to the disease, the native peoples had been forced to contend simultaneously with aggressive invaders and a virulent disease to which they had no time to build immune resistance."

Almost with the speed of Ukdena,
the sickness crossed the water between islands,
entered the low country of the Apalachee
rose into the mountains of the Tsalagi.
From the Tsalagi homeland
in the middle of the world
the disease spread
in all directions.

People died.
Young and old
they died.
Potawatomi and Kansa
Kiowa and Paiute
Shuswap and Shoshoni
Chiricahua and Azteca
they died.

That was during the first hell
of the Fifth World.
So many people died
That Turtle Island seemed empty.

But the ones who survived,
they were the strong human beings,
the ones the sickness couldn't easily kill,
and their children were also strong.
The disease kept coming back,
but every time
the people were stronger
and the disease could not kill
so easily.

"As opposed to Africa," the speaker said, "development of cultural exchange took a very different turn in the 'new' world, thanks to this pattern of successful resistance. Rather than cultural conquest or even cultural hegemony, the North American continent experienced something like a cultural marriage and an exchange between equals. Some of what was traded was tangible, as in the exchange of maize for wheat. Other trades were more subtle. Europeans learned how to hold the Forms of Peace. The Turtle Island Nations were introduced to the concept of the Nation State. It was this more subtle trade that effected the greatest change in both cultures. Europeans gradually stopped thinking of themselves as clever for accepting more gifts than they gave. There may be an objective sense in which it's true that, as the Ukdena priests say, this continent is built on the energies of Ukdena-mind."

The river of prophecy
is one river

The current weaves and divides,
but water always flows
downhill

Perhaps there is more
than one reality.

Spiral mind is wide enough
to contain another universe.

"I can sum up Indian history in the United States of America in very few words," said the keynoter at a conference in Washington, D.C., the nation's capitol. "The Trail of Tears. Sand Creek. Wounded Knee. We can imagine how things might have been different, but we're confronted nonetheless with how things were, and are. But I also want you to consider this. Where did the people of this continent go? They did not all die in the American genocide, though nine-tenths of them did. Their descendants are not all living on reservations, though many are, trapped there as a matter of public policy. But where are the rest?

"Let me frame it in another way. No conqueror is left unaffected by the conquest. Consider that in the United States of America today we have people who look like Europeans who will chain themselves to a tree and risk death for the sake of an owl. I'm talking about a process that goes both ways, of course. There are also people who look like Indians who will lease their tribal lands to strip miners. Who, then, is more Indian? Who is more white? Where are the Indians now? Where are the Europeans?"

Some would say that the effect of all those secret grandmothers, Indian women giving birth to and raising children in families that were designated "black" or "white," had been the **Indianization** of the majority culture. In this view, a lot of secret wisdom was passed down along with that secret blood. Proponents of this notion point out that the very attributes considered by the Europeans to be marks of savagery sound like a portrait of the still-evolving American culture: permissive child rearing; the habit of bathing more often than "necessary"; suspicion of "authority"; passionate pride; acceptance and empowerment of women and of more than one sexual norm; fluid class distinctions, or no such distinctions at all.

On Turtle Island
Arrow Mind and Spiral Mind
twine and twist
together.

It is one mind now.

In any version of the story,
it is one mind.

O, RARE AND MOST EXQUISITE

Douglas Clegg

Douglas Clegg was born in Virginia and lived in Los Angeles for eleven years before recently moving to Connecticut. He has published the novels *Goat Dance, Breeder, Neverland, The Dark of the Eye* and *The Children's Hour*. His short stories have been published in the magazines *Cemetery Dance, Deathrealm* and *The Scream Factory*, in the anthologies *Love in Vein, Little Deaths, Twists of the Tale: An Anthology of Cat Horror* and in *Best New Horror* and *The Year's Best Fantasy and Horror*.

When he was nineteen, Clegg relates, he worked in a nursing facility. He badly wanted to know elderly people, having had no grandparents himself past the age of five or six. So after his shift, he'd go and sit in someone's room and listen to their stories. What he heard was not always wonderful. Men and women would talk about their lives, and they'd complain bitterly about those who never loved them enough. What he sometimes heard through their stories was something they themselves did not know they were revealing—that these people speaking were the ones who had thrown away love, and trampled on it; had loved the ones who did not return their affection, and had abandoned the ones who did for shallow reasons. Clegg wanted to find a metaphor for the love, for the kind of young man who chases and cultivates love. And he has, in this gardener who adores flowers.

The story is reprinted from the anthology *Lethal Kisses*.

—E. D.

"What is human love?" I have heard my mother ask, when she was sick, or when she was weary from the rotted-wood dams of marriage and children. It's a question that haunts my every waking hour. I, myself, never experienced love, not the kind between a man and a woman. I once learned about it second-hand. When I was seventeen, I worked in a retirement home, in the cafeteria, and on my afternoons off I went up to the third floor. This was the nursing facility, and I suppose I went there to feel needed; all the elderly patients needed attention, often someone to just sit with them, hold their hands, watch the sun as it stretched down across the far-off trees heavy with summer green. I don't know why I was so taken with the older people, but I often felt more comfortable around them than I did around my peers. One day, an old man was shouting from his bed, "O, rare and most exquisite! O, God, O God, O, rare and most exquisite creation! Why hast thou forsaken me?" His voice was strong and echoed down the slick corridor; his neighbors, in adjacent beds, cried out for relief from his moans and groans. Since the orderlies ignored all this, routinely, I went to his room in order to find out what the trouble was about.

He was a ruffian. Bastards always live the longest, it was a rule of thumb on the nursing floor, and this man was a prince amongst bastards. Something about the lizard leather of his skin, and the grease of his hair, and the way his forehead dug into his eyebrows as if he were trying to close his translucent blue eyes by forcing the thick skin down over them. He had no kindness in him; but I sat down on the edge of his bed, patted his hand, which shook, and asked him what the matter was.

"Love," he said. "All my life, I pursued nothing but love. And look where it's gotten me." He was a rasping old crow, the kind my brother used to shoot at in trees.

"Did you have lunch yet?" I asked, because I knew that the patients would become irritable if they hadn't eaten.

"I will not eat this raw sewage you call food."

"You can have roast beef, if you want. And pie."

"I will not eat." He closed his eyes, and I thought he was about to go to sleep, so I began to get up off the bed. He whispered, coughing a bit, "Bring me the box under the bed."

I did as he asked. It was a cheap strong-box, the kind that could be bought in a dimestore. When I set it beside him, he reached under the blankets and brought out a small key. "Open it for me," he said. I put the tiny key in the hole, turned, and brought the lid up. The box was filled with what appeared to be sand. "Reach in it," he said, and I stuck my hands in, and felt what seemed to be a stick, or perhaps it was a quill. I took it out.

It was a dried flower, with only a few petals remaining.

"Do you know about love?" he asked me.

I grinned. "Sure."

"You're too young," he said, shaking his head. He took the dried flower from my hand, and brought it up to his nose. Dust from the petals fell across his upper lip. "You think love is about kindness and dedication and caring. But it is not. It is about tearing flesh with hot pincers."

I smiled, because I didn't know what else to do. I wondered if he were sane; many of the patients were not.

He said, "This is the most rare flower that has ever existed. It is more than seventy years old. It is the most valuable thing I own. I am going to die soon, boy. Smell it. Smell it." He pressed the withered blossom into the palm of my hand, and cupped his shaking fingers under mine. "Smell it."

I lifted it up to my nose. For just a second, I thought I smelled a distant sea, and island breezes of blossoming fruit trees and perfumes. Then, nothing but the rubbing alcohol and urine of the nursing floor.

"I will give this to you," he said, "to keep, if you promise to take care of it."

Without thinking, I said, "It's dead."

He shook his head, a rage flaring behind his eyes, a life in him I wouldn't have expected. "You don't know about love," he grabbed my arm, and his grip was hard as stone, "and you'll live just like I did, boy, unless you listen good, and life will give you its own whipping so that one day you'll end up in this bed smelling like this and crying out to the god of death just for escape from this idiot skin so that the pain of memory will stop."

To calm him, because now I knew he was crazy, I said, "OK. Tell me."

"Love," he said, "is the darkest gift. It takes all that you are, and it destroys you."

And he told me about the flower of his youth.

His name was Gus, and he was a gardener at a house that overlooked the Hudson River. The year was 1925, and his employer was an invalid in his fifties, with a young wife. The wife's name was Jo, and she was from a poor family, but she had made a good marriage, for the house and grounds occupied a hundred acres. As head gardener, Gus had a staff of six beneath him. Jo would come out in the mornings, bringing coffee to the workers. She was from a family of laborers, so she understood their needs, and she encouraged their familiarity. Her husband barely noticed her, and if he did, he wouldn't approve of her mixing with the staff.

One morning, she came down to Gus where he stood in the maze of roses, with the dew barely settled upon them, and she kissed him lightly on the cheek. He wasn't sure how to take this; she was wearing her robe, as she always did when she brought the coffee out to the men, although it revealed nothing of her figure. She was the most beautiful woman he had ever seen, with thick dark hair, worn long and out of fashion, a throwback to the long Victorian tresses of his mother's generation. She had almond-shaped eyes, and skin like olives soaked in brandy—he had never seen a woman this exotic in Wappingers Falls, which was his home town. She smelled of oil and rosewater, and she did not greet him, ever, without something sweet on her lips, so that her breath was a pleasure to feel against his skin. She drew back from him, and with her heavy accent, said, 'Gus, my handsome boy of flowers, what will you find for me today?'

When she kissed him on the cheek, he waited a minute, and then grabbed her in his arms, for he could no longer contain himself, and they made love there, in the morning, before the sun was far up in the sky.

Gus had girls before, since he was fourteen, but they had been lust pursuits, for none of the girls of the Falls, or of Poughkeepsie, or even the college girl he had touched in Connecticut, stirred in him what he felt with Jo. He called her, to his men, "My Jo," for he felt that, if things were different, she would not be with this wealthy man with his palsied body, but with him. Gus and Jo, he wrote it on the oak tree down near the river, he carved it into a stone which he had placed in the center of the rose garden.

He knew that she loved him, so he went that day to find her the most beautiful flower that could be had. It was a passion of hers, to have the most beautiful things, for she had lived most of her life with only the ugly and the dull. He wished he were wealthy so that he might fly to China, or to the South of France, or to the stars, to bring back the rarest of blooms. But, having four bits on him, he took the train into New York City, and eventually came to a neighborhood which sold nothing but flowers, stall upon stall. But it was mid-summer, and all the flowers available were the same that he could grow along the river. As he was about to leave, not knowing how he could return to his Jo without something very special, a woman, near one of the stalls said, "You don't like these, do you?"

Gus turned, and there was a woman of about twenty-two, he guessed. Very plain, although pretty in the way that he thought all women basically pretty. She was small and pale, and she wore no make-up, but her eyes were large and lovely. "I've been watching you," she said.

"You have?"

"Yes. Do you think that's rude? To watch someone?"

"It depends."

"I think it's rude. But then," she said, smiling like a mischievous child, "I've never been ashamed of my own behavior, only the behavior of others. I'm ashamed of yours. Here I've watched you for fifteen minutes, and you barely took your eyes off the flowers. How rude do you think that is? Very. You like flowers, don't you?"

"I'm a gardener. I take care of them."

"Lovely," she said wistfully, "imagine a life of caring for beautiful things. Imagine when you're very old, and look back on it. What lovely memories you'll have." Although she seemed forthright, the way he knew city people were, there was something fitful in the way she spoke, almost hesitant somewhere in the flow of words, as if all this snappy talk was a cover for extreme shyness. And yet, he knew, city women were rarely shy.

He had not come all the way to the city to flirt with shop-girls. "I'm looking for something out of the ordinary."

She gave a curious smile, tilting her head back. She was a shade beautiful in the thin shaft of daylight that pressed between the stalls. She was no Jo, but she would make some young man fall in love with her, he knew that. Some city boy who worked in the local grocer's, or ran a bakery. Or, perhaps, even a junior bondsman. She would eventually live in one of the boxcar apartments in Brooklyn, and be the most wonderful and ordinary bride. She would have four children, and grow old without fear. Not like Jo, who was destined for romance and passion and tragedy and great redemption, not Italian Jo of olive skin and rosewater. The woman said, "I know a place where you can find very unusual flowers."

"I want a beauty," he said.

"For a lady?"

Because Gus knew how women could be, and because he detected that he might get further along with this girl if he feigned interest in her, he lied. "No. Just for me. I appreciate beautiful flowers." He felt bad, then, a little, because now he knew that he was leading her on, but she seemed to know where the interesting flowers were, and all he could think of was Jo and how she loved flowers. Gus was considered handsome in his day, and women often showed him special attention, so he was used to handling them, charming them. "I need a beauty," he repeated.

"I'm not saying beautiful," she cautioned him, and began walking between the stalls, through an alley, leading him, "but unusual. Sometimes unusual is better than beautiful." She wore a kind of apron, he noticed, the long kind that covered her dress, and he wondered if she were the local butcher's daughter, or if she were a cook. The alley was steamy; there was some sort of kitchen down one end of it, a Chinese laundry, too, for he smelled the soap and the meat and heard someone shouting in a foreign language, but nothing European, for Gus knew how those languages sounded, and this must've been Oriental. The woman came to an open pit, with a thin metal staircase leading down to a room, and she hiked her apron up a bit, and held her hand out for him to steady her as she descended. "My balance isn't too good," she told him, "I have a heart problem—nothing serious—but it makes me light-headed sometimes on stairs."

"There're flowers down there?" he asked, as he went down the steps slowly.

"It's one of my father's storage rooms. He has a flower shop on Seventh Avenue, but there's an ice house above us, and we get shavings for free. They stay colder down here," she said, and turned a light up just as he had reached the last step. "There's another room three doors down, beneath the laundry. We keep some there, too."

The room was all of redbrick, and it was chilly, like winter. "We're right underneath the storage part of the ice house." As the feeble light grew strong, he saw that they were surrounded by flowers, some of them brilliant vermilion sprays, others deep purples and blacks, still more of pile upon pile of dappled yellows on reds on greens. "These are all fresh cut," she said, "you can have any you want. My father grows them underneath the laundry, and when he cuts them, we keep them on ice until we ship them. Here," she said, reaching into a bowl that seemed to be carved out of ice. She brought up tiny red and blue blossoms, like snowballs, but in miniature. She brought them up to his face, and the aroma was incredible, it reminded him of Jo's skin when he pressed his face against her breasts and tasted the brightness of morning.

The woman kissed him, and he responded, but it was not like his kiss with Jo. This woman seemed colder, and he knew he was kissing her just because he wanted the blossoms. He remembered the cold kiss all the way to the big house, as he carried his gift to his beloved.

Jo was shocked by the tiny, perfect flowers. He had left them for her in a crystal bowl of water on the dining-room table so that she would see them first when she came to have breakfast. He heard her cry out, sweetly, and then she came to the kitchen window to search the back garden for him. She tried to open it; but it had rained the night before and all that morning, so it was stuck. She rushed around to the back door, ran barefoot into the garden and grabbed his hand. "Sweetest—precious—blessed," she gasped, "where did you find them? Their smell—so lovely."

He had saved one small blossom in his hand. He crushed it against her neck, softly. He kissed her as if he owned her and he told her how much he loved her.

She drew back from him then, and he saw something change in her eyes. "No," she said.

When the flowers had died, he ventured back into the city, down the alley, but the entrance to the pit was closed. He rapped on the metal doors several times, but there was no response. He went around to the entrance to the ice house, and asked the manager there about the flowers, but he seemed not to know much about it other than the fact that the storage room was closed for the day. Gus was desperate, and had brought his month's pay in order to buy armloads of the flowers, but instead, ended up in an Irish bar on Horace Street drinking away most of it. Jo didn't love him, he knew that now. How could he be such a fool, anyway? Jo could never leave her husband, never in a thousand years. Oh, but for another moment in her arms, another moment of that sweet mystery of her breath against his neck!

He stayed in the city overnight, sleeping in a flop house, and was up early, and this time went to the Chinese laundry. The man who ran it took him to the back room, where the steam thickened. Gus heard the sounds of machines being pushed and pressed and clanked and rapped, as a dozen or more people worked in the hot fog of the shop. The owner took him further back, until they came to a stairway.

"Down," the man nodded, and then disappeared into the fog.

Gus went down the stairs, never sure when he would touch bottom, for the steam was still heavy. When he finally got to the floor, it dissipated a bit, and there was a sickly yellow light a ways off. He went towards it, brushing against what he assumed were flowers, growing in their pots.

Then, someone touched his arm.

"Gus." It was the woman from the week before. "It's me. Moira."

"I didn't know your name," he told her.

"How long did the flower last?"

"Six days."

"How sad," she said, and leaned against him. He kissed her, but the way he would kiss his sister, because he didn't really want to lead her on.

The mist from the laundry enveloped the outline of her face, causing her skin to shine a yellow-white like candles in luminaria, revealing years that he had not anticipated—he had thought she might be a girl in her early twenties, but in this steam, she appeared older, ashes shining under her skin.

"I loved the flowers."

"What else do you love, Gus?"

He didn't answer. He pulled away from her, and felt the edges of thick-lipped petals.

She said, "We keep the exotics here. There's an orchid from the Fiji Islands—it's not properly an orchid, but it has the look of one. It's tiny, but very rare. In its natural state, it's a parasite on fruit trees, but here, it's the most beautiful thing in the world."

"I never paid you for the last flower."

"Gus," she said, and reached up to cup the side of his face in the palm of her hand, "whatever is mine, is yours."

She retreated into the mist and, in a few moments, laid in the palm of his hand a flower so small that he could barely see it. She set another of its kind into a jewellery box, and said, "This is more precious than any jewel I know of. But if I give it to you, I want you to tell me one thing."

He waited to hear her request.

"I want you to tell me—no, promise me—you will take care of this better than those last ones. This should live, if cared for, for over a month. You do love flowers, don't you?"

"Yes," he said, and, because he wanted this tiny flower so much for his Jo, he brought Moira close to him and pressed his lips against hers, and kissed around her glowing face, tasting the steam from the laundry. He wanted it so badly, he knew this flower would somehow win his Jo. Somehow, she would manage to leave her husband, and they would run away together, maybe even to the Fiji Islands to live off mango and to braid beautiful Jo's hair with the island parasite flowers.

Yet, there was something about Moira that he liked, too. She wasn't Jo, but she was different from any woman he knew. When he drew his face back from hers, her face was radiant and shining, and she was not the middle-aged woman he had thought just a minute ago. She was a young girl, after all, barely out of her teens, with all the enthusiasm of fresh, new life. He wondered what his life would be like with a girl like this, what living in the city with her would feel like, what it would be like to live surrounded by the frozen and burning flowers.

There were tears in Moira's eyes when she left him, and he sensed that she knew why he wanted the beautiful flowers.

And still, she gave him the rare and exquisite ruby blossom.

The tiny flower died in fourteen days. Gus could not return to the city for over six weeks, because a drought had come down the valley, and he had to take special pains to make sure that the gardens didn't die. Jo did not come and see him, and he knew that it was for the best. She was married, he was merely the gardener, and no matter how many gorgeous flowers he brought to her, she would never be his. He thought of Moira, and her sweetness and mystery; her generosity was something he had never experienced before in a woman, for the ones he had known were often selfish and arrogant in their beauty. He also knew that the old man must suspect his over-familiarity with Jo, and so his days would be numbered in the Hudson River house.

One afternoon, he took off again for the city, but it took several hours, as there was an automobile stuck on the tracks just before coming into Grand Central Station. He got there in the evening, and went to the Chinese laundry, but both it and the ice house were closed for the day. He remembered that Moira had mentioned her father's shop, and so he went into the flower district and scoured each one, asking after her. Finally, he came to the shop of Seventh Avenue, and there she was, sitting behind a counter arranging iris into a spray-like arrangement. She turned to see him, and in the light of early evening, she was the simple girl he had seen the first day they had met. How the mist and the ice could change her features, but in the daylight world, she was who she was!

"Gus," she said, "I thought you weren't coming back. Ever."

"I had to," he said, not able to help his grin, or the sweat of fear that evaporated along his forehead, fear that he would not find her. It was like in the moving pictures, when the lover and his beloved were reunited at the end. He ran around the counter and grabbed her up in his arms, "Oh, Moira, Moira," he buried his face in her neck, and she was laughing freely, happily.

She closed the shop, and pulled down the shade. "Gus, I want you to know, I love you. I know you might not love me, but I love you."

Gus sighed, and looked at her. Here he was, a gardener, and she, a flower-shop girl, how could a more perfect pair be created, one for the other?'

"There's something I want to give you," she said.

"You've given me—" he began, but she didn't let him finish.

"Something I want to give you." She began unbuttoning the top of her blouse.

When she was completely naked, he saw what was different about her. "I told you I had a heart problem. I could never give my heart freely, knowing that I was like this. Different."

He stepped back, away from her.

"Who did this to you?" he asked, his voice trembling.

She looked at him with those wide, perfect eyes, and said, "I was born this way."

The threads.

There, in the whiteness of her thighs.

He was horrified, and fascinated, for he had never seen this before.

Her genitals had been sewn together, you see, with some thread that was strong, yet silken and impossibly slender, like a spider's web. She brought his hand there, to the center of her being, and she asked him to be careful with her. "As careful as you are with the flowers."

"It's monstrous," he said, trying to hide the revulsion in his voice, trying to draw back his fingers.

"Break the threads," she said, "and I will show you the most beautiful flower that has ever been created in the universe."

"I can't." He shivered.

Tears welled in her eyes. "I love you with all my being," she said, "and I want to give you this . . . this . . . even if it means . . ." Her voice trailed off.

He found himself plucking at the threads, and then pulling at them, until finally he got down on his hands and knees and placed his mouth there, and bit into the threads to open her.

There must have been some pain, but she only cried out once, and then was silent.

Her labia parted, curling back, blossoming, and there was a smell, no, scent, like a spice wind across a tropical shore, and the labia were petals, until her pelvis opened, prolapsed like a flower blooming suddenly, in one night, and her skin folded backwards on itself, with streaks of red and yellow and white bursting forth from the wound, from the pollen that spread golden, and the wonderful colours that radiated from between her thighs, until there was nothing but flower.

He cupped his hands around it. It was the most exotic flower he had ever seen, in his hands, it was the beauty that had been inside her, and she had allowed him to open her, to hold this rare flower in his hands.

Gus wondered if he had gone insane, or if this indeed was the most precious of all flowers, this gift of love, this sacrifice that she had made for him.

He concealed the bloom in a hat-box, and carried it back to the estate with him. In the morning, he entered the great house without knocking, and his heart pounded as loud as his footsteps as he crossed the grand foyer. He called boldly to the mistress of the house, "Jo!" he shouted, "Jo! Look what I have brought you!" He didn't care if the old man heard him, he didn't care if he would be without a job, none of it mattered, for he had found the greatest gift for his Jo, the woman who would not now deny him. He knew he loved her now, his Jo, he knew what love was now, what the sacrifice of love meant.

She was already dressed, for riding, and she blushed when she saw him. "You shouldn't come in like this. You have no right."

He opened the hat-box, and retrieved the flower.

"This is for you," he said, and she ran to him, taking it up in her hands, smelling it, wiping its petals across her lips.

"It's beautiful," she said, smiling, clasping his hand, and just as quickly letting go. "Darling," she called out, turning to the staircase, "darling, look at the lovely flower our Gus has brought us, look," and, like a young girl in love, she ran up the stairs, with the flower, to the bedroom where the old man coughed and wheezed.

Gus stood there, in the hall, feeling as if his heart had stopped.

"It was three days later," he told me, as I sat on the edge of the nursing room bed, "that the flower died, and Jo put it out with the garbage. But I retrieved it, what was left of it, so that I would always remember that love. What love was. What terror it is."

The old man finally let go of my arm, and I stood. He was crying, like a baby, as if there were not enough tears in a human body to let go of, and he was squeezing his eyes to make more.

"It's all right," I said, "it's just a bad dream. Just like a bad dream."

"But it happened, boy," he said, and he passed me the flower. "I want you to keep this. I'm going to die some day soon. Maybe within a month, who knows?"

"I couldn't," I said, shaking my head. "It's yours."

"No," he said, grinning madly, "it never was mine. Have you ever been with a woman, boy?"

I shook my head. "Not yet."

"How old are you?"

"Seventeen. Just last month."

"Ah, seventeen. A special time. What do you think human love is, boy?"

I shrugged. "Caring. Between people. I guess."

"Oh, no," his smile blossomed across his face, "it's not caring, boy, it's not caring. What it is, is opening your skin up to someone else, and opening theirs, too. Everything I told you is true, boy. I want you to take this dried flower—"

I held it in my hand. For a moment, I believed his story, and I found myself feeling sad, too. I thought of her, of Moira, giving herself up like that. "She loved you."

"Her? She never loved me," he said. "Never."

"How can you say that? You just told me—"

His voice deepened, and he sounded as evil as I have ever heard a man sound. "Jo never loved me."

I looked again at the dried flower. He plucked it from my fingers, and held the last of its petals in his open palm.

He said, "You thought that was Moira? Oh, no, boy, I buried her beneath the garden. This is Jo. She finally left her husband for me. And then, when I had her . . . O, Lord, when I had her, boy, I tore her apart, I made her bloom, and I left her to dry in sand the way she had dried my heart." He laughed, clinging more tightly to my arm so that I could not get away. "Her flower was not as pretty as Moira's. Moira. Lovely Moira." He sniffed the air, as if he could still smell the fragrance of the opening flower. "I made Jo bloom, boy, and then I stepped on her flower, and I kept it in darkness and dust. Now, boy, *that's* what love is." He laughed even while he crushed the dried blossom with his free hand.

"O, rare and most exquisite!" he shouted after me as I pulled away from him, and backed out of that madman's room.

"O, why," he laughed, "why hast thou forsaken me?"

NEVER SEEN BY WAKING EYES

Stephen Dedman

Stephen Dedman lives in Western Australia and has worked as a video librarian, game designer, actor, experimental subject, and manager of a science fiction bookstore. His short fiction has appeared in *The Magazine of Fantasy & Science Fiction, Pulphouse, Aurealis,* and the anthology *Little Deaths.* His first novel, *The Art of Arrow Cutting,* has recently been published.

Although there has been much speculation about Professor Charles L. Dodgson's interest in photographing little girls, he seemed to have done no harm. And as his shy, strange alter ego, Lewis Carroll, he created *Alice's Adventures in Wonderland* and *Through the Looking Glass,* two enduring literary works that have entertained scores of children since they were written. The following story was published in the August issue of *The Magazine of Fantasy & Science Fiction* and according to the author was inspired by "the nightmarish aspects and often macabre humor of the Alice books, *The Hunting of the Snark,* and the letters of Carroll; by the mystery posed in Dodgson's missing diaries, and by Elton John's song, 'All the Young Girls Love Alice.' "

—E. D.

They say that we Photographers are a blind race at best: that we learn to look at even the prettiest faces as so much light and shade; that we seldom admire, and never love.

—Lewis Carroll, A *Photographer's Day Out*

The Reverend Charles Lutwidge Dodgson, the logician and photographer and lesser-known mirror image of Lewis Carroll, first met Alice Liddell when she was three. John Ruskin, a fellow lecturer at Oxford, was also smitten with young Alice, and later became obsessed with twelve-year-old Rose La Touche. Edgar Allan Poe married his thirteen-year-old cousin Virginia. Dante fell in love with Beatrice when she was eight and a half.

If you expect me to add my name to this list, you're out of your mind.

"He was terrified of the night," she said, softly. "Terrified of dreaming, I think. Even beds frightened him."

I nodded. I don't remember any nighttime scenes at all in either of the *Alice* books, or *Snark*, or even *Sylvie and Bruno*, and the only mention of a bed to come to mind was "summon to unwelcome bed/A melancholy maiden!/We are but elder children, dear,/Who fret to find our bedtime near." The hunters of the Snark "hunted till darkness came on," with not a word of what happened afterward, and *Sylvie and Bruno Concluded* ends (and not a moment too soon) with the stars appearing in a bright blue sky. True, "The Walrus and the Carpenter" is set at midnight, and features an oyster-bed, but the sun stays up the whole time.

"How did you meet?"

Alice smiled prettily, without showing the tips of her teeth. "In London, outside a theater—the Lyceum, I think. I'd seen him before, but I had no idea who he was. When I told him my name, he said, 'So you are another Alice. I'm very fond of Alices.'"

"When was this?"

"Winter. I don't remember the year, but he was about thirty, and he hadn't written *Wonderland* yet, and I think Prince Albert was still alive. Eighteen sixty, maybe." I nodded. Dodgson was a compulsive diarist, but many of his diaries disappeared after his death, like his letters to Alice Liddell, and all of his photographs and sketches of naked little girls.

I suppose it started in the darkroom, at home: developing old, half-forgotten rolls of film is the safest form of time travel; you don't need a license, or even a seat belt. This roll had been in the Nikon for at least a year, and when I finally sat down with the proof sheet and a glass of Glenfiddich, I was ready to see anything. Forty minutes and two glasses later, I was still wondering why the hell I'd taken five shots of Folly Bridge. Granted that it's where the famous rowing expedition and the story of Wonderland started, and that I don't get up to Oxford as often as I'd like, it's been photographed more often than Capa shot "Death in the Afternoon."

There was nothing mysterious about any of the other shots, at least to me. On the proof sheet, they all look harmless enough—a busy street in Bangkok, far enough from Patpong to be safe; a beach near Townsville; a park in Tokyo; the Poe Cottage in Philadelphia; a slum in Brasilia or Rio. An extremely observant eye (such as Poe's) would notice a particularly beautiful little girl in almost every shot—never in the center, but always perfectly in focus. She isn't the same girl. She's always the same girl. She always has dark hair, black or almost black; pale skin; large eyes. Small, slight, almost elfin. The girl in Townsville is probably no older than ten; the girl in Bangkok may be twelve or twenty or anywhere in between. She isn't the same girl. She's always the same girl. And her name is—

I stared at the photographs of Folly Bridge; five shots, from slightly different perspectives, but all from the St. Aldates side. Long shadows—evening, probably just before sunset. And no girl. Where the hell did she go?

I slept badly that night, but without disturbing anyone. My dreams were obscene; you don't need the details, except that the girl from Folly Bridge was . . . there.

She was smaller than the ideal, with the creamy pallor of the Londoner who can't afford to buy a tan. Her hair was short, but extremely untidy. Her eyes were too dark, impossibly dark, and her smile remained long after the dream had ended. It was not the smile of a little girl. It was the smile of something older, and wiser, and very hungry.

I woke shivering, expecting to find the sheets drenched with sweat or worse. Instead, they were completely dry, and cold, as though no one had slept there at all.

Barbara is far and away the best secretary I've ever had. She's a law school dropout, efficient, intelligent, computer literate, multilingual, empathic, diplomatic, moderately ambitious, extremely attractive, and devoutly gay; we've been having breakfast together for four years now, without ever misunderstanding each other (well, not seriously). Two of the juniors, both avid prosecutors, were sitting at a table near the door discussing the latest batch of ripper murders that were splattered across all the papers. A pot of coffee and a cherry Danish were waiting for me in my booth, and so was Barbara.

"Rough night?" she murmured, as I sat down.

I nodded. "What have I got today?"

"Partners' meeting at eight, Druitt arriving at ten and the *Mirror's* lawyers at eleven, political lunch," she grimaced slightly, "at the Savoy at two—"

"Oh, God, is that today?"

"I've left the afternoon free."

"Good. What about tomorrow morning? Am I in court?"

"No. Not until Friday. You have two—"

"Postpone them."

She keyed something into her notebook without even blinking. "Where are you going?"

"Oxford."

Sullivan (okay, so that isn't his real name) was a numbers man for the Tories, known to his colleagues as the Lord High Executioner. If he ever invites you to lunch, hire a taster. I was still sitting down when he muttered, "I hear the *Mirror* settled."

He obviously had excellent hearing for a man his age; we'd signed the papers less than twenty minutes before. I merely grunted. "I hope it was expensive?" he probed.

"My client's reputation is worth a lot of money."

"So is yours, by now." He smiled. Like most of the people who run most of the world, Sullivan had managed to avoid the burden of a reputation; you probably still don't know who I'm talking about. A waiter appeared, and I ordered carpetbag steak and a good burgundy. Sullivan waited until he was gone, then asked, "Are you planning to stay in London long?"

"I go where the firm sends me," I replied, "but I think I'll be here for a few years yet. I'd certainly prefer to; it beats hell out of New York."

He smiled. "Good. I won't waste your time, or mine. Have you ever considered a career in politics?" I shrugged. "All right. What if I said there was going to be a safe seat vacant before the next election?"

"I'm not interested," I replied, without any hesitation.

"Think about it. This isn't America; you wouldn't have to quit your practice. I know what you're worth—believe me, I do—and all right, MPs' salaries are pitifully low: even the travel allowance isn't much of a compensation. But you wouldn't have to give any of it up. *I* haven't; you know that." I nodded; he'd been a client of ours for many years "Hell, you already give away more money than most rock stars, more than most people can even dream about. All those kids you sponsor, all those donations to UNICEF and refugees—oh, don't look so bloody surprised. You really thought nobody knew? Welcome to the twentieth century, or what's left of it."

I said nothing.

"I'm not going to bullshit you," he lied. "I don't know *why* you do it, what you get out of it, but I don't care, either, if it's what you want to do. But if you *really* want to help the street kids or starving Thais or whoever, you'll consider my offer very carefully."

"Why me?"

"Because I know you can win. You always do. You're the best libel lawyer in the business, you haven't lost a case in years; I've seen you convince juries that black is white and queer is straight. You're a born politician." He paused, leaning back in his chair. "And I'll be honest. I know the other parties haven't approached you yet, and I know they will, and I know we can double whatever they offer."

"You can relax," I assured him. "I'll tell them the same thing I told you. I'm not interested."

"Why not?"

"For one thing, I don't believe it'll be as easy as you make out. I'm single, and I've lived most of my life in the States. Secondly, it's not what I want to do. Thirdly, I've never intended to become a public figure; I prefer to keep my private life private."

Sullivan snorted. "Like I said, this isn't America; *we* don't expect politicians to be moral paragons. We've had too many kings, and far too many princes; nobody gives a damn if an MP's not married, or if he bonks his secretary occasionally. Besides, you were born here, your father was some sort of war hero, you grew up in Boston so you speak better English than half the BBC, and you're a Rhodes scholar to boot. As for your private life, all right, I know you can't give a lecture without bonking one of the students, but what does that matter? They're all *girls*, aren't they?"

I looked at him, and said nothing. He was probably right about English politicians' private lives; nobody's ever given *him* any shit about the curious resemblance between his twenty-seven-year-old second wife and his fifteen-year-old daughter. The wife's not brilliant, but I'm sure she's guessed which of them he really wants to fuck. "Yes, they're all girls."

"And all over sixteen." He waved his fat fingers dismissively, then shut up as the waiter returned with our lunch. "All right. At least consider it. I don't need an answer for another week."

I parked near the corner of Thames and St. Aldates, and stared at Folly Bridge, wondering if it had ever deserved its name so thoroughly before. The urge to turn the Jag around and return to London was almost palpable. Instead, I took a deep breath, unbuckled my seat belt, opened the door, and stepped out into the thin October sunshine. Having come this far, the least I could do was visit some of the booksellers. Besides, it was a week before Michaelmas term, and I could wander around the colleges again without hordes of undergraduates making me feel like a fossil.

It was past six and almost dark when I headed back to the carpark, footsore from the cobbles, with fresh catalogues from Waterfield's and Thorntons in my briefcase. There was a girl standing outside Alice's Shop, staring into the window, though the shop had been closed for over an hour. She turned when she heard me, and we stared at each other across the road.

I *knew*, even before I saw her face, that it was the little girl from my nightmare. She was small, maybe nine or ten years old, wearing ripped jeans, sneakers, and a very baggy sweatshirt; her shoulder-length dark hair might have been loosely curled or merely tangled. She leaned back against the window, her right hand cupped before her, in what must have been a deliberate imitation of Dodgson's photograph of Alice Liddell as a beggar-girl.

I stood there frozen for a moment, and then a tourist bus passed between us, blocking my view. Hastily, I turned and resumed walking south; when I looked back, over my shoulder, she was gone. I hurried along, not even wanting to wonder why.

She was five or six meters behind me when I reached the carpark, and she followed me all the way to the Jag. I fumbled for the remote and unlocked the door, almost expecting her to rush ahead of me and climb in. Instead, she disappeared while my back was turned, and I slid into the seat and locked myself in. I sat there for a moment, breathing heavily, then turned the headlights on. She was standing in front of the car, close enough that the lights illuminated the Oxford crest on her dirty sweatshirt but not her face. After a moment's hesitation, I reached across and unlocked the passenger side door, and waited. I heard the door close again, and she was on me; I felt her bite, and saw nothing.

The contents of my wallet were spread across the passenger seat when I opened my eyes again, but nothing seemed to be missing except the girl. I examined myself in the mirror; I looked bleary-eyed and slightly disheveled, and maybe a little pale, but not injured. I peered at my watch; 7:56. If I hurried, I could be back in London by nine.

I decided to work late on Thursday, finishing a paper for the *Harvard Law Review*, but sent Barbara home in time for her karate class as a reward for not asking any embarrassing questions. The words I needed, exactly the *right* words, seemed to appear on the monitor as soon as I knew what I wanted to say; normally, when I write, there seems to be a block between my head and my hands, and everything I try to say clunks and screeches, and I spend hours facing the window rather than stare at the screen. This night, I became so absorbed in my work that it was well after midnight when I looked at my watch and realized why my coffee was so cold and the chambers had become so quiet; everyone else (even the Hatter, who still lives on Eastern Standard Time) had departed, leaving me utterly alone. I looked out the window again, and shivered and reached for my overcoat and umbrella.

It was cold, and the rain had slowed to a drizzle, almost a mist. The whole city felt somber and slimy and strange. The streets were deserted, and the only noise was the faint growl of the Jag and the occasional short hiss as something or someone appeared from the gloom and I had to brake. The statue of Eros looked more like a vampire, and I thought I saw some shadows move beneath it as I passed, a huddle of junkies or a bag lady with a shopping trolley. Driving through London protected by tinted glass and electronic locks always feels *wrong*, somehow, even in filthy weather; on good days, I feel as though I'm cruising (or catacombing, as my Texan cousins call it); bad nights, I just feel like a voyeur.

As soon as I arrived home, I closed all the curtains and turned on all the lights, then chose a CD at random and turned the stereo up full blast. It wasn't enough to make the place feel like home (it's a company flat; even the paintings are investments), but at least it felt warm and relatively secure.

Most of the partners decorated their rooms with the inevitable Spy caricatures of judges; I prefer to leave the judges outside when I can, and my taste in art runs more to Brian Frouds and Patrick Woodroffes. My private library clashes with the rest of the leatherbound decor, but what the Hell. I collapsed on the couch, and reached for my much-thumbed copy of *Faeries*. The little girls scattered among the horrors and grotesquerie looked so clean, so innocent, so ethereal. A pretty elf looked back at me with almond-shaped night-shaded eyes, for all the world like—

I dropped the book, which fell open to the sketch of Leanan-Sidhe. "On the Isle of Man," the text read, "she is the blood-sucking vampire and in Ireland the muse of poets. Those inspired by her live brilliant, though short, lives."

There was a knock on the door.

I will drink to your health, if only I can remember, and if you don't mind—but perhaps you object? You see, if I were to sit by you at breakfast, and to drink your tea, you wouldn't like that, would you? You would say "Boo! hoo! Here's Mr. Dodgson drunk all my tea, and I haven't got any left!" So I am very much afraid, next time Sybil looks for you, she'll find you by the sad sea wave, and crying "Boo! hoo! Here's Mr. Dodgson has drunk my health, and I haven't got any left!"

—Lewis Carroll, letter to Gertrude Chataway, 1875

I looked through the peephole. It was her, of course, still in the same dirty sweatshirt and tattered jeans. I drew a deep breath, and then opened the door slightly. She smiled.

"Can I come in?" She had a little girl's voice, a rather thin soprano, but it was well-modulated, almost polished: Marilyn Monroe with a hint of Oxford accent. Her tone was curious, rather than arrogant or imploring; her eyes merely watchful.

"Can I stop you?" I asked, only half joking. The building was supposed to be impregnable; even if she'd managed to sneak through the lobby while the doorkeeper was busy, there were cameras in every lift and corridor. "How did you get here?"

"By coach, and bus. Your address was in your wallet."

"Why?"

"Aren't you going to invite me in?"

"Who are you?"

"My name's Alice," she replied, as though that were an answer.

"*What* are you?"

She paused, smiling with her eyes as though she were trying to invent something. "What do I look like?" she asked, finally. "Aren't you going to invite me in?"

"What will you do if I don't?"

"Go away," she replied, "and not come back."

I stood there, trying to convince myself that it was stupid to be scared of a little girl, barely half a meter high, no matter how dark her eyes were. I tried to imagine myself shutting the door, and going on with my life. And then I stepped back, and let her in.

"What do you want?" I asked, after she'd folded herself up on the chaise longue, her arms around her knees.

"What do *you* want?" she replied, still looking around curiously.

"I asked first."

"A place to stay during the day," she replied. "Some new clothes. An alibi, occasionally. And maybe you could drive me somewhere, sometimes. I don't know how long I'll want to stay; probably a couple of weeks, maybe a month. Your turn."

"Is that all?"

"What else are you offering?"

"What are *you* offering?"

Her eyes lit up, suddenly; she'd noticed the open book on the couch, and the rest of the library. "You've got a lot of *Alice* books. How many?"

"Forty-two."

"Holy shit—oh, sorry. Why?"

"Different illustrators."

She nodded. "You must know a lot about Lewis Carroll."

"No, not really. There's a lot about him that no one knows."

"I could tell you some of it. I knew him."

I sat down opposite her, and tried not to smile. "How old are you?"

"I don't really know. Eight or nine."

"He died in eighteen ninety-eight," I said, gently.

She looked at me, impatiently. "I know. He got sick just after Christmas, and died a couple of weeks before his birthday. Or so I heard, after he didn't come back. I was still in Oxford; he could hardly take me with him to his sisters' home, could he?

"Don't look at me like that; you *know* I'm not making this up."

"Then you must be a hundred years old, at least."

She shook her head indignantly; I think she would have stamped her foot, if she'd been standing up. "I'm eight years old, and I'll *always* be eight years old. That was what he wanted. That's why he loved me.

"I knew him," she repeated, "and I knew things about him that he didn't even tell his diary, things that no one else remembers. I can tell you what I know, and I've told you what I want in return. Do we have a deal?"

"How do you know it's what I want?"

She laughed. It wasn't a child's laugh, but the way one laughs at a child. "I saw you when you came to Oxford last summer—June, was it?"

"July."

"I saw you looking in Alice's shop, and in Christ Church, saw you looking up at his rooms. . . . And you took my photograph. You pretended you were just taking a picture of Folly Bridge. Have you printed that photo yet?"

"Yes."

"I wasn't in it, was I?"

"No."

She nodded. "*He* found that, when he brought me up to Oxford for some photographs. I didn't know; photographs were new and strange, then, almost magic, and *very* expensive. That's how he found out what I was. I'd never even seen myself in a looking-glass, and I didn't know that I never could; looking-glasses were for the rich, and clean water I could see myself in? In London, last century? Hah! I can't even remember seeing myself naked before—"

"You're a vampire . . ." I whispered.

She laughed, a little sadly. " 'This must be the wood where things have no names,' " she quoted. " 'I wonder what'll become of my name when I go in? I shouldn't like to lose it at all—because they'd have to give me another, and it would almost certainly be an ugly one.' " She looked at the mirror over the bar, and said, "You can call me a vampire, if you like. I always think of vampires as male. We usually call ourselves sidhe, or mara, or succubi, or even lamia. But don't worry; I promise not to bite."

"You bit me in Oxford."

She pouted. "Not *badly*; I didn't take any more than I needed. You'll be okay. We *do* live off the living, usually while they're asleep; they feel sick the next day, or depressed, but we don't leave any scars, and we try to give them time to recover. Nowadays, we mostly survive on suicides and roadkill and junkies who're going to die anyway; we leave before the ambulance arrives, and no one notices if the bodies are missing a pint or two of blood. . . . Maybe that's why they say suicides become vampires. Of course, they don't, or the world'd be full of them. Us.

"And there are the symbiotes, who know what we are—mostly artists or writers. They give us blood, and we give them dreams."

I slept badly that night. Knowing that there's a vampire in your guest room makes it difficult to relax, and I was terrified of what I might dream.

Why didn't I just throw her out? Maybe because I wasn't sure that I could, wasn't sure what she'd do to me if I tried. And she'd known Charles Dodgson for nearly forty years. Maybe she knew—

I had no experience buying clothes for little girls, but I didn't want to tell anyone about Alice (not even Barbara), and I couldn't take her shopping until she had something better than her Oxford rags. I stopped at a Marks & Sparks on the way home and bought a collection of garments that were roughly the right size. They looked wrong on her when she first tried them on, wrong as a gymslip on a page three girl, but she was a good enough actress to get away with it.

She spent the night telling me about her first encounter with Dodgson. "He asked if he could write to my mother, to get her permission. Anna, my teacher—another sidhe—was working at the theater, so I told him she was my mother.

"His rooms were full of books—and toys, of course, but I remember the books better. Anna was teaching me to read, but she wasn't very good at it. When he saw how fascinated I was, he gave me a few books, to keep. I don't think it was meant as a bribe, though he always regarded Londoners as horribly commercial—he was a terrible snob.

"He photographed me in his rooms—this was before they let him build a studio on the roof—and let me watch as he developed the plates in a closet. . . . I hadn't really known what to expect, and I think he was too surprised to be frightened. Every time I visited him, after that, he had more books on ghosts and things like that—*The Wonders of the Invisible World, The History of Apparitions, The Vampire* . . . most of it crap. They were easily gulled in those days. Arthur Conan Doyle even believed in *fairies.* . . .

"I met the Liddell girls a few times. They were snobs, too, especially Alice, but angels compared to their mother. Alice *should've* been an absolute brat: she was beautiful and knew it, and *everyone* loved her; men, women, even a prince . . ."

"You?"

"I liked her. I didn't expect to, but I did."

"And Dodgson?"

She shrugged. "Dodgson loved all of them, like he loved most pretty girls who were willing to trust him—until they became teenagers, anyway. Ina was twelve or thirteen when I met her, and already seriously built; I think she scared him a lot worse than I did."

Saturday was a typical London spring day, bleak and damp and gray—though Alice warned me that we'd have to come home if the sun appeared; it wouldn't kill her quickly, but a few hours worth would hurt and could crack her skin. Driving down Gower Street, she glanced through the window at a bag lady, and sat up. "You know her?" I asked.

"Yes. She's . . . she's one of us, but she doesn't know it. She doesn't even know she's dead, she can't remember being alive, she doesn't even know why the sun hurts her; she just does her best to hide from it. She's probably been living on cats, rats, all sorts of garbage."

We turned into New Oxford Street, and I asked her to keep an eye out for a parking spot. "You said, last night, that you drank blood. Need it be human blood?"

She shook her head. "It has to be human, but it doesn't really *have* to be blood; sperm will do, but we need much more of it than one man can make. Hundred years ago, some of the sidhe could fuck or suck enough men a night to stay alive that way, but not now. It takes too long, and it's not worth the effort unless all the men come to you. There are still some vampires in the beats and the bath-houses—never trust the boys who don't ask you to use a condom, some things are a lot worse than AIDS—but even *they* need blood sometimes. I don't know why. None of us are scientists. But it has to be human, too, or you start losing your mind. Or your soul, maybe. You lose you, anyhow; you become stupid, you start thinking like an animal, hunting animals, and then you die. Anna said that's how the stories about vampires turning into wolves and rats began—that, and the way we used to catch rabies from them, and them from us. *There's one.*"

I jumped, then realized she meant a parking spot, not a vampire. "Thanks."

The weekend passed much too quickly, and on Monday morning I returned reluctantly to Chambers and the negative nineties. The Hatter and I were dissecting a lease and trying to bore a large hole in the boilerplate when the phone rang. It was Sullivan, wanting to cancel our lunch. I agreed, and hung up, and enjoyed the feeling of relief for nearly a minute before I realized that Sullivan and I hadn't *made* an appointment for lunch, and that he would simply have told his secretary to phone my secretary if we had. I asked the Hatter to excuse me, and slipped out of the room. Barbara was sitting at her desk, staring intently at the screenpeace as it created mazes and blundered through them. "I just spoke to Sullivan," I said, softly.

"Yes, I know."

"We weren't having lunch today, were we?"

"Not that I heard."

"What's happened? Is he sick?" He *had* sounded a little strange—almost emotional.

"I don't think so," she said carefully. "I think it's his wife—and I think you'd better call him back."

I nodded, and ducked back into my room. The Hatter looked up from the photocopies he'd spread over my desk. He's a remarkably ugly man, with a distinct resemblance to a New College gargoyle—big hands and feet, big eyes, a huge nose, and frizzy ginger hair that no dye nor wig could conceal or con-trol—as well as being a hopeless advocate, but he has an excellent memory for precedents and a fetish for minute detail. He started gathering up the papers as soon as he saw my expression, and quickly disappeared. I slumped into my chair, and reached for the phone.

Sullivan told me the story with remarkable economy, for a politician; Sylvia, his wife, had gone out on Saturday night, and not returned. He hadn't reported her as missing (the police won't act, or even listen very hard, until someone's been gone forty-eight hours), and wanted the whole affair kept as quiet as possible. There was something decidedly strange about the way he said "affair," and I took a deep breath before asking, "What can I do?"

"If this gets out, I'm going to have to call a press conference. I'll need you there, just to make sure everybody minds their manners. Are you with me?"

If there was a threat in there, it was unusually quiet; he sounded more tired than anything else. If I'd said no, it probably wouldn't have cost me anything more than my job, maybe not even that. "I'll be there," I replied. "If necessary, that is. I'm sure she'll turn up before it comes to that."

He grunted. "Okay. Remember, if you get another offer, I'll beat it; that's a promise. I'll be in touch."

Alice was asleep when I returned home—or dead, maybe, but she *looked* asleep. She was lying on the bed in the guest room, curled up into a fetal ball, still wearing her jeans and anorak from the night before. Her eyes were closed, and her face had relaxed into a pretty, girlish pout. I stood in the doorway watching her for a few minutes, and then crept into the kitchen. I enjoy cooking, when I have the time, and I often suspect I make the best chili in England. Alice appeared, wrinkling her nose, while I was chopping garlic. "Sorry. Is this, ah . . ."

She shrugged. "Don't worry. It doesn't hurt me, it just fucks up my sense of smell. How was your day?"

"Pretty awful. I spent most of it helping a bank get away with knocking down an old building and replacing it with an office tower that looks uncannily like a giant refrigerator; the rest of the time, I helped a politician pretend to look for his wife. How about you?"

"Nothing exciting. Can you drive me down to Piccadilly, later?"

I nodded. She sat in the dining room and watched me cook, and chatted about some of Dodgson's other child-friends and models whom she'd met— Gertrude Chataway, Beatrice Hatch, Connie Gilchrist, Isa Bowman, Ina Watson, Xie Kitchin, others whose names she'd forgotten. He'd photographed all of them as near naked as they would allow, frequently with their mothers present; the child nude was a favorite subject of Victorian artists, and several of the girls had also modeled for Henry Holiday (then better known for his stained glass windows) or Harry Furniss. "I only saw most of them once or twice," she said. "He usually lost interest in them when they turned eleven or twelve—I remember he was particularly nasty to Connie, as though it were her fault that she was growing up—but he was still calling Gertrude 'dear child' when she was nearly thirty, and she let him; I guess she enjoyed it. I bumped into her when she visited in eighteen ninety-something, and she recognized me, and we had to pretend I was the daughter of the girl she'd met when she was eight." She laughed. "Of course, I didn't know any of them well; they were sunlight girls."

"He was lucky," I said, as I stirred the chili. "Nowadays, parents can be arrested for photographing their own children naked, even in the bath. So much for progress."

She looked at me coolly. "Have you ever read any Victorian porn? A hell of a lot of it's about old men fucking girls of ten or eleven, and that wasn't just a fantasy; it was common practice. There's been *some* progress; women and kids are better off, even if the men aren't."

"Sorry. It was a stupid thing to say."

"Yeah. It was. And okay, it's a stupid law, but where do you draw the line?" She shrugged. "You want to know if he fucked them, don't you? That's what everyone else asks—or if they don't ask, it's what they wonder. Do you want me to tell you?"

I didn't answer. She sat there silently for nearly a minute, then, softly, "He didn't even want to.

"No, that's a lie. Sometimes, he *did* want to—he dreamed about it, even fantasized about it, though he did whatever he could to distract himself from these fantasies—writing letters, inventing mathematical problems. . . . But I don't think he ever touched any of them, especially not when they were naked, and I think *that's* what matters.

"He never touched *me*, and I knew him for nearly forty years, and while I was physically as delicate and fragile and generally unsuitable for fucking as any of them, he knew I sure as shit wasn't innocent. He never let me touch him, either; and he hit me when I offered to fellate him. Knocked me across the room—he was a lot stronger than he looked—and apologized later. The thought really horrified him."

Which meant he'd probably had it before, I thought; a man confronted with a *new* idea, however horrific, has to think about it for a moment before he can react. But I didn't say anything.

"He wanted to be the White Knight, courteous and gentle and dreamy, and clumsy, and bad at his job . . . and he never removed his armor. I think what he *really* wanted was for sex not to matter. He wanted to be a boy again—no, a child. Even being a boy implied that sex existed."

" 'I am fond of children,' " I quoted, " 'except boys.' "

She nodded. "He grew up surrounded by sisters and younger brothers, until they sent him off to school, which he hated. He wanted to return home; I think he spent the rest of his life wanting to return to that home. He was never really cut out to be an adult; he stuttered whenever he spoke to adults, he wasn't even interested in *money*, let alone sex. He just liked studying, and solving mathematical problems, and writing little satires and nonsense, and surrounding himself with toys and books and children—all the things he'd done as a child. He never 'put away childish things,' as he once put it, and we loved him for it. Without him, *I* wouldn't have had a childhood at all."

I looked down at the skillet, and realized that I was burning my dinner. I rescued it as best I could, and asked, "Why didn't you make him a vampire?"

"I don't know how—Anna never taught me—and, anyway, he wouldn't have wanted it. It was too late; I couldn't make him a child again, couldn't give him back his innocence, and he wouldn't have wanted to be thirty or forty forever."

I nodded. There was something strange about the way she'd said "innocence," but there wasn't time for a cross-examination before the news, and I had to know if Sylvia Sullivan's disappearance had been noticed yet. There were stories about increases in the jobless and homeless figures, a small shipment of crack intercepted in the Chunnel, and massacres in Peru, Kowloon, Johannesburg, and Atlanta; I guess they were too busy to worry about a backbencher's wife, however photogenic. "What's happening in Piccadilly?"

"You wouldn't like it."

"I wasn't expecting an invitation. Meeting more sidhe?" It was two days before Halloween, which the British don't celebrate the way we do, but which might be Fourth of July for vampires.

"Yes."

"Going out for a bite?"

She looked at me coldly. "Do you really want to know?"

One of the first things they teach lawyers is never to ask a question unless they already know the answer. "No, I guess not."

That night, I dreamed about my childhood—something I hadn't done in years. It was my tenth birthday, and everyone was there; it wasn't until I'd woken up, still feeling good, that I began wondering what was wrong with that. I'd had a tenth birthday party, yes, and I *had* gotten my first real camera then, and my parents *were* still together and all my grandparents were still alive, so what was—

Alice was in the en-suite, brushing her teeth. I'd stopped wondering how she was getting in and out; she'd had more than a century to study burglary. "Is that what you meant when you said you give your victims dreams?"

"You're not one of my victims."

"Are you sure?"

She spat the toothpaste out of her mouth. Her eyes were blazing, and there was white froth on her chin; she looked horribly rabid. "You're a lawyer. I'm a vampire. There is such a thing as professional courtesy."

"I'm serious."

She shrugged, stuck the toothbrush back in her mouth, and glanced at the mirror; I could see my reflection, but not hers. Eventually, she said, "I didn't *give* you that dream; you dreamed it by yourself. I just helped you remember it. What's wrong?"

"Nothing."

"Bullshit. Nightmare?"

"No."

She smiled at the mirror. "Okay. So I screwed up. Sorry; you looked happier than you had in years, and I thought . . ."

"*Years?*"

"I remember when you were a student. You went to University College, right? Rooms on Logic Lane?"

I nodded. "Someone in admin must have had a twisted sense of humor. . . . You mean you've been *watching me for twenty years?*"

"No. Just while you were at Oxford. I liked you; hell, some of us even fall in love. And I remembered your face, the way you looked at me, and when I saw you again . . ."

"Did you bite me then? When I was a student?"

She looked away from me. "Not seriously."

"*Seven years and six months!*" Humpty Dumpty repeated thoughtfully. "*An uncomfortable sort of age. Now if you'd asked my advice, I'd have said 'Leave off at seven'—but it's too late now.*"

"*I never ask advice about growing,*" Alice said indignantly.

"*Too proud?*" the other enquired.

Alice felt even more indignant at that suggestion. "*I mean,*" she said, "*that one can't help growing older.*"

"One can't, perhaps," said Humpty Dumpty; "but two can. With proper
assistance, you might have left off at seven."
—Lewis Carroll, *Through the Looking-Glass and What Alice Found There*

There was nothing about Sylvia Sullivan in the news that morning, and, as
soon as the partners' meeting was finished, I asked Barbara to put a call through
to Sullivan; it'd be just like the pompous prick not to tell me if she'd come
back. She hadn't.

A moment later, Barbara walked in without announcing herself. I put down
the brief Midas had given me. "What's wrong?"

"You're looking for Sylvia Sullivan?"

I shrugged. As far as I knew, no one was. "Do you know where she is?"

"No . . ."

"But?"

She sat down, uncomfortably. "I've seen her around the bars before. . . ."

I blinked. "Gay bars?"

"Yeah. Not often—maybe once, twice a month. I think she's got some boyfriends, too. Nothing steady. Do you know her?"

Obviously not. "No."

"I don't know her well, either . . . we've had a few drinks, and talked, but
never fucked or anything. . . . I don't even know who *has* fucked her. For all I
know, she may be straight."

I had to think about that. It didn't help. "I don't understand."

"She was lonely. I don't think she was looking to get laid, but she probably
wouldn't have said no if that was the asking price. She just wanted to be
wanted; failing that, she got drunk, and took a taxi home. Do you know the
Elton John song 'All the Young Girls Love Alice'? From *Goodbye Yellow Brick
Road?*" I shook my head. "Pity. Sylvia . . . she's a good looking woman, married
to an old bastard who never fucks her without fantasizing he's fucking someone
else. Can you imagine what that's like?"

I tried. "Where do you think she is?"

"I don't know. I haven't seen her in weeks. There are lots of places she might
have been that night."

"Can you give me a list?"

She thought about it for a moment, staring out the window. "Maybe. Promise me you won't just give it to Sullivan?"

"Why?"

"If you find her, that's one thing. She may be running away, hiding, whatever, from the old shit; she may not want to be found. If you look for her, find
her, I can live with that—but I'm not handing her back to him on a platter. I
don't know her well, and I never fucked her, but I owe her that much."

"If she was trying to get away, wouldn't she just divorce him?"

She snorted. "Divorce Sullivan? Where would she find a divorce lawyer
who'd dare? Some kid straight out of school, if she was lucky. And he'd have
the Hatter doing the research, and you or Ashcroft or Midas if it ever got to
court. . . . More likely the old bloodsucker'd get some shrink to have her committed—"

I shuddered and stared out the window. London stared back at me, secure in her bulk, like a dinosaur that doesn't realize that it's being killed. "Could *you* go?"

"What?"

"Go to the clubs, or bars, or wherever. Take my card, and the Jag, and a photo, and ask if anyone's seen her. If they haven't, you don't even have to tell me where you went." I turned away from the window, and almost managed to look Barbara in the eye. "I'll pay you overtime, of course."

She hesitated, then nodded. "When shall I start?"

"Are they open this early?"

"A few of them . . ."

I tossed her the car keys, and she backed out of the room. I looked over at the window again, at the thick gray clouds and the thin gray sunlight. All the young girls love—

Barbara returned at five, and I handed her a wad of taxi vouchers. I didn't need to ask whether she'd had any joy. Getting lost in London is easy—you don't even have to try—and I had no good reason to believe that Sylvia was still in London. I'd tried to persuade Sullivan to report her as missing, and he said he'd think about it (Jesus, I hate being lied to, even if it's by a professional). At least he found her passport; her credit cards were still missing, but they hadn't been used since a visit to Harrods on Saturday morning, a fact that cheered him immensely.

I met Barbara for breakfast the next morning. Someone who *might* have been Sylvia Sullivan had been seen in a bar on Greek Street on Saturday night. She'd talked to, danced with, and accepted drinks from at least three men and one woman, but the barman hadn't noticed if she'd left with any of them. "What do you think?"

"I don't know what to think . . . but it doesn't sound as though she'd *arranged* to meet any of them."

I sipped at my coffee, forcing myself to wake up. "I agree."

"What now? The taxi drivers?"

I shook my head. "The old man can only cover up for so long; soon, someone's bound to notice that she's gone, and then it'll be the cops' baby. Or she might come back." I probably didn't sound very convincing.

I was ten years old again, looking through a viewfinder and waiting for the flash to recharge, and Irene was sitting on my bed reading, and someone touched my neck and shoulder—

I lay there, wide-eyed in the darkness, feeling as though I were trapped in a bed that was smaller than I was. My feet seemed incredibly far away, and the ceiling much too close, and the red-lipped girl standing beside the bed was—

"You were dreaming again," Alice said. "I thought I'd better wake you."

I sat up slowly, vaguely remembering that I was thirty-nine years old and six foot two. "Thanks . . . I think. What's the time?"

"About four."

I peered at her blearily, and tried to focus; my night vision isn't what it used to be (but then again, it never was). "Where've you been—no, forget I asked. Was it a nightmare?"

"Don't you remember?"

"I—" I blinked, and suddenly felt very cold. "I—no."

She stared at me, shook her head, and turned to walk out. "No. Please." I rubbed my eyes. "Look, I won't be able to get back to sleep, now. Tell me more about Dodgson."

She stopped, looked over her shoulder, said "No," and continued walking. "Why not?"

"You're lying to me."

I sat there, numb, and watched her leave. Finally, I muttered, "I'm sorry."

A moment later, she reappeared in the doorway. "Tell *me* a story," she suggested.

"What?"

"You're obsessed with a children's fantasist who's been dead for nearly a hundred years—even more obsessed than you were when you were seventeen. *Why?*"

"I liked his books a lot when I was a kid. My mother used to read them to me; she still loved them, probably because they were so English. When I went to Oxford, everyone seemed more interested in Charles Dodgson the pedophile than Lewis Carroll the fantasist . . . and it pissed me off, hearing them turn someone who'd written books that made so many kids happy into some sort of monster. I mean, there wasn't any evidence, none of the kids or even the parents accused him, *you* know it wasn't true. . . . I guess it became my first libel case, in a way. I did my damnedest to prove him innocent. . . ."

Alice stared at me, darkly, and then nodded. It was nothing but the truth, though she must have guessed it wasn't the *whole* truth . . . "Okay." She walked back into the room, and sat on the foot of the bed.

"There's a Dodgson story I don't think anyone else knows," she said, quietly. "A few people may have guessed—shit, *I'm* guessing most of it, but I had about thirty years worth of hints.

"Dodgson was always so nostalgic about his childhood that I don't think anyone's even *wondered* if he was abused as a boy. They don't know, or they forget, how much he hated his school days at Rugby. Maybe they know that he impressed the teachers, but they don't realize how much most of the boys hated him. They may have heard that he had a reputation for being able to defend himself, but they didn't hear him wishing that his school had given every boy a separate cubicle instead of putting all the beds in an open dorm. . . .

"Maybe it was an older boy; more likely, it was a lot of them, more than he could fight off. But I'm only guessing. . . ."

They found Sylvia Sullivan's Gucci handbag in a trashcan near Canary Wharf that morning. It gave them the clue they needed to identify the body they'd found between two of the half-empty office blocks on Sunday. The skull had been so shattered by the fall that even the dental records hadn't been enough.

No one knew how she'd gotten up to the roof without setting off a dozen alarms. I had a sneaking suspicion, but I didn't think the coroner would believe me.

> *There are skeptical thoughts, which seem for the moment to uproot the firmest faith; there are blasphemous thoughts, which dart unbidden into the most reverent souls; there are unholy thoughts, which torture, with their hateful presence, the fancy that would fain be pure.*
>
> —Lewis Carroll, *Pillow Problems*

I rushed home at lunchtime, and opened all the curtains in the house, except for the guest room. It was raining, of course, but I couldn't wait for the sun to reappear. Alice was asleep, or dead, and her clothes were scattered over the floor. I searched her pockets, finding nothing, and suddenly she rolled over and looked up.

I opened my wallet, removed a photograph of Sylvia, and flipped it at her. She caught it neatly, and flinched slightly.

"You *do* recognize her," I growled. "I'd hoped I was paranoid. Did you kill her?"

"What makes you—"

"I saw photographs of the body. There was hardly any blood at all. The coroner's trying to convince himself it was washed away by the rain. I've been trying not to wonder where you've been feeding, but now I have to know. *Did you kill her?*"

She shrank back, then shook her head slowly. "Me? No. She was already dead."

"You found her in the alley?"

"No. There was a feast on the roof." She smiled bleakly. "I was the guest of honor—the new kid in town, so to speak. I didn't know she was a friend of yours."

My knees buckled, and I pitched forward onto the bed, crying for someone I'd barely known.

"Kaarina found her," Alice continued. "She's good at spotting suicides before they jump. I don't know the whole story; she hangs around the bars and waits until she sees a jumper, usually has a few drinks with them, listens for a while, tells them that she's thinking of suicide too, suggests they both go along together. . . . Most of them chicken out. Sometimes they take her home, but she leaves before they find out what she is. Some of them . . . say yes."

I managed to lift my head and look at her. "For Christ's sake—" My voice cracked, and I tried again. "What sort of monster—"

"I'm a vampire," she replied. "You said so yourself. Or a sidhe. Or a boojum, maybe. I can't help what I am, what I need—"

"You can help what you *do*," I snarled. "You told me you can get the blood you need without killing anyone—"

"Sometimes. It's not always easy."

I rested my head on my hands, wearily. "Easy. How easy do you think it was for Dodgson? Hating boys, but never hurting them, just shutting them out of his universe? Loving little girls, but never touching them apart from the occasional kiss? Jesus, even *Sullivan*, who's as loathsome a human being as I've ever met . . . he wants to fuck his daughter, but he hasn't, and I bet he never will. It's not what you want, I'll forgive you that, we can't help what we want, even if it's wrong or obscene . . . but Jesus, what you *do!*"

We stayed there for what seemed like hours, me kneeling by her bed like a mourner, before she whispered, "What do *you* want?"

"I want the killing to stop."

"Is that all?"

I shrugged. Alice looked down at me, then reached out and touched my shoulder where it met my neck, and whispered, "Who's Irene?"

"What?"

"When you dream, you call out for 'Irene.' You did when you were at Oxford, too. Who is she?"

I looked at her. My eyes hurt like hell from crying, something I hadn't done in nearly thirty years, and all I could see was the dark hair and darker eyes. I knew it wasn't Irene, but it might have been. . . .

"Irene . . ." I began. "Irene was the first. The first girl I . . . She . . .

"She, uh, lived two houses away, when I was a kid. Year older than me. Beautiful girl, really beautiful . . . her mother died when she was, I don't know, seven or eight I guess, and she lived alone with her father. He was a . . . I can't remember. Doesn't matter."

I took a deep breath, and tried to start again. "She was the best friend I had, and the only one who lived nearby. Her father wouldn't let anyone visit the house, but she used to sneak over to mine before he came home in the evening. Mostly, she liked to borrow books—he wouldn't buy any, or give her any money—or just sit on my bed and read.

"When I turned ten—she was eleven and a half—I had a birthday party, and invited her, but her father wouldn't let her go. We kept hoping that he'd change his mind, or come home late, or whatever, so she was sort of guest of honor . . . but she didn't turn up. Jesus, I'd forgotten that party, until—anyway, my parents were splitting up, though I didn't know it then, and it was sort of my father's way of saying good-bye. He gave me a camera—a good one, a Nikon, with a zoom lens and flash. . . . I'd used his camera before, I was better with it than he ever was. . . .

"Irene came over the next afternoon. The rain was pissing down, I remember that . . . she was saying how sorry she was that she hadn't come to the party, and she hadn't been able to buy me a present. I showed her the camera, and she asked if I'd like to take some photographs of her. I took a few close-ups of her face, and then she started unbuttoning her blouse. She said it was okay, her father took photographs of her, like that, all the time. . . .

"I can still remember what she looked like: dark hair, like yours, big dark eyes; she was a little taller than me, but skinny, very small breasts, little pink nipples. . . .

"When I'd taken a few photographs, we . . ." I tried to talk, but there was a lump in my throat that I just couldn't swallow. Finally, I whispered, "did some of the other things she and her father did all the time. . . .

"It was nineteen sixty-six, I was ten, sex education was . . . well, my parents hadn't told me anything, and my teachers sure as shit hadn't. Besides, she kept saying it was okay, and I . . . I really liked her."

"Did your parents catch you?"

"No; I wish to hell they had. My father wasn't home yet, and my mother . . . I don't know. Irene dressed herself, and ran back home before her father got there. Of course, *he* knew what had happened, and when she told him that I'd taken photographs . . .

"He had a gun—it was supposed to be for scaring off burglars—and he went into the bathroom and shot himself in the head. But not before he shot her.

"I don't think we heard anything; if we did, we probably thought it was thunder. The rest of the story didn't come out for another few days. When it did . . .

"When it did, my mother took my camera, and ripped the film out, and burnt it. I don't remember what she did to me."

I took a deep breath, and threw up all over the bed.

Alice was waiting as I emerged from the shower. She'd closed the curtains, and the darkness was almost comforting, like a confessional. I suspect I still looked like hell, but at least I felt human. Almost. I tied a robe around myself, and collapsed onto the couch. "You said she was the first," said Alice.

"Yeah. Well. I didn't have sex with *anyone* else until I'd nearly finished high school—my mother made sure of that. Just before graduation, a few of my friends and I drove down to the Combat Zone, but that was a disaster; she was older than me, with big floppy breasts and badly dyed hair and . . . I didn't even *try* again until I won my scholarship and came to England.

"Soho was a nightmare. I'd been told it was London's answer to the Zone, or Times Square, but I could hardly find a picture of a naked girl who wasn't being spanked, caned, or whipped. It was like the London Dungeon—you know, the horror museum for kids—where it's okay to look at nudes, as long as they're being executed or tortured. Christ. Besides, most of the models looked old enough to be my mother.

"After that, it . . . became better. Easier. I met a few girls at Oxford who were still in their late teens . . . blondes were best, and redheads. They didn't look as much like Irene, I didn't have to worry about using the wrong name, and eventually I got used to them, but it was never as good as . . ."

Alice nodded. "But you never fucked any other little girls?"

"Once," I admitted. "In Bangkok. There was a child brothel that a client of ours knew about, out in the back streets, they had girls as young as seven. I picked one who looked about eleven; I don't know how old she really was." I shook my head. "I couldn't go through with it, and finally she gave up and I paid her and she said 'mai pen rai,' never mind. I've sent thousands of pounds to Thailand since then, sponsoring kids, but it hasn't made me feel any better.

"And I bought some kiddie porn, once, by accident. Honest. There's a group in America called the Lewis Carroll Collectors' Guild, and I sent them some money for an illustrated catalogue. I was expecting limited editions or something, not pictures of . . . anyway, I burnt it. Only time I've ever burnt a book. I guess that's when I started trying to clear the poor guy's name."

Alice nodded. "What do you *want?*" she repeated.

I thought about that, and finally replied, "Nothing I can have. I want Irene to have survived. Even *you* can't do that."

"No," she said. "I can't. Is there anything *else* you want?"

I stared into the darkness. I could barely see Alice, just a pair of eyes and a hint of sharp teeth. "Innocence. If not mine, then . . . I want there never to be another Irene. I don't want any more little girls hurt. I want the obscenity to *stop.*"

> *Long has paled that sunny sky;*
> *Echoes fade and memories die*
> *Autumn frosts have slain July.*
>
> *Still she haunts me, phantomwise,*
> *Alice moving under skies*
> *Never seen by waking eyes.*
> —Lewis Carroll, *Through the*
> *Looking-Glass and What Alice*
> *Found There*

Sullivan survived his wife's demise—politically, I mean—but I think it's put his challenge for the party chairmanship back a few years. His daughter, I'm happy to say, has been sent away to a boarding school.

There was a postcard from Bangkok in my In Tray this morning. Having a wonderful time; Alice. It's good to know things are going well; it wasn't easy (or cheap), sending a dozen sidhe to Thailand, finding flights that left and arrived at night, arranging passports for little girls who were born fifty, a hundred, or a hundred and fifty years ago.

I take another look at the article in the *Telegraph*, warning about tourists disappearing in Bangkok, and white male corpses being found in the back streets. *Bled* white. And then I fold the paper, and reach for the atlas, and wonder where I'm going to send them next.

WALKING THE DOG

Terry Lamsley

Terry Lamsley spent most of his childhood in the south of England. He has been living for seventeen years in Buxton, in Derbyshire, where many of his stories are set. For some time he's been employed by social services, working with disturbed adolescents and their families. He has recently had stories in the magazines *All Hallows* and *Ghosts & Scholars*, and the anthologies *Dark Terrors: The Gollancz Book of Horror*, and *Lethal Kisses*. His stories have been reprinted in *Best New Horror* and *The Year's Best Fantasy and Horror*. His self-published collection *Under the Crust*, was nominated for the World Fantasy Award and the title novella won the award in 1994. The book, out of print before the award was given, will be reprinted in a new limited edition by Ash-Tree Press. His second collection, *Conference With the Dead*, from which "Walking the Dog" is taken, was published by the same press. A third collection should be completed momentarily and he is finishing his novel *Dominion of Dust*.

Most of Lamsley's stories are ghost stories. "Walking the Dog" is a departure for him but no less disturbing for that. This might be considered a warning to readers who are considering jobs as dog walkers.

—E. D.

Opening a tin of cat food in the dark can be difficult and dangerous. Steve had cut the big muscle at the base of his thumb on a lid the first time he had tried, eleven days before. Now that he was more experienced and knew the moves to make, he had one open in seconds. Nevertheless, he was careful how he went about the task. He'd learned the hard way that preparing an animal's supper could be hazardous work.

He sliced the contents of the tin of "Liver-flavored Purrfect" with a fork and sprinkled the nauseating mess over the lawn. He still could not believe that hedgehogs could eat such stuff, but each night something did.

The hedgehogs, a whole family of them, were the obsession of an elderly couple who had gone on holiday for a month and who were scared the creatures would desert their garden if they were not regularly fed during their absence. They were paying Steve well to do the job. Easy money, as he had to pass the house at that time anyway, on his way home from his other engagements.

Tonight, though, it was not his last task of the day, as he had taken on an extra commitment for which, by his standards, he would be paid fabulously well. The hours were strange, from eleven at night until one thirty in the morning, but he didn't care about that. It was regular, permanent work and, with what he would get from it and his other jobs, he would just about make enough to live on. For the first time since he'd left school almost three years ago, he'd be independent of his parents. He would no longer be a burden. They wouldn't be able to give him such a bad time at home, and make him feel so useless and depressed.

He slipped the tin-opener into his leather jacket, dropped the empty can on a heap of others exactly like it in the wheely-bin by the side of the house, then stood for a few moments watching the vacant lawn.

So far, he had not seen one hedgehog. He had a suspicion they had taken off anyway, perhaps because their admirers were no longer there to make a fuss of them. Still, it wasn't his problem. He was doing what he was paid to do; it wasn't his fault if the ungrateful little buggers had upped and gone.

Something moved in the flower-beds surrounding the lawn, rustling the dry leaves of the dying annuals planted there. He watched and waited. The soft sounds continued, but nothing appeared. It was too dark to see much anyway.

"It's next door's moggy," he thought, "waiting for me to go away."

He dug his hands into his pockets and strode off.

He was due at his new job at Seaton House, on the other side of Buxton. Mr. Stook, his new employer, had asked him to "get there early, to receive instructions." The man spoke like that a lot; like a form from the Social Security. It worried Steve. He liked to get on well with the people he worked for. He hoped Stook wasn't going to be an awkward customer.

Steve had never been to Seaton House before. Mr. Stook had interviewed him at Steve's parents' house for some reason. He had asked a lot of probing questions, mostly about how fit and strong he was, and insisted on references from previous employers. It seemed a lot of fuss to make to hire the services of an animal-minder, which is what Steve called himself in the advertisements he put in the *Buxton Advertiser*.

He walked past the house twice before he found it. It was completely hidden from the road by a five foot wall backed by a hedge of tall black conifers.

It was a huge house. Steve knew nothing about architecture, but it looked old to him; older than most of the others surrounding it. It was enclosed in what amounted to a small wood. Only the silhouette of the roof and a number of chimneys, vaguely showing against the dimly moonlit clouds, made it visible at all. There was no knocker on the door, and Steve had trouble finding the bell. He discovered it by touch in the end; a big, old-fashioned button set in a circle of polished wood about six inches in diameter. He could feel letters cut in it under his fingers and guessed the order "PRESS" was written there. He pressed.

The door opened almost at once, which surprised him, but then he remembered he was expected.

A young woman looked down on him from the height of two steps. She clicked her tongue. The way she did it made it sound interrogatory, like a question.

"Steven Cave," Steve explained.

"The pet sitter?"

"Mr. Stook asked me to get here early."

"That's right," the girl agreed. "He did. Come in." As she walked away, he noticed she limped badly. She had trouble getting her right foot flat on the ground.

He stepped into the hallway. The girl preceded him up stairs that were steep and wide. The carpet was in tatters in places, and he tripped and almost fell.

The girl said, "Watch your step," which was easier said than done, as the bulbs above him gave nowhere near enough light for him to see his feet. He clung cautiously to the banister rail and thought, "Stook is some kind of miser, in spite of the money he's paying me."

She opened a door on the first floor and walked into a pitch-dark room. He followed her a little way, feeling suddenly uneasy, afraid he might bang his knees against something. The girl became quite invisible: then she must have found a switch, as her face suddenly appeared in a beam of pallid illumination that shone up from the circular aperture at the top of a shaded lamp. She glanced at him (confirming what he had suspected, that she looked odd, but attractive), said, "Wait here, he won't be long," and slipped out, closing the door behind her.

Steve dropped into an armchair and tried to relax. Not easy. The chair was covered in old, bone-dry black leather as hard as wood. There were no cushions. He stretched out his legs, and almost slid off. He pulled himself upright, and looked around. He was in a large, high-ceilinged room, sparsely furnished with big, blunt, graceless furniture. Not antique and interesting, like he'd seen in shops; just old, ugly and depressing.

He sensed there was something wrong with the room, but it took him a couple of minutes to work out what. Then he noticed there was not a single picture on the walls, nor any ornaments on the surfaces of the tables and cupboards. Acting on a hunch, he went and opened one of the cupboards. It was empty. They all were.

He got down on his knees and peered inside one. As he did so he felt a sensation on the back of his neck, as though something had jumped on it. For a moment, a sharp pain jabbed down his spine. He swore, stood up, and rubbed the affected area. A crick in the neck, he thought, whatever one of them is.

The pain quickly receded to almost nothing, but he still felt uncomfortable. He returned to the leather chair and sat waiting.

Somehow, the ugly furniture had a looming, brooding presence; it too seemed to be anticipating something. Steve glared round at it, but found it was more powerful than he was. Put out of countenance by a lot of dead wood, he looked away, down at his own crossed legs.

There were sounds out in the house somewhere, and footsteps passed by in the corridor.

Once he thought he felt a movement up behind the back of his head as if something was forcing its way between him and the chair. He swatted the area with his hand and jumped up. The chair was empty. He looked behind it. Nothing there.

He shook his head, and immediately felt a slight constriction round his throat, as though his shirt collar had tightened. He took off his jacket and rubbed his neck furiously, wagging his head up and down as he did so. To his relief, after a few seconds the sensation subsided.

He put his jacket back on and sat down again, feeling worried and slightly foolish.

Five minutes went by.

He remembered he had his Walkman in his pocket. He stuck the plugs in his ear and turned up "Happy in Hell" by The Christians very loud. At once he felt armed and ready to deal with the intimidating atmosphere about him in the room; the furniture shrank back, as well it might, and the place even seemed a bit brighter. He shut his eyes and sank into the music. When he pulled the tape out of the cheap machine to play the other side, he realized he was not alone any more.

Mr. Stook had joined him.

His employer was sitting at the table near the lamp, reading through a handful of documents. Steve recognized a CV he had put together and guessed the other papers were his references. He pulled out the ear plugs, switched off the hissing Walkman, and pretended to clear his throat. Stook stiffened slightly at the sound, but made no other response. He kept on reading. When he moved his head slightly, as he turned his attention to the next item in his hands, the light glistened and sparked on the silver frame and dark orange-tinted lenses of his spectacles. His face had a fuzzy, unfocused look. His features seemed to blend into each other with a smoothness that gave them an unfinished appearance, like a clay model awaiting the sculptor's final touches.

At last he finished reading, turned to Steve, and said, "Ah, there you are; the successful applicant." He hissed as he spoke, as though he had someone else's false teeth in. His voice had a querulous edge, suggesting he was not quite sure he had made the right choice. It was soft and barely audible. Steve thought if he was sitting a couple of feet further away, he would not have been able to understand what the man was saying. He found himself leaning forward, twisting slightly in his seat to point an ear towards his employer. He was suddenly alert, like a rabbit that had sniffed the scent of a fox.

"Thank you for attending early as requested," Stook continued. "I appreciate your compliance." He stood up, moving carefully, as though he was afraid he might break. He was at least a foot shorter than Steve, who was five eleven. He stooped from a point low down his back, forcing him to hold his head well back to look the boy in the eye. Because of the lack of definition in his features his face looked young; even, in a rather unpleasant way, infantile. In his tinted shades, he resembled a junkie baby. His little mouth was cherubic, enhancing this impression. The hands he held clasped together across his chest were thin to the bone. He was dressed in an oddly-cut suit with a tight fit that clung to his scrawny body. Steve guessed the man weighed about seven stone at most. He felt he could pick Stook up and throw him in the air, but behind this thought was the conviction that something very nasty would happen to him if he did. Stook looked capable of looking after himself, in spite of his slender corporality. He had a startling, powerful presence.

"Now, if you will accompany me downstairs, I shall introduce you to your colleague," Stook murmured, moving with slow, awkward steps across the room.

As he opened the door, light from the landing outside shone full on his face, and Steve saw Stook's flesh was covered in a fine, silvery, almost invisible down, as fluffy as the feathers of a newly-hatched chick. That explained why his features looked blurred. Steve had not noticed it before, when Stook had visited his house, because the man had worn a black trilby hat pulled down almost to the bridge of his nose, and had anyway kept his distance. The sight of the down was so peculiar that Steve found himself staring blatantly at what he could see of Stook's profile.

Stook must have realized this, because he turned, pulled back his lips, and bared his teeth slightly. It wasn't a smile; Steve didn't know what it was; it was not an expression he had seen before on any other face. It startled and confused him. He blushed.

Back on the ground floor, Stook led him through a succession of barely furnished rooms to the back of the house. The final room they went through was a kitchen containing a stone sink with a wooden draining board, a dented zinc wash-tub, and a large and ancient stove. There was no sign of any plates or food, and no cupboards to store such things. All was spotlessly clean. The air was sharp with disinfectant.

They went out into a large, dark, cobbled yard. In the distance, twenty yards away, a solitary light glowed over a door to an outbuilding.

Stook made towards it, moving slowly and with a peculiar, heavy-footed gait, as though he were wading through water. At times they hardly seemed to be making any progress at all but, if Steve stepped ahead, his employer made an irritable snatching motion in the air with his hand, ordering him back.

When they reached the door Stook rapped on it with his knuckles. The sound was dry, like bone on bone. A bolt was drawn back inside and the door was opened by the girl who had let Steve into the house. They walked into a bare, tiled room containing a long, scrubbed bench built over a drain, a selection of electric saws and knives hanging from hooks on the wall, a hose pipe jubilee-clipped to a tap, and not much else. The atmosphere was cold, as if the room was refrigerated in some way. Steve saw his breath in front of his face.

The girl was wearing a white apron over her skirt and blouse. Steve noticed there were russet stains on the apron which could have been dried blood. The girl's face was without expression or makeup, but her lips were bright red as were, to a lesser extent, her eyes. She looked as though she had been crying, or peeling a lot of onions. She looked wasted, as if she existed on coffee and cigarettes, or gin and Ecstasy. She was beautiful in a hard, macabre way that Steve found attractive, but the sight of her depressed him. These people are loonies, he thought, and they've got a bloody Rottweiler or a panther to exercise. They're going to make me earn my money.

"I know you two met briefly before," Stook whispered, "but it is necessary that you be properly introduced. You will be spending a lot of time in each other's company." He waved a finger in the air between them. "This—is Mr. Steven Cave and this—is Miss Amanda Osmond." Steve nodded, and the girl moistened her lips and blinked.

"Please," Stook insisted, urging them closer together with a gesture, "shake hands."

Steve held his hand out and the girl slipped hers into it. Steve grasped her fingers, waggled them up and down, looked into her face, and smiled hopefully. He felt no response against his palm, but the girl did look him in the eye briefly. She gave no sign she liked what she saw.

"Time, now, for one more introduction," Stook said, with a certain relish. He seemed to like introductions. "I regret I must leave you, Mr. Cave, but if you would be so good as to follow Miss Osmond . . . ?" He stepped back and gave a farewell wave.

Suddenly, Steve had a hundred questions needing answers. The first was: Could he go away and think if he really wanted the job? He wasn't sure he could handle it.

But the man was going, almost gone.

"Oh, by the way," Stook said, "I want you to realize that Miss Osmond is your senior. I hope you will work in happy partnership, but she will be, at all times, in charge." He stopped, waiting for an answer.

"Yes," Steve said, "of course."

And felt a sudden twinge of pain at the top of his back; a return of the sensation he had experienced when he had opened the cupboard in the house. He rubbed his neck vigorously, giving it the treatment that had proved partly successful before.

"Good," said Stook, "that is *most* satisfactory," and made his exit.

Steve realized Amanda was watching him with a strange expression on her face. He read it as a mixture of pity, distaste, and maybe something else, like fear. She said, "What's wrong?" but sounded incurious, as though she knew the answer.

"What?"

"With your neck."

"Nothing, just a crick."

"You think that's nothing?" she said. "Well, you just wait and see." She tossed her head, gazed up at the ceiling, and echoed again, "Nothing . . ."

Steve was seriously confused. He seemed to have upset her, but couldn't think how.

Anyway, the pain in his neck had gone again.

Amanda didn't seem in a hurry to get on with the introduction. She stared out of a window into the yard for a minute or so. She looked tired and bored, as though she was waiting for something not very interesting to happen. She made Steve nervous. He wanted to break the silence, to ask some of his questions, to quell his doubts and anxieties, but he sensed small talk would get short shrift from her. Perhaps he ought to keep his mouth shut as much as possible until he knew her better. He wondered if she was a bit . . . disturbed.

Working with Amanda, he decided, was not going to be easy. She was a chilly number.

Even so, he fancied her.

Then, suddenly, as though a bell had rung, the girl became active. She had a bunch of keys in her hand. She set about unlocking a complicated mechanism on a door at the rear of the room.

When it opened, Steve saw it was four inches thick and faced with steel on the inside.

They walked through it into a little closed-up cage. The girl shut the heavy door behind them and, as she did so, a section of the cage, on some automatic mechanism, swung up and out. They entered a room even colder than the last. It was lit by clumps of peculiar shell-shaped lamps along the walls that gave an illumination like none Steve had come across before; a sharp, pearly-pink glow that seemed to hover round its source, rather than spread wide. It reminded Steve of dentists' surgeries, or operating theaters, for some reason, though it certainly would not have been suitable for either kind of establishment. The room itself summoned up images of instruments used in such places; scalpels and drills and suchlike.

Before Steve had a chance to take in details of the tidy, clinical, but dingy room something big, an animal, rose up from the floor. It was mostly charcoal grey, with dark green stripes, and had short hair over its head, back and tail. Its legs and underside were naked greenish flesh. It was almost four feet high. It had a flat face, with eyes that looked forward. It had, Steve saw at once, oddly beautiful, expressive eyes, but expressive of what? He had no idea. The creature stared at him frankly, and seemed to be trying to see into his head.

It's giving me the once over, he thought. It's trying to read my mind. It looks as though it could, too. God knows what it is! They can't expect me to walk a thing like that.

"That's not a dog," Steve objected.

"Obviously. Did Mr. Stook mention a dog?"

Steve couldn't remember that he had, during his interview, but somehow he had assumed that was what he was being asked to deal with. He shook his head.

"He's dog-like, though, as you can see. Out at night, in the dark, he is easily mistaken for a dog. You don't have to worry about that."

She must have misinterpreted the expression of doubt on his face, because she said, "He's harmless most of the time. He won't hurt you. Touch him; put your hand on his head."

Steve looked from the animal to Amanda. She was watching him very closely, with a slight smile that could have been the start of a sneer.

He stepped towards the thing and scratched between its ears. It had little round ears. It made a gurgling noise in its throat, perhaps indicating contentment.

"What's its name?" he said.

"It hasn't got one." Amanda brushed her hands together briskly, impatiently. "And now we'd better get going," she added decisively.

Something touched the back of Steve's leg. The animal. It was looking up at him with its strange eyes. Its irises were a pattern of tiny black and white diamond shapes, like a harlequin's costume. The outer parts were sea-green, a very deep-sea-green.

It was, on the whole, an ugly bugger, but not unfriendly.

So why didn't it have a name? The anonymity seemed pointless, heartless. People even gave their pet goldfish names!

He decided he would christen it; but what to call it?

He'd have to think about that.

"Okay," he said, "let's go walkies. Show me the ropes, Amanda."

"We go in the van," she said.

"Is this it?" Steve said, looking out at the black night all around.

Amanda lit her third cigarette in half an hour and killed the lights and engine. "It's as far as we go tonight." The windows were shut and the front of the van was full of stale smoke.

Steve opened the side door and stuck his head out. A skeletal moon hung precariously above him, washing the landscape with a pale, sick lumination.

"Are we anywhere in particular?"

"In the middle of the moors north of Leek." She stretched wearily, then clambered out of the van, lowering herself carefully onto her damaged foot.

Steve joined her at the back of the vehicle and helped push the sliding door open. A light in the sealed-off rear compartment came on automatically, revealing the creature sitting on a water bed. Steve had asked about the bed and Amanda told him it was full of cold water. It helped to keep the temperature down. Steve had said, "Ah," and thought, "It's a bloody cold night anyway."

Earlier, they had loaded the "dog" on board without any trouble. It had been placid and cooperative. It had made a few noises that had alarmed Steve at first, but the girl had ignored them.

He was beginning to think that the job might be easy after all.

Amanda pulled a set of steps down out of the back of the van and said something incomprehensible to the animal. It approached them, reversed itself and, to Steve's astonishment, descended backwards. Its coordination was nothing like that of any animal he had ever seen. He noticed it had long, crudely prehensile claws that it used to grip the steps one at a time. It looked clumsy in motion, but seemed surefooted enough. Once on the ground it sniffed eagerly about, like a cartoon pooch tracking game.

Amanda flung her cigarette end away and lit up another.

"You trying to burn your lungs out with those?" Steve asked.

"Perhaps."

"Mr. Stook won't let you smoke in the house?"

She shrugged.

"He probably worries about your health."

For the first time, he heard her laugh. It was a painful, hacking sound that turned into a cough. When it finished she said, "He certainly likes to keep his employees going as long as possible," then coughed again. Steve thought he could hear other sounds in her chest, something glugging and gurgling. He was about to ask her if she was okay, but she gave him a look that shut him up.

The animal croaked softly, as though to draw attention to itself.

"Right," Amanda said, "this is where you do your bit." She clipped an extending lead on a collar round the creature's neck and handed Steve the other end. The lead was slightly luminous, emitting a weird green light. "So you can see where it's gone," she explained. She climbed back into the van. "Okay, beast-master, get walking. Have you got a watch?"

"Yes."

"Time?"

"Almost midnight."

"You give it an hour."

"But where do I take it?"

"Where it wants to go."

She said a mumbo-jumbo word to the animal, and it was off. It jerked the lead, nearly pulling Steve over. As he stumbled after it, he heard her say, "Your eyes soon get used to the dark, and there's plenty of starlight. It's easier if you give it plenty of lead. Just press the button to run it back. Keep it tight or it gets snagged."

And Steve's nightmare began.

The thing trotted off fairly slowly at first. It moved in a peculiar way, pawing the ground like a high-stepping pony with its front legs, but somehow trotting with its back ones. Steve seemed to remember seeing poodles in ballet skirts making similar motions in a circus. Right from the start he had to walk fast to keep up, but the creature soon accelerated, and he found himself running. He let out more lead and tried to slow down, but his charge had other ideas. He saw the grey shape ahead of him getting smaller and smaller on the end of its thin strip of green light.

The ground underfoot was uneven and dangerous, riddled with rabbit holes and lumps of sharp rock. He fell after five minutes, without harming himself, then got up and plunged ahead again. The thing had paused when he tripped, but only for seconds.

The rest of the hour was hell. After twenty minutes he called out to the creature to slow down, even though he didn't think it understood orders in English. If it did hear him, it ignored him. It found something to interest it at one point, and began snuffling frantically. As soon as he realized it had stopped, Steve flopped to the ground flat on his back, wound in some of the lead, and gazed up at the stars, gasping for air while his chest heaved almost to bursting point. His heart beat like the bass at a Guns 'n' Roses concert. After just a few minutes a small animal, probably a rabbit, screamed with pain again and again, as though it was being dismembered slowly. Steve looked in the direction of the sounds and saw his charge up on its back legs against the curtain of stars, seemingly dancing. It was hurling some misshapen lump of a living creature into the air, catching it in its jaws, then tugging at it with its paws. Hence the screams. The thing was obviously enjoying itself.

It soon wanted to move on, however. Too soon for Steve, who needed more time to get his breath back. He hauled on the lead, yelled at the creature, and refused to get up. The thing pulled hard, and started jerking at the lead. It was very strong. Steve found himself being dragged along in spite of his considerable weight. He tried to dig his heels into the bracken but failed to get a grip. He slid uncomfortably for a few yards until he came up against a large boulder. He managed to get his end of the lead round the rock in a loop which held. The thing stopped. It made angry, frustrated noises, like the cawing of a giant rook. Steve hung on, feeling triumphant. He had scored a point. It was finding out who was boss.

Then he felt a painful stab in the back of his head. The skin at the sides of his neck was drawn forward, as though something was reaching round towards his chin. Whatever it was grasped the flesh above his breast bone and began to crush his windpipe. At the same time his head was being pulled up and back. It was impossible to breathe.

He was holding the lead with both hands but he let go with one of them to feel around his neck for whatever was strangling him. There was nothing there that he could touch. There were indentations in his skin where the pain was greatest, however, as though something invisible was digging in.

He let go of the handle of the lead altogether and jumped to his feet. He saw the glowing green stripe slipping away from him like an electric snake. The animal, realizing it was free, became silent.

Steve hung onto his head as though he feared it might be torn off his shoulders. He was in agony, and quite unable to get air into his lungs.

Out of the corner of his eye he saw the creature come prancing swiftly towards him. It stopped a few feet in front of him and stared at him. It reared up on its hind legs and, as it did so, the pain Steve was experiencing became, for a second, much more intense. Then the thing took a leap in the air and sank down onto its belly.

At once, Steve felt himself released. The constriction round his neck was no longer there; the cause of the pain had gone. He gasped air, and fell to his knees. He was violently sick. He found himself on all fours. He closed his eyes, and moaned. His whole body was quaking with spasms of nausea.

When he opened his eyes again, he found the creature had moved closer. They were almost nose to nose. The thing's remarkable eyes were inches from his.

It was looking straight into him, or seemed to be. It moved a fraction closer and blinked. For an instant, the pain flashed on and off in the back of Steve's head. Then the animal turned, trotted off a little way, and sat down, obviously waiting.

Steve understood.

Meekly, he went and found his end of the lead.

He looked at his watch. It was almost one, time to get back to the van.

Then he realized he had no idea where he was. He was completely disorientated.

He staggered about lost for three or four minutes, while the creature trotted calmly behind him, almost at heel. Then, not very far away, the van's headlights flashed twice.

When he reached it, the girl was standing at the back with the door open. She slipped the collar and lead off the creature's neck, and it jumped on board.

They got into the van.

"How did it go?" Amanda said.

"A few problems." Steve's neck was so sore, it hurt to speak.

"Yeah, so I heard. You two fell out?"

"That sort of thing."

"You won't do *that* again, will you?"

"I won't have anything to do with it again," he said angrily.

"Oh yes you will." She lit a cigarette, started the engine, and turned to look at him. "It won't let you go."

"We'll see about that."

She started driving cautiously back, with the headlights dipped. "You don't understand, do you? You're hooked. You've got a monkey on your back."

Steve didn't answer.

They drove back in silence.

Steve had too much on his mind to notice how cold it was.

"I don't understand. Why do I have to walk it anyway?"

"I used to take it," Amanda said, "but my legs got broken once too often, and they won't heal properly any more. Then we got another girl to do it. . . ."

"No," Steve insisted, slightly embarrassed at causing her to mention her game legs. "I mean, how come we have to take it out at all?"

"It needs exercise. Can you imagine letting that creature out the back door to roam around for the night? To wander round town on its own?"

"But why do I have to walk *with* it? Why can't we just take it somewhere and leave it to run for an hour?"

"It gets lost. It's got no sense of direction. And it's short-sighted. I don't think it can see more than a few yards."

"Even with those amazing eyes?"

"Perhaps it sees things with them we can't see. Maybe, where he comes from, he can see perfectly."

"And where do you think that is?"

She paused, lit a cigarette from the last half-inch of her previous one, and said, "Who knows? Another dimension? Another planet? Hell? Your guess is as good as mine. One thing's certain, it's not part of the indigenous population."

They were driving out for Steve's fourth night on the job. Each time they went to a different spot, just in case they'd been seen the night before, and someone was waiting for them to return. There had been articles in the local papers about a strange animal in the district during recent weeks, and a couple of eye-witness descriptions had been close to the mark. Mr. Stook had got to hear about them, and had not been pleased with Amanda. She'd been disciplined, she told Steve. She didn't say how, but her "monkey" had played a part in the procedure, so now she was selecting the sites for the creature's exercise with particular care.

On their second trip out, she'd explained that she had a "passenger" on her back, the same as he did. It wasn't really a monkey, but the phrase "a monkey on the back," used by junkies back in the 40s and 50s as a euphemism for addiction, seemed to describe their own predicament exactly.

Even then, in spite of the evidence of his experiences on the first evening,

Steve couldn't quite believe her; he thought it was more likely there was something wrong with *him*.

That was what he wanted to believe.

When he'd tried to stay at home on the second night, when it was time to go to work, and the pains had started at the top of his spine, and had only eased when he had left his parents' home and set off in the direction of Seaton House, he had clung to the idea that it might be due to something that was wrong inside his head. He knew nothing about psychology, but was aware that the mind could make you do strange things.

Whatever it was, however, it hurt. It forced him to get to the job on time.

The next evening, at ten, he'd jogged as far and as fast out of Buxton as he could.

His "monkey" had almost throttled him by the time he had gone two miles, and he'd had to turn back. At home again he had run up to his room, stripped off his shirt, and looked in the mirror. At the front of his neck, just above his breast bone, were bruise marks the shape of two little three-fingered hands. The fingers had dug in deep enough to draw blood.

He'd gone to work then—in a hurry.

The fourth night, tonight, he had turned up on time: In fact, he'd been early.

The creature had not given him too many problems after their first trip out together, though walking it was still hard work. Instead of running wild for an hour, and dragging him after it, it had conformed to more dog-like ways for some of the time, trotting a few yards ahead of him at a reasonable speed and sticking mostly to sheep tracks and established paths. Steve was glad to find the thing ignored sheep. He had half expected it to kill and eat one every night for supper.

Amanda had explained when asked (she hardly ever volunteered information) that his first evening on the job had been the creature's first outing for months, so it had had a lot of steam to let off. It never went out between the start of June to the end of September because it didn't like the hot nights.

"It sort of hibernates in reverse in the room we collect it from. It's air-conditioned. It gets as cold as a witch's tit in there some times."

As to sheep for supper? "It eats when we get back, after you've gone. Stook sees to that. He's in charge of the pantry."

"What does he feed it?"

"Don't worry about that," she said. "Believe me, you don't want to know."

He mentioned the rabbit it had caught on the first night.

"It must have been a very stupid rabbit," she said, "or a sick or injured one."

"I don't think it ate it; just pulled it apart."

She nodded. "You won't see rabbit on its menu," she said. "It's a big game gourmet."

They reached some God-forsaken place and stopped. Steve opened the rear door of the van and stood aside as the thing stuck its backside out and reversed down the steps. Not for the first time, he wondered what his monkey would do to him if he gave the creature a kick in the rump. Something very painful, he was sure.

He still thought of the animal as "it." He had dropped the idea of giving it a name. Anonymity seemed to suit it.

So things continued for some months.

Stook told Steve to learn to drive, and paid for lessons.

The money Steve was earning was ridiculous, enough for him to be able to drop most of his other jobs. His standard of living soared. He started buying clothes to spruce up his image.

He had always had trouble with girls. They didn't seem to see him. Steve stared at girls a lot, he couldn't help it, but somehow, for some reason, they never so much as glanced back. It was as if he was invisible. They just looked through him.

He spent a lot of time in front of the mirror, trying to work out why. He thought he was handsome enough. Okay, he had a slightly podgy face. But his features, considered in isolation, were good. He looked . . . reasonable. Lots of worse-looking men his age were walking about with delicious girls on their arms, were sleeping with them. Steve's sex life was almost non-existent, and took place with the few girls who were attracted to him. For some reason, these were never girls he fancied. Something was wrong, he felt; he wasn't getting across to the right women.

So he started buying show-off clothing and having expensive haircuts. He thought girls would be more likely to notice him. He'd be more obvious.

But his new look wasn't having much effect.

Certainly not on Amanda.

She attracted him a lot. But she was an enigma; hard to get on with, and difficult to know. She didn't reveal much about herself.

He dreamed about Amanda.

They were foolish dreams, with him as a sort of white knight, saving her from the evil Stook.

The trouble was that, in reality, she didn't seem to realize she needed saving. She put up with what Steve perceived to be an abject, slavish existence.

And she always had her guard up. She had a weary, cynical attitude and way of speaking that somehow put her away at a great distance, out on her own. Steve felt she was beyond him, that he couldn't reach her, though sometimes he thought she was beginning to thaw out towards him just a little.

He was not sure how she spent her days, but he suspected she acted the skivvy for Stook and the creature, as the place where it lived was kept ultra-clean, as though scrubbed and scoured by a germ-phobic fanatic. The air around the house always stank of disinfectant, dust never seemed to get to settle on any surface in the outbuilding where the thing was kenneled, and you could see your face in the gloss paint and polished tiles on the walls. The inside of the house, though furnished with ancient and, in some cases, worn, dilapi-dated items, was also kept fastidiously neat and clean, and Steve was sure Stook didn't do the work himself.

So it had to be Amanda.

Steve began to think of her as a kind of doomed Cinderella. Cinderella with a monkey on her back.

His own monkey didn't trouble him much. For days he would forget it was there. Then he'd do something wrong when he was out with the creature, and it would give him a tweak, a jolt of pain that knocked him rigid, and he would remember.

And, often, he felt strangely tired. In recent weeks a lassitude had been creeping over him, as if his energy was draining away through the soles of his feet. Things that had once been easy were getting difficult. He'd been a body builder for almost two years, and had got himself very fit. But suddenly it was a strain to lift weights. He kept away from the gym because he was finding it harder and harder to keep up with his friends down there, and his shorts and t-shirts were starting to hang loose on him. People noticed, and made comments.

Also, he'd been sleeping like a dead thing recently, was getting up later and later, but still wasn't feeling refreshed.

And he was eating like a pig! His appetite was getting out of hand; his mother told him he must have worms.

Steve had a suspicion it was something worse than worms. A couple of times, in the mirror, he had caught an expression on his face that he had seen on Amanda's. A look that he was beginning to understand.

Frequently Amanda seemed to be trying to warn him about something; her conversation, sparse and elliptical as it was, was full of hints and allusions, suggested as much by her tone of voice as the meaning of the words she used. At times, when he thought she was trying to get through to him at some subliminal level, her normally blank, expressionless face would almost come alive. Feelings of frustration, fear, despair, and a terrible isolation would register briefly behind her eyes and in the lines at the corners of her mouth, to be wiped away at once by a grimace of pain, as though she had been whipped.

Reading between the lines of what she said, Steve came to understand that her monkey could somehow read her mind, even control her thoughts to some extent. Only occasionally, perhaps when it was dozing or otherwise occupied, could she communicate obliquely some of what Steve wanted to know. He got the impression she had been its victim for a long time: It had almost total mastery over her, and he would end up in the same condition. His own monkey was growing into him. It was getting to know him, to understand him. It had command of his body; one day it would have his soul. Or so Amanda seemed to be saying. From all this he deduced that he was still, to some extent, free to think and act in ways that she was not. Perhaps there was some way he could get the monkey off his back and then help Amanda deal with hers. Perhaps.

But there was also Stook to contend with. Steve wished he knew more about his employer. He became obsessed with a need to find out just what kind of eyes the man hid behind the impenetrable orange-tinted spectacles that always masked his out-of-focus face. He hardly ever had contact with Stook except at the end of each week, when he went to receive his pay. That, in itself, he found disturbing. And he realized he had never seen the man and his pet (if that was what the creature he took for nocturnal rambles was) together, not even once. Also, Stook never asked about its welfare or showed any concern about it at all, which was not natural. Steve was used to being questioned closely about the animals he cared for by their owners, as though the creatures were their own flesh and blood.

A suspicion evolved in Steve's mind that the dog-thing he exercised was just that, however; Stook's own flesh and blood!

"What does Mr. Stook do all day?" he asked Amanda one evening, as they drove to some remote, chilly location. It was almost Christmas, and a couple of inches of snow had fallen on top of a skim of frozen rain during the day. The girl was driving with greater concentration than usual.

"Goes out," she said from behind the cigarette that waggled at the side of her mouth. "Every day. In the van."

"Are you sure? Where to?"

"Looking for food to feed—it." She jerked a thumb over her shoulder towards the creature in the back compartment.

"And that takes all day?"

"It can do."

"You never did tell me what it eats," he said.

She shook her head and glanced sideways at him. For a few moments she was silent; then she said, apparently apropos of nothing, "Every day, you know, people go missing. Particularly kids. It's a sign of the times."

"That's right," Steve agreed, unsure where the conversation was leading. "You read about it in the papers."

"All the time. It's surprising how many of them never do get found."

"Perhaps no one bothers to look for a lot of them."

"Someone does."

Steve grunted encouragingly, thinking he was perhaps beginning to understand. "And when he finds them, they stay missing?"

"Definitely. And sometimes, if he has to, he makes them go missing in the first place," she said, and turned the van off the road along a dark track to nowhere. "If he can't find what he wants, he takes what he can find. He's a good hunter. He knows how to set traps."

The full meaning of Amanda's words skipped over the surface of Steve's mind for a while, refusing to sink in. But what he was hearing, what he thought she was saying, did not came as a total surprise. It was a bit like remembering fragments of an old nightmare. He had formulated wild theories and fantasies about Stook and his "pet" at least as disgusting as the girl's story.

After another short silence he said, "And the thing eats every day?"

"It has to have very fresh meat four or five times a week at least."

"Very fresh?"

"Lively. Still on the hoof. It likes to do its own slaughtering, though it will take the pre-butchered option if it has to."

For once, she seemed to be able to speak relatively freely, perhaps because her monkey knew if it gave her a jolt, she might lose control of the van on the snow and ice.

Suddenly, extrapolating, Steve understood something more. "So the meal is made to walk into the cage, then out into the room, is that it?" he said, trying to sound casual and inconsequential. "The cage opens automatically. It's a feeding hatch! The metal plating on the inside of the door is to stop dinner, not the creature, escaping?"

She nodded too hard, and set herself off coughing. Her cigarette fell from her lips to the floor. A stink of burning drifted up into the van. Steve bent down to find and extinguish the little fire, prodding around with the heel of his right shoe. Amanda slowed the van's speed to a crawl. As he fumbled he said, "Did you ever see Stook and that thing together in the same place?"

Then his own monkey woke up. He felt pain screw across the back of his eyes. He went blind. It was as though his eyes had been put out; there was that much pain. Black anguish filled his mind for an instant. He jerked back into his seat in one great spasm. He heard Amanda say something like "Drop it" or, maybe, "Stop it;" then he passed out.

When he came to he had a searing headache, but he could see again.

The van had stopped. Amanda, looking gray-faced and ill, had got out and opened the door at his side. Fluffy snow was blowing in and settling on his face. The girl was shaking him by the shoulder. He heard a noise behind him, slightly muffled, like the cry of a monster crow trapped in a sack. The thing in the back was getting impatient.

He dragged himself through the door down onto the frozen ground. Amanda gave him the lead and opened the rear door.

The creature was angry. It snarled at him before it reversed out. It charged off as soon as he got its collar on, dragging him behind.

Then it led Steve a grotesque and terrible dance.

It was a bleak place they had come to. The murky night sky was veiled by drifting nets of wet, swirling snow. He slipped on iced-over puddles a number of times in the dark. Once he landed awkwardly on his left arm and felt something give in the wrist. His hand went numb, then started to pulse with pain. He couldn't move the fingers of his left hand, and was forced to hang onto the lead with only his right. The creature dragged him along sideways, causing him to stumble and fall a dozen times.

He felt like a sailor, sinking in a storm and sighting a lifeboat when, at last, he saw the van lights flash.

He got Amanda to drop him off at the Cottage Hospital on the way back to Seaton House. She was very reluctant to do so. She would not, or could not, stop the van, and insisted he jump out while she cruised slowly past the drive that led up to the Accident Unit.

He caught a glimpse of her contorted features as she leaned across the passenger seat to slam the door behind him. Her monkey, he guessed, was going to give her hell when she got back.

Steve woke up shortly after noon next day. He opened his eyes and saw his left arm, in plaster up to the elbow, rising and dipping on his chest. He'd spent most of the night in hospital. X-rays had revealed chipped and broken bones in his hand and wrist. The radiographer had told him it could be months before he got full use of the hand again.

When he *had* finally got to bed, he had not been able to get to sleep for thinking about how the accident would affect his prospects with Stook. Strangely, he was anxious he might lose his job. It somehow seemed like a desirable occupation to him, in spite of the fact that most of his working hours were a walking nightmare. Maybe he had become addicted to money or, more sinisterly, perhaps his monkey was influencing his thinking. Either way, like it or not, he was worried.

He dragged himself out of bed. He dressed slowly, like a sleepwalker, then went to the kitchen and chomped through a breakfast of three bowls of Shredded Wheat, a fry-up big enough to hide most of the surface of a dinner plate, half a loaf of toasted bread, and a pint-and-a-half of milk. Then he felt tired again, and was tempted to return to bed for a few more hours, as he often did. But today he had urgent things to do. He had to let Stook know about the condition of his hand. The man was not on the phone, or was ex-directory, so Steve would have to pay him a visit. The idea appealed to him. He had been looking for an excuse to call at Seaton House during daylight hours for weeks.

A lot more snow had fallen. Probably for reasons of economy, the roads had not been salted, and traffic was sparse. Everywhere was eerily quiet; all sound was baffled, trapped in the banks of drifting white flakes. The town had a deserted feel, as though the population had been lured away overnight by the saucer-people.

Steve walked slowly, picking his way with care, not wanting to fall and damage his arm still further.

The first thing he saw when he trudged up Stook's drive was the van, parked where it never was left, at the front of the house. The front end was caved in from some considerable impact. The left tire was in shreds, and the windows were smashed. There were traces of an extra set of wheels nearby in the snow, suggesting the vehicle had been towed home.

He went and rang the doorbell and shouted through the letter box, got no response, and wandered round to the back of the house.

The rear courtyard was surrounded by two-storied outbuildings and a wall eight feet high. The one door, bolted on the inside, was impenetrable without the aid of a battering-ram and a rugby team to operate it. On his own, with a duff hand, there was no way Steve could force an entry. He didn't even bother to try. He went among the trees all round the house, aware that he was leaving an obvious trail of prints in the snow, and snooped in the windows. He learned nothing about Stook's way of life, however, as all the rooms he saw were barely furnished and looked unused. He came to the conclusion that Stook chose to live at Seaton House because the building was well hidden, yet close to the center of town, rather than because he needed a big establishment. It was probably easier to remain incognito, concealed in the community, than it would be if he inhabited some remote place where his activities, or lack of them, would become the object of speculation for farmers and other country dwellers, who commonly possess an insatiable curiosity about their neighbors' doings. Steve had been brought up on such a farm, and the same instinctive nosiness was born in him.

He wandered back into town, called the local hospitals from a telephone box to see if an Amanda Osmond had been admitted anywhere, and got negative replies from all of them. Then he sat in a pub for a couple of hours drinking lager, doing the quizzes on beer-mats, and listening to the barmaid's conversation. She was telling one of the customers (in fact, the only other customer), a sullen, silent man she seemed inordinately fond of, about her various *grand guignol* relationships. She obviously had lots of boyfriends. Steve thought she was beautiful. He fell in love with her. He normally never drank alcohol, but kept on drinking so he could stay and look at her. He thought, if he downed enough quickly, he might pluck up the courage to get talking to her himself. He stared at her shamelessly for minutes on end. She didn't seem to notice him, even when he went to the bar, even though he was dressed in one of his coolest, cost-a-packet outfits.

"I'm invisible," he thought. "I don't register with her. I suffer from negative charisma."

Then, suddenly disgusted with himself, he gulped down the last of his drink and got up to go. On the way out he walked to the bar, set his empty glass down in front of the object of his lust, and almost shouted, "See ya, then!"

"Ta, duck," she said, without turning. The customer in receipt of her monologue glanced askance at him, and raised an eyebrow.

"They think I'm pissed," Steve thought. "Perhaps I am, after five (or was it six?) pints of Special."

When he got outside and found his feet flailing about in the snow, he realized how drunk he was. Not far from the pub he slipped, fell on his backside, and bounced back up. "Ah ha," he thought, "I feel no pain!" and wanted to laugh. He stumbled back to Seaton House, lighter and happier than he had been for weeks.

When he got there he saw a new set of footprints leading up the drive. A woman's; almost certainly Amanda's. They stopped at the front door, and whoever had gone in was still there. There were no prints going back out.

He rang the bell, waited, then hammered with his fist. After a while the door opened slowly about six inches. It was on a chain. Round the edge of the door, thin, dry, scaly fingers appeared, clutching the wood with a crab-like pincer movement. Above them, a slice of Stook's furry face, half-hidden behind one lens of his dark orange-tinted spectacles, pressed forward into the gap.

Partly through shock (he had been sure Amanda would answer the door) and partly because he did not want to waft lager-polluted breath towards his employer, Steve stepped backwards. He nearly fell off the step. He regained his balance, but not his composure. He could not think of anything to say. Stook broke the silence.

"Why are you here at this time?" he asked, in a tight, tiny, snarling voice. "What do you want?" His fussy manner of speech and fastidious politeness had deserted him.

"He looks like an insect," Steve thought, "with that fuzzy face and those shades. He even sounds like one. A giant house fly, or a bluebottle. He wants swatting!"

"I had an accident last night. Perhaps Amanda told you." Steve held up his plastered arm. "I fell over when I was walking the . . ."

"I know all about it," Stook snapped. "It doesn't matter."

"Oh, and I forgot to tell you, I passed my driving test the day before yesterday."

Stook grunted; a sound that may have expressed satisfaction.

Steve suddenly felt stupid with drink. His brain became confused, then blank.

"I don't want you here now," Stook said.

"But what about tonight?"

"Come at the usual time."

"I've broken my arm."

"That doesn't concern me."

"I've got to rest it; take things easy."

"You've got a job to do. You'll be here on time."

"But what about the van?"

"That's my problem." Stook glared at him for a few seconds, during which Steve felt contempt emanating from the man like a powerful smell.

"I want to speak to Amanda," Steve said at last.

"Why?"

"Well . . ." Steve inwardly cursed the lager that seemed to have anaesthetized his tongue.

"She's not here," Stook said, in what could have been a taunting tone.

Then he hissed, "Go away," and shut the door.

Steve stood looking at the varnished wood in front of his nose and became very, very angry. He hardly ever was angry, about once or twice a year, but when he was, it made up for all the times he wasn't, and should have been.

He kicked the door, hurt his toe, and shouted, "You bastard, you know how I broke my wrist last night because *you were there when it happened.* I've got you worked out, you and your bloody pet."

Then he felt something stirring at the back of his neck. A dull, wavering ache moved out of his spine and across his shoulders. His monkey was trying to push and punish him, and not making a good job of it. He could feel its hands groping to reach round to his throat, but they had no strength, and seemed to fumble. At one point, they lost hold altogether, as though the monkey had fallen backwards.

Gleefully Steve recognized, in the parasite's powerless confusion, a reflection of his own drunkenness.

"It's more pissed than I am," he thought. "It feeds off me, and somehow it's got alcohol in its system, and it can't take it. It's got a weak head. It's rat-assed; legless! It can't hurt me."

Finding himself truly free for the first time for months, Steve felt bold.

And he was still angry, deep inside.

And he was still very drunk.

"Time to get things sorted," he mumbled, as he started plodding through the snow to the rear of Seaton House. "Bugger the money. I'll not work for that thing any more. And I'll find Amanda, and tell her to get her monkey drunk. That's the way to beat it. Then Stook can go and take himself for a walk."

He had noticed, during his prowl through the miniature woods growing round the perimeter of the house earlier in the day, a tree, growing close to the wall, whose branches reached out above the courtyard. Then, it had not occurred to him that he might be able to use it to get over the wall, especially as he only had the use of one arm; now, thanks to alcohol, it looked an easy climb.

Steve rose up the trunk, branch by branch, as though he was ascending a ladder, using the weight of his plastered wrist as a balance. He stepped out along an overhanging branch with all the confidence of a champion tango dancer leading his partner onto a ballroom floor. The branch dipped gracefully lower as Steve moved along it. When, after he had got the wall behind him, it snapped, depositing him in a drift of snow that had formed inside the courtyard, he didn't so much feel he was falling, as flying! He was so relaxed when he hit the ground that he was able to roll over onto his feet in one unbroken movement.

It was dank and dark in the courtyard. The snow, caught in eddies of wind trapped by the surrounding buildings, spun in frantically ascending circles around him.

Looking about he saw a vertical strip of light at the edge of the door leading into the outbuilding where the creature had its "kennel." There was a sound, a high, grinding, mechanical whirring, coming from behind the slightly open door, that had been muffled by snow and the wall when he had been in the garden on the other side.

A beam of light stretched across the snow towards him from the slightly open door. He walked along its diminishing width warily, as though he were walking the plank. The noise continued, rising to a sheer metallic screech, then sinking back to an even, angry snarl.

When it was at its loudest, Steve gave the door a shove and peered round it into the room.

Then drew back at once in horror.

Stook was in there, naked except for a pair of green Wellington boots and a brick-red rubber apron that almost formed a tube around his body. In it, he looked more than ever like some kind of bug. He had his back to Steve. He held an electric saw in his hands and was using it to cut up a carcass stretched out on the long wooden bench in front of him. The top end of the corpse had been jointed into unidentifiable chunks of meat. It was headless, but something heavy, about the size of a head, hung in a plastic Marks and Spencers bag from a nail driven into the edge of the bench. The lower section of the cadaver, partly concealed under a sheet of thick plastic, was untouched and obviously human. Two feet, lolling apart at the ankles at an angle of forty-five degrees, stuck out from under the sheet and over the end of the bench.

And Steve though he had seen a hand on the floor by Stook's boots. The hand was moving, sliding down a gutter near the bench, caught in the jet from a hose pipe that was snaking restlessly from side to side under the pressure of water it was ejecting.

The shock of what he had seen, far from sobering Steve up, flung his mind into a debilitating stew of incredulity, revulsion, and blind anger. He wanted to act, to strike against Stook, to *swat him down*, but he didn't do anything of the sort. He stood rooted to the spot, gasping and howling, softly but passionately, along with the sighing of the wind, frozen in an enchantment of disgust and revulsion. He remained like that for a couple of minutes, long enough for the snow to settle as a light crust on his shoulders and head, and for his feet to start to freeze in his sodden canvas trainers.

Then a new sound came from inside the outhouse. The deeper, harsher grinding of a bigger saw. His employer was getting down to work in earnest, making the final cuts. Presumably, soon, the meal would be ready, and the creature would eat.

The thought was enough to break the icy spell that Steve was under. He turned back, pushed open the door, and walked determinedly into Stook's private abattoir. Stook did not hear him enter; he would not have heard if Steve had shouted his name, against the noise of the machine.

Wondering if he might need a weapon, or something to defend himself with, Steve looked about for something heavy he could swing. As he did so, his monkey roused itself and tried, ineffectually, to cause him pain. It seemed to be sprawling inside his head, scratching at the back of his eyes with blunted talons, and gnawing his cerebellum with toothless gums. It was desperate, but almost helpless. Steve ignored it.

He got to within a couple of feet of Stook's back when he saw something hanging on the wall that brought him up short.

There was a row of hooks for the overalls and waterproofs that he and Amanda took with them when they went out on wet nights. Stook's clothing had been flung over one of these, and next to it hung the skirt and blouse that Amanda had worn the previous night, when Steve had broken his wrist in the snow. The girl's clothing was covered in blood stains, and there were streaks of red down the wall below.

Previously, dominated as he was by alcohol-enhanced emotions, Steve had not given a thought to the possible identity of the cadaver Stook was dismembering.

But his main motivation for invading his employer's domain had been to locate Amanda, and somehow to rescue her, as he had many times in his dreams. Now it seemed he had found her, but too late.

He glanced again at the corpse. It was about the right size, what remained of it. The proportions were Amanda's. The hand, which was now spinning in a whirling current of crimson water outflowing down the drain, was narrow and delicate, like Amanda's. He even thought he could see nicotine stains on the fingers.

Then Stook must have become aware that he was no longer alone. He switched off the screaming saw and turned awkwardly round. He was crouching low, bent forward in his habitual stance, with his chin jutting up almost in line with his breast bone. He looked absurdly sinister and repellent with his wasted, gray, downy arms swinging ape-like by his sides, and his knotted knees showing in the gap between the tops of his boots and the bottom of his apron. He still held the electric saw in his right hand, and he whipped the tip of the blade back and forth in a tiny arc, in a tense, threatening movement. His eyes, invisible behind his tinted shades, nevertheless drove into Steve's like corkscrews.

Stook said something in a language Steve couldn't understand. It sounded like a question. Stook's tone was demanding, querulous, mystified. As if in answer, Steve felt his monkey stir again; vague waves of discomfort pulsed weakly through his brain.

Stook moved a few inches closer to Steve, and spoke again. Now he sounded angry.

But Steve's monkey seemed to give up. It faded out. Steve thought it might have gone to sleep.

Stook raised his feeble voice and mouthed more incomprehensible words.

"It's no good shouting," Steve said. "Your little mate's passed out. He's sleeping it off."

"You're drunk," Stook observed.

"Right," Steve agreed. "And I'm going to stay drunk."

Shook's lips curled, but he didn't speak.

"That way, we're more or less equal," Steve said, feeling more confident by the second. He had begun to sober up, but now he felt a surge of elation, like a shot of spirit, from the certainty he had disarmed Stook and his minion. "I don't work for you any more, Stook. I know what you are, and I'm going to do something about you. I'm going to destroy you. Christ knows where you came from, but I'm going to send you to a worse place."

Stook made a buzzing noise with his tongue against his teeth, like an insect at a window. He sounded more impatient and irritable than scared. Hearing him, Steve experienced a moment of self-doubt, of anxiety that he had, perhaps, underestimated his employer, and assumed victory too soon.

Stook straightened up a little, and seemed to turn away almost derisively.

Thinking he was going to walk off, Steve was about grab him, by the throat perhaps, when Stook struck. He swung up his right arm, switching on the saw as he did so, and lunged forward at Steve's chest. The little man moved with unexpected agility. The saw blade bit something, and shrieked as it cut.

Steve thought he had been hurt, but felt no pain. He staggered back and, as he did so, Stook moved quickly forward to strike again. Then Steve understood *why* he felt no pain. He had automatically held up his left arm to protect himself, and the saw had hit the plaster close to his elbow and lopped off a slice. He had raised the injured arm defensively high above his head, out of the way, and it was still there, poised, waiting to be brought down. It felt very heavy.

Perhaps Stook recognized the danger because he snarled, adjusted his position, and side-stepped hurriedly. He lost his balance, and was on one foot when Steve's plaster-of-Paris club landed just above his right ear. The saw, on a dead-man's switch, went off.

There was a crack as Stook's neck broke, and he flew back against the bench sideways, smashing his head on its wooden top as he did so. His skull cracked open like an egg. Inside it, there were things Steve had not expected to see. There was no blood or brain. Instead, Stook's head was stuffed with what looked like dust, ashes, and blackened, shapeless objects that could have been lumps of charcoal, the remains of an ancient fire that had long ago gone out.

Steve stood motionless over his employer's body, staring incredulously as the contents of the man's head crumbled in a miniature landslide onto the surface of water splashing round it from the nearby hose. The ash-like substance floated swiftly away in dark, swirling streaks towards the drain.

Stook's dark glasses had stayed on in the struggle, as though welded to his nose. Steve reached down to remove them.

As he bent forward, someone grasped him by the shoulder and said, "For God's sake, what have you done?"

It was Amanda's voice. Steve jerked upright and turned slowly, dreading what he was about to see. He half expected to find behind him a dismembered corpse, hastily reconstructed perhaps, and topped by a dead but talking head.

Amanda looked battered and bruised. She had a bandage round her head, and a long, stitched-up cut across her forehead. Her face, where it was visible, was dove grey, and her skin had the texture of tightly stretched shiny paper.

"You're alive," Steve said, and looked across at the lumps of flesh on the bench. "I thought that was you. I saw your clothes; the blood stains . . . ?"

"I smashed the van last night, soon after I'd dropped you at the hospital. I got hurt."

"Then who has Stook cut up?"

"The girl who used to do your job. She didn't last long. She fell into a quarry in the fog one night. She died. Stook made me bring her back. He put her in the freezer as emergency rations for the creature. He couldn't get out today so . . .

"She's still not thawed out, or there would be a lot more blood everywhere. The tools Stook used made a mess of a fresh corpse."

"Anyway, *Stook* is dead," Steve blurted tipsily, as though to reassure himself. "That animal will have died with him. And the monkeys can't hurt you if you get drunk. I've worked it all out. We're free of the lot of them."

"What do you mean, the animal will have died with him?" she said.

"Christ, you must know *that*. You *must* have realized. Stook and that creature were one and the same. Stook was a werewolf, or something of the kind. It's bloody obvious."

The girl gave Steve an agonized look that made his heart sink into his gut. She shook her head. "He was just a man, or what was left of one. As to the creature . . ."

"Oh, *come on*, Amanda. You never saw the two of them together, ever, because they were the same thing in different forms." He gestured towards the sprawling corpse with the toe of a soggy trainer. "And you can't tell me *that* is just a man. His whole body is covered with hair, and see what he's got in his head! It looks like the inside of an oven after somebody burnt the dinner. And let's take a look at his eyes . . . !"

The girl stooped and removed Stook's tinted shades.

To reveal two red but human eyes set in dark tunnels deep behind the man's brow.

"I thought his eyes would be like the creature's," Steve said. "I was sure of it."

"He couldn't stand bright light, that's all. He was a man," Amanda insisted. "An incredibly old one, but that," she pointed into Stook's now half-empty skull, "is what happens to you when you have been preserved, kept alive for a very long time."

"From the look of him, he was in his seventies at most!"

"Stook was over two hundred and fifty years old. He was born in 1741."

"I don't believe it."

She glared angrily at him and snapped, "Tell me then; what age do you think I am?"

"Late twenties. No more."

"I *was* twenty-five, when Stook first employed me."

"When was that?"

"In 1926."

Steve slapped his head with his right palm. "It hurts me to say it, Amanda, but I think you're very confused. I've noticed before. You've got a real problem."

She almost laughed. "I've got plenty of them, and so have you. Even more, now Stook is dead."

"Exactly; so he can't harm us, or make us do anything we don't want to. And like I said, if you get pissed, the monkeys . . ."

"Forget that. You may be drunk now, but you can't stay drunk forever. You'll have to sleep, and then, when you've sobered up, your monkey won't repeat the same mistake. Alcohol was something new, something it hadn't come across before. But it won't ever let you near drink again."

"Why should it bother with me, now Stook's gone? There's no one to work for. And I tell you; that creature *will* have disappeared. I *know* it."

Amanda sounded at the edge of her patience. 'What makes you think the monkeys worked for Stook? He had his own monkey. It must have got him when he was middle-aged, over two hundred years ago.

"I found out a lot about him. He was famous once, and very rich, born into a family of fabulously successful merchants. He stayed in the business, and twice went exploring in Asia, looking for rare spices, and anything else he could sell. On the first voyage, he did well. On his second trip, an expedition to Tibet and God-knows-where beyond, he must have found more than he bargained for, or it found him, because he came back with that creature and, unknown to anyone but himself, a monkey on his back.

"The animal itself was a seven day wonder. There were all manner of strange things turning up in England then, in 1783; animate and inanimate items brought back to civilization from all over the world, and Stook's companion was just another outlandish oddity among many. Nobody knew about its peculiar appetite then, or perhaps someone *did* as, shortly after his return, Stook faded from the limelight, retired to the country, and became a recluse. He vanished. And there's no record anywhere that he ever died. I'm sure of that; I've looked. So I know what I'm talking about. I know my man."

Steve frowned. The implications of what Amanda was saying were beginning to sink in. She knew what she was talking about. It all sounded true. Suddenly, she didn't seem crazy at all. And he was sobering up fast. And getting scared.

"But I thought Stook was in charge," he said. "You're telling me he was just a slave," he pointed to the bolted door at the end of the room, "to that *thing?*"

"Just like you and me; you've got there at last," said Amanda, bleakly ironic. "The creature runs the monkeys, and the monkeys run us. It's what's known as a symbiotic relationship and, from one point of view, it works almost perfectly."

"The creature's?"

"Not ours." She put a cigarette between her lips and lit it awkwardly, her lighter wavering in an unsteady hand. She smoked it quickly, in silence, while Steve absorbed what she had told him.

Then the creature in the room beyond began to howl, and Amanda's monkey gave her neck a jolt that threatened to tear her head off. She went out of the room and came back immediately, pushing a stainless steel trolley. She rolled up her sleeves and began loading hunks of Steve's predecessor onto the trolley. He watched her limping painfully about round the butcher's bench. She banged against the bag with the head in it, causing it to swing on its nail like the pendulum of some squat, cumbersome clock. He tried to find the courage to go and help her, but his mind was full of horror and a descending, impending monster headache. He was sober now, and feeling very bad. He remembered why he had always avoided drink; because he got terrible hangovers.

"Any moment now," he thought, "my monkey will wake up. It's going to feel sick too, and it will want to make me suffer. It's time to get out of here while I can. I need more drink to keep the monkey quiet while I work out what to do next."

He explained his plan to Amanda, who did not respond. Her face had twisted into a grotesque mask of pain. Blood seeped from the cut across her forehead, and her movements were jerky and uncoordinated. Steve guessed her monkey was giving her a hard time, pushing her faster than she could go in an effort to get the creature fed quickly.

He wondered if there was any way the hungry thing, locked in the room where it lived, could get itself out. He doubted it. How long would it take to starve in there? Amanda had said it had to have fresh meat four times a week. Perhaps, like certain rodents, it consumed energy very quickly! It might burn itself out in a few days.

If he and Amanda could both stay drunk for a week or more, they would have a chance. . . .

"Amanda," he shouted. "We have to get out of here *now*."

She gave no indication she had heard, and seemed to be struggling to work even faster. Most of the joints of human meat were on the trolley. Suddenly she started to wheel it to the door that let into the creature's room.

Steve ran towards her. "I'm taking you out of here," he yelled, "if I have to carry you. Your monkey will hurt you, but don't try to stop me. Try to relax."

She had her back to him when he reached her. He grabbed her right shoulder with his good arm, and attempted to pull her round. As he touched her, two small hard hands grasped the top of his jacket, and something invisible jumped from her onto him and began clambering up his chest.

At the same moment, the monkey lodged within him jerked awake. It squawked like a mad macaw inside his head. For the first time, an image of its face—savage, alien, birdlike, with a blunt but serrated-edged beak instead of jaws, and tiny, cold, furious eyes—projected onto the screen of his mind's eye.

It began to thrash and peck and kick. It hit with its fists at the back of his eyes as though it were trying to punch them out. It reached down with its back legs towards his heart to grasp it, to stop it beating.

And the one on his chest had him by the throat. It was digging its taloned fingers into the flesh, forcing his head ever further back, threatening to snap his spine.

Steve could do nothing about the two monkeys that were tearing him apart from within and without, but somehow he got his arm round Amanda's waist and lifted her off her feet. She would not, or could not, cooperate. She squirmed and twisted as he lurched towards the door with her under his right arm. She weighed next to nothing and her struggles were weak, but even so, Steve found he couldn't hold her. The monkey in his head, which seemed to be trying to back its way out through his eye sockets, was blinding him. Also, it was affecting his balance. It somehow twisted his brain like a steering wheel, so he lost all sense of direction. It got to the point where he was unable to differentiate between up and down. The room seemed like a huge sphere that he was trapped in. Then he realized he no longer had hold of Amanda, and that he was falling. He thought he had walked off the edge of a cliff. The thing in his head gave a scream of triumph.

And something hit him in the belly, like a kick from a vast boot.

And then: Nothing!

Amanda swayed back as the dismembered head in the plastic shopping bag bounced off Steve's stomach. She had snatched the bag off the nail at the end of the bench and swung it at him hard, in desperation. There was no other weapon in the room she could have used except the electric saws, and she might have killed him with them. She wanted to, *had to*, keep him alive.

As Steve doubled forward, clutching his middle, Amanda swung the head again, battering Steve's own face with it. He slumped forward like a shot deer, and landed face down in the drain near the bench. She knelt down and tugged his right shoulder up, to twist his nose and mouth up out of the water. He mustn't drown. She checked that he was still breathing, then sat down next to him in the wet.

The creature in the next room was calling for food with its harsh, crass, rook-like call.

Amanda's monkey, which had jumped back off Steve and onto her when the boy had been trying to carry her away, sent a stab of pain down her spine, to urge her to make one last effort to get up and push the trolley through to its master. But Amanda couldn't even get to her feet. She was breathless, and all her energy was spent. Her monkey, that had known and preserved her for more than sixty years, understood, and allowed her a brief respite to regain some strength.

Amanda fumbled in her pockets, found a battered packet of cigarettes, stuck one in her mouth, and lit up. She drew as much smoke as she could into her diseased, rotten lungs, exulting in the self-damage she was doing, in the knowledge that her ruined, broken body could not take much more abuse. She knew the creature and its servants, the monkeys, would keep her going as long as she was at all useful to them, or until she fell apart.

As it was, she was only just able to get around on her legs, which contained so many badly mended broken bones, souvenirs of the years she herself had spent walking the "dog." Now she was barely able to drive the van. The accident the night before had been her fault. She had been too weak and clumsy to control the vehicle. Anyone else would have been able to avoid the accident. Unfortunately, she had not been killed in the smash.

Anyway, soon, when his wrist had healed, Steve would be able to drive the van.

Then, presumably, she would not be needed. They would let her die.

The creature beyond the door croaked again impatiently.

She got to her feet, pushed Steve's unconscious body over onto its back, and flicked her cigarette end into the drain.

She looked down at the boy for a moment, then said aloud, "Congratulations, Steve, you've been promoted. You'll have to advertise to get someone to replace you. You've got Stook's job. You're the hunter now. Tomorrow, the van will be repaired, and I'll have to drive you out to look for game. The creature will need fresh meat, and heaven help you if you don't come back with some."

Briefly it occurred to her that if Steve *was* unsuccessful, she might be on the menu herself.

Then her monkey gave her mind a tweak. She pushed the meat trolley to the door, and started to open the locks.

THE GOATBOY AND THE GIANT
Garry Kilworth

British author Garry Kilworth has published more than one hundred stories, as well as several novels for adults and for children (including *Archangel, A Midsummer Nightmare* and *House of Tribes.*) He won the World Fantasy Award for "The Ragthorn" (co-written with Robert Holdstock) in 1992. Although Kilworth has spent much of his life living abroad, his family roots (part Gypsy) are in rural Essex, England—where he and his wife now live.

"The Goatboy and the Giant" is a charming original fairy tale, reprinted from the equally charming children's anthology *Fantasy Stories,* edited by Mike Ashley and published in England.

—T. W.

There was a giant, full-limbed and fabulous, sleeping in the sun. The goatboy approached him warily, standing half as high as one of the enormous feet, whose bare soles looked like the bottom of a dry riverbed. When the young man walked past the towering feet, he observed that the translucent moons of the creature's toenails gleamed like topaz and the veins just beneath the surface of his delicate skin were rivers of the palest blue.

The youth began the journey from feet to head, marveling at the paleness of the giant's body, even though it had been exposed to the fierce Turkish sun, day over day, and the abrasive sandstorms of the Turkish wilderness, night under night.

When the goatboy reached the giant's head, by way of his muscled left leg and sinewy arm, he found it to be bald. This was an old giant, one who had lost his pigtail to the passing centuries. Such ancient titans passed their final years in sleep until death came to filigree their fingers with webs and powder their pates with fine dust.

The giant's face was turned towards the goatboy and though the creature's breath swhooshed over the wasteland, raising dustclouds and whirling widdershins, he could see it wore gentle features. The next time the giant breathed in through his nose, the youth threw sand up his nostrils, in order to wake him.

The giant coughed, sat up, and rubbed his face. His eyes opened wide, then they shut tight as he gave out the most enormous sneeze, which ripped shrubs from the earth and sent them rolling like tumbleweed across the desert. Finally, the giant blinked twice and looked around him.

"What time is it?" he asked, on seeing the goatboy.

"Almost the end of the century," said the lad.

And the giant said, "I've overslept again."

He rose and stretched himself, then began digging, scooping out handfuls of desert sand each large enough to bury a house. The hole grew to a great pit whose sides kept flowing like a flood into its depths, but finally the giant reached water and bent his great head to suck the liquid into his mouth. When he had finished drinking, the giant pulled fistfuls of cactus from the ground and chewed them to mush before swallowing. He gave one tremendous belch, wiped his mouth on his arm, then smiled at the goatboy.

"That was good," he said, and then lay himself down once more.

"Wait!" cried the goatboy. "You're not going back to sleep again?"

The giant sat up and blinked.

"Well, I was thinking of it, yes. I've had food and water, so what else is there to stay awake for? Can you give me a shake if you come by here in a few decades?"

The goatboy folded his arms and shook his head. His goats milled around his legs bleating, as he contemplated one of the last giants left on the earth. In fact, he told himself, no one had seen such a creature for at least a hundred years. He himself was familiar with them only through stories told him by his grandfather, back in the old township of Yozgat. He saw in this giant the potential to fulfill his ambition.

Now, the problem with goatboys was they had too much time to daydream. Once upon a century, way back before this goatboy's time, they had to fight with lions and bears, keep wolves from descending like Assyrians on the fold, defend their herd against lost armies of ravenous Greeks. When they were not looking after the goats, they were practicing with their slingshots or cutting new staves. Goatboys of old had no time to daydream.

Since lions, bears, wolves and confused Greeks were no longer a threat, the goatboy idled his hours away wishing he was a great rock star, like Michael Jackson, who sang to the most primitive of bushmen through the medium of transistor radios. At night the goatboy would lie under heavens glistening with distant suns and think not of the wonders of the universe, but of the marvelous world beyond Turkey where a boy with something unusual to offer might become rich and famous. Goats earned him a living, but they smelled and would never lead to the kind of life a rock star followed.

"Listen," said the goatboy to the giant, "you and I could make a team. I bet you're the last living giant on the earth. People would pay a fortune just to look at you. We could become rich and famous together."

"Rich and famous," repeated the giant, using the same tremulous tones employed by the boy, "is that a good thing?"

"Is it a *good?* Why it's the *only* worthwhile ambition in this world. Once you're rich and famous you can do anything. I expect you could buy a bed to support your weight and drift to your final rest on a raft of duck down and goose feathers."

The giant patted the desert sand.

"This is pretty soft," he murmured.

"Not as soft as a mattress stuffed with feathers," replied the boy.

"Well, what do we have to do, to become rich and famous?" asked the giant. "Is it hard work?"

"Certainly not. You only earn a living by working hard, or providing the necessities of life, like food and water. To become rich you must peddle luxuries. You just find something people don't really need but *desire* above all else, then you sell to them at extortionate prices. I'm sure people would want to see *you*, because you're unusual in this day and age."

"Am I?"

"Yes, and if you like, I'll help you get your riches. I'll have to charge you, of course, being a professional giant manager is not an easy task. What do you say to something in the region of seventy percent of the gross receipts?"

The giant's brow furrowed and he hugged his knees.

"What's a receipt? How many's a gross? I don't know anything about percentages. Are they the same as fractions?"

"I'll explain all that later," said the goatboy, "but in the meantime how about it?"

"That seems fair," he said. "After all, I have no idea about how to get rich and famous and you're an expert."

"Precisely," said the goatboy.

"However," said the giant, "I have no wish to leave this pleasant spot, even for a feather bed," and he bid the goatboy farewell.

Stunned for only a moment, the youth invented a tale which only giants, the most gullible creatures on the earth, would believe. Unfortunately it is a quirk of supernature, a paradox of the cruellest kind, that whatever giants believe becomes their truth.

"What was your last job?" asked the boy, knowing full well that giants never do manual work and haven't the intellect or dexterity required for other types of employment.

The giant shook his head.

"I've never had one of those."

The goatboy opened wide his eyes in mock concern.

"You mean you've never earned anything in your life?"

"Not a penny," confirmed the giant.

"Oh, that's really sad!"

"Now why should that be?"

"Because," lied the boy, "everyone knows that Og the King of Bashan, the first giant, who walked beside Noah's Ark with his head still above water, decreed that since giants were bound to be big lazy fellows who lay around in the sun all day, those who did no work and earned nothing during their stay on earth would not be permitted to enter heaven."

"He said that?"

"Everyone knows."

The giant sat up and held his face in his great hands, looking down through his fingers at the tiny goatboy below. His eyes were like lakes with no finite depth. His brow was a furrowed field. His pink lips trembled with worry.

"I haven't earned a penny," he cried, "so I shall never get to heaven."

In believing the tale it had become the truth.

"You still have time, before you die," said the goatboy, "to redeem yourself. Follow me!"

So the giant got to his feet and carried the goatboy down to the coast, striding out across the wasteland, each stride being twenty-one miles in length. Once they reached the sea, the goatboy instructed the giant to go into the water and follow the shoreline round to Istanbul, where he hoped they would be able to start making their fortune. It was not possible for the giant to walk over the land because there were cities, towns, villages and farms scattered all over the countryside and there was a danger someone might be crushed beneath those great soles. Even so, they had to keep a sharp lookout for ships, cruising along in the shallows, and fisherfolk collecting their lobsterpots out on the mud.

When they reached Istanbul, the giant was amazed at the amount of building that had gone on while he had been away.

"This was only a village last time I was here," he said. I can't even recognize it. Are you sure this is Byzantium?"

"It was called that," said the boy, "but they changed the name to Constantinople and now it's Istanbul."

"I'd never have believed it," said the giant.

"What can I say?" replied the goatboy. "You've been a bit of a sluggard in the past."

"I suppose that's true, but I do like my sleep."

"Well, that's going to change for a while, but eventually it will be worth it. You'll have your feather bed to float to heaven on and I can start my career as a rock star with a solid financial backing. What we'll do is sound out the city's businessmen. You'll have to wait here, while I go and make some arrangements."

"All right," said the giant, who was up to his waist in harbor water, the ships circumnavigating his girth. He folded his arms, to keep his hands from doing any damage, and set himself four-square in the mud. It began to rain, something the giant had not experienced out in the desert, but he did not complain. He knew the goatboy was helping him to a better way of rest.

It drizzled for days on end and the winds were from the north, but the giant merely shivered and hugged his beautiful body with his arms, trusting that the boy would soon return and help him earn some money so that Og would let him into heaven.

The goatboy left his fabulous creature and went to the big corporations, saying he had something quite extraordinary to offer them in the way of show business. Eventually he found himself in a plush office confronted by an array of the most wealthy persons in Istanbul. He explained his proposition to them.

"What I have here is probably unique," he said. "A giant, ladies and gentleman, in an age when technology is becoming old hat. People are beginning to get bored with video games and computers and are starting to look to the past, the golden age, the antique era, the ancient civilizations. What we have here is a wonder of the old world, when fables and folk tales were live entertainment."

He paused to see how his speech was affecting his audience.

They did not appear spellbound.

In fact, someone yawned.

"Just what," rumbled one bearded moneyman, "do you propose to *do* with your giant?"

"Why," cried the goatboy, "people will pay just to look at him."

The old gentleman nodded towards the window overlooking the harbour.

"Why should they? They can see him for free. You can't miss him, can you? He's the tallest thing for miles."

"Well, we have to hide him, in a building, so that they can't see him for free," said the boy frantically, feeling that things were not working out as well as he had planned, and his millions were slipping away from him. "I mean, if they can't see him, they'll pay then, won't they?"

"It'll take years to build something to contain your giant," snapped one of the other financiers in the room, "and where would we put him in the meantime? There'll be tourists descending on Istanbul like locusts before we get him hidden from sight, which will be good for the city but not for the owners of the giant. The Japanese and Americans and Germans will all have seen him by the time we get him under cover. The British think they've got the most interesting weather in the world, and don't bother with any other wonder of nature. The Scandinavians and Russians are too phlegmatic to concern themselves with fabulous creatures. The French don't like anything they haven't discovered themselves. The Koreans would pirate holograms of him all over the world. The Swiss prefer clockwork giants about six inches high that they can sell to the toyshops. The Chinese haven't got any money and the Africans don't like to travel. The rest of Asia is too busy trying to catch up with the century. That leaves the Australians and New Zealanders, who don't amount to more than a handful of backpackers who prefer cheap boarding houses and food from the stalls in the all night markets. Need I go on? Good morning to you, young man."

And so, to his dismay, the goatboy was dismissed.

Instead of returning to the giant and reporting his failure to the creature, he went on a tour of all the major cities in Turkey, trying to drum up enough enthusiasm to take the giant on a roadshow. He wrote to the Rolling Stones, telling them the giant would make a wonderful backdrop to their next concert. He tried to call David Bowie, who might have been able to suggest some zany use for the muscled colossus. He visited local radio and TV stations and went on the air with news of his find. All ended in failure.

"Can he sing?" asked the agents. "What does he play?"

Finally, defeat bearing down on him with its distinctively heavy and lumpy form, the goatboy returned to the Istanbul harbour.

There he found that his living wonder had caught a cold from standing in the wet, in the wind and the rain, which had turned to pneumonia. The poor giant had expired, slipping down into the waters of the Bosporus and floating away on the tide out into the sea of Marmara, where he drifted finally into the Mediterranean itself. His beautiful big body was washed up on the shores of a land whose inhabitants had stopped believing in giants and they were both amazed and confounded by his presence on their beach. For a while the people took to traveling down to the coast to view his remains and have their photographs taken standing between his fingers. A famous writer came to write descriptive notes on how the drowned giant affected the local population.

In time, his great ribs were used as bridges to cross ornamental streams, his pelvis became a skateboard park for the young and agile, his spinal cord became a tunnel down which youngsters would slide, his legbones and armbones were trestles for swings, his hands and feet seats for the elderly.

There was a small charge for the use of these facilities.

GOURD

Olive Senior

Jamaican author Olive Senior has published three collections of short stories and two collections of poetry, as well as nonfiction on Caribbean culture. Her most recent books are *Discerner of Hearts* (stories) and *Gardening in the Tropics* (poetry). The following mythic poem is reprinted from *Conjunctions* #27, the bi-annual fiction journal published by Bard College.

—T. W.

g
o
g o u r d
r
d
hollowed dried
calabash humble took-took
how simple you look. But what
lies beneath that crusty exterior?
Such stories they tell! They say O packy,
in your youth (before history), as cosmic
container, you ordered divination, ritual
sounds, incantations, you were tomb, you were
womb, you were heavenly home, the birthplace of
life here on earth. Yet broken (they say) you
caused the first Flood. Indiscretion could release
from inside you again the scorpion of darkness that
once covered the world. The cosmic snake (it is said)
strains to hold you together for what chaos would ensue
if heaven and earth parted! They say there are those
who've been taught certain secrets: how to harness the
power of your magical enclosure by the ordering of sound
—a gift from orehu the spirit of water who brought the

first calabash and the stones for the ritual, who taught
how to fashion the heavenly rattle, the sacred Mbaraká,
that can summon the spirits and resound cross the abyss
—like the houngan's asson or the shaman's maraka. Yet
hollowed dried calabash, humble took-took, we've walked
far from that water, from those mystical shores. If
all we can manage is to rattle our stones, our
beads or our bones in your dried-out container,
in shak-shak or maracca, will our voices
be heard? If we dance to your rhythm,
knock-knock on your skin, will we
hear from within, no matter
how faintly, your
wholeness
resound?

hollowed
dried
calabash
humble
took-took

how simple

you look

THE PHOENIX
Isobelle Carmody

Australian writer Isobelle Carmody has published several magical novels for children including *The Obernewtyn Chronicles, Scatterlings,* and *The Gathering.* She is also a journalist and radio interviewer, and lectures around the world on creative writing, dividing her time between her home on the Great Ocean Road in Australia and travels abroad. Carmody has won the Children's Literature Peace Prize and the CBC Book of the Year Award.

"The Phoenix" is a jolting dark fantasy tale—engrossing and unforgettable. It falls on the borderline between adult and children's fiction, between fantasy and horror. It comes from Carmody's new collection of stories, *Green Monkey Dreams,* published in Australia.

—T. W. and E. D.

"Princess Ragnar?"

Ragnar turned to William and tried to smile, but her hatred was so great that it would allow no other emotion. She did not feel it as heat but as a bitter burning cold flowing through her, freezing her to ice, to stone. Driven by such a rage, a princess might unleash her armies and destroy an entire city to the last person. She might command the end of a world.

"Princess? Are you cold?"

She barely heard William's words, but when she shook her head, before he turned away to keep watch for Torvald, she saw in his pale-green eyes the same blaze of devotion that had flared three summers past when he had pledged himself to her.

Her mind threw up an image of him making that pledge, the words as formal as the words from an old Bible.

"Princess, I, William, am sent by the Gods to serve and guard you in this strange shadowland, until we are shown the way home by such signs and portents as I am trained to recognize. I pledge my life to you."

Twelve years old, with one slightly turned eye, a broken front tooth, ripped shorts and a too large cast-off T-shirt advising the world to "Be happy," and here he was pledging his life to her.

He had a collection of T-shirts abandoned by the drug addicts and drunks who came to stay at Goodhaven to dry out. The weird thing was that those T-shirts always seemed to have something pertinent to say about what was happening when he wore them, and in the end, she came to see them as signs, just as William saw as signs a certain bird flying overhead, or a particular rock resting against another.

Hearing his absurd pledge, she had experienced a fleeting instinct to laugh out of nervousness or incredulity. That would have changed everything. Life could be like that sometimes—hinging on one tiny little thing or other. But she hadn't laughed because underneath the urchin dirt and crazy talk, she had seen a reflection of her own aching loneliness.

"Are you sure you have the right person?" she had said, instead of, "Are you crazy?" But it was close. They even started with the same words.

"You are Princess Ragnar," he had said.

Those words sent a shiver up her spine, even after so much time. Because she had never seen him before. Then there was *how* he said her name—as if he was handling something infinitely precious. No one had said it like that before in her whole life except maybe her mother, though perhaps that was just a memory born of wishful thinking.

"How do you know my name?" she had demanded.

He had grinned, flashing the chipped tooth that she later learned had been broken when he'd happened on a drying-out drunk who had managed to drink a whole cupboard-full of cough medicine. The Goodhaven people stocked up on everything because they thought the world was going to end any day now and they wanted to be prepared. Though how a hundred tins of baked beans and a cupboard full of cough medicine was supposed to help you survive the end of the world was beyond Ragnar. The drunk's back-handed slap had left William with the chip in his tooth that his aunt called God's will. In fact, that was what William had told her when she'd asked what had happened to his front tooth.

"It was God's will." As if God had slapped him one.

The chip was wide enough to make him talk with a lisp, but since he could still use his teeth, fixing it would have been cosmetic and his aunt and uncle eschewed worldly vanity, believing it to be one of the things that brought most of the human debris they called Poor Lost Souls to Goodhaven in the first place.

Besides that, William was simple and it would hardly matter to the poor addled child that he had a chipped tooth when his brain was all but cracked clear through.

Those words came to her in William's mimicked version of his aunt's high-pitched folksy voice. That was how she explained him away to occasional government visitors and fund-raising groups concerned about a child being exposed to the sort of people who came to Goodhaven.

"Oh, he has seen much worse than anything he could ever see here," William had mimicked his aunt. "Why his brain cracked under the pressure of seeing his mother and father murdered before his very eyes. He was there all alone a good two years before someone found him wandering around mad as a hatter."

William had been looked after by the same people who had murdered his parents, though no one could figure out why they would bother. Maybe it was because he was so young. He was four when his relatives had agreed to take him on.

He was no simpleton. Ragnar had seen that right off, but he was sure as heck one strange piece of toast, and no wonder. Seeing your parents murdered would be enough to make anyone a little crazy.

Of course, she had known nothing at all about that the first time they'd met.

She had been swimming and had come out of the water wearing nothing but her long red hair. There was never anyone around during the week and she had been pretending to be the mermaid; trying to make up her mind whether the love of a prince would be worth the loss of her voice and the feeling that she was standing on knives every time she took a step. Especially when her father said love did not last, or else why had her mother run off and left them?

She was trying to figure out where she had left her clothes when William walked out carrying them. He had his eyes on her face and he did not once let them drop. He just held out her clothes and she snatched them up and pulled on jeans and a sloppy paint-stained windcheater, her face flaming.

Then he had suddenly fallen to his knees.

Her embarrassment evaporated since she was clothed now and anyway the boy clearly had no prurient interest in her nakedness.

She put her hands on her hips. "Who the heck are you?"

"The gods have seen that you are lonely, Ragnar, and so I was sent to be your companion."

Anything she would have said was obliterated by astonishment. For she was lonely beyond imagining. Her father had forbidden her to let anyone at her school know they were living illegally in the boathouse, which made it easier to have no friends than to make up believable lies. They had been squatting since the owner had moved to America, having told her father he could use the boathouse for his dinghy if he kept an eye on it. Her father took the dinghy out maybe three times a year and she was always convinced he would drown because he never took any of the things you were supposed to take like flares or lifejackets. He didn't have to fish since his Sickness Benefit paid for food and cask wine. He worried her sick when he went out, and she could never understand why he did it. It wasn't even as if he ever caught anything big enough to be legal or good eating.

Once, while they were keeping vigil for his return, William told Ragnar matter-of-factly that her father fished because he remembered when he had been a real fisherman.

"He was never a real fisherman," Ragnar snorted. "He was some sort of mechanic."

"In his past life he was a fisherman and he slept with one of the goddesses.

She took you away with her, but because you were part human, the gods made her send you here. As a punishment to her because she broke the rules."

"Seems to me the gods and goddesses do nothing but break rules. Look at Prometheus and Pandora."

"They are lesser gods," William had said with a lofty kind of pride. "My princess comes from an older and greater race of gods. And if he was not a fisherman once, then why does your father fish?"

As usual his habit of suddenly circling and darting back on an argument left her gasping like a fish out of water. The thing was she did not know why her father had brought them here to this spit of flat sand between an industrial wasteland and a whole lot of salt pans and wetlands. Nor why he fished.

Ragnar had known no other life. Not really. She sometimes remembered a mother who did not seem to have much to do with the mother her father muttered and cursed about. William had an answer for that as well. He thought that she was remembering not her mother in this life, but the goddess mother of her other life.

"Then how come my father remembers me being born?"

"The gods can make anyone remember or forget. They made your father remember his wife having a child—and maybe she did have a baby." His eyes flashed as he warmed to this theme. "Maybe she took their real child with her and the gods just stepped in and put you here, so he would think she left his baby. So he would take care of you and keep you out of the eye of the world."

William was as worried about the eye of the world as her father. William, because of his uncle and aunt's fear of negative publicity that might affect Goodhaven's funding sources, and her father because he did not want to be thrown out of the boathouse, or have Social Security people poking around. Sending her to school worried him because if he didn't They would be after him—They being the Government—but if he did, people would find out where they were living. He had solved the problem by sending her to school, but telling her that if anyone figured out where she lived, she would be taken away to an orphanage and locked up. That had frightened her so much she said so little at school that people thought there was something wrong with her. Fortunately integration policies, and her own consistently normal marks, kept them from trying to send Ragnar to a special school of the sort William told such horror stories about. His relatives had tried a whole lot of schools before he had managed to convince them he was too far gone for school.

"I like people thinking I'm crazy. It's easier, and I know what I am inside so what they think doesn't matter."

Of course as she grew older, Ragnar's fear of the authorities was diluted to wary caution, but her father sealed her silence. He said they would never allow her to take Greedy away with them.

Greedy was a crippled seagull William had rescued and given to her as a gift, saying that in the realm of the gods, the seagull was her personal hawk. It was so devoted, William told her solemnly, that it had followed her to this world, but in order to come to her the gods offered the proud hawk only the form of a lowly scavenger. He told her the hawk's real name was Thorn, but secretly she nicknamed it Greedy, because it was.

"Thorn is hungry because in his previous life he was starved by the gods to try to make him forswear his allegiance to you," William had told her reproachfully the one time he heard her calling the bird Greedy.

William had an answer for everything. Truth was, he was a lot smarter than most of the kids and the teachers at school, at least in ways that mattered. He did not read, but he could tell stories better than any book, and he had built around the two of them a fantasy that was far more wonderful than life could ever offer. In the years since they had first met, he had been her companion and everything else she had wanted—slave, brother, confidant, friend. He had shed blood to seal his pledge though she had not wanted or asked for it, and he had promised to serve and obey, honor and protect her—with his own life if necessary.

He had watched her for a long time to make sure she was truly the one, he told her earnestly one time as they were baking mussels in a battered tin pot of salty water on a small fire. The water had to be salty or the crustaceans tasted vile.

"But how did you know in the end?"

He shrugged. "I found a sign and I knew—a ring of dead jellyfish on the beach in the shape of a crown."

It was easier to obey William's odd instructions than to try to understand why he thought a toilet brush in seaweed was a warning that you were being discussed, or how walking a certain way round an overturned shell could avert an accident. It was very rare that he wanted her to do anything troublesome, though once when he said they must walk along the railway lines for so many paces, she worried a lot because, if they were caught, they would end up in the children's court. But they had done it and William claimed that was what had stopped a council van coming down to Cheetham Point to check out rumors of people living there.

Did he manipulate events as he claimed? Mostly, Ragnar figured not, but it never hurt to take out insurance. Because there were many times when William knew things he could not know. Sometimes she would be going to catch the train and he would tell her that she would miss it, so he would wait for her in their secret place. And the train mysteriously would not come. Other times he would tell her it was going to rain when she was dressed lightly and, sure enough, by the end of the day, it would be pelting down.

Coincidence? Maybe. Ragnar did not believe she was a princess in exile. Not really. Though she did feel as if she had been born for more than this bit of barren land. One part of her looked at her father when he was drunk with his mouth open, a thin ribbon of drool falling from his lips, and knew she had been born of nobler blood. Sometimes when she was sitting in class, knowing the answers, but never speaking out because being too smart could bring you into the Public Eye even more than being too dumb, a little voice would whisper to her that she was special and destined for greatness, just as William said.

Sometimes when she and William sat at the very end of the land watching the sun fall in a haze of gold into the ocean, he would ask her if she felt the magic, and she would nod, lifting her chin and holding back her shoulders as regally as a princess, proud even in exile. Greedy would shiver on her lap, as if for a moment remembering his life as a mighty hawk hunter, bane of mice and small birds and even of cats.

It had been through such a sunset of molten gold that Torvald came to them. The day was uncommonly still, and a sea-mist was shot with bloody gold and red lights as the sun fell. Ragnar saw something shimmer and all at once could see a young man with golden hair flying in the wind, and a proud handsome face, coming on his boat out of the mist, and her lips had parted in breathless wonder. Then she heard the whining stutter of the speedboat engine and realized he was coming across the water to Cheetham Point from the Ridhurst Grammar School jetty.

She felt foolish the way she always did when she entered a little too deeply into William's world of myth and magic. Just the same, sitting in the back of the boat with one hand lightly on the tiller, long pale hair about his face, there was no denying he looked marvelous. She wished she could see what color his eyes were, for her daydreams, but of course he would turn back before he reached the Point because of the shallows.

Only he did not turn. For a moment she thought he had miraculously managed to sail over the sandbar even with the tide out, but then he had come suddenly to a grinding halt, beached until the tide rose again. After making some useless attempts to get the boat off the sandbar, he looked back, obviously concluding it was too far to swim. Then he turned to face the Point.

I will always see him that way, Ragnar thought. Him turning that first time to face them, so tall and handsome, the sky all gold and glorious behind him.

"We must help him, Princess," William had announced.

Ragnar had been shocked, because one of the rules was that they should never seek out the Public Eye or any other eye. During the holidays when boat people came, they stayed away from the Point during the day, mostly within Goodhaven grounds. And they always stayed away from the rich spoiled Ridhurst students who would do anything for a dare, including tormenting a small boy.

"He's from Ridhurst," Ragnar hissed, remembering how William had shivered when he told her how a group of students had ridden around and around him in ever smaller circles on their roaring motorbikes.

"He is one of us," William had announced, though he looked paler than usual.

Ragnar stared at him incredulously. "One of us?"

"Aye, Princess. He is the golden-haired voyager from over the sea whom you are destined to wed. His coming is a sign that the way will open soon for us to return. We must save him because there will only be one chance for all of us to cross."

"William, he is not from over the sea. He came from Ridhurst. . . ."

But he was running across the sand and shouting to the young man to wait and that they would help him. The handsome stranger waved back, and sat on the edge of the boat.

"We'll get the Longboat," William cried out over his shoulder.

The Longboat was a slim wooden boat to which its owner hitched his larger boat when he came to the Point each Christmas. It was bolted to a post outside the shed that housed his bigger boat, but William discovered that with a bit of wriggling you could get the chain off in spite of the lock. They often used the Longboat to fish or to go for short jaunts, but never in broad daylight.

"William, stop, I . . . order you to stop!" She only used her Royal prerogative to stop William from his most dangerous schemes, because it did not seem fair to take advantage of his illusions that way. But on this occasion he seemed not to hear her. He was wriggling the chain out from its bolt and dragging it towards the water, straining his skinny arms.

"Oh, for heaven's sake!" Ragnar muttered, then bent and helped him. The sooner they got this over with the better. They rowed out to the sandbar and up close Torvald was as handsome as he had been from the distance. His teeth were perfectly straight and white and his eyes as blue as the sweetest summer sky. He was a picture-book prince, which may have explained what happened next.

"Hi," he said, smiling right into her eyes. "Thanks for the rescue. No one warned me about the sandbar."

Ragnar had melted at the sound of his voice, deep and soft, with just a touch of an accent. But she managed to say, "It wasn't me . . . I mean, William got the boat."

"I meant thanks to you both. William, is it?" He held his hand out but William bowed.

"I am William and I am the pledged protector of Princess Ragnar in her exile."

Ragnar could have died. Her face felt as if it had third-degree burns.

"Really? Well, I am Torvald the Curious from over the seas," the stranger answered and bowed low to William and then to Ragnar. "I am pleased to make the acquaintance of the beauteous Princess Ragnar."

William gave Ragnar an "I told you so" look as Torvald the Curious stood up and smiled at them both.

"Come aboard our humble craft, my Lord Torvald, and we will bear you to shore and give you what humble sustenance we can offer in this place of exile until the waters allow you to depart," William said.

Torvald's smile deepened and without further ado, he gave their boat a push to free it from the sandbar, and climbed in. William rowed them back and Ragnar looked steadfastly towards the shore, refusing to look at Torvald whom she could see staring at her out of the corner of her eye.

The humble sustenance turned out to be her leftover school lunch and a rather shriveled-looking trio of apples that was William's offering. Torvald lowered himself to sit in the sand, stretching his long legs out in front of him, and when William solemnly offered him their picnic, he smiled a little and chose one of the apples.

"It looks as if you were expecting me. And this . . ." He held up the apple. "This seems appropriate, somehow."

"Truly," William agreed. "Eve offered the apple of knowledge to Adam, and Aphrodite offered an apple to Paris."

"Ah, but he should have taken the apple from the Goddess of Wisdom, shouldn't he?"

"Perhaps," William said. "But some things are cast in the stars and love is one of them. It will have its way, no matter what tragedy it calls in its wake."

Torvald's smile faded properly for the first time then. Perhaps that was the moment he realized this was no game to William. His eyes shifted to Ragnar questioningly, and she forced herself to meet his gaze with no expression, because to show what she felt would be to betray William, and to act as if she believed what William believed would be to betray herself. Also if she started talking, this golden-haired young man would begin to ask questions.

Torvald's expression of puzzlement grew more intense. "So . . . you are both in exile?" he said at last.

"Truly your name fits you," William said.

Torvald looked confused until he remembered the name he had announced himself with. "I am afraid I am curious to the point of rudeness. My father said I will never make a politician unless I learn to tell lies sweetly."

"No," William said. "You will not be a politician."

Torvald frowned at him. "You think not?"

William shook his head. "Politicians cannot afford to be curious. You will always be a seeker of the only true beauty which is truth."

Torvald blinked, much as Ragnar thought she must have done the first time she encountered William the Sage. That, he told her, had been his role before he was sent to her. He had been a seer of things to come. A Merlin.

"You are a strange boy," Torvald said. "Do you live here?"

Ragnar plunged in hurriedly. "No. We just came down for the day. We live over in Calway." That ought to put him off since it was a Housing Commission area.

"That is a long way. Did you walk?"

"We came around the beach." She pointed vaguely to the route she walked after catching the train from town on school days.

"Past Ridhurst?"

She nodded. "You go there, don't you?" Better to turn the talk back on him. She found that a useful way of dealing with curiosity.

But he just nodded and said, "You are brother and sister?"

"I am the servant and protector of Princess Ragnar," William said calmly.

Ragnar wanted to strangle him. "We're friends," she said.

"I have that honor also," William agreed.

Torvald looked from one of them to the other.

"Your father is a politician?" Ragnar asked, somewhat desperately.

"He is a politician of sorts. A diplomat." His eyes crinkled deliciously into a smile again. "He lies for his country rather than for a political party." Now his eyes were on William and they were serious. "But why did you say I will not be a politician? It is what my father wishes and I am not averse to the idea. He sent me here so that I will make important connections for the future. The sons and daughters of many influential people come to Ridhurst but it seems to me they worry about cricket and parties and the right clothes more than important matters. But perhaps I misjudge them as trivial and shallow because I arrived only last week. When I know them better, things might be different."

"Maybe," Ragnar said, thinking of the young women in their pale uniforms lifting their brows at her high school uniform when she got off the bus at their stop. The trouble was it was the closest stop to home, and even then it took a good half hour to walk round the beach to Cheetham Point.

Somehow, she had managed to get him talking about his father the diplomat and his appointment to Australia. His father was in Canberra but he had decided to send Torvald to the highly recommended Ridhurst as a boarder, at least until his mother, a doctor, followed a year later.

Ragnar was relieved when William announced suddenly that they must go back out or the Ridhurst boat would float free of the sandbank without him.

The trip back was conducted in relative silence, but as Torvald climbed out of the boat, he smiled at them both. "I thank you again for saving me from sitting like a fool in the boat until now. No doubt that is what was intended by the students who suggested I might enjoy a boat ride across to Cheetham Point."

"It was our pleasure to help you thwart your tormentors, Lord Torvald. Farewell."

"Perhaps we will meet again?" Torvald's eyes shifted to Ragnar and she felt the blood surge in her cheeks.

"I don't think so," she said. "Come on, William."

"As you will, my princess."

Ragnar cringed.

She thought that would be the end of that, but Torvald proved true to his name. He waited on the path a number of days and even wandered around Calway in the hope of bumping into his two off-beat rescuers. She, having some inkling perhaps, had gone a roundabout way through the wetlands to avoid the walk by the school, but one afternoon came home to see Torvald and William deep in conversation in the dunes near the boathouses.

Her heart lurched in sick fear.

"Princess Ragnar," Torvald said, getting to his feet.

Ragnar's fright was swamped with rage at the thought he was mocking William.

"What are you doing here?" she snarled.

William looked worried. "It is well, Princess. Truly. He will bring you no harm. He is your . . ."

"What do you want?" Ragnar demanded, cutting off whatever William would have said for fear he would start talking about future weddings.

"I am Torvald the Curious."

Ragnar did not know what to say in the face of that, especially with William sitting there beside her looking stricken. She calmed herself because maybe he had not said anything to this Ridhurst student about where they lived. Though it must look queer for them to come down here again like this.

"My father owns a boathouse and we were planning to camp out for the night, but it's not allowed. I'm sorry if I snapped at you."

"William is right. I mean no harm to you, Princess Ragnar."

"Don't call me that!"

"Being noble-born you may address the princess by her name if she is willing," William interpreted.

Ragnar sat down, speechless.

"Then I shall call you Ragnar and you will call me Torvald, or Tor. I prefer the latter."

"Thor . . ." William muttered.

Oh great, Ragnar thought. She glared at Torvald and asked William to leave them alone for a moment.

He rose at once, saying he would look for Thorn.

"Thorn?" Torvald asked.

"A crippled seagull that William thinks is a reincarnated hawk. Just like he thinks I'm a princess and you're some sort of lord," she said angrily. "What are you doing here sucking up to him and pretending to believe what he says? Are you going to write a paper for Ridhurst on the local feral kid?"

"William is a very interesting boy. I think he can see into the future sometimes. It's often the way with those society deems to be mad or simple. They see what most people do not. You are angry because you fear I will harm him, but I am not a student with a motorcycle and no brains or compassion." Torvald's voice was mild and serious.

"He told you about that?"

"He told me many things, and he was right when he said I will not harm either of you."

Ragnar was frightened again. "What did he tell you about me?"

"Nothing that I would ever use to harm you. I swear it on the honor of Torvald the Curious."

"Don't mock him!"

"I do not mock. You mistake me. I have honor and I have sworn by it. And who is to say that William is not right?"

"What?"

"He says we are destined for one another, and that my soul was the soul of a god who loved you, and has followed you into exile."

Ragnar's face was burning. "You don't love me."

He did not answer for a long moment, but only let his eyes hold hers. Then he said, "How do you know I did not fall in love with you the first moment I saw you coming towards me in that little boat, your red hair gleaming like molten copper and your face as fair as any goddess's? How do you know that the moment I saw you all the hungers and longings of my life were not answered?"

Oh, his words were as beautiful as his face, and they had gone through her defenses like a hot knife through butter. And in those months that followed she had come to love him body and soul; she had come to believe that William saw a different reality and in it, she was truly a princess and Tor her destined love.

And then two nights past, she was on the train dozing, catching the late train home from school because she was rehearsing for a school play in which she was one of the King of Siam's lesser wives. She woke out of a deep sleep to hear Tor's beloved voice, and for a moment she reveled in the sweetness of it, until she realized she was not dreaming and his words were anything but sweet.

"I am telling you, Rosco, you or any of your friends mess this up for me and

I will throttle you. I have a sweet set-up for myself and that red-haired peach is ripe and ready to drop into my hands. I gave her romance with a capital R and she ate it up along with her ferrety little friend."

"Should've run right over the gruesome little creep, cursing us, and two days later I broke my arm and Tristam fell over and slipped a disc."

"Yes, well, I think William the Wacko loves me enough to kill for me. He thinks I am some sort of king which means he has class even if his brains are scrambled."

"Just so long as you're not getting soft on them. If it wasn't for you playing the girl out, I would've reported the soak of a father for living in the sheds weeks back."

"Idiot." Tor's voice held a serrated edge of scorn Ragnar had never heard before. "I said the girl pleased me. I did not say I would introduce her to my parents or bring her to a school dance. She is a pig, but I prefer her in her shack where I can get at her—until I am bored. After that you may have what revenge you want on the boy."

"After you finish shacking up with the Pig Princess, eh? Ha ha ha."

Torvald had laughed too. Hard cruel laughter from a Torvald she had been too blind to see. Ragnar sat there in her corner as the train pulled up, praying they would not spot her. She stayed on until the East Potter stop, and then walked the seven kilometers back along the highway to the Cheetham Point turnoff, driven by the viciousness of her self reproaches and taunting echoes of Torvald's words.

"*I loved you the first moment I saw you. . . .*"

"*She is a pig but I prefer her in her shack where I can get at her. . . .*"

"*I will never harm you. . . .*"

"*I would not introduce her to my parents. . . .*"

She might not have told William, but he was waiting for her in a T-shirt that said "Shit Happens." It does, she thought, savage and half-mad with despair. She let William encircle her with his thin hard arms, and told him everything. And when there were no more tears, and the ice had begun to form over her emotions, she looked up into his face and found his pale eyes curiously blank.

"He proved too weak to withstand the darkness of this world and we should leave him to it. That would be the greatest torment for such as he," William said distantly. "Yet he is one of us and he must be punished for a betrayal that must make the gods weep when they learn of it. As they will when we return."

"Return?"

William nodded. "It is time. Two nights from now when the sun sets, a way will open to the realm of the old gods by their grace. This once and once only. I have dreamed it and I have read the signs. If we turn from it, we will be trapped here forever in this land of cruelty and darkness."

Ragnar had been too distraught to really listen. All she understood was that William had a plan that would punish Torvald for his seduction and betrayal.

"What do you want me to do?"

William asked her to send Torvald a message to come over the water to them on Sunday afternoon. It was Friday, and normally he would not come on weekends for fear he would be spotted and followed by Ridhurst students who might discover the truth. Or so he had told her, she thought bitterly. William told her to write that the tide would be high enough for him to negotiate the sandbar in the Ridhurst dinghy.

Coldly Ragnar wrote the note and slipped it into the internal mailbox in Ridhurst after dark while her father snored in his bed. She had not known what William planned then or now. She didn't care as long as Torvald suffered.

"He comes," William breathed.

Ragnar squinted through a rising sea-mist and saw Torvald launch the heavy school boat. She sat, stiff-backed and still as a statue as the boat came over the water and William ran to meet him and bring him back to where a picnic feast was laid out.

"Ragnar, my love," Tor said and bowed as he always did. But now Ragnar saw the gallant gesture for the mockery it had always been and her hatred weighed in her stomach, heavy as a stone.

"Tor." She forced her lips to shape a smile but there must have been something wrong in it, because instead of smiling back, Torvald frowned questioningly at her. He would not ask aloud what was wrong though, because of William. He would wait as always until William withdrew and they could speak freely.

Ragnar bent her head to hide the rage bubbling within her and stroked Greedy with fingers that trembled. He would not settle—no doubt he sensed the turmoil in her.

"Now we shall drink a toast, my lord, for this very night the way opens to the realm of the gods from whence we all came," William said, and passed a chipped enamel mug to Torvald.

"What?" Torvald asked.

"Drink," William said and handed a plastic mug to Ragnar, who was staring at Torvald with such longing and loathing that her soul felt as if it were curdling in her breast.

"Tonight we drink to the joy of William the Sage, who returns to the realm of the gods where he is an honored Merlin." William drank and, like an automaton, so did Ragnar. Torvald shrugged and drank.

William spoke again with an almost hypnotic solemnity, holding up his own jam jar as if it were a jeweled goblet. "Tonight we drink to Thorn the mighty hunter as he returns to his airy realms. . . ." He drank again and so did Ragnar and Torvald.

"Tonight the Princess in Exile returns to claim her kingdom. . . ."

Ragnar drank her father's cheap red wine, and found her head spinning because she had barely eaten for the last two days. But Torvald had not taken another drink.

"You are leaving?" he asked worriedly. "Would you go without me?"

"I am not finished, my lord," William said sternly. "We drink the bitter dregs to you for a betrayal that will sunder you forever from the princess. We might have let that be torment enough, were you a creature of this dark world."

But you are of the golden realms and so your treachery is too deep for us to let you live—even here in this shadow world."

"What?" Torvald asked, but his words slurred so badly they could barely understand. "Princess Ragnar?"

Ragnar's confusion over William's words dissolved in a boiling lava of bitter despair. "Don't you mean Pig, Tor? Don't you mean Ragnar the Pig whom you would never introduce to your parents or bring to a dance?"

His eyes widened in shock. "But, Ragnar . . ." His eyes clouded and he fell forward, catching himself on one hand. He stared at the spilled wine seeping into the pale sand. "The . . . drink?"

"Not poison but enough tranquilizer from the Goodhaven store to kill a horse, or a lord who betrayed his true land and his deepest love," William said sadly.

Fear flowed over the handsome features, then acceptance. "William . . . I do not blame you for this." He looked at Ragnar. "I was trying to divert Roscoe and his friends from reporting your father when I spoke . . . as I did on the train. They would . . . never be held back by compassion or . . . honor, so there was no point in speaking of such things to them . . . had . . . had to . . . to play their game." He coughed and fell forward onto his elbow, twisting his head so that he could look into Ragnar's horrified eyes.

"Had to play . . . a cruel game they could understand and sympathize with. Even admire. I . . . did not want to tell you the truth until I had thought of a . . . solution. You see, in a way, I did betray you. They . . . they followed me, you see. . . ."

"Torvald!" Ragnar screamed and gathered him into her arms, her terror too deep for words. Surely William had been joking. Surely he had only been trying to frighten Torvald.

"I should have told you the truth sooner . . . my love. Shouldn't have tried . . . being a hero. . . ."

His eyes fell closed. Ragnar shook him and knelt to press her head to his chest. She could find no heartbeat nor breath in him. She tried mouth to mouth resuscitation, letting herself think of nothing but the rhythm of breathing and pushing on his chest. How long she tried she could not have said but when William's hand fell on her shoulder and she sat up, her head spun.

"Bring him to the boat, Princess. They will be able to revive him perhaps in the sunlit realm of the old gods where all things are possible."

Ragnar stared at him hopelessly, thinking that she had let one of the two people she loved in all the world kill the other. It was not poor battered William's fault, for he had never known any sort of normality. It was her fault Tor was dead, her fault William was a murderer.

"I have made you a murderer. . . ." she whispered, stricken.

But William's eyes met hers steadily. "Tor's is not the first death at my hand in this dark world."

"What?" Ragnar whispered.

"I killed my father. He was trying to scalp my mother when I woke. So I took the gun he had thrown down and I killed him."

All the horror of the night coalesced around the bleak dreadful image of a small boy forced to shoot his father, and Ragnar's heart swelled with pity.

"Ah, William . . ." she whispered, blinded by tears. "What are we going to do?"

He reached out and took her hand in a surprisingly strong grip. "I have never lied to you, Princess. We belong to a world where there is hope and this is a world where there is none. Only come now, and help me get Lord Torvald's body into the longboat."

Ragnar stumbled to her feet and took Torvald's feet as William instructed. She did not know or care what he wanted to do. She had brought him to murder. Now she supposed they would dispose of the body.

The body. They half-dragged Tor over to the side of the Longboat which was anchored close to the water and, straining and pushing, heaved him over the edge. Ragnar felt sick at the thumping sound his body made as it landed in the bottom of the boat. She climbed in beside him, gagging at a queer acrid smell as she lifted Torvald's golden head onto her knees.

"Thorn!" William called, and Ragnar looked up in time to see the seagull stagger hippity-hop over the sand to his feet with a creaking caw of delight. He scooped the bird up and put it in the boat and then pushed it off into the water and climbed in beside them. Ragnar stared up at him as he lifted a plastic bottle from the bottom of the boat and tipped what looked like water over Torvald's unconscious form. Greedy squawked as he was drenched, and the smell was intensified as William sprinkled it over Ragnar's legs and dress.

"What is it?"

"It is the test," William said, emptying the last of the liquid over himself and the boat.

Ragnar watched him throw the bottle into the water and rummage in his pockets, before withdrawing something. "A test?" she asked dully.

William lit a match that flamed the color of the clouds on the horizon all shot through with the bloody brightness of the sun's death, and smiled at her.

"Do not be afraid, Princess. It is the last test of courage required by the gods—to know that we are worthy to dwell in their realm."

"William . . ." The clouds in Ragnar's brain dissolved as the match fell onto Torvald's body. Flame made a feast of him, but he did not move because he was beyond pain.

She watched the flames play over him and William came to sit beside her. He took her hand, sticky with tears and petrol, in his own thin strong fingers and kissed it reverently.

"What comes will be a moment of pain before the gods pluck us from the crucible." He looked down at Torvald. "Love was first born where we journey, Princess. Hold fast to that, for all love in this world is but the palest shadow of it. Where we go, love has magical properties and there may be a way to bring him back."

"We will die. . . ."

"No. It only seems so, else there would be no testing. But hold fast, Ragnar, for you are a princess and the gods are watching."

Ragnar wondered if she was mad but as the flames tasted the petrol on her dress and licked along the hem almost teasingly, she felt a surge of hope, for it seemed to her she could hear the brassy call of a horn, peeling out an eldritch welcome for a long-lost princess.

She stroked Torvald's face as flame licked flesh, and steeled herself not to scream, for she was a princess among the gods, and she was bringing her beloved home.

As flame rose around them like a winding sheet, Thorn the hunter lifted himself on crippled wings and flew.

CARIBE MÁGICO
Gabriel García Márquez

Nobel Prize–winning author Gabriel García Márquez is considered by many (myself included) to be the world's foremost writer of magic realist fiction. His enchanted, incisive, compassionate portrayals of life in Latin America have influenced a whole generation of younger writers throughout the world. Márquez has published many novels, story collections, and nonfiction works, including *One Hundred Years of Solitude*, *Love in the Time of Cholera*, *The General in His Labyrinth*, and *Of Love and Other Dreams*—all books no fantasy reader should miss. Born in Colombia, the author now lives in Mexico City and Bogotá.

The following little piece speaks quietly of the magic one encounters in the simpest details of life. It comes from *Conjunctions #27: The Archipelago, New Caribbean Writing*.

—T. W.

—Translated from Spanish by Edith Grossman

Surinam—as few in the world know—is an independent nation on the Caribbean, a Dutch colony until a few years ago. It has 163,820 square kilometers of territory and a little over 384,000 inhabitants of many backgrounds: East Indians, local Indians, Indonesians, Africans, Chinese and Europeans. Its capital, Paramaribo (in Spanish we pronounce it with the accent on the "i," while the natives stress the third "a"), is a dismal, clamorous city, its spirit more Asian than American, where four languages and numerous indigenous dialects are spoken in addition to the official language, Dutch. Six religions—Hinduism, Catholicism, Islam and the Moravian, Dutch Reform and Lutheran churches—have their adherents. At the moment Surinam is ruled by a regime of young military men about whom very little is known, even in neighboring countries, and chances are no one would pay attention to the place if not for the fact that once a week it is a scheduled stop for a Dutch airline that flies from Amsterdam to Caracas.

I've known about Surinam ever since I was very young, not because of Surinam itself (in those days it was called Dutch Guiana) but because it bordered French Guiana, whose capital, Cayenne, had once been the site of the infamous penal colony known in life and in death as Devil's Island. The few who managed to escape that hell—and they could as easily have been brutal criminals as political idealists—fled to the many islands of the Antilles to wait until they could return to Europe, or else changed their names and settled in Venezuela and along the Caribbean coast of Colombia. The most famous of these was Henri Charrier, author of *Papillon,* who prospered in Caracas as a promoter of restaurants and other, shadier enterprises, and who died a few years ago on the crest of an ephemeral literary glory as merited as it was undeserved. The glory, in fact, should have gone to another French fugitive, René Belbenoit, who described the horrors of Devil's Island long before *Papillon,* though today he has no place in any nation's literature and his name cannot be found in encyclopedias. Belbenoit had been a journalist in France before he was sentenced to life in prison for a crime no contemporary reporter has been able to discover; he found refuge in the United States, where he continued to practice his profession until he died at an honorable old age.

Other fugitives came to the Colombian town on the Caribbean coast where I was born, during the time of the "banana fever," when cigars were lit not with matches but with five peso bills. A few assimilated and became very respectable citizens who were distinguished by their heavy accents and hermetic pasts. One, Roger Chantal, whose only trade when he arrived was pulling teeth without anesthetic, mysteriously became a millionaire overnight. He celebrated with a Babylonian fiesta (in an improbable town that had little reason to envy Babylon), drank until he could no longer stand and shouted in his jubilant collapse: *Je suis l'homme le plus riche du monde.* In his delirium he displayed philanthropic qualities no one had seen in him before, and donated to the church a life-size plaster saint that was enthroned with a three-day bacchanalia. On an ordinary Tuesday three secret agents arrived on the eleven o'clock train and headed straight for his house. Chantal was not there, but the agents made a meticulous search in the presence of his native-born wife, who offered no resistance until they attempted to open the enormous armoire in the bedroom. That was when the agents smashed the mirrors and found more than a million dollars in phony bills hidden between the glass and the wood. Roger Chantal was never heard of again. Later, the legend was born that the million counterfeit dollars had been spirited into the country inside the plaster saint, which no customs agent had been curious enough to inspect.

This all came back to me in a rush just before Christmas 1957, when I had an hour stopover in Paramaribo. In those days the airport consisted of a flattened earth runway and a palm hut whose central wooden post held a telephone like the ones in cowboy movies, whose handle had to be cranked many times, and with a great deal of force, before an operator came on the line. The heat was scorching, and the heavy, dust-choked air carried the smell of sleeping caymans that identifies the Caribbean when you come there from another world. On a stool propped against the telephone post sat a young black woman, very beautiful and well built, with a many-colored turban like the ones used by women in certain African countries. She was pregnant, almost at term, and in silence she smoked a cigarette as I've seen it done only in the Caribbean: she held the lit end inside her mouth and puffed smoke out the other end as if it were a ship's smokestack. She was the only human being in the airport.

After fifteen minutes a decrepit jeep drove up in a cloud of burning dust, and a black man in shorts and a pith helmet climbed out carrying the papers that would send the plane on its way. As he handled the documents he spoke on the phone, shouting in Dutch. Twelve hours earlier I had been on a water-front terrace in Lisbon, facing the enormous Portuguese sea, watching flocks of gulls that came into the port taverns to escape the icy wind. At that time, Europe was a worn, snow-covered land, the days had no more than five hours of light and it was impossible to imagine the reality of a world of burning sun and overripe guavas, like the one where we had just landed. And yet the only enduring image of this experience, the one I still preserve intact, was of the beautiful, imperturbable black woman whose lap held a basket of ginger root to sell to the passengers.

Now, on another trip from Lisbon to Caracas, with another stopover in Paramaribo, my first impression was that we had landed in the wrong city. Today the airport terminal is a building with bright lights, huge glass windows, sub-dued air conditioning, the odor of children's medicine and the same canned music that is repeated without mercy in all the public spaces of the world. There are as many well-stocked duty-free shops selling luxury goods as in Japan, and in the crowded cafeteria one finds a lively mix of the country's seven races, six religions and countless languages. The change seemed one of several cen-turies, not twenty years.

My teacher, Juan Bosch, the author of a monumental history of the Carib-bean, among many other works, once said in private that our magic world is similar to the unconquerable plants that come back to life beneath the con-crete, breaking through and destroying it, to bloom again in the same spot. I understood this as never before when I walked through an unexpected door in the Paramaribo airport and found an impassive row of old women, all of them black, all of them wearing many-colored turbans and all of them smoking with the lit end inside their mouths. They were selling fruit and local handicrafts, but none of them made the slightest effort to attract buyers. Only one, not the oldest, was selling ginger root. I recognized her right away. Without really knowing where to begin or what to do about my discovery, I bought a handful of roots. As I did so, I recalled her condition the first time and asked straight out how her son was. She did not even glance at me. "I had a daughter, not a son," she said, "and at the age of twenty-two she's just given me my first grandchild."

THE WITCH'S HEART

Delia Sherman

Delia Sherman is no stranger to the pages of *The Year's Best Fantasy & Horror*. She's one of the best writers working today with the "imaginary world" and "historic fantasy" forms—and she's back again this year with another strong, engrossing, beautifully crafted tale. "The Witch's Heart" comes from Neil Gaiman's *Sandman* anthology, based on the Sandman comic book series (a huge cult hit, particularly on college campuses around the nation).

Sherman is the author of two fantasy novels, *The Brazen Mirror* and *The Porcelain Dove*, numerous short stories, and a forthcoming children's time-travel novel. She is the co-editor of *Horns of Elfland*, a collection of tales about magic and music, as well a part-time Consulting Editor for the fantasy line at Tor Books. Sherman and her partner live in Boston, Massachusetts, and in New York City.

—T. W. and E. D.

"I have killed."

The girl took two steps into the room and halted nervously, brushing the brindled hair from her eyes to glance at the cocoon of wolf pelts huddled by the fire and then away.

"Are you clean?" A woman's voice, resonant as an oboe, but without emotion.

The girl examined her hands back and front. "Yes," she said.

"Come, then." A long, delicate hand extended from the cocoon of furs and beckoned to the girl, who padded obediently to the woman's side and curled down at her feet.

"I left it at the kitchen door for the cook," said the girl. "It's chewed. I was hungry."

The woman laid her hand on the girl's hair. The girl leaned into the touch. "What was it, Fida? A rabbit?"

"A deer."

"Did you gut it?"

The girl Fida stilled, then shook her head vigorously. The woman's fingers tightened in her hair, gave it a small, sharp tug. "Bad cub," she said.

"Yes." Fida's mouth opened in an embarrassed grin, baring pointed teeth. She began to pant. The woman tweaked her hair again. "I'm hot," said Fida apologetically.

It was no wonder. The room was at blood heat from the fire and seemed hotter still; for it was red as the inside of a heart. Turkey carpets blanketed the floor, crimson hangings muffled walls and bed. The clock on the cherry wood mantel was made of red porphyry. Its hands stood at half past one—whether morning or afternoon was impossible to tell, the windows being both shuttered and curtained.

"I'm hot," said Fida again, and shifted, restless and uncomfortable. "I'm going out."

"You just came in."

"I'm going out again."

The woman withdrew her hand into her furs and shivered. "Of course," she said. "You must do as you please."

In one swift heave, Fida was on her feet and padding to the door. She paused with her hand on the knob. "Will you watch me go?" she asked.

"The moon's full," said the woman.

"I'm going to the Mountain," said Fida.

The figure in the chair went very still. "To the Mountain," she said, laying down her words like porcelain cups. "I will watch you go."

Fida grinned, and was gone.

No need to go to the window immediately, thought the woman. *Just sit a moment longer by the fire while the girl readies herself.* But even as she thought it, she was up, pulling back the curtain, unlatching the heavy wooden shutters, folding one of their panels into the thickness of the stone wall, pushing the casement window open to the night.

It had snowed, snow on deep snow. The clearing between the manor house and the forest was a silver tray polished to brilliance by a full moon riding the Mountain's shoulder. A beautiful night, all black and crystal white, and very, very cold. The chill flooded the woman's lungs, stung her cheeks and her eyes, cut through her layers of wool and fur and velvet as though they were thin silk. She clenched her chattering teeth and endured until a lean pale she-wolf trotted out around the side of the manor and toward the wood, pausing halfway across the clearing to look up at the window.

The woman raised one hand in a bloodless salute; the wolf howled.

As she watched the wolf's shadow lift its pointed chin against the snow, the woman felt time slip. The moonlight fell just as it had a year ago, the night she'd heard a noise outside her bloodred room. An owl, she'd thought at first, or a wolf howling. But when it came again, she thought it was a voice, shouting a word that might have been her name.

She was curious—no one had come near manor or Mountain for more years than she could count—so she had unshuttered the window and looked out. She saw naked trees groping at the edge of a dense wood, snow-draped Mountain brooding beyond, full moon glaring down on the courtyard, and nothing else. But as she shrank back into the room, away from the moon's cold gaze, a wolf had slid across her vision like a shadow.

Two shadows, really. The wolf's shadow was darker than the wolf itself, long and black as a shard of night fallen into the courtyard, stretching out from the wolf's forepaws, shoulders hunched, head tilted curiously, arms splayed just a little too wide for grace: the shadow of a young girl, as human as the wolf was not.

The woman had thrown wide the casement and leaned out into the frigid night.

"Come!"

Her voice rattled the air like a flight of pheasants; the wolf disappeared under the trees before the echo of it faded.

The woman closed the window with stiff, blue fingers and fumbled the shutters and the curtains shut. Then she blew up the fire and crouched beside it to thaw her hands among the darting flames. A young wolf, she thought, still a cub, to judge from the outsize paws and the lean, gangling body. A wolf with a human shadow.

A strange sight. But the woman was a witch, and she had seen strange sights before. A brown man with branching horns and dainty, cloven feet bending gravely above her to offer soup in a silver tureen. A small, sleek woman with apple-seed eyes, who swayed like grass in the wind when she walked. A Lady whose face shone coldly among her dark hair like the moon among clouds, and the Witch's father weeping at her feet. This wolf with a human shadow was not the strangest of them, nor the most unexpected. Once her father's Lady had shown it to her, trotting unsubstantially over the face of the moon. "Tinder," she'd said, and, "A two-edged blade." Then she'd smiled and gone away.

The Witch had not understood the Lady's words at the time, being young and passionate and unacquainted with blades and their uses. But she'd had time to consider them over the long, cold years, and she'd decided they meant that such a wolf was a promise of heat, like tinder, and that fire could burn as well as comfort. Now it was come, she was forewarned. All she need do was bring herself to step out under the moonlight, the starlight, the shadow of the Mountain, and she would be warm.

A flame caught her finger, caressed it to rosy life. She closed her long, dark eyes. "I cannot," she murmured. "I cannot go outside."

"Then you must stay inside." The voice was the Witch's own, and the face to which she raised her eyes. Both voice and face were cast over with a silver brilliance like the moon's.

"You," said the Witch.

"You," agreed the other.

"The hour has come."

"But you can't seize it." The fluting voice was both despairing and mocking. "You're afraid."

The Witch curled herself into the scarlet cushions of her chair and gathered a black shawl around her shoulders. Her visitor laid one arm along the mantel and gazed down at her, smiling slightly. Meeting her eyes, the Witch thought that she saw the moon in them, dead and leering; she shivered, but did not look away.

"I cannot feel fear," she said.

"No," said her visitor. "Nonetheless, you will not go out. Out is too cold, too hard, too bright. You have not been out in years. Besides, it would have pleased your father."

The Witch reached for a cup of tea—peppermint—fragrant and steaming to warm her hands and her cold, empty belly, and found one ready on the table. "What," she said when she had taken a careful sip, "could my father's pleasure have to do with my going out?"

"Very good," approved her twin. "The tea is a nice touch. Haven't you noticed that you never do anything you think would have pleased your father?"

"But breaking the spell would not please him. That was the bargain, wasn't it? That I should live like this forever?"

"That's what I said." The other turned to admire her reflection in the over-mantel mirror. "Pretty. I like the earrings. But you should do something new with your hair."

The Witch put her hand to her hair. It poured over her chair like carved and polished wood, deep brown, with a red glint in its depths. "I like it," she said.

"You're afraid to change it," said her visitor. "Your father liked it loose, you know. I remember him saying so."

"I did not call you," said the Witch. "I do not need you. Begone."

"Ungrateful bitch. I was just trying to help."

"I do not need your help."

The other began to laugh, showing small, white teeth that lengthened as she laughed and grew sharp and yellow until they filled all her mouth, and her tongue between them grew long and flat and red, and her laughter slid up into a shuddering howl. And then she was gone, taking the fire with her.

The next night the Witch watched for the wolf in the library from a French door that gave onto the courtyard.

The moon had paced across the sky before the wolf finally appeared, silent as smoke and close enough for the Witch to see the wet gleam of its eyes and its vaporous breath rising. Its shadow on the snow was sharp and clear as a black paper silhouette, blocky and awkwardly configured, yet unmistakably human.

The Witch forced herself to push the door ajar, then her nerve failed her. Shivering, she called:

"Come!"

The wolf started at her voice and loped back into the wood, pausing under the first trees and looking back over its brindled shoulder before taking itself and its shadow to the shelter of the wood.

The Witch ran after it, a step and then another crunching over the pathless snow, carrying her out of the shadow of the manor and into the moonlight. It dazzled her, so that she reeled and lifted both hands to her face and staggered backwards with the snow dragging at her feet like quicksand. Tripping over the threshold, she fell hard upon the library's carpeted floor, where she sat with her fingers pressing hard against her lids until stars appeared in the darkness there, and a milky light like moonrise. Hastily, she opened her eyes. The French doors were closed and shrouded, as they ought to be. But a silver chill was upon her.

In her chamber, she blew up the fire and wrapped herself in the wolf pelt from her bed. Half-expecting the Lady to appear, black-eyed and mocking, she brooded over the fire. The porphyry clock chimed meaningless hours. The flames were scarlet and gold, with coals glowing below them, hot and alive as the sun. One coal was larger than the rest, dull red in the fire's ice-blue heart, drawing her eye until it filled all her vision: a carbuncle encased in faceted crystal. The logs shifted, and the coal flared into whiteness marked with red, like the red mouth in a woman's face—her own face, the Lady's face, salt white, with blind stone eyes turned inward and two lines carved between the brows. The stone eyes twitched and opened on stars in a sky so black that it sucked into itself the soul of anyone gazing upon it. Into its deeps fell the Witch's soul, flying among adamantine knives that pricked her toward the moon, which looked upon her with loving eyes and stretched its bearded lips to engulf her.

The Witch seized one of the adamantine knives. It was all blade. Her hand scattered rubies from her wounded fingers, but she felt no pain as she sliced the star across and across the moon's face, only cold.

"That didn't work the last twenty thousand times you tried it," the Lady remarked. "Can't you try something else?"

The Witch gave a strangled mew, sat upright in the cushioned chair, put her hand out for a glass of wine. Her fingers groped in empty air. "Red wine," she said aloud. "In a golden cup. Set with rubies. Now."

"You must be mad," said the Lady cheerfully. "What you really need is meat. You haven't eaten anything in ages."

"Red wine," said the Witch decidedly, and lifted a brimming goblet to her lips. The wine was warm and fragrant with cinnamon and cloves; it burned in her hands and feet and behind her eyes. She drained the goblet, then dressed herself in a crimson velvet riding dress and little heeled boots lined with wolf fur, wrapped herself in pelisse and shawls, veiled her face against the wind and the cold gaze of the moon and stars. She unbolted the front door, opened it, and stepped outside to wait on the snow while the moon rose over the Mountain, bringing with it the she-wolf and her human shadow.

Seeing the woman, the wolf stopped. The Witch took a step forward. The wolf hesitated, lowered her tail, advanced one paw and then another. Step by slow step, wild-eyed and shivering, wolf and Witch left the safety of manor and forest, approaching the exposed and brilliant center of the clearing, approaching each other. They met. The she-wolf sat on her haunches; the Witch knelt before her and put back the veil, trembling like a bride. "You are Fida," she said. "You are my faithful servant."

The wolf shuddered all over, quick and hard as a death throe, then rolled onto her back and sprawled her back legs, offering the Witch her soft, pink belly. The Witch laid her gloved hand in the furry hollow, stroked upward to the furry chin, and stood.

"Come," she said, and this time the she-wolf obeyed, following at her heel like a well-trained dog back across the clearing through the open door, stopping only to mark the threshold with her scent. She looked about her, with ears pricked curiously, until the Witch closed the door and barred it. The cold, clear scents of pine and game and night and her pack drowned in a hot miasma of dusty wool and woodsmoke. The she-wolf sat down on the Turkey red rug and howled.

The Witch grasped her muzzle in both hands. "I don't like that noise," she said, shaking her gently. "Bad cub."

The wolf drooped her ears and whined; but when the Witch released her, she howled again: a long, panicked ululation.

Cold prickled up the Witch's spine. She needed utter devotion, and here was Fida, scrabbling frantically at the heavy oak door, snuffling at the thread of clean air, telling her that home was on the other side.

Laughter echoed in her ears like a silver bell. "Your father would be very pleased," it rang, mocking.

The Witch stamped her foot. "Bad cub," she shouted, to drown the bell. "Stop that at once and come with me."

The wolf raised her head and fixed her with moonstone eyes. Her nose wrinkled, her lip lifted from her sharp, yellow teeth; she rumbled threateningly. The Witch kicked her sharply in the ribs. She gave one startled yelp; the Witch kicked her again. Whining, the wolf offered her belly as she had in the courtyard. The Witch bent to accept her submission. "Good cub."

The ritual chamber was in the cellar, as far as possible from the open sky and the stars. The stairs leading down to it were cold and smelled of stale earth, like a long-abandoned den. The she-wolf marked them with her scent, and the chamber door and the high stone table that was its only furnishing. In one corner, she discovered a long, lumpy shape covered by a heavy carpet. Her nose pronounced the carpet dusty and the bones beneath it dry and fleshless and long, long dead. She sneezed, then leaped onto the table and sat, ears flicking back and forth, panting anxiously.

She whined when the Witch swept her front paws from under her and flipped her awkwardly on her back, but made no other objection. She even stretched her neck when the Witch put the knife to her underjaw and began to slit her skin away.

The Witch herself had never performed this ritual, but she had watched her father countless times, skinning the pelts from wolves and deer and bears to create servants to wait on him and her. After he died, she had made no more. She needed no servants; she preferred to do things for herself. If she knew absolutely that there would be wood for her fire and bread for her table, it would be so. That was the way of her magic, to work by absolute knowledge. Now, she knew absolutely that the she-wolf would lie still and trustful under her knife, and it was so. She knew she must cut only so deep and no deeper, must cut surely, without hesitation. A moment's doubt would kill the wolf and all the Witch's hopes of warmth. Once she might have doubted. But her father's bargain with the Lady had neatly excised disgust, compassion, and fear, leaving behind nothing but her absolute knowledge and a steady hand upon the knife.

There was no blood. The edges of the pelt were white and dry in the knife's wake, the flesh under it pink and whole and hairless. The pain, the Witch knew, would not be great unless by chance she pierced too deep. As the thought brushed her mind, the knife faltered, leaving a slender, scarlet track just over the breastbone. The she-wolf cried out in a voice neither human nor wolf, and the Witch sucked her breath in hard between her teeth. So easy to slip, to let out life and let in death—the ultimate coldness. Somewhere in the back of her mind a memory stirred, of blood hot on her cold hands, peat brown eyes wide with terror, and a thin, high scream like a dying rabbit's. Annoyed, she began to mutter the ritual aloud, the fluid words drawing the knife with them down the belly to the tail, then sideways between skin and pelt, working the wolf loose from the girl-form beneath.

The ritual took all night, and when the Witch was done, her hands ached with pulling and cutting, her lip bled where she had bitten through it, her eyes and knees twitched and strained. A brindled wolf pelt lay piled at one end of the stone table at the feet of a naked girl.

She wasn't pretty, not as humans measure beauty, being thin-hipped and shallow-breasted, her torso too long for her legs and arms, her hands and feet broad and stumpy, with horny palms and soles. Her hair was brindle gray like her pelt, and stood out in a wild aureole around her sharply planed face. Her nose was long and blunt, and her lips were very thin. Along her breastbone was a scar, red and raised like a whip welt.

"Fida," the Witch called her, and she opened eyes like winter moons. The thin, mobile lips twitched and worked, parted for the long, pink tongue to explore them. She made a tentative huffing noise, sneezed and sat up, eyeing the Witch with her head tilted awkwardly to one side.

"Mistress," she said, her voice rough and deep. She looked down at herself, lifted her hands one by one, licked between her stubby fingers, twisted to examine her altered body. She even tried to smell her crotch, at which the Witch laughed, cracking open the cut on her lip. The wolf-girl's head came up at the sound. Seeing the blood dribbling down the Witch's chin, she licked at it as she would lick the blood from a packmate's jaws. The Witch drew back from the touch of her tongue, hand to mouth, eyes showing white around the starless pupils.

"Bad cub?" the wolf-girl inquired anxiously.

The Witch shook her head slowly, then reached out to tousle the rough, brindled hair. "No," she said. "Good cub."

That day, Fida slept and woke and slept again, curled at the foot of the Witch's bed. When she woke at dusk, the Witch returned her pelt to her so that she could hunt. Following old habit, Fida searched out her pack. But she smelled wrong now—of woodsmoke and hot wool and dust and magic and humanity—and they soon drove her away again. For a little while, she licked her nipped haunches and whined before hunger drove her to hunt alone. She caught a rabbit and ate it, and then caught another to carry home to her new den. The rabbit was a little torn and chewed about the throat and back, but the Witch laughed when Fida laid it at her feet. She picked it up and smoothed the fur matted with blood and saliva, then knelt to caress the wolf's dripping jaws. "Good cub," she said. "I need meat."

"That's what I said." The Lady's voice was smug. Fida growled.

"Be still," said the Witch, and carried the rabbit into the dining room, where she laid it on the dark oak table, seated herself, and looked thoughtfully into the bog-brown eyes of her father's portrait hanging over the sideboard. "Stewed rabbit with dried apricocks and cinnamon," she said, and picked up silver-gilt cutlery. But when she looked down at her first real meal in a hundred years, the rabbit was still whole: laid out on the golden plate she'd imagined for it, mangled and cold.

"Eat," urged a hoarse voice behind her.

"I can't," whispered the Witch. The candle flames reflected in the rabbit's jet-bead eye were chips of diamond, or stars. A broad hand jerked the rabbit off the plate.

"Rabbit *good*," said Fida, and set her teeth to its soft belly to demonstrate. The Lady began to laugh, and the Witch put her hands over her ears and ran down the stairs to the ritual chamber, where the Lady never went.

When she emerged, she tripped over Fida, naked in her girl-shape, stretched out across the threshold.

"Bad cub," she said, and rolled over onto her back.

The Witch lifted her slippered foot and rested it lightly on the girl's hollow belly, at the end of the scar. "Bad cub," she agreed. "Bring me a deer, alive and unharmed, and I'll think you a very good cub indeed."

"Alive?"

"And unhurt."

It took Fida until spring, but she did it in the end, catching the deer in a trap she'd rigged in a shallow cave at the Mountain's tumbled hem. The Witch followed her into the wood to retrieve it, feeling for the first time in centuries the spring of grass and moss and pine needles under her feet, the weave of bark under her hand, the prick of pine scent and decaying leaves in her nose. Fida's shaggy presence at her knee warmed her through; as she led the spell-tamed buck back to the manor, she threw off her heavy shawl and loosened her gown at the neck.

In the front hall, the Lady was waiting for her. "What's this?" she inquired. "Following in Daddy's footsteps?"

"You said I needed meat," said the Witch defensively.

"Did I?" The Lady surveyed the buck. "How obedient of you. Do you intend to eat it alive?"

"I'm going to make a cook out of him." The Witch giggled suddenly. "I think his speciality should be venison stew, don't you?"

The Lady put out her hand to Fida, who advanced stiff-legged and bristling to sniff it. "Clever doggie," she said. Fida began to growl, the hair on her crest rising upright as her lip drew away from her fangs. The Lady snapped slender fingers under her nose. "A two-edged blade," she said, and disappeared.

All that summer of warmth and light and dappled sunshine, the Witch stalked the wood with the wolf padding beside her, silver-gray and graceful through the long evenings. She discovered the joys of the hunt, of blood hot on her hands and coppery on her tongue, and the sweet warmth of Fida's breath on her neck in the black hours between midnight and dawn. Sometimes she slept, and when she slept, she dreamed.

Walking in an ice cave, blue-white and cold as the stars, with one warm spot in the heart of it: a carbuncle in a crystal coffer. The carbuncle was carved in the shape of a human heart, two-lobed, veined delicately with blue. As she approached, it swelled slowly, contracted, and swelled again, warming as its beating strengthened, filling all the crystal cave with blood and heat and life. All save one corner, where a white-faced figure stood, robed in impenetrable black.

So the summer passed and autumn came. The days grew shorter, the nights longer, deeper, brighter with stars, and much, much colder. When the snows came, Fida wandered for a week in her wolf-form, sniffing at old dens and the bones of old kills, howling her frustration to the moon. The moon did not answer her, nor did the Witch, who greeted her return with black silence. Her body was bloodless and white with cold, but she thawed when Fida curled around her in the crimson-hung bed, and closed her eyes and sighed. With her mahogany hair folded across her throat, her unfathomable eyes veiled, her red lips half-open upon her small, sharp teeth, she was like a cub fallen from the teat. Fida nuzzled her neck, smooth and white and hairless, and the Witch turned to her and licked her mouth, petting her shoulders and her soft, shallow breasts. Their legs scissored together, thighs interlaced. Fida whined and nipped at the Witch's lips. The Witch whined too, then scrabbled from Fida's embrace to huddle against the bedpost, shivering and clutching her hair around her like a cloak. There was blood on her lower lip.

"Go away," she told Fida. "I'm cold."

Fida held out her arms. "Let me warm you, then."

The Witch gave a convulsive shudder. "No! No. You're making me cold. Go away."

Fida slipped out of the bed and padded naked to the door.

"Poor doggie," said the Lady.

Fida's eyes narrowed and her lips twitched.

"You don't like me, do you, doggie? Well, I like you. But I like your mistress better." Fida growled, as deep as her human throat would allow. The Lady smiled. "Jealous? I won't touch her, I promise. Now. Run away."

As the door closed behind Fida, the Lady settled herself comfortably in the Witch's cushioned chair. "Lazy girl," she said. "Tsk, tsk. Your father would be so ashamed of you. Don't you want your heart back?"

The Witch searched among the covers for her bed gown. "Of course I want it," she said.

"You're getting fat," said the Lady. "Must be all that venison stew. Or maybe it's love."

The Witch wrapped herself in fur-lined velvet. "I have no heart," she said sulkily. "You have to have a heart to love anything."

"I always thought so, certainly," the Lady agreed. "I don't know why your father was so *surprised* when you killed him. I told him he shouldn't have removed it."

The Witch clutched the bed gown, the fur rough against her icy skin. She was beyond shivering. "You removed it," she said. "That was the bargain."

"It was his bargain. He paid me for it, anyway. Which reminds me. We haven't discussed payment."

"Payment? But there's no bargain between us."

"Yes, there is. I remember it clearly. We discussed it just before you killed your father. You wanted to be free of him and you wanted your heart back. You said you'd give me anything I asked for."

"My heart is still in the Mountain," said the Witch.

"The were-girl can get it for you, if you're afraid to go yourself," the Lady said. "And you've been free of your father for eons. You owe me."

The Witch got out of bed and knelt by the fire. She didn't like being so close to the Lady, but the flames whispered comfort, and she was cold, so cold. "What do you want?" she asked.

"That would be telling, wouldn't it? You just have to be willing to give it to me. Are you willing?"

"I am not your creature," said the Witch.

"Aren't you?" The Lady widened her eyes. "You're mad as a hatter, mad with fear."

"I cannot feel fear," said the Witch.

"You are fear," said the Lady. "Bone to skin, hair to nail, you are made up of fear. Just like your father."

She laughed then, her eyes black and leering and full of stars, her mouth gaping wide on her merriment. The Witch seized the fire irons in icy fingers and slashed them across the Lady's face. The force of the blow sent bright blood spattering over her hand, her face, her gown, and hissing into the fire. The Lady gave a thin, high scream like a dying rabbit's. Her eyes were bright and mocking.

"How many times will you try that?" she said around the fire irons wedged in among teeth and red-stained bone. "It doesn't work. It doesn't work with me. It didn't work with your father. Not that I care; but it does make a mess."

The Witch covered her face with sticky hands. "Go away," she mumbled. "Take anything you want. Anything. Just go away."

"Very well," the Lady said. "I will."

When the Witch unblinded herself, the chair was empty and the blood was gone. So were the fire irons and the fire. The Witch dressed, braided her hair around her head, and called Fida.

Fida had clothed herself in a gown the Witch had imagined for her, loose leaf brown wool made high to the neck and tight to the wrists. She came in shyly and knelt at the Witch's feet, head low, shoulders hunched. The Witch took her by the chin, forced her head up, and looked long into her moonstone eyes.

"Do you love me?" she asked.

"Like hot blood," said Fida, unblinking. "Like the fresh marrow of bones."

"Good. Will you prove it?"

Fida looked puzzled. "I hunt for you. I sleep with you. What more do you want of me?"

The Witch caressed her hairless cheek. "There's a cave at the top of the Mountain," she said. "I want you to go there and bring me back something that I lost a long time ago."

"No," said Fida.

The Witch's hands dropped numbly. "You must."

"I will not. The Mountain is dangerous."

The Witch shivered, little tremors like ripples in still water. "You must, Fida. It's why I made you—to find my heart and bring it back to me, my heart that lies frozen in a cave at the Mountain's peak."

Fida ducked her head stubbornly. "The Mountain belongs to the White Wolves," she said. "They let no living thing pass."

"The Lady set them there to guard my heart from any who would harm me," said the Witch. "You love me. Surely they'll let you by."

"No."

"They're shadows, I tell you. They're for humans to fear, not for a wolf. Not for you."

"I am not afraid. I am not stupid." Fida touched the Witch's knee. "You have power and beauty and endless life. What do you need with a heart?"

"I need a heart," the Witch whispered. "I need *my* heart. I need it to love. I need it to hate. I can feel pain, nothing else. Oh, and cold. I can feel cold."

She began to weep, huddled in her wolf pelt, shuddering with dry, soundless sobs. Fida, reaching up to the blue-white hand, found it cold as snow or death. "You cannot love?" she asked sadly. "You don't love me?"

The Witch stilled. "You warm me," she said at last, and put her fingers to Fida's mouth.

The girl licked them until they were supple and ivory white and held them against her cheek. "I must think," she said.

"You will do it, then?"

"I don't know," said Fida. "I must think."

Sitting still by the open window, the Witch shuddered and wrapped an end of her black shawl around her throat. A year. Four hundred days, or a little less, since she'd first seen Fida; two days since she'd asked her to retrieve her heart from the Mountain. And before that, how long? Ten years? Fifty years? A hundred? What meaning does time have when there is nothing by which to measure it?

Fida had brought time into the Witch's life, marking the hours and days by her presence, by her absence. The Witch felt she had lived a lifetime in that year, two lifetimes in the two days Fida had oscillated restlessly between manor and wood. Now she was gone and the Witch did not know what to think. One moment, she knew, as she knew there would be wine at her hand, that Fida would not return, that the cold centuries would unfold year by year with the Witch at the heart of them, frozen and unchanging. The next moment she knew that Fida would bring her heart to her, awaken her like the Sleeping Beauty, to joy and warmth and peace.

Long after Fida had disappeared into the wood, the Witch sat staring out over the chiaroscuro of snow and forest, watching the shadow of the Mountain nibble at the manor and growing colder and colder until, had she had a heart, it would have stopped beating forever.

In that cold and in that silence, she remembered how lovely she had once found the moon's silver spell cast over Mountain and wood. She remembered loving the stars, and begging her father to teach her the patterns of their celestial dance. Those had been her first lessons in magic, conducted in the observatory her father had built in the manor's attics. They'd had human servants then, and people had come to visit from time to time—men in long black robes and ruffs and woolen caps tied under their spade-shaped beards, men whose skin was like unbleached linen, who smelled like old books. They had talked with her father of the stars, of the Philosopher's Stone that could turn lead into gold and confer eternal life. She'd had a little maid to wait on her, and a little dog to sleep at her feet, and her father had called her his heart's delight. The maid's name was Gretchen. The dog had been Sweetheart. Had she had a name? She must have. But she could not remember it.

The moon was full. Fida trotted up silent, silver glades toward the Mountain, her paws crunching on the frozen snow. She'd been as far as this the night before, to challenge the White Wolves, whose territory began where the trees thinned and the rocks grew thickly together. They'd answered her with growls and bared fangs. She'd fled downhill before them, but she'd learned that they had neither smell nor shadow. Perhaps they were like her mistress's bread, which filled the mouth and left the belly grumbling—shadows of wolves, with only the power that shadows have, to raise the ruff at nothing.

The trees began to dwindle in number and size, bowed by the wind, stunted by the cold, their roots twisted under boulders and down cracks in search of soil and water. Suddenly a wolf appeared, bright as mist in her path, his pack drifting near behind him like snow. Fida bristled and rumbled and cocked her ears forward. The White Wolf stretched his jaws and howled.

Had Fida worn her human form, she would have laughed aloud. No wolf howls at the edge of battle. She shook down her ruff and walked forward to meet him, wary but unafraid. The shadow-wolf howled louder, and his pack echoed him, scattering froth from their jaws like a snowstorm. As Fida approached, their howling grew more frantic, and they themselves more insubstantial, until she walked blindly through a cacophonous mist, following the slope of the ground upward step by step, while around her the White Wolves yammered like terrified puppies.

When the mist stilled, she was almost at the top of the Mountain, her nose against a slit in the rock barely wider than her shoulders. She sniffed deeply, smelled rock and water and something else, something that made her think of a white face and black eyes and sweetly curved red lips. Head warily low, she pushed into the slit and entered the Mountain.

The cave was very cold, colder than a frozen river, and so damp that Fida's bones ached with it. The moonlight crept in behind her, silvering the icy rocks, picking out odd gleams and sparks from the cave's shadowy throat. Slowly the wolf-girl paced into the darkness, her fur bristling.

Ice-rimed rock gave way to a tunnel carved out of blue ice, crazed and clouded like old crystal. At the end of the tunnel, a diamond spark glittered unnaturally, beckoning her forward. The walls breathed an arctic chill that froze her fur into an icy armor and her thoughts into silence, and still she advanced, her pads slipping on the glazy floor toward the ice cave, where the Witch's heart was hidden.

The cave itself was as bright as the tunnel was dark, carved facets of ice reflecting light back and forth to adamantine brilliance. The wolf narrowed her eyes against the glare and padded forward to the center and source of the light.

It was a casket of ice, set with moony jewels and bound with silver bands, fantastically carved and faceted to set off the scarlet heart that rested in its clear depths like an uncut ruby. The air around it shivered with waves of painful cold. The wolf bowed her head and whimpered.

In her blood-hot room, the Witch paced. She knew she must be patient, and yet she could not be still, but strode from hearth to window, from window to hearth, in a fever of restlessness. She wiped irritably at her hairline and her upper lip; her hand came away damp.

The wolf circled the casket, eyeing it as if it were a stag at bay. Her paws and tongue were bleeding and torn from her attack. Her brain was numb with magic and cold. Yet she was hopeful. It seemed a little warmer in the cave than it had been, and the surface of the casket was no longer perfectly flawless. It seemed to her, pacing and watching, that the heart had begun to beat a little, feebly, in time to her stiff-legged strides. Her own heart beat faster.

The Witch stood at the undraped window. Wood and Mountain were mantled in ermine, their image subtly distorted by the rippled window glass. She laid her hands flat against the icy pane. Heat caught in her chest and throat, dragging at each breath. She unbuttoned her woolen bodice and undid her boned lace collar, stroked her chilled hands down her face and neck. It felt nice; not as nice as Fida's coarse fur, damp after a run in the snow or the mist, but nice. She had a sudden image of Fida's head tucked into her shoulder, the brindled hair rough against her skin, the moony eyes hidden. She shivered, but not with cold.

"Well? Are you warm yet?" The Lady's voice was teasing. It was a lovely voice, the Witch thought, resonant as an oboe. Odd she'd never noticed. She turned to it as to a fire.

"I am warmer than I was," she said.

"Good. I hope you like it. Heat's expensive." The Lady was examining herself in the mantel mirror. The Witch saw both reflections, the Lady's and her own, near and distant, side by side. Feature by feature, they were identical: mahogany hair coiled like sleeping snakes around shapely heads, long, slanting eyes, high cheeks, crimson mouths, white throats.

The Witch stepped closer. "Who are you?"

The Lady settled a jeweled pin at her nape. "You," she said.

"No," said the Witch. "You are beautiful and I am not." She took another step. "Your lips are fire and your neck is snow. There are mysteries in the folds of your hair and the curve of your mouth." She was very near now. The two faces, one intent, one detached, watched her hand rise and hover toward the Lady's shoulder.

The Lady stepped aside and turned in one smooth movement. "Do you want to kiss me? There's a price on my kisses."

"Who are you?" asked the Witch again.

"Your father kissed me. He gave all he had for the privilege."

"I will give you everything I have."

"I have that already. You have nothing left to give me. Except everything you might have had. You could give me that."

Fida put off her wolf's pelt as the Witch had taught her, and wrapped it around her shoulders. Gently, she touched one torn finger to the casket, leaving a smear of blood on its clear surface, which slicked and shone for a moment, as if the blood had melted it to liquid. She lifted her finger to her mouth and ripped at the nail with her teeth until blood welled from the wound and dripped onto the casket. A fat crimson drop trembled a moment, cabochon, then collapsed and ran off the casket's side. Where it had been was a tiny pit.

Fida tore at her wrist then, sharp wolf teeth shearing through thin human skin as easily as knives. The resulting stream of blood was strong, pulsing over the icy casket in thick waves that thinned as they sheeted down the sides, melting the facets and the fantastic carving to rose-tinted smoothness, releasing the silver bands and the moony jewels to lie among rocks and pools of ice melt. Her arm grew heavy; she rested her hand on the ice, which burned her fingers, clung to them and to her wrist, freezing her to itself. Still the wound bled sluggishly as Fida knelt by the casket, her pelt slipping from her shoulders, watching her blood soak through the ice toward the Witch's glowing heart.

"Well?" said the Lady. "Is it a deal or isn't it? Your father knew what he wanted, and the last deal we made, you did too." A paper appeared in her hand, one line of small black type printed neatly across the middle and, beneath it, a blotched signature scrawled in brown ink.

"Here it is, in living color," she said. "I help get rid of your father and give you a chance to get your heart back, and you give me your name, your life, and your mind. Signed with your heart's blood, which is a neat trick for someone who doesn't have one."

The Witch reached for the paper; the Lady snatched it away. "Uh-uh," she said. "You'll just have to trust me. Come on, have I ever lied to you?"

"I don't know."

"So you don't," said the Lady cheerfully. "That's the beauty of it. But I always keep my bargains. Just ask your father."

"My father! My father! Why must you always be talking of my father? He's gone."

The Lady looked apologetic. "Well, that's the problem, you see. He isn't. When you cut out his heart, you simply covered him up with a rug and left him in the corner of the ritual chamber." The Witch's eyes shifted away, blank as stones. The Lady smiled and said, "I promised him you'd always be together."

"But what of your promise to me?" the Witch wailed.

"It hasn't been easy, I can tell you. Now. What about that kiss?"

The Witch felt her hair clinging stickily to her cheeks and brow, and lifted her hand to push it back. The movement brushed her loosened gown against her nipples, which hardened. There was sweat trickling down between her breasts, and, beneath the layers of her petticoats, she felt a moist heat between her thighs. The room pulsed around her, quick and hard. She stepped forward, close enough to see the thread of a healing cut on the Lady's lower lip.

Had Fida bitten the Lady, too? She fingered her own mouth, felt the faint ridge Fida's tooth had left there. It hadn't been a bite at all; it had been a kiss. And it had burned her. She recognized the heat now. It was desire for Fida. Fida of the wild smell and the bristly, brindled hair, Fida who never taunted her, Fida who was willing to brave the White Wolves for her. Fida who loved her.

"Yes," said the Lady, "she loves you. She's yours, by her own free gift. As you are mine."

"I am not yours," said the Witch.

"Very well, then; you're not. Save your chilly charms for your little pet, if she returns. She could meet a young dog-wolf on her way back through the wood—winter is mating season for wolves, did you know? And she-wolves are notoriously horny. Or she could run off with your heart, or eat it. You haven't been very kind to her, and she's still a wolf. Everyone knows that wolves are by nature cruel and crafty and mean."

"No," said the Witch. "She'd never do that. Would she?"

"Of course she wouldn't. She'd bring it back, or die trying. Wolves are notoriously faithful. And then you'd be whole again, mistress of your name, your life, and your mind. You'd feel warmth again, and love and fear and desire, and all sorts of other things you've forgotten about. Grief. Remorse. Loneliness. Oh, and you'll grow older. White hairs, some of them growing from your chin, and lines around your eyes and mouth. Loose teeth, droopy breasts. I can't guarantee you'll be able to imagine food and drink and fuel from thin air anymore, either. There are certain kinds of magic only I can give you."

The Witch made a little whimpering noise. Her reflection in the mirror flushed and paled as waves of heat and cold chased one another up her throat and licked her cheeks.

"Ah," said the Lady. "You don't like that, do you?"

"I want my heart," said the Witch. "That was the bargain."

"You can't have both your heart and me," said the Lady.

Fida lay white and unmoving in a puddle of pinkish ice melt, her hand cupped protectively around a quivering human heart. The cave was like a cloudy night, dark and close and featureless. In one corner, a shadow flickered black against black and drifted toward the wolf-girl. Shaking long sleeves from its star white hands, it touched her head. Fida's head stirred on her pillowing arm; she opened one eye and sighed. All was well. Her mistress had come to her.

"Good cub?" she whispered.

Her mistress giggled. Fida squinted up at the long face set in the depths of the cowl. No, not her mistress. Like, as a deadly mushroom is like an edible one, but not the same. Her eyes had no white, but were black from lid to lid; and where her mistress smelled of wool and woodsmoke and fear, this woman smelled faintly of peaches. Fida growled.

"Ah, you know me," said the Lady. "Well, never mind. It will be our little secret. You have something that belongs to me, I believe."

Fida closed her hand around the heart. It throbbed and burned in the hollow of her palm like a wound or a living coal.

"Don't be silly," said the Lady. "You can't fight me." Her white face filled the cave, round and unbearably white. "I am everything. I am wiser than heaven and more powerful than a pack leader in his prime. Truth itself is my creature and my slave."

Fida contracted on her sodden pelt, clutching the Witch's heart to rest against her belly, shielding it from the Lady's pitiless eyes with her wide hands and her bony knees.

The Lady's face waned, dwindled to a pale curve of cheek veiled by a drifting wrack of hair. "You can't fight me," she whimpered. "I am nothing. I am more ignorant than dirt and more powerless than a day-old cub. Truth passes through me as though I didn't exist."

Fida closed her eyes. Resting against her belly, the heart pulsed slowly, each beat sending warmth through her, and a trickle of strength.

In the blood-red chamber, the Witch sweated and shivered.

"It's the bitch-girl or me," murmured the Lady, soft as snow falling. "You can't have both. Why are you hesitating? She's an animal, not like you and me. She'll be dead in twenty years or so, just like the rest of them, and who knows whether I'll still want you by then? What do you know about this wolf-girl? How do you know you can trust her? Don't you want to know what she's doing right now?"

The Witch put her hands to her burning forehead, pressed it between them until the pain stopped her. "No. Yes. No. She loves me. I trust her."

"Suit yourself. She might be in trouble, be hurt, even dying. You could help her. But I guess you don't care."

"No! I do care. If she's hurt, I want to see."

The Lady smiled, a feral baring of the teeth. "Very well," she said. "You asked for it." She nodded at the mirror, which clouded and resolved into a dark painting of a naked girl curled on a wolf pelt. The girl was nursing something against her belly. Bending above her was the Witch, her proud face pleading, her hand beseechingly outstretched. The wolf-girl's lips were drawn back, snarling. Her eyes were wild.

"Does she look hurt?" asked the Lady.

"She looks . . . angry."

"Mad as hell," agreed the Lady.

"Why won't she give me the heart?"

"She wants it for herself," said the Lady.

The Witch screamed and, lifting her fists, shattered the vision into a thousand glittering shards. She turned to the Lady, sobbing, the tears hot on her cheeks, bloody hands begging an embrace. "You," she said thickly. "Who are you?"

The Lady opened her arms. "I am whatever you wish me to be," she said. "I am Desire."

But the Witch was still speaking and did not hear her. "You are Love," said the Witch. "You are Family and Home and Safety. You are my Heart."

Then she stepped into the embrace of Desire, which was as cold as the moon, and raised her lips to the lips of Desire, which sucked from her all warmth and hope of warmth. As they kissed, the fire in the hearth burned blue and white as ice, filling the room with a deadly chill. And far below, in the ritual chamber, her father's corpse shuddered and sighed.

In Fida's grasp, the heart throbbed wildly and unevenly, gave a wild, shuddering beat, and was still. Fida cradled it to her, willing it warm again, lifting it to her mouth and licking it. It lay cool and elastic in her fingers, dead meat.

"It's no use," said Desire. "She doesn't love you. She can't love you. She belongs to me."

"But I love her," said Fida passionately. "I love her more than my life."

"Die then," said Desire.

Not long after, Desire took the Witch's heart from between Fida's torn and bloody paws and set it back on the rocky spur where it had reposed for the past three hundred years. She spat upon it and smoothed the spittle into a casket of ice, faceted and fantastically carved, bound in silver bands and set with moony jewels. Then she pulled her cowl up around her face, shook down her long, dark sleeves, and drifted back into the corner.

The Witch sits in her blood-red room, cocooned in wolf pelts. The hands on her porphyry clock stand at half past one—whether morning or afternoon is impossible to tell, for the windows are shuttered and curtained. So are the Witch's eyes, lids closed against the ruddy firelight and veiled by the mahogany hair hanging loose over her face. Stone and glass and wood and cloth stand between her and the moon, but she can feel it nonetheless, cold and hungry outside her chamber window, riding above the Mountain where her heart lies frozen in ice. Someday she'll get it back. All she needs is someone who will brave the moon and the Mountain and the Lady's White Wolves, to break the spell and get it for her. Someone who will not betray her. Someone who will love her. A wolf with a human shadow. The Lady has promised.

PLUMAS (Feathers)

Patricia Preciado Martin

Patricia Preciado Martin is the author of *Songs My Mother Sang to Me: An Oral History of Mexican American Women* and *Images and Conversations: Mexican Americans Recall a Southwestern Past.* Her first fiction collection, *El Milagro and Other Stories*, is mystical, sensual and beautifully-crafted, inspired by the author's history, her family traditions, and the rich Mexican-American culture of Arizona's Sonoran Desert. "Plumas" is a gentle, haunting work of magic realism, painting a young woman's everyday world with the bright colors of old Aztec myth. It comes from *El Milagro*, published by the University of Arizona Press. Martin lives in Tucson, Arizona.

—T. W.

Banish care; if there are bounds to pleasure, the saddest life must also have an end. Then weave the chaplet of flowers, and sing thy songs in praise of the all-powerful God; for the glory of this world soon fadeth away. Rejoice in the green freshness of thy Spring; for the day will come when thou shalt sigh for these joys in vain; when the sceptre shall pass from thy hands, they servants desolate in thy courts, thy sons, and the sons of thy nobles shall drink the dregs of distress, and all the pomp of thy victories and triumphs shall live only in their recollection.... The goods of this life, its glories and its riches, are but lent to us, its substance is but an illusory shadow, and the things of today shall change on the coming of the morrow. Then gather the fairest flowers from thy gardens, to bind round thy brow, and seize the joys of the present, ere they perish.
—Nezahualcoyotl, Aztec emperor and poet king
William Prescott, The Conquest of Mexico

Paloma Flores stepped nimbly off of the 7:00 A.M. crosstown bus at the corner of Glenn and Palo Verde Streets. She was a few minutes late for work as usual, and she walked hurriedly through the chain-link fence that led past the football field to the high school parking lot. She darted among the parked cars as fast as her slender muscular legs and sensible shoes could carry her. When she reached the "Employees Only" entrance at the back of the brick cafeteria building, she ran up the concrete steps, fumbled with her key, and opened the heavy, steel security door slowly. She was careful not to close it too noisily lest her tardiness be noticed. The supervisor of the cafeteria staff, Sister Fredericka, was a stout German nun with a ruddy face, a quick temper, and a strident voice. She ran the kitchen with the military precision of boot camp and maintained the discipline with religious fervor. She tolerated no lapses in punctuality, efficiency, cleanliness, or order. The last thing that Paloma Flores wanted was any extra attention from Sor Fredericka or a scolding from her in her thick Teutonic tongue.

Paloma Flores hung her plain, gray cloth coat on a hook in the staff lounge and slipped a clean white smock from the bin of freshly laundered linen over her shapeless cotton frock. She then carefully stretched a hairnet over her thickly braided tresses—her hair was ebony, radiant, but she wore it modestly in a sleeping coil on top of her elegant head. Over the hairnet she drew a cap of fine gauze to ensure that every strand was in place and tucked out of sight. It was a health department requirement, and any errant lock would be scrutinized by Sister Fredericka until she matched it with its hapless owner. Then she would mark demerits next to the guilty party's name in the little black book that she carried in the oversized pockets of her black smock. Ten demerits and one's pay could be docked; too many demerits and one could be dismissed.

Paloma Flores slipped as quietly and unobtrusively as possible into the work line at the stainless-steel counters in the cafeteria kitchen. Her coworkers, all women, chattered in Spanish as they worked—chop, chop; slice, slice; stir, stir. Plática y plática:[1] of sweethearts and husbands and children and friends and in-laws; of fears and illnesses and remedies; of love and disillusionment; of recipes and herbs and fashion and fiestas. Plática y plática, mincing onions; plática, cubing meat; plática, peeling carrots and potatoes; plática, kneading dough; plática.

Paloma Flores had become accustomed to the good-natured teasing about her tardiness from her work companions—the curious glances, the questioning raised eyebrows, the knowing smirks—especially from Carmen García, who stood opposite her at the work counter. Carmen seemed out of place in the cafeteria kitchen assembly line with her pompadour, enormous dangling earrings made of peacock feathers, stiletto heels, false eyelashes, and exotic perfume. She was a sharp contrast to plain and unadorned Paloma Flores. But Carmen had a heart of gold and meant well. She was determined simply to draw out the shy and reticent Paloma, who was the only one of the women who rarely spoke or shared any details with her companions about her solitary life.

"Late again?" Carmen García would tease when Sor Fredericka, her oversized rosary beads rattling on her waist, had passed out of earshot on her inspection tour. "What's going on? Do you have a boyfriend that you're keeping a secret from us? Is someone hiding under your bed who makes you late?"

---

[1]chatter; gossip; conversation

Paloma Flores' nimble fingers never faltered in their culinary tasks as she endured Carmen's good-natured ribbing with a quiet smile and a flush on her cheeks. She kept her silence; she had no choice. How could she tell them about the dream?

The recurrent dream startled her bolt upright in her narrow, single bed in her modest, neat room in the boarding house of Doña Amparito on Convent Street. The dream left her wide-eyed and sleepless, her heart pounding, her forehead damp with excitement, her lungs choking with a perfumed smoke, her body trembling, her ears ringing with the faraway haunting sound of drums and flutes and conch shells.

The massive oak clock at the far end of the cafeteria ticked off the minutes brassily—countdown to the lunch hour and the swarm of noisy, hungry teenagers who would invade the dining hall at precisely 12:05 P.M. The echo of the ticking clock was lost in the din of students scraping chairs, banging trays and utensils, slurping milk and juice, and chattering in excited, high-pitched voices. They were as hungry and efficient as locusts, and it would not be long before the cafeteria was again quiet, the horde of adolescents surging out the double-wide glass doors onto the school grounds.

The kitchen staff, famished by now, would hurriedly eat lunch—the leftovers of today's menu, the fruit of their own labors. Then the clamor and chatter would begin again: plática, plática, the clink of glasses and clatter of plates and utensils; plática, the racket of metal pots and pans; plática, the rattle of plastic trays; plática, the steam rising from the hot, sudsy wash and rinse water like the vapors from an ancient volcano. Then the cafeteria workers—their backs aching, their feet tired and swollen from standing at their labors, their hands reddened—would ebb out the back door and surge like a wave across the parking lot en route to the shores of their own private lives.

Carmen García removed the detested hairnet and gauze cap and placed a bright-green bandanna over her pompadour to protect her hairdo from the fickle breezes. She tied a knot under her chin and touched up her lipstick, rouge, and cologne. "Okay, Paloma," she teased, "now don't be late tomorrow or you might get caught by Sister Fredericka. Boy, I sure would like to meet this novio of yours; I'll bet he's quite a looker. Maybe I should steal him from you!" She smiled a wide grin, her gold-capped teeth glinting. They strolled together through the parking lot until they reached Carmen's vintage Chevrolet. Carmen blew rings of smoke out her heart-shaped "Cherries in the Snow" mouth, then tapped the ashes from her cigarette with her long, red fingernails that shone like jewels in the sun. "Anyway, Honey," she added as she struggled with the car door, "you can always talk to me and let me know what's really going on." Paloma Flores' cheeks reddened, but she kept her counsel.

Her name was Xochitl, which meant "flower bird" in Nahuatl. She was a Cihuateopixque, a female priest dedicated to the Aztec goddess Tonantzín, the creator goddess, the earth and harvest goddess, the goddess of young growth and beauty.

Xochitl wore her midnight-black hair long to her waist, free and flowing, and the locks were interlaced with strips of colored cloth and feathers. Her face was decorated with red, yellow, and white paint and her breasts, arms, and shoulders were perfumed with a liquid amber called *isataisatahte*. Attached to her waist was a thick, black strap anointed with a sweet-smelling balsam. In her right hand she carried an enormous burden basket of fragrant herbs and flowers, for spring was the time for the offering of flowers to Tonantzín.

In her left hand Xochitl carried a fan of feathers and a little flag of beaten gold topped with the feathers of the macaw. She wore earplugs of coral and jade, a necklace of gold with pearls and amethysts, and bracelets and anklets of gold, turquoise, and emeralds that were trimmed in feathers. Her lower lip was pierced and set with pieces of rock crystal, within which were stuck blue feathers of the hummingbird that made them seem like sapphires. She wore these ornaments hanging as if they came out of her flesh, and she also had golden half-moons hanging from her lips. Her nose was pierced and therein was inserted fine turquoise. Her sandals were of jaguar fur adorned with gold and precious stones; the thongs were of gold thread embellished with trogon feathers from the deep forests.

She had a crown of feathers called a *tlauhquecholtzontli*, which was made of the feathers of the roseate spoonbill. She wore it with the *thauhquecholeuatl*, a jacket of spoonbill feathers, and the *tzapocueitl*, a petticoat of green feathers from the Quetzal bird. The garments lapped over one another like tiles. In addition, she wore a headband called the *quetzalallapiloni*, an adornment of beaten gold with the feathers of the Quetzal bird.

She ascended the thousand steps to the summit of the pyramid where the altar of Tonantzín was located. Xochitl was attended by a hundred vestal virgins who chanted solemnly. At the summit awaited a score of priests. Their bodies were horrible with tattoos, their faces covered with the *coa-xayacacatl*, the snake mask of mosaic turquoise. The priests were resplendent in feather headdresses and capes of brilliant plumage. They carried in their right hands the *chicahu-aztlei*, an elaborately carved staff adorned with feathers and bells. Around their waists they wore hooves, fruit, shells, and cocoons, and dried nuts, seashells, bones, and metal bells were strung on a string sewn to a leather band that was decorated with feathers.

A hundred brazier fires were burning, and an incense called copal ascended in fragrant clouds to the starlit heavens. Exceedingly large drums were brilliantly painted and bedecked with gold bands and gay feather ornaments, and they were elaborately carved with the reliefs of the eagle and jaguar warriors. There were many other drums made of all manner of snake and animal skins, tortoise and armadillo shells, and horns, flutes, and conch shells.

The singing and the chanting of the priests, the music from the instruments, the rhythms and swaying of the dancing attendants, the crackling of the fires and the roar of the winds, the sound of it all together was so haunting that it seemed to be a sound from the very center of the earth. One could hear it at a distance of twenty leagues, and it was said that it could wake those in the deepest slumber. Even the dead.

*   *   *

Chop, chop. Slice, slice. Stir, stir. Plática, plática. The women are busy at their kitchen stations, their foreheads furrowed, their heads bent in concentration. There is an empty space at the workspace opposite Carmen García. Paloma Flores has not been to work for over a week. She has sent no word. Her phone goes unanswered, her mail returned.

Chop, chop. Slice, slice. Plática, plática. "So, Carmen, what ever happened to la Paloma?" asks a concerned Doña Antoñita, a gray-haired grandmother of six who is working diligently at the station next to Carmen. "Why isn't she coming to work anymore? She hasn't been in for days."

Carmen García pauses, then flutters her hands excitedly and fingers her brooch made of butterfly wings. "I'm not sure I know exactly what's going on." She leans over dramatically and speaks in a voice a little louder than a whisper. There is silence in the assembly line as the cooks pause at their tasks, their utensils suspended in midair, straining to hear every word. "I heard that she was fired by la Sister Fredericka and won't be coming back."

"Ay, pobre, for heaven's sakes, why?" asks Doña Antoñita. "Tan buena y tan trabajadora."[2]

Carmen's false eyelashes flutter like fans, but her eyes shine with a flame dark and deep. "Yeah, I know," she says sympathetically. "It's too bad. But I guess la Sister got mad or something. I overheard her saying something to the fry cook, something about how she just couldn't tolerate it. Rules are rules. Something about she had never in all her years seen anything like it. Something about how Paloma's feathers kept getting in the soup."

---

[2] So good and such a good worker.

CROW GIRLS
Charles de Lint

Canadian author Charles de Lint is one of the primary pioneers of "urban fantasy," a contemporary form of the literature that brings ancient mythic themes to modern urban life. His work has been increasingly centered in the imaginary city of Newford, using an evolving cast of characters including the young punk artist Jilly Coppercorn, her fiddle-playing pal Geordie, and the "crow girls" of the following tale. De Lint's most recent Newford novels are *Memory and Dream* and *Trader*—both highly recommended. A novel about the crow girls, *Someplace to be Flying*, will come out next year. This story is reprinted from a limited edition chapbook published in Canada by Triskell Press.

In addition to writing, De Lint is a Celtic folk musician, book critic, folklore scholar, and visual artist. He and his wife live in Ottawa, Ontario.

—T. W.

I remember what somebody said about nostalgia, he said it's okay to look back, as long as you don't stare.

-Tom Paxton, from an interview
with Ken Rockburn

People have a funny way of remembering where they've been, who they were. Facts fall by the wayside. Depending on their temperament they either remember a golden time when all was better than well, better than it can be again, better than it ever really was: a first love, the endless expanse of a summer vacation, youthful vigor, the sheer novelty of being alive that gets lost when the world starts wearing you down. Or they focus in on the bad, blow little incidents all out of proportion, hold grudges for years, or maybe they really did have some unlucky times, but now they're reliving them forever in their heads instead of moving on.

But the brain plays tricks on us all, doesn't it? We go by what it tells us, have to I suppose, because what else do we have to use as touchstones? Trouble is we don't ask for confirmation on what the brain tells us. Things don't have to be real, we just have to believe they're real, which pretty much explains politics and religion as much as it does what goes on inside our heads.

Don't get me wrong; I'm not pointing any fingers here. My people aren't guiltless either. The only difference is our memories go back a lot further than yours do.

"I don't get computers," Heather said.

Jilly laughed. "What's not to get?"

They were having cappuccinos in the Cyberbean Café, sitting at the long counter with computer terminals spaced along its length the way those little individual juke boxes used to be in highway diners. Jilly looked as though she'd been using the tips of her dark ringlets as paintbrushes, then cleaned them on the thighs of her jeans—in other words, she'd come straight from the studio without changing first. But however haphazardly messy she might allow herself or her studio to get, Heather knew she'd either cleaned her brushes, or left them soaking in turps before coming down to the café. Jilly might seem terminally easy-going, but some things she didn't blow off. No matter how the work was going—good, bad or indifferent—she treated her tools with respect.

As usual, Jilly's casual scruffiness made Heather feel overdressed, for all that she was only wearing cotton pants and a blouse, nothing fancy. But she always felt a little like that around Jilly, ever since she'd first taken a class from her at the Newford School of Art a couple of winters ago. No matter how hard she tried, she hadn't been able to shake the feeling that she looked so typical: the suburban working mother, the happy wife. The differences since she and Jilly had first met weren't great. Her blonde hair had been long then while now it was cropped short. She was wearing glasses now instead of her contacts.

And two years ago she hadn't been carrying an empty wasteland around inside her chest.

"Besides," Jilly added. "You use a computer at work, don't you?"

"Sure, but that's work," Heather said. "Not games and computer screen romances and stumbling around the Internet, looking for information you're never going to find a use for outside of Trivial Pursuit."

"I think it's bringing back a sense of community," Jilly said.

"Oh, right."

"No, think about it. All these people who might have been just vegging out in front of a TV are chatting with each other in cyberspace instead—hanging out, so to speak, with kindred spirits that they might never have otherwise met."

Heather sighed. "But it's not real, human contact."

"No. But at least it's contact."

"I suppose."

Jilly regarded her over the brim of her glass coffee mug. It was a mild gaze, not in the least probing, but Heather couldn't help but feel as though Jilly was seeing right inside her head, all the way down to where desert winds blew through the empty space where her heart had been.

"So what's the real issue?" Jilly asked.

Heather shrugged. "There's no issue." She took a sip of her own coffee, then tried on a smile. "I'm thinking of moving downtown."

"Really?"

"Well, you know. I already work here. There's a good school for the kids. It just seems to make sense."

"How does Peter feel about it?"

Heather hesitated for a long moment, then sighed again. "Peter's not really got anything to say about it."

"Oh, no. You guys always seemed so . . ." Jilly's voice trailed off. "Well, I guess you weren't really happy, were you?"

"I don't know what we were anymore. I just know we're not together. There wasn't a big blow up or anything. He wasn't cheating on me and I certainly wasn't cheating on him. We're just . . . not together."

"It must be so weird."

Heather nodded. "Very weird. It's a real shock, suddenly discovering after all these years, that we really don't have much in common at all."

Jilly's eyes were warm with sympathy. "How are you holding up?"

"Okay, I suppose. But it's so confusing. I don't know what to think, who I am, what I thought I was doing with the last fifteen years of my life. I mean, I don't regret the girls—I'd've had more children if we could have had them—but everything else . . ."

She didn't know how to begin to explain.

"I married Peter when I was eighteen, and I'm forty-one now. I've been a part of a couple for longer than I've been anything else, but except for the girls, I don't know what any of it meant anymore. I don't know who I am. I thought we'd be together forever, that we'd grow old together, you know? But now it's just me. Casey's fifteen and Janice is twelve. I've got another few years of being a mother, but after that, who am I? What am I going to do with myself?"

"You're still young," Jilly said. "And you look gorgeous."

"Right."

"Okay. A little pale today, but still."

Heather shook her head. "I don't know why I'm telling you this. I haven't told anybody."

"Not even your mom or your sister?"

"Nobody. It's . . ."

She could feel tears welling up, the vision blurring, but she made herself take a deep breath. It seemed to help. Not a lot, but some. Enough to carry on. How to explain why she wanted to keep it a secret? It wasn't as though it was something she could keep hidden forever.

"I think I feel like a failure," she said.

Her voice was so soft she almost couldn't hear herself, but Jilly reached over and took her hand.

"You're not a failure. Things didn't work out, but that doesn't mean it was your fault. It takes two people to make or break a relationship."

"I suppose. But to have put in all those years . . ."

Jilly smiled. "If nothing else, you've got two beautiful daughters to show for them."

Heather nodded. The girls did a lot to keep the emptiness at bay, but once they were in bed, asleep, and she was by herself, alone in the dark, sitting on the couch by the picture window, staring down the street at all those other houses just like her own, that desolate place inside her seemed to go on forever.

She took another sip of her coffee and looked past Jilly to where two young women were sitting at a corner table, heads bent together, whispering. It was hard to place their ages—anywhere from late teens to early twenties, sisters, perhaps, with their small builds and similar dark looks, their black clothing and short blue-black hair. For no reason she could explain, simply seeing them made her feel a little better.

"Remember what it was like to be so young?" she said.

Jilly turned, following her gaze, then looked back at Heather.

"You never think about stuff like this at that age," Heather went on.

"I don't know," Jilly said. "Maybe not. But you have a thousand other anxieties that probably feel way more catastrophic."

"You think?"

Jilly nodded. "I know. We all like to remember it as a perfect time, but most of us were such bundles of messed-up hormones and nerves I'm surprised we ever managed to reach twenty."

"I suppose. But still, looking at those girls . . ."

Jilly turned again, leaning her head on her arm. "I know what you mean. They're like a piece of summer on a cold winter's morning."

It was a perfect analogy, Heather thought, especially considering the winter they'd been having. Not even the middle of December and the snowbanks were already higher than her chest, the temperature a seriously cold minus-fifteen.

"I have to remember their faces," Jilly went on. "For when I get back to the studio. The way they're leaning so close to each other—like confidantes, sisters in their hearts, if not by blood. And look at the fine bones in their features . . . how dark their eyes are."

Heather nodded. "It'd make a great picture."

It would, but the thought of it depressed her. She found herself yearning desperately in that one moment to have had an entirely different life, it almost didn't matter what. Perhaps one that had no responsibility but to draw great art from the world around her the way Jilly did. If she hadn't had to support Peter while he was going through law school, maybe she would have stuck with her art. . . .

Jilly swiveled in her chair, the sparkle in her eyes deepening into concern once more.

"Anything you need, anytime," she said. "Don't be afraid to call me."

Heather tried another smile. "We could chat on the Internet."

"I think I agree with what you said earlier: I like this better."

"Me, too," Heather said. Looking out the window, she added, "It's snowing again."

Maida and Zia are forever friends. Crow girls with spiky blue-black hair and eyes so dark it's easy to lose your way in them. A little raggedy and never quiet, you can't miss this pair: small and wild and easy in their skins, living on Zen time. Sometimes they forget they're crows, left their feathers behind in the long ago, and sometimes they forget they're girls. But they never forget that they're friends.

People stop and stare at them wherever they go, borrowing a taste of them, drawn by they don't know what, they just have to look, try to get close, but keeping their distance, too, because there's something scary/craving about seeing animal spirits so pure walking around on a city street. It's a shock, like plunging into cold water at dawn, waking up from the comfortable familiarity of warm dreams to find, if only for a moment, that everything's changed. And then, just before the way you know the world to be comes rolling back in on you, maybe you hear giddy laughter, or the slow flap of crows' wings. Maybe you see a couple of dark-haired girls sitting together in the corner of a café, heads bent together, pretending you can't see them, or could be they're perched on a tree branch, looking down at you looking up, working hard at putting on serious faces but they can't stop smiling.

It's like that rhyme, "two for mirth." They can't stop smiling and neither can you. But you've got to watch out for crow girls. Sometimes they wake a yearning you'll be hard-pressed to put back to sleep. Sometimes only a glimpse of them can start up a familiar ache deep in your chest, an ache you can't name, but you've felt it before, early mornings, lying alone in your bed, trying to hold onto the fading tatters of a perfect dream. Sometimes they blow bright the coals of a longing that can't ever be eased.

Heather couldn't stop thinking of the two girls she'd seen in the café earlier in the evening. It was as though they'd lodged pieces of themselves inside her, feathery slivers winging dreamily across the wasteland. Long after she'd read Janice a story, then watched the end of a Barbara Walters special with Casey, she found herself sitting up by the big picture window in the living room when she should be in bed herself. She regarded the street through a veil of falling snow, but this time she wasn't looking at the houses, so alike, except for the varying heights of their snowbanks, they might as well all be the same one. Instead, she was looking for two small women with spiky black hair, dark shapes against the white snow.

There was no question but that they knew exactly who they were, she thought when she realized what she was doing. Maybe they could tell her who she was. Maybe they could come up with an exotic past for her so that she could reinvent herself, be someone like them, free, sure of herself. Maybe they could at least tell her where she was going.

But there were no thin, dark-haired girls out on the snowy street, and why should there be? It was too cold. Snow was falling thick with another severe winter storm warning in effect tonight. Those girls were safe at home. She knew that. But she kept looking for them all the same because in her chest she could feel the beat of dark wings—not the sudden panic that came out of nowhere when once again the truth of her situation reared without warning in her mind, but a strange, alien feeling. A sense that some otherness was calling to her.

The voice of that otherness scared her almost more than the grey landscape lodged in her chest.

She felt she needed a safety net, to be able to let herself go and not have to worry about where she fell. Somewhere where she didn't have to think, be responsible, to do anything. Not forever. Just for a time.

She knew Jilly was right about nostalgia. The memories she carried forward weren't necessarily the way things had really happened. But she yearned, if only for a moment, to be able to relive some of those simpler times, those years in high school before she'd met Peter, before they were married, before her emotions got so complicated.

And then what?

You couldn't live in the past. At some point you had to come up for air and then the present would be waiting for you, unchanged. The wasteland in her chest would still stretch on forever. She'd still be trying to understand what had happened. Had Peter changed? Had she changed? Had they both changed? And when did it happen? How much of their life together had been a lie?

It was enough to drive her mad.

It was enough to make her want to step into the otherness calling to her from out there in the storm and snow, step out and simply let it swallow her whole.

Jilly couldn't put the girls from the café out of her mind either, but for a different reason. As soon as she'd gotten back to the studio, she'd taken her current work-in-progress down from the easel and replaced it with a fresh canvas. For a long moment she stared at the texture of the pale ground, a mix of gesso and a light burnt ochre acrylic wash, then she took up a stick of charcoal and began to sketch the faces of the two dark-haired girls before the memory of them left her mind.

She was working on their bodies, trying to capture the loose splay of their limbs and the curve of their backs as they'd slouched in towards each other over the café table, when there came a knock at her door.

"It's open," she called over her shoulder, too intent on what she was doing to look away.

"I could've been some mad, psychotic killer," Geordie said as he came in.

He stamped his feet on the mat, brushed the snow from his shoulders and hat. Setting his fiddlecase down by the door, he went over to the kitchen counter to see if Jilly had any coffee on.

"But instead," Jilly said, "it's only a mad, psychotic fiddler, so I'm entirely safe."

"There's no coffee."

"Sure there is. It's just waiting for you to make it."

Geordie put on the kettle, then rummaged around in the fridge, trying to find which tin Jilly was keeping her coffee beans in this week. He found them in one that claimed to hold Scottish shortbreads.

"You want some?" he asked.

Jilly shook her head. "How's Tanya?"

"Heading back to L.A. I just saw her off at the airport. The driving's horrendous. There were cars in the ditch every couple of hundred feet and I thought the bus would never make it back."

"And yet, it did," Jilly said.

Geordie smiled.

"And then," she went on, "because you were feeling bored and lonely, you decided to come visit me at two o'clock in the morning."

"Actually, I was out of coffee and I saw your light was on." He crossed the loft and came around behind the easel so that he could see what she was working on. "Hey, you're doing the crow girls."

"You know them?"

Geordie nodded. "Maida and Zia. You've caught a good likeness of them—especially Zia. I love that crinkly smile of hers."

"You can tell them apart?"

"You can't?"

"I never saw them before tonight. Heather and I were in the Cyberbean and there they were, just asking to be drawn." She added a bit of shading to the underside of a jaw, then turned to look at Geordie. "Why do you call them the crow girls?"

Geordie shrugged. "I don't. Or at least I didn't until I was talking to Jack Daw and that's what he called them when they came sauntering by. The next time I saw them I was busking in front of St. Paul's, so I started to play 'The Blackbird,' just to see what would happen, and sure enough, they came over to talk to me."

"Crow girls," Jilly repeated. The name certainly fit.

"They're some kind of relation to Jack," Geordie explained, "but I didn't quite get it. Cousins, maybe."

Jilly was suddenly struck with the memory of a long conversation she'd had with Jack one afternoon. She was working up sketches of the Crowsea Public Library for a commission when he came and sat beside her on the grass. With his long legs folded under him, black brimmed hat set at a jaunty angle, he'd regaled her with a long, rambling discourse on what he called the continent's real first nations.

"Animal people," she said softly.

Geordie smiled. "I see he fed you that line, too."

But Jilly wasn't really listening—not to Geordie. She was remembering another part of that old conversation, something else Jack had told her.

"The thing we really don't get," he'd said, leaning back in the grass, "is these contracted families you have. The mother, the father, the children, all living alone in some big house. Our families extend as far as our bloodlines and friendship can reach."

"I don't know much about bloodlines," Jilly said. "But I know about friends."

He'd nodded. "That's why I'm talking to you."

Jilly blinked and looked at Geordie. "It made sense what he said."

Geordie smiled. "Of course it did. Immortal animal people."

"That, too. But I was talking about the weird way we think about families and children. Most people don't even like kids—don't want to see, hear, or hear about them. But when you look at other cultures, even close to home . . . up on the rez, in Chinatown, Little Italy . . . it's these big rambling extended families, everybody taking care of everybody else."

Geordie cleared his throat. Jilly waited for him to speak but he went instead to unplug the kettle and finish making the coffee. He ground up some beans, and the noise of the hand-cranked machine seemed to reach out and fill every corner of the loft. When he stopped, the sudden silence was profound, as though the city outside was holding its breath along with the inheld breath of the room. Jilly was still watching him when he looked over at her.

"We don't come from that kind of family," he said finally.

"I know. That's why we had to make our own."

It's late at night, snow whirling in dervishing gusts, and the crow girls are perched on the top of the wooden fence that's been erected around a work site on Williamson Street. Used to be a parking lot there, now it's a big hole in the ground on its way to being one more office complex that nobody except the contractors want. The top of the fence is barely an inch wide at the top and slippery with snow, but they have no trouble balancing there.

Zia has a ring with a small spinning disc on it. Painted on the disc is a psychedelic coil that goes spiraling down into infinity. She keeps spinning it and the two of them stare down into the faraway place at the center of the spiral until the disc slows down, almost stops. Then Zia gives it another flick with her fingernail, and the coil goes spiraling down again.

"Where'd you get this anyway?" Maida asks.

Zia shrugs. "Can't remember. Found it somewhere."

"In someone's pocket."

"And you never did?"

Maida grins. "Just wish I'd seen it first, that's all."

They watch the disc some more, content.

"What do you think it's like down there?" Zia says after awhile. "On the other side of the spiral."

Maida has to think about that for a moment. "Same as here," she finally announces, then winks. "Only dizzier."

They giggle, leaning into each other, tottering back and forth on their perch, crow girls, can't be touched, can't hardly be seen, except someone's standing down there on the sidewalk, looking up through the falling snow, his worried expression so comical it sets them off on a new round of giggles.

"Careful now!" he calls up to them. He thinks they're on drugs—they can tell. "You don't want to—"

Before he can finish, they hold hands and let themselves fall backwards, off the fence.

"Oh, Christ!"

He jumps, gets a handhold on the top of the fence and hauls himself up. But when he looks over, over and down, way down, there's nothing to be seen. No girls lying at the bottom of that big hole in the ground, nothing at all. Only the falling snow. It's like they were never there.

His arms start to ache and he lowers himself back down the fence, lets go, bending his knees slightly to absorb the impact of the last couple of feet. He slips, catches his balance. It seems very still for a moment, so still he can hear an odd rhythmical whispering sound. Like wings. He looks up, but there's too much snow coming down to see anything. A cab comes by, skidding on the slick street, and he blinks. The street's full of city sounds again, muffled, but present. He hears the murmuring conversation of a couple approaching him, their shoulders and hair white with snow. A snowplow a few streets over. A distant siren.

He continues along his way, but he's walking slowly now, trudging through the drifts, not thinking so much of two girls sitting on top of a fence as remembering how, when he was a boy, he used to dream that he could fly.

After fiddling a little more with her sketch, Jilly finally put her charcoal down. She made herself a cup of herbal tea with the leftover hot water in the kettle and joined Geordie where he was sitting on the sofa, watching the snow come down. It was warm in the loft, almost cozy compared to the storm on the other side of the windowpanes, or maybe because of the storm. Jilly leaned back on the sofa, enjoying the companionable silence for awhile before she finally spoke.

"How do you feel after seeing the crow girls?" she asked.

Geordie turned to look at her. "What do you mean, how do I feel?"

"You know, good, bad . . . different . . ."

Geordie smiled. "Don't you mean 'indifferent?' "

"Maybe." She picked up her tea from the crate where she'd set it and took a sip. "Well?" she asked when he didn't continue.

"Okay. How do I feel? Good, I suppose. They're fun, they make me smile. In fact, just thinking of them now makes me feel good."

Jilly nodded thoughtfully as he spoke. "Me, too. And something else as well."

"The different," Geordie began. He didn't quite sigh. "You believe those stories of Jack's, don't you?"

"Of course. And you don't?"

"I'm not sure," he replied, surprising her.

"Well, I think these crow girls were in the Cyberbean for a purpose," Jilly said. "Like in that rhyme about crows."

Geordie got it right away. "Two for mirth."

Jilly nodded. "Heather needed some serious cheering up. Maybe even something more. You know how when you start feeling low, you can get on this descending spiral of depression . . . everything goes wrong, things get worse, because you expect them to?"

"Fight it with the power of positive thinking, I always say."

"Easier said than done when you're feeling that low. What you really need at a time like that is something completely unexpected to kick you out of it and remind you that there's more to life than the hopeless, grey expanse you think is stretching in every direction. What Colin Wilson calls absurd good news."

"You've been talking to my brother."

"It doesn't matter where I got it from—it's still true."

Geordie shook his head. "I don't buy the idea that Maida and Zia showed up just to put your friend in a better mood. Even bird people can get a craving for a cup of coffee, can't they?"

"Well, yes," Jilly said. "But that doesn't preclude their being there for Heather as well. Sometimes when a person needs something badly enough, it just comes to them. A personal kind of steam engine time. You might not be able to articulate what it is you need, you might not even know you need something—at least, not at a conscious level—but the need's still there, calling out to whatever's willing to listen."

Geordie smiled. "Like animal spirits."

"Crow girls."

Geordie shook his head. "Drink your tea and go to bed," he told her. "I think you need a good night's sleep."

"But—"

"It was only a coincidence. Things don't always have a meaning. Sometimes they just happen. And besides, how do you even know they had any effect on Heather?"

"I could just tell. And don't change the subject."

"I'm not."

"Okay," Jilly said. "But don't you see? It doesn't matter if it was a coincidence or not. They still showed up when Heather needed them. It's more of that 'small world, spooky world' stuff Professor Dapple goes on about. Everything's connected. It doesn't matter if we can't see how, it's still all connected. You know, chaos theory and all that."

Geordie shook his head, but he was smiling. "Does it ever strike you as weird when something Bramley's talked up for years suddenly becomes an acceptable element of scientific study?"

"Nothing strikes me as truly weird," Jilly told him. "There's only stuff I haven't figured out yet."

Heather barely slept that night. For the longest time she simply couldn't sleep, and then when she finally did, she was awake by dawn. Wide awake, but heavy with an exhaustion that came more from heartache than lack of sleep.

Sitting up against the headboard, she tried to resist the sudden tightness in her chest, but that sad, cold wasteland swelled inside her. The bed seemed depressingly huge. She didn't so much miss Peter's presence as feel adrift in the bed's expanse of blankets and sheets. Adrift in her life. Why was it he seemed to have no trouble carrying on when the simple act of getting up in the morning felt as though it would require far more energy than she could ever hope to muster?

She stared at the snow swirling against her window, not at all relishing the drive into town on a morning like this. If anything, it was coming down harder than it had been last night. All it took was the suggestion of snow and everybody in the city seemed to forget how to drive, never mind common courtesy or traffic laws. A blizzard like this would snarl traffic and back it up as far as the mountains.

She sighed, supposing it was just as well she'd woken so early since it would take her at least an extra hour to get downtown today.

Up, she told herself, and forced herself to swing her feet to the floor and rise. A shower helped. It didn't really ease the heartache, but the hiss of the water made it easier to ignore her thoughts. Coffee, when she was dressed and had brewed a pot, helped more, though she still winced when Janice came bounding into the kitchen.

"It's a snow day!" she cried. "No school. They just announced it on the radio. The school's closed, closed, closed!"

She danced about in her flannel nightie, pirouetting in the small space between the counter and the table.

"Just yours," Heather asked, "or Casey's, too?"

"Mine, too," Casey replied, following her sister into the room.

Unlike Janice, she was maintaining her cool, but Heather could tell she was just as excited. Too old to allow herself to take part in Janice's spontaneous celebration, but young enough to be feeling giddy with the unexpected holiday.

"Good," Heather said. "You can look after your sister."

"*Mom!*" Janice protested. "I'm not a baby."

"I know. It's just good to have someone older in the house when—"

"You can't be thinking of going in to work today," Casey said.

"We could do all kinds of stuff," Janice added. "Finish decorating the house. Baking."

"Yeah," Casey said, "all the things we don't seem to have time for anymore."

Heather sighed. "The trouble is," she explained, "the real world doesn't work like school. We don't get snow days."

Casey shook her head. "That is *so* unfair."

The phone rang before Heather could agree.

"I'll bet it's your boss," Janice said as Heather picked up the phone. "Calling to tell you it's a snow day for you, too."

Don't I wish, Heather thought. But then what would she do at home all day? It was so hard being here, even with the girls and much as she loved them. Everywhere she turned, something reminded her of how the promises of a good life had turned into so much ash. At least work kept her from brooding.

She brought the receiver up to her ear and spoke into the mouthpiece. "Hello?"

"I've been thinking," the voice on the other end of the line said. "About last night."

Heather had to smile. Wasn't that so Jilly, calling up first thing in the morning as though they were still in the middle of last night's conversation.

"What about last night?" she said.

"Well, all sorts of stuff. Like remembering a perfect moment in the past and letting it carry you through a hard time now."

If only, Heather thought. "I don't have a moment that perfect," she said.

"I sort of got that feeling," Jilly told her. "That's why I think they were a message—a kind of perfect moment now that you can use the same way."

"What *are* you talking about?"

"The crow girls. In the café last night."

"The crow..." It took her a moment to realize what Jilly meant. Their complexions had been dark enough so she supposed they could have been Indians. "How do you know what tribe they belonged to?"

"Not Crow, Native American," Jilly said, "but crow, bird people."

Heather shook her head as she listened to what Jilly went on to say, for all that only her daughters were here to see the movement. Glum looks had replaced their earlier excitement when they realized the call wasn't from her boss.

"Do you have any idea how improbable all of this sounds?" she asked when Jilly finished. "Life's not like your paintings."

"Says who?"

"How about common sense?"

"Tell me," Jilly said. "Where did common sense ever get you?"

Heather sighed. "Things don't happen just because we want them to," she said.

"Sometimes that's *exactly* why they happen," Jilly replied. "They happen because we need them to."

"I don't live in that kind of a world."

"But you could."

Heather looked across the kitchen at her daughters once more. The girls were watching her, trying to make sense out of the one-sided conversation they were hearing. Heather wished them luck. She was hearing both sides and that didn't seem to help at all. You couldn't simply reinvent your world because you wanted to. Things just were how they were.

"Just think about it," Jilly added. "Will you do that much?"

"I . . ."

That bleak landscape inside Heather seemed to expand, growing so large there was no way she could contain it. She focused on the faces of her daughters. She remembered the crow girls in the café. There was so much innocence in them all, daughters and crow girls. She'd been just like them once and she knew it wasn't simply nostalgia coloring her memory. She knew there'd been a time when she lived inside each particular day, on its own and by itself, instead of trying to deal with all the days of her life at once, futilely attempting to reconcile the discrepancies and mistakes.

"I'll try," she said into the phone.

They said their goodbyes and Heather slowly cradled the receiver.

"Who was that, mom?" Casey asked.

Heather looked out the window. The snow was still falling, muffling the world. Covering its complexities with a blanket as innocent as the hope she saw in her daughters' eyes.

"Jilly," she said. She took a deep breath, then smiled at them. "She was calling to tell me that today really is a snow day."

The happiness that flowered on their faces helped ease the tightness in her chest. The grey landscape waiting for her there didn't go away, but for some reason, it felt less profound. She wasn't even worried about what her boss would say when she called in to tell him she wouldn't be in today.

Crow girls can move like ghosts. They'll slip into your house when you're not home, sometimes when you're only sleeping, go walking spirit-soft through your rooms and hallways, sit in your favorite chair, help themselves to cookies and beer, borrow a trinket or two which they'll mean to return and usually do. It's not break & enter so much as simple curiosity. They're worse than cats.

Privacy isn't in their nature. They don't seek it and barely understand the concept. Personal property is even more alien. The idea of ownership—that one can lay proprietary claim to a piece of land, an object, another person or creature—doesn't even register.

"Whatcha looking at?" Zia asks.

They don't know whose house they're in. Walking along on the street, trying to catch snowflakes on their tongues, one or the other of them suddenly got the urge to come inside. Upstairs, the family sleeps.

Maida shows her the photo album. "Look," she says. "It's the same people, but they keep changing. See, here's she's a baby, then she's a little girl, then a teenager."

"Everything changes," Zia says. "Even we get old. Look at Crazy Crow."

"But it happens so fast with them."

Zia sits down beside her and they pore over the pictures, munching on apples they found earlier in a cold cellar in the basement.

Upstairs, a father wakes in his bed. He stares at the ceiling, wondering what woke him. Nervous energy crackles inside him like static electricity, a sudden spill of adrenaline, but he doesn't know why. He gets up and checks the children's rooms. They're both asleep. He listens for intruders, but the house is silent.

Stepping back into the hall, he walks to the head of the stairs and looks down. He thinks he sees something in the gloom, two dark-haired girls sitting on the sofa, looking through a photo album. Their gazes lift to meet his and hold it. The next thing he knows, he's on the sofa himself, holding the photo album in his hand. There are no strange girls sitting there with him. The house seems quieter than it's ever been, as though the fridge, the furnace and every clock the family owns are holding their breath along with him.

He sets the album down on the coffee table, walks slowly back up the stairs and returns to his bed. He feels like a stranger, misplaced. He doesn't know this room, doesn't know the woman beside him. All he can think about is the first girl he ever loved and his heart swells with a bittersweet sorrow. An ache pushes against his ribs, makes it almost impossible to breathe.

What if, what if . . .

He turns on his side and looks at his wife. For one moment her face blurs, becomes a morphing image that encompasses both her features and those of his first true love. For one moment it seems as though anything is possible, that for all these years he could have been married to another woman, to that girl who first held, then unwittingly, broke his heart.

"No," he says.

His wife stirs, her features her own again. She blinks sleepily at him.

"Wha . . . ?" she mumbles.

He holds her close, heartbeat drumming, more in love with her for being who she is than he has ever been before.

Outside, the crow girls are lying on their backs, making snow angels on his lawn, scissoring their arms and legs, shaping skirts and wings. They break their apple cores in two and give their angels eyes, then run off down the street, holding hands. The snow drifts are undisturbed by their weight. It's as though they, too, like the angels they've just made, also have wings.

"This is so cool," Casey tells her mother. "It really feels like Christmas. I mean, not like Christmases we've had, but, you know, like really being part of Christmas."

Heather nods. She's glad she brought the girls down to the soup kitchen to help Jilly and her friends serve a Christmas dinner to those less fortunate than themselves. She's been worried about how her daughters would take the break from tradition, but then realized, with Peter gone, tradition is already broken. Better to begin all over again.

The girls had been dubious when she first broached the subject with them— "I don't want to spend Christmas with *losers*," had been Casey's first comment. Heather hadn't argued with her. All she'd said was, "I want you to think about what you just said."

Casey's response had been a sullen look—there were more and more of these lately—but Heather knew her own daughter well enough. Casey had stomped off to her room, but then come back half an hour later and helped her explain to Janice why it might not be the worst idea in the world.

She watches them now, Casey having rejoined her sister where they are playing with the homeless children, and knows a swell of pride. They're such good kids, she thinks as she takes another sip of her cider. After a couple of hours serving coffee, tea and hot cider, she'd really needed to get off her feet for a moment.

"Got something for you," Jilly says, sitting down on the bench beside her.

Heather accepts the small, brightly-wrapped parcel with reluctance. "I thought we said we weren't doing Christmas presents."

"It's not really a Christmas present. It's more an everyday sort of a present that I just happen to be giving you today."

"Right."

"So aren't you going to open it?"

Heather peels back the paper and opens the small box. Inside, nestled in a piece of folded Kleenex, are two small silver earrings cast in the shapes of crows. Heather lifts her gaze.

"They're beautiful."

"Got them at the craft show from a local jeweler. His name's on the card in the bottom of the box. They're to remind you—"

Heather smiles. "Of crow girls?"

"Partly. But more to remember that this—" Jilly waves a hand that could be taking in the basement of St. Vincent's, could be taking in the whole world. "It's not all we get. There's more. We can't always see it, but it's there."

For a moment, Heather thinks she sees two dark-haired slim figures standing on the far side of the basement, but when she looks more closely they're only a bag lady and Geordie's friend Tanya, talking.

For a moment, she thinks she hears the sound of wings, but it's only the murmur of conversation. Probably.

What she knows for sure is that the grey landscape inside her chest is shrinking a little more, every day.

"Thank you," she says.

She isn't sure if she's speaking to Jilly or to crow girls she's only ever seen once, but whose presence keeps echoing through her life. Her new life. It isn't necessarily a better one. Not yet. But at least it's on the way up from wherever she'd been going, not down into a darker despair.

"Here," Jilly says. "Let me help you put them on."

RAPUNZEL'S EXILE

Lisa Russ Spaar

Spaar's brief prose piece, "Rapunzel's Exile," has an impact far greater than its length might suggest. It is a dark and horrific rendering of the familiar fairy tale, speculating on the complex nature of the relationship between foster daughter and witch. "Rapunzel's Exile" is reprinted from *Ploughshares*, Vol. 22, #4. This piece also appeared in her book, *Rapunzel's Clock*, which won the Virginia Commission for the Arts Award in 1996.

—T. W. and E. D.

I was told to lie down in the cart, and I did. My braided hair mixed with straw under me to catch the blood I seeped. Then she covered me with heavy furs and brush. The night was stark and cold, the stars close and multiplying like cells as we creaked along under them a long time. We crossed several creeks, water hissing up through shelves of ice. She pulled the whole time. She was a strong woman.

When I'd first felt the blood darken my skirt in the garden, I knew she'd cursed me for my new game, tossing stones over the wall, and someone— who?—tossing them back. All that day, she paced while I lay in her bed, waiting to die. All that night we traveled.

At dawn we were deep in a forest, so tangled we had to ditch the cart and pick by foot through roots and brambles. Ravines pitched and rose. We waded thigh-deep in leaves and water. I watched her tough haunches, the rope around her waist that tethered my neck. The sky grew heavy with pent snow, and still we walked in woods so old and dark at noon the owls cried.

The one who'd held my face, called it her "sun," had turned to me her wordless back. Behind her, I had no choice but follow, twelve years old, bent and sopping wet with shame and terror. Even when we came, finally, to the cleared place where the tower rose dully in weak moonlight, and I gasped "Godmother!," she would not turn to look at me. Her knife flashed quick to cut the rope, then pointed through the low door. I cried and said "No, no"—I pleaded and grasped for her—but the bright blade held me back. On my knees inside, I groped the stairs. The cellar draft above me fell upon my face, and I knew that this place had been made ready for me all the years that she had loved me. And I guessed that this was love, too—not the seesaw play of stones lopped over a garden wall, but my lonely climb upward, and the thick scrape of mortar over shoved and piled stones, behind.

THE WITCHES OF JUNKET
Patricia A. McKillip

One of the fantasy field's finest writers graces our pages once again, this time with an engaging contemporary tale about a unique American family of witches. World Fantasy Award winner Patricia A. McKillip is the author of *The Forgotten Beasts of Eld*, the "Riddlemaster" trilogy, *Stepping from the Shadows, Something Rich and Strange, The Book of Atrix Wolfe* and other luminous books that no lover of fantasy (or of beautiful prose) should miss. Her short fiction has been published in several anthologies, including *Xanadu, Full Spectrum, Snow White, Blood Red* and *The Armless Maiden.* "The Witches of Junket" comes from *Sisters in Fantasy 2,* a collection of original fantasy tales by women writers (edited by Susan Shwartz and Martin H. Greenberg.)

—T. W.

Granny Heather was out on the lawn digging up nightcrawlers by flashlight when she saw the black spot on the moon. She heard the tide, though the sea was twenty miles away, and she saw the massive rock just offshore south of Crane Harbor open vast black eyes and stare at her. Three huge birds flew soundlessly overhead, looking like pterodactyls, glowing bluish-white, like ghosts might. She didn't know if she was in the past or future. In the future, the sea might eat its way through the wrinkled, old coast mountains across the pastures where the sheep grazed, to her doorstep. In the past, those dinosaur birds might have flown over Junket, or whatever was there before the town was. She stopped tugging at a nightcrawler that was tugging itself back into its hole, and she turned the flashlight off. She made herself as small as possible, hunkering down on her old knees in the damp grass. Her hair felt too bright; she wondered if, under the moonlight, it glowed like the ghost birds. She heard her thin blood singing.

"So," she whispered, "you're awake."

For a moment she felt stared at, as if the full moon were an eye. It could see into her frail bones, find the weakest places where a tap might shatter her. She felt luminous, exposed, her old bones shining like the bones of little fish down in the darkest realms of the sea.

Then it was over, she was disregarded, the moon was no longer interested in her.

She stood up in the dark, tottery, her heart hammering, and made her way back into her house.

The next morning, she took her pole and her nightcrawlers and her lawn chair down the road to where the old pumphouse straddled a branch of the Junket River, where the bass liked to feed. She pleated a worm onto her hook and added an afterthought: a green marshmallow. No telling, she thought. She cast her line into the still water.

A trout rose up out of the water, danced on its tail and said: Call Storm's children.

It vanished back into the water as she stared, and took the worm clean off the hook, leaving the marshmallow.

She reeled in, sighing. "It's easy," she grumbled to the trout, "for you to say. You don't have to put up with them."

But she had to admit it was right.

Still and all, Storm's children being what they were, she got a second opinion.

She drove her twenty-year-old red VW Beetle over to Poppy and Cass's house, adding another 3.8 miles to the 32,528.9 she had turned over in twenty years. Cass was in the yard, polishing a great wheel of redwood burl. His work-shed, which was a small warehouse left over from when the nearly invisible town of Raventree actually had a dock for river traffic, was cluttered with slabs of redwood and smaller, paler pieces of myrtle. He smiled at Heather, but he didn't speak. He was a shy, untidy giant, with hair that needed pruning and a nicotine-stained moustache. He jerked his head at the house to tell Heather where Poppy was, and Heather, feeling damp in her bones, creaked to the door, stuck her head inside.

"Poppy?"

Poppy came out of the kitchen, wiping her hands on a dish towel. "Why, Heather, you old sweet thing, I didn't hear you drive up. Come on in and sit down. I'll get us some tea." Turning briskly back to the kitchen, she caused whirlwinds: plants moved their faces, table legs clattered, framed photos on the wall slid askew. Heather waited until things quieted, then eased into one of Cass's burl chairs. It had three legs like a stool and a long skinny back with a face, elongated and shy, peering out of the wood grain. A tea kettle howled; Poppy came back out again carrying mugs of water with mint leaves floating in them. Heather preferred coffee, but she preferred nearly anything to Poppy's coffee. Anyway, she liked chewing on mint leaves.

Poppy settled into a chair with wide arms that had holes for plant pots; delicate strings-of-hearts hung their runners over the sides almost to the floor. Poppy was a tall, big-boned woman who wore her yellow-grey hair in a long braid over one shoulder. Her eyes were wide-set, smokey grey; her brows were still yellow in her smooth forehead. She favored eye-smacking colors and clunky jewelry. Abalone, turquoise, hematite, and coral danced on her fingers. She wore big myrtle-wood loops in her ears; a chunk of amber on a chain bounced on her bosom. She was the age Storm would have been, if Storm hadn't skidded into a tree on a rainy night. Heather had looked to Poppy after that, someone for her bewildered eyes to rest on after Storm had vanished, and Poppy had let her, coaxing her along as patiently as if Heather had been one of her ailing plants.

Heather took a sip of tea and spent a moment working a mint leaf out from behind one tooth, while Poppy meandered amiably about her married daughter and her new grandson. "Chance, they named him," she said. "Might as well have named him Luck or Fate or—Still and all, it's kind of catching."

"Poppy," Heather said, having finally swallowed the mint leaf, "I got to send for Storm's children."

Poppy put her mug down on the chair arm. Her brows pinched together suddenly, as if a tooth had jabbed her. "Oh, no."

"I've been told to."

"Who told you?"

"A trout, under Tim Greyson's pumphouse."

"Well why, for goodness sake?"

Heather sighed, feeling too old and very frail. "You know what's inside Oyster Rock." Poppy gave a nod, silent. "Well, it's not going to stay there."

Poppy swallowed. She stared at nothing a moment, her sandal tapping—she preferred the cork-soled variety, that lifted her up even taller and slapped her feet as she walked. "Oh, Lord," she muttered. "Are you sure? It's been down there for eight hundred years, ever since that Klamath woman drove it into the rock. You'd think it could have stayed there a few more years."

"You'd think so. But—"

"Maybe we don't have to send for Storm's children. Maybe we could handle it ourselves. Still, Annie's up north with her daughter and Tessa has to get her legs worked on, and Olivia's at the mud caves in Montana, rejuvenating her skin—"

"That leaves you and me," Heather said dryly. "Unless you're busy, too."

"Well—"

"The point is, that thing's not going to ask us if we have time for it. It's not going to wait around for Annie to get home or Olivia to get the mud off her face. It's coming out. I felt it, Poppy. I saw the warnings. None of us was around eight hundred years ago to know exactly what it does, so if a trout says get help, how're you going to argue with it?"

Poppy drew a breath, held it. "Did you catch the trout?" she asked grimly. "No."

"Pity. I'd like to deep-fry it." She kicked moodily at the planter again; the ficus in it shivered and dropped a leaf. "Are you sure what's inside the rock isn't the lesser of the two evils?"

"Poppy! Those are my grandchildren you're talking about. Besides," she added, "they're older now. Maybe they've settled down a little."

"Last time they came, they threw a keg party in the church parking lot."

"That was seven years ago and, anyway, it was at Evan's funeral," Heather said stubbornly. She kicked at the planter herself, feeling the chill at her side where Evan wasn't anymore. "And it was more like a wake. Even I had a sip of beer."

Poppy smiled, patting Heather's hand soothingly, though her brows still tugged together. "Evan would have enjoyed the party," she said. "It's a wonder he didn't shuffle back out of his grave."

"He always was an irreligious old poop. Poppy, I got to do it. I can't ignore what I saw. I can't ignore advice given by water."

"No." Poppy sighed. "You can't. But you can't bring Storm's children back here without explaining why, either. We'd better have a meeting. I'd like to know what we're dealing with. Inside the rock, that is. It had another name, that rock, didn't it? Some older name . . . Then people settling around Crane Harbor renamed it; the old name didn't make any sense to them."

"I don't remember."

"Well, of course, it was years before even you were born—Mask. That's what it was. Mask-in-the-Rock."

Heather felt her face wrinkle up, in weariness and perplexity. "Mask. They were right—it doesn't make much sense." Her legs tensed to work herself to her feet. But she didn't move. She wanted to stay in Poppy's house, where the chairs had shy faces and lived in a green forest hidden away from anything called Mask. "Things get old," she said half to herself. "Maybe this Mask-thing got a little tired in eight hundred years."

"More likely," Poppy said, "it had an eight-hundred-year nap." The door opened; Cass came in, and her face changed quickly. She rose, smiling, flashing amber and mother of pearl, chattering amiably as she picked up Heather's mug. "Heather and I are going to take a little ride, honey. Maybe do a little shopping, go watch some waves, have a bite to eat at Scudder's. Is there anything you want me to pick up for you?"

"I don't think so," Cass said, smoothing his moustache. His hand, broad, solid, muscular, like something he might have carved out of wood, moved with deliberation from his mustache to Poppy's purple shoulder. He smiled at her, seeing her a moment. Then his eyes filled up again with burls, boles, shapes embedded in wood grain. He gave her shoulder an absent pat. "Have fun."

"Fun," Poppy said, grim again, as she fired up Heather's VW and careened onto the two-lane road that ran along the Junket River into Crane Harbor. "Heather, I feel like I'm sitting in a tin can. Is this thing safe?"

"I've had it for twenty years and I never even dinged it," Heather said, clutching the elbow rest nervously. "You be careful with my car, Poppy McCarey. If you land us in the river—"

"Oh, honey, this car would float like a frog egg."

"Maybe," Heather said grumpily. "But you don't got to go so fast—that thing's been in there for eight hundred years."

The road hugged the low, pine-covered mountain on one side and gave them a view of the Junket Valley on the other, with the slow river winding through green fields, the sheep on them white as dandelion seed. Occasionally, they passed small herds of cows, which made Heather remember the old farm back in Nebraska, before the drought boiled the ground dry as a rusty pot.

"There's that Brahma bull," she said as they rounded a curve. She liked looking at it, humpy and grey among the colored cows.

"There's llamas," Poppy said, "over by Port James. Have you seen them?"

"Over by the cranberry bogs?"

"Yeah."

"Yeah."

Poppy weighed down on the gas suddenly to pass a pickup pulling a horse trailer, and Heather closed her eyes. She must have taken a little nap, with the sun flicking in and out of the trees, light and dark chasing each other over her face, for when she opened them again, they were passing the slough and there were no more hills left in front of them. Then there was no more land left; they had come to the edge of the world. She put her window down to smell the sea.

The air was chilly; the sea, its morning mist rolling away in a dark grey band across the horizon, looking turquoise. The tide heaved against the pilings along the harbor channel; foam exploded like bed ticking into the bright air.

"Tide's in." Poppy turned away from the harbor onto a road that ambled along the cliffs and beaches toward Oyster Rock. Fishers stood at the edge of the tide, casting into the surf.

"Bet the perch are biting now," Heather said wistfully. Poppy, who hated to fish, said nothing. They passed the Sandpiper hotel, pulled into a viewpoint parking lot behind it. Poppy turned off the engine.

They sat silently. From that angle on the cliff, they could see the grassy knoll on top of Oyster Rock, and the white-spattered ledges where the cormorants nested. The tide boiled around the rock, tried to crawl up it. Gulls circled it, like they circled trawlers and schools of fish, wheedling plaintively. To Heather, their cries seemed suddenly cries of alarm, of warning, at something they had felt stirring beneath their bird feet, inside the massive rock.

"Looks quiet enough," Poppy said after a while.

"Maybe," Heather said, feeling small again, cold. "But it doesn't make me quiet in my bones. Always did before, always whenever we'd drive here to look at it—me and Evan, or me alone after Evan died—in the morning, in the moonlight. You watch the waves curling around that old rock with the birds on its head and you feel like as long as that rock stands there, so will the world. Now, it don't feel that way. It just feels—hollow."

Poppy nodded, the myrtle loops rocking in her ears. "The cormorants have all gone," she said suddenly, and Heather blinked. So they had. The dark shadows on the splotched wall where the birds had nested for years, were nothing but that—splits in the rock, or maybe shadows of the birds that the birds had left behind, escaping. Poppy's mouth tightened; her ringed hand fiddled nervously with amber. She reached out abruptly, and started the engine. "We've got to make some phone calls."

"Where we going to meet?"

"Your house, of course. Nobody but the cats there to listen in."

"You better get me home then. I got to dust."

Poppy spun to a halt in the gravel. She stared at Heather a second before she laughed. "Listen to you! I swear you wouldn't go to your own funeral unless you cleaned out your refrigerator first."

"I probably won't," Heather retorted. "Now, between this and that and Storm's children coming, I'll never get my tomatoes planted."

"That's another thing you have to do."

"What?"

"Call Storm's children."

"Oh, fiddle," Heather said crossly. "Damn!"

Sarah Ford came that night, and Tessa walking with her canes, and Laura Field, who was even older than Heather, from the Victorian mansion across the street, and Dawn Singleton, who was only nineteen, and Rachel Coulter, who always found the thread on the carpet, the stain on the coffee cup, the dust on the whatnot shelf. Heather took oatmeal cookies out of the freezer, and jars of Queen Anne cherries from her tree out of the pantry. Olivia Bogg was out of state, Vi Darnelle was down with the flu, and Annie Turner had gone to Portland to visit her daughter. But, considering the notice they'd been given, it was a good gathering, Heather thought. She watched Rachel turn a cookie over to examine a burned spot on it, and she wanted to take one of Tessa's canes and smack Rachel in the shin. Rachel bit into the cookie dubiously; her heavy, frowning face quivered like custard. How Poppy, in an orange sweater, orange lipstick, tight jeans, high-heeled sandals, and what looked like half the dimestore jewelry in Junket, managed to look remotely glamorous at her age was more than Heather could understand.

They finished their coffee and dessert and gossip; little pools of silence spread until they were all silent, curious faces turning toward Poppy, who was perched on the arm of the sofa and toward Heather, who was gazing at an old oval black-and-white picture of Evan as a little boy, wearing a sailor suit and shoes that buckled like a girl's. How, she wondered, always with the same astonishment, did he get from being that little long-haired boy to that old man in his grave? How does that happen?

Then the cuckoo sprang out of its doorway nine times and Heather blinked, and saw the faces turned toward her, waiting.

"Who called this meeting?" Tessa asked in her deep, strong voice.

"I did," Heather said.

"For what reason?" Dawn Singleton's young voice wavered a little out of nervousness; her black hightops stirred the nap on Heather's carpet.

"I've been warned."

"By what?" old Laura Field asked, her voice as sweet and quavery as Dawn's. Poppy almost hadn't got her; she'd been on her way out the door to visit her husband, who had been in a coma at the Veterans Hospital in Slicum Bay for nine years.

"By the moon. By birds. By water."

There was a short silence; even Rachel was looking a little bug-eyed. Then Rachel cleared her throat. "What warning was given?"

"The thing inside Oyster Rock is coming out."

Even the cuckoo clock went silent then. It seemed a long, slow moment from the movement of its pendulum back to the movement of its pendulum forth. Dawn's hightops crept together, sought comfort from each other. Poppy moved, fake clusters of diamonds sparking in her ears. It was her turn to ask one question.

"What must be done?"

They came to life a little at her voice. Rachel blinked; Laura Field cleared her throat softly; Sarah Ford, her mouth still open, shifted her coffee cup.

"I have been advised."

"What advice was given?" Sarah asked faintly. Middle-aged, plump, pretty, she looked constantly harried, as if she were trying to catch up with something always blown just out of reach. Having half a dozen boys would do that, Heather guessed. The cuckoo clock stretched time again, suspending Heather's thoughts between its tick and its tock.

"I got to call Storm's children."

Somebody's cup and saucer crashed onto the floor. Heather opened her eyes. Dawn's hands were over her mouth; her eyes looked half-shocked, half-smiling. Rachel, of all people, had dropped her coffee on the floor. Luckily she was sitting over in the kitchen area, where there was nothing to spill it on. Laura Field's eyes looked enormous, stricken; she was patting her hair as if a wind had blustered through the room. Tessa closed her own eyes, looking as if she were praying, or counting to ten.

"Who in hell," Tessa demanded, "gave that advice?"

Rachel, standing beside Poppy while Poppy wiped up the mess, gave Tessa a reproving glance. But no one else seemed to think the profanity unjustified. Heather sighed. Storm had been born out of blistering sun, dust-storms, blizzards so thick they swallowed houses, barns, light itself. But Storm had been the aftermath, the memory of what had passed. She had swallowed the storms, had them inside her, returned them as gifts her children carried—lightning bolts, icicles, streaks of hot brown wind—across the threshold of the world.

"A fish," Heather said.

Tessa pressed her lips together. She was ten years younger than Heather, but heavy and slow: the veins in her legs nearly crippled her. She had kept books for the lumber mill for thirty years. Whenever it closed down, depending on whether the political outcry was for live trees or lumber, she fiddled with an article about how things got named up and down the river between Junket and Crane Harbor, along the coast between Port James and Slicum Bay. She'd be fiddling in her grave, Heather thought privately; she viewed bits of information as suspiciously as she might have viewed something furry in her refrigerator.

Dawn opened her mouth, her young face looking perplexed, as well it might. "What is inside Oyster Rock?" she asked. There was a short silence.

"Don't know; nobody knows. Mask, it's called. Legend is a woman from over Klamath way faced it down and drove it inside the rock."

"If one woman did that," Rachel said tartly, "why do we need to send for Storm's children?"

"Because the trout said," Heather answered wearily. "That's all I know. Advice given by water."

Poppy, rattling fake pearls in one hand, asked Heather resignedly, "Where are they?"

"South," Heather said. "Somewheres. California. Texas, Lydia called me a year ago on Evan's anniversary. She gave me a number to call if I needed them. Said she changed her name to—oh, what was it? Greensnake. She never said where she was calling from exactly. Number's in my book. . . ." She leaned her head back tiredly, closed her eyes, wanting to nap now that she'd fed and warned them. She lifted her head again slowly at the silence, found them all watching her, as still and intent as cats. She shifted. "I suppose—"

"Quit supposing," Rachel said sourly. The phone on its long line was making its way toward her, hand to hand. "Do it."

"Call me Lydia again," Lydia said sweetly. Her hair was green; she wore a short black dress that fit her body like a snakeskin and black heels so high and thin she probably speared a few nightcrawlers on her way across Heather's lawn. Georgie, hauling bags out, turned to give Lydia a sidelong glance out of glacier-cold eyes. Georgie had hair like a mown lawn, quick-bitten nails, flat, high, craggy cheekbones like her grandfather's, and a gold wedding band on her left hand that flashed like fire as she heaved a suitcase into the porchlight. Poppy had driven her old station wagon to pick them up at the airport in Slicum Bay. Joining Heather, she seemed unusually thoughtful. Heather, counting heads anxiously in the dark, said, "Where's—" And then the third head came up, groaning, from between the seats.

Lydia said brightly, "Grace is a little shaken."

Grace hit the grass hands first, crawled her way out of the car. She was skeleton thin, with hair so long and silvery she looked a hundred years old when she stood up, haggard and swaying. "I threw up," she whispered.

"In my car?" Poppy said breathlessly.

"Georgie'll clean it up. I can't travel in anything with wheels. Not even roller skates. It's because I'm so old."

Poppy's agate necklace clattered in her hand. "Oh," she said, and stuck there.

"You can't be more than twenty-five," Heather guessed, calculating wildly.

"Twenty-nine," Georgie said succinctly, and clamped her thin lips together again.

"I mean older than the wheel. Deep in my . . . in my spiritual life," said Grace.

Lydia hiccuped in the silence. "Oh, I beg," she said. She leaned down from a great height, it seemed, to kiss Heather's cheek. As she straightened, Heather caught a waft of something scented with oranges. Her head spun a little: Lydia seemed to straighten high as the moon, as long as the Junket river in her black stockings and heels.

They settled in the living room finally, cups of coffee and tea fragrant with that smell of oranges from Lydia's flask. Heather had some herself; a sip or two and she could swear orange trees rustled at her back and she could almost see the fire within Georgie's cold, granite face. In his photo, the last taken, Evan seemed to smile a tilted smile. Poppy, who never drank, had a healthy swig in her cup.

"Oyster Rock," Lydia mused, sliding a heel off and swinging it absently from her toe.

"Mask," Poppy said, "they called it back then." She tapped an agate bead to her teeth, frowning. "Whenever then was, that you call back then whenever they were."

"Uh," Grace said with an effort. She held onto her cup with both hands, as if it might leap onto the carpet. A strand of her white hair was soaking in it. "I'll find out."

"Tessa might know more."

"Tessa the one sounds like a sea lion in heat?"

Poppy pushed the agate hard against a tooth. "You might say."

"Uh. She goes back, but not as far."

"As far as—"

"Me. She goes back to when it had a name. I go back to when it didn't."

Grace started to sag then. Lydia reached out deftly, caught her cup before she fell facedown on the couch. Lydia ticked her tongue. "That girl does not travel well."

"She all right?" Heather asked, alarmed.

"Toss a blanket over her," Georgie said shortly. "She'll be back before morning."

Lydia watched Grace a moment. She looked dead, Heather thought, her face and hair the same eerie, silvery white, all her bones showing. Lydia's green head lifted slowly. She seemed to hear something in the distance, though there wasn't much of Junket awake by then. She made a movement that began in her shoulders, rippled down her body to end with a twitch that slid the shoe back on her foot. When she stood up, she seemed taller than ever.

"That place," she said to Heather. "What's its name? Tad's. That still alive?"

"Tad's?" Heather sought Poppy's eyes. "I guess."

"I left something there."

"You—But you haven't been here for seven years!"

"So it's been there seven years. I like a night walk."

"Honey, you can't go in Tad's! You can't go among truckers and drunks with that hair and them shoes. Whatever you left, let it stay left."

"I left a score," Lydia said. She flicked open a gold powder case, smoothed a smooth green brow with one finger, then lifted her lip to examine an eyetooth. "I left a score to settle at Tad's." She snapped the powder case shut. "Coming, Georgie?"

Heather closed her eyes. When she opened them and her mouth, there was only Grace looking like a white shadow on the couch, and Poppy wandering around collecting cups. She stared, horrified, at Poppy.

"We got to do— We can't just let— You call Cass, tell him to get down to Tad's and help those girls—"

"No." Poppy shook her head; shell and turquoise clattered with emphasis. "No, ma'am. Those aren't girls, and they don't need our help, and I wouldn't send Cass down there tonight if Tad was singing hymns and selling tickets to heaven. Stop fussing and sit down. Have some more tea."

Heather backed weakly into her rocker, where she could keep an eye on Grace, who looked as if she had bought a ticket and was halfway there. Heather dragged her eyes away from the still face to take a quick look around the room. She said hopefully, "Don't suppose Lydia left her flask. . . ."

Poppy gave her a tablespoon of Lydia's elixir in her tea; she was asleep and dreaming before she finished it.

Grace sat upright on the couch. The house was dark. It wasn't even the Junket house, Heather realized; it was more like the old farmhouse where Storm had been born.

"Shh," Grace said, and held out her hand. She had color in her face; her hair glowed in the dark like pale fire. For some reason she was wearing

Heather's old crocheted bedroom slippers. "You can come with me but don't talk. Don't say a word. . . ."

Heather took her hand. Grace led her into the bedroom where she and Evan had slept over fifty years ago. The bed, under its thin chenille spread, glowed like Grace's hair. Then it wasn't a bedspread at all—it was the sea, foaming pale under the moon. Heather nearly stumbled at a blast of wind. She opened her mouth but Grace's hand squeezed a warning; she put a finger to her lips. She turned her head. Heather looked in the same direction and nearly jumped out of her skin. The old rock heaved out of the ocean like a whale in their faces, as black against the sea and stars as if it were an empty hole.

Then she knew it wasn't an emptiness. It was a something looking for its face. It was a live thing that couldn't be seen—it needed a face to make it real. Then its eyes could open; then its vast mouth could speak. Heather clung like a child to Grace's hand, her mouth open wide. The wind pushed into her so hard she couldn't make a noise if she'd wanted.

Heather, the emptiness said. *Heather*.

She jumped. She opened her eyes, saw Grace rising up on the couch, her hair glowing like St. Elmo's fire, her eyes white as moons. Then her hair turned red. Then blue. Heather, too stunned to move, heard Poppy say, "Guess they finished at Tad's."

It was after one in the morning. Flo Hendrick's son Maury was standing on Heather's lawn talking, while his flashing lights illumined her living room through the open curtains. She couldn't move. Then she heard a strange sound.

Laughter. From Maury Hendrick, who hadn't smiled, Flo said, since his pants fell down in a sack race in the third grade.

Poppy sucked in her breath. Then she grinned a quick, tight grin that vanished as soon as Heather saw it. Maury's car crunched back out over the gravel. Lydia strolled in, carrying a beer bottle.

"Well," she said lightly, "I feel better. Don't you feel better?"

"What happened?" Poppy asked.

"Where's Georgie?" Heather asked.

"Oh, Georgie's still down there helping Tad. Georgie likes tidying things. Remember how she cleaned up the church lot after Grandpa's funeral?"

"What happened?" Poppy asked again. She was so still not a bead trembled; her eyes were wide, her mouth set, the dimples deep in her cheeks. Lydia looked at her, still smiling a little. Something in her eyes made Heather think of deep, deep water, of dark caves hollowed out, grain by grain, by the ancient, ceaseless working of tides.

"A lot of women in Junket suddenly had an urge to drink a beer at Tad's tonight. Funny. There was some trouble over comments made. But as I said, Georgie's helping clean up."

Poppy moved finally, groped for her agates. "Did Tad call Maury in?"

"Nobody was called. It was a private affair. Maury was just cruising Main. He stopped to chat about open containers on public sidewalks. Then he gave me a ride home."

"What'd you say to make him laugh?" Heather demanded. Lydia's smile slanted upward; she turned away restively to Grace, who was sitting motionless on the couch. Heather followed Lydia, still not finished about Tad's, wanting to comb through all the details to get the fret out of her. The wide, moony look in Grace's eyes chilled her.

Lydia stood in front of Grace, gazed down at her silently. Evan, in his sailor suit, looked innocently at them both. Heather wondered suddenly if Evan could have seen them coming, his storm-ridden granddaughters, he would have passed on down the road to peaceable Mary Ecklund and married her instead.

"Grace," Lydia said, so sharply that Heather started. "Where are you?"

"In the dark," Grace whispered. "Watching."

"Watching when? Then? Or now?"

"Shh, Lydia. Whisper."

Lydia softened her voice. "How far back are you?"

"Then. Tide's full. Rock was bigger then. Moon's behind clouds. Seagulls floating on the high tide, little cottony clouds you can barely see. Now—they're all flying. They've all gone. It came out."

Heather's neck crawled. Poppy, walking on eggs, came to stand beside her. Heather clutched at her wrist, got a charm bracelet that clanged in the silence like cowbells. The faint, reckless smile was back in Lydia's eyes.

"What is it?"

Grace was silent a long time. She whispered finally, "I know you." Heather's knees went wobbly. "I know you. I saw you under a full moon ten thousand years ago. You were sucking bones."

Heather sat down abruptly on the floor. For a moment the house wavered between light and shadow; the light from the kitchen seemed to be running away faster and faster. The cuckoo snapped open its door, said the time, but time seemed to be rushing away from her as fast as light. Dark was the only thing not running; it was flowing into the emptiness left by light and time, a great flood of dark, separating Heather from the little, familiar thing that counted off the hours of her life.

Cuckoo, said the clock.

Heather, said the dark.

Cuckoo.

Her eyes opened; light was back in bulbs and tubes where it belonged. "It's two in the morning," she protested to Poppy, who was lifting up the phone receiver. "Who're you waking up?"

Poppy hesitated, receiver to her shoulder, and gave Heather a long look. "I was calling an ambulance."

"I'm all right. I got to go to bed is all."

Lydia was kneeling beside her. Heather groped wearily at her proferred arm. Thin as she was, Lydia pulled Heather to her feet as if she were made of batting.

"Don't be scared, Granny."

"It was eating up everything."

"That's why you called us. We'll handle it, me and Grace and Georgie. But we need you to help."

"I'm too old."

"No. We need you most of all. It's old, too. So's Grace. You get a good night's sleep. Tomorrow you call everyone, tell them to meet us at Oyster Rock at sunset. Georgie, you're back." She smiled brightly at Georgie, who, carrying a couple of empty cans, a flattened cigarette carton, and an old church bulletin, looked as if she had started to tidy up Junket. "Have a good time?"

"Smashing," Georgie said dryly, and did so to a soda can.

"Good. We're about to make another mess."

Between Tessa hobbling on her canes and Lydia wobbling on her spikes, they looked, Heather thought, about as unlikely a gathering as you might meet this side of the Hereafter. They stood on the cliff overlooking the beach and Oyster Rock; they had chosen the Viewpoint Cliff because the sign was so well hidden under a bush that nobody ever saw it. Poppy, wearing stretch jeans and a bubblegum-pink sweater and enough makeup to paint a barn, had driven Heather in the VW. She hovered close to her now, for which Heather was grateful. Georgie had just driven up. She had borrowed Poppy's station wagon earlier and asked directions to the dump. Heather wondered if she had spent the afternoon cleaning it up.

In the sunset, the rock looked oddly dark. The birds had abandoned it; maybe the barnacles and starfish had fled, too. The grass on its crown was turning white. Heather shivered. The sun was sliding into a fogbank. The fog would be drifting across the beach in an hour.

"You all right?" Poppy said anxiously for the hundredth time.

"I'm all right," Heather kept saying, but she wasn't. Her hands felt like gnarled lumps of ice and her heart fluttered quick and hummingbird-light. She could feel the ancient dark crouched out there, just behind where the sun went down, just waiting. It was her face it wanted, her frail old bones it kept trying to flow into. She was weakest, she was easiest, she was closest to the edge of time, she was walking on the tide line. . . .

Maybe I should, she thought, clutching her windbreaker close, staring into the sinking sun. It's about time anyway, with Evan gone and all, and it would save some fuss and bother. . . . Wouldn't get much out of me anyway, I'm so slow; it wouldn't have a chance between naps. . . .

She felt an arm around her, smelled some heady perfume: Lydia, her hair a green cloud, her eyes narrowed, about as dark as eyes could get and not be something other.

"Granny?" she said softly. "You giving up without a fight? After all those blizzards? All the drought and dust storms and poverty you faced down to keep your family safe and cared for?"

"I was a whole lot younger, then. Time ran ahead of me, not behind."

"Granny? If you don't fight this, you'll be the next thing we'll all have to fight. You'll be its face, its eyes, you'll be hungry for us." Heather, stunned, couldn't find spit to swallow, let alone speak. "Am I right, Georgie?"

Georgie picked up a french fry envelope, shook out the last fry to a gull and wadded the paper. She didn't say anything. Her eyes burned through Heather like cold mountain water. Then she smiled, and Heather thought surprisedly, *There's Storm's face. It's been there all along.*

"Granny'll be all right," she said in her abrupt way. "Granny's fine when she's needed."

The sun had gone. The fog was coming in fast. Waves swarmed around the base of the rock, trying to heave it out of the water or eat it away before morning. But the rock, black as if it were a hole torn through to nothing, just stood there waiting for the rest of night.

Tessa banged on the VW fender with her cane, which must have brought Evan upright in his grave.

"Gather," she commanded in her sea-lion voice, and Poppy snorted back a laugh. Heather poked her, glad somebody could laugh. They circled on the rocky lip of the cliff: Tessa in one of the bulky-knit outfits she wore so constantly that Heather couldn't imagine her even in a nightgown; Dawn chewing gum maniacally, wearing a skirt as short as Lydia's and hightops with red lips on them; Laura, fragile and calm, wearing her Sunday suit and pearls; Sarah in a denim skirt and a windbreaker, looking like she was trying to remember what was on her grocery list; Rachel, dyspeptic in sensible polyester; Poppy, her hand under Heather's arm; Lydia in red lipstick; Georgie in jeans; and Grace, who looked like she just might live after all, her hair blown wild in the wind and livid as the twilight fog.

Storm's children revealed what they had brought.

Lydia fanned the assortment in her hand and passed around the circle, giving them to everyone but Heather.

"I don't know what this is," Dawn whispered nervously, holding up what looked to be a size J.

"It's a crochet hook."

"But I don't know how."

"It'll come," Lydia said briskly, handing Laura the daintiest. Poppy was looking dubiously at hers. Tessa gave one of her foghorn snorts but said nothing. Lydia surveyed the circle, smiling. "Are we all armed? Granny, you're empty-handed. Georgie, give her your fishing pole."

"I can't cast in this wind," Heather said anxiously. "It's only got one little bitty weight on it. And the water's way over there. And it's too dark to see—"

"Oh, hush, Heather," Tessa growled. "Nobody came here to fish. You know that."

"Granny did," Lydia said sweetly. Her green hair and scarlet lips glowed in the dusk like Grace's hair; so did Georgie's hands, paler than the rest of her, moving like magician's gloves through the air. The sky was misty, bruised purple-black now, starless, moonless. They could still see something of each other—an eye gleam, a gesture—from the lights in the motel parking lot. "Granny's going fishing. It's Georgie's favorite pole, so whatever you catch, don't let go of it. You just keep reeling in. We'll take care of the rest. Ready, Grace?"

Grace held a bone between her hands.

It was some animal, Heather thought uneasily. Cow or sheep shank, some such, big, pearly-white as Grace's hair, thick as her wrist. Thick as it was, Grace broke it in two like a twig.

She held both pieces out toward the rock. Her eyes closed; she crooned something like a nursery song. Heather felt her back hairs rise, as if some charged hand had stroked the nape of her neck. The bone dripped glitterings as hard and darkly red as garnet.

Dawn bit down on her crochet hook. Poppy held hers upright like a candle; her other hand gripped Heather as if she thought Heather might take to the air in the sudden wind that pounced over the cliff. Heather heard it howl a moment, like a cat fight, before it hit. It smashed them like a high wave. Heather wanted to clutch at the sparse hair she had left, but Poppy held one arm, and she had the pole in her other hand. She tried to say something to Poppy, but the wind tore her words away and then her breath.

Heather, the dark said, a mad wind crooning in Grace's voice. *Heather*, it said again, a wave now, rolling faster and faster in the path of the wind. *Heather*, it said, sniffing for her like a dog, and she froze on the cliff while it stalked her, knowing she had no true claims to life or time, nothing holding her on earth, even her bones were wearing down, disappearing little by little inside her while she breathed. The circle of shadowy faces couldn't hold her; Poppy's hand couldn't protect her; she was a lone, withered thing and if this dark didn't get her, the other would soon enough, so what difference was there between them?

"Granny?" Lydia didn't even have to shout. Her voice came as clear and light as if her red neon lips were at Heather's ear. "You can cast any time, now."

She could feel Poppy's hand again, hear Grace's meaningless singsong. But Poppy's hand felt a thousand miles away; she was just clinging to skin and bone, she could never reach deep enough to hang onto anything that mattered. She couldn't anchor onto breath or thought or time.

"Granny?"

And time was the difference between this dark and death. This thing had all the time in the world.

Heather.

"Granny?"

"Honey, it's just no use—" She heard her own cracked, wavery voice more inside her head than out, with the wind shredding everything she said. "I can't cast against this—"

"Granny Heather, you get that line out there or I'll let this wind snatch you bald."

Heather unlatched the reel, caught line under her thumb, and flung a hook and a weight that wouldn't have damaged a passing goldfinch into the eye of the dark.

The line unreeled forever. It took on the same eerie glow as Lydia's lips, Georgie's hands, and it stretched taut and kept unwinding as if something had caught it and run with it, then swam, then flew, farther and farther toward the edge of the world. It stopped so fast she toppled back out of Poppy's hold; Poppy grabbed her again, pulled her upright.

What she had caught turned to her.

She felt it as she had felt it looking out of the moon's eye. She went small, deep inside her, a little animal scurrying to find a hiding place. But there was no place; there was no world, even, just her, standing in a motionless, soundless dark with a ghostly fishing pole in her hands, its puny hook swallowed by something vast as fog and night, with the line dangling out of it like a piece of spaghetti. Lightning cracked in the distance; fine sand or dust blew into her face. The wind's voice took on a whine like storms that happened in places with exotic names, where trees snapped like bones and houses flung their rafters into the air. The line tightened again; Heather's arms jerked straight. She felt something fly out of her: the end of her voice, her last breath. She heard Georgie say, "Don't lose my pole, Granny. Grandpa gave it to me."

Evan's old green pole he caught bluegill with, this storm aimed to swallow, along with her and the cliff and most of Crane Harbor. It sucked again; she tottered, feeling her arm sockets giving. Poppy, crochet hook between her teeth, was hanging on with both hands, dragged along with her.

"Heather!" It was Tessa, bellowing like a cargo ship. "Quit fooling around. You've been fishing for seventy years—bring it in!"

She was breathless, her heart bouncing around inside her like a golf ball, smacking her ribs, her side. The line tightened again. This time it would send her flying out of Poppy's hold, over the cliff, and all she could do was hang on, she didn't have the strength to tug against it, she had no more strength, she just didn't—

"Remember, Granny," Lydia said, "not long after Storm was born, when you walked out into the fields with her to give Grandpa his lunch, and halfway back, all the fields lifted off the ground and started blowing straight at you? You couldn't see, you couldn't breathe, you couldn't move against the wind, but you had to get Storm in, you had to find the house, nothing—not wind or dirt or heat—was going to get its hands on Storm. You pushed wind aside to save her, you saw through earth. And then when you got to the house, the wind shoved against the screen door so hard you couldn't pull it open. You didn't have any more strength, not even for a screen door. You couldn't pull. You couldn't pull against that wind. But you did pull. You pulled. You pulled. You pulled your heart out for Storm. And the door opened and flew away and you were inside with Storm safe."

"I pulled," Heather said, and pulled the door open again, for Storm's children.

It gave so fast Poppy had to catch her. Line snaked through the air, traced a pale, phosphorescent tangle all over the ground. For a second Heather thought she had lost it. Then she saw the end of the line, hung in the air at the cliff edge just above them. She sagged on the ground, her mouth dry as a dust storm, her blood crackling like lightning behind her eyes. She felt the wind change suddenly, as if the world were going backward, and startled, she looked up to see Lydia's blood-bright, reckless smile.

"Georgie?"

Georgie reached behind her to Poppy's station wagon and pulled open the back end. Half the garbage in the Junket dump whirled out, a flood of debris that swooped in the wind and tumbled and soared and snagged, piece by piece, against the thing at the cliff edge. Old milk cartons, bread wrappers, toilet paper rolls, styrofoam containers, orange peels, frozen dinner trays, used Kleenex, coffee grounds, torn envelopes, wadded paper, magazines, melon rinds skimmed over their heads and stuck to the dark, making a mask of garbage over the shape that Heather had hooked. She saw a wide, lipless, garbage mouth move, still chewing at the line, and she closed her eyes. Dimly, she heard Lydia say, "Tessa will now give us a demonstration of the basic chain stitch."

"Dip in your hook," Tessa said grimly. "Twist a loop, catch a strand on the hook and pull it through the loop. Catch a strand. Pull. Catch. Pull."

"Funny," Heather said after a while. Lydia, green hair and lips floating in the dark, knelt down beside her.

"What's funny, Granny?"

"I never knew crocheting was so much like fishing."

"Me, neither."

"You catch, then you pull." She paused. She couldn't see Lydia's eyes, but she guessed at them. "How'd you know about that dust storm? About how the screen door wouldn't open? I never remembered that part. You weren't even born. Your mama was barely two months old."

"She remembered," Lydia said. "She told us."

"Oh." She thought that over and opened her mouth again. Lydia's red floating lips smiled. Might as well ask how she could do that trick, Heather thought, and asked something else instead.

"What's going to happen to it?"

"Georgie'll clean it up."

"She going to put it back inside the rock?"

"I think she has in mind taking it to the dump with the rest of the garbage. It'll take some time to untangle itself and put the pieces back together."

"Will it?"

"What, Granny?"

"Put the pieces back together?"

Lydia patted her hand, showing half a mouth; she was looking at the huge clown face that was loosing bits of garbage as the flashing hooks parted and knotted the dark behind it. She didn't answer. Poppy, at the cliff edge, drawing out a chain of dark from between a frozen orange juice can, an ice cream container, and a fish head, looked over at Heather.

"You all right, honey?"

"I think so." Beside Poppy, Laura was making a long fine chain, her silver needle flashing like a minnow. Waiting for nine years for her husband to open his eyes gave her a lot of time on her hands, and she could crochet time faster than any of them. Sarah, with a hook as fat as a finger, was making a chain wide enough to hold an anchor. Dawn did a little dance with her hightops whenever she missed a beat with her hook. Rachel, of all people, broke into a tuneless whistle now and then; Heather didn't know she could even pucker up her lips.

"Nice fishing," Tessa boomed. "Good work, Heather."

"I had help," Heather said. "I had my granddaughters."

Georgie lifted her head, gave Heather one of her burning smiles, like spring wind blowing across a snowbank. Grace had gone to sleep against Georgie's knees, looking, with her hair over her face, like a little ghostly haystack. Heather leaned back against Lydia's arm. She closed her eyes, listened to her heart beat. It wouldn't win any races, but it was steady again, and it would do for a while, until something better came along.

THE CRUEL COUNTESS
Chris Bell

Chris Bell was born in North Wales; he now lives in Hamburg, Germany, where he works for a music publisher. He is the author of surrealist and realist fiction published in magazines in England, Wales, Ireland, Germany, Finland, New Zealand, Canada and the U.S. Bell's stories, like his publication credits, have a distinctly international flavor— as evidenced by the following haunting tale, set in a German cemetery. "The Cruel Countess" was published in *The Third Alternative* (a small English magazine) and in Bell's first story collection, *The Bumper Book of Lies*. Two other stories from Bell's collection are also recommended: "Dream Me an Island" (set in the Caribbean) and "This Shining World" (based on Maori myth).

—T. W.

I am riding a bicycle through the biggest cemetery in the world; cycling downhill, the past rushing up towards me. The last rays of the setting sun shine through the glass set into the memorial column, silhouetting row upon row of urns; sky scrolling overhead and the light behind the mullioned panes phosphorescent in its intensity.

These urns contain the ashes of victims from German concentration camps and the countries occupied during the Third Reich. The trees race by. I feel as if I am flying. The sky is dramatic. There should be music. I start to pick out the shapes of letters on the inscriptions.

Bonfires of burning leaves spice the chilly air. I feel uneasy without my Star of Solomon talisman jingling against my chest. Yet, as the wind polishes my face, I thank God. I am grateful to be alive.

I accelerate recklessly, oblivious of the potential hazards: other cyclists appearing from my left and right, rushing out from the side paths and joining the slope down which I am flying. My surroundings render this sense of "danger" quite absurd.

It is almost a year since Opal Hush left me.

I leave the cemetery by the main gate, steering around enticingly oblique female skaters in spray-on shorts and knee-protectors, hair fluttering like horsetails. On the way back up the hill towards my flat, a fast car pulls in to the curb, and an elegant young woman at the wheel hoots her horn and beckons to me. I do not recognize her. She is dressed in black and is exceptionally pale; as though her face is thickly powdered. Her eyes are heavy, dim-lidded; like the back windows of a hearse.

"Where's the main entrance to the Ohlsdorf Cemetery?" she asks in a flustered yet exceptionally feminine voice.

I explain that she is already there; all she needs do is to turn right. I walk on, turning my head back to her car, eager to see her striking face again. She points agitatedly in the direction of the main cemetery gate with raised eyebrows and a questioning look on her face. I nod.

Late for a funeral? As deathly as she is, it could be her own. She is as pale as the girl in the sculpture I discovered on the western edge of the cemetery—indeed, the likeness is quite disturbing.

She also reminds me of Opal.

Winter it was, a brittle Hamburg daybreak shrouded in frost and all the gravestones huddled under hibernating rhododendrons. Unexpectedly came hurtling out of the mist, dragging two figures by their hair, the statue of a woman, a grotesquely pensive woman, with a curved pattern of ice veiling her naked body.

I stopped my bike to take a closer look.

She stood on a rough pedestal in front of a spray of ferns. One of the figures she was dragging was a young boy, the other the girl. Both faces bore tortured expressions.

The sculpture radiated an emotive burden of distress and the air around me felt weighted down by it. I could not imagine what nadir of grief could have generated such a stony vision.

I had moved to Hamburg from London in December 1987. I could not take any more of Margaret Thatcher's economic miracle; characterized for me by standing in a snaking queue at Chiswick Post Office waiting to cash my social security check.

I came to live with my German girlfriend, Opal Hush, on an estate whose buildings are cracked like chunks of stale gingerbread in memory of the Royal Air Force air raids, situated on the main road to the airport. Next door is the cemetery. The estate, when built before the war, was considered to be a model. A model of what I am still not quite sure.

I had met Opal Hush about three years before. She had been the lithe, good-humored assistant in the optician's shop where I bought some glasses during a particularly strenuous business trip. Either through vanity or absent-mindedness I had left my own in London. My short-sightedness was worsening rapidly with each session at the computer monitor, in inverse proportion to my soaring conceit.

I remember the German exactitude of *Blickkontakt*, the shop where she worked ("Eye Contact!"), the vanilla scent of her breath and the closeness of her face as she checked the frames for their fit around my ears. "What do you think?" she asked as our eyes met.

"I think you're beautiful," I admitted.

"Perhaps you need stronger lenses after all."

For a time, life with her was as modest and straightforward as our first conversation. So much so, that I did not even notice I was living it. I took for granted that it would go on forever. Now I can't remember exactly what it was I thought we had.

I keep telling myself: no more thinking—just be there. But fate is unavoidable. It is the school timetable of life and, as it turned out, Opal Hush was just waiting for her destiny to be completed.

The streets around the Ohlsdorf Cemetery are not served by commonplace shops and stores. For a radius of a mile, one finds only tombstones, caskets and wreaths. Ordinary neighborhoods have roadside displays of fruit and vegetables; these shops specialize in the accoutrements of Death.

Ranks of diversely-clad marble headstones parade in pavement plots, decorated with a biblical abundance of quotations and pithy inscriptions. The dozens of florists deal mostly in tributes. Even the shops in the station entrance will not allow you to forget that life is a one-way ticket. My personal favorite has a sign reading: "A funeral doesn't have to cost a fortune—DISCOUNT COFFINS HERE."

On Sundays and the special days Germany has set aside for her dead (I cannot think of many that are set aside for the living), coach-loads of old women in hats invade Ohlsdorf. They hunt for bargain caskets and inhabit the tea-rooms. Undertakers terrorize the pedestrians in their high-powered hearses.

It's a morbid place to go about the business of living, you might think, but a reassuring one if you are on your last legs, in the knowledge that there isn't far to go.

Some nights, when I am lying awake in bed, I see the cemetery gates in my mind's eye; ornately curved under a full moon.

Two years ago, in October, I arrived back from a short trip to Nashville that had thrown me like an unbroken stallion. On the flight I took a trembling pledge to give up drinking. Opal was there to greet me at Hamburg airport. I remember being overwhelmed by strange faces as the automatic doors slid open and I emerged at "Arrivals Terminal 4." I had brought Jean-Paul Gaultier perfume for her and a bottle of duty-free Glenfarclas whiskey for myself.

There would be time for abstinence, I persuaded myself, in the winter months to come.

Opal was driving. "It matures in sherry casks," I said. She was wearing one of her shortest skirts and I slid my left hand with a gentle hiss along her thigh at the traffic lights.

"How about you, Sam?" she asked. "Any danger of you maturing in the foreseeable future? A couple of years back we talked about having children. Ring any bells? What about getting married?"

I just grinned and rolled my hand over the contours into the warmth between. "What would I go and do a thing like that for? You've never done me any harm. But since you mention sex—let's go and see Antonio at Wa-Yo. I haven't had any decent sushi for weeks."

Over sushi and sake, Opal spoke her mind. "I entrusted you with my love and you lost it. I never wanted to be anything but a friend to you, to be with you sometimes; no more than that. And I didn't want you to expect any more of me than that. I gave you love because that's what I felt for you. So we both had some of it; we shared it like friends. But you got complacent. You began to think of my love as a matter of course. And you've corrupted not only yourself with your drinking; you've corrupted my love with it, too."

She was not only eloquent, she was right. I had taken her for granted; as the coming winter is betrayed by the harsh laughter of ravens in the cemetery.

It has an autumnal aspect, the cemetery, regardless of the season. Leaves fall, winter through summer. Ravens hop churlishly about the litter bins. The horizon has that half-surprised look; *stillness!* The scent of turned earth hangs on the air. There are bone-bare branches and cinnamon browns; crunching paths and unevenly rusted railings, blistering under black paint. Occasionally, a lost glove is to be found hanging from an ornamented railing spike, damp and forlorn.

Night and day the silence is cracked by the desperate cacophony of sirens— ambulances and emergency doctors in ambulances on their way to and from Barmbek General Hospital. There is no music in it, only peril.

It was quite difficult to find a book about the cemetery, in spite of it being the biggest in the world. The author of a two-volume reference work in the city library had this to say about the statue of the bare-breasted woman:

> *Fate (in folklore also known as the "Cruel Countess"). 1905, Hugo Lederer. Shell-limestone. Figure 200 cm, pedestal 20 cm. "H. Lederer 1905." A group consisting of three persons. "Fate"—a goddess with bared breasts and a flowing gown—drags a youth and a girl by their hair behind her. The girl, with closed eyes, has given up the struggle; the boy, pain distorting his face, claws at the ground. This Pre-Raphaelite-style sculpture originally stood in its own small pavilion in the garden of the Eduard Lippert family house at 107 Harvesterhuder Weg. She came to Ohlsdorf in 1956.*

I had a vision of her journey: dragging the boy and girl behind her through the night, all the way from *Harvesterhuder Weg* (seven kilometers away, as the crow flies), shells and limestone grating on the tarmac, leaving a trail of coarse sand.

Lederer was also the sculptor of two large family graves at Ohlsdorf. I sought them out but neither had the quality of "Fate," a truly terrifying work—in spite of the goddess' flattened face and unflattering Pre-Raphaelite hairstyle, which gives the impression that she has walked many miles in the pouring rain and could use a good towel-down and blow-dry.

There were so many discoveries to make in the Ohlsdorf cemetery: the masked, bandaged eyes of the woman in relief on the Thörl grave with its chained posts; the boy and girl sculptures at the Gaiser grave; the prone lion guarding the Dalmann tombstone; silvery, shredded bark glinting in the winter sun; prismatic drops of occulting melted snow on branches; the ornate water tower on *Cordes-Allee*, a forgotten turret of Mervyn Peake's crumbling Gormenghast, flickering like a candle in Time's yawn.

By now it had become a place of magic as well as a garden of rest; full of life, no necropolis.

At a shop full of trinkets in that part of Hamburg disparagingly referred to as *Little Istanbul*, Opal bought me a bronze talisman from a grinning Turk. It featured the five-pointed Star of Solomon, and promised to bring me wisdom, intuition and understanding—which apparently she felt I sorely needed.

I remember being quite crestfallen upon opening the little plastic bag because a complicated ritual was required before the talisman would be "charged" with the protective qualities it was designed to emit.

Exchanging my recalcitrance for energy, I gathered a glass of water, a white candle, poured some salt into a saucer, found a white tablecloth and salvaged some sandalwood joss-sticks that had been lying in the bottom of a drawer for years.

In the living room I dragged the coffee table out into the middle of the floor and turned out the lights. Spreading the tablecloth, I placed the candle in the middle and lit it. From the candle, I lit the incense sticks. Closing my eyes, I thought for a few minutes about what I hoped to achieve with the talisman: that, in future, I would display the wisdom and the intuition to accept Opal on her terms; to be more tolerant and understanding.

The air swiftly became fogged by the cloying sweetness of the incense.

I took a pinch of salt and sifted it through my fingers into the water. For a moment, nothing happened, but then the water began to seethe with a nebulous golden light. The silence in the room turned in on itself, cresting as anticipation in my stomach.

Surprisingly, I remembered the words on the instructions that accompanied the talisman—the kind of thing (like names and phone numbers) I usually require prompting on: "With salt I bless this water, may all it touches with light be blessed, also."

As instructed, I sprinkled the talisman with water and spoke the words: "With this holy water I bless the talisman so that, through the wisdom attained, Opal Hush and I may be happier together."

I passed the talisman through the smoke from the joss-sticks, pronouncing the words: "With this burning incense I charge the talisman so that, intuitively, Opal Hush and I may learn to treat each other more fairly." Finally, I passed the talisman through the candle flame, saying: "With this holy flame, I cleanse the talisman, so that Opal Hush and I may live in better mutual understanding."

I closed my eyes and held the talisman in my right hand. After a few moments, I seemed to sense a ray of light above me, radiating in all directions. I attempted to concentrate upon it and it became a perfect sphere. Gradually, a channel of white light extended downwards from it, meeting my head. Its energy flowed down my neck. The top of my spine filled with warmth that radiated to my throat and solar plexus. I felt strengthened by it and, because

it had all been described so precisely in the instructions, not in the least sceptical about what was happening.

With the energy inside me, I sensed light flowing throughout my body and
into the talisman in my hand. I relaxed for a moment, thinking about how
blissful my life with Opal could be in future.

My body seemed to become heavier, to re-connect with the earth and the
present moment. I threaded the talisman onto a leather thong and wore it to
bed.

The following day, I cycled around the cemetery's western perimeter road. The
previous night there had been a force-eleven gale with gusts of up to 135-
kilometers an hour. I slept through it. In its aftermath, the litter bins and
gutters were full of crippled umbrellas; bent spokes and ragged fabric poking
out of them. There was a pink one in a puddle on the main road that looked
like a dead animal or the aftermath of a traffic accident. Dead leaves had been
swept into sodden heaps. The trees looked torn and naked.

I cycled past old family vaults; felt as if I was on the surface of a ball rolling
within a ball, the great curved sky caressing the earth. There was a profound
tranquillity; grass and graves bathed in an uncanny light.

The silver of fall was turning to winter gold and Hamburg—garlanded in
frosted leaf-mold—was nostalgically familiar. There was a yearning in its colors;
all I needed now was the sound of snow underfoot and Hamburg's traditional
smells (sugared almonds, liquorice, smoked fish) and I would be back in 1984
at the beginning of my relationship with Opal Hush.

The low rumble of a passing bus faded into the distance. A raven sprang like
a hooded thief into the undergrowth.

Over the hilltop trudged a ragged, bedevilled figure, bent to the wind. She
crossed the road in front of me.

It was the Cruel Countess. She was some way off but I could hear creaking
and the shearing of limestone; the friction of straining limbs. She was alone.
And she was singing Bessie Jackson's *Shave 'em Dry* in a croaky voice, humming
the tune and weaving the mumbled lyrics in between: "I got nipples on my
titties big as the end of my thumb, I got somethin' 'tween my legs'll make a
dead man come."

I felt the urge to call after her: "Just tell me the truth! What's going to
happen to Opal and me?" She did not acknowledge my presence and, by the
time I had reached the point where she had crossed, there was no sign of her.

A little farther on was the empty limestone plinth upon which I had first
seen her. Where was the wretched couple, the boy and girl?

Next Sunday, I persuaded Opal to take a walk with me. As so often, we ended
up at the entrance to the cemetery. We stopped to read the blue enameled
sign at the main gate:

MAIN CEMETERY OHLSDORF

*This 'Central Cemetery' established in 1877—the biggest in the
world—replaced the parish cemetery outside the gates of old-Hamburg.*

The park-like design is the work of the Cemetery's director Wilhelm Cordes. The layout was archetypal and often imitated. Otto Linne, Cordes' successor, began to create the new section in 1920, according to architectural principles. Apart from the 12 chapels and the crematorium, there are also mausoleums, numerous artistically designed graves and 2 museum areas. Many well-known personalities are buried here.

This kingdom of the dead was ruled by trees. We savored their fragrances and, in our aimless wandering, came upon an enormous cross of rough-hewn stone. The dead ferns at its base looked as though they were of burnished gold. Chewed by moss and crowned by leaves of ivy, the inscription carved on its transverse beam read:

"The Lord command your ways and set your hopes on Him, He will surely take care of things." J. RIEPER.

Jim Rieper? The Grim Reaper? The grave looked old and uncared for. The silence was overwhelming; we could have been deep in the forest. Nothing to startle us, no passing people. I copied out the inscription and we continued north, between rhododendrons capsuled in brown where flowers had once been.

"I'm so frustrated!" said Opal suddenly, clinging to me with tears surging in her throat. "I feel so small and unimportant. Nobody seems to give a damn about what I think. You don't even listen to me any more."

I tried to reassure her, told her not to doubt herself; to demand the right to fail and to be proud of her actions; never to look back and think, "I should have done that differently."

This was not what she wanted to hear.

The irony is that I was her biggest problem. I didn't sense it. On the contrary; I was calm. I felt that I could give good counsel. I was dull enough to think that perhaps the concentration of departed souls in the air was helping me; the natural stillness making it easier for me to think clearly; that I was being soothed by the very inscriptions on the tombs. It all seems pathetic now, although I would still swear that a powerful convergence of energies occurs at this cemetery.

All she had wanted of me were the few short words I felt it unnecessary—even wasteful—to speak. Instead, I rambled on until, eventually, her grip on my arm softened. Perhaps the monotony of my voice had lulled her into equanimity.

"Where would I be without you?" I asked her, only half rhetorically.

"Probably somewhere better," said Opal, only half jokingly.

"More likely in Llandudno Junction," I replied gratefully. No more half measures.

When she hugged and held me, I thought I had achieved something; that things would again be as they had been in the old days. I loved her and took it for granted that she knew.

It dulled the words to have to keep repeating them, I thought.

Hysteria has a way of repeating itself; my pledge to stop drinking was well-meant but not well-kept. This did not go unnoticed.

"There has to be an end to it, Sam," she said, seeming to sway obscurely in the peaty mists of my consciousness. "I don't even believe I can find love for myself any more. I want to go away, not be with anybody for a while."

Before she had a chance to be with herself, Fate caught her by the hair.

I first remember her complaining about headaches while we were out Christmas shopping. I thought it was the cold. They always seemed to be at the same point at the side of her head, above her ear. Then she starting forgetting appointments and the due dates of orders she had placed at work. She would relate the same anecdote several times within the space of a day. It was unlike her; she had always been so organized.

In early January, Opal was diagnosed as having a brain tumor. Surgery was obviously risky, but the doctors rated the chances of successful removal of the non-malignant tumor as excellent.

The operation was arduous, but went well. I visited her in hospital. She was in a two-bed room with a view of the ambulances arriving at the neurological ward of the University Hospital. They had shaved her head and dressed it with an elasticized bandage. It looked like an ill-fitting ski-mask. Her eyes had sunken into a greyness that had conquered her face. She was wan and poorly nourished, as if something was eating her instead, but she smiled at me as I entered.

They had put her on morphine sulphate. It killed the postoperative pains but, in turn, caused her mood to swing precariously between euphoria and despondency.

I bought her a Sony CD Diskman and "Citizen Dan," the complete, digitally-remixed Steely Dan collection. "Even *Here At The Western World* is on it," I said, pointing the song out on the credits. We had often joked that the "skinny girl" in its lyrics was a cryptic reference to her.

She glowed, briefly, and kissed me dryly on the cheek.

They kept her in intensive care. After three weeks it was clear that something had gone wrong. The surgeon, one of the world authorities on cerebral tumors, told us that if they were to operate again they would be able to remove a remnant of the tumor they had failed to reach the first time. The dangers of anaesthetizing her for longer had been too great, he said. Provided they were successful, Opal would be able to live quite normally again.

Opal was so ebullient and optimistic that there was really no discussion. She wanted an end to the uncertainty, she said, presenting me with a small envelope and telling me not to open it unless something happened to her.

Surgically, the second operation was successful. But then, in the weeks that followed, Opal's behavior became increasingly erratic. Her short-term memory dwindled and, although she always recognized me, she erased nurses and doctors within moments of their introduction.

Eventually, she was admitted to a closed hospital in the suburbs of Hamburg. One night, she managed to get out and was found by the police in the village, wearing only her night-gown and slippers, looking for a chemist's shop.

*   *   *

What the medical world patronizingly refers to as "complications" had set in.

Opal died on Monday, May 15th, while I was in Bavaria at an on-line communications conference.

We never had a chance to talk, to say goodbye properly. The second operation had been her decision. She went into it with her customary optimism, aware of the risks but willing to take a chance. Perhaps it was the morphine that had made her so fey.

I am ashamed to admit that my immediate grief was no more profound than that upon draining a particularly fine bottle of whiskey. Soon, though, I found myself nursing a curious emptiness far worse than the variety of hangover that simply does not want to get better.

Death connects us, all races—it is the universal quantity.

As Opal was keen on reminding me—and I always hear the words in the voice of Joni Mitchell—"Something's lost, but something's gained in living every day." Bereavement was a revelation to me and, without irony, I thanked Opal for another new experience.

The funeral was on a beautifully warm spring day. I arranged with the pastor for a tape to be played at the end of the service—John Martyn's version of *Over The Rainbow*—knowing it would end in tears. As the casket left the chapel-of-rest on a conveyor belt, it wobbled alarmingly. Its movement was horribly vaudeville; like a prop in some cheesy conjuring trick. In faltering German, I read out the paragraph that Opal had placed in the mysterious envelope, written in hospital specially for this occasion:

> *"Death belongs to life as does birth. It is not life's enemy—we must learn to treat it as a friend. Now that I am gone, I shall try to give you a sign, something unambiguous, to let you know that there is a next stop after life. On that day you will hear from me again. I'll wait for you all a while, somewhere close by. All is well."*

All is well.

At the grave-side my knees grew weak and I felt in danger of joining the casket. For a while I stood nearby, propped against a tree, but when some disinterested mourners began to slope off in the direction of the nearest watering-hole, I headed into the depths of the cemetery.

I found The Cruel Countess, sitting on an isolated bench in the shadows near a lake haunted by flitting butterflies. Bulrushes hushed the grazing geese. Dragonflies daubed themselves on the afternoon: some red, some blue; darting, humming to the tune of the spring. She seemed to be staring at four fir trees in a row of diminishing height at the opposite side of the lake. She was not holding anyone by the hair; neither the boy nor the girl with the tortured expressions was anywhere to be seen.

She looked so at home on her bench that it seemed more natural to talk to her than to the mourners at Opal's grave side; each a stranger in their private grief.

"Where are your two young friends?"

"I am a sculpture. I am by no means obliged to answer sarcastic questions, you know." Her voice was not as you might expect for a statue; it was warm and vaguely polyphonic, as if accompanied by a faint soprano boy choir; variations in a minor key.

"I didn't mean to be sarcastic. I'm in mourning."

"Death is in the nature of things. There are only a limited number of souls to go around, you know."

"It's funny you should mention that, I thought it might be that way. I often hear a voice while I'm shaving or showering, or caught up in insecure, destructive thoughts. It cries, in a kind of yelled whisper, 'Let me out! Get me out of here.' Does that make any kind of sense to you?"

The Cruel Countess crossed and uncrossed her legs, studied her non-existent wristwatch. "I don't find it difficult to sympathize with your prisoner. You might at least have the common courtesy of introducing yourself to me."

"The name's Sam Kite."

"Fate."

"Pleased to meet you." It's not every day you bump into Fate at the cemetery. "I've abandoned my search for the truth," I said. "I am now looking for a good fantasy. Any suggestions?"

The Cruel Countess chuckled in the recesses of my Inside Head. "For the past few moments you've been talking to a statue. I'd say that wasn't bad for a start. Let it come naturally, or you won't feel the benefit."

"May I come back and see you again?"

"I will be here. I shall decide in due course whether or not you see me."

The clangor of Hamburg's Sunday morning church bells is like a summons to the service at the end of the world. Behind their accelerating cacophony, in the ululating counterpoint in the background, is the ever-distant wail of an ambulance siren. These bells lament; are never uplifting. They fill me with dread. It is the rocking of the earth, the clanging of the universe pulling itself apart.

I rise and leave. On days like these there is only one place to be in Hamburg.

The rhododendron leaves in the cemetery are rolled together like miniature Christmas tree angels; wrapped up in their wings, to protect themselves.

Lazy drivers are out in force, misusing the cemetery as a bypass, driving as recklessly as owners of high-performance cars can afford. We live too fast. We want to cram as much life into this short span of years as is humanly possible and so not live out our few moments. The present becomes lost in the flickering of days, months, years. Decades pass and we realize that we have not lived them. Our angels remain rolled up, wrapped in their winter wings, heedless of the passing seasons.

An icy rain is falling relentlessly now.

At the West Ring, Fate has resumed her customary lookout point at the roadside. With bosom bared and gown flowing, she drags boy and girl brutally behind her, prone bodies grating over the pedestal's shells and limestone, leaving a trail of coarse sand. The boy, pain distorting his face, claws the ground; the girl, eyes closed, has succumbed to the struggle.

She has the same long hair, of course, this skinny girl, and reveals her handfuls of half-spherical breast; the same full, sensuous calves and—although her expression is exquisitely pained—her beautiful face. Because the girl being dragged across the biggest cemetery in the world is Opal Hush and she is a prisoner both of Hugo Lederer's sculpture, *Das Schicksal,* and of Fate.

"Wisdom, Intuition and Understanding," I say, and Opal Hush's sallow cheeks are pearled with raindrops as I hang my Star of Solomon talisman around her stone-cold neck.

As the thaw extends itself to me, Hamburg's evening windows are burnished copper in the setting sun; an alloy of nostalgia and anticipation. The colossal wonder of every living day takes on the form of a gentle prayer around my heart.

In that coppering of windows lie my memories of Opal Hush. Everything can be reduced to its essence; the essence of her is coppered glass against the verdigris on Hamburg's roofops.

Well-being never gets closer than just out of reach. I do my best to leave it there; Fate always comes when least expected.

LITTLE BEAUTY'S WEDDING
Chang Hwang

"Little Beauty's Wedding," a fantasy story that draws upon Chinese "death" folklore, is haunting, disturbing, and oddly moving. It comes from the winter issue of *Story* magazine.

—T. W.

"That's all?" the Mamasan screamed into Mr. Un's face. "That's all? She's worth more than that. Just look at her. Look how fresh and young she is. She's only sixteen. That's worth a little extra. She's hardly been touched. I've only had her here for a few months. A girl like that should be easy for you to handle. Just look at her."

Mr. Un gazed down at the young girl's tender white face. She was lying quietly at his feet with her eyes closed and her mouth slightly parted as if she was still taking in air in her sleep.

"What's her name?" he asked the Mamasan. He leaned down to touch the girl's cold hands. They were still soft.

"We called her SaiMei, Little Beauty," the Mamasan answered. "As you can see, I took very good care of her. No bruises anywhere."

"How long have you had her?"

"Only a couple of months."

"How did she die?" Mr. Un inquired.

"Don't know. She's always been sickly, ever since her brother sold her to us. Half the time, she was in bed sick instead of in bed with our customers. You will give me a bit more, won't you? I still haven't recovered her cost."

Mr. Un stood up and looked at the Mamasan with a solid face and unblinking eyes. In the past years, he had seen his business almost disappear, but he knew he wouldn't have much trouble in selling Little Beauty. He wanted the girl, but he also knew that the could not surrender to the Mamasan's demands so quickly and easily. If he did, however strongly he felt about the girl, the Mamasan would lose her respect for him and he would never be able to deal fairly with her again.

"She's getting hard already," Mr. Un started.

"You must be mistaken," the Mamasan answered. "I guarantee you that she is fresh. She died only yesterday morning. My customer found her just as you see her. It almost gave him a heart attack."

"But her hands are cold and stiff."

"You are such a big man, and your hands are so big and rough and strong. It makes it very difficult to feel such small tender hands like hers. It's only the cold morning air. Winter is coming. We all get stiff. Besides, the cold winter air should keep her nice and fresh-looking."

"I've already got two girls."

"But none as young and pretty as my Little Beauty. Look at her. She's only fifteen. Where will you be able to find another girl who died so young, yet unmarked by some horrible accident?"

"Business is bad," Mr. Un continued.

"So is mine. Ever since the government started cracking down, it's become very expensive to keep the police outside our doors. Before, we just had to give them free time with the girls. Now they want money, and a lot of it," the Mamasan added.

"Do you remember Mr. Keoung?" Mr. Un asked.

The Mamasan nodded. "I haven't seen him in a long time."

"That's because he was executed last month. They caught him. Confiscated all his merchandise. He was taking care of a couple of my girls for me while I was up north. I took a huge loss. Business is getting more dangerous."

"Only a few yuan more. She's definitely worth it. She could pass for fourteen, or even thirteen. You can even take those clothes she's wearing. They are new. I bought them for her just last week."

Mr. Un knew the Mamasan was lying because he had seen another girl wearing the same dress in the previous month when he had made his regular visit to see if any of the Mamasan's girls had died. She always kept them for him.

"I'll give you ten more yuan." Mr. Un pulled out his money and counted twenty bills in front of the Mamasan, making sure that he counted slowly and loudly.

Giving an extra ten yuan was more of a gesture than anything else. Another ten yuan was nothing to Mr. Un but it would give the Mamasan the feeling that she had received something for her efforts.

"One, two, three," he said as he waved the bills under the Mamasan's wide round eyes. "Say yes and the money is yours. Say no and you can bury the girl," Mr. Un said as he slowly began to return the two hundred yuan back into his pocket.

The Mamasan grabbed Mr. Un's hand.

"You're always too kind," she said as she carefully pulled the twenty bills out of Mr. Un's hand.

Mr. Un smiled at the Mamasan. "You're always a tough customer."

"But never as good as you," the Mamasan replied, and both gave each other a smile to confirm that the business had been concluded in a satisfactory manner to both of them.

That the girl would have been sold to Mr. Un was a foregone conclusion.

Mr. Un wanted the girl and the Mamasan would have taken anything rather than bury her. But if the business arrangement had not been to either of their satisfactions, Mr. Un would have had to look for a new source of supplies and the Mamasan would have lost an extra source of income.

Mr. Un pulled forward his mule-driven cart. The Mamasan called two of her boys to help Mr. Un load Little Beauty into the cart. First they removed the stacks of fresh wooden branches that covered a square wooden coffin big enough to hold two bodies. The two boys slid Little Beauty into the coffin and Mr. Un carefully placed the branches over it, making sure that Little Beauty could not be seen.

In the early years of his business, Mr. Un could drive his cart down the main town roads with the bodies exposed and in full view for the customers. He remembered the times when all the townspeople would gather in the streets whenever they heard the bells tied around his mule. Children would escort him to the town center and the people would examine what he had to sell with keen eyes, offering praise and criticism. Many would give him advice on choosing better merchandise and on keeping the bodies looking fresh and alive.

Now, Mr. Un had to hide his merchandise. If the police were to catch him traveling the roads with dead bodies, Mr. Un would find himself praying before the barrel of an executioner's rifle. An honored business had been driven into the dark, a casualty of the new vision of the government.

Mr. Un climbed aboard the cart and drove his mule away from the whorehouse and out of town. He kept his head low to avoid the winter wind and to keep from being noticed or recognized by the others traveling the same road.

Mr. Un continued on until near twilight. He stopped on a short, narrow wooden bridge that spanned the width of a dry stream and tied his mule to the iron post of the bridge. He looked around to make sure no one was approaching from either end. When he was satisfied that he was alone, he climbed down to the bank of the stream and crawled under the bridge.

Just under the planks of the bridge and out of sight was an opening for an old sewage line. Mr. Un crawled inside and into the dark. Like a blind man navigating through his own house, Mr. Un adeptly made his way and lit a lantern hanging a few yards from the opening.

The lantern lit up a small tunnel that had been enlarged just high enough for a man to stoop. Mr. Un had excavated this place into a cave six years ago. He had many such places strewn around the countryside. They were his secret warehouses. Only one had ever been discovered.

The lantern was weak and lit only a portion of the cave. Mr. Un carried it to the corner and lifted a tarp of woven straw. There lay the body of a woman in her early thirties, still wearing the nightgown in which she had died two weeks ago. She lay like a stiff board against the wall of the cave, arms by her sides like two skinny wooden poles. In the light of the lantern, the clear herbal paste that Mr. Un had carefully smeared all over the woman's body to keep it from decaying gave her face and arms a wet and glossy red glow, a haunting appearance in the darkness.

Mr. Un knew that the woman would be hard to sell. He rarely bought anyone over thirty, but she had been given to him for almost nothing. Her husband had chased him for three days, begging him to purchase his dead wife. Mr. Un learned, only after buying the woman, that the husband had used the money to purchase a dress for his new girlfriend.

Mr. Un ran the flickering light down the length of the woman's body like an artist admiring his own work. He checked to make sure there were no spots or crevices he might have missed when he applied his secret herbal paste. The body still looked fresh. He estimated he would have another four weeks before the paste would wear away, exposing the body to the air and starting decay.

Mr. Un replaced the straw tarp over her. He blew out the light and let the darkness consume him as he retraced his steps and pulled himself out of the tunnel.

It was dark outside. The sun had given its last breath for the day and had fallen below the horizon. Now the stars and the moon were taking their turn to have their voices heard.

Mr. Un climbed back to the road and onto his cart. He swung his leather whip high into the sky and brought it down hard against the back of the mule, which jumped awake from his sleep and galloped a few yards before easing into a brisk walk.

Mr. Un and his mule traveled all night using the light shining through the holes in the black blanket above. They would travel as the sun awoke and through the morning until the sun started its descent over the horizon again. That would be their notice that they had reached their destination.

It was a small mud house located at the foot of a mountain path. It was the only house for several miles in all directions. Mr. Un's father had lived here all his life, and Mr. Un had followed into his father's business and life.

Mr. Un liked the house. He liked the isolation and the knowledge that all the land around him was his to do with as he pleased. There was no one from the government to tell him where to plant his crops, where to build his ditches, and where to place his home. The isolation also provided him with the privacy his business required.

Mr. Un tied his mule to a post next to the door. He removed the wood from the cart and stacked it neatly beside the post where he could easily reach it from inside the house through the window. He liked this convenience of retrieving his firewood. It gave him a feeling of being in control of his home and a feeling of modernity that he was constantly hearing about every time he went into the cities.

His mule-driven cart was a reminder of a past era that everyone in the cities wanted to leave behind. To the city people who saw bicycles give way to motorcycles and cars and saw television and refrigerators come into their homes, the mule and the cart were terrible reminders of the ignorant country folks and where they had come from. And like all who are ashamed of their past, the city people sneered and laughed and spat on Mr. Un as he drove his lonely mule between the honking cars and roaring motorcycles.

Mr. Un didn't give much credence to the city people. He saw them as lost souls who had forgotten the path behind them, forgotten their birthplace, and had been blinded by the need for material goods that seemed to burn brightly like fool's gold at the end of a very short and narrow road to the cliff's edge.

Mr. Un didn't need any of that. He had everything he wanted, a simple life and a simple job, providing for those who still believed in the history of the past and the need to soothe loved ones' souls.

Mr. Un carefully pulled Little Beauty out of the coffin. He lifted her gently so that her pretty dress would not be torn by the raw edges of the wooden cart. He carried her into the house and laid her on his worktable in the center of the room.

The sun had already disappeared, and the room was completely dark. Mr. Un walked blindly as he had done in the cave and carefully lit four candles, placing them at the corners of the table. Little Beauty was completely lit from all sides. Mr. Un could have waited until the morning to do his work but Little Beauty had already been dead two days. He was afraid that if he delayed any longer Little Beauty would start losing the tenderness in her skin and the appearance of life that still prevailed in her face.

Mr. Un pulled a large jar from under the table and placed it next to Little Beauty. He untied the lace of her dress, carefully unfastened the buttons, lifted her head, and pulled her arms out of the sleeves. He then slid the dress to her waist and down her legs until Little Beauty was naked. There were no underpants or undershirt. The Mamasan had not given him anything more than what was needed to sell her.

Mr. Un stood back and admired Little Beauty's soft white body. It was delicate and beautiful. Her small breasts lay gently to the side, and except for the patch of black hair below her navel, she appeared pure and clean. There was no sign of the illness that had taken her life.

He stood staring at the body that would have tempted any man. But Mr. Un was getting old now. Had he been many years younger and many women less experienced, he may have taken delight and pleasure in Little Beauty's body. But now, he just admired her radiance and felt a duty to preserve it with all his skill and craftsmanship.

He opened the jar, reached inside, and pulled out a fist of clear herbal paste. He dropped it onto Little Beauty's chest and with both hands gently massaged the paste into her skin. He continued to add more paste until he was sure he had covered her entire body, which shone in the candlelight like a doll encased in a plastic shell.

Mr. Un placed more candles around the body to speed the drying process. He would have to wait until the paste was dry before adding another layer. He repeated the process four times during the night and finished just before morning.

He then dressed Little Beauty and went to a small bed in the corner of the room. He looked once more at Little Beauty's lovely face and collapsed into sleep until that evening.

When Mr. Un awoke, he examined Little Beauty to make sure she had been preserved properly. He had been exhausted while working through the night and wanted to make sure that he had not missed a spot. If he had, the skin would begin to rot, attracting insects and worms that would get in through the opening to eat away at the body from the inside.

After he was completely satisfied with the results, Mr. Un placed Little

Beauty back in her coffin and onto the mule-driven cart. He returned to his house and brought out a second coffin. Inside was another girl about the same age as Little Beauty. He covered both of them with wooden branches.

He went into the house once again and brought out two small red lanterns that he lit and hung on the front corners of the cart. This was his advertisement to the villagers that he would be visiting tonight. The two lanterns represented the two bodies he was carrying. The size of the lanterns and the red color would tell anyone looking for him that he had two young girls for sale.

Mr. Un drove his cart north into the mountains. It was a road he had often traveled, and it was this path and every little chirp and howl of the night that gave him companionship and familiarity on a long two-day trip. To Mr. Un the mountain path represented a road to the comforts of the past. It kept the changes going on in the city from crossing into the mountains and preserved the history and customs of the past. Mr. Un traveled by night and found himself a large sheltering tree away from the road to sleep under during the day.

He arrived at the first village early the second evening. The villagers heard his bells ringing through the streets, but very few came out, and those who did just wanted to see the corpses. No one intended to buy. Many of them re-marked at the beauty of the corpses, but few could afford them or had any use for them. Mr. Un left the village without disappointment. He knew that it would be more and more difficult to find buyers. He expected that he would have to go further into the mountains before he would be able to find people still willing to buy his merchandise.

Mr. Un continued on his journey, traveling by night. He passed through three more villages and was met with the same result. People were curious to see the remnants of the past coming down their streets, but no one wanted to purchase Mr. Un's merchandise.

It was on the fifth night of his journey and in the eighth village that Mr. Un finally found fortune smiling at him. He had barely rounded the corner of a mountain path leading into the village's main road when the sound of his bells brought out a man and his wife. They ran up to him when he approached and begged him to stop. They were desperate. Mr. Un liked the sound of their voices because he knew he would be able to demand any price for his girls.

The couple ran to the back of the cart, and without waiting for Mr. Un, flung away the branches that covered the coffins. They lifted the lids, looked inside, and fell into each other's arms in a fit of joyful tears. The gods had answered their prayer, they cried out to Mr. Un. They shook his hand vigorously and invited him to their home for dinner and to discuss the matter of his merchandise.

Mr. Un, who for the past five days and nights had been living on bread and dried fruit he had brought from home, gladly accepted the invitation. He finally felt like he was being given the treatment he had almost forgotten. He remem-bered his early years when he could always find invitations waiting for him at every village he visited. Mr. Un grabbed the reins of the mule and walked with the couple as they told him their sad story and of their need for one of his girls.

The man was thirty-seven and his wife was thirty-five. They had met for the first time on their wedding night, which was arranged by their parents, the richest families in this and the adjoining villages. In nine months the wife gave birth to their only child, a beautiful son. With the vast farmland that was given to them from their parents, the couple and their son led a comfortable and rich life.

The only tragedy that befell their happy lives was the sudden and unexpected death of their seventeen-year-old son. The parents had just finalized the arrangements for him to wed the daughter of a rich landowner in a village not too distant from their own. They waited for their son to return from the fields to tell him of the good news. But evening came and darkness fell over the village, and their son never returned.

In a state of panic and worry, the parents sent all the village men to the fields to search for him. They soon found him lying dead in the middle of the field. There were no injuries or any signs of murder. He had just collapsed on the way home. No one knew the cause.

Beyond the sadness of his death and all the arrangements that would have to be made for their son's funeral, the parents' greatest worry was that their son had died before marriage. They could send him to the other world with all the wealth he would need, but they worried that their son would be alone and would live his centuries in the next world in loneliness.

That had been three days ago. Since then, the parents had been waiting for Mr. Un. They knew of his trade and had prayed he would arrive before they would be forced to bury their son alone. They desperately sought a wife for him.

When Mr. Un and the parents reached the house, Mr. Un was treated to a grand dinner of minced beef, chicken, vegetable, and rice, during which the father complimented him on his wisdom and knowledge while his wife sought Mr. Un's advice on the care of the dead bodies until the burial. Mr. Un, who was seldom the center of attention and was infrequently questioned so intensely about his knowledge and job, found the entire evening very satisfying to his ego. In between the cups of rice wine he imbibed too often, he freely gave suggestions on the care of their dead son's corpse. He even gave them a small jar of his secret herbal solution.

When the dinner was finished, the father and Mr. Un sat outside in the night and discussed the price for Little Beauty. The parents had decided on her the moment they saw her. The father inquired about the girl's family and cause of her death. Mr. Un told him a story he had invented a long time ago and often used with the young girls he sold.

Little Beauty was the daughter of a small farm family. She had been raised in the strictest of rules, learning to be a good woman and wife. Because her mother was sick in bed, Little Beauty was already an able housekeeper who could cook, clean, wash, and garden. But most of all she was obedient. She was the prize of her village and every family sought her for their sons. However, she took ill one night and died in her sleep. People said that she was so wonderful, the gods felt that no man was worthy of her and took her away. Her father and mother loved her and did not wish to part with her; however, the mother was still ill and they needed the money.

The father listened with an approving nod. He was happy to hear that Little Beauty would be a good obedient wife for his son. When Mr. Un finished his story, the father turned to him and asked what it would take to place Little Beauty next to his son.

Mr. Un began by thanking the father for the dinner and hospitality. He told him how rare it was that he was treated so generously or with so much respect for his profession. He told the father how he wanted to help the family, and how he would take less than his normal fee for Little Beauty.

The father quickly answered, "We have not done enough to honor you. Your job is a hard and arduous one. You should not take less than you deserve. We do not want to feel like we had taken advantage of your generosity. Please, you should take everything due the wonderful service you are providing our son."

Mr. Un gave out a joyful laugh. "It is no problem. I will ask the price of only one thousand yuan for Little Beauty."

The father was shocked but did not show it. He thought the price was very high but quickly said, "That is too generous of you, Mr. Un. How can we thank you? Will you please attend our son's wedding? We will hold it tomorrow night. We have already made all the preparations in anticipation of your arrival."

Mr. Un smiled and nodded. He knew that the price was high, but after seeing their home and the desperation in their faces, he knew that the couple would pay him. The house, unlike most in the mountains, was built of bricks. Wooden shingles covered the roof, and the grounds around the house had been laid with concrete. There was also a fish pond filled with goldfish. These were all things that had to be brought up from the city and showed the family's wealth. In the house, Mr. Un had also noticed a television, and the moment he saw it, he had decided to double his fee.

After Mr. Un helped the father carry Little Beauty into the house, the father paid him and abruptly said good-bye without mentioning the wedding again. The father was angry at the extortion for Little Beauty.

But Mr. Un didn't care and said he would come to the wedding the next night before driving off again. He set up his camp just outside the village on the family's land and stayed awake longer than usual, dreaming about what he would do with the large sum of money he had received for Little Beauty. It was more than he had expected to get for both girls.

He was woken up early by the cries of children running down the road with their hands filled with flowers. There were many more children than Mr. Un had expected to see in a mountain village. One young girl stopped for a moment to stare at the stranger there.

"Do you need some money, mister?" she asked. "They're giving money for the flowers. Here, you can take one." She handed him one stem and ran after the other children.

Mr. Un looked at the flower and then at himself. The first thing he would do with his money was buy himself a new set of clothes. He did not like having a child take pity on his appearance.

Mr. Un spent the rest of the day sitting under the tree. He anticipated another week of traveling before he would be able to sell the second girl. He wanted to give himself and his mule time to relax before continuing on.

When the sun completed its day-long journey and the sky was leaving an orange tail towards the horizon, Mr. Un climbed back onto his cart and drove to the house. The road was empty, as if the whole village had suddenly disappeared. It was only when he reached the house did Mr. Un see anyone. Gathered around the house seemed to be the entire population of the village. A path bordered by bright colorful lanterns had been created from the road to the rear of the house where the wedding was to be held. There were two women walking down the path lighting each lantern.

Mr. Un left his mule on the road and walked through the crowd, introducing himself and offering everyone the remaining girl in his cart. People smiled at him but quickly distanced themselves. No one wanted to be there but everyone felt obliged to come to the wedding of the son of the biggest landlord of the village. Many worked for him and many more owed money and favors to the family.

At the rear of the house, a large tarp had been raised above bamboo poles to create a canopy for the wedding couple. The poles had been adorned with the beautiful flowers the children had picked in the morning. Everyone stayed outside the canopy, standing at the edges admiring the spectacle and watching the ceremony.

On one side, the mother had set up pictures of their ancestors and surrounded them with hundreds of candles set in perfect rows on three raised steps. The candles burned brightly, and except for the lanterns, provided the only source of light under the canopy.

In the center were two chairs, and on the chairs were placed the son and Little Beauty. They were both dressed in the traditional colorful wedding clothes. A veil had been placed across Little Beauty's face, hiding it from those gathered around the edges of the canopy. The father and the mother, who sat in their traditional clothes to the right side of the couple, proceeded with the wedding.

The ceremony had already begun by the time Mr. Un arrived. With the help of two villagers who played the parts of the bride and groom like actors in a large theatrical play, the wedding vows were exchanged. The two actors then presented the serving of the ceremonial tea to the parents. At the end of the nuptials, the father rose and invited the villagers to meet their son and daughter.

People lined up and approached the wedding couple. One by one, they offered their best wishes for the couple's new life in the next world and their best wishes to the father and mother. Each drank from the cup offered from the father and stepped aside for the next person in line.

Mr. Un approached the newlyweds and extended his best wishes. He looked at Little Beauty but could not see her face through the thick veil. He felt sorry that, after spending so much time preserving her, the parents hid her from the rest of the world. Mr. Un turned to the parents and extended his best wishes to them. They thanked him for his wishes and for bringing Little Beauty for their son.

When all the villagers had wished the family well, they brought forward two sedan chairs. Four women carefully moved the corpses from under the canopy and sat them in the chairs. They tied their arms and legs to the chairs to prevent the corpses from falling. Eight men, four to a chair, raised them to their shoulders and carried the couple down the lantern-lit path and into the road. The parents followed behind and the people followed the parents, creating a long procession that wound down the road like the tail of a kite.

At the end of the short trip was a hut that had been carefully built and beautifully decorated. The men placed the sedan chairs on the ground and the same four women moved the wedding couple inside the hut. They closed the door, locked it, and placed two men outside the door to guard the hut while the others returned to the house for the banquet feast.

At the house, a small fire was created, and the family brought out replicas of all the gifts they would have given their son if he was still alive. First was a house and four servants made from thin bamboo shoots and colored papier-mâché. The house was about six feet high and six feet wide on all sides. It had been meticulously built, even to the details of the door and the windows. The parents had gone to great expense to have these objects made for the ceremony. The servants were four feet high and bore the same handsome workmanship as the house.

The father and the mother carefully lifted the house and placed it into the fire, letting the flames consume it. Everything burned in the fire would be sent to the next world and brought into being for their son and daughter. When the house had completely turned to ashes, the servants were thrown into the flames. The four servants turned to ashes would appear in the next world for the newlyweds.

When all of these were burned, the parents brought out smaller items made from the same bamboo shoots and papier-mâché. One by one, they burned every item. There was a car, something they had seen in the cities but could never own. Then came the television, two horses, a dozen cows, pigs, chickens, ducks, and money. Through the night they burned two baskets full of paper money. They wanted to make sure that their son and new daughter would have a royal life, and that their son would establish an estate ready for them once they also entered the next world.

While the parents were busy burning gifts, the villagers each threw a small token into a separate fire and went to the tables to enjoy the wedding feast.

Mr. Un gathered extra food for the journey and left while the parents were still burning paper money. The wedding had been short, and after the feast, people returned to their homes. Mr. Un, feeling out of place, climbed into his cart and drove away, passing by the hut still being guarded by two men. They were probably guarding the hut from people like him. Maybe the parents were afraid Mr. Un would attempt to steal Little Beauty. Mr. Un never stole bodies, but he never questioned the source of the bodies sold to him.

Though Little Beauty had been only slightly more than a very good business deal for Mr. Un, he was still glad that she had been sold to a family of wealth. He was happy that she would have a better life in the next world than she had been offered in this one. Mr. Un turned his mule toward the dark road and drove forward to sell another girl.

EATEN (SCENES FROM A MOVING PICTURE)

Neil Gaiman

Neil Gaiman is a transplanted Briton who now lives in the American Midwest. He is the author of the award-winning Sandman series of graphic novels, coauthor (with Terry Pratchett) of the novel *Good Omens*, and most recently author of the novel and BBC TV series *Neverwhere*. He also collaborated with artist Dave McKean on the brilliant book *Mr. Punch*. In addition, Gaiman is a talented poet and short story writer whose work has been published in *Snow White, Blood Red; Touch Wood: Narrow Houses 2; Ruby Slippers, Golden Tears; Midnight Graffiti* and *Black Swan, White Raven*. The collection *Angels and Visitations* reprints some of his shorter work.

"Eaten" is a poem in iambic pentameter and was inspired, we've been told, by a dream. It is generally more raw than most of Gaiman's work, although one reviewer described it as "humorous." Depends on your point of view, I guess. It's from *Off Limits: Tales of Alien Sex* and is not for the faint of heart.

—E. D.

INT. WEBSTER'S OFFICE. DAY
As WEBSTER sits
reading the LA Times, MCBRIDE walks in
and tells in

FLASHBACK
how his SISTER came
to Hollywood eleven months ago
to make her fortune, and to meet the stars.
Of how he'd heard from friends that she'd "gone strange."
Imagining the needle, or far worse,
he travels out to Hollywood himself
and finds her standing underneath a bridge.
Her skin is pale. She screams at him "Get lost!"
and sobs and runs. A TALL MAN DRESSED IN BLACK

grabs hold his sleeve, tells him to let it drop
"Forget your sister," but of course he can't . . .

(IN SEPIA
we see the two as teens,
a YOUNG MCBRIDE and SISTER way back when,
giggles beneath the porch, "I'll show you mine,"
closer perhaps than siblings ought to be . . .
PAN UP
to watch a passing butterfly.
We hear them breathe and fumble in the dark:
IN CLOSE-UP now he spurts into her hand,
she licks her palm: first makes a face, then smiles . . .
HOLD on her lips and teeth and on her tongue).

END FLASHBACK
WEBSTER says he'll take the case,
says something flip and hard about LA,
like how it eats young girls and spits them out,
and takes a hundred dollars on account.

CUT TO
THE PURPLE PUSSY. INT. A DIVE,
THREE NAKED WOMEN dance for dollar bills.
WEBSTER comes in, and talks to one of them,
slips her a twenty, shows a photograph,
the stripper—standing close enough that he
could touch her (but they've bouncers on patrol,
weird steroid cases who will break your wrists)—
admits she thinks she knows the girl he means.
Then WEBSTER leaves.

INT. WEBSTER'S CONDO. NIGHT.
A video awaits him at his home.
It shows A WOMAN lovelier than life
Shot from the rib cage up (her breasts exposed)
Advising him to "let this whole thing drop,
forget it," promising she'll see him soon . . .

DISSOLVE TO
INT. MCBRIDE'S HOTEL ROOM. NIGHT.
MCBRIDE'S alone and lying on the bed,
He's watching soft-core porn on pay-per-view.
Naked. He rubs his cock with Vaseline,
lazy and slow, he doesn't want to come.
A BANG upon the window. He sits up,
flaccid and scared (he's on the second floor)

and opens up the window of his room.
HIS SISTER enters, looking almost dead,
implores him to forget her. He says no.
THE SISTER shambles over to the door.
A WOMAN DRESSED IN BLACK waits in the hall.
Brunette in leather, kinky as all hell,
who steps over the threshold with a smile.
And they have sex.

THE SISTER stands alone.
She watches as THE BRUNETTE takes MCBRIDE
(her skin's necrotic blue. She's fully dressed).
THE BRUNETTE gestures curtly with her hand,
off come THE SISTER'S clothes. She looks a mess.
Her skin's all scarred and scored; one nipple's gone.
She takes her gloves off and we see her hands:
Her fingers look like ribs, or chicken wings,
well chewed, and rescued from a garbage can—
dry bones with scraps of flesh and cartilage.
She puts her fingers in THE BRUNETTE'S mouth . . .
AND FADE TO BLACK.

INT. WEBSTER'S OFFICE. DAY.
THE PHONE RINGS. It's MCBRIDE. "Just drop the case.
I've found my sister, and I'm going home.
You've got five hundred dollars, and my thanks."
PULL BACK on WEBSTER, puzzled and confused.

MONTAGE of WEBSTER here. A week goes by,
we see him eating, pissing, drinking, drunk.
We watch him throw HIS GIRLFRIEND out of bed.
We see him play the video again . . .
The VIDEO GIRL stares at him and says
she'll see him soon. "I promise, Webster, soon."

CUT TO
THE PLACE OF EATERS, UNDERGROUND.
Pale people stand like cattle in a pen.
We see MCBRIDE. The flesh is off his chest.
White meat is good. We're looking through his ribs:
his heart is still. His lungs, however, breathe,
inflate, deflate. And tears of pus run down
his sunken cheeks. He pisses in the muck.
It doesn't steam. He wishes he were dead.

A DREAM:
As WEBSTER tosses in his bed.
He sees MCBRIDE, a corpse beneath a bridge,
all INTERCUT with lots of shots of food,
to make our theme explicit: this is art.

EXT. LA. DAY.
WEBSTER's become obsessed.
He has to find the woman from the screen.
He beats somebody up, fucks someone else,
fixated on "I'll see you, Webster, soon."

He's thrown in prison. And they come for him,
THE MAN IN BLACK attending THE BRUNETTE.
Open his cell with keys, escort him out,
and leave the prison building. Through a door.
They walk him to the car park. They go down,
below the car park, deep beneath the town,
past shadowed writhing things that suck and hiss
and glossy things that laugh, and things that scream.
Now other feeder-folk are walking past . . .
They handcuff WEBSTER to A TINY MAN
who's covered with vaginas and with teeth,
and escorts WEBSTER to

THE QUEEN'S SALON.

(An interjection here: my wife awoke,
scared by an evil dream. "You hated me.
You brought these women home I didn't know,
but they knew me, and then we had a fight,
and after we had shouted you stormed out.
You said you'd find a girl to fuck and eat."

This scares me just a little. As we write
we summon little demons. So I shrug.)

The handcuffs are removed. He's left alone.
The hangings are red velvet, then they lift,
reveal THE QUEEN. We recognize her face,
the woman we saw on the VCR.
"The world divides so sweetly, neatly up
into the feeder-folk, into their prey."
That's what she says. Her voice is soft and sweet.
Imagine honey ants: the tiny head,
the chest, the tiny arms, the tiny hands,

and after that the bloat of honey-swell,
the abdomen enormous as it hangs
translucent, made of honey, sweet as lust.

THE QUEEN has quite a perfect little face,
her breasts are pale, blue-veined; her nipples pink;
her hands are white. But then, below her breasts
the whole swells like a whale or like a shrine,
a human honey ant, she's huge as rooms,
as elephants, as dinosaurs, as love.
Her flesh is opalescent, and she calls
poor WEBSTER to her. And he nods and comes.
(She must be over twenty-five feet long.)
She orders him to take off all his clothes.
His cock is hard. He shivers. He looks lost.
He moans "I'm harder than I've ever been."
Then, with her mouth, she licks and tongues his cock . . .

We linger here. The language of the eye
becomes a bland, unflinching, blowjob porn,
(her lips are glossy, and her tongue is red)
HOLD on her face. We hear him gasping "Oh.
Oh, baby. Yes. Oh. Take it in your mouth."
And then she opens up her mouth, and grins,
and bites his cock off.

                              Spurting blood pumps out
into her mouth. She hardly spills a drop.
We never do pan up to see his face,
just her. It's what they call the money shot.

Then, when his cock's gone down, and blood's congealed,
we see his face. He looks all dazed and healed.
Some feeders come and take him out of there.
Down in the pens he's chained beside MCBRIDE.
Deep in the mud lie carcasses picked clean
who grin at them and dream of being soup.

Poor things.

We're almost done.

We'll leave them there.

CUT to some lonely doorway, where A TRAMP
has three cold fingers up ANOTHER TRAMP,

they're starving but they fingerfuck like hell,
and underneath the layers of old clothes
beneath the cardboard, newspaper and cloth,
their genders are impossible to tell.

PAN UP

to watch a butterfly go past.

(ENDS)

ANGEL

Philip Graham

Philip Graham has published fiction in *The New Yorker, The North American Review, The Washington Post Magazine,* and *The Norton Book of Ghost Stories.* He is the author of one novel, *How to Read an Unwritten Language,* two story collections, and a memoir of Africa cowritten with his wife, Alma Gottlieb, an anthropologist. He teaches creative writing at the University of Illinois, and lives in Urbana with his wife and two children. The following beautifully written story, "Angel," comes from Graham's most recent collection, *Interior Design.*

—T. W. and E. D.

Bradley already knew by heart the tales of the lonely angels who hovered at busy street corners and watched careless children; of angels whose tears for all the unconfessed sins of the world created the mountain streams that emptied into the oceans; and of angels who lived in upholstered chairs and waited for lapsed believers to settle unsuspectingly into a suddenly renewed faith. Yet as he sat in the front row of the nearly empty catechism class, resisting as always the impulse to stare at the wispy hint of pompadour that dangled from Father Gregory's forehead, Bradley still listened carefully as the priest said, "Celestial beings have no bodies of their own and need none, for they are clothed in thought. But they love to assume the human form, and this they can do instantly."

The Father looked up at the ceiling, away from Bradley and the other remaining student, that young girl named Lisa who always sat in the last row. Only two left, he thought. "Some angels," he half-mumbled, "let their fingers, hands, and limbs fill out slowly, with voluptuous grace, quietly erupting from nothing into a diaphanous shape."

Though Bradley knew most of these words, he wished Father Gregory would spell the hard ones so he could look them up. But he was afraid to interrupt the Father, who, regarding his hands as if he were alone, said, "Others spend hours inventing a perfect face for their angelic temperaments." Then the Father held one hand before his lips as though suppressing a cough and continued, very softly, "There is some dispute as to whether angels invent clothes for themselves." Bradley suppressed a giggle and glanced back at Lisa. He was shocked to see her indifferent face.

At the end of all those empty rows of folding chairs, Lisa watched the Father's bulbous lips move, which she imagined slapped together. She was glad she wasn't close enough to hear, so she could decide what to make up about today's class—the last time she had told the truth about Father Gregory's stories her dad had smacked her for lying. But right now she couldn't concentrate; instead she wondered why the Father still called out the long class roll even though only two kids were left.

"It is of course well known that angels can read a person's thoughts," Father Gregory said, "but some angels will do this only briefly, for they are too easily lost within that thicket of desires and fears, strange opinions and unspoken urges—so unangel-like!" He looked down at the two students and wondered how long it would take before they too stopped coming to class, so his afternoons would finally be free. "*All* angels—the seraphim and cherubim—are addicted to us," he now whispered, "and they hover not so much to protect, but to experience us." Bradley, straining to hear this, felt uneasily that he had just heard a secret. He didn't care if he couldn't always understand; he loved being spoken to as if he were an adult.

Bradley stood beside Lisa under the church eaves and pretended, because it was raining, that his parents would be picking him up too. He wanted to ask Lisa why she kept coming to class if she didn't appreciate the Father, but she stood away from him and offered no opening for his curiosity.

Jonah and the whale, that's what we talked about, Lisa thought, watching the station wagon pull up to the curb and stop. The dim figure of her mother leaned over in the car and the window slowly slid down. "Hurry up, dear, you'll get wet," she called. Lisa's fingers scraped at her skirt. Finally, she walked to the car slowly, still not sure how long Jonah had been in that whale's stomach.

"I want to hear all about your class, sweetie," Bradley heard, and he envied such attentiveness. Then the glass rose up and the car pulled away. He remained at the church entrance and waited. His parents were probably home from work by now, and maybe one of them might actually be on the way. But the wet street was empty.

He held his school satchel over his head and walked quickly, imagining that the rain fell through his angel hovering alongside him. If only he had a bicycle. Remembering the Father's words, he tried to express himself clearly and calmly, so his angel would listen longer than usual to his unangel-like thoughts, and slowly enumerated all the special features he wanted: ten speeds, orange-and-black trim, a bell and adjustable seat. But he wanted this bicycle only if his parents gave it to him—this would be a sign that his angel had heard.

Opening the front door, Bradley could smell dinner cooking and he walked to the kitchen. There were his parents, leaning over the stove, his father stirring a wooden spoon in the pot, his mother shaking salt into the rising steam. They stood so closely together that Bradley couldn't imagine a space for himself.

"Mom, Dad."

Jill and Bud turned to see their son standing in the doorway, holding his catechism. "Hello dear," his mother said, bending down and offering her cheek for his kiss. She rested her hand on his damp shirtsleeve. "Oh, is it raining?"

"Just a little."

Unsettled that her son had walked in the rain, Jill decided to offer Bradley his daily treat early. "Have you been a good boy today?" she asked.

Bradley nodded.

"Then here's your potato chip," she said, reaching for the counter, and she placed the chip in his waiting mouth. Her son stood still with his mouth closed, for he wasn't allowed to chew. This was their own home-grown communion: if Bradley was becoming religious, Jill couldn't see why she shouldn't exchange a greasy wafer for some quiet.

Bud said, "Well, Brad ol' boy, dinner is on the way, so why don't you take in some TV?" Bradley turned and walked down the hall to the den. Bud watched him disappear. His son's recent piety was yet another example of the inexplicability of childhood. He was pleased he could restrain himself from criticizing this latest addition to Bradley's recent manias: handwriting analysis, when his son searched the desk drawers for even the shortest note, and then that oatmeal box telephone system, with strings leading from room to room. It was so hard to be a good father in the face of such perplexing enthusiasms.

In the den, Bradley settled himself into a chair. The television was already on and waiting for him, busy with laughter and applause. Even with his eyes closed he could barely make out the indistinct murmur of his parents' voices. He wondered if their angels spoke to each other, revealing secrets about his parents that he would never know. Then he felt a salty twinge, and he concentrated on the potato chip dissolving on his tongue. Angels don't like to eat, he remembered Father Gregory once saying, because the thought of mixing food with their angelic form upsets them. But they like for us to eat, and they try to imagine taste, they try not to think of digestion. In an effort to endear himself, Bradley decided to describe his experience for his angel. First it's very salty, he thought, your tongue wants to curl up, and it's hard not to chew. When the chip starts to go mushy, you can press it—very softly—against the roof of your mouth with your tongue, and then little pieces break away. They melt very, very slowly.

Jill called her son to dinner; when he didn't answer she entered the room quietly. She regarded her son's small body, framed by the upholstered arms of the chair. His eyes were closed, and his obedient silence in front of the blaring TV was so total that he seemed about to disappear. She couldn't stop watching him, and she remembered his alarming cries as an infant, his tiny arms raised, pleading to be held.

The hardest part, Bradley thought, is to let the last piece melt instead of swallowing it. He was able to restrain himself, and soon the last bit of chip disappeared. It was terrifically difficult, he felt, to pay such close attention, and he wondered how angels could do this every instant. Suddenly his mother was before him, repeating again and again how she was going to take him to the old amusement park before it closed down. Bradley stared up at her, amazed: this wasn't a bicycle, but it was good enough.

*   *   *

Alone in the Ferris wheel, Bradley felt weightless circling so high up. He still didn't quite believe he was here, and the rust and the loud groans of the ancient rides couldn't spoil his pleasure. He picked at the chipped paint in his cabin, watched the little flecks flutter down, and he tried to make out his parents in the crowds below.

Jill and Bud waited below while their son spun above them. Though they had intended to come alone, Jill had managed to convince Bud to bring Bradley along. Better bumper cars and greasy food, she said, than genuflection, genuflection, genuflection. They had first met here while standing in some long line, and it was so romantic now, holding hands in this amusement park for one last time before it closed forever at the end of the season. Jill could remember Bud smiling at her in the extraordinary heat and then holding his jacket over her for a little shade.

All afternoon Bradley rode on the Loop-A-Loop, Tumble Buckets, and The Space Twister. On the boardwalk he aimed ineffectually at stacked wooden bottles, he was drawn to the pervasive promise of pizza and hot dogs wafting from the open stalls. He especially loved the sticky sweetness of cotton candy, the way it clung to the edges of his mouth and stuck to his fingers when he touched his cheek. He closed his eyes, about to describe this to his angel as a way of thanks, but then his mother bent down to wash the glistening smudges from his face.

As Bradley watched her scrape the last bit away, he heard the happy screams from the nearby roller coaster ride. He looked up at the cars making such swift, tight turns above them. Jill watched too, remembering how she'd clutched Bud's jacket on that ride so long ago.

Bud bought the tickets and fingered them with pleasure. But when they approached the seats he and Jill hesitated—the run-down roller coaster didn't fit their memories. Finally they sat together in one of the last cars, and Bradley could see that there was no room for him, although his mother patted the bit of cushion beside her. "That's okay," he said and he settled in the car behind them. The leather seat was cracked with age, and he picked at the tiny, pliable pieces while the conductor collected tickets.

The roller coaster slowly ascended the sharp rise of track with a ratchety, metallic groan. Regretting that he had ever entertained the slightest desire to be on this ride, Bradley imagined his angel was beside him. Rather than recount how the people on the ground began to shrink, however, he simply wished he had squeezed in with his parents. Bradley rattled his safety bar and hoped one of them would look back just once.

The first cars rushed down the steep slope with a curling roar and the howls of passengers. Even his parents screamed and Bradley joined in as the roller coaster hurtled to the bottom of the slope, and at each curve of track it twisted improbably one way, then another. Bradley was sure the cars would lurch from the tracks and he tightened his grip on the clattering bar. But another steep rise suddenly appeared and the roller coaster swiftly rose and fell and spurted toward another sharp turn. It tilted precipitously again, and Bradley heard a loud snap.

His parents were in the air in awkward disarray, hands clutching at their broken safety bar. They swiftly fell from sight and the roller coaster rushed down the next slope. Unable to believe what he had seen, Bradley struggled to stand in his seat, hoping his parents were somehow still in the car before him. His body trembled with the shuddering roller coaster, the wind rushed against his face and filled his open mouth, and his howls continued well past the final screeching halt at the end of the ride.

Bradley's aunt and uncle had no children after too many years of trying and they were secretly, guiltily happy to take in their favorite nephew. They fed him little treats, hoping cookies layered with tempting jams would defeat his sadness. They always made room for him on the couch, allowing any channel change he requested, and they avoided any topic concerning his mother and father.

Under the dimmed overhead lights of the dining room, Bradley watched Aunt Lena pass the cucumber salad to Uncle George while they talked of common memories that he didn't share, of neighbors he didn't know. When his uncle sipped ice water and squinted from the cold, Bradley recalled his father's features, and sometimes even his aunt's crisp footsteps to the refrigerator reminded him of his mother. Bradley stared past the chicken cutlets and wondered if his parents ever thought of him in heaven. Were their angels still with them? Bradley hated the thought that those angels, with all their memories of his parents, might be hovering next to strangers. Or did angels forget? Bradley almost envied the idea.

Though Bradley's aunt and uncle weren't religious, they remembered his parents' complaints and so they took him to church. But now he disliked having to stand and kneel all the time, and why hadn't his angel somehow warned him and his parents away from the roller coaster? While the thin priest—so unlike Father Gregory—droned the Mass, Bradley tried to recall what he could of the Father's confiding words: how angels envelop us with rapt attention; how they only want to experience us, not protect us. Bradley pictured his parents smashed on the ground, their angels hovering over them without sadness, simply satisfying their curiosity about death, while his own angel calmly examined his terrible grief.

Bradley squirmed in the pew and imagined *he* was falling through the air while his parents were safe in the roller coaster. Then, his body twisted on the pavement, dead but somehow still aware, he watched the roller coaster speed to the end. His mother and father left the ride undisturbed and walked over his body as if he weren't lying broken beneath them. They seemed like giants, and this image of his mother and father, resurrected and enormous, their indifference implacable, followed him out the church and back to his new home.

That evening he sat on the couch with his aunt and uncle in front of the television. "Tonight it's your Aunt Lena's night to choose the programs," his uncle announced with a wink. "What do you say, hon?"

She patted her nephew's knee. "I think I'm in the mood for Bradley's favorite show."

Bradley smiled up at her, sure that his angel would enjoy a description of the one-liners, even the commercial breaks, though when he turned to the television Bradley found himself once again imagining that he lay sprawled on the fairgrounds after tumbling through the sky. But this time, at his parents' approach he forced himself to rise up despite the great pain in his shattered bones. They stopped, then fled. Bradley watched their figures growing smaller and smaller, yet he felt oddly happy, for they had *seen* him. He repeated his fall, and when his parents arrived again he reached up and held their wrists. Their faces strangely impassive, they struggled until they broke away and fled again.

With each battle his parents became less substantial, and Bradley remembered that his angel must be hovering nearby, watching. Why won't it help me? he thought. Then shimmering fingers burst out of nothing and his angel reached out: slowly it loosened his grip on his straining parents until they were able to tear away. Stunned, Bradley crumpled back to the ground. His angel was a *jealous* angel and wanted no rivals.

Bradley rose from the couch, surprised to see his aunt and uncle laughing at the blaring television. "Sweetie?" his aunt began.

"I have to go to the bathroom," he said, almost running away.

He locked himself inside. It was the smallest room in the house, so small that his angel couldn't escape. "Keep away, keep away from me!" Bradley shouted, and he swung his arms wildly, hoping he struck through his angel's shape, bursting apart its invisible presence. Yet he suspected that, unlike him, it could easily heal itself, so he spun his arms about him even more and he screamed until his throat ached, his anger beyond words. His aunt and uncle pounded on the door, but he didn't let them in until he was dizzy and exhausted.

Aunt Lena held him, unable to hush his wailing, and Uncle George, alarmed at such unhappiness, reached out and awkwardly stroked his nephew's hair. "Hey, Brad ol' boy, hey Brad," he murmured.

Bradley listened to his uncle's voice, so similar to his father's, and he eased into his aunt's anxious grip. *They* wanted to comfort him, even if his angel didn't. What Father Gregory had said was true: his angel wanted only to observe him and his thoughts. Suddenly he wanted to protect his aunt and uncle from this same fearsome angel that had kept him from his parents. Remembering the intense calm he had felt when detailing the potato chip, Bradley hoped that more such careful communications might appease his angel. Slowly pushing his aunt away, he began to silently describe the crinkled look of hurt on her face.

Bradley's aunt and uncle grew accustomed to the sight of him fingering the ridges of a lampshade, the interior of a mailbox, and they were puzzled by his almost constant paging through the dictionary, since he rarely spoke. Aunt Lena ached for the sound of his voice, and whenever she touched Bradley his hesitant, endearing hug turned into a sudden breaking away, and she was left alone in a hall, the kitchen.

One afternoon as Bradley tried to sneak outside, his aunt called from the living room, "Where are you off to, Bradley?"

He pretended not to hear, but when he pushed open the creaking screen door she said, "Would you like a little snack first?"

"No thanks," he managed, though he was hungry.

Standing outside, he knew from the directions of the subtle, shifting winds that a storm was approaching. All those grasping branches above him shook and his hair swept across his forehead like the softest of touches. He bent down and thrust his hand into one of the last small piles of late snow. Its crystals were larger and harder than he expected. Then he squeezed some in his fist and felt the cold throb against his warmer skin. After the bit of snow dissolved, Bradley slowly swept his tongue over the lines of his palm, silently describing each ticklish ripple. The rain began to fall. Bradley stood there as it soaked his hair and drained down his face, its taste vaguely metallic against his parted lips, and he recorded scrupulously how his increasingly wet clothes matted against him, how an oddly pleasurable chill spread over his body.

Aunt Lena dropped the cauliflower she was washing in the sink when she glanced out the window and saw Bradley standing drenched in the middle of the backyard, his face turned up into the rain. She ran outside, wailing his name.

That night Lena and her husband sat beside Bradley's bed, alarmed at their feverish nephew's smile while he touched his forehead carefully with his fingers, as if for the first time. When Bradley recovered three days later, Uncle George bought him a bicycle. They sat together in the driveway and attached baseball cards to the spokes for an intricate, ratchety sound, and Uncle George patiently ignored those unnerving moments when his nephew sat still, his eyes distant, his hands working at nothing.

But Bradley was rarely at home. Instead he ranged through the neighborhood, discovering the patterned silences between bird calls, the new green shoots and their clusters of buds within buds. Dizzy and oppressed by the seemingly endless supply of the world, he doubted he could ever chronicle it all for his angel, and one evening, while listening to his uncle's faraway voice calling him, Bradley stood transfixed beneath an evergreen tree lit by a street lamp. In the odd light its needles were an unearthly green. Detailing the ascending, branched pattern of the thin needles, which resembled an odd spiral staircase, he realized that the convoluted spaces between the branches were passages for the wind. But he could only see these spaces by looking at the branches, which in turn held no pattern without the surrounding emptiness, and Bradley was reminded of his own invisible, complementary presence.

After years of plumbing the hidden corners of dictionaries, words had become for Bradley exquisite bearers of comfort, yet by high school the frequent sight of boys and girls necking furtively in the school hallways filled him with a strange longing for which there were no words. He found brief solace in gym class, deftly kicking a soccer ball that seemed to float endlessly in the air before suddenly eluding the goalie, or exulting in a basketball's intricate, rhythmic music as he sped down the court.

Despite his sometimes unnerving solitude a few girls thought he was cute; Debby Wickers, who seemed to always appear by his hall locker, adjusting the pile of books under her arm, thought he was handsome. But after so often standing near his locker with nothing to say or do, Debby was almost ready to give up on Bradley ever acknowledging her.

One day Bradley was pressing his hands against the side of his locker door, mutely describing the touch of metal and how its edges are almost sharp enough to cut—anything to avoid facing the girl who always stood so close to him, to suppress his curiosity about her constancy. But when he heard the sound of her patient sigh, there was something final in it that made Bradley turn and look at her steady dark eyes, her thick brown hair. "What's your name?" he asked, so quietly, and Debby felt he was staring at her face as if he were trying to memorize it.

The next evening he was at Debby's house, helping her with algebra. They sat on the carpet in her room, books open and paper scattered, while her parents called up regularly to ask how their homework was coming along. Bradley stammered out the solutions to the problems, and Debby was pleased—his nervousness was so flattering. When she had enough of answers she already knew, she stretched out on the floor, yawned, and then glanced up at Bradley. The night before she had made a long-distance call to her sister in college. "Let him take off just one thing," her sister had said. "He'll be chained to you after that, he'll want to know what's under the rest of your clothes." Debby put her hand on his knee and smiled before she turned away.

Bradley wanted to touch the back of her neck where her dark hair seemed to burst out of nowhere, but he was at the center of an invisible stage, his curious angel the audience. Debby looked over her shoulder and reached for Bradley. Though he knew he shouldn't touch her, he tried to convince himself that her beckoning hand had just waved his angel away. He tentatively stroked her wrist and she snuggled against him. Instead of pushing her away, he gently touched Debby's neck and she arched her back. After a long moment he finally cupped his hand and slowly placed it over a breast, the cloth of her blouse softly tickling his palm.

Bradley let Debby lead his hands to one button after another until the thought of his angel, capable of anything, returned. Debby saw his face blank over. Shocked that he was resisting what she offered, she coaxed him into unfastening her belt, and before long she forgot everything her sister had advised.

When Debby was finally, stunningly exposed beside him, Bradley felt the habitual urge to describe what he saw. *Never* any privacy, *never* alone? he thought. He closed his eyes, refusing to explicate Debby, but already he could sense the presence of an angry, invisible hand. "No!" Bradley shouted, "No!" Debby sat up, frightened by Bradley's cries, by the sound of steps up the stairs. The door to her room opened. Debby held her skirt against her, but she could tell from her father's brief, horrified glance that he could see right through it. And then he was after Bradley, who was still shouting, his eyes still closed.

In college Bradley majored in Accounting and immersed himself in long spreadsheets, half hoping that his angel would eventually grow bored by the regularity of numbers. But that intimate presence had become a habit he couldn't cast out; Bradley sometimes wondered if Father Gregory had felt this way. He tried to remember the Father's long-ago words but could only see his lips moving: a silent, distant performance.

He always sat by himself in the dormitory dining hall, tired from programming long columns of audits and inventories, and though he was proud of his secret eloquence, Bradley listened with envy to the chaotic accumulation of speech and laughter that rose and fell in the large hall. He understood grimly that he had forgotten how to talk to other people, and he tried to imagine how his voice might sound as part of those alien give-and-take rhythms. But he spoke directly to no one, for he was afraid *not* to believe in his angel's possessive will, and when he felt words brimming up he panicked: he released them as sudden laughter, great huffing gulps of sound that held no happiness.

Soon Bradley couldn't stop these cheerless bursts, and he began to haunt the local comedy club whenever he felt the need to speak. Sitting alone at the bar, he held back a welter of words and hoped his awkward laughter blended in with the hearty convulsions of the strangers around him. He stared at the rows of bottles lined up beneath the mirror, those almost transparent bodies filled with clear or strangely colored liquids: how he envied the way they could be so easily emptied.

One night he arrived for the Open Mike Spotlight, the least entertaining show of the week, and he had to endure long stretches before he could join in with any appreciative guffaws and snorts. Yet he couldn't stop watching the painfully amateur failures who grasped at even the most modest reward from the audience. That night's barmaid, frightened by his desolate laughter, considered refusing him another beer—whatever tormented the poor guy, no drink would drown it.

Finally, after a middle-aged man's ten-minute repertoire of personal noises, the MC announced "Last call." Bradley finished his beer, edged off his stool, and was alarmed to discover he was walking toward the stage. He wanted to stop, but he felt the same as when that roller coaster had started its slow climb and there was no turning back. He stepped into the spotlight, absolutely uncertain of himself. As he adjusted the mike he listened to the loud, amplified crunks, the murmur of distant and unfamiliar voices. They were waiting, listening, and Bradley remembered his parents' funeral, when he had been the mute center of everyone's attention. His throat constricted—if he didn't speak right now he might never speak again. A few people in the audience began to applaud ironically.

"Better be careful," Bradley heard himself say, "God doesn't like irony." Where is *this* coming from? he thought, but more words rose up and he released them. "Irony introduces ambiguity, which undermines the power of God's Word, and His punishment is the Angel of Irony."

There were a few hoots, and the MC began to edge toward the stage. They think I'm a fanatic, a crank, Bradley realized with alarm. "No, wait," he said, "I'm only trying to be helpful. You see, the Angel of Irony is drawn to irony but, ironically enough, can't understand it. Maybe one day that angel will float nearby when you say something like, 'It sure would be great to live in this little dump for the rest of my life.' Then it'll grant you your wish and you'll be stuck in that dump no matter what you try to do."

Bradley paused, struck by the fluidity of his strange thoughts and the booming sound of his amplified voice. He looked out at the audience, their faces pale disks in the dark. Were they waiting for a punch line? He had none, so he plunged on.

"And what about your personal angel? There's one sitting right beside you now and yet somehow taking up no space at all. Since an angel has no substantial presence it can compress itself to the size of a synapse, can follow the extraordinarily swift and winding ways of a thought. But it must have *some* weight: imagine that this extra bit of almost nothing attaches to a memory or the beginning of a thought and subtly alters its forward motion, veering it, however slightly, to another neuron. Could our daily indecisions," he continued, exhilarated, "be the contrast between what we truly want and where our concentrated knot of angel has taken us? Maybe we're compositions, evolving works of art for angels, and they're attracted to the elegant patterns they make of our fates."

The audience was terribly quiet, but Bradley felt more words forming and he could hold nothing back. "It's late. Maybe you'd like to leave, right now, and get away from all my idiotic words, but your angel swerves you away from such a thought. Your angel is vain. Trained by a life of eavesdropping, it can't resist listening to such delicious talk. And maybe it's anticipating the pleasure, when everyone applauds, of its transparent body fluttering in the small explosions of the surrounding air."

Finally emptied, Bradley felt almost weightless, actually released from that burrowing presence, and this purging was pleasurable, a loss that was simultaneously gain. But then the oppressive need to describe returned, and he couldn't help listening carefully to the applause, that indecisive clapping of hands that was both restrained and enthusiastic, conveying at the same time curiosity, appreciation, and resistance.

Although no one could really call his monologues comedy, Bradley became a regular at the club, and soon he was known informally as the Angel Man. Ignoring the clink of glasses, the whoosh of the tap at the bar, he held on to the microphone stand as if it tethered him to the stage, and the intensity of his concentration quieted the occasional heckler. He was immediately filled with words that metamorphosed into phrases and sentences, hungry for that exhausted moment after a performance when, briefly emptied of his angel, he had to clutch the plush curtain backstage and ease into its swaying.

But often his eloquence didn't seem his own, and Bradley suspected that his angel was confessing its inexplicable qualities. "Consider this," Bradley found himself saying one evening, "since an angel has no voice, it assumes the vocal inflections of its human companion, and what we sometimes believe to be private thoughts are actually communications from our angels." Yet as he listened to himself—or was it to his angel?—Bradley wondered if he might be able to pour out all those words inside until they couldn't be replenished, if one night he might finally be deserted.

He returned to the club as often as possible, pushing his impromptu inventions and never repeating himself. "Imagine how different angels are from us," he said one evening, "because what we can't do without, angels don't need:

food, clothes, houses, doorways, or cars. . . ." For one dizzy moment Bradley had nothing to say, and he was filled with a wild thought: Could this really be the last emptying?

Bradley closed his eyes, and in the dark he briefly created he saw a young girl's face appear, a dot of memory he immediately knew belonged to Lisa, that girl who sat in the back during catechism class. She regarded Bradley with total disinterest, and then her features altered and multiplied into his mother's and father's, both imperturbably facing him. He reached out to prevent their escape, but there were no wrists to grasp.

Hearing nervous coughs, Bradley opened his eyes and simply stood there, searching foolishly through the audience for his parents' faces. Then he noticed a young couple sitting at a front table: the man smiled a steady, peculiar smile, but it was the woman's impassive gaze, which seemed not to see Bradley at all, that drew him. He needed to speak to her, only to her, and at once he felt a great stillness inside him.

"Imagine a being who shares your secrets," he began, leaning forward on the stage, "the ones you manage to conceal from everyone. Compared to your angel, your intimacy with your spouse is similar to your occasional dealings with a salesclerk. Are you here tonight with a husband, a wife? Look at that stranger beside you, so unable to challenge the secret knowledge of your angel."

Diane didn't dare glance over at her relentlessly devout husband who had come here just because he loved to be appalled. All evening she'd had to pretend she was bored, but now the Angel Man seemed to speak directly to her, and Diane was afraid he saw past her false face and knew how stunned she was by his words.

"Remember, to angels we are both storm and ballast," Bradley said, anxious for even the barest flicker of interest on the woman's face. "We're a promising harbor for an angelic grip, but we are also the most turbulent of passages, the tightest of squeezes for an angel once it truly wants to slip inside us."

Diane watched the Angel Man, his face so peaceful in the spotlight. She thought of her husband's angel: twisted in his heart, its wings crushed and worthless, its sad contortions resembling his fist on the table. She could sense him stirring angrily in his seat, aware of the attention she was receiving. She dreaded going home, where she was helpless before the unyielding injustice of his opinions, where even her dreams couldn't escape the sound of his angry voice. She kept her face a blank.

"We're sometimes too voluminously primitive," Bradley continued, "a catalogue of imperfections, for angels to truly enjoy us. I sometimes wonder why angels hover beside us if we're such an inexpressibly crude version of themselves, for they have more facets than we can imagine, each one lit by a light we can't see. Perhaps our angels are prodigiously unfaithful and temporarily leave us, from boredom or exhaustion, to enter the mind of a new and excitingly unfamiliar human. Perhaps my own angel has done this. Perhaps it will someday leave me forever for someone new."

He stopped and stared at the woman's stiff face. She isn't even listening, he thought, at best she's holding back a yawn. He looked out over the rest of the faces in the audience, but they all seemed to recede from him.

Diane imagined his angel speeding toward her, whispering the sorts of secrets she had listened to all evening. The lone spotlight dimmed and she could just make out, "Whoever receives my angel, you're welcome to every dogged attention it's capable of, and may it give you better fortune than it ever gave me." She looked up in gratitude, but the Angel Man had turned his back on her and the rest of the audience. As he walked offstage, Diane felt dangerously, deliciously weightless, and her lips tingled with forbidden words. And what *could* her husband do, she thought, if her words were not her own, how could he possibly reply if she howled out at him in an angelic rage? Already she saw him open-mouthed and speechless before her.

Bradley stopped backstage, giddily empty, and he clung to the heavy folds of the curtain. He kept repeating to himself those last words, hoping to stave off his angel's possible return. Through the curtain he could hear the rasp of chairs pushing back, murmuring voices, footsteps. He envied that crowd out there, leaving to return to their own lives. Then he thought, I'm the only life my angel has. And this seemed to be its own strange comfort, one that might forever help him to endure his companionable loneliness. But this insinuating idea also alarmed Bradley, and he checked an urge to describe the dark curtain, even though it shimmered along its length from his slightest touch.

ELK MAN

Amy Breau

The "Elk Man" is a fascinating figure found in Native American lore, particularly in the tales of the Lakota Sioux. This supernatural creature would sometimes take the form of a handsome young man, wild in his ways and utterly irresistible to women. Although he was deemed a dangerous figure, disruptive to the tribal way of life, "elk magic" was sometimes sought by men of certain tribes to aid in courtship. This poem looks at elk seduction from a woman's point of view. This poem is from *Prairie Schooner*, Vol. 70, number 4.

—T. W.

> *And then it was clear*
> *that the young man was really an elk,*
> *and so it was beyond their power to subdue him*
> *by killing him; neither could they put a stop*
> *to his attraction for women.*
> —Ella Deloria's *Dakota Texts*

A branch snaps
at your passing. Dusk drapes
your dark shoulders through trees.

I've seen the black bands around aspen
your teeth tattoo, the red warm earth you hoof free
from snow, and in spring, coming over the hill,
a pool of water still cloudy, your cloven heart
prints fresh in sand.

All my family frowns when I step into night
to find you. Women you've drawn within your
cloak
say I'm better off without you, and certainly

I've had better luck with porcupine,
whitetail, and hawk

but Wapiti, strong heart, I hear you
the clearest midnights when I stand deer-still
and you sound the distance between us
all muscle and lung—
my heart's white rootthreads shiver
in the clearsoil dark.

BECKONING NIGHTFRAME
Terry Dowling

Terry Dowling lives in Sydney, Australia, and is one of that country's most respected writers of speculative fiction. His short fiction has been published in Australian magazines such as *Aphelion*, *Eidolon* and *Australian Short Stories*, and in the U.S. magazines *Strange Plasma* and *The Magazine of Fantasy & Science Fiction*, and in the anthologies *Urban Fantasies*, *Matilda at the Speed of Light*, *Terror Australis*, *Intimate Armageddons* and *The Year's Best Fantasy and Horror*. His novels include *Rynosseros* and *Blue Tyson*. His science fiction collection, *Wormwood*, won the Readercon Small Press Award for Best Collection in 1991. His horror stories have been collected in *An Intimate Knowledge of the Night*.

Dowling's horror fiction is remarkably varied—he has written an excellent historical ghost story, "The Daemon Street Ghost Trap," and a frightening contemporary tale of supernatural revenge called "Scaring the Trains." "Beckoning Nightframe," set in a self-aware contemporary urban society, is a story of obsession and monomania peopled by those who should (and do) know better. This knowledge, to me, is what makes the story so frightening. It was originally published in issue 22/23 of the Australian magazine *Eidolon*.

—E. D.

Corinne Kester had once been described as a knife. Hard, sharp, bright, relentless, yes, and penetrating, that's what George Faye had said, both in his review of her first book and on some TV talk show.

It had brought her a certain cachet at the time, had led in fact to her latest project and to George being one of the twenty-two guests at her combined launch and thank-you party. Had led too to Corinne's renewed determination never to let their one-time attraction for each other have any kind of resolution—a sort of revenge by nostalgia and lost opportunity.

Perhaps George had reached the stage where he wanted more, could even deliver more, but there'd been too many years where it was obvious he was just trying to ground her mystique, to satisfy his curiosity and be gone. So now he would die wondering. She would remain shiny bright, hard and, yes, penetrating.

That's what Corinne Kester was thinking when she first noticed the curtains beckoning to her.

All twenty-two guests were out on the terrace—the six psychiatrists who'd helped her profile the Harborside Killer, and their respective wives, husbands and partners, several of the editorial people, several publicists, some closer friends. George, of course, careening from one to the next like some lonely planet. Planet and knife. It seemed apt.

It was a mild autumn evening, darkening quickly after a splendid sunset and a successful alfresco dinner, certainly warm enough to use the spacious deck, though a cool breeze had come up and they would go inside soon. Her apartment in the four-storied, tiered apartment building was higher than the houses across Victoria Place. There was a view of the bay across low rooftops, framed at the top by a rich lapis blue, at the sides by black tree silhouette and adjacent apartment buildings, at the bottom by the white house with its warm lighted windows and the path leading down its northwestern side to what looked like a semi-detached shed with its long window of two square panes.

Curtained, never lighted that she could remember. House, shed, long window, all noticed a thousand times, part of the view, the nightframe.

And now that frame was beckoning. True, standing there with Doctors Michael Castley, Samantha Crewe and Dan Truswell, listening to Dan speak of some recent developments in the Hunter, she just looked casually, contentedly, out at the night, had her eye caught by the lights across the bay, by the boats moored there, the merging blues, then by the black sideframe of trees, down to the bottom frame-edge of house, warm lights, path, long window, to where the dull white curtains were, yes, beckoning to her.

Someone who lived there had opened the top-hinged casement window a bit, pushed it out so wind sliding under a door formed a draft, causing the curtains to belly out, to ripple and lift, to make swift scalloping edges of darkness under the dull white.

It was just something you noticed when it wasn't your turn in conversation, then noticed again, then kept noticing, a visual refrain to the evening, a flicker of movement in the splendid stillness, soothing, relaxing in a way.

Checking on other guests, pouring drinks, letting Max Jobarth take some final publicity shots with her advisory "team" of experts, took her away from it for a while, but the beckoning effect was there when she stepped back onto the deck twenty minutes later, just keeping an eye on things.

The whole scene was darker, of course. Little of the blue was left in the sky; now it was a starfield above and intense blacks all around, distant light-points, barest hints of boats, cables slapping masts and, there at the bottom, like peering down a tunnel of flaring, hooding trees (one on the street, one in the front yard of the house), focused by a security light on that side path, was the long double-paned window still raised, the curtains still rippling, scalloping, offering hints of darkness beyond.

No longer soothing or relaxing, Corinne found. Mesmerising, an unexpectedly dramatic centerpiece to the night now that the sky had gone dark, withdrawn the last of its sunset glory. Hypnotic, those edges rippling at her.

"Corinne?"

It was George Faye, the planet on its sad orbit, hunting, reaching out, expecting nothing.

"George. Hi."

"Wondered where you were."

"It's a nice night."

"It's a good party. Interesting party, with your hand-picked boffins in there. Everyone's sure they're coming over as prats." George was "eroded" English. His language sometimes gave it away.

"As what?" Corinne said, though she'd heard well enough.

"Spill a drink, stand a certain way and you feel those psychiatrists of yours taking you apart."

"Like novelists and journalists. Everything is grist."

"Then I've been through the mill twice over. Castley and Crewe just put hands to their chins and nod at whatever I say. I feel I'm being dissected."

"They were essential for the book, George. Gave it respectability."

"Doubled the advance too, I bet."

"Something like that. I don't think I betrayed their trust."

"I'm sure."

Corinne saw he was going to stay around, was about to say "Better join the others", when he noticed the curtains too.

"Now that's weird."

"What is?"

"That house across the street down there. That window down the side. The way the curtains are moving."

"It's just the wind."

"Yeah, but eerie, you know. Like they're reaching out."

Beckoning. Reaching out. It didn't help Corinne's mood. She resented George being part of it, finding her out at something that had found a place in her mind. It was one more unwanted intimacy. After the months of research and writing, the endless interview transcripts, revisions, proofing and editing galleys, the media gauntlet, she was in shut-down mode, ready for private head space, solitary moments, everyone to be gone. Curtains reaching out! It was George reaching out, needful as ever, trying to connect. She resented it with a vehemence that surprised her.

"We should go in."

"Corinne?"

"George, I'm host. Let's go."

The night wound down from there—probably inevitable with her panel of experts lending an air of implied scrutiny to everything, as George said, giving even the smallest lapse or gaffe a curious weight of significance. It remained a fascinating party but not an altogether comfortable one. By the time the first guests began leaving at 9:45, Corinne had decided she'd never try it again.

George Faye posed his usual problem, tried to linger, but one of the psychiatrists read the situation for what it was and stayed to lend an avuncular hand.

"Corinne," Dan Truswell said in George's hearing. "You still want to go over those latest interview briefs? If you're too tired . . ."

"No, let's get it over and done with. Then I'm turning in."

George took the hint and left with good grace, promised he'd call.

Corinne didn't mention the curtains to Dan, the oddly compelling signature they made on the night. "Thanks for that, Dan."

"He looked needy. You didn't."

"Yeah, well. I invited him."

"Going for closure, I'd say. He's been part of your professional life."

"Where I have to keep him, Dan. Not too vindictive, I hope."

"We ritualize our lives according to our needs, Corinne. I imagine you know that better than anyone after the Harborside business."

"We did good, Dan."

"You've done an excellent job."

"You truly don't mind staying on for the interviews?"

Dan Truswell smiled. "We've been through this, what, four times now? I'll see you Tuesday at 11 A.M., then Friday at 10. You've got my mobile number."

"I appreciate it. Rebecca says it really will help sales. Lend respectability."

"Of course it will. We've discussed this, Corinne. The level of responsibility you showed makes it a pleasure to help. See you Tuesday."

When she had her apartment to herself at last, Corinne didn't go out on the deck. She understood the sequencing of pathological behavior so much better after reconstructing a putative mindset for the Harborside Killer, knew the difference between psychotic and psychopathic conduct, how a rather routine MO could be so bizarrely anchored yet not be a psychotic disorder, rather the fruits of dissociation and childhood conditioning fraught with trauma resulting in compensation exactly as Dan had said. The rituals.

Time to let it go, she resolved, though she ran the sequence in her mind: casual preoccupation to fixation to neurosis, obsession and monomania, the *idee fixe* becoming everything.

So, none of the casual checking to see if the front door was locked (she'd locked it after Dan), to check her alarm was set (she'd set it before the guests arrived), to see if she'd put detergent in the dishwasher (she had); none of those things people do, a lack of focusing on the moment producing the first glimmers of anxiety. She spent forty minutes cleaning up, then went to bed.

And woke at 3:40, lay blinking in semi-darkness, watching tree-shadow on the ceiling, running through the Harborside MO as she had so many other nights: the painstaking, incredible things Jenko had done to those fourteen people. She got up for a glass of water to wake herself enough to push those thoughts aside, stood looking out her window as she drank it, and saw the curtains again. Rippling at her. Swelling out, waving. Hi, Hi!

She smiled, laughed out loud once.

"No you don't," she said, closed the blinds and returned to bed, took some time sleeping but managed.

The window was closed on Sunday and Monday nights. On Tuesday and Wednesday it was open but there wasn't enough wind. The curtains hung off-white and unmoving in the tunnel of the night, set about and around with twinkling streetlight, flaring house-light, distant and near—like a kaleidoscope fixed on a still image but whose sides were bright, fractionated and changing. Yes, a peripheral kaleidoscope focused on a set, intriguingly still center: a window one and a half meters long, fifty centimeters or so deep, top-hinged, with twin square panes and dull white curtains. The heart of a kaleidoscope of night.

Or better yet, like the dioramas she'd made as a girl. A peephole in a shoebox, giving a view of a tiny room or a single image made compelling and dynamic by the false perspectives, miniature light sources and intense focus. Its framing effect.

Just a chance arrangement of things. A nightframe, yes. With that diorama, kaleidoscope sort of intensity.

On Thursday it was closed again, which reinforced the idea that the shed was a sleepout for someone, though Corinne had never seen a light behind the window that she could remember.

On the Friday night it was open, and the chill southerly that came up around 7:15 had the curtains rippling and fluttering at her. When she got back from dinner with Paul and Chloe after 11, the window was closed, just part of the larger world again and, though it again suggested habitation, she had never seen a light and still felt it was deserted.

On the Saturday afternoon the window was open, the curtains bellying slightly in a mild breeze. When she saw the elderly couple who lived there getting into a cab shortly after 1:15 P.M., she realized two things: that this was her chance to go down and see it all up close and that the whole thing was a lot more important to her than she wanted to admit.

She stood deciding. It was a warm quiet Saturday afternoon; the couple had gone out; the house seemed deserted; the gate, the side path, the shed were all in sunlight.

She'd say she was looking for a missing cat, knock on the front door first, say a few "kitty kitty"s in case anyone was looking, make it all seem casual.

Within minutes she was out in bright sunshine, walking round the front of her large apartment block, crossing Victoria Place to the white house. She began her "kitty kitty" routine almost immediately, though no one seemed to be watching.

Soon she was on the sidewalk before the low cast-iron gate with one of the "frame" trees at her back, looking down the path as if for a lost pet, but really noting the window and the curtains as they stirred gently, ever so slightly. Then she was at the front door, ringing the bell. She waited an appropriate few minutes, then walked around the side.

The curtains stirred lazily, languidly, bellied at her just enough behind the two square panes.

"Pablo! Here kitty! Here kitty!" she said, and kept walking, reached where the path turned left toward the back door, dog-legged right. She followed it, saw the deserted backyard, lawn, bushes, fences, and moved down the long front of the shed.

The brown wooden door was closed. Whatever breeze moved the curtains was slipping in underneath or perhaps just lifting in under the panes.

But locked? She had to try.

Maybe her cat had been locked in by mistake—that would be her excuse.

Acting concerned, she turned the knob, pushed the door back on a cluttered interior, a dusty gloom dispelled as she opened the door wider, then stepped inside. The curtains bellied away from her in the sudden draft, pushed and curled against the panes, flared briefly and settled back.

Corinne saw boxes and tools, a lawnmower, an old bicycle, what was possibly covered furniture. No bed, no signs that it was used as a flat. Just a shed. A storage shed.

She moved to the window, felt the curtains, lifted the unlined fabric between her fingers, moved it, felt its texture, let it fall back.

There, she thought, smiling. *Done.*

Corinne felt so much better. She stepped out into the yard, pulled the door closed behind her, then moved back up the path to the street.

Done. Done. Done.

Back in her apartment, she set the kettle going, made coffee, then, only then, went out on the deck to look down at where she'd been—at the quiet house, the sunny path, the shed with its barely moving curtains. She imagined herself there and how she would have looked, going to the front door, moving down the side, disappearing to the left. The few minutes in the shed.

Then Corinne noticed it. There was hardly any wind, barely a breeze, but now at one corner of the window there was a solitary spot of darkness, as if the curtain were hitched up there, caught on something or—yes—as if someone had lifted it to peek out, and was now watching her.

Corinne stared in dread at that point of darkness, saw it vanish as the curtains bellied and shifted.

Just a corner hitched up. Just a coincidence.

But it was so silly, so amusing to the rational part of her, yet at the same time so—what?—potent, vividly disturbing, that she told Dan Truswell about it over coffee when he dropped by the next day, keeping it light, simple, not mentioning the visit. She just sketched it in as something noticed, something intriguing, even compelling, intruding now and then but hardly a serious preoccupation.

Dan listened, smiled, nodded, finally said exactly what she expected. "You of all people, Corinne, understand how profound things can be at the level of perception."

It was such a relief to hear it said she found she wanted to say more, take it further.

"It doesn't feel like misperception, Dan."

"I didn't say *mis*perception. Don't twist my words. The individual is the only reality. Whatever is, is. For you it may be a feeling of uncommon sensitivity, even intense focus, but an important stimulus nonetheless, even profound recognition. You may feel the anxiety of not being able to convey to another what you've *recognized*. I'm saying I accept your reaction to this stimulus, your response to it as a psychoactive agent. How could it be misperception?"

"You see it as a clinical condition?"

Dan smiled. "Only inasmuch as it's my profession to process experience this way. It can be reported on this way. We're a consensus society. You know me well enough to know I accept the normality of the subjective truth while advocating consensus. My appropriate reaction is to accept what you're telling me at face value, match it with cause and effect, then be fair observer."

"It's not enough."

"Of course not. I'm agreeing totally. I see the window and the curtains, but *I* don't feel the stimulus or have the recognition; therefore it's hearsay, reported phenomena. Because I'm cast as a champion of consensus, I comment on you, not it. How could I comment on it? I'm not qualified."

"It seems to be real."

"That 'seems' is important. But see it as hypersensitivity, a kind of hyperaesthetic reaction, a glitch in perception. My first concern is that you allow a false recognition, a miscuing of perceptual functions."

"Like déjà vu."

"Just like déjà vu. And *idees fixes* are like that. Why don't you go visit the residents. Ask to see the inside of the shed. Say you're . . ."

"I've done that." Corinne felt a rush of guilt.

"And?"

"It's just a storage shed. Tools, furniture, boxes and stuff. Not a flat or anything. No one lives there."

"Good. That was probably hard to do. What did they say?"

"I didn't get permission."

"Oh."

"I've only ever seen an older couple, a guy and his wife. Yesterday I waited till they'd gone out and went over. Pretended I was looking for a missing cat. Just went down the side."

"Okay. The window was up?"

"Yes. But there was hardly any wind. The curtains weren't moving much."

"The door was open?"

"No. But it wasn't locked. I looked inside."

"You went inside?"

"Yes. I touched the curtains. Dusty unlined cotton. Just ordinary curtains. I looked round a bit then went back out, kept up my 'kitty kitty' routine till I was back here."

"How do you feel?"

"Better. Better now I've done it. Know the mechanism involved."

"Mechanism?"

"Yeah. That it's wind under the shed door helping make the draft. That it's just boxes and stuff in there. Dan, it was like a visual thing, you know? You look at something a thousand times, then suddenly it resolves into something distinctive you haven't noticed before and now can't help noticing. Like those paranoiac-critical paintings Dali did—*The Invisible Man* and that one with the bust of Voltaire. When you see the hidden images or they're pointed out to you then it's all you see. Like those tests you use in perception testing. Those Rorschach inkblots."

"You feel you're going to be okay with this?"

"Sure. What do you think?"

"I think you've been through a lot. For the better part of a year you've been involved in the profiling of a dangerous psychopath. You've followed the trial, had access to transcripts and case details that are, well, harrowing to say the least. We're in a society just coming to grips with things like post-natal depression and attention deficit disorder, all kinds of compensation and denial behavior. I don't have to tell you. Of course we can allow severance phenomena."

"That's what you call it? Severance phenomena?"

"That what I'm calling it here today, Corinne, yes. It's up there with recently bereaved people seeing deceased loved ones, all manner of anomalous perceptions that are part of normal life. Just do what you need to and put it behind you as soon as you can."

And they spoke of other things. Corinne very carefully made sure they did so.

She knew it was full-blown obsession, sweet monomania, a week or so later, the night she arrived home from a publicity dinner organized by Dennis and Gillian, stepped out onto the deck just to look at the night (of course) and saw the security light wasn't on across the street. There was only blackness at the side of the house, an unseen tunnel of darkness, a black hole in the night she couldn't see but knew was there, pulling at her.

With dismay she realized she wasn't able to see the nightframe as complete without it. Most of it was there—the twinkling lights in the lustrous blue-black expanse, the deeper framing blackness of the trees and roofline silhouette. But it was incomplete; worse, it was as if the long window, the curtains, sat in darkness like something watching again. It was what you did to watch someone, wasn't it? Switched off lights and stood back in darkness to look out?

But she didn't think of the double window-panes as eyes, no, not even as a spider waiting or fingers beckoning, not even as some sinister, snaring flower. (Deadly nightshade. Such a term. Deadly nightframe.) No anthropomorphizing at all. She saw it (some detached, clinical part of her realized) as the curtains she had *touched*. Cued. Given *her* scent to.

And being locked into obsession, being so irrationally focused and finding it so suddenly rational, eloquent unto itself, she had to know what was down that unseen flue of darkness. Window open or closed? Curtains blowing or still? There was wind. But enough wind? There'd been wind on so many other occasions and the curtains had hung unmoving behind the open panes.

Corinne laughed at the recollection—the distant, observing part of her did. *God, I'm losing it and here I am pondering weather anomalies and microclimates.*

She had to know. The cat routine would probably cover it, but she did have to know. Like someone checking the car headlights were switched off for the second or third time, that the alarm was set, that a fax had gone through, she had to go down and see. Just did.

She put on casual clothes, got the flashlight from the kitchen drawer, let herself out into the windy darkness, went round the side of the apartment block into Victoria Place, crossed to the white house, passed under parts of the nightframe, again passed *into* it, she noted, stepped under the tree, stood on the sidewalk with the tree behind her right shoulder and the slough of darkness right there, leading down.

There was a glitter of glass. Nightsighted, nightframed, she could make out the twin panes glinting in hints of streetlight. She stepped over the low gate, getting ready to call "Here, kitty kitty" if an automatic security light came on, though she doubted it would. There hadn't been a night she'd looked out and not seen the light on and the double panes and curtains clearly. The globe had gone. Or they'd forgotten to turn it on. Deliberately hadn't?

But she was ready with her alibi call as she moved down past the front windows, raising her torch, finger on the switch. It wasn't a long walk—eight, ten meters at the most—and she was darksighted enough to see familiar detail, to almost see enough.

Still, she had to know.

She flicked on the torch, saw the curtains bellying, scalloping, rippling at her, right there, the wind getting in under the door, drafting up, saw them so much closer, so urgently working their window dance in the thin light, in the thick dark, saw in the small lunate flickers, in the parings of darkness the curtains made at her, something standing back, staring back, the sense of something, someone, an immanence in those flecks and spatterings of deeper black.

She turned and ran, must have cried out because the front houselights came on as she leapt the iron gate and turned to the left, slipped beyond the tree, hurried beyond the street. By the time she was staring down through her own dark window, the side light was on too, the nightframe intact again, restored to its full configuration. When the bedroom lights went off, Corinne went to bed with a strange sense of peace, of having won some kind of test. And though she woke at least twice, she didn't get up to check. She could hear the wind and see the tree-shadow on her ceiling and knew that down there the light was on and she was safe, everything in its place, no matter how the curtains might beckon during the long night.

"I'm well into it," she told Dr. Dan when he dropped by the next day and they were chatting over coffee again. He was down in Sydney on business, he said, but she felt it was probably his way of keeping an eye on her too.

"Tell me."

"Started out keeping it to myself. Only told you the other day, no one else. But I'd ask people about fixations they might have. Building a normality horizon."

Dan smiled kindly. "We hate to be alone. Did many admit to having some?"

"Only a few. Most of us keep our rituals secret. We don't like to say we recite a lucky word or touch a jade Buddha or avoid a particular street or color. What's that Asian concept: public face, private face, secret face?"

"Add day face and night face. Japanese, I think. Some societies don't even have the concepts."

"That's it, Dan. That's exactly it. We do need terms like that French one for thinking of what to say too late."

"L'esprit d'escalier?"

"I think that's it. We need terms for the moment when we're talking with someone and we know *they* know we're lying."

"Or we know, incontrovertibly, that a relationship, a marriage, is over. Yes. Do you have such a term for me, Corinne?"

And there she was—exposed at the very point she sought the term for.

"Yes. Or rather no, not a single term. But I feel anchored, you know? Right here and rational. Sane and focused. Yet it's the moment nothing I say can win back your belief that I'm wholly sane. I've passed into clinical for you. Convictions, anxieties are now being read as part of a pathology. I can sense you tracking me, regarding me differently, storing your perceptions differently."

"I disagree. I'd say it's the moment you *fear* that has happened. We're friends, Corinne. You're a smart, gifted lady coming out of an intense period in your life, an overloaded, supersaturated period, if you like. The difference is that you're admitting to something others can regard as obsessive . . ."

"Aberrant."

". . . ritualized behavior, to use that valuable term. Aberrant doesn't cover it."

"But it is morbid fascination."

"You haven't hallucinated, have you? You don't hear voices?"

She shook her head.

"You don't seem to be displaying undue paranoia or loss of self-control, just reasonable concern. I don't see much evidence of flattened or inappropriate affect."

"Dan . . ."

"Corinne, you must know why we avoid using clinical terminology with 95 percent of our subjects. People imagine things while they're under incredible stress. Seize on terms *they* think account for their condition. It's the worst trap. We carefully avoid talking about mental 'disease.' People resist the idea of the brain being ill like any other organ, susceptible to disease. We say 'disorder.' We're well beyond the days of tidying it all up into neat categories like hebephrenia and catatonia and prescribing pherothiazine. Just look what you've been through with the book, steeped in the deeds of a late-onset schizophrenic who displayed little of the usual disorganized behavior. You learned the facts. You were locked up with theories and terminology and an intense and informed scrutiny. Of course there might be a residual hyperawareness. We all need to be de-briefed after this sort of thing. Barbara, Mark and Jay have to talk me down all the time. It's part of it. I could give you dozens of cases from psychotherapy and forensic psychiatry where gifted and experienced professionals have been harmed by the nature of the task. If you're not prepared to go on a holiday or re-locate for a while, I suggest you enjoy the curtains while you can. Take a mild sedative at bedtime and consider yourself lucky it hasn't been worse. I'll monitor your conduct; you just let me know about anything else."

"If I hallucinate or hear directives from the soul."

"Correct."

"Dan, this has the intensity of hallucination."

"Yes, but pull over and turn off your car engine in a forest glade and a natural silence will seem preternatural, even uncanny. I was studying those slate tiles out on your deck last week and saw a fossilized fern leaf, realized it was, what, 140 million years old. That made me notice every damn tile there. Little packages of frozen time. I didn't mention it but it was profound. Humans move through this sort of stuff all the time, trivializing the living of life which is both intrinsically so marvelous yet so natural and mundane."

Corinne laughed, was so glad to laugh, to have Dan's words, his humanity. "So just go with it, you reckon?"

Dan laughed too. "Just go with it. We desensitize so quickly, so damn quickly."

"Come on, curtains! Do your stuff!"

"Indeed. And keep me away from those deck tiles for a while! Get 'em back to mundane as soon as possible, thank you very much!"

Dan's words helped. His easy, encompassing wisdom, born of grief and suffering, of witnessing worlds breaking down and reality remade, gave her a handle on it, let her go out on the deck in bright sunlight and study the bits of what she could see—the so much larger, infinitely extended dayframe. The window, the curtains, didn't intrude. It was all to do with visual effect after all, and there were so many windows, so many things vying for consideration. The curtains hung white and still and didn't stand a chance.

Journeys in light, she remembered someone saying, perhaps Jenko, the Harborside Killer. *We are designed for journeys in light.*

So she sat through the late afternoon doing an outline for an article, making and taking phonecalls, even told Dan what she was doing when he phoned. She watched the gradual darkening of the land around 4:30, saw the nightframe shadowing into being: a lessening of light in the space between two apartment blocks, the gloom forming in that backyard as bush- and fence-shadow lengthened, stole definition, stole the light, just wore it away.

She had it all in its increments and installments, how bits of night slipped in, so much of it unnoticed—one minute, dayframe, the next time she looked, something else, some interstitial wearing down of light, darkness glooming up. It was marvelous and relentless; natural, mundane and utterly terrifying. She laughed in unexpected wonder and fear and relief.

Then, at 5:30 when the streetlights came on, it was almost fully in place, needing only a deepening of colors already there, needing only subtleties of wind and the security light to be added.

When Dan phoned again at 6:30 (granting the importance of her ritual), she had a question.

"Dan, what if the brain *likes* the effect of something more than it should? More than *I* am aware? What if it notices phenomenal elements and, independently of what I consciously know, chooses to find significance?"

"It's still you," Dan said.

"I know it is. Of course it is. But it's also aesthetics, isn't it? Like a piece of art? We're predisposed to things, to natural things meaning something. Do you allow that the mind can find something profoundly beautiful, compelling, important that the conscious self doesn't know about, doesn't have a conscious grasp of?"

Dan barely hesitated. "Of course. That has to be how it is. We said it the other day: any human society is just consensus reality. We withhold things. Conceal things. Orthodoxy is just generally sanctioned consensus reality."

"So it has to do with paradigms. Patterns. How we *agree* to model what we perceive."

Again Dan hesitated, reading beyond her words. "Ultimately that's all it is, yes."

"Like the Japanese notion of *tenko*. A government fiat decreeing how the populace is to regard something. Determined consensual reality."

"Controlled paradigms, yes. Quite a crime against humanity. But it goes deeper. Corinne, look . . ."

"It's what I'm saying, Dan. I rationally accept what I'm responding to. It's just that I'm allowing that some part of *me* has identified something meaningful, and is trying to place it in a consensus paradigm that doesn't altogether work. Bits are left hanging out. My question is, should I be dishonest about a felt imperative just because an arbitrary, conventionalized thing called 'normal reality' doesn't have room for it? Or because it might be seen as clinically suspect?"

And with a stab of alarm, Corinne heard how she sounded, what she was saying, heard Dan's silence.

"Sorry," she said. "I'm just waxing lyrical, Dan."

Dan Truswell's tone had shifted to the careful, considered timbre she'd heard in his Jenko interview tapes, every word measured for ambiguity and its ability to be evaded.

"You are, and I'm agreeing. There's not one of us hasn't got alarming, astonishing secrets, yearnings, convictions. It is what we do, just as we do match the *idios kosmos* of the self with the shared *koinos kosmos* of consensus society and use that as a standard for regulating conduct and expectations. We can talk paradigms any time you want, Corinne, and I'll be right there listening to you and agreeing. We did it with Jenko, saw how a fundamental paradigm shift and some powerful ritualized and subjective reality patterning led to those terrible deaths. What I'm hearing, and what you're now hearing me responding to in my best professional tone, is someone behaving in an anxious, overstimulated way, yes, with obsessive, stressed and fixated responses. Any disordering I hear from you is only in degree, in the extent to which it troubles you and obsesses you. In other words, this matters and I care. I take my first position as your friend, my second as a caring professional who has given most of his life to allowing for vital alternative paradigms in others as the result of illness and injury, not automatically as this intense existentialist package you're experiencing. It's the difference between Jenko and Sartre. Charles Manson and Picasso."

"What should I do?"

"You've said no to a holiday and relocating, so go where it takes you. But listen, Corinne, just let me know if you hallucinate."

Corinne laughed. "Because I won't let you know if I feel paranoid delusions or follow inner voices, will I?"

And Dan's voice warmed. "Remember that old saying: be careful what you resemble. I'll be phoning in."

"Monitoring my affect. I'll have to be good, won't I?"

"I've known you long enough to know."

"Lines like that kill conversation."

"So do lines like that. Speak to you soon, okay?"

She did well for a while, but it *was* as if part of her knew something the rest of her didn't. She found herself checking on the curtains—in between publicity outings and signings, while working on various freelance articles, planning follow-up projects to capitalize on her current high profile.

It was a holding pattern in a sense, a kind of status quo. In the mornings the light was wrong; rather that there was just too much light. In the afternoon it began happening, the consolidation, the languid building of the frame. It got so she scheduled appointments elsewhere for the mornings, had people visit her at her apartment after midday rather than going out, tried not to miss the last few hours of daylight. There were evenings with friends, a few dates—though now she finally had time for them she found herself disinclined, distracted, yes, preoccupied. She did good saves: she was still coming up out of a major project, still putting together a viable social life not made up of medical and publicity professionals.

She told herself she just liked being around the apartment. So, her mind might be sorting through a perceptual something, trying to find homeostasis—psychostasis?—but on the surface (how it was with so much life, consensus or private) she didn't check the window too often, wasn't constantly jumping up from her desk or her deck chair to see if the curtains were blowing. She just let it be, let it complete whatever it was, wherever it was happening in her, submitted to Dan's phonecalls and occasional visits with composure and pleasure.

The Monday phonecall marked the change.

"How am I doing?" she asked for the fiftieth, probably the hundredth time.

"Fine as always," Dan said. "A darn sight better than your old admirer, George."

"George Faye? What's happened?"

"I saw him last week, just by chance. He looked terrible. Haggard. Wasn't sleeping. Couldn't seem to concentrate on things. I recommended him to someone local."

Corinne wasn't aware she'd left a silence till Dan said her name.

"Corinne?"

"You're going to hate this, Dan."

"Speak."

"That night of the launch celebration. He was there, remember?"

"Of course. We worked as a team to save your honor."

"Yeah, well he came out on the deck. Saw me watching the curtains."

"And? Don't go careful on me, Corinne. Just say it."

"He commented on them too. Said they looked weird."

"And your perception is?" (Dan never said, "What's your point?")

"Remember with Jenko, one of the hardest things the authorities faced was predicting methodology. One time the blue paint, the next time the melted coins, then the soft toy stuffing. We did finally allow what was obvious all along, that particular things were psychoactive for him—just randomly affecting. Can this be psychoactive, Dan? Can it? I've seen it. George saw it."

"I've seen it too, Corinne. Lots of your guests have."

"So it's not automatically psychoactive. Some people respond, others don't."

Dan made a thoughtful sound. "I'm resisting this."

"*I'm* resisting this! Neither of us can afford to though. Do you think I like going on like this at you? *George* mentioned it! *He* remarked on it! Now you say he's showing signs."

"Professionally he'd already lost it, Corinne. Apparently drinking too much. Missing deadlines."

"This is different."

"Not part of something already happening?"

"You saw how he was. You're the one who spoke to him. Would you say altered affect?"

Dan hesitated, tellingly, damningly. "Yes. But Corinne . . ."

"Dan, I can't possibly convey something that's personally, dynamically psychoactive to someone who hasn't felt the imperative."

"Corinne . . ."

"You've got to speak to George! Ask him about dreams, preoccupations. See if anything matches."

"If he thinks of the curtains, you mean. Has dreams. Senses something."

"Dan, why not? I may be wrong, sure, but this takes it beyond me. You must allow how important this is for me."

"He may not remember. Like you say, a wholly unconscious thing."

"It takes it beyond me, Dan! Either way I'd be grateful."

"I'll see what I can do."

And when Dan had rung off, for the first time she felt she'd been pretending, feigning much more control than she really had. But the important thing was that he'd gone, left her with the news of George, lonely planet spinning away, deflected, wobbling toward ruin.

She could deal with Dan. She'd maintain her calm demeanor, urge him to consider the possibility of what? Psychoactive loci? Chance alignment of objects, arrangements of line, light and angle? Get him to experience the assembly of its parts, perhaps the delivery of some superrational agenda.

God, these terms. Where were they coming from?

But no hallucinations. No inner directives. Not yet.

No new legacies from interviewing Jenko or too much time spent considering psychopathology.

It had been weeks, carefully negotiated days. She'd maintained homeostasis, a psychostasis. She'd passed Dan's assessment of her or he'd be phoning, pounding on her door.

Dear deflected Dan. (No, that was George Faye. Deflected George.)

Part of her rallied, some part made for reason and orthodoxy; she calmed herself.

Dan would call. Good.

She'd display for him, show she could connect.

And she'd also keep an open mind: accept the possibility of something given, recognized only for its possibility, but working in her mind and following, what? Its template, agenda, superrational logic? Whatever.

The options? Without Dan, despite Dan, Corinne considered some. This chance directive fading, the agenda working itself away, eroded by orthodoxy. Or would it catalyze? Volatize? Commandeer more of her mind?

Well, Dan would be watching, keeping an eye on her. Being a lifeline.

And it was natural, not supernatural. Preternatural maybe, by its nature. Hyperaesthesia. Intense seeing. Intense focus. A chance triggering that was surely ghosting away even now, worn down by too much else.

Corinne put it aside, went back to her article.

The trap was sprung that night.

Corinne had enjoyed a pleasant, comfortable, safely ordinary dinner with a publicist, Tony Ashcroft, had flirted just enough to keep him interested, and was back at her apartment at 11:15. She got ready for bed, then stepped out on the deck to check the nightframe.

Street. House. Bay. Boats and twinkling streetlight, all there in a glance. Then, taking it slowly: blue-black night and starpoint, down to the bay, hints of boats, the streetlight beyond standing reflected on the water, then the black trees stirring in the night wind and, across Victoria Place, the house, its side security light on at this hour, the window sitting at the end of its channel of light, window open but the curtains not moving.

Corinne went to bed, read a while, slept.

Woke at 12:40 to tree-shadow on the ceiling, found herself wondering, went to the window, saw that the curtains were rippling at her, blowing out, half-moons of utter black in the scalloping white, fluttering at her. Hello. Hello. Awake now.

It was eerie but something known, familiar and mundane, part of orthodoxy, just chance elements, suggestions.

Corinne smiled and went back to bed.

Woke at 1:50, sighed to find it becoming such a long night. Looked out the window again, saw the security light was off. The window had vanished in a mass of darkness. She imagined it there, couched in black, curtains fluttering at her, watching.

No you don't. Oh no. We've done this before.

Corinne made herself go backo to bed, even slept for a while, but woke at 2:14, went to the window, needing to see.

It was hard to know what she expected. The streetlights off? Everything dark and focused on that black rippling center?

The security light was on again and, though there was wind, a strong and cool southerly, and though the window was definitely open, the curtains hung still behind the twin, angled panes.

She knew she had to go down there. Find out why.

The security light was on. No flashlight was needed though, when she'd dressed, she grabbed it just in case.

Once again she went around the front of her apartment building down to Victoria Place, crossed the street, stood on the sidewalk at the top of the path looking down at rest of the tableau.

Wind blew around her, had the trees churning and heaving. The curtains hung still.

Corinne stepped over the low iron gate, began down the path.

Was there movement? Had the curtain on the left twitched at her, stirred slightly?

She strained to see, *did* see a movement there. A bellying out, a settling back.

Perhaps it had been there all along. She just hadn't see it, had imagined the stillness.

Another few steps. Again they bellied toward her. And again, though this time the edge scalloped once, showed a black edge, quickly gone.

Microclimates. Anomalies of airflow. A draft getting in. Just ordinary things. Orthodoxy.

Two more steps. Then she paused, waited.

Your turn. Your turn.

Sure enough, the curtains bellied, scalloped, beckoned twice this time, cautioning, two vents of darkness, offered, stolen away.

Your turn.

Corinne took her step, waited.

Nothing. The dead hang of fabric. Nothing.

Another step.

The curtains bellied, flared out in a sudden shuddering ripple, a gust of wind, gave four, six black hearts or more, settled back.

Corinne smiled. She hadn't screamed, hadn't cried out. The window had done its best, screamed at her silently, but she had managed.

So close now. She took two more steps. Three.

They bellied, heaved, showed a solitary twist of black and settled.

Corinne smiled. She had won.

She reached the window, could have touched the twin panes, with another step could have felt the curtains, but turned aside instead, left then right, moved down to the door of the shed.

Would it be occupied? she wondered. Decided no. Just knew.

She grabbed the knob, opened the door, shone her flashlight into the gloom. Saw the same clutter as before, and the curtains hanging. Just boxes and junk and, yes, a view of her apartment if she cared to look back up the tunnel of light, back through the nightframe. Line of sight. Line of night. The other part of it.

She'd have that view, she decided, would look out, complete the equation, perhaps even see herself gazing down, waving, beckoning, an absurdity, a fancy.

Corinne went to the window, pushed the curtains aside and looked out, felt them struggle around her as the wind surged in through the open door and the security light went out. She was inside the frame.

And as the edges settled, folded, sank in and the warmth flowed, Corinne knew that behind the shock, the panic, the terrible fear, what she really felt was incredible relief, and that though her final word was "No!", what she was saying with every part of her being was "Yes!"

THE DEAD COP

Dennis Etchison

Dennis Etchison has been selling stories since the late 1960s and is one of the horror genre's most respected and distinguished practitioners. He has won three British Fantasy Awards and two World Fantasy Awards. His short fiction has been collected in *The Dark Country*, *Red Dreams* and *Blood Kiss*. He has published four novels, *Darkside*, *Shadowman*, *California Gothic* and the recently released *Double Edge*. Etchison also edited several acclaimed anthologies, including *Cutting Edge*, three volumes of *Masters of Darkness*, *Lord John Ten* and *MetaHorror*. And he has written extensively for film and television.

Los Angeles, once supremely confident in its isolation from "bad things happening," has been shaken up in the past few years by the reality of earthquakes, gang warfare and riots, creating a paranoia among its residents and fodder for Mr. Etchison's fertile imagination. The stories that have been birthed of this milieu (including "The Dog Park," reprinted in The Seventh Annual Collection of this series) are among his best. "The Dead Cop" is one of them, inspired by the real, titular character in this story. The story was first published in *Dark Terrors 2: The Gollancz Book of Horror*.

—E. D.

Standing in the red glow, Decker watched a pattern emerge at the center of the paper. It appeared to be a horizon broken by several jagged vertical lines. A few seconds more and the lines sharpened into what might be swords or spears. He waited for something else to take form, anything at all that might provide a clue, but there were no surrounding details in this frame, either. And it was impossible to remember exactly what he had caught in his viewfinder that night.

As he leaned over the tray, squinting in the metallic fumes, he heard a ringing. He reached for the timer, then realized he had not bothered to set it for this print. The ringing came again, a faint chirping, as if a small bird had found its way into his studio on the other side of the thin wall. He slid the sheet of paper into the stop bath and opened the door, flooding the darkroom with light from the overhead windows. It was no good, anyway; the pattern had come up too fast and was already turning black.

His telephone rang again.

"Hello?"

"Pete? Thank God."

"Hi, honey." The glare from the panes in the skylight blinded him. "What's wrong?"

"Nothing. I mean—I was about to hang up. I thought you'd left."

"Not yet."

"Are you okay?"

"Sure."

"You sound so far away."

He turned the receiver so the mouthpiece was closer to his lips. The stubble on his chin caught in the tiny holes, magnifying what sounded like a scraping in his ear. "I was in the darkroom."

"Oh, sorry."

"That's all right. I'm finished."

"You are? Well, tell me!"

"Tell you what?"

"How did it go?"

The bare white walls took on texture, first the rows of dark rectangles, favorite enlargements he had mounted for display over the years, then the corkboard filled with test prints from his new assignment: closeups of burgers and fries and soft drinks in cups, all suspended in space on a folded paper swing. The pale yellow fries fanned out from their container like the severed fingers of children caught in the mouth of a cornucopia.

"The job? It went fine."

"Really?"

"I had trouble with the Monster Gulp. The ice melted, but the guy from the Feed Bag wanted to be sure it looked cold. So I had to spray the cup. The water kept beading up and running off. I tried mineral water and corn syrup, and I finally got it."

"Congratulations!"

"They still have to see the proofs. Everything is supposed to be high-key. Bigger than life."

"I'm so proud of you! So—what were you doing? When I called, I mean. You said you were in the darkroom."

"Just cleaning up."

"Oh." She paused, as if allowing for a delay in the phone lines. "So you can go home now. Unless you have—something else to work on."

"No."

She sighed, a white hissing like steam released inside the plastic earpiece. "That's good. I mean, I'll see you at home, then."

"Okay."

The conversation did not seem to be over. He waited.

"Oh," she said, "I almost forgot. The shoe repair, on Pico. They have my Ferragamos. Could you stop by? He closes at six."

"I thought you get off at five."

"It's Counselors' Night. I have to stay till seven-thirty."

His throat tensed. "It'll be dark by then."

"We have a lighted parking lot. It's safe. I promise."

He didn't say anything.

"Are you okay?" she said.

"Sure. I'll get the shoes. Don't worry about it."

"Thanks. You may as well go ahead and eat. There's half a barbecued chicken left."

"Okay. Or I'll pick up something on the way."

"The Apple Pan?" she said.

"Maybe the Feed Bag. I could strap on a burger."

She laughed.

"Be careful, Cory," he said, very seriously.

"You, too."

"I feel fine now. Honest."

"I *know* you do," she said with an unnatural emphasis. "Love you."

"Me, too," he said, and hung up.

He looked at his watch. It was only a little after five. If he worked fast he could print one more frame from the nightclub. He would need as much contrast as possible to hold the details; #6 paper, full-strength developer, and maybe some dodging. But there was still time.

When he turned out of the parking lot on to Venice Boulevard, the traffic was bumper-to-bumper. A diffused glaze hung over the cars and trucks pointing east; in the opposite direction the light was more intense, as though bounced off aluminized reflectors somewhere above the haze while the sun prepared to sink into the ocean several miles to the west. He joined the flow eastward, but only for a few blocks. At the first corner, a crowd of Hispanic workers gathered under the American shield of the old Helms Bakery building, waiting with bowed heads for buses that would take them deeper into the city. He tried not to look at them as he inched forward to La Cienega, where he finally made a left, heading home.

The route was a relentless grind at this time of day, jammed with workers on their way back to Washington and Jefferson and the ghettos of South Central. Eyes shone white and fixed behind dirty windshields as large hands gripped steering wheels with grim determination. He moved over for another left at Pico so he could stop by the shoe repair shop. Then he noticed that it was already after six.

He had taken too long with the last batch of prints. There was nothing usable in the envelope; but it was important to be sure. A promise was a promise, especially to his son. He would tell his wife that he had spotted some flaw in the proofs for the Feed Bag and decided to do them over. As for Gary's pictures, at least he had tried. He hoped the boy would understand.

Beneath the Santa Monica freeway, the hard bass rhythms of gangsta rap shook his Mercedes, reverberating in the underpass like the aftershocks of a temblor. He should have taken Robertson. There was nothing to do about it now. He rolled his window up tightly and waited for the traffic to move again.

Another tense mile and the pale, white-gold lettering of the Great Western Bank building wavered into view through the mist. Now the letters spelled out the name of the new owner, a publisher whose sexually graphic magazines sold so well that he had bought the property outright. Years ago, when John Wayne served as the bank's television spokesman, a larger-than-life bronze statue of the late actor on horseback was erected by the entrance, like a sentinel protecting the Westside from attack by outsiders. The statue was still there. What would the conservative cowboy think, knowing that he now guarded an upwardly mobile pornographer's beachhead on the corner of La Cienega and Wilshire, inside the once secure boundaries of Beverly Hills?

He drove Wilshire to Rodeo, a street lined with the world's most expensive shops, some so exclusive that they required advance credit approval before granting admission. An Asian couple left Gucci's and crossed in front of Decker's car, unaware that jaywalking was a crime in this city, while groups of young men and women with unfamiliar brand names on their jeans strolled past Fendi and Van Cleef & Arpel's, their European accents sounding oddly appropriate amid the many foreign-owned businesses here. The tourist section was only a few blocks long, but he found himself stuck behind a Gray Line bus that paused at every storefront in order to give its passengers a chance to focus their cameras through the tinted windows. By the time he came to Sunset Boulevard the lights of the Beverly Hills Hotel were on, throwing smudged shadows of tall palm trees across the pastel façade. Now, this close to home, he should have begun to unwind. But there was something about the shadows that held his attention and would not let go. He tried to ignore the angular verticals against the uneven horizon as he waited for the line of taillights to make their turns, then continued across and up into Beaumont Canyon.

The last mile was the hardest. After only a few days off work he was shocked to find traffic in the canyon dramatically worse, with so many trucks and oversized sport utility vehicles that he could see no more than a single car length ahead. It took twenty minutes to creep a few hundred yards. In front of him a Mexican gardener's pickup groaned and shuddered, brakes squealing every ten feet. An Isuzu Trooper rode his bumper, its elevated headlights burning holes in his rearview mirror, then began to honk. Other vehicles took up the call until the canyon sounded like New York City at high noon. When a Range Rover cut out of line and tried a J-turn at the first cross street, downhill drivers flashed their high beams and made obscene gestures, only their thrusting fingers visible in the glare. Decker thought he heard the crunch of a fender somewhere ahead, followed by angry voices, and for the next several minutes all movement ceased. The Trooper boiled over in front of a mansion protected by an electrified fence, the gardener's pickup vibrated as it lurched and rolled backward, dropping leaves and clods of dirt on to Decker's hood. He cleaned his windshield with a few passes of the wipers. As the blades came to rest, he noticed a police car parked at the side of the road.

How did it get here so fast? he wondered. He saw no sign of a wreck, no broken glass. Perhaps there had not been an accident and the mere sight of the police car had caused the slowdown, its very presence a deterrent. He thought of giving the officer a wave and a smile, but the patrol car's windows were dark and misted over. He drove on past.

By the time he got home it was after eight o'clock. Cory was not there yet.

*   *   *

When he called her school there was no answer. He told himself that she was probably stuck in traffic on the other side of the hill.

He sat down at the kitchen table and opened the envelope.

With such badly underexposed negatives there was not much to see in the prints, despite his best efforts to retain an image. Even on high-contrast paper the frames had gone black with almost nothing in the shadows. The dodging left an opaque halo at the center, ghostly against the surrounding darkness.

He would tell Gary that he had screwed up. It was embarrassing. The boy had only asked him to take a few publicity photos of the concert. That was easy enough. But something had gone wrong.

He tried to remember.

Somehow, in the noise and the crush of bodies, he had loaded his Leica with a slower portrait film instead of Tri-X. When he discovered his mistake later, he pushed it as far as he dared in the darkroom, but all that gave him was a series of exposures with severely blocked-up highlights and the remaining areas unprintably thin. They might make for some interesting abstract blow-ups, something that would work in a gallery show, but that was not what his son wanted. It was a shame; the night had been special. The word was that there were important people in the audience, people whose opinions could decide the band's future. So they had gone for it, jamming retro Goth at an earsplitting level, amps cranked up to the point where dogs howl and chase their tails, Gary's fingers raking the metal strings until what looked like drops of blood flew from the guitar, as the air grew heavy and began to crackle like an electrical storm. A performance that would never come again. And Decker had blown it.

He studied the prints one last time.

There was the name of his son's band under the ceiling, the letters an un-readable snowstorm of grain in the spotlights. Below, Gary and Mark and the rest of the group were only blurred shadows. Then the false horizon line that was the edge of the stage, and below that blackness. Decker remembered the audience rushing forward in a dark wave, pressing closer. They must have had their arms raised, because there were the vertical lines again, extending up from the bottom half of the frame.

He got out his magnifying glass.

Now he saw rounded silhouettes rising out of the darkness—closed fists, cheering the band on. But what were the lines *above* the hands? Though it had happened only a week ago, he had trouble remembering. The lines were so sharp they could be horns or the ears of wild animals.

He would have to ask Gary.

He picked up the phone, started to dial his son's number. He'd tell him that the pictures were no good, but maybe there was another gig coming up soon. And the next time he'd get it right.

Wait.

This was Thursday. Gary would be rehearsing. Where? At Mark's, just like every Tuesday and Thursday since junior high. He was probably there now. Decker carried the cordless phone to the living room and flicked on the lamp as he dialed Mark's number.

"Hello, this is the Fordham residence. . . ."

"Hi, Jack." Why was the lamp so dim? He found the remote, turned on the TV. "Are Mark and Gary—?"

"No one can come to the phone, but if you'd care to leave a message, we'll return your call as soon as possible."

Decker broke the connection.

He poured himself an inch of Scotch. Onscreen, a sitcom about a minority family was in progress. The program had just started but the members of the family were already trading insults like a neighborhood gang playing the dozens. He kept the sound low and sat down on the sofa.

Maybe Gary and Mark were over at the new drummer's. What was his name? Cory would know. He'd ask her, as soon as she got home. He took a sip of the Scotch and tried to relax while he waited.

Seated under the lamp, he felt detached from the rest of the room, as though it were receding even as he gazed across it, at the carpet and furniture and the photographs mounted in windowbox frames along the walls. There was the one of Cory by candlelight, then Cory and little Gary waving by the tree in the yard, Gary playing his first guitar, Gary's high school graduation. Their faces smiled back as always from the richly gradated prints, but now his own technique began to irritate him. The background areas in each image were so dark that in this light the faces appeared to be no more than pale reflections, as if he had forgotten to fix them in acid and they were now fading to black, about to disappear. Only the television family shone clearly out of the shadows, striking obvious poses and waiting for laughs from an unseen audience. Then the program dissolved to a series of commercials.

He focused on the screen as images flickered across it, products so brightly lighted that they seemed more alive than anything else in the room. He wondered if there would be a spot for the Feed Bag, its oozing burgers and fries supported by disposable cardboard neck trays, as he had shot them for the layout this morning. But it was too soon; the drive-thru chain had only just opened, with LA as the first test market. Soon his photographs would pop up on billboards all over the city and he would have more assignments than he could handle. It was good to be working again. He felt as if he had taken off much more than a week.

He drained the Scotch and got up to pour another as a live teaser for the evening news came on. There were unconfirmed reports of another drive-by shooting. A special Eyeball Report on gang violence was promised at eleven.

Where did it happen this time? Decker wondered.

He thought uneasily of Cory and her class in the East Valley, an area known for gang activity. And tonight she had stayed late for a meeting there. He imagined his wife on the way to her car, after. Then other cars, low-riders, cruising into the empty lot and calling out, taunting her, and the doors flying open, the weapons in their dirty hands, the tight-lipped smiles and the catcalls and their brown eyes turning black as a single weak security light fickered by the back of the building. . . .

It was another two-and-a-half hours till the newscast.

As he picked up the phone to call the school again, headlights flashed outside and a tall, pointed shadow fell across the windows. He hurried to the front door in time to see a car pass on the lane, the silhouette of the old pine tree sweeping the front of the house. Then there was only the darkness. He went back inside.

He decided to try the police. He punched 911 and got a busy signal. He pressed redial, as someone opened the back door.

"Cory?"

In the kitchen, she stumbled and almost fell as she stepped over the threshold. Her books and papers flapped to the floor. He ignored them and held her, gripping her arms.

"Hey," she said, "take it easy. . . ."

"Are you all right?"

"Of course I am. You're hurting me. Pete. . . ."

He hugged her.

"Hi," she said.

He let her go. "Hi."

"Sorry I'm late. You wouldn't believe how many parents showed up. Have you been home long?"

He took a deep breath. "No."

"Did you eat?"

"Not yet."

"You're supposed to eat, remember?"

"I was waiting for you."

"I couldn't help it, Pete!"

"It's all right."

"Well, I guess I can make us something. Just let me get out of these shoes. . . ."

"I'm not very hungry."

"Did you get my new heels?"

"I didn't have time. The traffic was unbelievable."

She walked through to the living room, taking off her coat. "Well, I'll just have to get them on the way to work. If he's open that early . . ."

"I was thinking. Maybe you should quit, Cory. It's not like we need the money."

"It's not about the money."

"What *is* it about?"

"Those kids. It matters to them."

"Does it?"

"Why?" she snapped. "Because they're Chicanos?"

"That's not what I mean."

"What *do* you mean?"

He backed off and sank on to the couch. "I was worried, that's all."

She turned to him, one side of her face in shadow.

"You don't have to," she said gently. "Please." She came over and stood before the couch. Now her features were lost completely to the backlight, only a few sharp strands of her hair outlined against the lamp. "We're doing fine. You're back at work, and so am I. It's better this way. Isn't it?"

He took her hand and drew her down next to him. Cory was naive but she meant well. Over her shoulder, he saw the TV family collapse together on to their sofa, convulsed with laughter, knowing that their day was coming. At least it was not here yet.

"Sure," he said.

"There. See? So what are we talking about?"

Outside, at the end of the lane, the rush-hour traffic in the canyon had ended. A lone car with a broken muffler sped toward Mulholland, radial tires screaming around the hairpin curves.

"I tried to get to Pico," he said, "but it's like a war zone out there."

"I know. Ever since they closed the Sepulveda Pass."

"When did they do that?"

She looked at him peculiarly. "It's been a while."

"Oh."

She lowered her head and squeezed his hand.

"At least we've got a traffic cop now," he said.

"Do we?" she said distantly.

"He was parked by Tremont Road. I passed him on the way up. I hope it does some good."

"I hope so, too." She studied his eyes. Then she said, "Hey, when do I get to see the pictures?"

She meant the Feed Bag layout. Of course. "It's only burgers and fries. Not exactly art."

"Well, I'm proud of you, anyway. You know that, don't you?"

He put his arm around her shoulders and drew her close. He felt her cold skin and her warm breath against the side of his neck. They sat that way for a minute.

"I was wondering," he said. "What was that drummer's name?"

She pulled away. "What drummer?"

"In Gary's band. The new one."

"What are you talking about?"

"I thought I'd give him a call. Do you have the number?"

"No, Pete," she said after a long pause. "I don't."

She stood abruptly and went into the kitchen. He wondered if there was trouble in the band, possibly a falling out that he did not know about. For the moment he decided not to pursue it. He heard her open the refrigerator and set something heavy on the table. Then it was quiet. Another TV program began, the latest installment of *Unanswered Questions*. Tonight's episode was about the recently discovered missing pages from the diary of a dead film actress. The pages purportedly contained the solution to an unsolved murder. Decker found the remote control and raised the volume, as Cory said something unintelligible.

From the kitchen doorway he saw her seated at the table, the leftover barbecued chicken now in a Pyrex dish, and next to that the photos from the concert. She had removed them from the envelope.

"What are these?" she said.

"Nothing."

"I asked you a question, Peter."

He started toward her. "Please, don't look at them."

"Why not?"

"They're from Gary's last concert. At the Box Club. But they didn't come out."

"Then," she said, "what are you going to do with them?"

He took the photos from her and slipped them back into the envelope. "Burn them, I guess."

"Good."

She turned away and began making the dinner.

They hardly spoke for the rest of the evening. When the eleven o'clock news came on, she was already asleep. He sat up and watched the report about the drive-by shooting. Witnesses claimed it had happened in South Gate, miles from here, but no body had been found yet. In bed he listened to her breathing next to him and thought about her job in the Valley, where conditions were just as bad. The Chief of Police called it an isolated incident but he had taken the precaution of ordering a tactical alert throughout the city. That means it's spreading, thought Decker. He fell asleep dreaming of a parking lot very much like the one behind her school, or what he imagined it to be like. Something was going on there, but he could not see what it was through the fog.

In the morning he had a meeting at the ad agency. Fortunately it was not until eleven o'clock, well after the rush hour. On the way down the hill he tuned to the classical music station, but FM reception here was so weak that the strings sounded like keys scraping the side of his car. He switched to the AM band for the news. There was a late-breaking story about another disturbance, this time in the Crenshaw district. They were getting closer.

He was relieved to see another squad car on Beaumont. It was parked in roughly the same location as the one last night, between Tremont and Huffington Place. The motor was off and the tinted windows were rolled up so that once again he could not see the officer inside. But it was good to know that the LAPD had finally heeded the Westside's pleas for more protection. The canyons were especially vulnerable, with the Valley to the north and the rest of the LA basin to the south, not to mention the Mexican border beyond.

The meeting went smoothly. The rep from the Feed Bag wanted more light and color in the photos. That would be easy enough; it was simply a matter of printing them up. Decker explained that losing the shadows would mean less depth and realism, but apparently they wanted their product to appear two-dimensional, with nothing left to draw the eye beyond the surface of the picture. No problem, he told them. He knew that he could do it in an afternoon. He also knew that he would put it off as long as possible, now that the job had become even less interesting.

He came home early enough to beat the worst of the traffic, though more than a few commuters were already starting their trek up and over the hill. He passed the electrified fence where the Trooper had overheated last night; the mansion was guarded by an iron servant with outstretched hand, its enameled face painted an inaccurate but politically correct pink. A zippy young businessman with cell phone drifted over the line in his BMW, a divorcée chauffeured her blonde daughters in an aging Rolls Royce, a private shuttle full of tourists turned up a sidestreet in search of movie-star homes. At the first big curve the traffic slowed to a second-gear crawl. Now, at this time of day, he realized how many non-residents used the canyon as a freeway alternate. Ahead he saw plumbers and electricians in company vans, day laborers in rusty Fords and Chevys, college students in unwashed Toyotas and Nissans, teenagers cruising in ragged convertibles and four-wheel-drives. He was sure that none of them were from around here.

When he got home he watched the early news. A local reporter was at the site of the latest incident. In the background, gang members in knit caps and baggy clothes mugged for the camera with raised fists, some making the sign of the horns with their fingers.

He called his son's number, but there was no answer.

In the evening, *Unanswered Questions* presented Part Two of its story about the late actress's secret diary. The missing pages had turned up in an estate sale at a home once owned by an actor who died of alcoholism years ago.

Decker spent the next hour searching his house for the blow-ups from the concert, and finally decided that Cory must have thrown them out.

Perhaps there was a problem between her and the boy, something that she had kept from him. Why was she angry? He knew better than to press her on the subject. She would tell him in her own time. Meanwhile, he would let the problem work itself out, whatever it was. The prints were not that important, as long as he had the negatives.

A teaser for the Eyeball News promised more coverage of the unrest, which appeared to be escalating. Shots from several live remotes around the city featured interviews with spokesmen for various gangs, including blacks, Hispanics, Koreans, even a few tattooed skinheads.

He realized that Cory had not come home yet. It was late enough for him to feel uncomfortable but too early to panic. There was no point in calling the school with the switchboard closed. He could go there and try to find her, but what if she was already on her way?

Now there were unconfirmed reports of more trouble, including a firebombing in Culver City, only a mile or so from his studio.

He couldn't just sit here.

He left a note for her on the back door.

A mist had moved down from Mulholland and into the canyon. The houses were milky and indistinct behind the trees, cars glistening and silvered in the driveways. Diffused headlights swung past like lanterns in fog. He was surprised to see that the police car was still here. As far as he could tell it had not moved. For the first time he wondered if it might be a movie prop, with location shoots so common in this area. He slowed down, pausing at the curb for a better look.

The shield on the side appeared to be authentic, down to the seal of the city of Los Angeles. If it was a fake it was perfect. Too perfect. But if it was the real thing, why would the LAPD leave one of their cars in the same spot for days on end?

He tuned to an all-news station as he left the canyon. A ten o'clock curfew had just been declared for much of greater LA. Decker glanced at the dashboard clock and decided there was time.

He took Beverly Glen to Pico, turned right at 20th Century-Fox and continued up Motor. The Cheviot Hills Tennis Center was dark except for a pair of white shorts and a disembodied arm swinging a racket through the mist. The neon sign for D. B. Cooper's glowed like faint landing lights near National, and then the mist cleared and he made out the tall water tower that had always reminded him of a Martian spacecraft standing above the old MGM backlot, now owned by Sony.

If there had been a fire anywhere nearby there was no sign of it now. At the corner of Motor and Venice, two patrol cars blocked off the parking lot of the Versailles Cuban Restaurant while officers stood by the exit, checking IDs. As he approached the Helms Bakery building he slowed, preparing to turn into the tenants' lot, and discovered that the sidestreet was barricaded. An officer in a riot helmet waved him on, his eyes hidden behind the protective visor.

The next news bulletin announced a bombing in the garment district, near downtown LA.

That was where Gary had his loft.

The horizon to the east swirled with mist heavy enough to be smoke. Decker wished for a car phone so that he could warn his son. Where was the nearest telephone booth? The gas stations at Robertson and at La Cienega were closed off with wooden sawhorses and the fast food restaurants up and down Venice had all shut down early.

He would have to drive there.

But the entrance ramp to the I-10 was blocked by more barricades. The surface streets between here and the dark heart of the city would be unpredictable. Olympic passed directly through Koreatown, and every other major east-west artery intersected at least one ethnic stronghold. La Cienega was already closed to the south, in the direction of Washington and Jefferson and the black neighborhoods. Soon the western section would be cut off on all sides, effectively isolated.

Had Gary tried to call?

Cory would know.

If she had made it home.

He cut back up National to Pico, heading north. The mist thickened again and he had to use his wipers, sweeping away what appeared to be fine ash as well as moisture. As he neared Sunset the traffic grew congested. Beverly Glen, Benedict and Beaumont Canyons were all freeway alternates and late commuters now searched for any route still open to the Valley. Through the glass he heard blips of competing radio stations in other cars, each with a different version of the news. There had been a minor disturbance or a full-scale riot in East LA or Watts, with no serious injuries, mounting casualties or dozens dead. The police had the situation contained or the city was under siege and the Mayor had called for the National Guard. He kept his window closed and his door locked.

He knew now that he was on his own. They all were. LA was not a city but a freeway system that mixed together tribes with nothing in common except an overlapping geography, directed and distributed by the grid. That was why the traffic was out of control wherever people crossed each other's turf. They had no sense of community, no respect for the routes they were forced to share, and everything not part of one's neighborhood was enemy territory, a no-man's-land to be trashed. Decker finally understood the appeal of sport utility vehicles. With their high cabs and reinforced bodies, they were like tanks ready for the battlefield. He pounded the wheel and leaned on the horn.

Halfway up the canyon he found himself idling next to the abandoned police car. He wondered if it belonged to an officer who lived on this street, or one who came here at all hours for private reasons, perhaps to visit a girlfriend. Now, against the line of descending headlights, he thought he saw someone in the driver's seat. The head was cocked at an odd angle, as if the officer were sleeping it off. But before he could get a closer look, there was a break in the bottleneck and the traffic began to move again.

Cory's car was parked in back but the house was dark. He rushed through to the living room and found her waiting by the sofa in the light of the television set. She threw her arms around his neck and clung to him. He kissed her as an Eyeball News reporter conducted a live interview. Onscreen, firefighters picked through the charred remains of a convenience store, while round-eyed children with dirty fingers waved at the camera from behind police barricades.

"I'm sorry," she said. She felt his face carefully with her hands, as if he were fragile. "I had to stay with the children. Nobody could get through, not even the buses."

Over her shoulder, the TV coverage continued.

"What's happened?" he said.

"They're still looking for the body. The Crips say it's in Watts. The Brown Brotherhood says East LA. So far, it's just a rumor. But all the gangs are taking credit."

"Why?"

"It was a cop. At least that's what they say. It's just an excuse to loot and burn. I go to work every day so the children will have a chance, and now they're destroying their own neighborhoods! It's stupid, so stupid. . . ."

"They know what they're doing."

"What do you mean?"

"They want the city, this time."

Her eyes were enormous in the semidarkness. "That doesn't make sense."

"Doesn't it?" He had hoped she would see the handwriting on the wall, but apparently she did not, even now. He started for the kitchen. "Did Gary call?"

She did not answer.

He turned on the kitchen light, looking for the phone. "He might be trying to get us. I tried, but there's never any answer. What did he do, change the number?"

Behind him, he heard her make a sound in her throat. When he turned around her eyes were full of tears.

"Oh, God," she said.

"What's wrong? Did something happen to Gary?"

She regained control of herself and went to him. "I thought you were all right. But you're not. Jack Fordham's been getting calls. He said it was a prank. . . ."

"Tell me, Cory."

He attempted to push her away but her hands tightened, forcing him to look at her.

"We'll be okay," she said. "You'll see. I'll take care of you. . . ."

"Tell me!"

"You've been sick. You don't remember the last year, not anything at all, do you?"

"It's been a week, Cory. I've been off work for a week!"

"Pete, I want you to listen to me."

He felt strangely calm. He knew what she was going to say, as if he had heard it before, in a dream. He saw the pictures in his mind again, of the parking lot and the gang, the confrontation. It was not about Cory, after all.

"Honey, Gary's dead."

No, he thought, not yet. Somehow she knew what he had been dreaming. But that did not mean it had to happen. There was still time to stop it, to get the boy out of there before it was too late.

"You're lying," he said.

He went outside and started the Mercedes, dropped into gear and clicked on the headlights. He wiped a clear spot on the fogged windshield and rolled forward over wet leaves, low branches slapping the glass. For a moment all he could see was a wall of mist. Then he heard a scream. He looked at the rearview mirror. A shadow reached out to the car, red in the glow of the taillights.

He unlocked the passenger door.

"Are you coming or not?" he shouted.

She stood there, her face crawling with rivulets of water, then got in.

The canyon was empty of traffic as far as he could see. The mist that had collected in the hills now poured down like smoke, heavy with moisture, a glittering whiteness that his headlights could not penetrate. He turned right, toward Sunset and the city.

"Will you tell me where we're going?"

He ignored her. Even with the defroster on the windshield did not stay clear. Beads of moisture began to collect on the inside of the glass as he leaned forward, following the double line. The fog thinned briefly and he saw the lights of houses twinkling behind the trees. Then the white wall closed around the car and he was driving blind again. He pressed harder on the accelerator. With visibility so limited he felt alert to any possibility. The familiar landmarks would only have lulled him into an illusion of security, leaving him more vulnerable. That was the danger of believing in surfaces, in what showed. Now, aware of how much he could not see, he was ready for anything. It was more than an aesthetic preference. It was a matter of survival.

"Please," she said, "where—?"

"To get Gary." He felt her shocked eyes on him, heard the sharp intake of breath above the pulse of the wipers. "If you can't handle that, get out now."

"I thought it was good that you forgot everything," she said softly, "but now . . ."

A car passed them, speeding downhill from Mulholland.

"At least let me drive!"

He knew she was trying to trick him so that she could turn around and go home. The tires hissed over the wet pavement, trees sagged and waved in front of lampposts. Somewhere above the fog great wings flapped, marking the pace. Then the fog blew aside, like curtains parting on a stage, and in the spotlight he saw the police car.

She opened her window and leaned out, signalling for help. He pulled her roughly back into the seat.

"Forget it," he told her. "There's never anybody in that car."

The flapping became a roar. The sky grew brighter and the fog blew aside, as a helicopter hovered overhead with its searchlight trained on the abandoned car.

As they pulled abreast of it he saw again the form inside, illuminated clearly now in the circle of light from above. There was a head and shoulders, leaning precariously to one side in the seat, about to topple over.

Not even the Westside is safe, he thought. They must have killed him right here, in Bel Air, but we were all too busy to notice.

"There's your dead cop," he said. "They don't know where he is? Well, they do now!"

He climbed out of the Mercedes and raised his face to the light, holding his arms up.

"Here!"

She ran to him and dragged him over to the police car, digging her fingers into his hair to make him see what was inside. It was a department-store mannequin dressed in a uniform with badge and hat, propped up behind the wheel. She shouted in his ear as the blades sliced the air.

"Look, Pete, it's a only a dummy! For traffic control! They call it passive law enforcement . . . !"

She was right, but what did that matter? Someone had seen it, one of the cars passing through, a gardener or a workman or a transient, and the rumors had started.

No cars had passed them going uphill. Did that mean Sunset was blocked off?

He hoped so. Because the gang would come back, the ones who had done it, to show the way so others would know who was to lead them. Then they would all come, from Compton and Inglewood and Huntington Park and South Gate, from Monterey Park and El Sereno and Silverlake and Little Saigon, swarming across the basin in a united front, a tide that would sweep away everything in its path. They had been sitting tight in their ghettos, waiting for someone to fire the opening shot so they could move in force. For years they had hit and run with small strikes, a convenience store, a mall, even picking off members of rival gangs, feeding on each other as the frustration grew. Now all that was over. Their time had come at last.

The helicopter banked and rose higher, flapping away.

"Come home with me, Pete," he heard her say in the sudden silence.

"Who killed my son?"

"He was my son, too. It doesn't matter now. It's over. . . ."

"You're wrong," he said.

He squinted, struggling to see the details, as the mist returned. He had captured a piece of it in his viewfinder that night, just before it started. . . .

Under the track lights was a banner with the name of his son's band, and below that the blur that he knew to be Gary on lead guitar. Then the horizon line of the stage, the heads of the crowd, and the thrusting verticals. He stared into the swirling particles of fog as if studying the grain pattern in a frame of film, and this time he refused to look away until he saw it all.

The pattern began to move.

Beyond the edges of the frame were bouncing heads, the bare-chested boys with shirts tied around their waists. The music assaulted his eardrums so that he had to shut his eyes but the image remained clear.

There, in the middle of the crowd, several figures were not moving to the music. They had slipped past the security guards after the set started and made their way down front. He had no trouble spotting them because they were wearing jackets with emblems on the back, their colors. He felt bodies pressing closer and hot breath on his neck, and realized that Cory was clinging to him.

He lowered the camera long enough to free himself from her. The night air chilled him. He opened his eyes and saw her standing in front of him, about to disappear into the mist.

"The name," he said. "What was the name of Gary's band?"

"Please . . ."

"Say it!"

"The New Goths," she told him, and began to cry again.

Yes, he thought, that's it. The same as the emblem on the jackets. They came to the club to see who had stolen their name. That was why the weapons came out, at first only a few thin, jagged lines in his viewfinder, as still as swords at rest. When the song ended they put them away and did not take them out again until the parking lot. They were the last things Decker saw that night, the last things Gary ever saw.

Now the fog behind Cory became white, so bright that the outline of her body seemed a part of it. He saw her disembodied head turning to look behind her, as the helicopter reappeared above the horizon at the top of the canyon. The blades beat the air and the fog cleared and he saw the jagged lines of dead trees and the legs of a water tower against the sky, and then the rounded shapes of heads rising up in the beam of the searchlight.

"They forgot," he said.

She turned back to him, confused.

He thought of how Beaumont Canyon continued on up to Mulholland and then all the way down the hill to the Valley on the other side, to Panorama City and Pacoima and San Fernando and the gang enclaves there.

"They stopped them at Sunset," he told her. "But they forgot about Mulholland."

"What . . . ?"

"It's too late now," he said. "They're here."

They came marching down the hill, ignoring the police helicopter. He saw the blond stubble of their hair shining in the searchlight and the swastikas tattooed on their skulls, and he knew that it was not the Crips or the Bloods or the New Goths, not this time. They were skinheads, whatever they called themselves.

The helicopter boomed a warning but they kept coming, the lines of their sharp, splintered baseball bats held high. Their eyes shone like the eyes of wild animals, like raccoon eyes, yellow and terrible. When they saw Decker and his wife and the Mercedes they started running and yelling.

He pushed her behind him and stood his ground, stepping out into the center of the pavement to meet them.

URSUS TRIAD, LATER

Kathe Koja and Barry N. Malzberg

Kathe Koja is the author of *The Cipher, Bad Brains, Skin, Strange Angels* and *Kink. The Cipher* was cowinner (with Melanie Tem's *Prodigal*) of the Horror Writers Association's Bram Stoker Award for Superior Achievement in a first novel; *The Cipher* also won the *Locus* Poll in the same category. Koja is the author of many short stories, several of which have appeared in best of the year anthologies. She lives with her husband, artist Rick Lieder, and her son in the suburbs of Detroit.

Barry N. Malzberg is the author of more than seventy novels, among them *Herovit's World, Beyond Apollo* (winner of the John W. Campbell Memorial Award), *Underlay, The Men Inside* and *The Remaking of Sigmund Freud*; the essential essay collection *Engines of the Night*; and numerous fiction collections including *The Man Who Loved the Midnight Lady, The Many Worlds of Barry Malzberg* and *The Passage of the Light: The Recursive Science Fiction of Barry N. Malzberg.*

Kathe Koja and Barry N. Malzberg have collaborated on one novel and over thirty short stories during the past few years. Their stories have appeared in *Omni* magazine, *Alternate Outlaws, Dinosaur Fantastic, Little Deaths* and other anthologies.

"Ursus Triad, Later" is a difficult piece both stylistically and in content. The reader is thrust into the middle of an endless nightmare inspired by an innocent classic fairy tale. The story was first published in *Off Limits: Tales of Alien Sex*. Let me be clear: this is *not* a fairy tale, but a story of graphic, brutal horror.

—E. D.

Now the door, the knob on the door, the small sliver of light dense, concentrated, aiming from the room behind: where the bears nested. The splinters of the floor, the brutal surfaces upon which she had rolled, scrambled, been pawed and lumbered over, half-suffocated between fur and ragged blanket and fear of the splinters, pointed always but always somehow missing puncture: of her eyes, the worn but tender skin beneath; her suffering lips.

Once her perspective had been larger, once—she thought, or believed she had thought—she had seen the house entire, light everywhere: the gleam of glass and porcelain, the glimpse of cages through transparent walls, but that must have been a long time ago or perhaps some trick of perspective, some dull accident of sensibility, for now she could see only that door, that knob, the light, the floor from the position to which she had sunk: the dainty ord- nance of paws, the heavy intake of the bears' breath somehow framing condi- tions without providing illumination. The cages had come open some time ago, were never closed now; the keeper—if there had been a keeper, a jailer, some master who had schooled them (and if so for what extravagant enjoyment, who under God's sun could train animals to purposes like these?)—now fled, the house the bears' alone, she the intruder, she the peeping, curious, external force crushed now to this sullen, sunken wood and the creaking sound of their inhalations as one by one, solemnly, they played with her: over and over, open- ing her up like a wound, their paws and fur the ancient sutures drawn by that wound, bleached and stanched and then somehow magnified by their with- drawal as one by one, each by each they left her on the floor: to gather her own breath and breathing wounds together before another one returned to rend her now anew.

Somewhere through all of this she must have eaten, drunk, found a way to eliminate; slid into coma and emerged; there must have been some kind of passage in which the common tasks of consciousness were conducted but she knew—and it was all that she knew—that she had no knowledge of those times, could remember it as little as her initial swim in the womb: it was literally some other life because now everything was the bears, the tumbling conjoin- ment, the snaffle from their muzzles and the cascading, indifferent light which at odd angles swooped over, swooped through her; the dazed and cavernous surfaces of her sensibility sometimes roused briefly by that light, only to plunge again in the tumble and harsh necessity of their breath. She had become emp- tiness, and they filled her again and again.

Bach, Beethoven, and Brahms: her names for them, her three assailants, masters and dumb slaves as she herself was a slave. Dumb and sullen, beneath or beyond language, but she had to try to assign some meaning to the situation, had given them names to suit what she took to be their personalities in that time before this time when she must have come here, must have had reasons— what were they?—to enter this strange and damaged cloister, this space beyond redemption, to emerge as if from death or fever into the circling stare of the bears: eyes dull and compliant, slow struggle of limbs as they balanced on hind legs, ready to begin the dance anew; and she their silent partner, pink and breathing on the wood.

There was no real communication amongst them; they seemed to her to work within circumscription, intersecting only to bump as one left, another came to snort and root around her stricken body. She had known from the first that appeals, cries, struggles, resistance of any kind would only have at- tenuated her situation; the animals were beyond command, beyond whatever powers of humanity she had then been still able to summon and so: the splin- ters: the fur: the paws and the breathy stink. Her agony. Their arabesques. Submitting to them, over and over, submitting to Bach now, the largest of them and the most regular, the most rhythmic, the most metronomic: Bach because this B seemed to believe in order, in a kind of regulation of movement which rattled and thrust in clearly identifiable rhythms, rhythms as solid and inescapable as Bach, Beethoven, and Brahms, as the distorted perspective of this floor, this light, this distance inside and out.

Now Bach yawed and steamed against her, the smell of the beast in her head, on her lips like some dry unguent, his huge body seeking, seeking, humped and breathing, gigue and largo and then subsiding, guiding himself away from her, the turgid genitals of the metronomic bear refracted in the shadows, those shadows already diminishing as Bach moved slowly from her in an odd, abbreviated limp, humping his way into the darkness. The shadows seemed lifeless even in motion, even as she seemed lifeless there on the wood of the floor.

In this silence, in this momentary partition, she thought she might be spared for a while, that Bach had now had his ceremonial fill and that Beethoven and Brahms were in the upper room, casting circles of darkness, silent beyond bearish grunts and small explosions of fathomless feeling, but even as she turned in this moment's relief, moved to gather the ragged blankets, to press that sleeve of insubstantial protection against herself, she felt them eased from her grasp and then Brahms, a huge, sordid mass was settling himself against her. Brahms: the autumnal bear, the bear of sneezes and sighs and small, absent groans, passion expended, fallen desire and she, too, groaned with the futility, the hopelessness of the bear's attributed despair as on her stomach he cast circles with a paw, then clumsy in wintry desire straddled her at last. Sinking slightly beneath the bear, resigned to assist as much as possible; unlike the others Brahms seemed to her to appreciate some kind of gesture, to have a sense of her presence and collaboration whereas the others, so locked into their own spasms and black rhythms, gave no sense of recognition or response at all. Snorts, sighs, the press of fur against her as she raised her hands, grasped the bear to draw him to a kind of crooning concentration as deep underneath the fur the small shudders, foreshadowed expenditure and then the bear's yelp, a human sound, a high, girlish shriek as he rolled away from her to lie, streaked by light, a wheezing heap: damp fur, sweat, soot, and for her again that dim shudder within her thighs, sensibility risen and draining from her just as she had drained from this house that which she had found before her.

She must have found something before her, must have been outside this house at one time, brought into it by accident of desire or curiosity now denied recollection: there was a past beyond and before this house, that smell, those shudders creeping like insects up and down her helpless legs, thighs, spread and spraddled, and she would have wept, great groaning tears against the wood, wood pressed to her lips, splinters like the wafer of God himself between her teeth, but here there was if not godlessness then the orbit of no salvation, here was the constellation, the great cross of heat, sour stink, black upon black upon fur upon flesh; nothing and everything, here in this room. Reeking, aseptic cavern, drawn and enthralled and diminished like the vessel that drains but is not emptied, there must have been *something* prior to this but it was closed to her now, closed forever like the doors of nascence, slammed like the gates of death on the yearning faces of the living: there is no going forward nor back, there is nothing. This is what is: this floor, these animals, the faint metallic scent of her own fluid, her body pinned in rags and speckled with old blood; and the door; and the light.

Brahms sobbed in a corner, again she reached for the blankets but the great sounds of imminence flooded the room and she knew before the collision that Beethoven, the most jolting and demoniac of the three, had come to seek in her his own fulfillment; Beethoven of the sudden, shuddering strokes, the silences, the storms, the great uneven swings of the body: the one she feared most in those broken unleashings of spine and heat grabbing her, grabbing her, the alternating cycles of some unknowable need seizing the hammer and tongs of the bear's body as it rammed against her and this, now, was the present, the animal against her, great in its need but curiously empty and tentative for all that; at the core the same uncertainty and brokenheartedness of Brahms but the shell was hard, hard, and she felt Beethoven pass through, over, above her like a storm, his hoarse grunts of emission, and she thought, eyes closed, *no more, no more* as she sank beneath fur, paws, breath, spasm, eaves, and darkness of the house collapsing around her and all around the darkening trot of the beasts as at some time later or perhaps this was earlier—smashed chronology, chronology smashed—they gathered to confer.

It was the feast she remembered, if memory gave her any gifts at all: some telescoping of circumstance found her seated high in the room, a table of fruits and desserts before her, all of the spices and jellied treats and cakes smeared lascivious with icing spread on a table the size of an altar, a table larger than any she had ever seen and she leaned toward that feast, thinking *I want this*, the food enormous in her hand, her hand spreading to encompass the feast entire: and in the moment before enjoyment, before even its possibility she heard them: there at the far side of the room, their small, luminescent eyes fixed upon her, the shaggy blackness of their fur not harbinger but frankest truth: and the seizure of breath, the cakes toppled, the fruit rolling and smashing as she rolled and smashed, pulped and tore, juices everywhere as in that new posture of dreadful and fixed attention they came, one by one, upon her, for the first of an endlessness of times.

Reaching for Brahms' tail as he rooted and muttered around her, lifting herself to some less strenuous accommodation, she felt that she in some way was sinking toward some kind of new, ursine splendor, had somehow—by pain, by terror, by the pink pity of her ravaged limbs—dissolved the barrier between herself and the beast atop her. Picking and poking at the secret heart of the great animal she found herself served as well as serving, become more than sheer receptacle: it was a kind of way out, perhaps: it was the method of escape that sinks one more fully into the pit, and as the bear commenced its familiar, groaning adumbration of expenditure she shouted something, hoarse and guttural, *caw* like the bark of an animal, something before language which was itself language and gripping that fur tried to come *up* with Brahms even in the bear's descent: and the long, pivoting drop which in its suspension and calamitous nature seemed in some way to mimic her confused ideas of escape, to *be* escape: go farther in: become: belong. Sunk into slivers, vaulted into light, she felt herself as one with Brahms even as the seizure squirted to the expected silence and the bear shambled away as if she did not exist at all.

> The dream of the feast: their waiting eyes.
> She waited, too.
> All feasts are one.

In the rapid metronomic shudderings of Bach, she now found—earlier or later, but *now*—that some deepened surge of her own entrails, her own wordless wants was smoothed, engaged to rhythmic response by the motions of the bear and so it was no surprise at all when, yielding in sudden spasm, Bach broke from that complex rhythm and, balancing perilously on one paw, began a fragmented, syncopated movement which she first accommodated and then seemed to pass through, as light passes through a window, as semen passes through the tubing flesh and in that passing she ascended, risen as Bach, like Brahms, fell to snuffling and somehow troubled silence beside her, before himself rising to shamble away in unaccustomed ursine muttering.

And now she, beyond language but not gesture, beckoned from the floor to Beethoven, beckoned in the light: *Come on,* she said to the beast, *come on then, you too* and again the clasp, the enclosure, the idea bursting in her mind: becoming one with them, grunting and heaving as Beethoven grunted and heaved, her own fur rising in small shreds and hackles as she rotated her knees, her long scarred open legs against the spiteful silence of the bear against her, the gigantic hammer of the bear against her, and this time she took it without a cry, without sound at all until Beethoven's own grunt of sudden and arrhythmic expenditure from which he fell as the others had fallen, shambled as they had shambled, sat now as they sat: staring at her, clumps of soot and sweat, muzzles uplifted as if to scent on the air the smell of her change and she watched them back, watched those brooding and immobile shapes as if she were in control of this situation, which in no real sense could ever be the case. She had abdicated all control in her greed for the feast: very well. Let greed be her master, then; let escape be entrance; let in be furthest in of all.

She had entered in curiosity and hunger, bedazzled by that unexpected house in the shattered woods, untroubled by the warnings of those with whom she had traveled before she had embarked, alone, on this more rigorous journey; and in what measure had they cared, to allow her the journey at all? And so the door, the house, the feast on the table one soaring poem of satiation: *this: here: take: eat:* and reaching beyond the sweetmeats, reaching toward some gorging fulmination which would have been, she knew, as close to ecstasy as she would ever come in the lonely and desperate life which was all that had been granted her, in that reach and grasp she had heard only the marveling thunder of her heart, that aching engine of greed in the presence of fulfillment: but she had not gone far enough, it seemed, had wanted but not fully, had reached but not taken, grasped, eaten, become: had only raised her eyes to see their eyes, little and bright, empty and full, to hear above the bewildered crooning of her own empty breath their breath murmurous, the sour and tangible entry into the world of the door, the floor, the light, the slivers, the odd varying rhythms of the beasts. You wanted to be filled? their postures asked her as they came upon her. Then *be* filled. To bursting.

But that was the secret, was it not? after all? The floor, yes, the slivers and the pains, yes, but yes, too, her own new knowledge, sieved from degradation, obtained from going all the way in: take the bears, receive them, *be* a bear, the Queen of the Bears, the queen of the magic forest and the empty house, daughter of the night born to gambol in stricken and ecstatic pleasure with those three refracted selves restored to her through pain: the autumn, the pedant, and the hammer, all three dense with need, her own need, her own greed as she raised herself on her elbows, there on the floor, there at the feast, and she bared her stained and filthy teeth to say *Come: come to me now*, and as if in their first true moment of attention came the hawking groans, the motions of the bears: turning, first toward one another, then to form a circle, a unit, one lumbering and dreadful mass as all three, as one, advanced upon her: to receive her benediction: to pour and fill and to become.

JFK SECRETLY ATTENDS JACKIE AUCTION

Robert Olen Butler

Robert Olen Butler won the Pulitzer Prize for his story collection A *Good Scent from a Strange Mountain* (1993). He is also the author of seven novels, including *They Whisper*. Butler lives in Lake Charles, Louisiana, with his wife, novelist Elizabeth Dewberry, and teaches at McNeese State University.

"JFK Secretly Attends Jackie Auction" is an "alternate history" fantasy from the October issue of *Esquire* magazine. The story is also included in Butler's new collection, *Tabloid Dreams*—a witty, wise, wonderful collection. I recommend it highly.

—T. W.

When we turned onto Seventy-second Street and saw what awaited us, my handler flinched, and he tightened his grip on the wheel. I suspect he wanted to accelerate on by and abort the whole plan. But he knew the Director had okayed it and he looked at me.

"Are you sure, Mr. President?" he said.

The only thing you could see of Sotheby's was a white awning. The front of the building had completely disappeared behind television trucks and satellite dishes. It was a risk, of course. But things that Jackie and I had lived with were disappearing into the hands of strangers, and it made me feel as if I were dead. The CIA could get me in only on this third day, and I knew well enough already that the four thousand dollars I'd been able to scrape together from my ration of pocket money probably wouldn't allow me to buy back even a tie clip. But there were other things working on me. I had to go.

We passed an NHK satellite truck beaming to Tokyo and then a BBC truck, and I said to my handler, "Let every nation know, whether it wishes us well or ill, that we shall pay any price."

"Mr. President?" he said, pressing me to prove I wasn't rambling. He was a very young man.

"You probably never even read my inaugural address," I said.

He was reaching for his cellular phone.

"Dave, you don't have to call. I'm just having a little joke. It's all right. The Director and I talked it over. There's no better place to hide than the glare."

Dave pulled his hand back to the steering wheel. "I'm sorry, Mr. President."

"That's okay, Dave. In case of domestic insurrection, the president has contingency plans to go to a safe house in Arlington, Virginia."

His hand went for the phone again.

"Chill out, Dave. That was President Johnson's plan. Old news. I said that on purpose as a joke."

"I respectfully request that you don't joke like that, Mr. President."

My handler is right to be nervous. After all, loose talk is why I'm in the position of having to sneak into the public auction of the effects of my late wife. It's why my long-suffering Jackie was led to live, unaware, as a bigamist, the wife of a Greek who had a face that could stop a thousand ships.

The bullets fired on that fateful afternoon in Dallas killed only the editor in my brain. After that moment, I could not hold my tongue about anything. I woke up on the gurney rolling into the hospital and began at once to disclose all the state secrets of that very secretive time. Of no use now. But it's far too late to explain any of this to a world that the Agency determined quite quickly must never have even momentary access to me.

I completely agreed with the decision. It's only the editor that's gone. My powers to reason are still completely intact, and this was the only reasonable course. Anyone who came near me would become a security risk. And of no import to the CIA but critical to me, I would have talked endlessly to Jackie about the things that we agreed would never be spoken. Along with the secret details of our foreign policy, the smells and sights and tastes of all the women I'd ever known would come tumbling out. There was no choice but to bury the wax dummy in my place. Not only is my faculty of reason untouched, so are my powers to remember. Sweet memory. It's been the great comfort of my confinement.

Still, I'm very glad now to be sliding to a stop in front of this white awning. I know I can meet my commitment to silence. I realize that it's still important. I say that what I know is of no use. But I suspect that if I were to speak now of the doomsday rocket silo twenty miles north by northeast of Burgdorf, Idaho, in the Gospel Hump Wilderness, I would be speaking of something still in place, though perhaps the target agenda of Moscow, Peking, Pyongyang, and Hanoi would have changed slightly. But I am determined to withhold even the faintest allusion to these things.

As I pointed out to the Director, I never asked to go to the funerals or the weddings. I didn't ask to go to Teddy when he left that girl in the dark water at Chappaquiddick or to my nephew, who never even had a chance to know me, when it was clear to me that he needed to speak honestly of what he'd done to that girl in Florida. I didn't even ask to go to John-John to warn him about the magazine business. But this auction was a different thing.

I step out of the car. I suspect the Director has watchers in the crowd. I am never out of sight. But for a moment I feel alive again. I feel that I am living in my body, in the present moment. How sweet that is, I've come to realize in these thirty-two years of exile. How often in the life I used to lead was I in a place that could have filled me with memories, but my mind carried me elsewhere. I missed the moment. Now, on the sidewalk in front of Sotheby's, I head to the end of a long line of people whose faces once would have turned to me, whose hands would have come out to touch me. It took me a long time to get used to that touching. I never quite did. But I crave it now. They touch me now in my dreams. Hands trembling faintly from excitement, warm with the flush of desire. I touch them back, each one.

But here, the TV lights glare and the crowds line up and they yearn to touch only the things I touched. I think this is similar to what Abraham Lincoln dreamed the week before he was killed. He dreamed that he awoke from a deep sleep and he heard distant sobbing. He arose and made his way through the empty hallways of the White House to the East Room, where he found a great catafalque draped in black. A military guard stood there and Lincoln asked, "Who is dead?" The man replied, "It is the President." I could ask anyone now in this line, "Whose French silver-plated toothbrush box with cover is this, being auctioned off to strangers?" And the reply would be, "It is the President's."

I pass all these hands stuffed in pockets or clutching purses or fluttering in conversation. I pass all these faces turned away from this bearded man with close-cropped hair and the faint line of a scar on the side of his skull and the hobble of a very bad back. And I know I should be glad that there is not the tiniest flicker of recognition. The Director and I are in complete agreement. He's stuck his neck out for me. Pity for an old man and his past. Trust that old age has slowed my tongue, which it has, somewhat. But part of me is ready to tell, at the slightest glance from a stranger, how Mayor Richard Daley found fourteen thousand votes in the cemeteries of Chicago to swing a state and elect a president. And I would point out the debt of gratitude the whole planet owes those dead voters. None of us knew at the time of the missile crisis of 1962 that the Soviet general in charge of troops in Cuba was authorized to use tactical nuclear weapons. After the Soviet Union broke up, the general appeared on TV—I get all the cable channels—and he said if the American President had chosen to send troops to the island, they would have been nuked. If Richard Nixon had been the President, he certainly would have sent those troops. What does this mean? It means those dead Chicagoans prevented a nuclear holocaust. My impulse to talk about these things aside, credit should be given to this necropolis of American heroes.

But no stranger gives me a glance. I go to the end of the line and my back is hurting, but out here in public, the pain reassures me somehow. A woman up ahead in the line turns her face idly toward me. She has hair the color of the old Red Grange model football we used in Hyannis the same autumn I made love on the overstuffed chair in my Senate office, to a woman who was all bones and freckles and teeth and her thick hair was the same color, a roan color, and she sat on my lap and thrashed her hair around me. She has spent time with me often these past years, in my memory. And this woman in line turns her eyes briefly to me and then her attention passes on. She is perhaps thirty-five. In my memory I am thirty-five, but this woman before me now sees only an old man. But I'm still sitting on that overstuffed chair and the leather squeaks beneath me and I'm sweating and smelling the woman's hair and I tell her about its color, the color of a Red Grange football, and she laughs. The woman in line laughs now. She is with someone near her, but I don't look to see who it is. I watch her face dilate sweetly in laughter and if she were standing next to me, I know I would speak to her of this other woman, whose name I can't remember and whose eyes I can't remember, though I've often tried in these years of exile. I would like to remember her eyes, because remembering these other things as vividly as I do makes me feel as if the memory of her eyes should be there too but it got put aside and then sold off or given away and it was a big mistake. I want it back.

I want my Harvard-crest cuff links back, too. I'm thinking of them as I finally make it through the front door of Sotheby's and a young Negro woman in a uniform holds out her hand to help me through the metal detector. I would not call her a Negro to her face—I know the language has changed—but I am still a creature of my time and Martin called himself that. I will always remember where I was on the day Martin was shot. I was in the little stone-walled garden in the cottage in the compound in Virginia. I was about to launch a putt across the fifteen-foot green whose one hole has pulled me to it ten thousand times a year for all these years. I was just aligning the head of my putter— I want my old putter back, too, by the way, though it's sure to draw a small fortune—I was just squaring up the head of my putter when whatever aide it was assigned to me at that time—I don't remember him except that he was young—stepped out of the back door and he said "Mr. President" with a rasp in his throat and I knew that it was something terrible. Poor Martin. How nice it would have been if only his editor had been shot away and they thought to bring him to me. We could have told each other so many things we never had sense enough to talk about when we were living our public lives. And Bobby too. We three could live together and I'd talk with Martin and I'd wrestle my little brother to the ground—even with my back—and with his editor shot off Bobby could tell me what he really thinks of me, and that would do him good.

So this young Negro woman reaches out to the old man she sees in front of her, an old man having trouble straightening up, having just gone up some steps with a very bad back, and her hand clutches me beneath my forearm. And though there are two sleeves between me and her flesh, I thrill at her touch. I straighten up, not wanting her to be touching the arm of a stooping old man, and there must be pain but I don't feel it. She looks me in the eyes, just before I step through, and I think there is some flicker of recognition there.

"Do you know me?" I ask.

"No sir," she says.

I realize I'm on the verge of telling her about the perfect hit man we'd hired to kill Fidel Castro in 1963. Pedro Antonelli. I don't know why I think she'd be interested in this. But I know I'm not supposed to say anything. So I step through the arch of the metal detector, and the machine cries out as if it had seen a ghost. The woman who touched my arm is beside me and I'm ready to confess.

But before I can speak, she says, "Do you have anything metal, sir?" and I understand.

I tap the side of my head, on the tight ridge of scar tissue, and I say, "Metal plate. From service for my country." I think she can hear the ring of it beneath my knuckle.

"I'm sorry, sir," she says, and I'm hoping she will reach up to touch the place herself. But her hand goes to my arm again and urges me toward a desk. "Thank you," she says. "Show your registration slip over there."

I move away from her and there is still a ringing in my head and at the desk they give me my bidding card, and from the push of people behind me I'm going up more steps, made of stone, and my back is hurting again and I'm growing older by the moment, though I can still feel her touch on my arm.

The Director has not been very good in recognizing my desires as a man. I've always understood the risks. There weren't very many women with the highest Agency clearances who were prepared to open themselves to me. One or two over the years. And there was always a drug to slow my tongue, because even the highest clearance is still bound tight by the need-to-know test. I presume the rest of me was slowed as well by the drug, certainly my awareness was, for I remember these women only very faintly. I wish there had been another way, a safer way, a fully conscious way, for me to feel the touch of a woman. But I did not ask what more they could do for me. I only asked what I could do for my country.

The room is very large and I struggle toward the front, but the rows of padded beige chairs are filled more than halfway back already. I look around and I straighten again, this time with clear pain, but a pain put aside. I see Jackie down the row. She has not yet sat down. She has a pillbox hat and that stiff bouffant hairdo. But I remind myself that she couldn't be that young. And she's dead. I look again. Her eyes—she is smoothing her hot-pink dress and looking around the room—her eyes are Asian. Her gaze fixes and hardens and I follow it and coming down the aisle is another Jackie, a Caucasian one, dressed in mint blue, unaware still of her rival.

I sit. I am on the aisle and breathing heavily. I suspect there are several of me in the room as well, though I hope not to catch even a brief sight of them. I can't help but look up, and the second Jackie, with a slightly longer hairdo, twirled up at the bottom, brushes past me. Her face turns and her eyes fall and she looks straight at me. She doesn't show any sign at all of sensing who I am. As false as she is—her eyes are much too close together and her mouth is too thin—I'm briefly disappointed that she doesn't recognize me. I look away and I close my eyes. Jackie has been with me, as well, all these years.

When John and Caroline were sleeping in the afternoons, I'd clear half an hour in the affairs of state and tell my staff to leave us alone, and Jackie and I would make love in the room where they all made love, the presidents of the United States. And I'd ask her to talk to me about art while we touched. I wanted her mind in this act, and her voice, breathy as a starlet. I've been slandered over and over in the books. Smathers was way out of line telling those things about our Senate bachelor days. I might've talked like that about women with him—men have always talked stupidly about women with each other. And it's true that my mind was often elsewhere when I touched the women who always seemed to be there, open to me. But not because I didn't value them. Not because they were objects to me, taken up and cast off even more coldly than the objects for sale in this crowded room. There are suddenly too many things in my head at once. This happens sometimes. The voice of a woman now. "New bidder on my right at sixty thousand." I don't know what it is that's for sale but I have only four thousand and I clench inside, a little desperate for a reason I can't quite identify, Jackie would rise naked above me as I lay delicately still, trying not to let my back distract me. She would rise into a column of sunlight from the window and her skin was dusky and her voice was soft and she would be wearing a single strand of pearls, the only thing left on her body, and she would speak of the geometry of Attic pottery in the tenth century B.C., and the bands of decoration were drawn in black on cream-colored clay and there would be meanders and chevrons and swastikas and then, gradually, as the ninth century B.C. passed and the eighth began, there was an advent of animal forms. She spoke of all these wonderful vessels: the amphora with its two great handles and the krater with its fat belly and wide mouth and the skinny lekythos, for pouring. Jackie would throw her head back and her mind would make my breath catch and now the eighth century B.C. was in full flower with horsemen and chariots and battle scenes crowding these clay pots, and scenes of men and women lamenting the dead, and her eyes would tear up, even as we touched and she fell forward and I put my hands on her back and felt her bones.

"No, m'am, it's not your bid." A long, sweetly handsome face, a Boston sort of face, to my eye, is floating over the lectern at the front of the room, rolling out numbers. "It's at a hundred and ten on the phone. Now a hundred and twenty in the front. Yes, m'am, now it's yours, at a hundred and thirty. A hundred and thirty thousand dollars. A hundred and forty at the back of the room." I look away from her and I think for a moment that it must be a Grecian krater for sale, something I'd always hoped Onassis would buy for her but that she would never speak of with him. Then on a TV monitor to the side of the room I see a triple strand of pearls. A hundred and forty and now fifty and now sixty and I squeeze my eyes shut. Jackie crosses the White House bedroom to me, her clothes strewn behind her and the pearls tight at her throat, and they make her nakedness astonishing to me, as if no woman has ever been this naked before, and it takes the contrast, the failed covering of the thin string of pearls, to show me this.

The room has burst into applause. I look up. And the second Jackie, her eyes too close together but rather large, very dark, is looking at me. She is in the aisle seat directly across from me and she is looking at me intently.

"Now lot number 454A," the woman at the front says.

This Jackie in blue won't look away. She knows me. She knows.

"A single-strand, simulated-pearl necklace and ear clips."

I drag my attention away from the simulated Jackie's gaze and on the TV screen is the necklace my wife wears in my memories of our lovemaking. Perhaps not that very one. Perhaps some other necklace. She wore a single strand of pearls at our wedding, too. When Jackie wore pearls, I felt her nakedness always, even beneath her clothes. I stare at this necklace on the television screen and it could well be the pearls of any of a hundred memories I've taken out and handled on countless nights of what has been my life. I feel myself rise up slightly, briefly, from my chair. I hold back my hands which want to lift to the screen, to this image of her pearls. I want these pearls very badly.

"The opening bid is ten thousand dollars," the woman with the long face says.

I cry out. My cry is in anguish, but there are twenty cries at the same moment and they are all saying "Ten thousand." So no one hears. Except perhaps the Jackie across the aisle. This necklace is beyond my reach already. All the fragments of my life in this place are beyond my reach. I look to the right and she is fixed on me, this thin-lipped faux first lady. Her mouth moves.

I stand up, I turn, I drop my bidding card and push my heavy legs forward, the pain in my back flaring at each step. Twenty thousand. Thirty. The bidders' hands fly up, flashing their cards, the dollars pursue me up the aisle. Forty thousand from the phones. Fifty from the front row. I touch her there, at the hollow of her throat just below the pearls. Jackie rises up straight, nestled naked on the center of me, and I lift my hand and put my fingertips on the hollow of her throat. And I am out the main door of the auction room, breaking through a hedge of reporters who pay no attention to me. I stop, my chest heaving and the pain spreading all through me, and I look over my shoulder and just before the reporters close back up, I see her. She's coming toward me. The Jackie in blue has risen and is following.

The bodies of newsmen intervene but I know she will soon be here. Now I wish for the Director's men. I want their hands to take my elbows and I want them to whisper, This way, Mr. President, and I want them to carry me away, back to the empty garden and a patch of sunlight where I can just sit and sort out the strange things going on inside me. But I am on my own, it seems. The main staircase is before me, but there are more reporters that way and the faux Jackie will catch me just in time for them.

I turn blindly to the right, I go along a corridor, my face lowered, trying to disappear, and another staircase is before me, a modest one, linoleum, a metal handrail. My hand goes out to it, I take one step down and her voice is in my ear.

"Please," she says.

I stop.

"I recognized you," she says.

I turn to her.

"But I didn't mean to drive you away."

Her eyes are very beautiful. The brown of them, like the earth in the deepest hole you could dig for yourself, like a place to bury yourself and sleep forever, is like the brown of Jackie's eyes. I want to tell her secrets. About myself. About missile silos. About anything. All the secrets I know.

"I thought I read somewhere you were dead," she says.

She sounds charmingly ironic to me. But there is something about her eyes now, a little unfocused. And she is dressed as my wife, who is dead.

"I didn't believe it," she says.

"Good," I say, struggling with my voice which wants to speak much more.

Then she says, "I've seen all your movies."

There is a stopping in me.

"*The Grapes of Wrath* is my favorite."

"Thank you," I say. "Hurry back to the auction now. You must buy some of Jackie's pearls."

She tilts her head at the intensity of my advice.

I turn away from her, move myself down the steps.

"Yes," she calls after me. "I will."

I am out the side entrance now, on York Avenue. It is quieter here. No one looks at me. I am a ghost again. I turn and walk away, I don't know in what direction.

But this I do know: I love Jackie. I know because inside me I have her hands and her hair and her nipples and her toes and her bony elbows and knees and her shoes and belts and scarves and her shadow and her laugh and her moans and her simulated-pearl necklaces and her yellow gypsy bangle bracelets and her Gorham silver heart-shaped candy dish and her silver-plated salt and pepper shakers. And somebody has my golf clubs. And somebody has my cigar humidor. And somebody has my Harvard-crest cuff links. And somebody has a single strand of Jackie's pearls, a strand that I also have. And what is it about all these things of a person that won't fade away? The things you seek out over and over and you look at intently and you touch. You touch with your own hands. Or you touch with the silent movement of your mind in the long and solitary night. Surely these things are signs of love. In a world where we don't know how to stay close to each other, we try to stay close to these things. In a world where death comes unexpectedly and terrifies us as the ultimate act of forgetting, we try to remember so that we can overcome death. And so we go forth together in love and in peace and in deep fear, my fellow Americans, Jackie and I and all of you. And you have my undying thanks.

... WARMER

A. R. Morlan

A. R. Morlan lives in northern Wisconsin. Her short fiction has been published in magazines such as *Night Cry, The Twilight Zone, Weird Tales, Worlds of Fantasy and Horror, The Horror Show,* and *Phantasm* and in the anthologies *Cold Shocks, Obsessions, Women in the West, The Ultimate Zombie, Love in Vein, Deadly After Dark: The Hot Blood Series, Sinestre, Twists of the Tale* and in several volumes of *The Year's Best Fantasy and Horror.* She is the coeditor of a forthcoming anthology, *Zodiac Fantastic,* from DAW Books.

Morlan is a flexible and talented stylist. Here she takes a poke at the sometimes sleazy world of rock and roll, in a story that, belying its title, gives the reader quite a chill.

—E. D.

Before Edan Westmisley faxed his summons to my agent, my only legitimate (as in you could see my face) claim to semi-demi-fame was the Steppe Syster's "Love Victim" video where I licked the tattoo off the chest of their lead guitarist, Cody Towers.

Yeah, that was me. Not that anyone makes the connection between the big-hair, tits-swaying-in-a-bikini-top, thong-bottomed retro pre-AIDS bimboid slithering up the paint-drizzled riser toward Cody's semi-desirable, love-handled bare torso, tongue out and lashing against candy-apple lips, just before he notices me, slings his Stratocaster behind his pimply back and hoists me up by the armpits, so I can lovingly slurp off his licorice-icing tattoo (painted on over his Dermablend-smeared real phoenix-in-flames tattoo by a bandanna-covered bald-pated tattoo artist) in slo-mo close up, and what I am now, thanks to Edan Westmisley and his once-in-a-career offer—

—the offer he didn't share with my agent, or with anyone employed in his hidden/not hidden studio; the offer which held out the promise of me becoming something far more spectacular and memorable than just a tattoo-devouring bimbo. . . .

"Thaaat's riiight, kiddo, Edan West*mis*ley, Gran' Poo-*bah*-supremo at Genius Productions, as in get your mini-skirted bum down to his office, *pronto*—"

It wasn't unusual for my agent Gerhard Berbary to speak in italics, but for him to even come close to swearing (he was Canadian, which made 'bum' synonymous with 'ass' or worse), something much bigger than just another metal video shoot or frontal nude body-doubling part was at stake here, especially as far as Gerhard's cut was concerned. And at this point in my "career," considering how few videos, walk-ons and tit-'n'-ass insert shots he'd been able to round up for me, I knew that he would've sold my corpse for morgue gape shots if it would've netted him a commission. . . .

Not that being dead could've made me feel any less uneasy than Gerhard's wake-up call about Westmisley wanting me to come to his studio early that afternoon; while I didn't consider myself an "insider" when it came to the music scene, I did have subscriptions to *Billboard, Variety, Rolling Stone* and *Spin* . . . and with all my free time, especially after the "Love Victim" shoot, I'd had the opportunity to learn more than I actually cared to about Mr. Westmisley, formerly of the sixties Fluxus movement (a well-to-do group of what Gerhard dubbed "art-farts" which included Yoko Ono and her bare-buttocks-in-a-row film, really classy shit like that), and currently sole owner, stockholder, president and producer-in-residence at Genius Productions Ltd., a record company that produced hard-core industrial, techno, alternative and speed metal acts (like Steppe Syster), almost none of which ever charted higher than 150 on the *Billboard* Album Chart, but which were killers on the college charts— all the more ironic because Westmisley had supposedly (if the unauthorized bios reviewed in *Rolling Stone* could be believed) been all-but-bodily-thrown out of every university in Europe and the East Coast, for a little more than simply flunking out or missing dorm curfew—

(—as in things even pay-to-say journalists like Kitty Kelly were afraid to reveal after one unauthorized bio writer turned up belly-bloated on the Nantucket shoreline after interviewing some ex-Vassar co-ed in her nursing home bed . . . the bed she'd been confined to after dating soon-to-be-ex-Harvard alumni Westmisley—

—one of the same universities he'd later endow with trifles like libraries, gymnasiums and radio stations during the early eighties, after he'd finished the last round of chemo-and-radiation for his near-fatal bout with skin cancer.

He'd contracted said skin cancer during a two-year round-the-world junket in his favorite yacht in the mid-seventies, when he was on his collecting binge . . . and he'd sped home across two oceans with close to a dozen countries breathing down his burnt-to-jerky neck, threatening legal action for whatever illegal/endangered baubles he'd "bought." . . .)

And now Edan Westmisley wanted me to drive to his office, for a reason even my agent didn't know—

I asked Gerhard twice, "You mean to meet *with* him, like face-to-face?" and both times, his answer was the same . . . and as maddeningly vague:

"You want me to *read* you his fax? Here it is: 'Ger*hard*, please send your client from the Steppe Syster 'Love Victim' shoot to my office for a private meeting, noon to*day*.' *Hear* that, dear*heart*? The man said 'Please.' . . ."

"He didn't mention me by name," I'd countered both times, as the phone cord wrapped itself around my wrist like a curly python, but Gerhard was adamant—I was his only client to appear in a Steppe Syster video.

"But Ger, Westmisley only produces records, as in musicians . . . his *people* handle videos, he just oversees what they come up with." As I pleaded with him, I squeezed the receiver anxiously, my skin crawling under the remembered pressure of Westmisley's smoke-glass-shielded eyes.

I suppose people who saw the "Love Victim" video assumed that my tattoo-slurping cameo was morphed, but that wasn't "Edan's *style.*" Or so said Kenny, the director, while everyone waited for Mr. Bandanna to finish embellishing Cody's chest as he stretched out like a fallen Christ on the drum riser, bitching about how much the black paint-thin icing tickled as the glumly sweating tattoo guy spent an hour of studio time painting faux needlework between Cody's nipples. There was only so much butt-wiggling for Kenny to do in that hour, so eventually he confided, "Great Scarface's into sens*a*tion, albeit visually simulated sensations . . . *he* can't feel a damn thing any more." Kenny whispered in his irresistible Capote-esque drawl, glancing toward the rear of the studio, past the terminator of on-set lights, between every word. After the third or fourth glance, I looked back toward what he was staring at . . . Edan Westmisley, or some of him. He was a featureless, dark slice of shadow against the murky studio shadows, with only the plump, convex ovals of his sunglass lenses reflecting the arc-light glare.

"Looks like roadkill before it's run over," I whispered in Kenny's hoop-lobed ear; he whispered in my thrice-pierced ear, "Oh no, Edan's not roadkill . . . he's an immobile, hulking *beast* that smashes and twists grillwork, before sending your car into the fucking *ditch,*" just as the suspended-in-darkness lenses drifted away to the *clup-clup* of his retreating lizard-skin boots. Once Kenny seemed sure that he was out of range in the huge studio, he added, "I've developed 'shoulder eyes' while working for him . . . all Edan has to do is stare at me, and my skin *writhes* . . . like getting a sunburn while staying dead-fish-*white.*"

I thought Kenny was just blissfully melodramatic, but once Bandanna-Guy was finished, and Kenny started flat-clapping his hands, begging for "*Qui*-et," as he cued the lights and the assistant director set the electronic clapboard, I heard that steady, rhythmic *clup-clup* echoing in the far reaches of the studio, a staccato wooden-heeled counterpoint to the fuzzed-out tape the band was syncing to . . . and while I could barely see those disembodied shimmering discs of reflected light hovering behind Kenny's muscular, T-shirted back, they began to bore down on my exposed skin, the way light rays exert a trace of real weight—an unseen, yet measurable pressure. If Kenny endured "shoulder eyes," I endured "body eyes" . . . and by the time I snake-slithered up that riser, and tiny splinters dug into my exposed midriff, my skin felt as if it were being smothered, each pore screaming for air, and once Cody's sweating, calloused hands hoisted me up for my tattoo-tonguing close-up—Kenny barked orders at the Steady-cam operator, but his voice seemed filtered, as if unable to penetrate Edan's suffocating stare—I forgot Kenny's directions about keeping my eyes open, and began furiously lapping and slurping up bitter black icing, not caring where or how furiously I licked, until Cody jerked back, yelping, 'Hey! Watch the nipple ring, wouldja?' after my left incisor snagged the gold ring jutting out from his raisin-like nipple, and Kenny soothed, "*Go* with it, Cod*eee*, make it *work* for you," but all the while I couldn't shake that hand-firm pressure all over me, as if Westmisley's eyes were doing a King Kong on my Fay Wray skin, so I wound up licking Cody's Adam's apple before Kenny burbled, "Cut! *Per*-fect . . . it's a wrap. *Hon* . . . Hon*ey*, time to get up—"

Only, I didn't want to get up, not with Edan still there, behind Kenny; I stayed on my knees until Cody hoisted me up by the armpits, roughly, and whispered, "Get lost, wouldja?" then stalked off for his dressing room, whining to Kenny, "She almost yanked my ring out, man." I still couldn't open my eyes, though, until Kenny shot back, "Just as long as it wasn't in your dick . . . not that *that's* big enough *to* pierce," and under those playfully drawled words, I heard the ever-more-distant *clup-clup* of Edan's boot heels, as he left the studio.

"Don't mind that pimpled *twit*, dear, he'll never stop you from working," Kenny began as I opened my eyes, as if it was Cody I was so obviously scared of; not wanting to spoil Kenny's fantasy about Edan being hung up on him, I just smiled, nodded, and took the hand-down he offered me, before stepping off that riser and out of the studio, into the fading-but-*real* touch of sunlight on my oxygen-starved flesh.

"—listen, *kiddo*, do *I* question Edan Westmisley and still expect to make any more deals in *this* charming burg? If he faxed me a request that I *personally* swab out his private vomi*torium* with my *tongue*, I'd glaaadly *do* so—am I speaking *English* to you, or am I jabbering in fucking *Greek?*"

Privately replying, "No, Gerhard, *you'd* gladly do *him* if he'd stoop to dropping *his pants for a third-rate wanna-be like* you," I mumbled, "English, Ger," before asking (even as my brain protested), "When did he want me there?"

"Noon . . . do you realize that any *other* of my clients would already be *at* Westmisley's as I speak, doing the knee-dance under his *desk* in gratitude? And swallowing every damn *drop*? If he hadn't of asked for *you* in particular, I'd have called one of my other clients . . . what's the matter, you scared of the *stories* about him?"

Even though he had no way of seeing me, I shook my head of would-be-video-queen big-hair *No*; crazy producer stories were as commonplace as urban legends—didn't Tina Turner once see Phil Spector pick up an apple core coated with cigarette ash out of a tray and eat it? The quirks and foibles of producers were the stuff of *Rolling Stone*'s "Random Notes" column, weren't they? But the underground zines, the grungy hand-photocopied jobbies sold at the bigger book stores, they had the real, fresh dirt on No-Eyes Westmisley: the over-lord attitude with his engineers; the sudden, blackball firings; the kinky stuff his ex-lovers only hinted at; the way he circumvented customs with whatever fetishes or artifacts he'd glommed onto during that cancer-causing last jaunt of his; and how he'd beaten said cancer by going to Third World doctors who'd try anything, from whatever source, to heal what should never be healed . . . yet, despite all the weirdness he'd indulged in from the sixties on (long past the time when his fellow Fluxus members went respectable—like when Yoko made huggy-kissy with McCartney at the Rock and Roll Hall of Fame induction), Edan Westmisley was the original Teflon Dude, and never mind Ronbo Reagan.

No union could touch him. No woman—no matter what bed or cell or worse she occupied—could blackmail him. Whether it was out of fear, or because he was so well insulated (old-money rich, from a peerage in England), no one knew for sure, save for knowing that Edan Westmisley was about as close to a god as a man could be and still need to shake his dick after pissing (or so Kenny advised me during a chance meeting outside of Spago).

Yet, as powerful as Westmisley was, he'd said "Please" to the cut-rate agent of a would-be actress . . . someone who couldn't do a tattoo-licking shot without almost removing a guy's nipple ring the hard way.

To get a "Please" from Westmisley was far rarer than gobs of manna dripping on the Walk of Fame . . . a courtesy he wasn't obliged to give to anyone, for anything. But as Gerhard gave me directions to Westmisley's office-cum-studio, I wondered just what sort of price-tag—be it actual or something less tangible—was attached to that unexpected show of civility. . . .

Now, I realize that Edan's adding "Please" to that fax had nothing to do with politeness, or any normal human civility, but was perhaps meant only to forestall suspicion.

Genius Productions Ltd. was located out in the Hills, or almost past them, to be exact; to this day, I can't find the spot on any map. But then again, since I've never driven near the place again, let's just say it's Out There. Anyhow, if you were to drive past it unknowingly, you'd never realize that you'd just whizzed past the entire complex—not that the building was hidden by trees or by a fence (Edan detested the obvious, in all things). It was just that the place was so unassuming that it barely registered. Oyster-white stucco exterior, minimal smoke-tinted windows, three squat stories, flat tile roof, superbly earthquake-proof in that there was nothing to break off (and reinforced from within by double-strength I-beams, as Edan proudly informed me), with only a bizarre metal sculpture adorning the brownish stubble of grass directly in front of the entrance to indicate that it wasn't a warehouse or sweatshop garment factory.

Yet, the sculpture itself was the key to both the identity of the building and the mentality of the man who designed and built it; from every angle but one, it resembled randomly staked Christian and Coptic crosses, of varying heights and widths, fanned out in a crescent shape across the lawn. But once a car was almost past the entire building, if you happened to look just so in the rearview mirror, the assemblage would suddenly meld together into a concave, seemingly smooth unbroken surface—save for the open spaces which read (in reverse, since it was *meant* to be read in a mirror):

GENIUS PRODUCTIONS LTD.

It was so perfectly executed it was chilling; even if a motorist noticed the solid version of the sculpture (including the squared-off words), it only remained solid-looking long enough to barely register the words before dissolving into a scattering of haphazard steel as soon as the car sped forward.

But I didn't feel privileged to have caught on to Edan's single-glimpse-only sign, as I backed my Escort up and then drove into the nearly empty parking lot to the east of the building; the *selectiveness* inherent in the design of that sculpture/sign galled me, perhaps because it gave no concession to unavoidable, human things like an eyelash getting in one's eye, or someone blinking at that exact second, or something going wrong with the car, or with traffic. Happen to miss that fraction of a second of the sign's wholeness, and a person might spend hours combing the freeway, searching for the elusive edifice just passed.

But the true pre-eminence of Edan Westmisley was waiting to be revealed to me; the double-paned smoked doors in front of the building were operated by a sensor, like those in a store, so that in itself didn't spook me . . . but the lack of anyone—security guards, receptionists, cleaning men with big sloppy galvanized metal buckets, wanna-be recording artists hoping to get *past* the non-existent receptionists—I-mean-*any*one, inside that stucco, steel and glass edifice did get to me. In a major way . . .

All I saw was a quarter mile of empty hallway, carpeted in the sort of plushy beige carpeting that mats down if you sneeze at it, extending in a straight line from where I stood to the back of the building. Which culminated in another door, this one industrial-steel-with-pneumatic-hinges (the emergency-only type usually seen in the rear of by-the-highway chain stores), and surmounted by a red-lit EXIT sign.

"You're quite cold, yaw'know, just standing there."

The voice was without a definable source; just simply *there*. But I was clued in enough to realize that it was Westmisley's languid, English-accented upper-class-twit voice (I'd seen that MTV interview Kurt Loder did with him just before he'd gone on that ill-advised yacht voyage and brought home a little more than a hold full of illegal goodies), and nervy enough not to want him to realize how badly he'd frightened me, so I drew myself up to my full five nine plus heels, smiled my toothiest should've-been-a-model smile, and forced myself to purr (didn't Gerhard tell me how *lucky* I was to *be* here?), "And I don't like being cold—"

"Start moving and you'll begin to warm up—" At least the disembodied voice had a slight hint of warmth in it by then. When he stopped speaking, he began humming, a tuneless, one-note drone that allowed me to figure out that he'd planted speakers in the walls, ceiling, even *under* the carpeting . . . which made me feel as if I was walking down his throat. As I walked, casually swinging my arms with each step (even though I would've rather hugged myself by then, purely for the security of it) down that diffusely lit hallway—recessed fluorescents that cast less than forty watts per fixture—I noticed there were doors set into the cream-colored Lucite walls; the pin-thin outlines were unmistakable . . . as was the lack of knobs.

Twenty steps down that runner of carpeting.

"Warmer."

Ten more steps, slowing down near each door outline.

"*Much* warmer—"

Glance up, but still no cameras visible. *Maybe in the fixtures?*

"*Waaarrrmmmmah*—" The humming became a throaty growl.

Two steps forward. Then one back. *There.* Just like with the statue outside, I didn't see the unadorned embossed lettering over the one doorway until I'd almost passed by:

"Timeo Danaos et dona ferentes"—Virgil

I might've been only a model-without-portfolio, an ass-or-boobs-for-hire body-double for straight-to-video flicks whose sole claim to semi-fame came during the increasingly infrequent airings of the "Love Victim" video, but I didn't consider myself an uneducated bimbo, no matter what Gerhard thought. I'd finished high school, top third of my class, and had done a year and a half of college, too. I couldn't read Greek, but I'd heard of Virgil—not that I was ready to let Westmisley know *that* much about me yet.

"Verrry waaarm—" I moved a foot sideways, to the right.

"Hot—" The door slid open before me, gliding into the wall with a muted *schwoosh* of Lucite rubbing Lucite. Beyond me was yet more unmatted plush carpet, culminating in another blank cream wall. *Smartass bastard.* I trotted up to the unopened pocket door so fast Westmisley barely had time to blurt out "Boiling!" as the door opened, and I strode through the newly revealed opening—

—into what looked, felt, and even smelled like a pit, like a droppings-piled bat cave, or some ransacked ancient tomb still swirling with the dust of disturbed mummified remains . . . the contrast between creamy-bright *nothingness* and prodigal *fullness* finally smashed the last shards of my pseudo-hip LA woman veneer; I stopped so abruptly I almost fell forward onto the swirling arabesques of his Persian/Oriental carpet from the built-up momentum.

As I steadied myself, I became aware of—

—Eyes. Everywhere around me. Square-and-triangle Kachina doll eyes, tight-lidded slits in the faces of African fertility figurines whose bodies were little more than knee-to-chin engorged vaginal lips. Glass and plastic orbs set in the nappy heads of mounted game animals, more than a few of them from extinct or endangered species. Pin-prick gargoyle eyes, unblinking in their stony intensity. Wrinkled, fine-lashed lids drawn tight over the sunken orbs of several shrunken heads which hung by frazzled, beaded topknots. Bland concave pup-illess eyes in chipped Grecian and Roman statuary fragments. Frosting-bright sockets in Mexican sugar skulls. And peep-holes set in the gold and silver irises of the rows of gold and platinum records which formed dividing lines between the shelved antiquities and oddities covering the walls of Westmisley's office.

And reigning supreme in that silent, frozen freak show was Edan Westmisley himself, his purple-wattled, burst-capillary red and mottled-grayish tan full moon of a face suspended over a bridge of semi-clawed, tortuously linked fingers under his ill-defined chin, his eyes protected with those oval smoky glasses, his carefully brushed and dry-sprayed graying hair (a wig, perhaps?) a glowing nimbus over his ruined features . . . but despite the almost heavenly way his neatly side-parted hair seemed lit from within, the effect wasn't angelic in the least.

His immaculate gray Italian silk suit, starched-till-it-shone white shirt, and

burnished pewter-tone tie didn't register on my consciousness until a few dis-
oriented seconds had passed (I did know his boots were lizard skin, as Kenny
had claimed); precious seconds during which he was able to survey and . . .
catalogue me with those near-hidden, impartial, *appraising* eyes of his. As if I
was yet another *item* he could buy, then mount on those cluttered walls of
his. . . .

That much I realized when he smiled; not a friendly, glad-to-meet-ya smile,
but a stiff rictus of those purple-tinged lips, which parted to reveal a fence-like
double row of white, flat surfaced teeth . . . seeing that pseudo-smile, I knew
that whatever words came through those bloated lips, past those hard-edged,
perfect teeth, wouldn't convey one iota of whatever a jaded, world-weary man
like Westmisley might still be capable of *feeling*, if, indeed, he felt anything
for anyone at all.

I think I smiled in reply; I don't recall much besides him pointing out a
chair, and me easing into its spongy depths, unable to speak . . . unable to *think*,
actually. Drumming his blunt-tipped, crescent-clawed fingers (each ridged nail
perfectly manicured, save for the tip of the left forefinger, which was missing
above the last joint) on top of his empty, black-wood-surfaced desk, Westmisley
said without preamble:

"Lovely . . . how you licked away that buffoon's tattoo . . . I could almost hear
the uppermost layers of flesh parting from his chest . . . an exquisitely painful
moment, especially the way the chap winced until his eyes fairly *watered*—"

"I snagged his nipple ring with my incisor," I blurted out, my face flushing
at the memory. "Kenny said he'd edit it out, but—"

"But he didn't . . . I assume you can figure out why." There was no question
mark punctuating his voice, as if positing that I should know such a thing.
Directly behind his left shoulder, a particularly rabid-looking Indonesian carved
mask leered at me until I felt incredibly exposed, vulnerable, and found myself
babbling, "Not really . . . Cody seemed to be so piss-upset about it, I just figured Kenny *would* edit it out—"

"As he intended to do, until I told him not to. That flash of pain in the
guitarist's eyes was precisely what I wanted. The object, as it were, of the entire
tattoo-removing scene. The act leading up to it was only a means to a most
specific end . . . after all," he added, his Twit-of-the-Year tone growing softer,
yet darker, with each carefully enunciated syllable, "I could have had that sequence morphed in less than half the time it took that tattoo *artiste* to em-
bellish that blubbery fool's epidermis with frosting, and probably at a
comparable expense. The resulting faux tattoo, and you as well, were fungible
. . . all I ever had in mind was seeing that unfeigned twinge of agony in the
chap's eyes, accompanied by an unrehearsed grimace of pain about the lips.
Nothing more than what might've been accomplished by a swift, clean thrust
to the uncupped groin . . . but via a more aesthetic route. A small tidbit for
the visually jaded."

His short speech finished, Westmisley laced bent fingers into a fleshy shield
before his lower chest, and stared at me until I could almost make out his eyes
behind the infernally reflecting lenses . . . slow-blinking, turtle-wattled eyes,
small shiny balls set in a webbing of crinkled, oddly shiny skin. Those eyes were

so unnaturally bland, so removed from pain or any sort of inner suffering, I wondered if they were cosmetic contact lenses, perhaps to cover sun-induced discoloration or disease; no one who had gone through such indisputably painful treatments for cancer should've possessed such calm, untroubled eyes.

Oh, I'd heard of people with no threshold of pain, who never felt as much as a headache, but that was a rare condition; what could the odds have been of such a rich, worldly man also being blessed with freedom from external or internal agony? Yet, for him to intentionally inflict pain on another—

"But it was an accident . . . I didn't mean to hurt him," I countered, as I shifted around in the chair, trying to assume a more upright position, but the chair (a modernistic, nubby-surfaced marshmallow perched on a stem-like base) seemed to have no internal framework . . . just layer upon layer of spongy softness, with no hard core to pull myself up on. So there I sat, legs slightly splayed, arms loosely akimbo, head just barely supported by the high back of the stupid seat, yet still trying to hang on to whatever dignity I possessed.

"All the better for the desired effect . . . why do you think I told Kenny to hire a woman to devour Cody's tattoo? All the members of the group were similarly embellished, some with more pleasing designs . . . but only he sported pierced nipples. And the nipple is such a sensitive area of the anatomy . . . much more so than the earlobe, don't yew think?" He stared at my ears, with their trio of studs per lobe, and I reflexively pawed my hair over my ears before replying, "Yeah . . . I don't know how anyone could have that done—"

"Getting your ears pierced didn't hurt?" Behind those shining lenses, something flickered for a second in his pale eyes, something eager, hungry—

"No—wait, I mean, yeah, it hurt, y'know, but it wasn't a major thing . . . not enough to stop me from having more holes put in. But an earlobe isn't a nipple—"

"No, no, it isn't," he agreed, in a surprisingly regretful-sounding tone. Then shifting his voice from wistfulness to its former briskness, he went on, "You probably realize I didn't ask you here to discuss body piercing and tattoo removal . . . listen carefully to this, would you?" Nearly smiling for real, he unlaced his fingers and reached over to his left, where he pressed a slightly recessed portion of the desktop. A few seconds of hissing static followed, the sound coming out of every wall as well as the ceiling; white noise amplified and captured on ferrous oxide, then came this almost-familiar looped sample, its tune nearly buried in industrial drumbeats and fuzzed-out electric techno synths, with additional layers of reverb and redubs—

"Is that the intro to Fleetwood Mac's 'Tusk?' " I ventured timidly, having decided that Westmisley got off on whatever information he could glom onto from people; in reply, he said softly, "Luke-warm . . . it's the drumline from 'Goody-Two Shoes,' Adam Ant's solo effort—but *wait*—" With his right, whole index finger, he motioned for me to lean forward. Despite the squishiness of the chair, I *leaned*—

—and a fraction of a second later, this . . . *voice* cut through the beat, redubs and reverb; just a single sustained note that somehow grew stronger, louder and *needier* by the minute. When it seemed that no set of lungs could power a note for that long, that *energetic* a period of time, the voice swooped down to a shivery whisper, droning on and on in a rhythmic, chant-keen-*prowl* melody

without actual words . . . definitely not house, not quite speed metal caterwauling, nor thrash, and certainly not a grunge growl, but whatever this . . .
sound was, it was definitely hard-core. And miles beyond any alternative music
I'd heard before . . .

More like . . . *elemental.* Pre-primitive, but with a hybrid industrial/thrash/
techno back-beat swooping in and around every flutter and trill of that incredible, inexhaustible set of pipes.

And as I listened, I felt myself wanting, needing to *move*, to just free whatever
it was that made me *alive* in my body, to shake flesh and bones and pulsing
blood to that impossibly fast over 140 beats per minute melody . . . I can't
remember getting up, but a couple of minutes into the song, I *was* up and
dancing around the cluttered, musty-aired room, my limbs jerking from places
deep within me, my head rolling sinuously on my neck, my eyes almost but
not quite closed, as if I'd just dropped a cocktail of smart drugs, or "E"—

—but when I found myself face to face with one of *them*, it was like a switch
had been shut off in my brain, leaving me frozen in unblinking place before
the wall opposite Westmisley's ebony desk.

I was virtually eye to eye with a trio of the most gawdawful *ugly* . . . constructions I'd ever seen anywhere, be I sober or stoned, and as I gazed at their oddly
slick and slightly moist-looking surfaces, I wondered how their owner could
bear to look at them while sitting serenely behind his desk, especially since
their lidless eyes were all but locked on his shielded ones.

They were about twenty-some inches tall, like baby dolls, only no kid
would've taken one of *those* things to bed with her. Big bald heads, the skulls
ivory-pale with nary a hint of hair stubble, just filmy-thin shiny flesh, with gelid
glassy eyes set into the sockets, and open jaws filled with glistening over-sized
ivory teeth. No hint of flesh on the exposed arms; just finely carved bones
attached to each other with some sinewy-looking waxy amber threads. The rest
of the bodies were wrapped in quasi-mummy-style linen bandages, culminating
in a blunted point where the feet should've been. Repulsive as they were, I
couldn't stop staring at them; whoever fashioned these images did an ingenious
job of waxing or varnishing or . . . wetting the surfaces to make everything glis-
ten in a not-sunny-but-it-*should*-be manner, so that the skulls and their pencil-
thin arm bones shone like they were resting under clear, clean water instead of
being exposed to the drying, polluted LA air.

Just then, the song died away, culminating in a fevered, intense whisper
before the final triumphant *whoop*, and I was able to speak once more, now
that the song had released my body and mouth.

"Wha . . . what *are* those things?"

"What do you think they might be?" That same cold toying voice I'd heard
upon entering the building. Not wishing to be suckered in again by the sheer
power of his ability to possess things, to manipulate that which was just beyond
his reach, I concentrated on the middle figure, taking in the gelid yet hazy tan-
irised eyes, and began, "Uhm . . . representations of dead people—"

"Warm," he conceded.

"Or . . . life after death, like spirits?" After the intense work-out I'd just experienced, I still had trouble organizing my thoughts.

"Waaarmer . . ."

"Really *old* spirits," I ventured, to which he replied in a terse whisper, "*Hot*
... they're *Kakodiamones*. Ancient Greek for evil spirits. Very rare representations ... I acquired them three years ago or so—"

Without needing for him to explain further, I realized he was talking about
his final yacht voyage; within months of returning home, he'd haunted every
cancer clinic in the world, trying to halt the fast-spreading, disfiguring mela-
nomas which threatened to all but rot the flesh off his carcass—the indie zines
and even Loder on MTV attributed it to too much time spent lounging in
equatorial and Mediterranean sunlight, and not enough time spent smearing
on sunblock. As my gaze cautiously roamed his corrugated flesh, while I tried
to appear as if I were maintaining polite eye contact, I was struck by the irony
of such a powerful, old-money dude not bothering to shell out a few bucks for
a case of SFP 32 sunscreen, but then again, if what I'd read in those same
indie rags was true, parts of his body which didn't show in polite company
were still ... viable, according to those ex-mistresses who were willing or able
to say anything at all about him.

After taking in every ridge, wattle and unexpected contour of his face, I realized that the subject of his repulsive, spit-shined figurines might hit too close to
home, make him uncomfortable (or possibly invoke his legendary, quirky temper), so I took a conversational side-step and asked, "Isn't that inscription over
your outer door Greek too?" in an over-confident voice which made me cringe in
retrospect, for Westmisley's puce-mottled shining lips jerked into a chilly smile.
"Just warmish, if that. Actually, it's from the Latin ... Virgil was a Roman, after
all. It means, 'I fear the Greeks even when they offer gifts.' "

Glancing back at the stiff trio, I remarked, "Considering what *they* look like,
no wonder Virgil said—"

The puckered skin of his lips twisted into a full *moué* as he answered in a
slightly peevish tone, "I'm certain that Virgil wasn't referring to Katharine,
Kerenze and Kristine here—" Noting my puzzled expression, he elaborated
with a crêpe-lidded wink. "I've found the best way of dealing with the unknown
and the frightening is trivialization ... condescending pet names, inappropriately silly—"

" 'Silly,' " I found myself echoing with a dumb nod of my head, until Westmisley's expression shifted from indulgent to irritated; then, with a flick of his
clawed hand, he indicated the concealed tape deck in his desktop and asked,
"Well, what do you think of this?"

Giving Westmisley my most sincere would-be model smile, I began slowly,
while making my way back to that impossibly pneumatic chair, "The singer ...
god, she's *fabulous*. Just incredible ..." Then, remembering that Westmisley
had actually composed music, back in his Fluxus art-fart days, I backtracked,
"... I mean the music itself was fantastic, but that *voice* ... to sing like that,
she must've been opera-trained, like Pat Benatar, or Linda—"

At that, Westmisley again pursed his lips into a crooked *moué*, as if I'd
insulted his newest musical acquisition in an unknown way, so I quickly added,
while trying to lean forward, "But she blows them away, no contest. I'd *love* to
see the reaction of the first rave crowd who hears her—"

It was then, for just a fraction of a second, that he let down his guard—or
at least allowed whatever it was that he was thinking or feeling to change his

expression; no sooner had I uttered those last words than his features softened, as his eyes (through the tinted lenses) grew wistful, their surfaces sheened with unmistakable moisture, and, for a moment, he once again resembled the fairly-good-looking-in-a-snooty-British-fop-way producer he'd been before the low-hanging Mediterranean sun made his skin go supernova. It was like this song, this singer, meant so incredibly *much* to him; the pride he felt at that moment was all but palpable—

—and, watching his ruined features melt with inner warmth, something went slightly soft and vulnerable in me; looking back on it, I can only describe what happened to me as being like that . . . momentum thing which occurs when you lift up one of those hanging steel balls and let it strike the rest of the balls suspended from that rack of five or six balls, when the moment of impact causes the last ball in line to fly free of its fellow balls. You'd think the last ball in line moved in sympathy with the first ball, rather than it being a con-trolled, impersonal reaction. His changed expression was that first ball. And my feelings were free-flying far from reality when my eyes registered those shifting features. . . .

There was a beat of silence as I let my voice trail off, then, while I still flew high and loose, words tumbled out of my mouth.

"I've been to a few raves, but nothing they played matched *this* . . . it's . . . it's like you tapped *into* her, and put all of her there *is* onto a master tape . . . it's life, in a song. Something that sweeps you into it and doesn't let go until it's done with you—"

Cutting off my stream of babble with one slicing motion of his curved right hand, Westmisley leaned forward ever so slightly, and asked softly, his voice teasing in its insouciance, "What do you suppose she looks like, while singing?" Then, as if sensing that I'd need prompting in order to answer him, he thumbed on the tape player, albeit at a lower volume. I concentrated as I listened, letting my mind paint an image to match the voice before I spoke again.

"Wild . . . jerking like Janis Joplin, not holding back at all . . . sweating, she's *dripping* . . . hair's all spiked where she's run her hands through it as she sings . . . I see her dripping with chains, little rings digging into her skin between them . . . if she's wearing anything, it's mostly ripped off from all her flailing around . . . ribcage is heaving, the hollow of her throat is fluttering . . . she's just sweating and gleaming there—"

The silence which followed that wordless melody was painfully loud and echoing in my ears. I slumped back against the billowing padding of my chair, eyes half closed, and finished, more to myself than to him, "—then she just collapses in a shiny heap, panting softly. That's . . . that's what I see when I hear her. . . ."

"I suppose that's one way of picturing her," Westmisley reflected in a tone which somehow suggested that his mental image was far, far different from mine—but also one he was disinclined to share.

Before I could ponder his words (as I've done so, *so* many times since), he smiled again, then added, "How would you like to . . . act out what you've just described to me?"

That time, I needed no time to reflect on his words—or their implicit meaning. I'd been knocking around LA and the fringes of the music scene long enough to recognize his pitch for what it was, as my mind scolded me *What else did you think he'd want from you? Did you think you had any* talent *he could exploit?*

He was talking C & C Music Factory, Black Box, even Milli Vanilli time. As if I was some hick bitch who'd just stepped off the Greyhound from Bible-Belt, USA in search of instant fame-'n'-fortune.

"I won't lip-synch," I said tersely, remembering all the negative press those video body-doubles had accumulated so quickly—and so permanently. I was about to get up and leave when Edan replied softly, his voice almost seductive in its faux warmth, "But I know what you *do* do . . . you wait in an overpriced, undersized apartment, waiting for your barely-in-the-loop agent to come through with yet another crotch shot or back-of-the-stage-only video shoot. Between each ever-more-infrequent gig, you wait. Growing a little older, a little less firm, a little less 'in' and a lot more desperate. I've checked your . . . resumé. You've tumbled from B-flick body-doubling to Euro-market crotch-grinds for US made-for-TV films. And despite what our sweet friend Kenny assured you, that nipple-sore guitar god *has* spread the word about that wicked incisor of yours—"

"But it was what you had in mind when—you *used* me—"

"Shouldn't one use what is bought? And if so, isn't re-using it up to the owner, too?"

I stood up, ready to head for that Open Sesame door . . . knowing that what waited for me beyond that endless, empty plush-floored hallway was just as barren—and without any potential surprises lurking behind those paper-cut-edged doors. I knew I was meat . . . which meant being devoured or left to rot. I sat down again, biting my lips to keep quiet, while Westmisley purred, "Thought you'd agree . . . now, how limber are you? I expect more than a mere mouthing . . . *my* divas dance," he added with a spittle-flying burst of emphasis that made *this* slab of meat begin squirming on the plate, as if I'd been cut into steak but not yet placed on the sizzling grill—

Trying to remember if Genius Productions Ltd.'s client roster boasted any other high-profile diva types, I decided to buy mental sorting-out time by asking, in an off-hand tone, "Poor thing . . . she must be terribly fat, or homely, for you to go through all this trouble . . . I've seen how the press eats performers alive when word gets out about them doubling for a singer . . . but with a voice like hers, could she really be *that* bad-looking?"

Once the words were out of my mouth, I regretted them, for surely I didn't have enough clout to get away with a taunt like that with someone as hideous-looking as Edan Westmisley . . . but his reaction proved to be far more frightening than an unleashed flood of curses or show of temper could've been—

—he simply leaned back in his chair, laced his talon-like fingers behind the back of his had-to-be-wigged head . . . and began laughing, a deep, bubbling-from-his-toes chuckle that soon brought pearl-like tears to his shielded eyes, and exposed both rows of teeth back to the first molars. He rode his swivel chair like a bronco, while the laughter erupted from his heaving chest, as if he were mentally replaying Monty Python's "Killing joke" skit, prior to him keeling over in a spent heap of ruined flesh—then he simultaneously stopped rocking back and forth and placed his tight-skinned curved hands on the desk before him, while regarding me with a sly, I-know-something-*you*-don't smile.

"How bad do you sup*pose* she looks?"

Like you, *prick,* my mind raged, while I forced my lips to smile prettily before replying tentatively, as if this *were* simply another mind-game, "Oh, overweight, no tan . . . couch potato city—"

"Brrr . . . cold, cold, *cold,*" he teased in a voice that carried no hint of humor, while his eyes danced and glittered behind the dark convex glass.

Remembering some article in *Spin* mentioning that the only artists signed to his label were bands, all male bands—

(my *divas dance*)

—I shrugged my shoulders and tried, "Stringy hair and skin like the inside of an English muffin," not caring how he'd react; true, he may've just been referring to divas in general before, but that "my" was far too possessive to be figurative. . . .

"Hmmm . . . warmish, but not very." He still half-smiled.

Glancing at his wall-ensconced trophies for inspiration, I ventured, "Bug-eyed, or cross-eyed?" while staring at that Indonesian mask, and was rewarded with "Warmer . . ."

Wishing that this guy *was* into harmless quirks like chomping down on ash-breaded apple cores, I laced my fingers in front of my waist before suggesting, "Too skinny . . . like she'd make Kate Moss look like a blimp?"

"Uuummm, *waaarm*—"

Mentally tallying my "warm" score, I formed a mind-picture that looked teasingly familiar . . . even if it was too impossibly ugly to be seriously considered. *He has to be playing another Genius mind-game . . . like that sign outside. I'm just seeing pieces . . . all I have to do is step back a few paces to get it—*

Shifting slightly in that pillow-like chair, I looked around at walls that stared back at me, and asked, "Is it true that this studio is called 'Genius' in honor of your IQ score when you were a boy in England? I've read that in a couple of articles—"

"Which means more than one person has bollocked it up, doesn't it?" West-misley's smile was a lop-sided smirk, underscoring the peevishness of his voice, as he went on, "It's yet another reference to the Romans, *like* Virgil . . . they believed that just as each woman had her Juno, so a man had his Genius. A spirit which gives each person his or her being, a sort of . . . guardian angel, protecting them throughout their lives. Although sometimes said protection is very limited indeed," Edan mused, as his stub of a finger caressed one cratered cheek, "forcing the person to seek out other forms of protection."

"You're really *into* ancient cultures, aren't you," I asked as brightly and wide-eyed-video-queenly as possible; hoping that he'd dropped the "warmer" game for good. I thought that if I could pull his attention back to himself, to *his* all-consuming needs, he'd forget that I'd been gauche enough to ask *why* my services would be needed by him . . . especially after he'd taken such pains to remind me exactly why I couldn't turn down his offer. . . .

But I'd forgotten that meat shouldn't think or hope at all.

" 'Into ancient cultures,' " he echoed softly, each syllable eating into the room's silence like a drop of acid, leaning forward slightly and adding in that same stinging, biting whisper, "All of us, me, you, that spotty lout with the edible body ornament, my lovely friend Kenneth, every man-Jack of us, is the result *of* ancient culture. Nothing's new, *nothing*. No artwork, no song, no work of literature . . . nothing at *all*. Different configurations, that's all. Took me a long time to realize that, starting in the sixties, back when all my co-conspirators in artistic challenge were trying to set this bloody sphere of water and mud on its arse. Only then, I was content to haul out what was very old, and try to pass it off as new by changing bits of it around. Music as art form, or some self-deluding *rot* like that.

"But I wasn't any more profound than Yoko was with her bare bum—which included my vertical smile, by the way, before I broke free of the whole Fluxus movement. No one realized how far back I'd been digging for my work . . . probably because I didn't go back *far* enough. Nothing I'd done was old enough to be new. Which was *so* frustrating. The kind of frustrating one needs to get out of one's system in any way, any form . . . When I couldn't do what I needed to do, I switched gears, went the 'those-who-can't-do-teach' route, only for musicians, 'can't do' becomes 'can produce.' . . .

"*That* gave me credibility, additional power . . . as if I really needed more," he added, with an icy-toothed grin.

"Yet I never got over my love of what was old, what was exotic simply because it *was* old enough to be forgotten. Quite an addiction, actually. A bigger rush than the usual hands-on power games I'd played since I was in short pants . . . and if one can do that ferreting into the forgotten times, forgotten places, all on one's lonesome, *quite* unlike a curly-headed tot, that rush can be intoxicating. Better than dropping Ecstacy, or listening to derivative house-techno-thrash gibberish," he admitted with a self-deprecating wave of his hands.

"Although this last time around, I quite outdid myself . . . I certainly outstayed my welcome in the Mediterranean, at least as far as that curly-haired, cherubic former tot was concerned. . . . But," he confided with a wink in my too-confused-to-react direction, "the fact that my personal Genius chose that time to go on temporary holiday was outweighed by what I brought back with me—aside from my obvious 'gift' from Apollo, of course . . . you *do* realize that Apollo was the Greek sun god, no?"

"I'm not dumb," I whispered. "I've been to college—"

"So have I, so have I . . . tons of them. I suppose it was what I learned there that put me in this fix—" Again he tapped his lopped-off finger against his flesh, producing a drunk-like leathery *thonk* that turned my stomach and guts to mush. "—all those tales Thomas Bullfinch and Edith Hamilton translated from the Greek . . . all those marvelous creatures with unbelievable, fantastic attributes. What I wouldn't have given to have heard the melody of Pan's pipes, or the song of the Sirens luring sailors to their doom—can you imagine how captivating, how alluring, their voices must've been, for men to risk all, forsake all, just to continue listening to that deadly melody under that lethal sun? And think, not one of *them* lived long enough to find out what sort of throat produced such bewitching arias, alas—"

Unsuccessfully trying to sit upright in that adiopocere-squishy chair, I flicked a strand of hair out of my eyes and said, "But none of them died . . . the Sirens were just a myth, like the Cyclops and the witch who turned men into pigs and dogs, so nobody missed—"

All he did was smile at that, but the genuine nature of that smile, the eye-crinkling *completeness* of it, shut me up faster than a back-handed smack across the lips.

And think, not a one of them *lived long enough—*

My agent wasn't the only man in LA who literally spoke in italics . . . but Edan was no closet-queen, like Gerhard, or sweet, gentlemanly Kenny. West-misley used his verbal italics most sparingly . . . most pointedly—

And as he continued to smile at me, his vaguely reptilian flesh merrily crin-kled around those dancing eyes (my *divas dance*), I felt that burning pressure on my exposed back and shoulders, as if a steady gaze was being aimed my way, only Kenny's appellation "shoulder eyes" didn't cut it at *all*—what I felt was more like "shoulder daggers"—

Hundreds of painted, carved and inlaid eyes watched me impassively as I gracelessly clawed my way out of that cupped fleshy palm of a chair, dropping unceremoniously to my knees before I was able to regain my footing and make for that closed pocket door, my hands extended before me like those of the newly blind, as I tried to walk while peering through cast-down lids and capri-shell lashes, so as not to see those shiny-raw *things* Edan had so playfully named after collecting them—if, indeed, he'd merely *obtained* them at all—but just before Westmisley obligingly opened that sealed Lucite door, and it *shwicked* aside in a rush of sterile, unscented displaced air, I heard his soft, soft whisper behind me.

"*Much* waaarmer . . ."

Edan Westmisley's latest diva, capriciously dubbed "Cer-een," made her first and last appearance at a rave held in an abandoned warehouse on the outskirts of Santa Monica a few weeks later. And while the cops blamed what happened on some bad "E" which was passed out that evening and early morning, the fact that all the people who died were men more than told *me* what had really gone down. From what those who survived had to say to *Spin* and *Circus*, or (at much greater length, and in gorier detail) to the tabloids, Edan had actually listened to me that afternoon, in as far as what I'd said about what the singer looked like. Whoever the lip-syncher was, she'd been far more desperate than I was—word was she was pierced in places no sane person should allow them-selves to be pierced, and that her black spiked hair resembled bits of wire shoved in her scalp. Nobody mentioned how well she moved; after she opened her mouth behind the headset microphone, things like writhing and being limber didn't matter at all. But what went down in that strobe-lit warehouse didn't derail Westmisley's latest diva; he merely sidestepped the issue by using that *voice* as an uncredited sound-bite on other Genius records . . . which is probably what he meant to do all along. Or what he should've done, if he hadn't been consumed by his twisted need for revenge, after his own flesh went nova . . . the price paid for living through what no man before him had sur-vived.

The press almost found him out after one dance-mix engineer decided to isolate the voice from the rest of a bootleg tape made during the Santa Monica rave, but when his wife found him dead in his home studio, word was she only played so much of the tape before setting fire to it, and the studio itself.

Even that episode did nothing to stop Edan from blowing his own horn one last time . . . Just as he'd predicted, I was sitting in my overpriced, too-small apartment, watching my expanding waistline in my hall closet mirror and not really caring one iota about my increasing girth, when the Express Mail package came. There wasn't much in it, just a cassette, some photos in a plain manilla envelope, and a self-taped video. No note, no last verbal jab . . . although once I heard that naked, raw voice on the tape, torn free of the lulling, masking overdubbed music, and thumbed the eight-by-ten-inch black-and-white photos out of the envelope, I couldn't bring myself to watch whatever it was he'd videotaped, for I knew I wasn't nearly insane enough to live with myself after watching it. The way Edan was, or had become after his last voyage in the land of the Sirens. And before he'd turned the tables on them in memory of every other man they'd managed to kill.

I've since burned the photos, but removing the images from my mind isn't as easy as licking off a tattoo the hard way. He'd kept them as they originally were for a time, long enough to photograph them. Aside from being small, delicate, they were more or less human looking. Before he flayed them, taping their voices as he did so. But only above the waist; after they finally died, and were preserved with whatever it was he used to render them glassy-hard above, it was obvious from the lone shot of the unwrapped one that he'd taken pains to keep the flesh of the legs and what was between them soft enough to keep enjoying, perhaps in honor of those who'd died before being able to enjoy *them*.

After all, word was that the skin cancer didn't ruin all of *his* skin. . . . But, despite my own flabby body, and my descent into crotch shots, despite *all* that Westmisley did to ruin me, I've never needed or wanted personally to verify that rumor. . . .

NOT WAVING

Michael Marshall Smith

Michael Marshall Smith was born in England in 1965, lived in the United States, South Africa, and Australia for his first ten years, then returned to the UK. He now lives in North London, with his girlfriend Paula, two cats, and "enough computers to launch a space shuttle." His short fiction has been published in *Omni*, *Peeping Tom*, *Chills*, *Touch Wood: Narrow Houses 2*, *Dark Voices*, *Shadows Over Innsmouth*, *The Anthology of Fantasy and the Supernatural*, both *Darkland* anthologies, *Dark Terrors*, *Lethal Kisses*, *Best New Horror* and the last three volumes of *The Year's Best Fantasy and Horror*. He has won the British Fantasy Award for short fiction twice and the August Derleth Award for his critically acclaimed first novel *Only Forward*. His second novel, *Spares*, was published in the UK in 1996 and recently in the U.S. It has been bought for film by Steven Spielberg. He is currently writing the script for a mini-series of Clive Barker's *Weaveworld* and is working on other projects for the Smith & Jones Production Company.

"Not Waving" is about love, guilt and the choices that sometimes trap us. It was originally published in *Twists of the Tale*.

—E. D. and T. W.

Sometimes when we're in a car, driving country roads in autumn, I see sparse poppies splashed in among the grasses and it makes me want to cut my throat and let the blood spill out of the window to make more poppies, many more, until the roadside is a blaze of red.

Instead I light a cigarette and watch the road, and in a while the poppies will be behind us, as they always are.

On the morning of 10th October I was in a state of reasonably high excitement. I was at home, and I was supposed to be working. What I was mainly doing, however, was sitting thrumming at my desk, leaping to my feet whenever I heard the sound of traffic outside the window. When I wasn't doing that I was peeking at the two large cardboard boxes that were sitting in the middle of the floor.

The two large boxes contained, respectively, a new computer and a new monitor. After a year or so of containing my natural wirehead need to own the brightest and best in high-specification consumer goods, I'd finally succumbed and upgraded my machine. Credit card in hand, I'd picked up the phone and ordered myself a piece of science fiction, in the shape of a computer that not only went like a train but also had built-in telecommunications and *speech recognition*. The future was finally here, and sitting on my living room floor.

However.

While I had £3000 worth of Mac and monitor, what I didn't have was the £15 cable that connected the two together. The manufacturer, it transpired, felt it constituted an optional extra despite the fact that without it the two system components were little more than bulky white ornaments of a particularly tantalizing and frustrating kind. The cable had to be ordered separately, and there weren't any in the country at the moment. They were all in Belgium.

I was only told this a week after I ordered the system, and I strove to make my feelings on the matter clear to my supplier, during the further week in which they playfully promised to deliver the system first on one day, then another, all such promises evaporating like the morning dew. The two boxes had finally made it to my door the day before and, by a bizarre coincidence, the cables had today crawled tired and overwrought into the supplier's warehouse. My contact at Callhaven Direct knew just how firmly one of those cables had my name on it and had phoned to grudgingly admit they were available. I'd immediately called my courier firm, which I occasionally used to send design roughs to clients. Callhaven had offered, but I somehow sensed that they wouldn't quite get round to it *today*, and I'd waited long enough. The bike firm I used specializes in riders who look as if they've been chucked out of the Hell's Angels for being too tough. A large man in leathers turning up in Callhaven's offices, with instructions not to leave without my cable, was just the sort of incentive I felt they needed. And so I was waiting, drinking endless cups of coffee, for such a person to arrive at the flat, brandishing said component above his head in triumph.

When the buzzer finally went I nearly fell off my chair. The entry phone in our building was fashioned with waking the dead in mind, and I swear the walls vibrate. Without bothering to check who it was I left the flat and pounded down the stairs to the front door, swinging it open with, I suspect, a look of joy upon my face. I get a lot of pleasure out of technology. It's a bit sad, I know—God knows Nancy has told me so often enough—but hell, it's my life.

Standing on the step was a leather convention, topped with a shining black helmet. The biker was a lot slighter than their usual type, but quite tall. Tall enough to have done the job, evidently.

"Bloody marvelous," I said. "Is that a cable?"

"Sure is," the biker said indistinctly. A hand raised the visor on the helmet, and I saw with some surprise that it was a woman. "They didn't seem too keen to let it go."

I laughed and took the package from her. Sure enough, it said AV adapter cable on the outside.

"You've made my day," I said a little wildly, "and I'm more than tempted to kiss you."

"That seems rather forward," the girl said, reaching up to her helmet. "But a cup of coffee would be nice. I've been driving since five this morning and my tongue feels like it's made of brick."

Slightly taken aback, I hesitated for a moment. I'd never had a motorcycle courier in for tea before. Also, it meant a delay before I could ravage through the boxes and start connecting things up. But it was still only eleven in the morning, and another fifteen minutes wouldn't harm. I was also, I guess, a little pleased at the thought of such an unusual encounter.

"You would be," I said with Arthurian courtliness, "most welcome."

"Thank you, kind sir," the courier said, and pulled her helmet off. A great deal of dark brown hair spilled out around her face, and she swung her head to clear it. Her face was strong, with a wide mouth and vivid green eyes that had a smile already in them. The morning sun caught chestnut gleams in her hair as she stood with extraordinary grace on the doorstep. Bloody hell, I thought for a moment, the cable unregarded in my hand. Then I stood to one side to let her into the house.

It turned out her name was Alice, and she stood looking at the books on the shelves as I made a couple of cups of coffee.

"Your girlfriend's in Personnel," she said.

"How did you guess?" I said, handing her a cup. She indicated the raft of books on Human Resource Development and Stating the Bleeding Obvious in 5 Minutes a Day, which take up half our shelves.

"You don't look the type. Is this it?" She pointed her mug at the two boxes on the floor. I nodded sheepishly. "Well," she said, "aren't you going to open them?"

I glanced up at her, surprised. Her face was turned toward me, a small smile at the corners of her mouth. Her skin was the pale tawny color that goes with rich hair, I noticed, and flawless. I shrugged, slightly embarrassed.

"I guess so," I said noncommittally. "I've got some work I ought to do first."

"Rubbish," she said firmly. "Let's have a look."

And so I bent down and pulled open the boxes, while she settled down on the sofa to watch. What was odd was that I didn't mind doing it. Normally, when I'm doing something that's very much to do with me and the things I enjoy, I have to do it alone. Other people seldom understand the things that give you the most pleasure, and I for one would rather not have them around to undermine the occasion.

But Alice seemed genuinely interested, and ten minutes later I had the system sitting on the desk. I pressed the button and the familiar tone rang out as the machine set about booting up. Alice was standing to one side of me, sipping the remains of her coffee, and we both took a startled step back at the vibrancy of the tone ringing from the monitor's stereo speakers. In the meantime I'd babbled about voice recognition and video output, the half-gigabyte hard disk and CD-ROM. She'd listened, and even asked questions, questions that followed from what I was saying rather than to simply set me up to drivel on some more. It wasn't that she knew a vast amount about computers. She just understood what was exciting about them.

When the screen threw up the standard message saying all was well we looked at each other.

"You're not going to get much work done today, are you?" she said.

"Probably not," I agreed, and she laughed.

Just then a protracted squawking noise erupted from the sofa, and I jumped. The courier rolled her eyes and reached over to pick up her unit. A voice of stunning brutality informed her that she had to pick something up from the other side of town, urgently, like five minutes ago, and why wasn't she there already, darlin'?

"Grr," she said, like a little tiger, and reached for her helmet. "Duty calls."

"But I haven't told you about the telecommunications yet," I said, joking.

"Some other time," she said.

I saw her out, and we stood for a moment on the doorstep. I was wondering what to say. I didn't know her, and would never see her again, but wanted to thank her for sharing something with me. Then I noticed one of the local cats ambling past the bottom of the steps. I love cats, but Nancy doesn't, so we don't have one. Just one of the little compromises you make, I guess. I recognized this particular cat and had long since given up hope of appealing to it. I pointlessly made the sound universally employed for gaining cats' attention, with no result. It glanced up at me wearily and then continued to cruise on by.

After a look at me Alice sat down on her heels and made the same noise. The cat immediately stopped in its tracks and looked at her. She made the noise again and the cat turned, glanced down the street for no apparent reason, and then confidently made its way up the steps to weave in and out of her legs.

"That is truly amazing," I said. "He is not a friendly cat."

She took the cat in her arms and stood up.

"Oh, I don't know," she said. The cat sat up against her chest, looking around benignly. I reached out to rub its nose and felt the warm vibration of a purr. The two of us made a fuss of him for a few moments, and then she put him down. She replaced her helmet, climbed on her bike, and then, with a wave, set off.

Back in the flat I tidied away the boxes, anal-retentive that I am, before settling down to immerse myself in the new machine. On impulse I called Nancy, to let her know the system had finally arrived.

I got one of her assistants instead. She didn't put me on hold, and I heard Nancy say "Tell him I'll call him back" in the background. I said good-bye to Trish with fairly good grace, trying not to mind.

Voice recognition software hadn't been included, it turned out, nor anything to put in the CD-ROM drive. The telecommunications functions wouldn't work without an expensive add-on, which Callhaven didn't expect for four to six weeks. Apart from that, it was great.

Nancy cooked that evening. We tended to take it in turns, though she was much better at it than me. Nancy is good at most things. She's accomplished.

There's a lot of infighting in the world of Personnel, it would appear, and

Nancy was in feisty form that evening, having outmaneuvered some coworker. I drank a glass of red wine and leaned against the counter while she whirled ingredients around. She told me about her day, and I listened and laughed. I didn't tell her much about mine, only that it had gone okay. Her threshold for hearing about the world of freelance graphic design was pretty low. She'd listen with relatively good grace if I really had to get something out of my system, but she didn't understand it and didn't seem to want to. No reason why she should, of course. I didn't mention the new computer sitting on my desk, and neither did she.

Dinner was very good. It was chicken, but she'd done something intriguing to it with spices. I ate as much as I could, but there was a little left. I tried to get her to finish it, but she wouldn't. I reassured her that she hadn't eaten too much, in the way that sometimes seemed to help, but her mood dipped and she didn't have any dessert. I steered her toward the sofa and took the stuff out to wash up and make some coffee.

While I was standing at the sink, scrubbing the plates and thinking vaguely about the mountain of things I had to do the next day, I noticed a cat sitting on a wall across the street. It was a sort of very dark brown color, almost black, and I hadn't seen it before. It was crouched down, watching a twittering bird with that catty concentration that combines complete attention with the sense that they might at any moment break off and wash their foot instead. The bird eventually fluttered chaotically off and the cat watched it for a moment before sitting upright, as if drawing a line under that particular diversion.

Then the cat's head turned, and it looked straight at me. It was a good twenty yards away, but I could see its eyes very clearly. It kept looking, and after a while I laughed, slightly taken aback. I even looked away for a moment, but when I looked back it was still there, still looking.

The kettle boiled and I turned to tip water into a couple of mugs of Nescafé. When I glanced out of the window on the way out of the kitchen the cat was gone.

Nancy wasn't in the lounge when I got there, so I settled on the sofa and lit a cigarette. After about five minutes the toilet flushed upstairs, and I sighed.

My reassurances hadn't done any good at all.

A couple of days came and went, with the usual flurry of deadlines and redrafts. I went to a social evening at Nancy's office and spent a few hours being ignored and patronized by her power-dressed colleagues, while she stood and sparkled in the center. I messed up a print job and had to cover the cost of doing it again. Good things happened, too, I guess, but it's the others that stick in your mind.

One afternoon the buzzer went and I wandered absentmindedly downstairs to get the door. As I opened it I saw a flick of brown hair and saw that it was Alice.

"Hello there," I said, strangely pleased.

"Hello yourself." She smiled. "Got a parcel for you." I took it and looked at the label. Color proofs from the repro house. Yawn. She must have been looking at my face, because she laughed. "Nothing very exciting, then."

"Hardly." After I'd signed the delivery note, I looked up at her. She was still smiling, I think, though it was difficult to tell. Her face looked as if it always was.

"Well," she said, "I can either go straight to Peckham to pick up something else that's dull, or you can tell me about the telecommunications features."

Very surprised, I stared at her for a moment, then stepped back to let her in.

"Bastards," she said indignantly when I told her about the things that hadn't been shipped with the machine, and she looked genuinely annoyed. I told her about the telecom stuff anyway, as we sat on the sofa and drank coffee. Mainly we just chatted, but not for very long, and when she got to the end of the road on her bike she turned and waved before turning the corner.

That night Nancy went to Sainsbury's on the way home from work. I caught her eye as she unpacked the biscuits and brownies, potato chips and pastries, but she just stared back at me, and I looked away. She was having a hard time at work. Deflecting my gaze to the window, I noticed the dark cat was sitting on the wall opposite. It wasn't doing much, simply peering vaguely this way and that, watching things I couldn't see. It seemed to look up at the window for a moment, but then leapt down off the wall and wandered away down the street.

I cooked dinner and Nancy didn't eat much, but she stayed in the kitchen when I went into the living room to finish off a job. When I made our cups of tea to drink in bed I noticed that the bin had been emptied, and the gray bag stood, neatly tied, to one side. When I nudged it with my foot it rustled, full of empty packets. Upstairs the bathroom door was pulled shut, and the key turned in the lock.

I saw Alice a few more times in the next few weeks. A couple of major jobs were reaching crisis point at the same time, and there seemed to be a semi-constant flurry of bikes coming up to the house. On three or four of those occasions it was Alice whom I saw when I opened the door.

Apart from one, when she had to turn straight around on pain of death, she came in for a coffee each time. We'd chat about this and that, and when the voice recognition software finally arrived I showed her how it worked. I had a rip-off copy, from a friend who'd sourced it from the States. You had to do an impersonation of an American accent to get the machine to understand anything you said, and my attempts to do so made Alice laugh a lot. Which is curious, because it made Nancy merely sniff and ask me whether I'd put the new computer on the insurance.

Nancy was having a bit of a hard time, those couple of weeks. Her so-called boss was dumping more and more responsibility onto her while stalwartly refusing to give her more credit. Nancy's world was very real to her, and she relentlessly kept me up to date on it: the doings of her boss were more familiar to me by then than the activities of most of my friends. She got her company car upgraded, which was a nice thing. She screeched up to the house one evening in something small and red and sporty, and hollered up to the window. I scampered down and she took us hurtling around North London, driving with her customary verve and confidence. On impulse we stopped at an Italian restaurant we sometimes went to, and they miraculously had a table. Over coffee we took each other's hands and said we loved one another, which we hadn't done for a while.

When we parked outside the house I saw the dark cat sitting under a tree on the other side of the street. I pointed it out to Nancy but, as I've said, she doesn't really like cats, and merely shrugged. She went in first and as I turned to close the door I saw the cat was still sitting there, a black shape in the half-light. I wondered who it belonged to, and wished that it was ours.

A couple of days later I was walking down the street late afternoon when I noticed a motorbike parked outside Sad Café. I seemed to have become sensitized to bikes over the previous few weeks: probably because I'd used so many couriers. "Sad" wasn't the café's real name, but what Nancy and I used to call it, when we used to traipse hung-over down the road on Sunday mornings on a quest for a cooked breakfast. The first time we'd slumped over a Formica table in there we had been slowly surrounded by middle-aged men in zip-up jackets and beige bobble hats, a party of mentally subnormal teenagers with broken glasses, and old women on the verge of death. The pathos attack we'd suffered had nearly finished us off, and it had been Sad Café ever since. We hadn't been there in a while: Nancy usually had work in the evenings in those days, even at weekends, and fried breakfasts appeared to be off the map again.

The bike resting outside made me glance inside the window, and with a shock of recognition I saw Alice in there, sitting at a table nursing a mug of something or other. I nearly walked on, but then thought what the hell, and stepped inside. Alice looked startled to see me, but then relaxed, and I sat down and ordered a cup of tea.

She'd finished for the day, it turned out, and was killing time before heading off for home. I was at a loose end myself: Nancy was out for the evening, entertaining clients. It was very odd seeing Alice for the first time outside the flat, and strange seeing her not in working hours. Possibly it was that which made the next thing coalesce in front of us.

Before we knew how the idea had arisen, we were wheeling her bike down the road to prop it up outside the Bengal Lancer, Kentish Town's bravest stab in the direction of a decent restaurant. I loitered awkwardly to one side while she stood in the street, took off her leathers, and packed them into the bike's carrier. She was wearing jeans and a green sweatshirt underneath, a green that matched her eyes. Then she ran her hands through her hair, said "Close enough for rock and roll," and strode toward the door. Momentarily reminded of Nancy's standard hour and a half preparation before going out, I followed her into the restaurant.

We took our time and had about four courses, and by the end were absolutely stuffed. We talked of things beyond computers and design, but I can't remember what. We had a bottle of wine, a gallon of coffee, and smoked most of a packet of cigarettes. When we were done I stood outside again, more relaxed this time, as she climbed back into her work clothes. She waved as she rode off, and I watched her go, and then turned and walked for home.

It was a nice meal. It was also the big mistake. The next time I rang for a bike, I asked for Alice by name. After that, it seemed the natural thing to do. Alice also seemed to end up doing more of the deliveries to me, more than you could put down to chance.

If we hadn't gone for that meal, perhaps it wouldn't have happened. Nothing was said, and no glances exchanged: I didn't note the date in my diary.

But we were falling in love.

The following night Nancy and I had a row, the first full-blown one in a while. We rarely argued. She was a good manager.

This one was short, and also very odd. It was quite late and I was sitting in the lounge, trying to work up the energy to turn on the television. I didn't have much hope for what I would find on it but was too tired to read. I'd been listening to music before and was staring at the stereo, half mesmerized by the green and red points of LEDs. Nancy was working at the table in the kitchen, which was dark apart from the lamp that shed yellow light over her papers.

Suddenly she marched into the living room, already at maximum temper, and shouted incoherently at me. Shocked, I half stood, brow furrowed as I tried to work out what she was saying. In retrospect I was probably slightly asleep, and her anger frightened me with its harsh intensity, seeming to fill the room.

She was shouting at me for getting a cat. There was no point me denying it, because she'd seen it. She'd seen the cat under the table in the kitchen, it was in there still, and I was to go and throw it out. I knew how much she disliked cats, and anyway, how could I do it without asking her, and the whole thing was a classic example of what a selfish and hateful man I was.

It took me a while to get to the bottom of this and start denying it. I was too baffled to get angry. In the end I went with her into the kitchen and looked under the table. By then I was getting a little spooked, to be honest. We also looked in the hallway, the bedroom, and the bathroom. Then we looked in the kitchen again and in the living room.

There was, of course, no cat.

I sat Nancy on the sofa and brought in a couple of hot drinks. She was still shaking, though her anger was gone. I tried to talk to her, to work out what exactly was wrong. Her reaction was disproportionate, misdirected: I'm not sure even she knew what it was about. The cat, of course, could have been nothing more than a discarded shoe seen in near darkness, maybe even her own foot moving in the darkness. After leaving my parents' house, where there had always been a cat, I'd often startled myself by thinking I saw them in similar ways.

She didn't seem especially convinced but did calm a little. She was so timid and quiet, and as always I found it difficult to reconcile her as she was then with her as Corporate Woman, as she was for so much of the time. I turned the fire on and we sat in front of it and talked, and even discussed her eating. Nobody else knew about that, apart from me. I didn't understand it, not really. I sensed that it was something to do with feelings of lack of control, of trying to shape herself and her world, but couldn't get much closer than that. There appeared to be nothing I could do except listen, but I suppose that was better than nothing.

We went to bed a little later and made careful, gentle love. As she relaxed toward sleep, huddled in my arms, I caught myself for the first time feeling for her something that was a little like pity.

Alice and I had dinner again about a week later. This time it was less of an accident and took place farther from home. I had an early-evening meeting in town, and by coincidence Alice would be in the area at around about the same time. I told Nancy I might up having dinner with my client, but she didn't seem to hear. She was preoccupied, some new power struggle at work edging toward resolution.

Though it was several weeks since the previous occasion, it didn't feel at all strange seeing Alice in the evening, not least because we'd talked to each other often in the meantime. She'd started having two cups of coffee, rather than one, each time she dropped something off, and had once phoned me for advice on computers. She was thinking of getting one herself, I wasn't really sure what for.

While it didn't feel odd, I was aware of what I was doing. Meeting another woman for dinner, basically, and looking forward to it. When I talked to her my feelings and what I did seemed more important, as if they were a part of someone worth talking to. Some part of me felt that was more important than a little economy with the truth. To be honest, I tried not to think too hard about it.

When I got home Nancy was sitting in the living room, reading.

"How was your meeting?" she asked.

"Fine," I replied. "Fine."

"Good," she said, and went back to scanning her magazine. I could have tried to make conversation, but knew it would have come out tinny and forced. In the end I went to bed and lay tightly curled on my side, wide awake.

I was just drifting off to sleep when I heard a low voice in the silence, speaking next to my ear.

"Go away," it said. "Go away."

I opened my eyes, expecting I don't know what. Nancy's face, I suppose, hanging over mine. There was no one there. I was relaxing slightly, prepared to believe it had been a fragment of a dream, when I heard her voice again, saying the same words in the same low tone.

Carefully I climbed out of bed and crept toward the kitchen. Through it I could see into the living room, where Nancy was standing in front of the main window in the darkness. She was looking out at something in the street.

"Go away," she said again, softly.

I turned round and went back to bed.

A couple of weeks passed. Time seemed to do that, that autumn. I was very immersed, what with one thing and another. Each day held something that fixed my attention and pulled me through it. I'd look up, and a week would have gone by, with me having barely noticed.

One of the things that held my attention, and became a regular part of most days, was talking to Alice. We talked about things that Nancy and I never touched upon, things Nancy simply didn't understand or care about. Alice read, for example. Nancy read, too, in that she studied memos, and reports, and boned up on the current corporate claptrap being imported from the States. She didn't read books, though, or paragraphs even. She read sentences, to strip from them what she needed to do her job, find out what was on television, or hold her own on current affairs. Every sentence was a bullet point, and she read to acquire information.

Alice read for its own sake. She wrote, too, hence her growing interest in computers. I mentioned once that I'd written a few articles, years back, before I settled on being a barely competent graphic designer instead. She said she'd written some stories and, after regular nagging from me, diffidently gave me copies. I don't know anything about fiction from a professional point of view, so I don't know how innovative or clever they were. But they gripped my attention, and I read them more than once, and that's good enough for me. I told her so, and she seemed pleased.

We spoke most days and saw each other a couple of times a week. She delivered things to me, or picked them up, and sometimes I chanced by Sad Café when she was sipping a cup of tea. It was all very low key, very friendly.

Nancy and I got on with each other, in an occasional, space-sharing sort of way. She had her friends, and I had mine. Sometimes we saw them together, and performed, as a social pair. We looked good together, like a series of stills from a lifestyle magazine. Life, if that's what it was, went on. Her eating vacillated between not good and bad, and I carried on being bleakly accepting of the fact that there didn't seem much I could do to help. So much of our lives seemed geared up to perpetuating her idea of how two young people should live that I somehow didn't feel that I could call our bluff, point out what was living beneath the stones in our house. I also didn't mention the night I'd seen her in the lounge. There didn't seem any way of bringing it up.

Apart from having Alice to chat to, the other good news was the new cat in the neighborhood. When I glanced out of the living room window sometimes it would be there, ambling smoothly past or plonked down on the pavement, watching movement in the air. It had a habit of sitting in the middle of the road, daring traffic to give it any trouble, as if the cat knew what the road was for but was having no truck with it. This was a field once, the twitch of her tail seemed to say, and as far as I'm concerned it still is.

One morning I was walking back from the corner shop, clutching some cigarettes and milk, and came upon the cat, perched on a wall. If you like cats there's something rather depressing about having them run away from you, so I approached cautiously. I wanted to get to at least within a yard of this one before it went shooting off into hyperspace.

To my delight, it didn't move away at all. When I got up next to her she stood up, and I thought that was it, but it turned out to be just a recognition that I was there. She was quite happy to be stroked and to have the fur on her head runkled, and responded to having her chest rubbed with a purr so deep it was almost below the threshold of hearing. Now that I was closer I could see the chestnut gleams in the dark brown of her fur. She was a very beautiful cat.

After a couple of minutes of this I moved away, thinking I ought to get on, but the cat immediately jumped off the wall and wove in figure eights about my feet, pressing up against my calves. I find it difficult enough to walk away from a cat at the best of times. When they're being ultra-friendly it's impossible. So I bent down and tickled, and talked fond nonsense. I finally got to my door and looked back to see her, still sitting on the pavement. She was looking around as if wondering what to do next, after all that excitement. I had to fight down the impulse to wave.

I closed the door behind me, feeling for a moment very lonely, and then went back upstairs to work.

Then one Friday night Alice and I met again, and things changed.

Nancy was out at yet another work get-together. Her organization seemed to like running the social lives of its staff, like some rabid church, intent on infiltrating every activity of its disciples. Nancy mentioned the event in a way that made it clear that my attendance was far from mandatory, and I was quite happy to oblige. I do my best at these things but doubt I look as if I'm having the time of my life.

I didn't have anything else on, so I just flopped about the house for a while, reading and watching television. It was easier to relax when Nancy wasn't there, when we weren't busy being a Couple. I couldn't settle, though. I kept thinking how pleasant it would be not to feel that way, that it would be nice to want your girlfriend to be home so you could laze about together. It didn't work that way with Nancy, not anymore. Getting her to consider a lie-in on one particular Saturday was a major project in itself. I probably hadn't tried very hard in a while, either. She got up, I got up. I'd been developed as a human resource.

My reading grew fitful and in the end I grabbed my coat and went for a walk down streets that were dark and cold. A few couples and lone figures floated down the roads, in midevening transit between pubs and Chinese restaurants. The very formlessness of the activity around me, its random wandering, made me feel quietly content. The room in which Nancy and her colleagues stood, robotically passing business catchphrases up and down the hierarchy, leapt into my mind, though I'd no idea where it was. I thought quietly to myself that I would much rather be here than there.

Then for a moment I felt the whole of London spread out around me, and my contentment faded away. Nancy had somewhere to go. All I had was miles of finite roads in winter light, black houses leaning in toward each other. I could walk, and I could run, and in the end I would come to the boundaries, the edge of the city. When I reached them there would be nothing I could do except turn around and come back into the city. I couldn't feel anything beyond the gates, couldn't believe anything was there. It wasn't some yearning for the countryside or far climes: I like London, and the great outdoors irritates me. It was more a sense that a place that should hold endless possibilities had been tamed by something, bleached out by my lack of imagination, by the limits of my life.

I headed down the Kentish Town Road toward Camden, so wrapped up in heroic melancholy that I nearly got myself run over at the junction with Prince of Wales Road. Rather shaken, I stumbled back onto the curb, dazed by a passing flash of yellow light and a blurred obscenity. Fuck that, I thought, and crossed at a different place, sending me down a different road, toward a different evening.

Camden was, as ever, trying to prove that there was still a place for hippie throwback losers in the 1990s, and I skirted the purposeful crowds and ended up in a back road instead.

And it was there that I saw Alice. When I saw her I felt my heart lurch, and I stopped in my tracks. She was walking along the road, dressed in a long skirt and dark blouse, hands in pockets. She appeared to be alone and was wandering down the street much as I was, looking around but in a world of her own. It was too welcome a coincidence not to take advantage of and, careful not to surprise her, I crossed the road and met her on the other side.

We spent the next three hours in a noisy, smoky pub. The only seats were very close together, crowded round one corner of a table in the center of the room. We drank a lot, but the alcohol didn't seem to function in the way it usually did. I didn't get drunk but simply felt warmer and more relaxed. The reeling crowds of locals gave us ample ammunition to talk about, until we were going fast enough not to need any help at all. We just drank, and talked, and talked and drank, and the bell for last orders came as a complete surprise.

When we walked out of the pub some of the alcohol kicked suddenly in, and we stumbled in unison on an unexpected step, to fall together laughing and shh-ing. Without even discussing it we knew that neither of us felt like going home yet, and we ended up down by the canal instead. We walked slowly past the backs of houses and speculated what might be going on beyond the curtains, we looked up at the sky and pointed out stars, we listened to the quiet splashes of occasional ducks coming in to land. After about fifteen minutes we found a bench and sat down for a cigarette.

When she'd put her lighter back in her pocket Alice's hand fell near mine. I was very conscious of it being there, of the smallness of the distance mine would have to travel, and I smoked left-handed so as not to move it. I wasn't forgetting myself. I still knew Nancy existed, knew how my life was set up. But I didn't move my hand.

Then, like a chess game of perfect simplicity and naturalness, the conversation took us there.

I said that work seemed to be slackening off, after the busy period of the last couple of months. Alice said that she hoped it didn't drop off too much. So that I can continue to afford expensive computers that don't do quite what I expect? I asked.

"No," she replied, "so that I can keep coming to see you." I turned and looked at her. She looked nervous but defiant, and her hand moved the inch that put it on top of mine.

"You might as well know," she said. "If you don't already. There are three important things in my life at the moment. My bike, my stories, and you."

People don't change their lives: evenings do. There are nights that have their own momentum, their own purpose and agenda. They come from nowhere and take people with them. That's why you can never understand, the next day, quite how you came to do what you did. Because it wasn't you who did it. It was the evening.

My life stopped that evening, and started up again, and everything was a different color.

We sat on the bench for another two hours, wrapped up close to each other. We admitted when we'd first thought about each other, and laughed quietly about the distance we'd kept. After weeks of denying what I felt, of simply not realizing, I couldn't let go of her hand now that I had it. It felt so extraordinary to be that close to her, to feel the texture of her skin on mine and her nails against my palm. People change when you get that near to them, become much more real. If you're already in love with them then they expand to fill the world.

In the end we got on to Nancy. We were bound to, sooner or later. Alice asked how I felt about her, and I tried to explain, tried to understand myself. In the end we let the topic lapse.

"It's not going to be easy," I said, squeezing her hand. I was thinking glumly to myself that it might not happen at all. Knowing the way Nancy would react, it looked like a very high mountain to climb. Alice glanced at me and then turned back toward the canal.

A big cat was sitting there, peering out over the water. First moving myself even closer to Alice, so that strands of her hair tickled against my face, I made a noise at the cat. It turned to look at us and then ambled over toward the bench.

"I do like a friendly cat," I said, reaching out to stroke its head.

Alice smiled and then made a noise of her own. I was a bit puzzled that she wasn't looking at the cat when she made it, until I saw that another was making its way out of the shadows. This one was smaller and more lithe, and walked right up to the bench. I was, I suppose, still a little befuddled with drink, and when Alice turned to look in a different direction it took me a moment to catch up. A third cat was coming down the canal walk in our direction, followed by another.

When a fifth emerged from the bushes behind our bench, I turned and stared at Alice. She was already looking at me, a smile on her lips like the first one of hers I'd seen. She laughed at the expression on my face and then made her noise again. The cats around us sat to attention, and two more appeared from the other direction, almost trotting in their haste to join the collection. We were now so outnumbered that I felt rather beset.

When the next one appeared I had to ask.

"Alice, what's going on?"

She smiled very softly, like a painting, and leaned her head against my shoulder.

"A long time ago," she said, as if making up a story for a child, "none of this was here. There was no canal, no streets and houses, and all around was trees, and grass." One of the cats round the bench briefly licked one of its paws, and I saw another couple padding out of the darkness toward us. "The big people have changed all of that. They've cut down the trees, and buried the grass, and they've even leveled the ground. There used to be a hill here, a hill that was steep on one side but gentle on the other. They've taken all that away, and made it look like this. It's not that it's so bad. It's just different. The cats still remember the way it was."

It was a nice story, and yet another indication of how we thought in the same way. But it couldn't be true, and it didn't explain all the cats around us. There were now about twenty, and somehow that was too many. Not for me, but for common sense. Where the hell were they all coming from?

"But they didn't have cats in those days," I said nervously. "Not like this. This kind of cat is modern, surely. An import, or crossbreed."

She shook her head. "That's what they say," she said, "and that's what people think. They've always been here. It's just that people haven't always known."

"Alice, what are you talking about?" I was beginning to get really spooked by the number of cats milling softly around. They were still coming, in ones and twos, and now surrounded us for yards around. The stretch of canal was dark apart from soft glints of moonlight off the water, and the lines of the banks and walkway seemed somehow stark, sketched out, as if modeled on a computer screen. They'd been rendered well and looked convincing, but something wasn't quite right about the way they sat together, as if some angle was one degree out.

"A thousand years ago cats used to come to this hill, because it was their meeting place. They would come and discuss their business, and then they would go away. This was their place, and it still is. But they don't mind us."

"Why?"

"Because I love you," she said, and kissed me for the first time.

It was ten minutes before I looked up again. Only two cats were left. I pulled my arm tighter around Alice and thought how simply and unutterably happy I was.

"Was that all true?" I asked, pretending to be a child.

"No," she said, and smiled. "It was just a story." She pushed her nose up against mine and nuzzled, and our heads melted into one.

At two o'clock I realized I was going to have to go home, and we got up and walked slowly back to the road. I waited shivering with her for a minicab, and endured the driver's histrionic sighing as we said good-bye. I stood on the corner and waved until the cab was out of sight, and then turned and walked home.

It wasn't until I turned into our road and saw that the lights were still on in our house that I realized just how real the evening had been. As I walked up the steps the door opened. Nancy stood there in a dressing gown, looking angry and frightened.

"Where the hell have you *been?*" she said. I straightened my shoulders and girded myself up to lie.

I apologized. I told her I'd been out drinking with Howard, lying calmly and with a convincing determination. I didn't even feel bad about it, except in a self-serving, academic sort of way.

Some switch had been finally thrown in my mind, and as we lay in bed afterward I realized that I wasn't in bed with my girlfriend anymore. There was just someone in my bed. When Nancy rolled toward me, her body open in a way that suggested that she might not be thinking of going to sleep, I felt my chest tighten with something that felt like dread. I found a way of suggesting that I might be a bit drunk for anything other than unconsciousness, and she curled up beside me and went to sleep instead. I lay awake for an hour, feeling as if I were lying on a slab of marble in a room open to the sky.

Breakfast the next morning was a festival of leaden politeness. The kitchen seemed very bright, and noise rebounded harshly off the walls. Nancy was in a good mood, but there was nothing I could do except smile tight smiles and talk much louder than usual, waiting for her to go to work.

The next ten days were both dismal and the best days of my life. Alice and I managed to see each other every couple of days, occasionally for an evening but more often just for a cup of coffee. We didn't do any more than talk, and hold hands, and sometimes kiss. Our kisses were brief, a kind of sketching out of the way things could be. Bad starts will always undermine a relationship, for fear it could happen again. So we were restrained and honest with each other, and it was wonderful, but it was also difficult.

Being home was no fun at all. Nancy hadn't changed, but I had, and so I didn't know her anymore. It was like having a complete stranger living in your house, a stranger who was all the worse for reminding you of someone you once loved. The things that were the closest to the way they used to be were the things that made me most irritable, and I found myself avoiding anything that might promote them.

Something had to be done, and it had to be done by me. The problem was gearing myself up to it. Nancy and I had been living together for four years. Most of our friends assumed we'd be engaged before long: I'd already heard a few jokes. We knew each other very well, and that does count for something. As I moved warily around Nancy during those weeks, trying not to seem too close, I was also conscious of how much we had shared together, of how affectionate a part of me still felt toward her. She was a friend, and I cared about her. I didn't want her to be hurt.

My relationship with Nancy wasn't completely straightforward. I wasn't just her boyfriend, I was her brother and father, too. I knew some of the reasons her eating was as bad as it was, things no one else would ever know. I'd talked it through with her, and knew how to live with it, knew how to not make her feel any worse. She needed support, and I was the only person there to give it. Ripping that away when she was already having such a bad time would be very difficult to forgive.

And so things went on, for a little while. I saw Alice when I could, but always in the end I would have to go, and we would part, and each time it felt more and more arbitrary and I found it harder to remember why I should have to leave. I grew terrified of saying her name in my sleep, or of letting something slip, and felt as if I were living my life on stage in front of a predatory audience waiting for a mistake. I'd go out for walks in the evening and walk as slowly up the road as possible, stopping to talk to the cat, stroking her for as long as she liked and walking up and down the pavement with her, doing anything to avoid going back into the house.

I spent most of the second week looking forward to the Saturday. At the beginning of each week Nancy announced she would be going on a team-building day at the weekend. She explained to me what was involved, the chasm of evangelical corporate vacuity into which she and her colleagues were cheerfully leaping. She was talking to me a lot more at the time, wanting to share her life. I tried, but I couldn't really listen. All I could think about was that I was due to be driving up to Cambridge that day, to drop work off at a client's. I'd assumed that I'd be going alone. With Nancy firmly occupied somewhere else, another possibility sprang to mind.

When I saw Alice for coffee that afternoon I asked if she'd like to come. The warmth of her reply helped me through the evenings of the week, and we talked about it every day. The plan was that I'd ring home early evening, when Nancy was back from her day, and say that I'd run into someone up there and wouldn't be back until late. It was a bending of our unspoken doing-things-by-the-book rule, but it had to be done. Alice and I needed a longer period with each other, and I needed to build myself up to what had to be done.

By midevening on Friday I was at fever pitch. I was pacing round the house not settling at anything, so much in my own little world that it took me a while to notice that something was up with Nancy, too.

She was sitting in the living room, going over some papers, but kept glancing angrily out of the window as if expecting to see someone. When I asked her about it, slightly irritably, she denied she was doing it, and then ten minutes later I saw her do it again. I retreated to the kitchen and did something dull to a shelf that I'd been putting off for months. When Nancy stalked in to make some more coffee she saw what I was doing and seemed genuinely touched that I'd finally got around to it. My smile of self-deprecating good-naturedness felt as if it were stretched across the lips of a corpse.

Then she was back out in the lounge again, glaring nervously out of the window, as if fearing imminent invasion from a Martian army. It reminded me of the night I'd seen her standing by the window, which I had found rather spooky. She was looking very flaky that evening, and I'd run out of pity. I simply found it irritating, and hated myself for that.

Eventually, finally, at long last, it was time for bed. Nancy went ahead and I volunteered to close windows and tidy ashtrays. It's funny how you seem most solicitous and endearing when you don't want to be there at all.

What I actually wanted was a few moments to wrap a present I was going to give to Alice. When I heard the bathroom door shut I leapt for the filing cabinet and took out the book. I grabbed tape and paper from a drawer and started wrapping. As I folded I glanced out of the window and saw the cat sitting outside in the road, and smiled to myself. With Alice I'd be able to have a cat of my own, could work with furry company and doze with a warm bundle on my lap. The bathroom door opened again and I paused, ready for instant action. When Nancy's feet had padded safely into the bedroom, I continued wrapping. When it was done I slipped the present in a drawer and took out the card I was going to give with it, already composing in my head the message for the inside.

"Mark?"

I nearly died when I heard Nancy's voice. She was striding through the kitchen toward me, and the card was still lying on my desk. I quickly drew a sheaf of papers toward me and covered it, but only just in time. Heart beating horribly, feeling almost dizzy, I turned to look at her, trying to haul an expression of bland normality across my face.

"What's this?" she demanded, holding her hand up in front of me. It was dark in the room, and I couldn't see at first. Then I saw. It was hair. A dark brown hair.

"It looks like a hair," I said carefully, shuffling papers on the desk.

"I know what it fucking is," she snapped. "It was in the bed. I wonder how it got there."

Jesus Christ, I thought. She knows.

I stared at her with my mouth clamped shut and wavered on the edge of telling the truth, of getting it over with. I thought it would happen some other, calmer, way, but you never know. Perhaps this was the pause into which I had to drop the information that I was in love with someone else.

Then, belatedly, I realized that Alice had never been in the bedroom. Even since the night of the canal she'd only ever been in the living room and the downstairs hall. Maybe the kitchen, but certainly not the bedroom. I blinked at Nancy, confused.

"It's that bloody cat," she shouted, instantly livid in the way that always disarmed and frightened me. "It's been on our fucking bed."

"What cat?"

"The cat who's always fucking outside. Your little *friend*." She sneered violently, face almost unrecognizable. "You've had it in here."

"I haven't. What are you talking about?"

"Don't you deny, don't you—"

Unable to finish, Nancy simply threw herself at me and smashed me across the face. Shocked, I stumbled backward and she whacked me across the chin, and then pummeled her fists against my chest as I struggled to grab hold of her hands. She was trying to say something but it kept breaking up into furious sobs. In the end, before I could catch her hands, she took a step backward and stood very still. She stared at me for a moment, and then turned and walked quickly out of the room.

I spent the night on the sofa and was awake long after the last long, moaning sound had floated out to me from the bedroom. It may sound like selfish evasion, but I really felt I couldn't go to comfort her. The only way I could make her feel better was by lying, so in the end I stayed away.

I had plenty of time to finish writing the card to Alice, but found it difficult to remember exactly what I'd been going to say. In the end I struggled into a shallow, cramped sleep, and when I woke Nancy was already gone for the day.

I felt tired and hollow as I drove to meet Alice in the center of town. I still didn't actually know where she lived, or even her phone number. She hadn't volunteered the information, and I could always contact her via the courier firm. I was content with that until I could enter her life without any skulking around.

I remember very clearly the way she looked, standing on the pavement and watching out for my car. She was wearing a long black woolen skirt and a thick sweater of various chestnut colors. Her hair was backlit by morning light, and when she smiled as I pulled over toward her I had a moment of plunging doubt. I don't have any right to be with her, I thought. I already have someone, and Alice is far and away too wonderful. But she put her arms around me, and kissed my nose, and the feeling went away.

I have never driven so slowly on a motorway as that morning with Alice. I'd put some tapes in the car, music I knew we both liked, but they never made it out of the glove compartment. They simply weren't necessary. I sat in the slow lane and pootled along at sixty miles an hour, and we talked or sat in silence, sometimes glancing across at each other and grinning.

The road cuts through several hills, and when we reached the first cutting we both gasped at once. The embankment was a blaze of poppies, nodding in a gathering wind, and when we'd left them behind I turned to Alice and for the first time said I loved her. She stared at me for a long time, and in the end I had to glance away at the road. When I looked back she was looking straight ahead and smiling, her eyes shining with held-back tears.

My meeting took just under fifteen minutes. I think my client was rather taken aback, but who cares. We spent the rest of the day walking around the shops, picking up books and looking at them, stopping for two cups of tea. As we came laughing out of a record store she slung her arm around my back, and very conscious of what I was doing, I put mine around her shoulders. Though she was tall it felt comfortable, and there it stayed.

By about five I was getting tense, and we pulled into another café to have more tea, and so I could make my phone call. I left Alice sitting at the table waiting to order and went to the other side of the restaurant to use the booth. As I listened to the phone ringing I willed myself to be calm, and turned my back on the room to concentrate on what I was saying.

"Hello?"

When Nancy answered I barely recognized her. Her voice was like that of a querulously frightened old woman who'd not been expecting a call. I nearly put the phone down, but she realized who it was and immediately started crying.

It took me about twenty minutes to calm her even a little. She'd left the team-building at lunchtime, claiming illness. Then she'd gone to Sainsbury's. She had eaten two Sara Lee chocolate cakes, a fudge roll, a packet of cereal, and three packets of biscuits. She'd gone to the bathroom, vomited, and then started again. I think she'd been sick again at least once, but I couldn't really make sense of part of what she said. It was so mixed up with abject apologies to me that the sentences became confused, and I couldn't tell whether she was talking about the night before or about the half-eaten packet of Jell-O she still had in her hand.

Feeling a little frightened and completely unaware of anything outside the cubicle I was standing in, I did what I could to focus her until what she was saying made a little more sense. I gave up trying to say that no apology was needed for last night and in the end just told her everything was all right. She promised to stop eating for a while and to watch television instead. I said I'd be back as soon as I could.

I had to. I loved her. There was nothing else I could do.

When the last of my change was gone I told her to take care and slowly replaced the handset. I stared at the wood paneling in front of me and gradually became aware of the noise from the restaurant on the other side of the glass door behind me. Eventually I turned and looked out.

Alice was sitting at the table, watching the passing throng. She looked beautiful, and strong, and about two thousand miles away.

We drove back to London in silence. Most of the talking was done in the restaurant. It didn't take very long. I said I couldn't leave Nancy in the state that she was in, and Alice nodded once, tightly, and put her cigarettes in her bag.

She said that she'd sort of known, perhaps even before we'd got to Cambridge. I got angry then, and said she couldn't have done, because I hadn't known myself. She got angry back when I said we'd still be friends, and she was in the right, I suppose. It was a stupid thing for me to say.

Awkwardly I asked if she'd be all right, and she said, yes, in the sense that she'd survive. I tried to explain that was the difference, that Nancy might not be able to. She shrugged and said that was the other difference: Nancy would never have to find out if she could. The more we talked the more my head felt it was going to explode, the more my eyes felt as if they could burst with the pain and run in bloody lines down my cold cheeks. In the end she grew businesslike and paid the bill, and we walked slowly back to the car.

Neither of us could bring ourselves to small talk in the car, and for the most part the only sound was that of the wheels upon the road. It was dark by then, and rain began to fall before we'd been on the motorway for very long. When we passed through the first cut in the hillside, I felt the poppies all around us, heads battered down by the falling water. Alice turned to me.

"I did know."

"How," I said, trying not to cry, trying to watch what the cars behind me were doing.

"When you said you loved me, you sounded so unhappy."

I dropped her in town, on the corner where I'd picked her up. She said a few things to help me, to make me feel less bad about what I'd done. Then she walked off around the corner, and I never saw her again.

When I'd parked outside the house I sat for a moment, trying to pull myself together. Nancy would need to see me looking whole and at her disposal. I got out and locked the door, looking around halfheartedly for the cat. It wasn't there.

Nancy opened the door with a shy smile, and I followed her into the kitchen. As I hugged her and told her everything was all right, I gazed blankly over her shoulder around the room. The kitchen was immaculate, no sign left of the afternoon's festivities. The rubbish had been taken out, and something was bubbling on the stove. She'd cooked me dinner.

She didn't eat but sat at the table with me. The chicken was okay, but not up to her usual standard. There was a lot of meat but it was tough, and for once there was a little too much spice. It tasted odd, to be honest. She noticed a look on my face and said she'd gone to a different butcher. We talked a little about her afternoon, but she was feeling much better. She seemed more interested in discussing the way her office reorganization was shaping up.

Afterward she went through into the lounge and turned the television on, and I set about making coffee and washing up, moving woodenly around the kitchen as if on abandoned rails. As Nancy's favorite inanity boomed out from the living room I looked around for a bin bag to shovel the remains of my dinner into, but she'd obviously used them all. Sighing with a complete lack of feeling, I opened the back door and went downstairs to put it directly into the bin.

There were two sacks by the bin, both tied with Nancy's distinctive knot. I undid the nearest and opened it a little. Then, just before I pushed the bones off my plate, something in the bag caught my eye. A patch of darkness amid the garish wrappers of high-calorie comfort foods. An oddly shaped piece of thick fabric, perhaps. I pulled the edge of the bag back a little farther to look, and the light from the kitchen window above fell across the contents of the bag.

The darkness changed to a rich chestnut brown flecked with red, and I saw it wasn't fabric at all.

We moved six months later, after we got engaged. I was glad to move. The flat never felt like home again. Sometimes I go back and stand in that street, remembering the weeks in which I stared out of the window, pointlessly watching the road. I called the courier firm after a couple of days. I was expecting a stonewall and knew it was unlikely they'd give an address. But they denied she'd ever worked there at all.

After a couple of years Nancy and I had our first child, and she'll be eight this November. She has a sister now. Some evenings I'll leave them with their mother and go out for a walk. I'll walk with heavy calm through black streets beneath featureless houses and sometimes go down to the canal. I sit on the bench and close my eyes, and sometimes I think I can see it. Sometimes I think I can feel the way it was when a hill was there and meetings were held in secret.

In the end I always stand up slowly and walk the streets back to the house. The hill has gone and things have changed, and it's not like that anymore. No matter how long I sit and wait, the cats will never come.

THE LADIES OF GRACE ADIEU

Susanna Clarke

British author Susanna Clarke is a bright new light in the fantasy field—and a name to watch. The unusual, thoroughly magical story that follows is her first fiction sale; it is not difficult to predict that many more will be forthcoming. She has contributed a story to Neil Gaiman's Sandman collection (also highly recommended); she has a story forthcoming in the adult fairytale anthology *Black Swan, White Raven*; and she is working on a novel about the magician Mr. Norrell and his pupil, Jonathan Strange. "The Ladies of Grace Adieu" comes from Volume I of Patrick Nielsen Hayden's new speculative fiction anthology series, *Starlight*. Clarke lives in Cambridge, England, where she is an editor of cookbooks.

—T. W.

Above all remember this: that magic belongs as much to the heart as to the head and everything which is done, should be done from love or joy or righteous anger.

And if we honor this principle we shall discover that our magic is much greater than all the sum of all the spells that were ever taught. Then magic is to us as flight is to the birds, because then our magic comes from the dark and dreaming heart, just as the flight of a bird comes form the heart. And we will feel the same joy in performing that magic that the bird feels as it casts itself into the void and we will know that magic is part of what a man is, just as flight is part of what a bird is.

This understanding is a gift to us from the Raven King, the dear king of all magicians, who stands between England and the Other Lands, between all wild creatures and the world of men.

—*From the Book of the Lady Catherine of Winchester*
(late fifteenth century),
translated from the Latin by Jane Tobias (1775–1819)

When Mrs. Field died, her grieving widower looked around him and discovered that the world seemed quite as full of pretty, young women as it had been in his youth. It further occurred to him that he was just as rich as ever and that, though his home already contained one pretty, young woman (his niece and ward, Cassandra Parbringer), he did not believe that another would go amiss. He did not think that he was at all changed from what he had been and Cassandra was entirely of his opinion, for (she thought to herself) I am sure, sir, that you were every bit as tedious at twenty-one as you are at forty-nine. So Mr. Field married again. The lady was pretty and clever and only a year older than Cassandra, but, in her defense, we may say that she had no money and must either marry Mr. Field or go and be a teacher in a school. The second Mrs. Field and Cassandra were pleased with each other and soon became very fond of each other. Indeed the sad truth was that they were a great deal fonder of each other than either was of Mr. Field. There was another lady who was their friend (her name was Miss Tobias) and the three were often seen walking together near the village where they lived—Grace Adieu in Gloucestershire.

Cassandra Parbringer at twenty was considered an ideal of a certain type of beauty to which some gentlemen are particularly partial. A white skin was agreeably tinged with pink. Light blue eyes harmonized very prettily with silvery-gold curls and the whole was a picture in which womanliness and childishness were sweetly combined. Mr. Field, a gentleman not remarkable for his powers of observation, confidently supposed her to have a character childishly naive and full of pleasant, feminine submission in keeping with her face.

Her prospects seemed at this time rather better than Mrs. Field's had been. The people of Grace Adieu had long since settled it amongst themselves that Cassandra should marry the Rector, Mr. Henry Woodhope, and Mr. Woodhope himself did not seem at all averse to the idea.

"Mr. Woodhope likes you, Cassandra, I think," said Mrs. Field.

"Does he?"

Miss Tobias (who was also in the room) said, "Miss Parbringer is wise and keeps her opinion of Mr. Woodhope to herself."

"Oh," cried Cassandra, "you may know it if you wish. Mr. Woodhope is Mr. Field stretched out a little to become more thin and tall. He is younger and therefore more disposed to be agreeable, and his wits are rather sharper. But when all is said and done he is only Mr. Field come again."

"Why then do you give him encouragement?" asked Mrs. Field.

"Because I suppose that I must marry someone and Mr. Woodhope has this to recommend him—that he lives in Grace Adieu and that in marrying him I need never be parted from my dear Mrs. Field."

"It is a very poor ambition to wish to marry a Mr. Field of any sort," sighed Mrs. Field. "Have you nothing better to wish for?"

Cassandra considered. "I have always had a great desire to visit Yorkshire," she said. "I imagine it to be just like the novels of Mrs. Radcliffe."

"It is exactly like everywhere else," said Miss Tobias.

"Oh, Miss Tobias," said Cassandra, "how can you say so? If magic does not linger in Yorkshire, where may we find it still? 'Upon the moors, beneath the stars, With the Kings wild Company.' *That* is my idea of Yorkshire."

"But," said Miss Tobias, "a great deal of time has passed since the King's wild Company was last there and in the meantime Yorkshiremen have acquired tollgates and newspapers and stagecoaches and circulating libraries and everything most modern and commonplace."

Cassandra sniffed. "You disappoint me," she said.

Miss Tobias was governess to two little girls at a great house in the village, called Winter's Realm. The parents of these children were dead, and the people of Grace Adieu were fond of telling each other that it was no house for children, being too vast and gloomy and full of odd-shaped rooms and strange carvings. The younger child was indeed often fearful and often plagued with nightmares. She seemed, poor little thing, to believe herself haunted by owls. There was nothing in the world she feared so much as owls. No one else had ever seen the owls, but the house was old and full of cracks and holes to let them in and full of fat mice to tempt them, so perhaps it were true. The governess was not much liked in the village: she was too tall, too fond of books, too grave, and—a curious thing—never smiled unless there was some thing to smile at. Yet Miss Ursula and Miss Flora were very prettily behaved children and seemed greatly attached to Miss Tobias.

Despite their future greatness as heiresses, in the article of relations the children were as poor as church mice. Their only guardian was a cousin of their dead mother. In all the long years of their orphanhood this gentleman had only visited them twice and once had written them a very short letter at Christmas. But, because Captain Winbright wore a redcoat and was an officer in the ———shires, all his absences and silences were forgiven and Miss Ursula and Miss Flora (though only eight and four years old) had begun to show all the weakness of their sex by preferring him to all the rest of their acquaintance.

It was said that the great-grandfather of these children had studied magic and had left behind him a library. Miss Tobias was often in the library and what she did there no one knew. Of late her two friends, Mrs. Field and Miss Parbringer, had also been at the house a great deal. But it was generally supposed that they were visiting the children. For ladies (as every one knows) do not study magic. Magicians themselves are another matter—ladies (as every one knows) are wild to see magicians. (How else to explain the great popularity of Mr. Norrell in all the fashionable drawing rooms of London? Mr. Norrell is almost as famous for his insignificant face and long silences as he is for his incomparable magicianship and Mr. Norrell's pupil, Mr. Strange, with his almost handsome face and lively conversation is welcome where ever he goes.) This then, we will suppose, must explain a question which Cassandra Parbringer put to Miss Tobias on a day in September, a very fine day on the cusp of summer and autumn.

"And have you read Mr. Strange's piece in *The Review?* What is your opinion of it?"

"I thought Mr. Strange expressed himself with his customary clarity. Anyone, whether or not they understand any thing of the theory and practice of magic, might understand him. He was witty and sly, as he generally is. It was altogether an admirable piece of writing. He is a clever man, I think."

"You speak exactly like a governess."

"Is that so surprising?"

"But I did not wish to hear your opinion as a governess, I wished to hear your opinion as a . . . never mind. What did you think of the ideas?"

"I did not agree with any of them."

"Ah, *that* was what I wished to hear."

"Modern magicians," said Mrs. Field, "seem to devote more of their energies to belittling magic than to doing any. We are constantly hearing how certain sorts of magic are too perilous for men to attempt (although they appear in all the old stories). Or they cannot be attempted any more because the prescription is lost. Or it never existed. And, as for the Otherlanders, Mr. Norrell and Mr. Strange do not seem to know if there are such persons in the world. Nor do they appear to care very much, for, even if they do exist, then it seems we have no business talking to them. And the Raven King, we learn, was only a dream of fevered medieval brains, addled with too much magic."

"Mr. Strange and Mr. Norrell mean to make magic as commonplace as their own dull persons," said Cassandra. "They deny the King for fear that comparison with his great magic would reveal the poverty of their own."

Mrs. Field laughed. "Cassandra," she said, "does not know how to leave off abusing Mr. Strange."

Then, from the particular sins of the great Mr. Strange and the even greater Mr. Norrell, they were led to talk of the viciousness of men in general and from there, by a natural progression, to a discussion of whether Cassandra should marry Mr. Woodhope.

While the ladies of Grace Adieu were talking Mr. Jonathan Strange (the magician and second phenomenon of the Age) was seated in the library of Mr. Gilbert Norrell (the magician and first phenomenon of the Age). Mr. Strange was informing Mr. Norrell that he intended to be absent from London for some weeks. "I hope, sir, that it will cause you no inconvenience. The next article for the *Edinburgh Magazine* is done—unless, sir, you wish to make changes (which I think you may very well do without my assistance)."

Mr. Norrell enquired with a frown where Mr. Strange was going, for, as was well known in London, the elder magician—a quiet, dry little man—did not like to be without the younger for even so much as a day, or half a day. He did not even like to spare Mr. Strange to speak to other people.

"I am going to Gloucestershire, sir. I have promised Mrs. Strange that I will take her to visit her brother, who is Rector of a village there. You have heard me speak of Mr. Henry Woodhope, I think?"

The next day was rainy in Grace Adieu, and Miss Tobias was unable to leave Winter's Realm. She passed the day with the children, teaching them Latin ("which I see no occasion to omit simply on account of your sex. One day you may have a use for it,") and in telling them stories of Thomas of Dundale's captivity in the Other Lands and how he became the first human servant of the Raven King.

When the second day was fine and dry, Miss Tobias took the opportunity to slip away for half an hour to visit Mrs. Field, leaving the children in the care of the nursery maid. It so happened that Mr. Field had gone to Cheltenham (a rare occurrence, for, as Mrs. Field remarked, there never was a man so addicted to home. "I fear we make it far too comfortable for him," she said) and so Miss Tobias took advantage of his absence to make a visit of a rather longer duration than usual. (At the time there seemed no harm in it.)

On her way back to Winter's Realm she passed the top of Grace and Angels Lane, where the church stood and, next to it, the Rectory. A very smart barouche was just turning from the high road into the lane. This in itself was interesting enough, for Miss Tobias did not recognize the carriage or its occupants, but what made it more extraordinary still was that it was driven with great confidence and spirit by a lady. At her side, upon the barouche box, a gentleman sat, hands in pockets, legs crossed, greatly at his ease. His air was rather striking. "He is not exactly handsome," thought Miss Tobias, "his nose is too long. Yet he has that arrogant air that handsome men have."

It seemed to be a day for visitors. In the yard of Winter's Realm was a gig and two high-spirited horses. Davey, the coachman and a stable boy were attending to them, watched by a thin, dark man—a very slovenly fellow (somebody's servant)—who was leaning against the wall of the kitchen garden to catch the sun and smoking a pipe. His shirt was undone at the front and as Miss Tobias passed, he slowly scratched his bare chest with a long, dark finger and smiled at her.

As long as Miss Tobias had known the house, the great hall had always been the same: full of nothing but silence and shadows and dustmotes turning in great slanting beams of daylight, but today there were echoes of loud voices and music and high, excited laughter. She opened the door to the dining parlor. The table was laid with the best glasses, the best silver and the best dinner service. A meal had been prepared and put upon the table, but then, apparently, forgotten. Travelling trunks and boxes had been brought in and clothes pulled out and then abandoned; men and women's clothing were tumbled together quite promiscuously over the floor. A man in an officer's redcoat was seated on a chair with Miss Ursula on his knee. He was holding a glass of wine, which he put to her lips and then, as she tried to drink, he took the glass away. He was laughing and the child was laughing. Indeed, from her flushed face and excited air Miss Tobias could not be entirely sure that she had not already drunk of the contents. In the middle of the room another man (a very handsome man), also in uniform, was standing among all the clothes and trinkets and laughing with them. The younger child, Miss Flora, stood on one side, watching them all with great, wondering eyes. Miss Tobias went immediately to her and took her hand. In the gloom at the back of the dining parlor a young woman was seated at the pianoforte, playing an Italian song very badly. Perhaps she knew that it was bad, for she seemed very reluctant to play at all. The song was full of long pauses; she sighed often and she did not look happy. Then, quite suddenly, she stopped.

The handsome man in the middle of the room turned to her instantly. "Go on, go on," he cried, "we are all attending, I promise you. It is," and here he turned back to the other man and winked at him, "delightful. We are going to teach country dances to my little cousins. Fred is the best dancing master in the world. So you must play, you know."

Wearily the young lady began again.

The seated man, whose name it seemed was Fred, happened at this moment to notice Miss Tobias. He smiled pleasantly at her and begged her pardon.

"Oh," cried the handsome man, "Miss Tobias will forgive us, Fred. Miss Tobias and I are old friends."

"Good afternoon, Captain Winbright," said Miss Tobias.

By now Mr. and Mrs. Strange were comfortably seated in Mr. Woodhope's pleasant drawing room. Mrs. Strange had been shown all over Mr. Woodhope's Rectory and had spoken to the housekeeper and the cook and the dairymaid and the other maid and the stableman and the gardener and the gardener's boy. Mr. Woodhope had seemed most anxious to have a woman's opinion on everything and would scarcely allow Mrs. Strange leave to sit down or take food or drink until she had approved the house, the servants and all the housekeeping arrangements. So, like a good, kind sister, she had looked at it all and smiled upon all the servants and racked her brains for easy questions to ask them and then declared herself delighted.

"And I promise you, Henry," she said with a smile, "that Miss Parbringer will be equally pleased."

"He is blushing," said Jonathan Strange, raising his eyes from his newspaper. "We have come, Henry, with the sole purpose of seeing Miss Parbringer (of whom you write so much) and when we have seen her, we will go away again."

"Indeed? Well, I hope to invite Mrs. Field and her niece to meet you at the earliest opportunity."

"Oh, there is no need to trouble yourself," said Strange, "for we have brought telescopes. We will stand at bedroom windows and spy her out, as she goes about the village."

Strange did indeed get up and go to the window as he spoke. "Henry," he said, "I like your church exceedingly. I like that little wall that goes around the building and the trees, and holds them all in tight. It makes the place look like a ship. If you ever get a good strong wind then church and trees will all sail off together to another place entirely."

"Strange," said Henry Woodhope, "you are quite as ridiculous as ever."

"Do not mind him, Henry," said Arabella Strange, "he has the mind of a magician. They are all a little mad."

"Except Norrell," said Strange.

"Strange, I would ask you, as a friend, to do no magic while you are here. We are a very quiet village."

"My dear Henry," said Strange, "I am not a street conjuror with a booth and a yellow curtain. I do not intend to set up in a corner of the churchyard to catch trade. These days Admirals and Rear Admirals and Vice Admirals and all His Majesty's Ministers send me respectful letters requesting my services and (what is much more) pay me well for them. I very much doubt if there is any one in Grace Adieu who could afford me."

"What room is this?" asked Captain Winbright.

"This was old Mr. Enderwhild's bedroom, sir," said Miss Tobias.

"The magician?"

"The magician."

"And where did he keep all his hoard, Miss Tobias? You have been here long enough to winkle it out. There are sovereigns, I dare say, hidden away in all sorts of odd holes and corners."

"I never heard so, sir."

"Come, Miss Tobias, what do old men learn magic for, except to find each other's piles of gold? What else is magic good for?" A thought seemed to trouble him. "They show no sign of inheriting the family genius, do they? The children, I mean. No, of course. Who ever heard of women doing magic?"

"There have been two female magicians, sir. Both highly regarded. The Lady Catherine of Winchester, who taught Martin Pale, and Gregory Absalom's daughter, Maria, who was mistress of the Shadow House for more than a century."

He did not seem greatly interested. "Show me some other rooms," he said. They walked down another echoing corridor, which, like much of the great, dark house, had fallen into the possession of mice and spiders.

"Are my cousins healthy children?"

"Yes, sir."

He was silent and then he said, "Well, of course, it may not last. There are so many childish illnesses, Miss Tobias. I myself, when only six or seven, almost died of the red spot. Have these children had the red spot?"

"No, sir."

"Indeed? Our grandparents understood these things better, I think. They would not permit themselves to get overfond of children until they had got past all childhood's trials and maladies. It is a good rule. Do not get overfond of children."

He caught her eye and reddened. Then laughed. "Why, it is only a joke. How solemn you look. Ah, Miss Tobias, I see how it is. You have borne all the responsibility for this house and for my cousins, my rich little cousins, for far too long. Women should not have to bear such burdens alone. Their pretty white shoulders were not made for it. But, see, I am come to help you now. And Fred. Fred has a great mind to be a cousin too. Fred is very fond of children."

"And the lady, Captain Winbright? Will she stay and be another cousin with you and the other gentleman?"

He smiled confidingly at her. His eyes seemed such a bright, laughing blue and his smile so open and unaffected, that it took a woman of Miss Tobias's great composure not to smile with him.

"Between ourselves she has been a little ill-used by a brother officer in the ———shires. But I am such a soft-hearted fellow—the sight of a woman's tears can move me to almost any thing."

So said Captain Winbright in the corridor, but when they entered the dining parlor again, the sight of a woman's tears (for the young lady was crying at that moment) moved him only to be rude to her. Upon her saying his name, gently and somewhat apprehensively, he turned upon her and cried, "Oh, why do you not go back to Brighton? You could you know, very easily. That would be the best thing for you."

"Reigate," she said gently.

He looked at her much irritated. "Aye, Reigate," he said.

She had a sweet, timorous face, great dark eyes and a little rosebud mouth, forever trembling on the brink of tears. But it was the kind of beauty that soon evaporates when anything at all in the nature of suffering comes near it and she had, poor thing, been very unhappy of late. She reminded Miss Tobias of a child's rag doll, pretty enough at the beginning, but very sad and pitiful once its rag stuffing was gone. She looked up at Miss Tobias. "I never thought . . ." she said and lapsed into tears.

Miss Tobias was silent a moment. "Well," she said at last, "perhaps you were not brought up to it."

That evening Mr. Field fell asleep in the parlor again. This had happened to him rather often recently.

It happened like this. The servant came into the room with a note for Mrs. Field and she began to read it. Then, as his wife read, Mr. Field began to feel (as he expressed it to himself) "all cobwebby" with sleep. After a moment or two it seemed to him that he woke up and the evening continued in its normal course, with Cassandra and Mrs. Field sitting one on either side of the fire. Indeed Mr. Field spent a very pleasant evening—the kind of evening he loved to spend, attended to by the two ladies. That it was only the dream of such an evening (for the poor, silly man was indeed asleep) did not in any way detract from his enjoyment of it.

While he slept, Mrs. Field and Cassandra were hurrying along the lane to Winter's Realm.

In the Rectory Henry Woodhope and Mrs. Strange had said their goodnights but Mr. Strange proposed to continue reading a while. His book was a *Life of Martin Pale* by Thaddeus Hickman. He had reached Chapter 26 where Hickman discussed some theories, which he attributed to Martin Pale, that sometimes magicians, in times of great need, might find themselves capable of much greater acts of magic than they had ever learnt or even heard of before.

"Oh," said Strange with much irritation, "this is the most complete stuff and nonsense."

"Goodnight, Jonathan," said Arabella and kissed him, just above his frown.

"Yes, yes," he muttered, not raising his eyes from the book.

"And the young woman," whispered Mrs. Field, "who is she?"

Miss Tobias raised an eyebrow and said, "She says that she is Mrs. Winbright. But Captain Winbright says that she is not. I had not supposed it to be a point capable of so wide an interpretation."

"And if anything were to happen . . . to the children, I mean," whispered Mrs. Field, "then Captain Winbright might benefit in some way?"

"Oh, he would certainly be a very rich man and whatever he has come here to escape—whether it be debts or scandal—would presumably hold no more fears for him."

The three ladies were in the children's bedroom. Miss Tobias sat somewhere in the dark, wrapped in a shawl. Two candles bloomed in the vast dark room, one near to the children's bed and the other upon a little rickety table by the door, so that anyone entering the room would instantly be seen. Somewhere in the house, at the end of a great many long, dark corridors, could be heard the sound of a man singing and another laughing.

From the bed Miss Flora anxiously enquired if there were any owls in the room.

Miss Tobias assured her there were none.

"Yet I think they may still come," said Miss Flora in a fright, "if you do not stay."

Miss Tobias said that they would stay for a while. "Be quiet now," she said, "and Miss Parbringer will tell you a story, if you ask her."

"What story shall I tell you?" asked Cassandra.

"A story of the Raven King," said Miss Ursula.

"Very well," said Cassandra.

This then is the story which Cassandra told the children.

"Before the Raven King was a king at all, but only a Raven Child, he lived in a very wonderful house with his uncle and his aunt. (These were not really his relations at all, but only a kind gentleman and lady who had taken him to live with them.) One day his uncle, who was reading books of magic in his great library, sent for the Raven Child and enquired politely how he did. The Raven Child replied that he did very well.

" 'Hmmph, well,' said Uncle Auberon, 'as I am your guardian and protector, little human child, I had better make sure of it. Show me the dreams you had last night.' So the Raven Child took out his dreams and Uncle Auberon made a space for them on the library table. There were a hundred odd things on that table; books on unnatural history; a map showing the relative positions of Masculine Duplicity and Feminine Integrity (and how to get from one to the other) and a set of beautiful brass instruments in a mahogany box, all very cunningly contrived to measure Ambition and Jealousy, Love and Self-sacrifice, Loyalty to the State and Dreams of Regicide and many other Vices and Virtues which it might be useful to know about. All these things Uncle Auberon put on the floor, for he was not a very tidy person and people were forever scolding him about it. Then Uncle Auberon spread the Raven Child's dreams out on the table and peered at them through little wire spectacles.

" 'Why,' cried Uncle Auberon, 'here is a dream of a tall black tower in a dark wood in the snow. The tower is all in ruins, like broken teeth. Black, ragged birds fly round and round and you are inside that tower and cannot get out. Little human child, when you had this terrible dream, was you not afraid?'

" 'No, Uncle,' said the Raven Child, 'last night I dreamt of the tower where I was born and of the ravens who brought me water to drink when I was too young even to crawl. Why should I be afraid?'

"So Uncle Auberon looked at the next dream and when he saw it he cried out loud. 'But here is a dream of cruel eyes a-glittering and wicked jaws a-slavering. Little human child, when you had this terrible dream, was you not afraid?'

" 'No, Uncle,' said the Raven Child, 'last night I dreamt of the wolves who suckled me and who lay down beside me and kept me warm when I was too young even to crawl. Why should I be afraid?'

"So Uncle Auberon looked at the next dream and when he saw it he shivered and said, "But this is a dream of a dark lake in a sad and rainy twilight. The woods are monstrous silent and a ghostly boat sails upon the water. The boatman is as thin and twisted as a hedge root and his face is all in shadow. Little human child, when you had this terrible dream, was you not afraid?'

"Then the Raven Child banged his fist upon the table in his exasperation and stamped his foot upon the floor. 'Uncle Auberon!' he exclaimed, 'that is the fairy boat and the fairy boatman which you and Aunt Titania yourselves sent to fetch me and bring me to your house. Why should I be afraid?'

" 'Well!' said a third person, who had not spoken before, 'how the child boasts of his courage!' The person who spoke was Uncle Auberon's servant, who had been sitting high upon a shelf, disguised (until this moment) as a bust of Mr. William Shakespeare. Uncle Auberon was quite startled by his sudden appearance, but the Raven Child had always known he was there.

"Uncle Auberon's servant peered down from his high shelf at the Raven Child and the Raven Child looked up at him. 'There are all sorts of things in heaven and earth,' said Uncle Auberon's servant, 'that yearn to do you harm. There is fire that wants to burn you. There are swords that long to pierce you through and through and ropes that mean to bind you hard. There are a thousand, thousand things that you have never yet dreamt of: creatures that can steal your sleep from you, year after year, until you scarcely know yourself, and men yet unborn who will curse you and scheme against you. Little human child, the time has come to be afraid.'

"But the Raven Child said, 'Robin Goodfellow, I knew all along that it was you that sent me those dreams. But I am a human child and therefore cleverer than you and when those wicked creatures come to do me harm I shall be cleverer than them. I am a human child and all the vast stony, rainy English earth belongs to me. I am an English child and all the wide gray English air, full of black wings beating and gray ghosts of rain sighing, belongs to me. This being so, Robin Goodfellow, tell me, why should I be afraid?' Then the Raven Child shook his head of raven hair and disappeared.

"Mr. Goodfellow glanced a little nervously at Uncle Auberon to see if he were at all displeased that Mr. Goodfellow had spoken out so boldly to the human foster child, but Uncle Auberon (who was quite an old gentleman) had stopped listening to them both a while ago and had wandered off to resume his search for a book. It contained a spell for turning Members of Parliament into useful members of society and now, just when Uncle Auberon thought he had a use for it, he could not find it (though he had had it in his hand not a hundred years before). So Mr. Goodfellow said nothing but quietly turned himself back into William Shakespeare."

In the Rectory Mr. Strange was still reading. He had reached Chapter 42 where Hickman relates how Maria Absalom defeated her enemies by showing them the true reflections of their souls in the mirrors of the Shadow House and how the ugly sights which they saw there (and knew in their hearts to be true) so dismayed them that they could oppose her no more.

There was, upon the back of Mr. Strange's neck, a particularly tender spot and all his friends had heard him tell how, when ever there was any magic going on, it would begin to prickle and to itch. Without knowing that he did so, he now began to rub the place.

So many dark corridors, thought Cassandra, how lucky it is that I know my way about them, for many people I think would soon be lost. Poor souls, they would soon take fright because the way is so long, but I *know* that I am now very near to the great staircase and will soon be able to slip out of the house and into the garden.

It had been decided that Mrs. Field should stay and watch the children for the remainder of the night and so Cassandra was making her way back to Mr. Field's house quite alone.

Except (she thought) I do not believe that that tall, moonshiny window should be *there*. It would suit me much better if it were behind me. Or perhaps on my left. For I am sure it was not there when I came in. Oh, I am lost! How very . . . And now the voices of those two wretches of men come echoing down this dark passageway and they are most manifestly drunk and do not know me. And I am here where I have no right to be. (Cassandra pulled her shawl closer round her.) "And yet," she murmured, "why should I be afraid?"

"Damn this house!" cried Winbright. "It is nothing but horrid black corridors. What do you see, Fred?"

"Only an owl. A pretty white owl. What the devil is it doing inside the house?"

"Fred," cried Winbright, slumping against the wall and sliding down a little, "fetch me my pistol, like a good fellow."

"At once, Captain!" cried Fred. He saluted Captain Winbright and then promptly forgot all about it.

Captain Winbright smiled. "And here," he said, "is Miss Tobias, running to meet us."

"Sir," said Miss Tobias, appearing suddenly out of the darkness, "what are you doing?"

"There is a damned owl in the house. We are going to shoot it."

Miss Tobias looked round at the owl, shifting in the shadows, and then said hurriedly, "Well, you are very free from superstition, I must say. You might both set up as the publishers of an atheist encyclopedia tomorrow. I applaud your boldness, but I do not share it."

The two gentlemen looked at her.

"Did you never hear that owls are the possessions of the Raven King?" she asked.

"Do not frighten me, Miss Tobias," said Captain Winbright, "you will make me think I see tall crowns of raven feathers in the dark. This is certainly the house for it. Damn her, Fred. She behaves as if she were my governess as well."

"Is she at all like your governess?" asked Fred.

"I cannot tell. I had so many. They all left me. You would not have left me, would you, Miss Tobias?"

"I do not know, sir."

"Fred," said Captain Winbright, "now there are two owls. Two pretty little owls. You are like Minerva, Miss Tobias, so tall and wise, and disapproving of a fellow. Minerva with two owls. Your name is Jane, is it not?"

"My name, sir, is Miss Tobias."

Winbright stared into the darkness and shivered. "What is the game they play in Yorkshire, Fred? When they send children alone into the dark to summon the Raven King. What are those words they say?"

Fred sighed and shook his head. "It has to do with hearts being eaten," he said, "that is all I recall."

"How they stare at us, Fred," said Winbright. "They are very impertinent owls. I had always thought they were such shy little creatures."

"They do not like us," said Fred sadly.

"They like you better, Jane. Why, one is upon your shoulder now. Are you not afraid?"

"No, sir."

"Those feathers," said Fred, "those soft feathers between the wing and the body dance like flames when they swoop. If I were a mouse I would think the flames of Hell had come to swallow me up."

"Indeed," murmured Winbright, and both men watched the owls glide in and out of the gloom. Then suddenly one of the owls cried out—a hideous screech to freeze the blood.

Miss Tobias looked down and crossed her hands—the very picture of a modest governess. "They do that, you know," she said, "to petrify their prey with fear; to turn it, as it were, to stone. That is the cruel, wild magic of owls."

But no one answered her, for there was no one in the corridor but herself and the owls (each with something in its beak). "How hungry you are, dearest," said Miss Tobias approvingly. "One, two, three swallows and the dish goes down."

About midnight Mr. Strange's book appeared to him so dull and the night so sweet that he left the house and went out into the apple orchard. There was no wall to this orchard but only a grassy bank. Mr. Strange lay down beneath a pear tree and, though he had intended to think about magic, he very soon fell asleep.

A little later he heard (or dreamt that he heard) the sound of laughter and of feminine voices. Looking up, he saw three ladies in pale gowns walking (almost dancing) upon the bank above him. The stars surrounded them; the night wind took their gowns and blew them about. They held out their arms to the wind (they seemed indeed to be dancing). Mr. Strange stretched himself and sighed with pleasure. He assumed (not unreasonably) that he was still dreaming.

But the ladies stopped and stared down into the grass.

"What is it?" asked Miss Tobias.

Cassandra peered into the darkness. "It is a man," she said with great authority.

"Gracious heaven," said Mrs. Field, "what kind of man?"

"The usual kind, I should say," said Cassandra.

"I meant, Cassandra," said the other, "what degree, what station of man?"

Jonathan Strange got to his feet, perplexed, brushing straw from his clothes.

"Ladies," he said, "forgive me. I thought that I had woken in the Raven King's Otherlands. I thought that you were Titania's ladies come to meet me."

The ladies were silent. And then: "Well!" said Mrs. Field, "What a speech!"

"I beg your pardon, madam. I meant only that it is a beautiful night (as I am sure you will agree) and I have been thinking for some time that it is (in the most critical and technical sense) a magical night and I thought perhaps that you were the magic that was meant to happen."

"Oh," cried Cassandra, "they are all full of nonsense. Do not listen to him, my dear Mrs. Field. Miss Tobias, let us walk on." But she looked at him curiously and said, "You? What do *you* know of magic?"

"A little, madam."

"Well, sir," she said, "I will give you a piece of good advice. You will never grow proficient in the art as long as you continue with your outmoded notions of Raven Kings and Otherlanders. Have you not heard? They have all been done away with by Mr. Strange and Mr. Norrell."

Mr. Strange thanked her for the advice.

"There is much more that we could teach you . . . ," she said.

"So it would seem," said Strange, crossing his arms.

". . . only that we have neither the time nor the inclination."

"That is a pity," said Strange. "Are you sure, madam, that you will not reconsider? My last master found me to be a most apt pupil, very quick to grasp the principles of any subject."

"What was the name of your last master?" asked Miss Tobias.

"Norrell," said Strange softly.

Another short silence ensued.

"You are the London magician," said Cassandra.

"No, indeed," cried Strange, stung. "I am the Shropshire magician and Mr. Norrell is the Yorkshire magician. We neither of us own London as our home. We are countrymen both. We have that, at least, in common."

"You seem, sir, to be of a somewhat inconsistent, somewhat contradictory character," said Miss Tobias.

"Indeed, madam, other people have remarked upon it. And now, ladies, since we are sure to meet again—and that quite soon—I will wish you all a goodnight. Miss Parbringer, I will give you a piece of advice in return for yours (for I am certain that it was given in good faith). Magic, madam, is like wine and, if you are not used to it, it will make you drunk. A successful spell is as potent a loosener of tongues as a bottle of good claret and you will find the morning after that you have said things you now regret."

With that he bowed and walked back through the orchard into the house.

"A magician in Grace Adieu," said Miss Tobias thoughtfully, "and at such a time. Well, let us not be disconcerted. We will see what tomorrow brings."

What tomorrow brought was a courteous note from Mr. Woodhope, expressing his hopes that the ladies of Grace Adieu would do his sister the honor of meeting her at the Rectory that afternoon. On this occasion the invitation included Miss Tobias, although, in general, she did not visit in the village (and was no great favorite with Mr. Woodhope).

Despite the misgivings which all the ladies felt (and which Mrs. Field had several times spoken out loud), Mr. Strange met them with great good manners and a bow for each and he gave no hint to any one that this was not the first time he had seen them.

The talk was at first of the commonest sort and, to the ladies of Grace Adieu who did not know him, Mr. Strange seemed of an easy and sociable character, so it was a trifle unsettling to hear Arabella Strange ask him why he was so silent today. Mr. Strange replied that he was a little tired.

"Oh," said Mrs. Strange to Mrs. Field, "he has been up all night reading books of magical history. It is a bad habit that all magicians get into and it is that, as much as anything, which weakens their wits in the end." She smiled at her husband as if expecting him to say some clever or impertinent thing in return. But he only continued to look at the three ladies of Grace Adieu.

Halfway through their visit Mr. Woodhope rose and, speaking his great regret and looking at Miss Parbringer, begged that they would excuse him—he had parish business to attend. He was very anxious that Mr. Strange should go with him, so much so that Strange had no alternative but to oblige him. This left the ladies alone.

The conversation turned to the articles Mr. Strange had published in the quarterly reviews and, in particular, those passages where he proved that there could never have been such a person as the Raven King.

"Mrs. Strange," said Cassandra, "you must agree with me—those are most extraordinary opinions for a magician, when even our common historians write the King's dates in their history books—four or five times the span of a common life."

Arabella frowned. "Mr. Strange cannot always write exactly what he pleases. Much of it, you know, comes from Mr. Norrell. Mr. Norrell has studied magic for many years more than any other gentleman in England, and certainly with much greater profit. His opinion must carry great weight with anyone who cares about English magic."

"I see," said Cassandra, "you mean that Mr. Strange writes things which he does not entirely believe, because Mr. Norrell tells him to. If I were a man (and, what is much more, a magician) I should not do any thing, write any thing, if I did not like it."

"Miss Parbringer," murmured Miss Tobias, reprovingly.

"Oh, Mrs. Strange knows I mean no offense," cried Cassandra, "but I must say what I think and upon this topic of all things."

Arabella Strange smiled. "The situation," she said, "is not exactly as you suppose. Mr. Strange has studied for a number of years with Mr. Norrell in London, and Mr. Norrell swore at the beginning that he would not take a pupil, and so it was considered a great honor when he consented to take Jonathan. And then, you know, there are only two true magicians in England and England is at war. If those two magicians quarrel, what follows? What greater comfort could we offer the French than this?"

The ladies took their tea together and the only slight incident to disturb the remainder of the visit was a fit of coughing which seized first Cassandra, and then Mrs. Field. For several moments Mrs. Strange was quite concerned about them.

When Henry Woodhope and Strange returned the ladies were gone. The maid and Mrs. Strange were standing in the passageway. Each was holding a little white linen cloath. The maid was exclaiming loudly about something or other and it was a moment before Jonathan Strange could make himself heard.

"What is it?" he asked.

"We have found some bones," said his wife, with a puzzled air. "Small, white bones, it would seem, of some delicate little creatures, and two little gray skins like empty pods. Come, sir, you are the magician, explain it to us."

"They are mouse bones. And mouse skins too. It is owls that do that. See," said Strange, "the skins are turned quite inside out. Curious, is it not?"

Mrs. Strange was not greatly impressed with this as an explanation. "So I dare say," she said. "But what seems to me far more miraculous is that we found these bones in the cloths which Miss Parbringer and Mrs. Field had to wipe their fingers and their mouths. Jonathan, I hope you are not suggesting that these ladies have been eating mice?"

The weather continued very fine. Mr. Woodhope drove his sister, Mr. and Mrs. Field and their niece to ———Hill to see the views and to drink and eat by a pretty, hanging wood. Mr. Strange rode behind. Once again he watched all the party carefully and once again Mrs. Strange told him that he was in a grave, odd mood and not at all like himself.

On other days Mr. Strange rode out by himself and talked to farmers and innkeepers on the highways all around. Mr. Woodhope explained this behavior by saying that Strange had always been very eccentric and that now he had become so great and full of London importance, Mr. Woodhope supposed he had grown even more so.

One day (it was the last day of Mr. and Mrs. Strange's visit to their brother) Mrs. Field, Miss Tobias and Cassandra were out walking on the high, empty hills above Grace Adieu. A sunlit wind bent all the long grasses. Light and shade followed each other so swiftly that it was as if great doors were opening and closing in the sky. Cassandra was swinging her bonnet (which had long since left her head) by its blue ribbons, when she saw a gentleman on a black mare, come riding to meet them.

When he arrived, Mr. Strange smiled and spoke of the view and of the weather and, in the space of five minutes, was altogether more communicative than he had been in the entire past fortnight. None of the ladies had much to say to him, but Mr. Strange was not the sort of gentleman who, once he has decided to talk, is to be put off by a lack of encouragement on the part of his listeners.

He spoke of a remarkable dream he had had.

"I was told once by some country people that a magician should never tell his dreams because the telling will make them come true. But I say that that is great nonsense. Miss Tobias, you have studied the subject, what is your opinion?"

But Miss Tobias was silent.

Strange went on. "I had this dream, Mrs. Field, under rather curious circumstances. Last night I took some little bones to bed with me—I happened upon them quite recently. I put them under my pillow and there they stayed all night while I slept. Mrs. Strange would have had a great deal to say to me upon the subject, had she known of it. But then, wives and husbands do not always tell each other every thing, do they, Mrs. Field?"

But Mrs. Field said nothing.

"My dream was this," said Strange. "I was talking to a gentleman (a very handsome man). His features were very distinct in my dream, yet I am quite certain that I never saw him before in all my life. When we came to shake hands, he was very reluctant—which I did not understand. He seemed embarrassed and not a little ashamed. But when, at last, he put out his hand, it was not a hand at all, but a little gray-furred claw. Miss Parbringer, I hear that you tell wonderful stories to all the village children. Perhaps you will tell me a story to explain my dream?"

But Miss Parbringer was silent.

"On the day that my wife and I arrived here, some other people came to Grace Adieu. Where are they now? Where is the thin dark figure—whether boy or young woman I do not know, for no one saw very clearly—who sat in the gig?"

Miss Tobias spoke. "Miss Pye was taken back to Reigate in our carriage. Davey, our coachman, conveyed her to the house of her mother and her aunt—good people who truly love her and who had wondered for a long, long time if they would ever see her again."

"And Jack Hogg, the Captain's servant?"

Miss Tobias smiled. "Oh, he took himself off with remarkable speed, once it was made plain to him that staying would do no good at all."

"And where is Arthur Winbright? And where is Frederick Littleworth?"

They were silent.

"Oh, ladies, what have you done?"

After a while Miss Tobias spoke again. "That night," she said, "after Captain Winbright and Mr. Littleworth had . . . left us, I saw someone. At the other end of the passageway I saw, very dimly, someone tall and slender, with the wings of birds beating all around their shoulders. Mr. Strange, *I* am tall and the wings of birds were, at that moment, beating around my shoulders . . ."

"And so, it was your reflection."

"Reflection? By what means?" asked Miss Tobias. "There is no glass in that part of the house."

"So, what did you do?" asked Strange a little uncertainly.

"I said aloud the words of the Yorkshire Game. Even you, Mr. Strange, must know the words of the Yorkshire Game." Miss Tobias smiled a little sarcastically. "Mr. Norrell is, after all, the Yorkshire magician, is he not?"

"I greet thee, Lord, and bid thee welcome to my heart," said Strange.

Miss Tobias inclined her head.

Now it was Cassandra's turn. "Poor man, you cannot even reconcile what you believe in your heart to be true and what you are obliged to write in the quarterly reviews. Can you go back to London and tell this odd tale? For I think you will find that it is full of all kinds of nonsense that Mr. Norrell will not like—Raven Kings and the magic of wild creatures and the magic of women. You are no match for us, for we three are quite united, while you, sir, for all your cleverness, are at war, even with yourself. If ever a time comes, when your heart and your head declare a truce, then I suggest you come back to Grace Adieu and then you may tell us what magic we may or may not do."

It was Strange's turn to be silent. The three ladies of Grace Adieu wished him a good morning and walked on. Mrs. Field alone favored him with a smile (of a rather pitying sort).

A month after Mr. and Mrs. Strange's return to London, Mr. Woodhope was surprised to receive a letter from Sir Walter Pole, the politician. Mr. Woodhope had never met the gentleman, but now Sir Walter suddenly wrote to offer Mr. Woodhope the rich living of Great Hitherden, in Northamptonshire. Mr. Woodhope could only imagine that it was Strange's doing—Strange and Sir Walter were known to be friends. Mr. Woodhope was sorry to leave Grace Adieu and sorry to leave Miss Parbringer, but he comforted himself with the thought that there were bound to be ladies, almost as pretty in Northampton-shire and if there were not, well, he would be a richer clergyman there than he was in Grace Adieu and so better able to bear the loneliness.

Miss Cassandra Parbringer only smiled when she heard he was going and that same afternoon, went out walking on the high hills, in a fine autumn wind, with Mrs. Field and Miss Tobias—as free, said Miss Parbringer, as any women in the kingdom.

WILDERNESS

Ron Hansen

Ron Hansen is the author of five novels, including *Desperadoes*, *Mariette in Ecstasy* and *Atticus*. He has also published one collection of short stories, *Nebraska*, and one book for children, *The Shadowmaker*. He lives in northern California.

"Wilderness" is a powerful and gorgeously crafted tale of magic realism. The author makes skillful use of fairytale symbols to balance his story on the sharp edge between fantasy and horror. "Wilderness" is reprinted from the pages of *Epoch* magazine.

—T. W. and E. D.

On a green lake in the Adirondacks a tanned old man was rowing. It was six A.M., and the lake was glass, and fog lingered under the juniper trees. Milos swung the oars up and the rowboat glided. His right hand wiped his bald head and the gray hair on his chest. He looked at the sweat on his palm. His blue sweater was on the other seat and water drops from the oars darkly spotted it. A gray wolf slinked out of the fog through high, poking grass and stepped onto the painted white dock. His tongue hung long as he panted. Milos adjusted his direction and pulled toward the wolf. The bray of his oarlocks was the only sound.

Her name was Sylvia and she wrote poetry at a cottage table that thumped when she punched the typewriter keys. She was dark, rather pretty, and forty-two, a full professor of English at Williams, one of the foremost experts on the Romantic Age. She was Axel's second wife, the woman they said was too good for him. She drank iced tea from a jelly glass and slept in an extra-large gray sweatshirt with "Williams" lettered in purple on it. She smoked clove cigarettes and used the lid of a jelly jar for an ashtray. She stood on the porch of the island cottage and watched yellow-raincoated fishermen cast their lines into the green Atlantic as seagulls looped and dropped and climbed heavily out of the water with scraps. She read each day's product at night with a soft calico cat on her lap, a cat that she guessed belonged to a neighbor.

* * *

Her husband Axel was in Mexico with a second-year graduate student, Arietta, who meant more to him than his marriage now. He was a heavy man, fifty-five years old, with a gray crewcut and a white beard, a professor in the field of art restoration at Williams. He was gingerly excavating the ruins of what might have been a cooking room five hundred years ago, and if he looked up he could see gorgeous, sexy, too-admiring Arietta tenderly scraping intricate pottery with a fine sculptor's tool, the shade of a Panama hat around her pale neck like a scarf. Axel pried a root from the ground and without looking up inquired. "Tell me, do you know any opera, Arietta?"

Arietta held up a hand to shade her eyes and asked, "I beg your pardon?"

Axel said. "I find it funny that we've been together for so long, and yet I haven't asked you about—" He did not complete his thought for as he picked up a spade he saw a white cat with gray patches carefully licking its forepaw.

Milos poured honey from a jar onto a bowl of oatmeal and milk and centered the bowl on a place setting in the dining room. The teapot whistled and Milos made Earl Grey tea and sat in a green leather chair in his study. His soft white calico cat pounced up onto his lap. Milos petted it soothingly and spoke a foreign language into its ear. The cat thumped down to the carpet and oozily disappeared outside. Milos frowned into space.

Sylvia shut up the cottage and packed into a foreign car a typewriter, teapot, paperbacks, and string-tied boxes heaped with camping clothes, poems, and one hundred pages of scholarship that she could read only with great displeasure. She drove west with her wrist on the steering wheel, her mind preoccupied, uncoupled, even as she repeated the Spanish phrases spoken on the language tapes she listened to on a Walkman. And she was crossing the Adirondacks, past Lake Pleasant, when she pulled over to the roadside in order to unpack her husband's red wool hiking coat and walk among the junipers, eating one of the green apples she kept in a picnic basket. She heard on the Walkman, "I'm just passing through," and she said, *"Estoy solo de paso."* And she was listening hard to find out if she was right when she turned at a weird roadside noise and saw what may have been a wolfhound tearing at groceries in the front of her car.

She yelled, "Hey! How'd you get in there? Shoo!"

The wolfhound regarded her insultingly before retreating a little through the wide-open door and trotting off with a half-filled grocery sack in his jaws.

Sylvia yelled again and the wolfhound simply regripped his loot before loping down a woodcutter's road, stopping after fifty yards or so to get a new purchase on the grocery sack and to gaze back at the hurrying woman as if he were letting her catch up. She flung a stick that the hound dodged in a way she found sarcastic, and she looked back to her car on the highway and watched wild pages flap out the front window, looping high as seagulls into the air.

The cat approached Milos again upstairs as the man was slipping into a nightshirt. The cat roped between the old man's tanned legs and Milos moved a window curtain aside to peer out.

*   *   *

Arietta stood with one hand in a pocket of her khaki shorts while the other picked skin tissue off her upper arm. She was golden-haired and painfully sunburnt and she regretted every choice she'd made in the past six months. Axel was deep in a cellar he'd happened upon and she could only see his brown calves and ankle-high boots as he cleaned a room painting with a camel-hair brush. The white cat whined and wiled its way between her legs, and she gathered it up. She asked. "Do you see anything written?"

Axel paused before saying, "The script is unfamiliar." He looked up at Arietta, shading his eyes. "So our cat has reappeared."

"Do you want me to get the camera?"

"Please," said Axel. "And with a new roll of film, please."

She walked to the Jeep, petting the cat, and squatted down in the shade of the car in order to reload the camera. She smelled candle wax. She snapped on the flash attachment and heard the clinking of glasses. She stood in surprise but could see nothing except sunlight and pink foothills over a beige Mexican landscape. A man's voice said, "Do you think I would poison you?" and she let the cat fall out of her arms. She experienced a pressure against her breasts as if she were being petted. "Axel!" she screamed, but kisses smeared against her lips and cheek and she was being whispered to in a language foreign to her. She struggled away and got to the cellar, crying, "Oh, Axel; help me!" But when she looked down into the room, she saw only a gray hound that was large as a wolf, growling up at her.

Axel was strolling back from the Jeep as slow as a dawdler in a park. He grinned and dangled the camera down to her. "So!" he said. "Just as you ordered."

She combed her gold hair away from her eyes. The wolf, of course, was gone. Axel stooped to peer into the cellar, saying, "And now perhaps you'll let me see this marvelous painting?"

Sylvia was lost, by then, in wilderness. Her only thought was that the wolfhound would be going back to a cottage and she could get directions there. So she followed a path through the dark green foliage that was swiped awry with the animal's passing, and she had gone miles in a darkness that made midday seem night when she began to see sunlight dappling the upper leaves of the trees and then the path and then she emerged into a clearing of sponge grass where the hound was standing, swinging his tail, as seagulls dipped into the grocery sack and carried scraps to the porch of a large yellow house.

Sylvia called, "Hello? Is anybody home?" and instantly felt girlish and ignorant. She stamped away the seagulls and picked up the grocery sack as the wolfhound panted and looked to a porch swing that was rocking as though somebody had just gotten up.

The yellow house was a strange anthology of designs, with gables and spires and parapets, scalloped cornices, intricate porch posts, and red chimneys of miscellaneous heights. Sylvia looked through a window and saw a library of books that climbed so high that the owner used a step-ladder on wheels. She called again and looked though an oval glass at a dining table with a teapot and a place setting and one lighted candle. A phonograph was playing Bach, the Goldberg Variations. She rapped on the entryway door three separate times and then permitted herself to trespass, certain that she could explain the lapse in etiquette once the occupants returned.

Axel peered at contact prints under the shade of a flapping tent canopy. Arietta sat across from him, her chin in her hand, seeing now how old he was, how parental, how caught up in his project and incurious about her. He'd said, in the rigid English of a foreigner, "You have been getting too much sun, maybe." He'd said, "If there are guilty parties, there are always voices." Axel moved his magnifying glass over a photograph and said, "Such a disappointment, Arietta. Not Spanish, not Aztec, perhaps no more than a century old. The gods help a peasant girl to go to the court of the sun king. She makes love to a prince but then—I cannot tell why—flees the place, and the prince must spend many years looking for this girl. They meet and there is great happiness." Axel pushed the contact prints away and sat back in his fold-up chair. "Cinderella," Axel said. "Some children were playing a little joke, perhaps. I hope you are not too sorry."

Arietta budged forward and squinted at the photographs. "Do these diagonal lines mean anything?"

"They mean I made a particularly stupid mistake. I ought to punish myself so and so." He lightly slapped his cheeks and grinned as he got up to crouch over his graduate student. "Look you: a face appears here: next, a car, could it be a Mazda? And here, a yellow house, a gable, a gray-haired man—who it could be, I don't know. The roll is being used once before."

"And the woman is Sylvia," Arietta said.

Axel shrugged. "Naturally." He pulled Arietta up and chaperoned her over to the tent they'd pitched next to the Jeep. He said. "It is very comical, really. The prince is one time superimposed on me. And my dear wife is the golden-haired girl I am seeking."

"How silly," Arietta said.

Sylvia took off her red wool hiking coat and stood alone in every room in the house. She ate the oatmeal on the dining room table without knowing why and though she emptied the teapot she grew so sleepy that she went upstairs to one of the many beds and collapsed on top of the covers. She kept thinking, Why are you so unhappy? And she slept deeply until nightfall.

She could recall the clicking of the dog's claws on the glossy floorboards, the rapid gasps of the dog's respiration, the change in the mattress as the dog jumped up and flung his weight down next to hers, but Sylvia could do nothing but grant the dog his right to the room, and she only thought about his coming when she felt a change in the mattress again and got up on an elbow to see a man of some age in a wingback chair angrily glaring at her. "I'm sorry," she said, and the man's expression became one of pleasure.

"Don't be," Milos said. "You look so pretty sleeping."

"You must think me terribly impolite. I just couldn't help myself."

"Yes, but you must speak no more apologies, please. I get so little company up here. I will pretend you are one of my grandchildren having her nap before supper."

Axel was sitting outside, smoking a pipe, when Arietta came out of the tent in bluejeans and a wool pullover. "So many stars," she said.

"Do you hear the wolves?"

She looked to the darker inch of night where she knew the foothills were but she could only make out the sounds of the flapping canopy, plaintive insects, wind. "Do you think they'll come for our food?"

Axel shrugged. "If they're hungry." He got up, lighting his pipe again. "I'll go for my ax."

The soft calico cat meowed and Arietta crouched to encourage it to come forward, patting her thighs and calling "Kitty." The cat stepped closer and posed like a sculpture, peeking at Arietta without recognition as though its eyes were no more than gold marbles. Axel rummaged through the Jeep, singing opera phrases, and Arietta approached the cat, pretending it knew what she meant when she spoke about happiness, missing it, milk. The cat simply licked a gray patch on its chest and, as she knelt to scoop it up, hopped aslant of her, pausing just beyond her grasp and opening its mouth in an unvoiced reply. Arietta walked to it and the cat walked away; Arietta swooped it and stepped into the pit that Axel had happened upon, dropping into nothing at all and spinning like paper on air.

Milos sat opposite Sylvia and pinged his champagne glass against hers. "To my companion," he said, "who is writing such good poetry."

"To Milos," Sylvia said.

Milos said, "You will find me interesting." He peered at her as he sipped his champagne and she looked away at the many candles, the expensive red plates, the gold trays heaped with enough food for eight. "You are not eating," he said. He put his champagne glass down and ripped off a scrap of fish, pushing it into his mouth. "See? Do you think I would poison you?"

"I'd really prefer to get back to my car," Sylvia said, and without really knowing why she added, "People are expecting me."

"You are being particularly stupid."

The cat with the gray patches paid no attention to Axel as the man walked the perimeter of the camp yelling, "Arietta!" over and over again. The cat paid no attention even when the man approached with an ax, it simply gave itself pleasure in any way it could and was so preoccupied that it didn't jump aside when Axel shouted his rage or even when the ax chopped into it.

Axel gaped in surprise, for the ax was splitting a sheet of paper and the cat had disappeared. He ripped the paper from the ax and moved a match light over it, seeing Sylvia's handwriting on a typewritten poem. More pages were looping up from the pit so Axel jumped down into it, getting up from his hands and knees on sponge grass at the edge of a lake. A rowboat nodded at a painted white dock and water slapped and a dog that was as large as a wolf growled only briefly before it lunged.

* * *

Milos was wooing Sylvia by complimenting himself, saying his green eyes were meant for worshipping her, his ears were meant to indulge her, his arms were big even in his old age in order to gather her close to his heart, which was redder than her wool coat. He got up from his chair to put an opera on the phonograph and Sylvia attempted to push away from the dining room table and politely make an exit. Milos stopped over her, however, nuzzling his whiskered chin into her pale neck, crushing her breasts in his palms, smearing kisses over her lips and cheeks even as she slapped at him, whispering persistently, "Warum bist du so unglucklich?"

The dog yelped once and Milos stalled, looking toward the painted dock and the lakes as a cat might. He then yanked Sylvia into a side kitchen and put a match to the oven. The candlelight was extinguished.

Having slaughtered the dog, Axel crept to the porch of the large yellow house. The Mazda was parked on the sponge grass and seagulls were roosting inside it like teapots. He pulled open a porch door and crept inside and the floorboards made a speech about each step he took as if he wore spades for shoes. He stopped by a study and saw the white cat with gray patches sitting on a green leather chair, its gold eyes peering at him, and he heard a knife clatter in a porcelain sink—not as if it slipped off a plate, but as if a hand had simply let it go to provide him with information. Axel wiped the dog's blood off the ax and onto the carpet and then he passed through a room that smelled of candlewax and champagne and passion, on into a room with a porcelain sink and a pool of Sylvia's blood on the floor. His wife had been chopped into little pieces and Milos was eating the last scrap of her.

"So it's you, old sinner!" Axel said, as if he were greeting a man he recognized. And he swung the woodcutter's ax through the man's yielding neck, cleaving Milos from his body like a fish head from a fish so that he was gasping and attempting to speak as he rolled along the floor. Axel then split open the belly as quickly as one might unzip a bag and Sylvia reappeared in one piece just as the girls do in a magic show. She and Axel stuffed Milos with poetry before they sewed him up and they dropped him over the side of the rowboat into the accepting green lake, where Milos sank like an iron spike.

The cat with gray patches Sylvia kept and it paws at the typewriter from her lap as she taps a cigarette into a jar lid. Axel stamps his hip waders on the porch steps and opens the cottage door, saying, "Look what I caught," and he lifts aloft not a fish but a seagull, the fishhook poking out of its neck.

"Did you enjoy Mexico?" Sylvia asks, and Axel frowns at her. "Mexico?" for she's made him forget everything, as if it never happened.

OSHKIWIINAG: HEARTLINES ON THE TRICKSTER EXPRESS

Gerald Vizenor

Gerald Vizenor, of the Anishinaabe tribe, is a professor of Native American Literature at the University of California, Berkeley, and the acclaimed author of many books on tribal histories and literature. His novels include *Hotline Healers, Bearheart, The Heirs of Columbus, Dead Voices: Natural Agonies in the New World* and *Griever: An American Monkey King in China* (winner of the American Book Award.) He has also published *The People Named the Chippewa, Narrative Chance* (essays on Native American literature), and an autobiography, *Interior Landscapes: Autobiographical Myths and Metaphors.* In addition, Vizenor is the general editor of the American Indian Literature and Critical Studies series for the University of Oklahoma Press.

The wild, miraculous story that follows is simply a tour-de-force; it's a privilege to include it here. The story comes from *Blue Dawn, Red Earth,* a collection of new Native writing. Many other works in the collection also have a magical, mythical touch; I particularly recommend the mysterious tale by Yaqui author Anita Endrezze and the poignant, quietly magical story by Chippewa author Kimberly Blaeser.

—T. W.

THE ACUDENTURIST

Lake Namakan never hides the natural reason of our seasons. The wind hardens snow to the bone, cerements over the cedar ruins, and hushed currents weaken the ice under the wild reach of our winter.

Overnight, the wild heirs are in the birch, the chase of wise crows. Higher in the distance, the bald eagles brace their nests once more with wisps of white pine, the elusive censers of the summer.

Everywhere, silence is unnatural in our seasons. Listen, the rivers cut massive stones to the ancient heartlines. Memories are more precise on the borders of reservations, nations, and the turns of creation. Trickster stories are the hidden currents of the seasons, the natural reason of our independence.

Gesture Browne is a trickster of precise memories, an esteemed tribal acudenturist, and the founder of the first reservation railroad. He was born in the summer, on an island near the international border, at the same time that Henry Ford established a modern assembly line to build automobiles. That industrial gesture, the coincidence of his birth, and his railroad adventures as an acudenturist were cause to mention the course of natural reason in trickster stories.

Lake Namakan, the memories of our seasons, the crows and bald eagles, the creation of reservations, and the revolution of automobiles were connected in a common vision of unrest and mobility. Gesture reasoned, as he probed a carious lesion in a molar, that the assurance of tribal independence was not a crown decoration of discoveries and treaties, but a state of natural motion. He shouted out, as his father had done from the water tower on the reservation, that sovereignties were movable stories, never the inactive documents of invented cultures.

THE TREATMENT

Gesture told me that trickster stories come out of the heart, not the mouth. "My heart hears the silence in stones, but teeth rot in the mouth, and what does a wimpy smile mean that covers rotten teeth?" His words warmed the air and brushed my cheek as he leaned over me in the dental chair. He smiled as he leaned, but never showed his teeth. Later, he revealed his crown.

Gesture was an acudenturist in motion, an acute denturist with a singular practice on his very own railroad. The dental chair was located at the end of the train, at the back of the luxurious parlor car. The train had been built for a rich banker who traveled on weekends to his country estate near Lake Namakan.

The banker, by chance of an abscessed tooth and a wild storm on the lake, gave his entire private railroad to the acudenturist and created an endowment to sustain the operation of the train on the reservation.

Gesture was born on Wanaki Island in Lake Namakan. He could have been a child of the wind and natural reason. The otters heard his stories on the stones in the spring, and he was more elusive in the brush than cedar waxwings. The islands were heard in the stories of the seasons, and seen in the everlasting flight of tribal memories. His relatives and the shamans come to the island in summer and winter to hear stories, to hear the stones and heal their presence in humor. His father was exiled and never returned to the reservation of his birth.

Ashigan, his father, was born on an island near the border. Six years later, his family was removed by treaty to a federal exclave, and then the unscrupulous agents ordered him to leave forever the White Earth Reservation. The order was a paradox; banished, as it were, back to the very islands his family had been removed from eleven years earlier. The sentence was truly ironic, as he had removed the United States Indian agent for crimes against tribal sovereignty, and held him hostage in a water tower. He told his son that "one removal must beget another in a stolen nest."

Ashigan shouted out the names of the criminal agents and told trickster stories on tribal independence several times a day for three weeks. Some people listened under the tower, others laughed and waited for the agents to shoot him down. He was a scarce silhouette on the tower, smaller for his age than anyone in his family, but his mouth was enormous, and his loud voice had been hired more than once to announce the circus and Wild West shows. He was no more than seventeen at the time of the removal and had earned the nickname Big Mouth Bass for his stories about the heinous incursions, assaults, larcenies, and murders on the reservation by the federal government.

Big Mouth Bass moved to the border islands and never mentioned the removal, the wicked agents, the twisted mouths of missionaries, or those tribal emissaries who had weakened his revolution in the water tower. The islands were sacred stones in his stories, and the avian shadows his natural solace, but he never shouted about anything ever again. At last, in his eighties, he returned to the reservation with his son, at the controls of their own train. He said the tribal railroad, *ishkodewidaabaan*, or the "fire car" in translation, was his "island in motion."

Since then, tribal people with terminal teeth, some of them with abscesses bigger than the one drained on the banker, drank wild rice wine in the lounge and watched the landscape rush past the great curved windows. They waited in the sovereignty of the parlor car to have their teeth repaired by their very own acudenturist.

"So, lucky for you this is not heart surgery," he said and then leaned over me, the side of his thick hand on my right cheekbone. Lucky indeed, were my very thoughts, but my heart was in my molars that morning. The silence was ironic. No one else has ever had permission to enter my mouth with various instruments, inflict pain, and then ask me questions that were not answerable. No silence could be more sorely heard than the mute responses of a crossblood journalist to the intrusions of an acudenturist, his unanswerable queries of me in a dental chair on a tribal railroad.

Gesture poked and scratched with a dental probe at the ancient silver in my molars. Closer, his breath was slow, warm, and seductively sweet with a trace of clove and commodity peanut butter. The leather chair clicked, a clinical sound, leaned to the side, and shivered as the train rounded a curve over the river near the border of the reservation. "Loose here, and there, there, there, can you feel that?" He pounded on my molars and we nodded in silence on the curve. Then, with a straight chisel he scraped the rough edges of the silver. I could taste the metal, the cold instruments, and his warm bare fingers in my mouth.

"Tribal independence is motion, stories to the heartlines, not the mere sentences and silences of scripture, not the cruelties of dead words about who we might have been in the past to hear our presence," he said and we nodded as the train leaned in the other direction. "Museums iced our impermanence, and the cold donors measure our sovereignty in the dead voices of their own cultures." He snorted and then explained that he would not be able to use an anesthetic because he was an acudenturist, "not a drugstore doctor." The silver was already too loose in my molars to wait on a licensed dentist at the end of the line.

"Instead, here are some scents of the seasons on the islands," he said and turned a narrow cone toward my face. The rush of air was moist and cool, and the first scent was a thunderstorm, then wet wool, a dog, and later on the essence of sex, but that must have come from generations of sweat on the leather chairs in the parlor car.

We nodded in silence and he turned the dental chair from the curved windows and the landscape to the power instruments. The other patients in the lounge turned with me from the rush of birch and white pine to the instruments. He started the mechanical dental engine. The drill was archaic, but the sound of the drive cables created a sense of contentment, the solace of an acudenturist in his own trickster stories. He drilled and cleaned the lesion, and then pounded real gold into the central grooves of my molars.

"Now, you are truly worth more than you were last night on the reservation, and we are both still free," said the acudenturist as he turned the chair back toward the curved windows.

THE ABSCESSED BANKER

I was born on the reservation, but my father moved to the city in search of work. I quit school, bounced around for years, served in the military, and finally landed as a journalist for a large daily newspaper, the *Twin Cities Chronicle*. Naturally, the editors named me Big Cheep, a nickname they learned from me. A nickname based on the way Ishi, the Yahi man who lived in a museum at the University of California, said the word *Chief*, a personal reference to the anthropologist Alfred Kroeber.

I was assigned to cover any story that had the slightest hint of tribal presence, as if no one else could cover such events without a genetic connection to a reservation. For all that, and even the heartless celebration of essentialism over racial deverbatives, such as drinkers, drummers, and dancers, no one in my crossblood generation had a more exciting job. I would have it no other way, and was more than pleased to write about the unnamable tribes and such unbelievable characters as the acudenturist Gesture Browne.

My editors, however, as much as they liked my work from the unknown and exotic headwaters of the reservations, were never certain if my stories were true or not. The other reporters shouted out their rough humor in the newsroom when one of my stories landed on the front page. I heard their playful envy, to be sure, and the ironies of what was sold as daily news, but I would have laughed anyway at such racial quibbles as "You need tribal fishing rights to believe this story" or "The second coming of Christ is worth a page and a half, unless she's an Indian."

In the end, the distinctions between fact and fiction never really seemed to matter much to the editors or readers, and surely that must be the reason why tribal humor and trickster stories have endured the most outrageous abuses by missionaries and government agents and, above all other cruelties, the dominance of dead-letter anthropologists.

The city editor often said that my stories about tribal people on the reservation "may not be the truth, but his stories are truer than what we publish day after day about elected politicians all the way to the White House."

My editor bought the truth of the banker with the abscess who was lost in a thunderstorm, and he ran my story as a feature on the front page, but he would not believe the stories about my golden molars. These stories, and the leather dental chair in a parlor car, were not convincing. He even looked in my mouth, poked the bright molar with a pencil, and then shouted, "Fool's gold on a tribal railroad, now that is believable!"

He smiled, and then we nodded in silence.

Gesture never hides the natural reason of a thunderstorm on the islands at Lake Namakan. He waits on the massive stones for a burst of creation. I know, because when he hears that certain wind, the crash of thunder in the distance, he is transformed by the power of the storm. He told me that the most natural death is to be struck by lightning, "a crash of thunder and the human remains are a thunderstone."

Ashigan and his son were healed by the power of the west wind, the rush of water over the massive stones. Gesture looks at least ten years younger when he faces a thunderstorm. And it was a storm, one ferocious thunderstorm over the islands, that changed his life forever. Indeed, he was out in the wild wind, but he was struck by a banker, not lightning, in the end.

Cameron Williams, the wealthy banker, was out in a canoe that very afternoon, a chance to show his grandson the bald eagles near the international border. The banker had no sense of natural reason and, distracted by the rise of the eagles on the wind, he drifted on the rough water over the border and was lost in the many bays and islands of Lake Namakan.

Gesture saw a canoe turn over on the waves near the island. The banker was lucky that such a tribal man would stand in a storm and watch the lake catch the wind. The canoe tumbled on the waves, and then he saw the blue faces of children in the water, the faces that haunted him in dreams, the blue faces beneath the ice near the mouth of a river. He tied a rope to a tree and swam out to the canoe. The lightning hissed overhead, and the water was wicked on the rise in the wind. The child was ashen, blue around his eyes and mouth, and his ancient blue hands were closed on a miniature plastic paddle. The banker trembled—he was too scared to shout—but he held on to the canoe.

Gesture tied the rope to the canoe and towed the child to shore. Cameron nodded, the waves crashed over them, and lightning crashed in the trees on the island. Later, the child recovered near the fire, but the banker weakened; his eyes were swollen and lost color. The storm passed overnight, but the wind howled and the waves crashed on the stones for two more days. They could not paddle against the high waves.

Cameron was weakened because he had a canine abscess that distended his right cheek and ear and closed one eye. The swollen banker was delirious on the second night. He cursed women and the weather for his condition, and then he started to wheeze; his breath was slower, strained, and his thin hands turned inward to the silence.

Gesture heard the last stories in the old man. The lake was thunderous, and the waves were too high for a canoe, so he decided to operate on the banker, then and there on the island, and drain the abscess. That night he built a small sweat lodge and warmed the old man near the stones, and moistened his swollen mouth with willow bark soaked in hot water.

The next morning he moved the banker out to the boulders on the shore, turned his head to the sun, and told the child to hold his swollen mouth open with a chunk of driftwood. The child nodded in silence, and then Gesture wound a thin wire several times around the base of the canine, and with a wooden lever, braced in the seam of a stone, he wrenched the poisoned tooth from the banker's mouth.

Purulence and marbled blood oozed out around the tooth, ran down his chin and neck, and stained the stone. Then pure putrid mucus gushed from the hole of the abscessed canine. He choked and gurgled, but in minutes he could see. His swollen eye opened, and he turned to his side on the stone and moaned as the infection drained from his head. The child cried over the color of the poisoned blood, and then he gathered water and washed the pus from the stone.

Later, the child touched the dark hollow abscess with his fingers. That afternoon the banker laughed and said his mistake in navigation was "not much better than Columbus." Perched on the warm stones, he told stories about his childhood, and took great pleasure in his missing tooth, the natural imperfection of his weathered smile.

Gesture paddled the banker and the child in their canoe back to their vacation home on the luxurious western reach of the lake, a great distance on the other side of the border. The water was calm in the narrows, and the sun bounced over the scant waves. The eagles teased the wind and then circled closer and closer to the shallow water on the shoreline.

THE FEATURE STORY

I was a journalist and convinced at the time that my stories created a sense of the unusual in a real world, even more in feature stories. Alas, the politics of the real are uncertain, and stories of natural reason and survivance in the tribal world were scarcely heard, and seldom recorded as sure historical documents.

Cameron Williams was one of my real features, a banker in the blood who reared his own documents and caused histories that touched on natural reason and tribal survivance. I was a reservation crossblood with a shadow of chance and the sound of oral stories in my ears, and he was a rich banker with several vacation homes and his own railroad. He was a serious stockholder in the very newspaper that employed me, and he traced his ancestors to the founding families of Puritan New England.

My editors at the *Twin Cities Chronicle* were too liberal for the banker, so it was even more difficult for me to track down any good information about the extraction of his abscessed canine in a thunderstorm. One of his assistants told me that he would not be interviewed for any story, and "certainly not about his exodontist."

I think it was my simple savings account at one of his banks that opened the door the first time. He was a pragmatist, to be sure, and he must have judged me by my documents, a savings account in this instance. Later, however, it would take more than my meager savings to overcome his suspicion of crossbloods. He told me that my genes were "enervated" and the "inheritance of a racial weakness has never been an honorable birthright." Crossblood or not, my recognition of one of his distant relatives earned an invitation to travel with him on his plane and train.

Cameron was a descendant of John Williams, a minister at the turn of the eighteenth century in Deerfield, Massachusetts. His family was captured one winter night, and his daughter, touched by the communion of the tribes, never returned. Eunice Williams renounced the dominance of her puritanical father and married a tribal man, and that historical document could not be denied by enervation. Twelve generations later, the banker is an heir to that crossblood union of Puritans and Kahnawakes in Canada.

"Sir, at our best we are crossbloods."

"At your best, you are a listener," said the banker.

"Indeed, and the abscess is your story."

"So, this is what you want to see, the hole," said the banker. He removed a false canine with his fingers and then smiled to show the hole. "The first thing my grandson did was touch the bloody hole, and he still does it when we tell the story together."

"How does an abscess become a reservation railroad?"

"Pack for an overnight and meet me in three hours at the entrance to the garage," he said and waved me out of the conference room. The scent of mint, an executive insinuation of nature in the carpets, lingered on my clothes for several hours.

Cameron was silent in the limousine to the airport. He only gestured at scenes out the window as we flew in his private jet over the lakes and landed at airport near his vacation home. From there we boarded a pontoon plane and flew close to the peaks of red pines, circled the many islands, and then landed on the smooth sheltered bay near Wanaki Island.

Gesture should have been there to meet the seaplane. How could he not hear the engines, and how often does company arrive by air? There was no dock on the island, so we waded over the massive boulders to shore.

"We were caught in a vicious storm and rolled over right out there," said the banker. "And here, on this very stone, a stranger saved my life, and he asked nothing for his trouble."

Gesture was reading in his cabin, a precise response to the curiosities and uncommon praise of a banker. Not even his mongrels were moved to denounce our presence on their island. "We never challenge bears or humans," he told me later.

The modern cabin was constructed mostly of metal, not what we expected to find in the remote pristine wilderness of the border islands. There were other surprises, such as skylights, a toilet that generated methane, and water heated by solar panels.

Gesture explained that the modern accommodations were a contradiction of tribal rights and federal wilderness laws. He had the aboriginal right to live on the islands, but he could not crap on the land or cut the trees to build a house. "Not because the trees have rights—that would be natural reason—but because the trees are on a pristine reservation," he told me. "So, we can live here in a natural museum."

Gesture and his father, their wives and several children, saved their money from treaty settlements, and income as guides for fishing parties, to buy modular ecological homes that were airlifted to the island in large sections and assembled in less than a week.

"I tried several times to remember what your house looked like, but my memory lost the picture," said the banker. The mongrels sniffed his ankles and sneezed several times.

High Rise, the white mongrel with the short pointed ears, moaned and rolled over at the feet of the banker. He rubbed his wet jowls on his shoes and ankles. The banker raised his trousers, and reached down with one hand to touch his head, to push him aside, but the mongrel moaned louder and licked his hand.

Poster Girl, the mottled brown mongrel that looked like a cat, was very excited by the scent of the banker and the moans of High Rise. She barked and ran around the banker in tiny circles. Her nails clicked on the wooden floor, an ecstatic dance. The banker was not amused by the mongrels.

"High Rise must have a nose for bankers," said the banker.

"Maybe, but he goes for the scent of mint. Yes, lingering from the executive carpets," said Gesture.

"Gesture, could we get down to some business?" the banker asked.

"You mean the mongrels?" Gesture responded.

"Would you like a paid scholarship to dental school?" the banker inquired.

"Dental school?" asked Gesture.

"Yes, an even chance to turn a mere instinct into a real profession, and you could be the very first dentist in your entire tribe," said the banker. His manner was earnest, but the invitation was an obscure pose of dominance.

"You flew way out here to send me to dental school?"

"A measure of my respect," said the banker.

"The measure is mine," said Gesture. He pointed to the books stacked near the wooden bench, and the mongrels moved in that direction. There were several novels and a book on dental care and hygiene. "You see, out here we are denturists with no natural reason to be dentists, our teeth are never the same, but denturists never turn mouths into museums."

"You saved my life," pleaded the banker.

"Maybe," said Gesture.

"You owe me the courtesy to recognize my everlasting debt to you," said the banker. "My grandson admires you more than anyone else in the family right now, he thinks you are the dentist of the islands."

"Denturist, and you had the abscess, not me."

"You are an original," said the banker. He moved to the bench and read the titles of books in several stacks. High Rise nosed his ankles, and Poster Girl posed beside him on the bench. There were new novels by Gordon Henry, Betty Louise Bell, Louis Owens, and Randome Browne, and older novels by Franz Kafka, Herman Melville, and Yasunari Kawabata. He was distracted by a rare book, the *Manabosho Curiosa*, the very first tribal book, published in the middle of the seventeenth century. The anonymous tribal curiosa of human and animal sexual transformations were discovered a century later at an auction of rare books in France.

"Gesture, this is a very rare book," said the banker.

"Poster Girl is a healer," said Gesture.

"What does she heal?" asked the banker.

"Whatever you want?"

"What do *you* want?" shouted the banker.

"What do you have?" shouted Gesture.

High Rise raised her head at the tone of his voice and sniffed the distance in the air. Poster Girl watched the banker on the bench. He was distracted more by the *Curiosa* than the mongrels.

"Basically, it comes down to this," said the banker. He laid the *Curiosa* on the stack of books, leaped from the bench, and turned to the window. "What would you accept that would make me feel better about this?"

"Make me an offer," said Gesture.

"Come with me and see!" shouted the banker. He turned and marched across the room to the door. The mongrels followed him out. He ordered the pilot to make room for one more passenger, but not the mongrels.

"Would you consider a scholarship to study at the university?" asked the banker. The pontoon plane bounced several times and then lifted slowly from the water.

"Why the university?"

"Say, to study literature," said the banker.

"I already do that," said Gesture.

"Anthropology, then."

"Anthropology studies me."

"You have a point there," said the banker.

"Natural reason is the point."

"You could be a pilot and have your own business on the lakes," said the banker. The plane circled the islands near the border. The late sun shivered in wide columns on the water.

"Do you have a railroad?" asked Gesture.

"Yes, my own private line."

"Give me that, and we have a deal," said Gesture. He gestured with his lips toward the shoreline. Bald eagles turned their shadows over and over on Lake Namakan.

"Great idea, the first tribal railroad in the history of the nation," said the banker. He raised his hands and shouted nonsense in the air. "Did you hear that, Mister Crossblood, this is the return of the noble train."

THE TRICKSTER EXPRESS

The Naanabozho Express, a seven-coach train, lurched out of the casino station on the White Earth Reservation and thundered into the sacred cedars on the last wild run to the White House in Washington.

Gesture Browne, the founder of the tribal railroad, or *ishkodewidaabaan*, in the memories of the elders, negotiated with the national native art museum the installation of a mobile cultural exhibition on the train, and then he summoned his heirs to declare motion a tribal island, a natural sovereign tribal state.

The trickster express ran on borrowed rails with a new museum, a parlor dental car, an acudenturist, a nurse with several nicknames, and the crystal trickster of tribal parthenogenesis. The express train was natural reason in motion, a nomadic survivance from a woodland reservation to the national capital.

Gesture never surprised anyone on the reservation with his uncommon transactions. His words rushed and bounced, one over the other with no connections or closures, but with that visual sense of transformations in his stories. Natural reason never ended, never in trickster stories, and never in his natural invectives. He was a wind in the best seasons, and his humor healed those who heard his stories on the trickster train. The man who conceived the first railroad on the reservation would not be caught unaware by his heirs on a wise run to tribal sovereignty.

The others, the educated canons on the bungee lines of reason, were astonished that an old man, who said he was once a woman, had stolen the sacred treasures of his own culture from a museum. The curators, on the other hand, were the dead voices of native museums, burdened with their obsessions, discoveries, heartless recoveries, and their mean manners of terminations and post-indian tenancies.

Gesture reassured me that motion is autonomous, that natural reason and memories are motion, and motion can never be stolen. Bones and blankets are stolen; motion is a natural sovereignty. The museum commodities on the train had been removed, silenced, and unseen, as the tribes had been removed to reservations. He said the museum in motion was not stolen, but a revolution of native sovereignty. "Museums are the houses of thieves; the sacred objects were stolen in the name of civilization and are more secure than native communities on reservations. The museums are dead, and here we are, in revolution on a trickster train."

THE CRYSTAL TRICKSTER

Cozie Browne heard that the west wind was lost, an ominous situation to consider that winter on the reservation. She heard the crows too, and rushed outside to warn the birch near the river. The ice waited in silence, hard-hearted on the blue summer mire, and even the cedar waxwings were uncertain over the late turn of the seasons. She overheard these stories as a child, and no one has ever been the same in her memories.

Notice of the lost wind was delivered by her cousin who lived in a cold basement apartment in the city. She was nine years old at the time and enticed by his wild urban manners. The mere mention of cities, that sense of distance and urban vengeance, molded the seasons in her memories. He was older and wiser about obscure tribal traditions and the enchanted stories of creation, and avowed that he could hear stories on the weave and wander of the wind.

Cozie was born in the summer at the same time that the first nuclear-powered submarine sailed under fifty feet of polar ice. The wind touched her head at birth with an ovate bunch of blond hair, a sign that tribal elders were reborn in their children. She learned to hear the bald eagles and to carry a sprig of white pine. She mourned in the presence of spirits, not humans, and no one but tricksters dared cross her trail to the fire.

Trickster stories tease a tribal presence, a chance to be heard between the reservations and the cities; otherwise, unseen, she would have shivered in silence over the insinuations of natural reason. Her uncle, a wise man of motion, rushed the thunderstorms on the islands, but the stories she heard would mend the absence, not the presence, of the west wind that winter.

Cozie earned four memorable nicknames in the natural service of the seasons. One name at birth, the second was shortened and secular, and much later she secured two more names as the first permanent night nurse at the public health clinic on the White Earth Reservation.

When she was born, Gesture Browne named his niece Minomaate, a tribal word that means a good smell, like "something burning" in the language of the Anishinaabe. The shorter version of her name was *mino*, a word that means "good," and that was translated as "cozy" by the missionaries. The two time-release nicknames, the first such postindian names on the reservation, were given when she became the night nurse.

Cozie is her heartline name, a trace to the ancestors, but the two other nicknames are essential in the stories of those who heard the seasons and were healed by *oshkiwiinag*, the crystal trickster in the dead of night.

She is touched by the sound of the wind, the distance of shadows, that rare presence of creation as the dew rises over memories, and the natural ecstasies of ancient rivers. Later, she is morose as the sun haunts the ruins of the night. She hears the tricksters of creation overnight, not in the bright light.

Sour is her nickname at first light, and later, seen closer to the sunset, she is summoned as Burn. The dawn and sunset determine the mood and manner of her timeworn names in the clinic on the reservation. Sour in the morning. Burn as the night nurse.

Sour was summoned one morning to the clinic. "Some sort of emergency," the director said on the telephone. She was not pleased, but there was a reported medical crisis on the reservation at Camp Wikidin near Bad Medicine Lake. The Girl Scouts had been ravished and were rumored to be in a state of post-traumatic ecstasies.

"Ecstasies are a medical crisis?"

"City Scouts . . ."

"To be sure, and the bitter light of day is upon me," she said and leaned over his polished desk for instructions. Sour covered her eyes and told him to close the blinds.

"Sour, you know we would never bother you in the morning, but it might cloud over and rain, so we thought you could bear partial light and examine the campers," said the director. "Who else could answer the emergency?" He closed the blinds very slowly.

"Heat rash?"

"No, more serious," said the director.

"Poison ivy?"

"No, more serious than that, it seems."

"Hornets in the shower?" said Sour.

"No, more serious, some sort of ecstatic hysteria brought on by something they ate, some allergic reaction, or whatever," said the director. "The camp leader said it might have something to do with the discovery of a statue."

"What statue?"

"No, no, this is not that myth of the trickster who transformed all the tribal women one summer in ancient memory," he said and then raised his hands to resist the rest of the story. "No, no, this is not one of those trickster diseases, these are young white Girl Scouts from the city."

"Why not?"

"No, the trickster in that story was made out of crystal."

"*Oshkiwiinag*, and plenty more," said Sour.

"Right, hundreds of women were pregnant that summer."

"My grandmother told me those stories."

"Never mind, get out to the camp," said the director.

"My uncle said the crystal trickster was a man and a woman at a circus that summer, and somehow, he teased, the population doubled in one year on the reservation," said Sour.

Sour packed a medical case with calamine, ammonia, baking soda, various antihistamines, and epinephrine. She drove the shortest route over unpaved back roads to the Girl Scout camp. The first giant drops of rain burst in the loose sand, and the black flies wavered in the slipstream. Splendid foliage leaned over the road, a natural arbor that reduced the light north of Bad Medicine Lake.

Camp Wikidin was built on stolen tribal land, a sweetheart concession to the Scouts on land that had been ascribed to the tribes in treaties. "Maybe the Scouts are allergic to the reservation," she muttered on the last turn. The camp director and two anxious assistant Scout leaders were marching in circles in the gravel parking lot.

"This thing is something strange, something sexual!" shouted one leader. Her cheeks were swollen and bright red, her gestures were uncertain, and she watched the shadows at the treeline in the distance.

"Wait a minute," said Sour.

"Really, some kind of sexual thing," the leader insisted.

"No, no, stand back and let me park the car."

"Dark windows," said the other leader.

"I hate the light," said Sour.

"Allergic?" asked the camp director.

"No, no, just hate what the bright light does to faces and the natural play of shadows," said Sour. "So, now about this sexual thing, where are the girls who need medical attention?"

"We locked the girls in the main cabin to protect them for now," said the camp director. "We thought it best, as they had the very same symptoms."

"Why?" asked Sour.

"Because, this thing *could* be sexual," said the director.

"Do you mean a man?"

"Something very sinister has happened here."

"Doctor Sour . . ."

"Nurse Cozie Browne," said Sour.

"Nurse Browne, we thought you would be a doctor."

"Perhaps you need a surgeon from the city," said Sour.

"Never mind, we have all been touched by something overnight," said the camp director. She turned toward the nurse, her face narrowed by one wide crease down the center of her forehead. She turned the loose wedding ring on her finger. She was worried, but not frightened. "Something that *could* be sexual, but we cannot believe our own words."

The assistants were closer to panic than the director. Their hands were unclean and trembled out of control. The assistant with the big red cheeks chewed on her knuckles. She could not determine if the "sexual thing" was the beginning or the end of her career as a Girl Scout leader.

Sour moaned at the last turn to the main cabin. The campers were at the windows, their bright red faces pressed on the panes. Their sensuous bodies had overheated the building, and a wave of moist warm air rushed out when the director unlocked the door.

Sour examined every camper in a private office with pictures of prancing horses on the walls. She soothed the girls with gentle stories about nature, images of lilacs, pet animals, and garden birds, but could not detect any allergies, infections, or insect bites. Most of the campers were shied by the heat of their own bodies, and mentioned their dreams, the unnatural sensations of soaring over water.

Barrie, one of the campers, had the sense at last to consider what had changed in their lives that might have caused such ecstasies. The girl described, with unintended irony, their habits and activities over the past few days, and then she revealed the secret of the Scouts, that the campers had not been the same since they discovered a statue buried on the other side of the lake.

Later, when the campers gathered to clean and examine the figure, their secret tribal treasure, some of the girls swooned and fainted right at the table. The emotions were so contagious that the campers buried the statue and worried that they were being punished by some demon of the tribal land who hated outsiders from the cities. These were signs of post-traumatic ecstasies.

Barrie, who was a senior Scout, drew a very detailed map of the secret burial site. She blushed as she marked the trail to the burial site near a cedar tree. Then she fanned her cheeks with the map. The mere thought of the trickster statue caused her breasts to rise and her breath to shorten.

Cozie located the crystal trickster in a moist shallow grave. She bound the statue in a beach towel and returned to the clinic. She was ecstatic on the back roads, certain that the treasure was the very crystal trickster that had transformed the mundane in so many tribal stories on the reservation.

She locked the trickster in a laboratory and reported to the director that there were no diseases to treat at the camp, nothing but blushes, short breath, and "mild post-traumatic histaminic ecstasies." Later, the camp leaders reported that the girls were much better and that a cookout was being prepared. The Scouts swore that they would never reveal to anyone the stories of the crystal trickster.

Burn unbound the trickster that night when she had finished her rounds in the clinic. The room was dark, with an examination light on the statue. She soaked the trickster in warm water, and as the mire washed away, the pure crystal seemed to brighten the laboratory.

The crystal trickster was named *oshkiwiinag* in the stories she heard on the islands and the reservation. The ancient statue warmed her hands and face. The crystal was smoother than anything she had ever touched. Smoother than a mountain stone, human flesh, otter hair, smoother than ice cream.

Oshkiwiinag was about seventeen inches high, and each part of the crystal anatomy was polished with precision. The arms, legs, head, torso, and penis were perfect interlocking parts. For instance, the bright head could not be removed unless both arms were raised, and the arms could not be removed with the head attached. The pure crystal penis was the most precise and intricate part of the trickster. She could not determine how to remove the penis from the crystal body.

Burn polished each part with such pleasure that she lost her sense of time and place. She carried the shrouded trickster home in the front seat of her car and placed the statue in a locked closet. She would consider how to present the trickster to her uncle and grandparents at Wanaki Island.

Cozie and the thirteen Girl Scouts who had touched *Oshkiwiinag* were pregnant, and nine months later their trickster babies were born at almost the same hour. The coincidence became a scandal in the media, and hundreds of reporters roamed the reservation in search of wicked tricksters. The tribal government was cursed with nonfeasance, and the clinic was sued for malpractice by several mothers of the trickster babies. Cozie was portrayed as tribal witch on several radio and television shows, a nurse who hated the light and caused those innocent Girl Scouts to become pregnant.

Cozie was forced to leave the only job she ever loved at night. At the same time, she had a clever daughter and an incredible trickster who could conceive a child with a crystal touch. She trusted that *Oshkiwiinag* was the real father of her child, because she had not been with a man for three years, two months, and nineteen days. Her uncle taught her to be precise with memories, and he said that "trickster conceptions were natural reason on the heartlines."

"Natural is not the reason," said Cozie.

Several months later, the state medical examiners concluded in their report that the conceptions were curious cases of parthenogenesis. There is medical evidence that ecstasies and even terror have been the occasions of innocent conceptions. Such trickster stories were heard in tribal communities centuries before the medical examiners were overcome by the coincidence of parthenogenesis.

The Heartlines

The Naanabozho Express waited overnight at the station near the clinic. Gesture invited his niece to dinner in the parlor car. Cozie told him stories about *oshkiwiinag*, and the medical investigations on the reservation. He leaned back in the dental chair and insisted that she establish her own clinic on the train, "so you can practice trickster conceptions on women who would rather not bear the sensations and tortures of sexual intercourse."

Cozie moved to the train that very night and painted an announcement on the side of the parlor car. The sign read PARTHENOGENESIS ON THE NAANA-

BOZHO EXPRESS and, in smaller letters, SOVEREIGN CONCEPTIONS IN MOTION WITH NO FEARS, TEARS, OR DISEASES.

The trickster express circled the reservation for several months, and in that time thousands of people had their terminal teeth repaired free by the one and only acudenturist in motion, and even more women boarded the train for a short time to touch *oshkiwiinag* and conceive a child without sex. Some women had their teeth renewed and touched the trickster at the same time, ecstasy on one end and a better smile on the other. The crystal trickster soothed those who would fear the pain of dental instruments.

Gesture is precise about memories and his mission to show the nation that tribal independence is truer in motion than in the hush of manners, that natural reason is heard in heartline stories of chance and coincidence, not in the cultural weave and wash of silence.

The Naanabozho Express lurched out of that lonesome casino station on the last wild run of natural sovereignty from the White Earth Reservation to the White House in Washington.

PERSEPHONE SETS THE RECORD STRAIGHT

Shara McCallum

Shara McCallum has had poems in a number of literary journals, with works appearing in or forthcoming in *The Antioch Review, Chelsea, The Iowa Review,* and *Quarterly West,* among others. She was recently nominated for a Pushcart Prize for the 1997 anthology. In the following poem, "Persephone Sets the Record Straight" about what really happened when she swallowed those pomegranate seeds. McCallum's intriguing mythic poem comes from the pages of *The Iowa Review.*

—T. W.

You are all the rage these days,
mother. Everywhere I turn, I hear
Demeter in mourning, Demeter
grieving . . . poor Demeter.

Always craving the spotlight,
I know this is what you wanted:
your face on the front page
of all the papers; gossip

columns filled with juicy tidbits
on *what life was like before winter,*
old hags in the grocery store, whispering,
how she's let the flowers go,

while young women hover
in their gardens, fearing their hibiscus
will be next on your hit list.
After all these summers,

you still won't come clean.
Passing me iced tea, instead

you ask, *how's the redecorating?*
are you expanding

to make room for little ones?
Fanning away flies,
you avoid my eyes, saying,
I've so longed to be a grandma,

you know.
For God's sake, mother,
can't you tell me the truth now it's done?
Just once, tell me.

how you put me in that field
knowing he'd come,
that you made snow fall
everywhere to cover your tracks,

that the leaves die still
because you can't punish him
for confirming your suspicions:
not wanting you,

he took me instead.
Of course I ate those seeds.
Who wouldn't exchange
one hell for another?

CRUEL SISTERS
Patricia C. Wrede

"Cruel Sisters" is based on the old Scots-English folk ballad of the same title (popularized by Pentangle, Clannad, and other modern folk music groups). There are only two sisters mentioned in most versions of this tragic ballad: the dark sister and the light. When Patricia C. Wrede heard a version containing three sisters she was inspired to write a prose rendition of the tale. The third sister made only a brief appearance in the song, which set Ms. Wrede to wondering just what her role in the story might have been. . . .

Wrede is an author beloved by young readers for her hilarious Enchanted Forest series, and by adult readers for such lovely books as *Shadow Magic, The Harp of Imach Thysell, Snow White and Rose Red* and *The Raven's Ring*. She has also written numerous short stories, recently collected in *The Book of Enchantments*—from which the following story is reprinted.

—T. W.

The Harper would have you believe that it was all for the love of sweet William that my sisters came to hate each other so, but that is not true. They were bitter rivals from the time we were very small. His song misleads about other things, too; it does not mention me, for instance. "Two sisters in a bower," it says, not three, though the harp spoke of me and the harper himself stood beside my chair that day when he and his harp turned our clean grief to bitter poison. As for what the song says of William—well, the harper did not write that part himself, so he is not wholly to blame. I could forgive him for that, but not for what he said of my sisters.

Anne was the eldest of us three. Everyone who saw her said she was born to be a queen, with her long black hair and dark, flashing eyes, and her intelligence and force of will. When first they met her, people came away thinking that she was tall; it was always a shock to them to see her again in company and find that she was barely average woman-size. Eleanor was the tall one; after she passed Anne in height, she made me mark the lintel of our chamber every week for two years, until she finally tired of taunting Anne. In other ways, too,

497

Eleanor was Anne's opposite: her hair was golden, and her eyes a clear, corn-flower blue. If Anne was born to be a queen, Eleanor was meant to be a rich duke's pampered wife, carefree and merry.

And I? I am Margaret, plain Meg, in all things the middle daughter. My hair is thick, but it is an ordinary brown. My face is pleasant enough, I think, but that is a far cry from my sisters' beauty. My father calls me the quiet one, when he thinks of me; my mother says I am too much on the sidelines, watch-ing and thinking and saying little. By the common wisdom, it should have been I who was jealous of my sisters, but I loved both, and even when we were sisters, but I loved them both, and even when we were children it hurt me to watch the spiteful tricks they played on each other.

They loved me, too, in their own ways. Sometimes, rarely, one would even give up tormenting the other if I asked it, but such occasions grew less frequent as we grew older. The last time I tried to intervene was when Anne was fourteen and Eleanor twelve.

Eleanor had spilled ink on her best dress and laid the blame on Anne. Anne said nothing when our tutor punished her for it, but her lips were stiff and white about the edges. I did not know, then, that Eleanor had lied about the ink, but I knew that something was very wrong.

That afternoon, I missed them both, a circumstance so unusual that I went looking for them at once. I found them outside the curtain wall, in the far garden beside the river, where the briars are left to ramble as they will. Anne had Eleanor's favorite gown—not her best one, which had the ink spilled on it, but the blue silk the color of her eyes, with the white roses embroidered about the neck—and was waving it beside the thorns while Eleanor wept and snatched at it, trying to keep it from harm. Neither of them saw me as I came near.

"You lied to Master Crombie," Anne said, waving the dress. "Admit it."

"You know whether I did or not," Eleanor said. "Give me my gown!"

"Lies are beneath the dignity of our house," Anne said coldly. "One who bears our name ought not to lie."

"Eleanor!" I said, and they both turned to look at me. "Is it true?"

"Is what true?" she said, but her eyes slid away from mine, and I knew that Anne was right, that Eleanor had indeed made up the tale she told our tutor.

"She told Master Crombie that I had ruined her gown," Anne said in a grim tone. "It was not true when she said it, but I will make it true now." And she made to throw the fragile blue silk among the thorns.

"No!" I said, and she paused and looked at me.

"You take her side?"

I shook my head. "No. What she did was wrong. But what you would do will not make it right."

"I will tell Master Crombie the truth," Eleanor said suddenly, her eyes fixed on Anne's hands.

Anne turned, looked startled, and her grip loosened. Eleanor darted forward and seized the gown, then whirled away, laughing. "Silly, foolish, to be so tricked!"

Anne's lips went white, and she lunged forward. I was just too late to stop her. With all her might, she shoved Eleanor into the briars. Eleanor screamed in fright and pain as the thorns scratched her and tore her skirts.

"Now the things you told Master Crombie are true, after all," Anne said to her. "I have made them so."

"Anne!" I said. "How could you? Eleanor, be still! You will only hurt yourself if you thrash about."

"Let her hurt as much as I did when Master Crombie whipped me for her lies," Anne said.

"She might have been hurt far worse," I said as I went to help Eleanor out of the briars. "Men have been blinded in those thorns." I kept my voice as calm as I could, though I was deeply shocked by both their actions. I think they saw it, but neither would apologize, or admit to being in the wrong, and from that day, whatever power I might once have had to stop them hurting one another, I had no longer.

I do not know what tale Eleanor made to account for her scratches and the rips in two of her gowns, but I know it was not the truth, for neither she nor Anne was ever disciplined for it. Indeed, if I had not been there myself, I would not have known why Eleanor no longer wore her favorite blue gown. Perhaps I would not have noticed the increased tension between my sisters, either. No one else seemed aware of it, though to me the atmosphere in the schoolroom seemed to grow daily more fraught with anger and resentment.

So I was happy when Anne was finally old enough to put up her hair and move on to grown-up things, for it meant that the fights between her and Eleanor all but ceased. I thought their enmity must end with growing up, and for a few years it seemed to do so. I made my own transition to the world of feasts and dancing smoothly. I watched Anne with her suitors, but as befits a younger sister, I sought none of my own until she should have made her choice.

And then William came to court. "Sweet William," some of the verses say, and another song styles him "bonny William, brave and true." Well, he was bonny enough, with his gray eyes and hair like the silk on corn, and he had a tongue like honey, but from the first I did not like him. I had spent my early years watching my lovely sisters wound each other with comments no one else could see were barbed; perhaps it gave me a distrust of beauty and sweet words. But if that were so, Anne should have been armored even better than I, and she loved him from the moment he bent to kiss her hand before leading her out for their first dance.

"Isn't he handsome?" she said to me that night as we made ready for bed. "And kind. And a little shy, I think."

"He didn't seem shy to me when he was flirting with the serving maid," I said.

"Meg! He did no such thing." Anne sounded really distressed. "You're making it up."

"I know what I saw."

"He may have talked with her, but it was just to put her at ease," Anne said. "I told you he was kind. You must have misinterpreted it."

"I suppose I might have," I said, though I was sure I had not. Anne's expression lightened at once, and she went on singing William's praises until the maids came to put out the rushlights. She did not seem to notice my lack of response, or if she did, she put it down to tact or sympathy. But I do not think she noticed. She was too full of William.

"He is not the only man who courted you this evening," I said at last. "Robert brought you roses, and Malcolm—"

"Feh to Robert and Malcolm and all the rest," Anne said. "William is my choice, and I'll have him or no one."

"You can't mean that, Anne!" I said, appalled. "It is too sudden."

"Oh, I'll not be so hasty before the court," she said. "Did you think I meant to claim him tomorrow? We'll have a decorous courtship, and when he speaks to Father at last, no one will be amazed or put out. But I wanted you to know."

"You've not planned it out between you already?" I said. "After only one meeting?"

Anne laughed. "You are a goose. Go to sleep, and dream which of the men you will choose to look kindly on when I am settled. Robert, perhaps, since his roses made such an impression on you."

I threw a pillow at her. It was not until later, when she was asleep, that I realized she had not answered my question.

Anne was as good as her word. Over the next six weeks, she let her partiality for William begin to show, slowly but certainly, so that soon there was no doubt in anyone's mind that William was to be my father's first son-in-law. Before the court, she was discreet; when we were alone and private at night, she filled my ears with William's excellencies. They planned for William to make a formal request for her hand before the assembled May Day Court, in another month. And then Eleanor's birthday arrived, and she put up her hair for her coming-of-age feast.

I should have guessed what would happen. Gossip travels on the air in a king's hall; even in the schoolroom, Eleanor must have heard of Anne and William and their coming handfasting. Coming, but not yet concluded. Hating Anne as she did, as she had for so long, it was inevitable that she would try to spoil her happiness.

In all fairness, she did not have to try very hard. William took one look at Eleanor and fell as hard and far as Anne had fallen for him. And he was not in the least discreet about the change in the object of his affections. Indeed, it must have been plain even to Anne that he had never truly cared for her, for he had never treated her with half the tenderness he used toward Eleanor.

When I saw how it would be, I went to Eleanor and begged her to relent, for all our sakes. She smiled at me and shook her head. "It is too late for that. William loves me, not Anne."

"Yes, but the pair of you need not flaunt it before her," I said. I was angry, and sore on Anne's behalf, and I spoke more sharply than I had intended.

Eleanor looked startled. "Is that what you think? That we have been brandishing our affection apurpose?"

Then I saw that she had not; it was only her usual heedlessness. I said, "It is what Anne thinks."

"Oh, Anne. She has grieved me enough in my life; this time it is her turn."

"Do not say that," I said, distressed. "Love should not serve spite, and she is your sister, as much as I am." *And you have given her grief for grief, all your lives,* I could have added, but did not.

"Dear Meg," Eleanor said. "Always the peacemaker. Well, I suppose I can do that much for you. But I cannot give him up now, even if I would. He will not have it so."

"I know," I said. "I wish he had never come here."

So, on the first of May, before the assembled court, William asked my father for Eleanor's hand, not Anne's. It was scandalous, of course—the youngest daughter to be married before either of her sisters!—but there was already so much scandal about the match that it hardly mattered. Anne was pale as milk, but she kept her head high. Only I knew how she wept in the garden afterward, and only I seemed to notice the white stiffness around her lips, which I had not seen since that day when she pushed Eleanor into the briars.

It was that memory that sent me to Eleanor once again, to beg her to make peace with Anne. Yet I was surprised when she agreed; I had not expected her to hear my plea. I did not expect Anne to listen, either, but she did. I wonder, now, if things would have happened as they did, had I not interfered. Perhaps Eleanor wanted only to gloat over her latest and most final victory, and not to mend matters as she said she would; perhaps Anne wanted to vent her anger and pain, and not to ease her heart. There is no not way to know. I tell myself that if those things were true, what I did can have made no real difference. But I do not really believe it.

All the world knows what happened next: how Anne and Eleanor went walking by the river that ran dark and swollen with snowmelt, and how only Anne returned, her dress torn, her hands scratched, and her hair in wild disarray. She told us Eleanor had slipped and fallen into the torrent, and she had struggled through the briars along the bank, trying without success to pull her out.

My father sent his men off to search at once, of course. William was first among them, his eyes a little wild, and Anne looked away as he rode out. Then she collapsed, all in a heap. I was almost glad. Tending Anne gave me something to do while we waited for the men to return.

They returned without Eleanor. I heard one of them say that with the river swollen as it was, she had doubtless been swept out to sea. Anne heard, too, and we wept together. Father sent more men for boats, though he must have known by then that it was hopeless. "At least we can bring her back to the churchyard," he said, and his voice cracked when he spoke.

We were not allowed even so much as that. My father's men found nothing, though the fisherfolk, too, joined in the search. Three days later, there was a terrible storm, with wind and hail and lightning and the sea in a wild rage. Afterward, everyone could see that little likelihood remained of finding Eleanor's body. The priest said a memorial mass, and my father paid him for a year of daily prayers. Things began to slip back into the routine of ordinary days, save that when we glanced out at the kitchen garden, or in at the sewing rooms, or down the long high table, we did not see Eleanor's bright hair, nor thought we ever would again.

Anne took it hardest of us all. She picked at her food but ate little, and she slept hardly at all. After that first day, she never spoke of Eleanor but once.

"She was so frightened," Anne told me, "and I could not pull her out. I could not."

I did not know how to comfort her. Indeed, I was surprised that she should need comforting. The rest of the court might marvel at her devotion to her youngest sister, but I knew how little love had been lost between them. I thought it was the horror of watching Eleanor drown that shadowed Anne's eyes, and perhaps it was. Or perhaps she was lost without Eleanor to rail against. Perhaps.

A month went by, and the grief of Eleanor's passing was no longer a sharp knife in the heart, but a dull, heavy burden that ached the muscles and tired the spirit. William stayed at court, and now and then I saw him watching Anne covertly. He had loved Eleanor, I was sure, but Eleanor was gone and he still wished to marry one of my father's daughters. It was too soon for him to transfer his affections back. Nonetheless, he could watch and judge his chances.

I did not think they were good. Anne was not one to take such a slight as he had put on her and then return to him smiling when he crooked his finger. William did not understand that. Once, he tried to speak with her, and she walked away without answering. Later in the evening, I heard him telling Robert that it touched his heart to see how Anne grieved for his Eleanor. He knew that I was near, and he spoke louder than he needed; I think he meant for me to carry tales to Anne. But that I could not do, even if I would have. Anne spoke no more of William than she did of Eleanor. It was as if they had both died, together, in that swollen river.

And then, suddenly, Midsummer was upon us. As was the custom, my father planned a feast, though none of us rejoiced in the prospect. It was to be the first great feast since Eleanor's death, and everywhere we turned we were reminded anew that she was no longer there.

To turn our minds from the empty place at the high table, my father sent out word that any harpers who wished to join us would be welcomed and would have a chance to play before the king and queen and their daughters. Harpers are always guested and gifted, of course, for harpers are known to hold some of the old magic and it is ill luck to do otherwise, but in the normal course of things only the best perform in the great hall. My mother complained of it, when she heard. She said we would spend an evening listening to every bad and boring player who earned a bit of bread on the highways and in the taverns, but by then it was too late to take back the offer.

For the most part, she was right. The harpers nearly outnumbered the guests at our Midsummer feast, and though Father set a limit of two songs apiece, each seemed to have chosen the two longest and most boring pieces he knew. It was nearing midnight when the last man rose to take his seat and play for us.

He was a tall man, blond and full of bony angles. He did not move with the practiced grace of the other musicians, and he carried his harp case as if it were an infant.

"My lord king, I bring you a wonder," he said, and even in those simple words, his voice was gold and silk.

My father nodded. "Sit and play for us, harper."

"I shall not play, my lord, but you shall hear a song the like of which no man has heard before."

"If you do not play, why do you carry a harp?" my father asked.

"It is the harp that plays," the minstrel said. His voice deepened and seemed to call shadows from all the corners of the room. "Listen, O king! For this is no ordinary harp. I made it of the bones of a drowned maiden I found upon the seashore and strung it with her hair, and as I worked I sang the ancient songs of magic, that the harp might sing in its turn. And now, indeed, it does. Hear the tale, and marvel!"

With that, he opened the harp case with a flourish and set his instrument on the stone floor before him. He did not seem to notice the horror that dawned upon the faces of our guests at his bald claim, or the way my father's face had gone white when he mentioned the drowned girl, or how my mother swayed in her seat when he told what gruesome use he made of the body. His attention was all on the harp.

A moment later, so was ours, for as soon as the minstrel stepped back, the harp began to play itself. One after another, the strings sang in notes of piercing strangeness, sweeter and more biting than the music of any ordinary harp. They filled the hall and echoed in the flickering shadows. The notes ran up and down the scale, then began to play a simple song, a tune that all of us had heard a hundred times and more. But the words that sang among the notes were no song any of us had heard before, and the voice that sang them . . . the voice was Eleanor's.

> "Mother and father, queen and king,
> Farewell to you, farewell I sing.
> Farewell to William, sweet and true,
> Farewell, dear sister Meg, to you.
> But woe to my fair sister Anne
> Who killed me for to take my man."

The harp played its scale once more and then began to repeat the verse. We sat frozen, all of us—all of us but Anne. She rose, her lips white and stiff, and walked to the harp. As it reached the final lines, the lines that named her Eleanor's murderer, Anne picked up the harp and smashed it against the hearthstone with all her might.

The bone splintered, stopping the music in a jangling discord. The jarring noises hung in the air long after Anne turned to face the assembled guests once more. She stood there, her chin high, every inch a king's daughter, while the last lingering sounds died into silence and the silence stretched into dismay and horror.

It was the minstrel who broke the silence. "You have killed your sister a second time," he said to Anne in his beautiful, silken voice.

Anne looked at him coldly. "Then that much of what she sang is true, now."

My mother slid to the floor in a faint. My father stood, though he had to brace himself against the table to keep his feet without trembling. "Take her away," he said in a hoarse voice.

"No!" I said before I thought.

He turned to look at me. "Margaret, it must be," he said, and his tone was gentle, though I could see the effort it took for him to speak so. "You heard the harp. See to your mother." He turned back to the hall and repeated, "Take her away."

The guards moved forward jerkily, like ill-managed puppets. I looked away, for I could not bear to watch. They took Anne quickly from the hall, and as the door closed behind them, the guests unfroze and began to murmur in low, stricken tones. I could not bear that, either. My mother's ladies were all around her, leaving nothing for me to do. I rose to leave.

The minstrel stood beside the door, holding his empty harp case. He looked at me with sympathy. I think that under other circumstances, I might have liked him. "It is hard for you to compass," he said softly. "I am sorry for your hurt."

I am not so good as Anne at giving people a look or a glare that freezes them to the bone, but I did the best I could. "You desecrated my sister's body, and for what? To cut up our peace and raise doubts where there were none."

"To find out the truth," the minstrel said, but he sounded a little shaken.

"The truth? What truth? My sister Eleanor was a liar all her life, and all her life cast the blame for her own errors on Anne. Why should death have changed that?"

"The dead are beyond such pettiness."

"Are they?" I said. "For most of what the harp sang, I do not know, but this much you can hear from anyone at court: 'William, sweet and true' was true to neither Anne nor Eleanor. And if the harp lied about that, why not about the other matters?"

I left while he was still casting about for an answer. I was tired and sore at heart and much confused. I did not know what to believe. Eleanor was a liar, and I know better than anyone the lengths to which she would go to spite Anne. But Anne had a temper, and when it was roused . . . well, I could not help remembering the briars. She might have pushed Eleanor into the river the same way and regretted it after. She might have. But did she?

We buried the shattered remains of the harp, which were all we had of my sister's bones. The ceremony brought no one any peace or comfort. The memories of magic and possible murder clung too close, and the tiny coffin made everyone think of the minstrel plucking and coiling Eleanor's golden hair for harp strings, and shaping her finger bones into tuning pegs, and cutting apart her breastbone for the harp itself. It would have been better if someone had thought to use a coffin of ordinary size. At least then we could have pretended to forget what had been done to her.

They could not try Anne for murder on the strength of a harp song, and that was all the proof they had. Still, after such an accusation, made in such a way, something had to be done. In the end, my father sent her to a convent to do penance among the sisters. She died of a chill less than six months later. She never denied what the harp had said, any more than she had ever denied Eleanor's lies in public. But the sisters say that she never confessed her guilt, either.

And I? I am the only daughter now, and it is a hard position to fill alone. William, "bonny William, brave and true," gave the lie to the harp's description once more by making sheep's eyes at me almost before the convent doors had closed behind Anne. I sent him away, and I was firm enough about it that he has not returned, for which I am grateful. But there will be others like him soon enough.

Even those who see me, Margaret, and not merely the king's last daughter, do not understand. They say I grieve too long for my sisters, that I should put their tragedy behind me. I grieve for Eleanor and Anne, yes, but it is my own guilt that takes me to the chapel every morning. If I had spoken sooner, if I had made our nurses and our tutors and our parents see the depth of the rivalry between Anne and Eleanor, perhaps one of them could have put a stop to it before it ended in this horror. At the least, perhaps they would have listened when I tried to make them see that the harp was not to be believed without question.

It is too late to change what happened between my sisters, but I still hear more than others seem to, and I have begun to speak of what I hear. It is hard to break the habit of so many years, but I think that I am getting better at it. At least, my efforts now have met with more success than did my attempts to soothe my sisters. Lord Owen and Lord Douglas set their argument aside after I spoke with them last month. My father says I stopped a potential feud, and speaks of having me attend the next working court, to advise him about the petitioners. So much attention makes me uncomfortable, but I suppose I shall become accustomed in time. It is the price I must pay for saying what I know. And if I have learned anything from this, I have learned that it is not enough to see. One must speak out as well.

Even today, I do not know what happened that day beside the river. But I am the only one with doubts, it seems. The dramatic accusation persuaded nearly everyone, and those who were not satisfied by the harp's song were convinced when Anne smashed the harp to bits. She did it to silence her accuser, they say. But I remember her words to the minstrel: "Then that much of what she sang is true, now." And I remember her voice when she was fourteen, saying of Eleanor, "It was not true when she said it, but I will make it true now."

I tried to tell my father all my doubts before he sent Anne away, as I tried to tell the minstrel that night in the great hall. Father would not listen then; like everyone else, he believed the harp. The minstrel's hearing was better, I think. For though the song he wrote afterward tells only the story that everyone believes, and nothing of the doubts I shared with him, he has at least made no more magic harps from the desecrated bodies of the dead.

THE HOUSE OF SEVEN ANGELS

Jane Yolen

Jane Yolen is one of the most important writers of children's books in this country, as well as the author of lovely, mythical fantasy stories and novels for adults. She is the author of *Briar Rose; Sister Light, Sister Dark; Cards of Grief; Tales of Wonder* and over one hundred other fine books. She is also a folklore scholar, lecturer, storyteller, ballad singer, and poet.

The following exquisite little folk tale is drawn from the author's Jewish heritage, and comes from the pages of her most recent picture book for children: *Here There Be Angels* (with beautiful drawings by David Wilgus.) Yolen—who has won the World Fantasy Award among numerous other honors—lives with her husband in rural Massachusetts, and also St. Andrews, Scotland.

—T. W.

My grandparents lived in the Ukraine in a village known as Ykaterinislav. It was a sleepy little Jewish town near Kiev, but if you go to look for it now, it is gone.

The people there were all hardworking farmers and tradesfolk, though there was at least one poor scholar who taught in the heder, a rabbi with the thinnest beard imaginable and eyes that leaked pink water whenever he spoke.

These were good people, you understand, but not exactly religious. That is, they went to shul and they did no work on the Sabbath and they fasted on Yom Kippur. But that was because their mothers and fathers had done so before them. Ykaterinislav was not a place that took to change. But the people there were no more tuned to God's note than any other small village. They were, you might say, tone-deaf to the cosmos.

Like most people.

And then one autumn day in 1897—about ten years before my grandparents even began to think about moving to America—a wandering rabbi came into the village. His name was Reb Jehudah and he was a very religious man. Some even said that he was the prophet Elijah, but that was later.

Reb Jehudah studied the Torah all day long and all night long. He put all the men in Ykaterinislav to shame. So they avoided him. My grandfather did, too, but he took out his books again, which had been stored away under the big double bed he and Grandma Manya shared. Took them out but never quite got around to reading them.

And then one of the village children, a boy named Moishe, peeked into Reb Jehudah's window. At first it was just curiosity. A boy, a window, what else could it have been? He saw the reb at dinner, his books before him. And he was being served, Moishe said, by seven angels.

Who could believe such a thing? Though the number, seven, was so specific. So the village elders asked the boy: How did he know they were angels?

"They had wings," Moishe said. "Four wings each. And they shone like brass."

"Who shone?" asked the elders. "The angels or the wings?"

"Yes," said Moishe, his eyes glowing.

Who could quarrel with a description like that?

Of course the village men went to visit Reb Jehudah to confirm what Moishe had seen. But they saw no angels, with or without wings. Like Balaam of the Bible, they had not the proper eyes.

But for a boy like Moishe to have been given such a vision . . . this was not the kind of rascal who made up stories. Indeed, Moishe was, if anything, a bit slow. Besides, such things had been known to happen, though never before in Ykaterinislav.

And so the elders went back to Butcher Kalman's house for tea, to discuss this. And perhaps Butcher Kalman put a bit of schnapps in their cups. Who can say? But they talked about it for hours—about the possibility of angels in Ykaterinislav, and in the autumn, too.

It was *pilpul*, of course, argument for argument's sake, even if they quoted Scripture. After a while, though, their old habits of nonbelief reclaimed them and they returned to their own work, but with renewed vigor. The crops, the shops, even the heder were the better for all the talk, so perhaps the angels were good for something after all.

Reb Jehudah knew nothing of this, of course. He continued his studying, day and night, night and day, wrestling with the great and small meanings of the law.

Now, one day an eighth angel came to visit him, an angel dressed in a long black robe that had pictures of eyes sewn into it, eyes that opened and closed at will. There was a ring of fire above the angel instead of a halo, and he carried an unsheathed sword. He held the sword above Reb Jehudah's head.

It was Samael, the Angel of Death.

Reb Jehudah did not notice this angel any more than he had noticed the others, for he was much too busy poring over the books of the law.

The Angel of Death shuddered. He knew that as long as the rabbi was engaged in his studies, his life could not be taken.

All this Moishe saw, peeping through the window, for he had come every day to watch over Rabbi Jehudah instead of attending heder or working on his father's farm. As if he were another angel, though a bit grubby, with a smudge on one cheek and his fingernails not quite clean.

When Moishe saw the eighth angel, he shook all over with fear. He recognized Samael. He had heard about that sword with its bitter drop of poison at the tip. "The supreme poison," his teacher had called it.

"Reb Jehudah," Moishe called, "beware!"

The rabbi, intent on his studies, never heard the boy. But the Angel of Death did. He turned his awful head toward the window and smiled.

It was not a pleasant smile.

And before Moishe could duck or run, the Angel of Death was by his side.

"I will have one from this village today," said the angel. "If it cannot be the rabbi, then it shall be you." And he held his sword above Moishe's head.

Seized by terror, the child gasped, and his mouth opened wide to receive the poison drop.

At that very moment, the seven angels in Reb Jehudah's house set up a terrible wail; and this, at last, broke the good rabbi's concentration. He stood, stretched, and looked out of the window to the garden that he loved, it being as beautiful to him as the Garden of Eden. He saw a boy at his window gasping for breath. Without a thought more, the rabbi ran outside and put his arms around the boy to try and stop the convulsions.

Head up, the rabbi prayed, "O Lord of All Creation, may this child not die."

The minute the rabbi's mouth opened, the poison drop from the sword fell into it, and he died.

The Angel of Death flew away, his errand accomplished. He would not be back in Ykaterinislav until early spring, for a pogrom. But the seven angels flew out of the open window, gathered up Reb Jehudah's soul, and carried it off to Heaven, where Metatron himself embraced the rabbi and called him blessed.

All this young Moishe saw, but he knew he could not tell anyone in Ykaterinislav. No one would believe him.

Instead he became a great storyteller, one of the greatest the world has ever known. His tales went around the earth, inspiring artists and musicians, settling children in their cots, and making the evenings when the tales were read aloud as sweet as nights in Paradise. "It was as if," one critic said of him, "his stories were carried on the wings of angels."

And perhaps they were.

RADIO WAVES

Michael Swanwick

Michael Swanwick is one of the finest writers working in the speculative fiction field today. His first novel, *In the Drift*, was published as part of Terry Carr's prestigious Ace Science Fiction Specials series; more recently he published *The Iron Dragon's Daughter*, a hard-hitting, ground-breaking work of modern fantasy. He has won the Nebula, Hugo and World Fantasy Awards. Swanwick lives with his wife and son in Pennsylvania.

The tale that follows is a luminous work of contemporary fantasy, first published in the January 1996 issue of *Omni* magazine. "Radio Waves" won the 1996 World Fantasy Award for the best short story of the year.

—T. W.

I was walking the telephone wires upside-down, the sky underfoot cold and flat with a few hard bright stars sparsely scattered about it, when I thought how it would take only an instant's weakness to step off to the side and fall up forever into the night. A kind of wildness entered me then and I began to run.

I made the wires sing. They leapt and bulged above me as I raced past Ricky's Luncheonette and up the hill. Past the old chocolate factory and the IDI Advertising Display plant. Past the body shops, past A. J. LaCourse Electric Motors-Controls-Parts. Then, where the slope steepened, along the curving snake of rowhouses that went the full quarter mile up to the Ridge. Twice I overtook pedestrians, hunched and bundled, heads doggedly down, out on incomprehensible errands. They didn't notice me, of course. They never do. The antenna farm was visible from here. I could see the Seven Sisters spangled with red lights, dependent on the earth like stalactites. "Where are you running to, little one?" one tower whispered in a crackling, staticky voice. I think it was Hegemone.

"Fuck off," I said without slackening my pace, and they all chuckled.

Cars mumbled by. This was ravine country, however built up, and the far side of the road, too steep and rocky for development, was given over to trees and garbage. Hamburger wrappings and white plastic trash bags rustled in their wake. I was running full-out now.

About a block or so from the Ridge, I stumbled and almost fell. I slapped an arm across a telephone pole and just managed to catch myself in time. Aghast at my own carelessness, I hung there, dizzy and alarmed. The ground overhead was black as black, an iron roof, yet somehow was as anxious as a hound to leap upon me, crush me flat, smear me to nothingness. I stared up at it, horrified.

Somebody screamed my name.

I turned. A faint blue figure clung to a television antenna atop a small, stuccoed brick duplex. Charlie's Widow. She pointed an arm that flickered with silver fire down Ripka Street. I slewed about to see what was coming after me.

It was the Corpsegrinder.

When it saw that I'd spotted it, it put out several more legs, extended a quilled head, and raised a howl that bounced off the Heaviside layer. My non-existent blood chilled.

In a panic, I scrambled up and ran toward the Ridge and safety. I had a squat in the old Roxy, and once I was through the wall, the Corpsegrinder would not follow. Why this should be so, I did not know. But you learn the rules if you want to survive.

I ran. In the back of my head I could hear the Seven Sisters clucking and gossiping to each other, radiating television and radio over a few dozen frequencies. Indifferent to my plight.

The Corpsegrinder churned up the wires on a hundred needle-sharp legs. I could feel the ion surge it kicked up pushing against me as I reached the intersection of Ridge and Leverington. Cars were pulling up to the pumps at the Atlantic station. Teenagers stood in front of the A-Plus Mini Market, flicking half-smoked cigarettes into the street, stamping their feet like colts, and waiting for something to happen. I couldn't help feeling a great longing disdain for them. Every last one worried about grades and drugs and zits, and all the while snugly barricaded within hulking fortresses of flesh.

I was scant yards from home. The Roxy was a big old movie palace, fallen into disrepair and semiconverted to a skateboarding rink which had gone out of business almost immediately. But it had been a wonderful place once, and the terra-cotta trim was still there: ribbons and river-gods, great puffing faces with panpipes, guitars, flowers, wyverns. I crossed the Ridge on a dead telephone wire, spider-web delicate but still usable.

Almost there.

Then the creature was upon me, with a howl of electromagnetic rage that silenced even the Sisters for an instant. It slammed into my side, a storm of razors and diamond-edged fury, hooks and claws extended.

I grabbed at a rusty flange on the side of the Roxy.

Too late! Pain exploded within me, a sheet of white nausea. All in an instant I lost the name of my second daughter, an April morning when the world was new and I was five, a smoky string of all-nighters in Rensselaer Polytech, the jowly grin of Old Whatsisface the German who lived on LaFountain Street, the fresh pain of a sprained ankle out back of a Banana Republic warehouse, fishing off a yellow rubber raft with my old man on Lake Champlain. All gone, these and a thousand things more, sucked away, crushed to nothing, beyond retrieval.

Furious as any wounded animal, I fought back. Foul bits of substance splattered under my fist. The Corpsegrinder reared up to smash me down, and I scrabbled desperately away. Something tore and gave.

Then I was through the wall and safe and among the bats and gloom.

"Cobb!" the Corpsegrinder shouted. It lashed wildly back and forth, scouring the brick walls with limbs and teeth, as restless as a March wind, as unpredictable as ball lightning.

For the moment I was safe. But it had seized a part of me, tortured it, and made it a part of itself. I could no longer delude myself into thinking it was simply going to go away. "Cahawahawbb!" It broke my name down to a chord of overlapping tones. It had an ugly, muddy voice. I felt dirtied just listening to it. "Caw—" A pause. "—awbb!"

In a horrified daze I stumbled up the Roxy's curving patterned-tin roof until I found a section free of bats. Exhausted and dispirited, I slumped down.

"Caw aw aw awb buh buh!"

How had the thing found me? I'd thought I'd left it behind in Manhattan. Had my flight across the high-tension lines left a trail of some kind? Maybe. Then again, it might have some special connection with me. To follow me here it must have passed by easier prey. Which implied it had a grudge against me. Maybe I'd known the Corpsegrinder back when it was human. We could once have been important to each other. We might have been lovers. It was possible. The world is a stranger place than I used to believe.

The horror of my existence overtook me then, an acute awareness of the squalor in which I dwelt, the danger which surrounded me, and the dark mystery informing my universe. I wept for all that I had lost.

Eventually, the sun rose up like God's own Peterbilt and with a triumphant blare of chromed trumpets, gently sent all of us creatures of the night to sleep.

When you die, the first thing that happens is that the world turns upside-down. You feel an overwhelming disorientation and a strange sensation that's not quite pain as the last strands connecting you to your body part, and then you slip out of physical being and fall from the planet.

As you fall, you attenuate. Your substance expands and thins, glowing more and more faintly as you pick up speed. So far as can be told, it's a process that doesn't ever stop. Fainter, thinner, colder . . . until you've merged into the substance of everyone else who's ever died, spread perfectly uniformly through the universal vacuum forever moving toward but never arriving at absolute zero. Look hard, and the sky is full of the Dead.

Not everyone falls away. Some few are fast-thinking or lucky enough to maintain a tenuous hold on earthly existence. I was one of the lucky ones. I was working late one night on a proposal when I had my heart attack. The office was empty. The ceiling had a wire mesh within the plaster and that's what saved me.

The first response to death is denial. *This can't be happening,* I thought. I gaped up at the floor where my body had fallen and would lie undiscovered until morning. My own corpse, pale and bloodless, wearing a corporate tie and sleeveless gray Angora sweater. Gold Rolex, Sharper Image desk accessories, and of course I also thought: *I died for* this? By which of course I meant my entire life.

So it was in a state of personal and ontological crisis that I wandered across the ceiling to the location of an old pneumatic message tube, removed and plastered over some fifty years before. I fell from the seventeenth to the twenty-fifth floor, and I learned a lot in the process. Shaken, startled, and already beginning to assume the wariness that the afterlife requires, I went to a window to get a glimpse of the outer world. When I tried to touch the glass, my hand went right through. I jerked back. Cautiously, I leaned forward so that my head stuck out into the night.

What a wonderful experience Times Square is when you're dead! There is ten times the light a living being sees. All metal things vibrate with inner life. Electric wires are thin scratches in the air. Neon *sings*. The world is filled with strange sights and cries. Everything shifts from beauty to beauty.

Something that looked like a cross between a dragon and a wisp of smoke was feeding in the Square. But it was lost among so many wonders that I gave it no particular thought.

Night again. I awoke with Led Zeppelin playing in the back of my head. *Stairway to Heaven.* Again. It can be a long wait between Dead Milkmen cuts.

"Wakey-risey, little man," crooned one of the Sisters. It was funny how sometimes they took a close personal interest in our doings, and other times ignored us completely. "This is Euphrosyne with the red-eye weather report. The outlook is moody with a chance of existential despair. You won't be going outside tonight if you know what's good for you. There'll be lightning within the hour."

"It's too late in the year for lightning," I said.

"Oh dear. Should I inform the weather?"

By now I was beginning to realize that what I had taken on awakening to be the Corpsegrinder's dark aura was actually the high-pressure front of an approaching storm. The first drops of rain pattered on the roof. Wind skirled and the rain grew stronger. Thunder growled in the distance. "Why don't you just go fuck your—"

A light laugh that trilled up into the supersonic, and she was gone.

I was listening to the rain underfoot when a lightning bolt screamed into existence, turning me inside-out for the briefest instant then cartwheeling gleefully into oblivion. In the instant of restoration following the bolt, the walls were transparent and all the world made of glass, its secrets available to be snooped out. But before comprehension was possible, the walls opaqued again and the lightning's malevolent aftermath faded like a madman's smile in the night.

Through it all the Seven Sisters were laughing and singing, screaming with joy whenever a lightning bolt flashed, and making up nonsense poems from howls, whistles, and static. During a momentary lull, the flat hum of a carrier wave filled my head. Phaenna, by the feel of her. But instead of her voice, I heard only the sound of fearful sobs.

"Widow?" I said. "Is that you?"

"She can't hear you," Phaenna purred. "You're lucky I'm here to bring you up to speed. A lightning bolt hit the transformer outside her house. It was bound to happen sooner or later. Your Nemesis—the one you call the Corpsegrinder, such a cute nickname, by the way—has her trapped."

This was making no sense at all. "Why would the Corpsegrinder be after her?"

"Why why why why?" Phaenna sang, a snatch of some pop ballad or other.

"You didn't get answers when you were alive, what makes you think you'd get any *now?*" The sobbing went on and on. "She can sit it out," I said. "The Corpsegrinder can't—hey, wait. Didn't they just wire her house for cable? I'm trying to picture it. Phone lines on one side, electric on the other, cable. She can slip out on his blind side."

The sobs lessened and then rose in a most un-Widowlike wail of despair.

"Typical," Phaenna said. "You haven't the slightest notion of what you're talking about. The lightning stroke has altered your little pet. Go out and see for yourself." My hackles rose. "You know damned good and well that I can't—"

Phaenna's attention shifted and the carrier beam died. The Seven Sisters are fickle that way. This time, though, it was just as well. No way was I going out there to face that monstrosity. I couldn't. And I was grateful not to have to admit it.

For a long while I sat thinking about the Corpsegrinder. Even here, protected by the strong walls of the Roxy, the mere thought of it was paralyzing. I tried to imagine what Charlie's Widow was going through, separated from this monster by only a thin curtain of brick and stucco. Feeling the hard radiation of its malice and need . . . It was beyond my powers of visualization. Eventually I gave up and thought instead about my first meeting with the Widow.

She was coming down the hill from Roxborough with her arms out, the inverted image of a child playing a tightrope walker. Placing one foot ahead of the other with deliberate concentration, scanning the wire before her so cautiously that she was less than a block away when she saw me.

She screamed.

Then she was running straight at me. My back was to the transformer station—there was no place to flee. I shrank away as she stumbled to a halt.

"It's you!" she cried. "Oh God, Charlie, I knew you'd come back for me, I waited so long but I never doubted you, never, we can—" She lunged forward as if to hug me. Our eyes met.

All the joy in her died.

"Oh," she said. "It's not you."

I was fresh off the high-tension lines, still vibrating with energy and fear. My mind was a blaze of contradictions. I could remember almost nothing of my post-death existence. Fragments, bits of advice from the old dead, a horrifying confrontation with . . . something, some creature or phenomenon that had driven me to flee Manhattan. Whether it was this event or the fearsome voltage of that radiant highway that had scoured me of experience, I did not know. "It's me," I protested.

"No, it's not." Her gaze was unflatteringly frank. "You're not Charlie and you never were. You're—just the sad remnant of what once was a man, and not a very good one at that." She turned away. She was leaving me! In my confusion, I felt such a despair as I had never known before.

"Please . . ." I said.

She stopped.

A long silence. Then what in a living woman would have been a sigh. "You'd think that I—well, never mind." She offered her hand, and when I would not take it, said, "This way."

I followed her down Main Street, through the shallow canyon of the business district to a diner at the edge of town. It was across from Hubcap Heaven and an automotive junkyard bordered it on two sides. The diner was closed. We settled down on the ceiling.

"That's where the car ended up after I died," she said, gesturing toward the junkyard. "It was right after I got the call about Charlie. I stayed up drinking and after a while it occurred to me that maybe they were wrong, they'd made some sort of horrible mistake and he wasn't really dead, you know?

"Like maybe he was in a coma or something, some horrible kind of misdiagnosis, they'd gotten him confused with somebody else, who knows? Terrible things happen in hospitals. They make mistakes.

"I decided I had to go and straighten things out. There wasn't time to make coffee so I went to the medicine cabinet and gulped down a bunch of pills at random, figuring something among them would keep me awake. Then I jumped into the car and started off for Colorado."

"My God."

"I have no idea how fast I was going—everything was a blur when I crashed. At least I didn't take anybody with me, thank the Lord. There was this one horrible moment of confusion and pain and rage and then I found myself lying on the floor of the car with my corpse just inches beneath me on the underside of the roof." She was silent for a moment. "My first impulse was to crawl out the window. Lucky for me I didn't." Another pause. "It took me most of a night to work my way out of the yard. I had to go from wreck to wreck. There were these gaps to jump. It was a nightmare."

"I'm amazed you had the presence of mind to stay in the car."

"Dying sobers you up fast."

I laughed. I couldn't help it. And without the slightest hesitation, she joined right in with me. It was a fine warm moment, the first I'd had since I didn't know when. The two of us set each other off, laughing louder and louder, our merriment heterodyning until it filled every television screen for a mile around with snow.

My defenses were down. She reached out and took my hand.

Memory flooded me. It was her first date with Charlie. He was an electrician. Her next-door neighbor was having the place rehabbed. She'd been working in the back yard and he struck up a conversation. Then he asked her out. They went to a disco in the Adam's Mark over on City Line Avenue.

She wasn't eager to get involved with somebody just then. She was still recovering from a hellish affair with a married man who'd thought that since he wasn't available for anything permanent, that made her his property. But when Charlie suggested they go out to the car for some coke—it was the Seventies—she'd said sure. He was going to put the moves on her sooner or later. Might as well get it settled early so they'd have more time for dancing.

But after they'd done up the lines, Charlie had shocked her by taking her hands in his and kissing them. She worked for a Bucks County pottery in those days and her hands were rough and red. She was very sensitive about them.

"Beautiful hands," he murmured. "Such beautiful, beautiful hands."

"You're making fun of me," she protested, hurt.

"No! These are hands that *do* things, and they've been shaped by the things they've done. The way stones in a stream are shaped by the water that passes over them. The way tools are shaped by their work. A hammer is beautiful, if it's a good hammer, and your hands are, too."

He could have been scamming her. But something in his voice, his manner, said no, he really meant it. She squeezed his hands and saw that they were beautiful, too. Suddenly she was glad she hadn't gone off the pill when she broke up with Daniel. She started to cry. Her date looked alarmed and baffled. But she couldn't stop. All the tears she hadn't cried in the past two years came pouring out of her, unstoppable.

Charlie-boy, she thought, you just got lucky.

All this in an instant. I snatched my hands away, breaking contact. *"Don't do that!"* I cried. "Don't you *ever* touch me again!"

With flat disdain, the Widow said, "It wasn't pleasant for me either. But I had to see how much of your life you remember."

It was naïve of me, but I was shocked to realize that the passage of memories had gone both ways. But before I could voice my outrage, she said, "There's not much left of you. You're only a fragment of a man, shreds and tatters, hardly anything. No wonder you're so frightened. You've got what Charlie calls a low signal-to-noise ratio. What happened in New York City almost destroyed you."

"That doesn't give you the right to—"

"Oh be still. You need to know this. Living is simple, you just keep going. But death is complex. It's so hard to hang on and so easy to let go. The temptation is always there. Believe me, I know. There used to be five of us in Roxborough, and where are the others now? Two came through Manayunk last spring and camped out under the El for a season and they're gone, too. Holding it together is hard work. One day the stars start singing to you, and the next you begin to listen to them. A week later they start to make sense. You're just reacting to events—that's not good enough. If you mean to hold on, you've got to know why you're doing it."

"So why are *you?*"

"I'm waiting for Charlie," she said simply.

It occurred to me to wonder exactly how many years she had been waiting. Three? Fifteen? Just how long was it possible to hold on? Even in my confused and emotional state, though, I knew better than to ask. Deep inside she must've known as well as I did that Charlie wasn't coming. "My name's Cobb," I said. "What's yours?"

She hesitated and then, with an odd sidelong look, said, "I'm Charlie's widow. That's all that matters." It was all the name she ever gave, and Charlie's Widow she was to me from then onward.

I rolled onto my back on the tin ceiling and spread out my arms and legs, a phantom starfish among the bats. A fragment, she had called me, shreds and tatters. No wonder you're so frightened! In all the months since I'd been washed into this backwater of the power grid, she'd never treated me with anything but a condescension bordering on contempt.

So I went out into the storm after all.

The rain was nothing. It passed right through me. But there were ion-heavy gusts of wind that threatened to knock me off the lines, and the transformer outside the Widow's house was burning a fierce actinic blue. It was a gusher of energy, a flare star brought to earth, dazzling. A bolt of lightning unzipped me, turned me inside out, and restored me before I had a chance to react.

The Corpsegrinder was visible from the Roxy, but between the burning transformer and the creature's metamorphosis, I was within a block of the monster before I understood exactly what it was I was seeing.

It was feeding off the dying transformer, sucking in energy so greedily that it pulsed like a mosquito engorged with blood. Enormous plasma wings warped to either side, hot blue and transparent. They curved entirely around the Widow's house in an unbroken and circular wall. At the resonance points they extruded less detailed versions of the Corpsegrinder itself, like sentinels, all facing the Widow.

Surrounding her with a prickly ring of electricity and malice.

I retreated a block, though the transformer fire apparently hid me from the Corpsegrinder, for it stayed where it was, eyelessly staring inward. Three times I circled the house from a distance, looking for a way in. An unguarded cable, a wrought-iron fence, any unbroken stretch of metal too high or too low for the Corpsegrinder to reach.

Nothing.

Finally, because there was no alternative, I entered the house across the street from the Widow's, the one that was best shielded from the spouting and stuttering transformer. A power line took me into the attic crawlspace. From there I scaled the electrical system down through the second and first floors and so to the basement. I had a brief glimpse of a man asleep on a couch before the television. The set was off but it still held a residual charge. It sat quiescent, smug, bloated with stolen energies. If the poor bastard on the couch could have seen what I saw, he'd've never turned on the TV again. In the basement I hand-over-handed myself from the washing machine to the main water inlet. Straddling the pipe, I summoned all my courage and plunged my head underground.

It was black as pitch. I inched forward on the pipe in a kind of panic. I could see nothing, hear nothing, smell nothing, taste nothing. All I could feel was the iron pipe beneath my hands. Just beyond the wall the pipe ended in a T-joint where it hooked into a branch line under the drive. I followed it to the street.

It was awful: like suffocation infinitely prolonged. Like being wrapped in black cloth. Like being drowned in ink. Like strangling noiselessly in the void between the stars. To distract myself, I thought about my old man.

When my father was young, he navigated between cities by radio. Driving dark and usually empty highways, he'd twist the dial back and forth, back and forth, until he'd hit a station. Then he'd withdraw his hand and wait for the station ID. That would give him his rough location—that he was somewhere outside of Albany, say. A sudden signal coming in strong and then abruptly dissolving in groans and eerie whistles was a fluke of the ionosphere, impossibly distant and easily disregarded. One that faded in and immediately out meant he had grazed the edge of a station's range. But then a signal would grow and strengthen as he penetrated its field, crescendo, fade, and collapse into static and silence. That left him north of Troy, let's say, and making good time. He would begin the search for the next station.

You could drive across the continent in this way, passed from hand to hand by local radio, and tuned in to the geography of the night.

I went over that memory three times, polishing and refining it, before the branch line abruptly ended. One hand groped forward and closed upon nothing.

I had reached the main conduit. For a panicked moment I had feared that it would be concrete or brick or even one of the cedar pipes the city laid down in the nineteenth century, remnants of which still linger here and there beneath the pavement. But by sheer blind luck, the system had been installed during that narrow window of time when the pipes were cast iron. I crawled along its underside first one way and then the other, searching for the branch line for the Widow's. There was a lot of crap under the street. Several times I was blocked by gas lines or by the high-pressure pipes for the fire hydrants and had to awkwardly clamber around them. At last, I found the line and began the painful journey out from the street again.

When I emerged in the Widow's basement, I was a nervous wreck. It came to me then that I could no longer remember my father's name. A thing of rags and shreds indeed! I worked my way up the electrical system, searching every room and unintentionally spying on the family who had bought the house after her death. In the kitchen a puffy man stood with his sleeves rolled up, elbow-deep in the sink, angrily washing dishes by candlelight. A woman who was surely his wife expressively smoked a cigarette at his stiff back, drawing in the smoke with bitter intensity and exhaling it in puffs of hatred. On the second floor a preadolescent girl clutched a tortoise-shell cat so tightly it struggled to escape, and cried into its fur. In the next room a younger boy sat on his bed in earphones, Walkman on his lap, staring sightlessly out the window at the burning transformer. No Widow on either floor.

How, I wondered, could she have endured this entropic oven of a blue-collar rowhouse, forever the voyeur at the banquet, watching the living squander what she had already spent? Her trace was everywhere, her presence elusive. I was beginning to think she'd despaired and given herself up to the sky when I found her in the attic, clutching the wire that led to the antenna. She looked up, amazed by my unexpected appearance.

"Come on," I said. "I know a way out."

*   *   *

Returning, however, I couldn't retrace the route I'd taken in. It wasn't so much the difficulty of navigating the twisting maze of pipes under the street, though that was bad enough, as the fact that the Widow wouldn't hazard the passage unless I led her by the hand.

"You don't know how difficult this is for me," I said.

"It's the only way I'd dare." A nervous, humorless laugh. "I have such a lousy sense of direction."

So, steeling myself, I seized her hand and plunged through the wall.

It took all my concentration to keep from sliding off the water pipes, I was so distracted by the violence of her thoughts. We crawled through a hundred memories, all of her married lover, all alike. Here's one:

Daniel snapped on the car radio. Sad music—something classical—flooded the car. "That's bullshit, babe. You know how much I have invested in you?" He jabbed a blunt finger at her dress. "I could buy two good whores for what that thing cost."

Then why don't you, she thought. Get back on your Metroliner and go home to New York City and your wife and your money and your two good whores. Aloud, reasonably, she said, "It's over, Danny, can't you see that?"

"Look, babe. Let's not argue here, okay? Not in the parking lot, with people walking by and everybody listening. Drive us to your place, we can sit down and talk it over like civilized human beings." She clutched the wheel, staring straight ahead. "No. We're going to settle this here and now."

"Christ." One-handed, Daniel wrangled a pack of Kents from a jacket pocket and knocked out a cigarette. Took the end in his lips and drew it out. Punched the lighter. "So talk."

A wash of hopelessness swept over her. Married men were supposed to be easy to get rid of. That was the whole point. "Let me go, Danny," she pleaded. Then, lying, "We can still be friends."

He made a disgusted noise.

"I've tried, Danny, I really have. You don't know how hard I've tried. But it's just not working."

"All right, I've listened. Now let's go." Reaching over her, Daniel threw the gearshift into reverse. He stepped on her foot, mashing it into the accelerator.

The car leaped backward. She shrieked and in a flurry of panic swung the wheel about and slammed on the brakes with her free foot.

With a jolt and a crunch, the car stopped. There was the tinkle of broken plastic. They'd hit a lime-green Hyundai.

"Oh, that's just perfect!" Daniel said. The lighter popped out. He lit his cigarette and then swung open the door. "I'll check the damage." Over her shoulder, she saw Daniel tug at his trousers knees as he crouched to examine the Hyundai. She had a sudden impulse to slew the car around and escape. Step on the gas and never look back. Watch his face, dismayed and dwindling, in the rear-view mirror. Eyes flooded with tears, she began quietly to laugh.

Then Daniel was back. "It's all right, let's go."

"I heard something break."

"It was just a tail-light, okay?" He gave her a funny look. "What the hell are you laughing about?"

She shook her head helplessly, unable to sort out the tears from the laughter. Then somehow they were on the Expressway, the car humming down the indistinct and warping road. She was driving but Daniel was still in control.

We were completely lost now and had been for some time. I had taken what I was certain had to be a branch line and it had led nowhere. We'd been tracing its twisty passage for blocks. I stopped and pulled my hand away. I couldn't concentrate. Not with the caustics and poisons of the Widow's past churning through me. "Listen," I said. "We've got to get something straight between us."

Her voice came out of nowhere, small and wary. "What?"

How to say it? The horror of those memories lay not in their brutality but in their particularity. They nestled into empty spaces where memories of my own should have been. They were as familiar as old shoes. They *fit*.

"If I could remember any of this crap," I said, "I'd apologize. Hell, I can't blame you for how you feel. Of course you're angry. But it's gone, can't you see that, it's over. You've got to let go. You can't hold me accountable for things I can't even remember, okay? All that shit happened decades ago. I was young. I've changed." The absurdity of the thing swept over me. I'd have laughed if I'd been able. "I'm dead, for pity's sake!"

A long silence. Then, "So you've figured it out."

"You've known all along," I said bitterly. "Ever since I came off the high-tension lines in Manayunk."

She didn't deny it. "I suppose I should be flattered that when you were in trouble you came to me," she said in a way that indicated she was not.

"Why didn't you tell me then? Why drag it out?"

"Danny—"

"Don't call me that!"

"It's your name. Daniel. Daniel Cobb."

All the emotions I'd been holding back by sheer force of denial closed about me. I flung myself down and clutched the pipe tight, crushing myself against its unforgiving surface. Trapped in the friendless wastes of night, I weighed my fear of letting go against my fear of holding on.

"Cobb?"

I said nothing. The Widow's voice took on an edgy quality. "Cobb, we can't stay here. You've got to lead me out. I don't have the slightest idea which way to go. I'm lost without your help."

I still could not speak.

"*Cobb!*" She was close to panic. "I put my own feelings aside. Back in Manayunk. You needed help and I did what I could. Now it's your turn."

Silently, invisibly, I shook my head.

"God damn you, Danny," she said furiously. "I won't let you do this to me again! So you're unhappy with what a jerk you were—that's not my problem. You can't redeem your manliness on me any more. I am not your fucking salvation. I am not some kind of cosmic last chance and it's not my job to talk you down from the ledge."

That stung. "I wasn't asking you to," I mumbled.

"So you're still there! Take my hand and lead us out."

I pulled myself together. "You'll have to follow my voice, babe. Your memories are too intense for me."

We resumed our slow progress. I was sick of crawling, sick of the dark, sick of this lightless horrid existence, disgusted to the pit of my soul with who and what I was. Was there no end to this labyrinth of pipes?

"Wait." I'd brushed by something. Something metal buried in the earth.

"What is it?"

"I think it's—" I groped about, trying to get a sense of the thing's shape. "I think it's a cast-iron gatepost. Here. Wait. Let me climb up and take a look."

Relinquishing my grip on the pipe, I seized hold of the object and stuck my head out of the ground. I emerged at the gate of an iron fence framing the minuscule front yard of a house on Ripka Street. I could see again! It felt so good to feel the clear breath of the world once more that I closed my eyes briefly to savor the sensation.

"How ironic," Euphrosyne said.

"After being so heroic," Thalia said.

"Overcoming his fears," Aglaia said.

"Rescuing the fair maid from terror and durance vile," Cleta said.

"Realizing at last who he is," Phaenna said.

"Beginning that long and difficult road to recovery by finally getting in touch with his innermost feelings," Auxo said. Hegemone giggled.

"What?" I opened my eyes.

That was when the Corpsegrinder struck. It leaped upon me with stunning force, driving spear-long talons through my head and body. The talons were barbed so that they couldn't be pulled free and they burned like molten metal. "Ahhhh, Cobb," the Corpsegrinder crooned. "Now this is *sweet*."

I screamed and it drank in those screams so that only silence escaped into the outside world. I struggled and it made those struggles its own, leaving me to kick myself deeper and deeper into the drowning pools of its identity. With all my will I resisted. It was not enough. I experienced the languorous pleasure of surrender as that very will and resistance were sucked down into my attacker's substance. The distinction between me and it weakened, strained, dissolved. I was transformed.

I was the Corpsegrinder now. Manhattan is a virtual school for the dead. Enough people die there every day to keep any number of monsters fed. From the store of memories the Corpsegrinder had stolen from me, I recalled a quiet moment sitting cross-legged on the tin ceiling of a sleaze joint while table dancers entertained Japanese tourists on the floor above and a kobold instructed me on the finer points of survival. "The worst thing you can be hunted by," he said, "is yourself."

"Very aphoristic."

"Fuck you. I used to be human, too."

"Sorry."

"Apology accepted. Look, I told you about Salamanders. That's a shitty way to go, but at least it's final. When they're done with you, nothing remains. But a Corpsegrinder is a parasite. It has no true identity of its own, so it constructs one from bits and pieces of everything that's unpleasant within you. Your basic greeds and lusts. It gives you a particularly nasty sort of immortality. Remember that old cartoon? This hideous toad saying, 'Kiss me and live forever—you'll be a toad, but you'll live forever.' " He grimaced. "If you get the choice, go with the Salamander."

"So what's this business about hunting myself?"

"Sometimes a Corpsegrinder will rip you in two and let half escape. For a while."

"Why?"

"I dunno. Maybe it likes to play with its food. Ever watch a cat torture a mouse? Maybe it thinks it's fun."

From a million miles away, I thought: So now I know what's happened to me. I'd made quite a run of it, but now it was over. It didn't matter. All that mattered was the hoard of memories, glorious memories, into which I'd been dumped. I wallowed in them, picking out here a winter sunset and there the pain of a jellyfish sting when I was nine. So what if I was already beginning to dissolve? I was intoxicated, drunk, stoned with the raw stuff of experience. I was high on life.

Then the Widow climbed up the gatepost looking for me, "Cobb?"

The Corpsegrinder had moved up the fence to a more comfortable spot in which to digest me. When it saw the Widow, it reflexively parked me in a memory of a gray drizzly day in a Ford Fiesta outside of 30th Street Station. The engine was going and the heater and the windshield wipers, too, so I snapped on the radio to mask their noise. Beethoven filled the car, the Moonlight Sonata.

"That's bullshit, babe," I said. "You know how much I have invested in you? I could buy two good whores for what that dress cost." She refused to meet my eyes. In a whine that set my teeth on edge, she said, "Danny, can't you see that it's over between us?"

"Look babe, let's not argue in the parking lot, okay?" I was trying hard to be reasonable. "Not with people walking by and listening. We'll go someplace private where we can talk this over calmly, like two civilized human beings." She shifted slightly in the seat and adjusted her skirt with a little tug. Drawing attention to her long legs and fine ass. Making it hard for me to think straight. The bitch really knew how to twist the knife. Even now, crying and begging, she was aware of how it turned me on. And even though I hated being aroused by her little act, I was. The sex was always best after an argument; it made her sluttish.

I clenched my anger in one hand and fisted my pocket with it. Thinking how much I'd like to up and give her a shot. She was begging for it. Secretly, maybe, it was what she wanted; I'd often suspected she'd enjoy being hit. It was too late to act on the impulse, though. The memory was playing out like a tape, immutable, unstoppable.

All the while, like a hallucination or the screen of a television set receiving conflicting signals, I could see the Widow, frozen with fear half in and half out of the ground. She quivered like an acetylene flame. In the memory she was saying something, but with the shift in my emotions came a corresponding warping-away of perception. The train station, car, the windshield wipers and music, all faded to a murmur in my consciousness.

Tentacles whipped around the Widow. She was caught. She struggled helplessly, deliciously. The Corpsegrinder's emotions pulsed through me and to my remote horror I found that they were identical with my own. I *wanted* the Widow, wanted her so bad there were no words for it. I wanted to clutch her to me so tightly her ribs would splinter and for just this once she'd know it was real. I wanted to own her. To possess her. To put an end to all her little games. To know her every thought and secret, down to the very bottom of her being.

No more lies, babe, I thought, no more evasions. You're mine now.

So perfectly in sync was I with the Corpsegrinder's desires that it shifted its primary consciousness back into the liquid sphere of memory, where it hung smug and lazy, watching, a voyeur with a willing agent. I was in control of the autonomous functions now. I reshaped the tentacles, merging and recombining them into two strong arms. The claws and talons that clutched the fence I made legs again. The exterior of the Corpsegrinder I morphed into human semblance, save for that great mass of memories sprouting from our back like a bloated spider-sack. Last of all I made the head.

I gave it my own face.

"Surprised to see me again, babe?" I leered. Her expression was not so much fearful as disappointed. "No," she said wearily. "Deep down, I guess I always knew you'd be back."

As I drew the Widow closer, I distantly knew that all that held me to the Corpsegrinder in that instant was our common store of memories and my determination not to lose them again. That was enough, though. I pushed my face into hers, forcing open her mouth. Energies flowed between us like a feast of tongues.

I prepared to drink her in.

There were no barriers between us. This was an experience as intense as when, making love, you lose all track of which body is your own and thought dissolves into the animal moment. For a giddy instant I was no less her than I was myself. I was the Widow staring fascinated into the filthy depths of my psyche. She was myself witnessing her astonishment as she realized exactly how little I had ever known her. We both saw her freeze still to the core with horror. Horror not of what I was doing.

But of what I was.

I can't take any credit for what happened then. It was only an impulse, a spasm of the emotions, a sudden and unexpected clarity of vision. Can a single flash of decency redeem a life like mine? I don't believe it. I refuse to believe it. Had there been time for second thoughts, things might well have gone differently. But there was no time to think. There was only time enough to feel an upwelling of revulsion, a visceral desire to be anybody or anything but my own loathsome self, a profound and total yearning to be quit of the burden of such memories as were mine. An aching need to *just once* do the moral thing.

I let go.

Bobbing gently, the swollen corpus of my past floated up and away, carrying with it the parasitic Corpsegrinder. Everything I had spent all my life accumulating fled from me. It went up like a balloon, spinning, dwindling . . . gone. Leaving me only what few flat memories I have narrated here.

I screamed.

And then I cried.

I don't know how long I clung to the fence, mourning my loss. But when I gathered myself together, the Widow was still there.

"Danny," the Widow said. She didn't touch me. "Danny, I'm sorry."

I'd almost rather that she had abandoned me. How do you apologize for sins you can no longer remember? For having been someone who, however abhorrent, is gone forever? How can you expect forgiveness from somebody you have forgotten so completely you don't even know her name? I felt twisted with shame and misery. "Look," I said. "I know I've behaved badly. More than badly. But there ought to be some way to make it up to you. For, you know, everything. Somehow. I mean—"

What do you say to somebody who's seen to the bottom of your wretched and inadequate soul?

"I want to apologize," I said.

With something very close to compassion, the Widow said, "It's too late for that, Danny. It's over. Everything's over. You and I only ever had the one trait in common. We neither of us could ever let go of anything. Small wonder we're back together again. But don't you see, it doesn't matter what you want or don't want—you're not going to get it. Not now. You had your chance. It's too late to make things right." Then she stopped, aghast at what she had just said. But we both knew she had spoken the truth.

"Widow," I said as gently as I could, "I'm sure Charlie—"

"Shut up."

I shut up.

The Widow closed her eyes and swayed, as if in a wind. A ripple ran through her and when it was gone her features were simpler, more schematic, less recognizably human. She was already beginning to surrender the anthropomorphic.

I tried again. "Widow . . ." Reaching out my guilty hand to her.

She stiffened but did not draw away. Our fingers touched, twined, mated.

"Elizabeth," she said. "My name is Elizabeth Connelly."

We huddled together on the ceiling of the Roxy through the dawn and the blank horror that is day. When sunset brought us conscious again, we talked through half the night before making the one decision we knew all along that we'd have to make.

It took us almost an hour to reach the Seven Sisters and climb down to the highest point of Thalia.

We stood holding hands at the top of the mast. Radio waves were gushing out from under us like a great wind. It was all we could do to keep from being blown away.

Underfoot, Thalia was happily chatting with her sisters. Typically, at our moment of greatest resolve, they gave not the slightest indication of interest. But they were all listening to us. Don't ask me how I knew.

"Cobb?" Elizabeth said. "I'm afraid."

"Yeah, me too." A long silence. Then she said, "Let me go first. If you go first, I won't have the nerve."

"Okay."

She took a deep breath—funny, if you think about it—and then she let go, and fell into the sky.

First she was like a kite, and then a scrap of paper, and at the very last she was a rapidly tumbling speck. I stood for a long time watching her falling, dwindling, until she was lost in the background flicker of the universe, just one more spark in infinity.

She was gone and I couldn't help wondering if she had ever really been there at all. Had the Widow truly been Elizabeth Connelly? Or was she just another fragment of my shattered self, a bundle of related memories that I had to come to terms with before I could bring myself to let go? A vast emptiness seemed to spread itself through all of existence. I clutched the mast spasmodically then, and thought: *I can't!*

But the moment passed. I've got a lot of questions, and there aren't any answers here. In just another instant, I'll let go and follow Elizabeth (if Elizabeth she was) into the night. I will fall forever and I will be converted to background radiation, smeared ever thinner and cooler across the universe, a smooth, uniform, and universal message that has only one decode. Let Thalia carry my story to whomever cares to listen. I won't be here for it.

It's time to go now. Time and then some to leave. I'm frightened, and I'm going.

Now.

Honorable Mentions: 1996

Adams, Benjamin, "Second Movement," *Miskatonic University.*

Adams, Richard, "The Bommie and the Drop-off," *Shivers for Christmas.*

Addison, Linda D., "Little Red in the Hood," *Tomorrow* No. 23, Nov.

Aiken, Joan, "The Ferry," *Shivers for Christmas.*

———, "The Monkey's Wedding Night," *Night Terrors.*

Aldiss, Brian, "The Mistakes, Miseries and Misfortunes of Mankind," *Common Clay.*

Allen, Karen Jordan, "Mrs. Pomeroy," *A Nightmare's Dozen.*

Allen, Mike, "The Romantic Age," (poem) *Dreams of Decadence,* Spring/Summer.

Allison, Dorothy, "Ounces," *Swords of the Rainbow.*

Anderson, Colleen, "These Proud Trees," (poem) *Talebones* #3.

Arnason, Eleanor, "The Dog's Story," *Asimov's Science Fiction,* May.

Arnzen, Michael A., "Falling Back," *High Fantastic.*

Auerbach, Jessica, "Police Report," *Unusual Suspects.*

Bailey, Dale, "The Mall," *The Magazine of Fantasy & Science Fiction,* Jan.

Bardens, Ann, "Another Grimm Tale (poem) *Superstition, Myth and Magick: The Maguffin,* Vol. XIII, Number 11.

Barker, Lawrence, "Rile Fouts and Dead Jake Sorrell," *Lore* Vol. 1, Number 4, Spring.

Barker, Trey R., "When I Saw Your Eyes," *Dead Lines* #4.

Barszczewski, Jan, "The Head Full of Screaming Hair," *The Dedalus Book of Polish Fantasy.*

Bart, D. J., "Fever," *Alfred Hitchcock Mystery Magazine,* September.

Barwood, Lee, "Pyre," *Sisters in Fantasy 2.*

Bayley, Barrington J., "The Crear," *Interzone* No. 110, Aug.

Beagle, Peter S., "The Magician of Karakosk," *David Copperfield's Beyond Imagination.*

Bear, Greg, "The Fall of the House of Escher," Ibid.

Bell, Chris, "Dream Me an Island," *The Bumper Book of Lies: Stories by Chris Bell.*

———, "This Shining World," Ibid.

Bell, Christine, "The Second Order of Infinity," *The Seven-Year Atomic Make-over Guide: Stories by Christine Bell.*

Bennett, Debbie, "Carousel," *Chills* #10.

Better, Cathy Drinkwater, "applause," (poem) *The Silver Web* #13.

Bilotserkivets, Natalka, "A Hundred Years of Youth," (poem) *From Three Worlds: New Writing from the Ukraine.*

Bishop, Michael, "Allegra's Hand," *Asimov's Science Fiction,* June.

Blaeser, Kimberly M., "Growing Things," *Blue Dawn, Red Earth.*

Blevins, Tippi N., "La Morte D'Amoureuse," *La Morte D'Amoureuse.*

———, "Waterlover," (poem) Ibid.

Boston, Bruce, "A Stray Grimoire," (poem) *Contortions* #1.

Bostwick, Gene, "Jello and My Wife," *Tomorrow* No. 22, Aug.

Bowkett, Stephen, "Hobyahs," *Kimota* #5.

Boyle, T. Coraghessan, "Killing Babies," *The New Yorker,* Dec. 2.

———, "Termination Dust," *Playboy,* May.

Bradbury, Ray, "The Electrocution," *Quicker Than the Eye.*

———, "The Finnegan," *F & SF,* Oct./Nov.

———, "Free Dirt," *Quicker Than the Eye.*

———, "Hopscotch," Ibid.

———, "That Woman on the Lawn," *F & SF,* Aug.

Bradfield, Scott, "Men and Women in Love," *Buzz,* Nov.

Bradford, Arthur, "Room for Rent," *Epoch,* Vol. 45, Number 3.

Braunbeck, Gary A., "But Somewhere I Shall Wake," *White House Horrors*.
———, "The Eater of Filth," *Monster Brigade 3000*.
Brenchley, Chaz, "My Cousin's Gratitude," *Fresh Blood*.
Brewster, Kent, "Weed Seed," *Tomorrow* No. 20, Apr.
Brooke, Keith and Brown, Eric, "Sugar and Spice," *Interzone* No. 112, Oct.
Brown, Rebecca, "The Princess and the Pea," *What Keeps Me Here*.
Brown, Simon, "The Mark of Thetis," *Eidolon #21*.
Brown, Toni, "Immunity," *Night Bites*.
Brownworth, Victoria A., "Twelfth Night," *Night Bites*.
Brunner, John, "Amends," *Asimov's Science Fiction*, Mar.
———, "The Drummer and the Skins," *Interzone* No. 103, Jan.
Burke, Caitlin, "A Rose in Spanish Harlem," *Night Dreams #4*.
Burleson, Donald R., "Hopscotch," *Terminal Fright #11*.
Burleson, Mollie L., "Literary Remains," *Cthulhu Codex #7*.
———, "Corona Mundi,"(poem) *Lore*, Vol. 1, Number 5, Summer.
Burt, Brian, "Phantom Pain," *Talebones #3*.
Butler, Robert Olen, "Help Me Find My Spaceman Lover," *Paris Review #140*.
———, "Woman Struck by Car Turns into Nymphomaniac," *Tabloid Dreams*.
Byers, Richard Lee, "Office Space," *Dante's Disciples*.
Cacek, Patricia D., "Metalica," *The Hot Blood Series: Fear the Fever*.
Cadger, Rick, "Symphony," *The Third Alternative #9*.
Cadigan, Pat, "A Lie for a Lie," *Lethal Kisses*.
Cadnum, Michael, "The Man Who Did Cats Harm," *Twists of the Tale*.
———, "Touch Me Everyplace," *Lethal Kisses*.
Cady, Jack, "The Bride," *Century #4*.
———, "Kilroy Was Here," *F & SF*, July.

Calbert, Cathleen, "The Vampire Cat," (poem) *The Ohio Review* #54.
Campbell, Ramsey, "Out of the Woods," *Dark Terrors 2*.
Cannon, Melissa, "Fairy Tales and Gloss," (poem) *Ploughshares*, Vol. 22, Number 1.
Carmody, Isobelle, "The Pumpkin-Eater," *She's Fantastical*.
———, "The Red Shoes," *Green Monkey Dreams: Stories by Isobelle Carmody*.
Carr, Jan, "Apologia," *Night Bites*.
Carroll, David, "Wild Thing," *Rictus #8*.
Carroll, Jonathan, "Alone Alarm," *Interzone* No. 114, Dec.
———, "Crimes of the Face," *The Literary Insomniac*.
Carter, Angela, "The Scarlet House," *Conjunctions 26: Sticks & Stones*.
Casil, Amy Sterling, "Jonny Punkinhead," *F & SF*, June.
Casper, Susan, "A Night at the J Street Bar," *Sisters in Fantasy 2*.
Castro, Adam-Troy, "Family Album," *Darkside: Horror for the Next Millennium*.
———, "Locusts," *F & SF*, Feb.
Castro, Brian, "Shanghai Dancing," *Risks*.
Cawood, Anthony, "When No One Calls," *Psychotrope #4*.
Chadbourn, Mark, "Cold Comfort," *Kimota #5*.
———, "If I Should Die in a Combat Zone," *Phantoms*, Sept.
Charles, Renée M., "A Model of Transformation," *Women Who Run with the Werewolves*.
Charnas, Suzy McKee, "Beauty and the Opéra or the Phantom Beast," *Asimov's Science Fiction*, Mar.
Chase, Robert David, "The Monster Parade," *Monster Brigade 3000*.
Chesbro, George C., "The Lazarus Gate," *Ellery Queen's Mystery Magazine*, Sept/Oct.
Chetwynd-Hayes, R., "The Chair," *Worlds of Fantasy and Horror #4*.
Chizmar, Richard T., "Devil's Night," *Midnight Promises*.
———, "Midnight Promises," Ibid.

———, "The Silence of Sorrow," Ibid.

Christian, M., "Wet," Sons of Darkness.

Ciencin, Scott, "Cages," Phantoms of the Night.

Clark, George, "Seven Stories for All the Animals," Glimmer Train, Winter.

Clark, Simon, "The Burning Doorway," Squane's Journal #2.

———, "Expressed From the Wood," Kimota #4.

———, "Feed My Children," The Edge, May/June.

Clayton, Jo, "Patience," Sword and Sorceress XIII.

Clegg, Douglas, "The Five," Twists of the Tale.

———, "The Fruit of Her Womb," Phantoms of the Night.

———, "The Ripening Sweetness of Late Afternoon," Dante's Disciples.

———, "Underground," Phantasm, Spring.

Clemens, Sarah, "I Gatti di Roma," Twists of the Tale.

Cobb, Tony, "The Syndrome," Not One of Us #16.

Cohen, Lisa R., "Leuka and Phlego," Realms of Fantasy, Apr.

Coldsmith, Sherry, "The Lucifer of Blue," Off Limits.

Collingbourne, Huw, "Violator," Peeping Tom #22.

Collins, Nancy A., "Someone's in the Kitchen," The Ultimate Haunted House.

———, "The Thing From Lovers' Lane," It Came From The Drive-In.

Coney, Michael, "The Most Ancient Battle," Phantoms of the Night.

Connolly, Lawrence C., "Smuggling the Dead," Terminal Fright #13.

Constantine, Storm, "Of a Cat, But Her Skin," Twists of the Tale.

———, "Remedy of the Bane," Realms of Fantasy, Aug.

Coover, Robert, "Briar Rose," Conjunctions 26: Sticks and Stones.

Corn, David, "My Murder," Unusual Suspects.

Coulter, Lynn, "Swamp Water," F & SF, Feb.

Couzens, Gary, "Straw Defenses," Psychotrope #4.

Coville, Bruce, "The Japanese Mirror," A Nightmare's Dozen.

Cox, Andy, "Burn," The Urbanite #7.

Crawford, Dan, "Realistic Novel Library," AHMM, Feb.

Crofts, Terry, "The Phantom Hangman," All Hallows #11.

Crowther, Peter, "The Bachelor," Phantoms of the Night.

———, "Eater," Cemetery Dance, Winter.

———, "The Fairy Trap," Fantasy Stories.

———, "Forest Plains," chapbook.

———, "Surface Tension," Monster Brigade 3000.

Crumley, James, "Hot Springs," Murder For Love.

Daitch, Susan, "Storytown," Storytown: Stories by Susan Daitch.

Daniel, David, "Health Food," Fungi, Fall.

———, "The Whole Schmeer," Fungi, Spring.

David, Peter, "Moonlight Becomes You," Otherwere.

Davidson, Avram and Davidson, Ethan, "Sambo," Eidolon #21.

Day, Marlene, "A Man and His Dreams," Risk.

de Lint, Charles, "Held Safe by Moonlight and Vines," Castle Fantastic.

———, "Shining Nowhere But in the Dark," Realms of Fantasy, Oct.

Dean, Pamela, "This Fair Gift," Sisters in Fantasy 2.

Deaver, Jeffery, "Interrogation," AHMM, Apr.

———, "The Weekender," AHMM, Dec.

DeCirce, Paul, "If You Find Buddha on the Path, Kill Him," Stygian Articles #6.

Dedman, Stephen, "The Service of the Dead," Aurealis #17.

Deeds, Marion, "Madonna of the Mask," Night Terrors #1.

Dellamonica, A. M., "Homage," Crank! #7.

Denyer, Trevor, "The Edge of the Country," *Time Out Net Books*, Nov.

Devereaux, Robert, "The Slobbering Tongue That Ate the Frightfully Huge Woman," *It Came From the Drive-In.*

Doolittle, Sean, "October Gethsemane," *Darkside: Horror for the Next Millennium.*

Dorr, James S., "The Sidewalk," *Terminal Fright* #13.

Dougherty, Kathleen, "Bright Hopes, Dark Soul," *EQMM*, Aug.

Douglass, Sara, "Of Fingers and Foreskins," *Eidolon* #21.

Dreischarf, J. Spencer, "We're Late," *Cabal Asylum*, Winter.

DuBois, Brendan, "The Promise Squad," *EQMM*, June.

Ducornet, Rikki, "The Neurosis of Containment," *Conjunctions 26: Sticks and Stones.*

Duffy, Stella, "Uncertainties and Small Surprises," *Fresh Blood.*

Dumars, Denise, "Hardscrabble," (poem) *Heliocentric Net Annual 1996.*

Duncan, Andy, "Liza and the Crazy Water Man," *Starlight 1.*

Dunford, Caroline, "War Story," *Kimota* #4.

D'Ammassa, Don, "Kites," *Night Terrors* #2.

———, "Milk-Curdling Horror," *Deathrealm* #29.

———, "Sneak Thief," *Tomorrow* No. 21, June.

Eller, Steve, "Nursery Rhymes," *Terminal Fright* #13.

Ellison, Harlan, "The Lingering Scent of Woodsmoke," *Harlan Ellison's Dream Corridor.*

Emerson, Ru, "Call Him by Name," *Sisters in Fantasy 2.*

Emswiler, Tim, "The Law of Conservation of Pain," *Stygian Articles* #6.

———, "New Wounds," *Stygian Articles* #4.

Esrac, William, "Prodigal Son," *Tomorrow* No. 19, Feb.

Evans, Kendall, "The Mandala," *Lore*, Vol. 1, Number 6, Fall

Evenson, Brian, "The Polygamy of Language," *Conjunctions 26: Sticks & Stones.*

———, "The Revolution," *Magic Realism*, Spring.

Faust, Christa, "Envy," *Darkside: Horror for the Next Millennium.*

Feeley, Gregory, "The Drowning Cell," *The Shimmering Door.*

Filer, Damien, "Addict," *Buried Treasures.*

Files, Gemma, "Hidebound," *Transversions* #5.

Finnegan, Madeleine V., "Alchemy," *Night Dreams* #4.

———, "Fabulon," *Peeping Tom* #23.

Fitzgerald, Lauren, "Wasting," *Darkside: Horror for the Next Millennium.*

Ford, John M., "Chain Home, Low," *The Sandman: Book of Dreams.*

Foster, Jake, "A Zombie Named Fred," *Monster Brigade 3000.*

Fowler, Christopher, "Unforgotten," *Lethal Kisses.*

Fowler, Karen Joy, "The Elizabeth Complex," *Crank!* #6.

———, "The Queen of Hearts and Swords," *David Copperfield's Beyond Imagination.*

Francis, H. E., "The Children," *Prairie Schooner*, Vol. 70, Number 1.

Francis, Mark, "In the Language of Earth," *Cthulhu Codex* #9.

Fraser, Antonia, "A Witch and Her Cats," *Women on the Case.*

Friesner, Esther M., "Moonlight in Vermont," *Sisters in Fantasy 2.*

———, "Sparrow," *Return to Avalon.*

Frost, Gregory, "That Blissful Height," *Intersections: The Sycamore Hill Anthology.*

Fuller, Thomas E. and Strickland, Brad, "The God at Midnight," *Realms of Fantasy*, June.

Fuqua, C. S., "Undertaker I: Ashes and Dust," *Rictus* #7.

Gaiman, Neil, "The Goldfish Pool and Other Stories," *David Copperfield's Beyond Imagination.*

Galarneau, Peter, Jr., "Blood Barters," *Heliocentric Net Annual 1996.*

Gallu, Elizabeth, "Best Intentions," *The North American Review*, Vol. 281, Number 1.

Garratt, Peter T., "The Hooded Man," *Interzone* No. 104, Feb.

George, Stephen R., "How It Happens," *Cemetery Dance*, Spring.

Gertler, Nat, "Restin' Piece," *The Hot Blood Series: Fear the Fever.*

Gilbert, David, "Grafitti," *The New Yorker*, Sept. 23.

Gombrowicz, Witold, "Dinner at Countess Kotlubay's," *The Dedalus Book of Polish Fantasy.*

Good, Graham, "1994," *Dalhousie Review*, Vol. 74, Number 3.

Gordon, Graeme, "Friday Night," *Fresh Blood.*

Goren, Lester, "The Madonna of the Jukebox," *Tales from the Irish Club: Stories by Lester Goren.*

Gorman, Ed, "Eye of the Beholder," *The Autumn Dead/A Cry of Shadows* (omnibus).

——, "Famous Blue Raincoat," *Cemetery Dance*, Summer.

——, "The Man on the Third Floor," *Cemetery Dance*, Spring.

——, "Yesterday's Dreams," *F & SF*, Dec.

Grabinski, Stefan, "The Black Hamlet," *The Dedalus Book of Polish Fantasy.*

Grady, James, "Kiss the Sky," *Unusual Suspects.*

Graham, Philip, "Beauty Marks," *Interior Designs: Stories by Philip Graham.*

Green, Dominic, "Evertrue Carnadine," *Interzone* No. 112, Oct.

Gresh, Lois, "Sole Man," *The Hot Blood Series: Fear the Fever.*

Grey, John, "Suspect," (poem) *Freezer Burn Magazine* 4.0.

——, "Witches at the Crossroads," (poem) *Crossroads*, Oct.

Griffin, Peni R., "Goldfish," *Realms of Fantasy* Aug.

Griner, Paul, "Follow Me," *Follow Me.*

——, "Lindy," *Epoch*, Vol. 45, Number 2.

Griswold, Eliza T., "The Annunciation,"

(poem) *The Antioch Review*, Vol. 54, Number 2.

Guthridge, George, "Chin Oil," *David Copperfield's Beyond Imagination.*

Haber, Karen, "A Bone Dry Place," *The Sandman: Book of Dreams.*

Hannett, L. A., "Lead These Graces to the Grave," *Terminal Fright* #13.

Hansen, Annie, "Spirit Curse," *Blue Dawn, Red Earth.*

Harris, Steve, "Christmas Dinner," *Peeping Tom* #21.

Harrison, M. John, "I Did It," *A Book of Two Halves.*

——, "The East," *Interzone* No. 114, Dec.

——, "Seven Guesses of the Heart," *The Shimmering Door.*

Hartnett, John, "Jenny's Own Song," *Haunts* #31.

Harvey, John, "She Rote," *Fresh Blood.*

Hauser, Erik, "Nightwalk," *All Hallows* #13.

Hembree, Amy, "The Mark," *Dead Lines* #4.

Henderson, C. J., "Patiently Waiting," *The Cthulhu Cycle.*

Hensley, Chad, "Dark Entry III," (poem) *Deathrealm* #30.

Hoard, Christine B., "Mr. Sardonicus," (poem) Ibid.

Hodge, Brian, "Healing the Body Politic," *White House Horrors.*

——, "In a Roadhouse, Far Past the Edge of Town," *The Convulsion Factory.*

——, "Liturgical Music For Nihilists," Ibid.

——, "Naked Lunchmeat," Ibid.

——, "Stick Around, It Gets Worse," *Darkside: Horror for the Next Millennium.*

Hodgson, William Hope, "By the Lee," *Terrors of the Sea.*

——, "Demons of the Sea," Ibid.

——, "The Heathen's Revenge," Ibid.

——, "The Sharks of the St. Elmo," Ibid.

——, "Sailormen," Ibid.

Hoffman, Nina Kiriki, "Airborn," *F & SF*, May.

———, "Incidental Cats," *Twists of the Tale.*

———, "Inner Child," *Otherwere.*

———, "I Was A Teenage Boycrazy Blob," *It Came From the Drive-In.*

———, "Wonder Never Land," *A Nightmare's Dozen.*

Hoffman, Theodore H., "Their Silly Little Hands," *AHMM*, June.

Hokkaido, José de, "Me and You and a Dog Named (Clovis)," *Tomorrow* No. 19, Feb.

Holland, Richard, "Dust to Dust," *All Hallows* #13.

Hopkins, Brian A., "Dead Art," *Bones* #1.

Horne, Calvin, "The Stover Cut," *Realms of Fantasy*, Dec.

Houarner, Gerard Daniel, "Angel of Death," *Painfreak.*

———, "The Beast that Was Max," Ibid.

———, "Demons of Blood and Passion," Ibid.

———, "Hot Thing," Ibid.

———, "The Oddist," *Epitaph* #1.

———, "Safe Word," *Painfreak.*

———, "Tongue," Ibid.

Huberath, Marek S., "The Greater Punishment," *The Dedalus Book of Polish Fantasy.*

Hughes, Rhys, "Burke and Rabbit," *Night Dreams* #4.

———, "Ten Grim Bottles," *All Hallows* #13.

Hughes, Rhys H., "Loop," *Psychotrope* #4.

———, "A College Story," *Ghosts & Scholars* #21.

Hughes, Stuart, "Clock's Runnin', Mister," *Peeping Tom* #24.

Hyde, Gregory R., "Broken Bones," *High Fantastic.*

Ings, Simon, "Keeping Alice," *Lethal Kisses.*

———, "Swallow," *The Shimmering Door.*

Jackson, Shelley, "The Putti," *Conjunctions 26: Sticks and Stones.*

Jacob, Charlee, "The Diet of Hermits," (poem) *Frisson: Disconcerting Verse*, Summer.

———, "Dust Dancer," *Deathrealm* #30.

———, "The First Vampire," (poem) *In Darkness Eternal*, Winter.

———, "Permafrost," *Women Who Run with the Werewolves.*

———, "Renaud," *Floating Worlds.*

———, "The Seven Ambers," *Terminal Fright* #12.

Jacobs, Harvey, "Thank You for That," *Twists of the Tale.*

Jakeman, Jane, "Lock Me Out!," *Ghosts & Scholars* #22.

Jasieński, Bruno, "The Legs of Isolda Morgan," *The Dedalus Book of Polish Fantasy.*

Jennings, Paul, "Picked Bones," *Uncovered!*

Jensen, Jan Lars, "Slowly Opened Eyes," *Grue* #18.

Johnson, Greg, "The Chinese Box," *Chicago Review*, Vol. 42, Number 2.

Jonas, Gary, "The Blood on Satan's Harley," *It Came From the Drive-In.*

Jones, Bruce, "Feeding the Beast," *The Hot Blood Series: Fear the Fever.*

Jones, Suzanne, "The Last, Best Chance," *EQMM*, Apr.

Jordan, Ceri, "Chemical Dreams," *The Third Alternative* #10.

Joss, Colin W. J., "But None, I Think, Do There Embrace," *Footsteps*, Winter.

Joyce, Graham, "Horrograph," *Phantoms*, Dec.

———, "Phantom Beach," *Phantoms*, July.

Kaiine, John, "Dolly Sodom," *Off Limits.*

Kaufman, David, "In the Lake at Garlock's Bend," *Midnight Shambler* #4.

Kellings, Ashlei, "Saint Angelen," *Aurealis* #16.

Kelly, James Patrick, "Why the Bridge Stopped Singing," *F & SF*, Sept.

Kenworthy, Chris, "Another Friend," *The Third Alternative* #10.

———, "The Closing Hand," *Kimota* #4.

———, "Covering Up," *Will You Hold Me?*

———, "Despite the Cold," *Time Out Net Books*, Aug.

Lewis, D. F. and Pinn, Paul, "In the Belly of the Snake," *The Edge*, Feb/Mar.

Lifshin, Lyn, "Classical Music Nights," (poem) *Freezer Burn Magazine* 5.0.

Ligotti, Thomas, "The Clown Puppet," *The Nightmare Factory*.

———, "Gas Station Carnivals," Ibid.

———, "The Nightmare Network," *Darkside: Horror for the Next Millennium*.

———, "The Red Tower," *The Nightmare Factory*.

———, "Severini," Ibid.

Lillie, Brent, "The Morpheus Project," *Aurealis* #17.

Link, Kelly, "Flying Lessons," *Asimov's Science Fiction*, Oct/Nov.

———, "Vanishing Act," *Realms of Fantasy*, June.

Lispector, Clarice, "Gentle as a Fawn," translated by Giovanni Pontiero, *Selected Cronicas by Clarice Lispector*.

Long, Karawynn, "Discovering Water," *Century* #4.

———, "The Year of the Dragon," (poem) *Asimov's Science Fiction*, July.

Longhorn, David, "The Regulars," *Ghosts & Scholars* #21.

Lord, Nancy, "Call of the What?," *The North American Review*, Vol. 281, Number 3.

Lucas, Michael W., "Breaking the Circle," *Women Who Run with the Werewolves*.

Lumley, Brian, "Mandraki," *The Many Faces of Fantasy*.

Lupinetti, Jude, "His Looks Deceived Me," (poem) *Dreams of Decadence*, Spring/Summer.

Maclay, John, "Late Last Night," *Night Screams*.

———, "Lucky," *Cemetery Dance*, Fall.

Malm, Lynda, "The Wounding," *Prisoners of the Night*, Aug.

Manison, Pete D., "Lover in Chrome," *Tomorrow* No. 22, Aug.

mari, dayna, "a gathering of widows," *The Silver Web* #13.

Martin, George R.R., "Blood of the Dragon," *Asimov's Science Fiction*, July.

Martin, Rafe, "Urashima Taro," *Mysterious Tales of Japan*.

Massie, Elizabeth, "Dibs," *Shadow Dreams*.

———, "Shadow of the Valley," Ibid.

———, "White Hair, We Adore," Ibid.

Massie, Elizabeth and Pettit, Robert, "Ice Dreams," *Darkside: Horror for the Next Millennium*.

Masterton, Graham, "Jack Be Quick," *White House Horrors*.

———, "Underbed," *Dark Terrors* 2.

Mastous, James B., "The Meaning," *Heliocentric Net Annual 1996*.

Matheson, Richard Christian, "The Screaming Man," *Lethal Kisses*.

MB, "Things in Boxes," *Chills* #9.

McAllister, Bruce, "Captain China," *Off Limits*.

McAuley, Paul J., "Negative Equity," *Dark Terrors* 2.

McBride, D. R., "Sollie," *Not One of Us* #15.

McCaffrey, Anne, "The N Auntie," *David Copperfield's Beyond Imagination*.

McCormack, Mike, "A is for Axe," *Getting it in the Head*.

———, "The Gospel of Knives," Ibid.

———, "The Stained Glass Violations," Ibid.

McDevitt, Jack, "Holding Pattern," *Realms of Fantasy*, Dec.

McDonald, Ian, "Islington," *Dante's Disciples*.

———, "Stickman," *Deathrealm* #28.

McGarry, Terry, "Taibhse," *Terminal Fright* #11.

McLaughlin, Mark, "The Lady With Little Friends in Her Hair," (poem) *Chills* #10.

———, "Personal Mythology," (poem) *Talebones* #2.

McCleary, Rob, "Nixon In Space," *Crank!* #6.

McNaughton, Brian, "Ghoulmaster," *Miskatonic University*.

McPherson, Michael C., "Thirty-One," *The 1995 SPGA Showcase*.

Meacham, Beth, "Coyote," *Sisters in Fantasy 2*.

Meng, Wang, "String of Choices," translated by Zhu Hong, *Chairman Mao Would Not Be Amused.*

Miller, James, "Absolute Zero," *Dark Terrors* 2.

———, "The Comforts of Sleep," *Psychotrope #4.*

Miller, Leslie Ann, "Sun Dancer," *Sword and Sorceress XIII.*

Minnion, Keith, "Killer," *Night Terrors #1.*

Misha, "Memekwesiw," *Blue Dawn, Red Earth.*

Monteleone Thomas F., "Get It Out," *Diagnosis: Terminal.*

Moorcock, Michael, "Sir Milk-and-Blood," *Pawn of Chaos.*

Morgan, Christopher J., "Tiger, Tiger, Burning Bright," *Phantoms of the Night.*

Morlan, A. R., "Bringing It Along," *Night Screams.*

———, "No Heaven Will Not Ever Heaven Be . . . ," *Twists of the Tale.*

———, "The Realtor," *Phantasm, Spring.*

———, "A Subtle Shade of Sepia," *Night Terrors #2.*

Mosiman, Billie Sue, "Prosper Bane, 05409021," *Diagnosis: Terminal.*

———, "The Smile of a Mime," *Miskatonic University.*

Murphy, Pat, "A Flock of Lawn Flamingos," *Lethal Kisses.*

———, "Iris Versus the Black Knight," *F & SF,* Oct/Nov.

Murray, Will, "Rude Awakening," *The Cthulhu Cycle.*

Myers, Gary, "The Keeper of the Flame," *The New Lovecraft Circle.*

Navarro, Yvonne, "Pictures Within," *White Knuckles #5.*

———, "The Stranger Who Sits Beside Me," *Darkside: Horror for the Next Millennium.*

Naylor, Ray, "The Ropes of the Lasso Inn," *Deathrealm #30.*

Nelson, Dale, "Nails," *Fungi,* Fall.

Newman, Kim, "Where the Bodies Are Buried 2020," *Dark Terrors* 2.

Newman, Kim and Byrne, Eugene, "Citizen Ed," *Interzone* No. 113, Nov.

Newton, Kurt, "Nature Walk," *Rictus #7.*

Nicholls, Mark, "Another School Story," *Ghosts & Scholars #21.*

Nickford, Raymond, "A Musical Calling," *Heliocentric Net Annual 1996.*

Nickle, David, "Sick Reggie," *Sons of Darkness.*

Novakovich, Josip, "Yolk," *Yolk: Short Stories by Josip Novakovich.*

Oates, Joyce Carol, "At the Paradise Motel, Sparks, Nevada," *Murder For Love.*

———, "Demon," *Demon and Other Tales.*

———, "The Dream-Catcher," *Off Limits.*

———, "First Love," chapbook.

———, "Leave Me Alone God Damn You," *Lethal Kisses.*

———, "Nobody Knows My Name," *Twists of the Tale.*

———, "The Stalker," *Unusual Suspects.*

Olshaker, Mark, "Doorway to the Future," *Unusual Suspects.*

Olson, Jacci, "Souls Along the Meridian," *Bonescribes: Year's Best Australian Horror 1995.*

Ore, Rebecca, "Horse Tracks," *Sisters in Fantasy 2.*

———, "Stone Whorl, Flint Knife," *Sisters in Fantasy 2.*

Osier, Jeffrey, "For the Curiosity of Rats," *Darkside: Horror for the Next Millennium.*

Owton, Martin, "The Pond in the Woods," *Kimota #4.*

O'Brien, Tim, "Faith," *The New Yorker,* Feb. 12.

O'Connor, Michael, "The Head," *Footsteps #3.*

O'Driscoll, M. M., "Rare Promise," *Lethal Kisses.*

O'Driscoll, Mike, "The Future of Birds," *Off Limits.*

Palwick, Susan, "GI Jesus," *Starlight 1.*

Park, Paul, "The Last Homosexual," *Asimov's Science Fiction,* June.

Partridge, Norman, "Bad Intentions," *Bad Intentions.*

———, "Dead Man's Hand," (novella) Ibid.

———, "An Eye for an Eye," *The Ultimate Haunted House.*

Parvin, Roy, "The Ames Coil," *Epoch,* Vol. 45, Number 3.

Pashkovsky, Yevhen, "Five Loaves and Two Fishes," *From Three Worlds: New Writing from the Ukraine.*

Paul, Chris, "Third Floor," *All Hallows* #13.

Paxson, Diana L., "Black Water," *Phantoms of the Night.*

Pearson, Ridley, "All Over But the Dying," *Diagnosis: Terminal.*

Piccirilli, Tom, "Devotion," *Cemetery Dance,* Summer.

———, "Familiar Child," *Deathrealm* #30.

———, "Extreme Closeup—Frame Blood-Red," *Pirate Writings* #10.

Platt, John R., "A Hell-Fire Cure for Baldness," *Satire,* Vol. 3, Number 2, Autumn.

Powers, Tim, "Where They Are Hid," *Charnel House.*

Pugmire, Wilum H., "The Kiss of Alchemy," *The Urbanite* #7.

———, "The Baleful God," *Cthulhu Codex* #7.

Queen, Carol, "Silencer," *Noirotica.*

Ragan, Jacie, "New Breed of Monks,"(poem) *Contortions* #1.

Rainey, Stephen Mark, "To Be As They," *Miskatonic University.*

Rand, Ken, "With Forked Tongue," *Talebones* #4.

Rath, Tina, "Work Experience," *All Hallows* #11.

Rathbone, Wendy, "The Sinister Woods," *The Hot Blood Series: Fear the Fever.*

Reed, Kit, "Whoever," *Asimov's Science Fiction,* Dec.

Reed, Robert, "Decency," *Asimov's Science Fiction,* June.

Rendell, Ruth, "Clothes," *EQMM,* Feb.

———, "The Man Who Was the God of Love," *Blood Lines.*

Rich, Mark, "An Event on the Way to Boston," *Stygian Articles* #7.

———, "This Night of Fishing," *The Silver Web* #13.

Richerson, Carrie, "The Harrowing," *F & SF,* Dec.

Riley, Patricia, "Wisteria," *Blue Dawn, Red Earth.*

Roberts, Katherine, "Rubies," *Visionary Tongue* #3.

Roberts, J. M., "Blackwater," *Superstition, Myth and Magic: The Maguffin* Vol. XIII, Number 11.

Robertson, Laurel, "It's Time to Go," (poem) *Crossroads,* Feb.

Robertson, Robin, "Sheela-Na-Gig," (poem) *The New Yorker,* Apr. 15.

Robson, Justina, "The Bull Leapers," *Visionary Tongue* #4.

Robson, Ruthann, "Women's Music," *Night Bites.*

Roche, Thomas S., "Christianne's Ghosts," *Black Lotus.*

———, "Sisters of the Weird," *Women Who Run with the Werewolves.*

———, "Up for a Nickel," *Noirotica.*

Rodgers, Alan, "Her Misbegotten Son," *Miskatonic University.*

Rogers, Bruce Holland, "These Shoes Strangers Have Died Of," *Enchanted Forests.*

Rosen, Barbara, "The Figure," *Night Terrors* #2.

Royle, Nicholas, "Black Boxes," *Phantoms,* Nov.

———, "The Comfort of Stranglers," *Dark Terrors 2.*

———, "Skin Deep," *Twists of the Tale.*

Rufer-Bach, Kimberly, "Ancestral Culture," *Phantoms of the Night.*

Russo, Patricia, "Grandma's Gingerboys," *White Knuckles* #6.

Rzewuski, Henryk, "I am Burnin'!," *The Dedalus Book of Polish Fantasy.*

Sallee, Wayne Allen, "Another Face of Celandine," *With Wounds Still Wet.*

———, "Choirs," *Ibid.*

———, "Fiends by Torchlight," *Darkside: Horror for the Next Millennium.*

———, "Girly-Girl," *With Wounds Still Wet.*

———, "It Was Only a Dream," *Grue* #18.

———, "Skull Carpenters," *With Wounds Still Wet.*

Sallee, Wayne Allen and Doolittle, Sean, "The Kingsbury Technique," *Dante's Disciples.*

Soukup, Martha, "Alita in the Air," A
Nightmare's Dozen.
——, "To Destroy Rats," Twists of the
Tale.
Spriggs, Robin, "Mr. Aberysthwyth and
the Three Weird Sisters," Terminal
Fright #12.
Springer, Nancy, "Concrete Example,"
Castle Fantastic.
——, "The Way Your Life Is," Sisters
in Fantasy 2.
——, "Yeah, Yeah," A Nightmare's
Dozen.
Spruill, Steven, "Humane Society,"
Twists of the Tale.
——, "Sinister," Diagnosis: Terminal.
Stableford, Brian, "The House of
Mourning," Off Limits.
——, "The Lost Romance," The
Chronicles of the Holy Grail.
Stein, Donna, "Jack and the Beanstalk,"
(poem) The South Carolina Review,
Vol. 28, Number 2.
Storm, Sue, "A Century of Tears," Pirate
Writings #12.
——, "In the Elephant's Graveyard
Where Space Dances With Time,"
Writers of the Future XII.
——, "The Whisper of Feathers,"
Dreams From the Stranger's Cafe #5.
Strand, Mark, "Great Dog Poems 1 &
2," (poems) The New Yorker, Jan. 15.
Studach, Stephen, "The Evil that Men
Do," Unspeakable Crimes.
Sullivan, Rosemary, "In the Giant's
House," The 1995 SPGA Showcase.
Sutton, David, "How the Buckie Was
Saved," Chills #10.
Swanwick, Michael and Dann, Jack,
"Ships," Lethal Kisses.
Szcypiorski, Andrzej, "The Lady with the
Medallion," The Dedalus Book of
Polish Fantasy
Szczepaniak-Gillece, Jessica K.,
"Fairytales: Little Red Cap," (poem)
Talebones #2.
Taeko, Kono, "Snow," Toddler-Hunting
and Other Stories.
——, "Toddler-Hunting," Ibid.
Taff, John F. D., "Orifice," The Hot
Blood Series: Fear the Fever.

Tan, Cecelia, "The Nightingale," Once
Upon a Time.
Tanner, Jason A., "Deep in the Mojo,"
Valkyrie #11, July.
Taylor, Keith, "At the Edge of the Sea,"
Dream Weavers.
——, "The White Doe," Fantasy
Stories.
Taylor, Lucy, "Bundling," The Ultimate
Haunted House.
——, "The Five Percent People," The
Hot Blood Series: Fear the Fever.
——, "Real Blood," Noirotica.
——, "Scars," Darkside: Horror for the
Next Millennium.
——, "Walled," Twists of the Tale.
Tem, Steve Rasnic, "The Burdens,"
Dante's Disciples.
——, "A Cascade of Lies," David
Copperfield's Beyond Imagination.
——, "Close to You," Bones #1.
——, "Elena," Darkside: Horror for the
Next Millennium.
——, "Ghost in the Machine,"
Bloodsongs #7.
——, "The Hideaway Man," A
Nightmare's Dozen.
——, "The Rains," Dark Terrors 2.
Tennant, Peter, "The Boy in the Box,"
Night Dreams #5.
Terry, Jack, "Raining Hell," EQMM,
Dec.
Tessier, Thomas, "Ghost Music: a
Memoir by George Beaune," Dark
Terrors 2.
——, "A Grub Street Tale," Lethal
Kisses.
Theroux, Paul, "Warm Dogs," The New
Yorker, Sep. 16.
Thomas, Jeffrey, "Conglomerate,"
Midnight Shambler #4.
——, "The Face of Baphomet,"
Mythos Tales and Others #1.
Tilton, Lois, "Kneeling at His Side,"
Sisters in Fantasy 2.
Totman, Brandon W., "Yellow," (poem)
Not One of Us #16.
Travis, Tia, "The Yellers of Their Eyes,"
It Came From the Drive-In.
Trommeshauser, Dietmar, "Portrait of a
Ghost," (poem) Rictus #7.

Trotter, William R., "Big Game,"
Deathrealm #29.

Valdron, D. G., "Anomalous
Phenomena and the Inevitability of
Mass Murder . . . ," Bad Magic.

———, "Piggyback," An Atrocity of
Serial Killers.

———, "Time in a Bottle," A Solitude of
Monsters.

Van Camp, Richard, "Sky Burial," Blue
Dawn, Red Earth.

VanderMeer, Jeff, "Black Duke Blues," The
Silver Web #13/The Book of Lost Places.

———, "The Flower Vendor," Freezer
Burn Magazine 6.0.

———, "The General Who is Dead,"
Freezer Burn Magazine 5.0.

Vaughn, David, "The Prosecutor of
DuPrey," EQMM, Jan.

Volsky, Paula, "The Giant Rat of
Sumatra," The Resurrected Holmes.

Vukcevich, Ray, "Catch," Twists of the
Tale.

Wade, Susan, "The Tattooist," Off
Limits.

———, "White Rook, Black Pawn,"
Twists of the Tale.

Wade, Susan, and Webb, Don, "The
Return of the King," Realms of
Fantasy, Feb.

Wagner, Karl Edward, "Final Cut,"
Diagnosis: Terminal.

Wallace, Mary, "Delight in Sacrifice,"
Peeping Tom #22.

Ward, C. E., "Old Martin," Ghosts &
Scholars #22.

Wastling, Clinton, "The Burning Fool,"
The Third Alternative #9.

Wasylyk, Stephen, "The Nine O'Clock
Woman," AHMM, Mar.

Watkins, William Jon, "Bonebirds,"
(poem) Frisson: Disconcerting Verse,
Summer.

Watson, Brad, "A Blessing," Last Days of
the Dog Men.

Watson, Ian, "The Great Escape,"
Dante's Disciples.

———, "My Vampire Cake," Worlds of
Fantasy and Horror #4.

———, "Tulips from Amsterdam,"
Interzone No. 110, Aug.

Watt-Evans, Lawrence, "What the Cat
Dragged In," A Nightmare's Dozen.

Webb, Don, "The Fox Hunt," A Spell
for the Fulfillment of Desire.

———, "The Lamp," The Edge, May/
June.

Weisman, John, "There Are Monsterim,"
Unusual Suspects.

Wells, Heather G., "Headed Home," Not
One of Us #16.

Westgard, Sten, "Without Fear of
Rejection," Tomorrow No. 20, Apr.

Weston, David, "Miss Hedgethorn," All
Hallows #12.

Whitbourn, John, "A Binscombe Tale for
Summer," (chapbook).

Wideman, John Edgar, "Ascent by
Balloon from the Yard of the Walnut
Street Jail," Callaloo, Vol. 19, Number
1.

Wilder, Cherry, "The Curse of Kali,"
Interzone No. 103, Jan.

Wilhelm, Kate, "Forget Luck," F & SF,
Apr.

———, "Merry Widow," Mary Higgins
Clark Mystery Magazine, premier issue.

Wilkinson, Michael, "Cages," (poem)
The Third Alternative #10.

———, "Stalk," (poem) The Third
Alternative #9.

———, "The Stone," (poem) Dancing
Fish.

Williams, Conrad, "Something For
Free," Dark Terrors 2.

Williams, Gavin, "The Cold," Phantoms,
July.

Williams, Sean, "Passing the Bone,"
Eidolon #20.

Williams, Tad, "The Writer's Child,"
The Sandman: Book of Dreams.

Williamson, Chet, "Dr. Joe," Diagnosis:
Terminal.

Williamson, J. N., "Beasts in Buildings,
Turning 'Round," Night Screams.

———, "On the Late Train Through
Texas," Deathrealm #27.

———, "Two Hands Are Better Than
One," The Hot Blood Series: Fear the
Fever.

Williamson, Neil, "Postcards," The Third
Alternative #9.

Willis, Connie, "In Coppelius's Toyshop," *Asimov's Science Fiction*, Dec.

Wiloch, Thomas, "Each Octave of Her Pain is Stillborn and Beautiful," (poem) *Black Moon Magazine* #5.

———, "The Night Begins to Breathe," (poem) Ibid.

———, "She Has Fallen Asleep Beside a Mirror,"(poem) Ibid.

———, "A Thin Crown of Black Thorns,"(poem) *Frisson: Disconcerting Verse*, Summer.

Wilson, David Niall, "The Death-Sweet Scent of Lilies," *Dark Destiny III: Children of Dracula*.

Wilson, David Niall and Hopkins, Brian A., "La Belle Dame Sans Merci," *Deathrealm* #28.

Wilson, F. Paul, "The Wringer," *Night Screams*.

Wilson, Gahan, "Best Friends," *Twists of the Tale*.

Winstead, Tom, "Seven Steps to Heaven," *The Silver Web* #13.

Wolfe, Gene, "The Man in the Pepper Mill," *F & SF*, Oct./Nov.

———, "Try and Kill It," *Asimov's Science Fiction*, Oct./Nov.

Womack, Craig S., "The Witches of Eufaula, Oklahoma," *Blue Dawn, Red Earth*.

Woodworth, Stephen, "Purple Hearts and Other Wounds," *The Hot Blood Series: Fear the Fever*.

Wornom, Howard, "Puppy Love Land," *F & SF*, Apr.

Woroszylski, Wiktor, "The White Worms," *The Dedalus Book of Polish Fantasy*.

Wrede, Patricia C., "Utensile Strength," *Book of Enchantments*.

Wu, William F., "Grid of Ice," *Phantasm*, Spring.

———, "Nairich," *Realms of Fantasy*, Oct.

Yolen, Jane, "Bolundeers," A *Nightmare's Dozen*.

———, "Flattened Fauna Poem #37: Cats," *Twists of the Tale*.

———, "Lady Merion's Angel," *Here There Be Angels*.

———, "Sphinx Song," *Realms of Fantasy*, June.

York, J. Steven, "The Unmarked Crossing," *F & SF*, Feb.

Zimmerman, Michael Ryan, "Saliva, Sunburn, & the Scum of the Earth," *Deathrealm* #27.

The People Behind the Book

Horror Editor ELLEN DATLOW is fiction editor of *Omni* magazine and has edited numerous anthologies including *Blood Is Not Enough, Alien Sex, Little Deaths, Off Limits* and *Twists of the Tale: Stories of Cat Horror*. She has won five World Fantasy Awards for her editing. She lives in New York City.

Fantasy Editor TERRI WINDLING, five-time winner of the World Fantasy Award, developed the innovative Ace Fantasy line of books in the 1980s and is a consulting editor for the Tor Fantasy line in the 1990s. As an anthologist, she has published more than twenty books including *The Armless Maiden*, the Snow White, Blood Red adult fairy-tale series (with Ellen Datlow), and the "Borderland" series for teenagers. As a writer, her publications include *The Wood Wife*, a contemporary fantasy novel, and a folklore column for *Realms of Fantasy* magazine. As a painter, she has exhibited work in museums and galleries around the US and Britain. She divides her time between homes in Tucson, Arizona and Devon, England.

Packager JAMES FRENKEL edited Dell Books's science fiction and fantasy in the late 1970s and early 1980s, was the publisher of Bluejay Books in the 1980s, and has been a consulting editor for Tor Books for the past ten years. Along with James Minz and a legion of student interns, Frenkel edits, packages, and agents books in Madison, Wisconsin.

Media Critic ED BRYANT is an award-winning writer of science fiction, fantasy and horror. He has had short fiction published in numerous magazines and anthologies. He has won the Hugo Award for his fiction. His work also includes writing for television. He lives in Denver, Colorado.

Comics Critic SETH JOHNSON grew up surrounded by comics and books. He is a freelance writer living in Madison, Wisconsin.

Artist THOMAS CANTY is the winner of the World Fantasy Award for Best Artist. He has painted illustrations for innumerable books, ranging from fantasy and horror to suspense and thrillers. He is also an art director, and has designed many books and book jackets during a career that spans over twenty years. He has painted and designed the jackets/covers for every volume of *The Year's Best Fantasy and Horror*. He lives outside Boston, Massachusetts.